SAS
STORIES OF HEROES IV

DAVID MONNERY
SHAUN CLARKE
PETER CAVE

BLITZ EDITIONS

This edition published in 1995

Reprinted 1998

Published by Blitz Editions
an imprint of Bookmart Limited
Registered Number 2372865
Trading as Bookmart Limited
Desford Road, Enderby
Leicester, LE9 5AD

A CIP record for this book is available from the British Library

ISBN 1 85605 302 4

Typeset by Hewer Text Composition Services, Edinburgh
Printed in Great Britain by Clays Limited, St Ives plc

SOLDIER K: SAS

MISSION TO ARGENTINA

David Monnery

1

There had not been a silence so complete in the public bar of the Slug & Sporran since Rangers won an 'Old Firm' match at Parkhead in injury time. Every head in the bar was turned towards the TV, and every right arm seemed suspended between mat and mouth with its cargo of beer. On the screen the aircraft carrier *Invincible* was moving slowly out towards the Portsmouth harbour entrance, past quaysides lined with cheering, weeping, laughing, flag-waving crowds. The British were not just going to war; they were going in style.

James Keir Docherty could hardly believe any of it. He could not believe such rapt attention from a bar more used to toasting the IRA than the English overlord; he could not believe the Government was actually standing up to the Argentinian generals; and he could not believe his unit, B Squadron, 22 SAS Regiment, had merely been placed on permanent standby. Those lucky bastards from D Squadron were already on their way to Ascension Island, with G Squadron next in the queue.

At this moment in his life Docherty was even more disposed to military adventure than usual. A couple of miles away to the south, in one of the developments built on the grave of the Gorbals, his father was slowly dying of emphysema. And it looked like the old bastard was intent on taking with him any last chance of a meeting of minds between father and son.

Docherty was not needed at the bedside, that was for sure. His mother, his two sisters, half the block, probably half the city's trade-union officials, were all already there, drinking tea, swapping yarns, reliving the glorious defeats of the past. His father would be a candidate for best-loved man in the city, Docherty thought sourly. He would leave this earth on a river of good will, arrive at the heavenly gates with enough testimonials from the rank and file to make even St Peter feel inadequate.

He took the penultimate swig from his pint. The ships were still sailing out of the harbour, the crowds still waving. Every now and then the cameramen would find a particularly sexy-looking woman to zoom in on. Several seemed to be waving their knickers round their heads. Sex and death, Docherty thought.

He sighed, remembering those weeks on the beach at Zipolite, both bowed down by grief and lifted up by . . . by just sun and sea really, by the wonder of the ordinary. The best decision he had ever made, buying that air ticket; one of the few he had not regretted. 'My life's a fucking mess,' he murmured into his glass. A dead wife, a dying father, and he could not come to terms with either of them. Why the fuck hadn't they called up B Squadron?

Should he have another drink? No – getting pissed in the afternoon was never a good idea. Getting pissed alone was never a good idea. He drained the glass and got to his feet.

Brennan Street was wreathed in sunshine. A good-looking girl walking down the opposite pavement – long legs in black tights and big silver earrings dancing in dark red hair – reminded him how long it had been since he had had a woman. It was almost two years since his self-appointed mission to screw every whore in Glasgow had fizzled out in the near-bankruptcy of both pocket and soul.

It would be a while longer before he broke his fast, Docherty decided. He grinned to himself. He would go and see Liam McCall instead. After all, what else was religion but a substitute for sex?

He walked down Brennan Street, cut across Sauchie-hall Street, and worked his way through the back streets to the Clyde. Every time he came back to Glasgow he was surprised by the speed with which it seemed to be changing, and mostly for the better. Sure, the shipyards were almost a memory, but new businesses seemed to be springing up everywhere, along with new eating places and theatres and galleries and leisure centres. There seemed to be so much more for young people to do than there had been when he was a boy.

But it was not all good news. The Gorbals of his youth – 'a jungle with a heart of gold' as one wit had named it – had simply been wiped away, and replaced by a desert. One without even the pretence of a heart of gold.

And unemployment was still going up and up, despite all the new businesses. If he had taken his father's advice when he was sixteen he would be on the scrap heap by now, a thirty-one-year-old with skills no one wanted any more. But would his father ever admit that? Not till fucking doomsday, he wouldn't. Joining the Merchant Navy had been irresponsible, joining the Army something close to treason, getting into the SAS about as kosher as screwing Margaret Thatcher and enjoying it.

Why did he care what his father thought? Why was he in Glasgow when he could be enjoying himself at any one of a hundred other places in Britain? He knew he had made good decisions. His life was a fucking mess despite them, not because of them.

He crossed the river. At least he was in good physical shape, no matter what the state of his psyche might be. A couple of drunks were happily throwing up on the bank below. Two leather-jacketed teenagers with outrageously greased quiffs were watching them from the bridge and laughing. They had empty Chinese food cartons all around them, probably bought with the spoils of a mugging. A walk across Glasgow in the early hours of Sunday morning might be a good SAS training exercise, Docherty thought. Requiring stamina, unarmed combat skills and eyes in the back of your head. Not to mention a sense of humour.

Another couple of miles brought him to his friend's parish church, which stood out among its high-rise surroundings rather like the Aztec pyramid Docherty had seen half-excavated on the edge of Mexico City's central square. Father McCall, whom even the schoolkids simply called 'Liam', was standing on the pavement outside, apparently lost in thought. He looked older, Docherty thought. He was nearly sixty now, and his had not exactly been a life of ease.

'Hello, Liam,' he said.

The frocked figure turned round. 'Jamie!' he exclaimed. The eyes still had their sparkle. 'How long have you been back? I thought you'd be gone, you know, on duty or whatever you call it.'

'Duty will do. But no. No such luck. There aren't enough ships to transport all the men who want to go. I'm on twenty-four-hour standby, but . . .' He shrugged and then grinned. 'It's good to see you, Liam. How are you? How are things here?'

'Much the same. Much the same.' The priest stared out across the city towards the distant Campsie Fells, then suddenly laughed. 'You know, I was thinking just now – I think I'm beginning to turn into a Buddhist. So much of what we see as change is mere chaff, completely superficial. And deep down, things don't seem to change at all. Of course,' he added with a quick smile, 'as a Catholic I believe in the possibility of redemption.'

Docherty smiled back at him. He had known the priest since he was about five years old. Liam would have been in his early thirties then, and the two of them had begun a conversation which, though sometimes interrupted for years on end, had continued ever since – and seemed likely to do so until one of them died.

'Do you have time for a walk round the park?' Docherty asked.

Liam looked at his watch. 'I have a meeting in an hour or so . . . so, yes. 'And you didn't answer my question. How long have you been here?'

'I didn't answer it because I felt guilty. I've been here almost a week. My father's dying and . . . well, I always seem to end up dumping all my problems on you, and, you know, every once in a while I get this crazy idea of trying to sort them out for myself.'

Liam grunted. 'Crazy is about right. Are you trying to put me out of business? How long would the

Church last if people started sorting out their own problems?'

Docherty grinned. 'OK, I get the message. You . . .' He broke off as a football came towards them, skidding across the damp grass. The priest trapped the ball in one motion, and sent it back, hard and accurately, with a graceful swing of the right leg. 'Nice one,' Docherty said. Maybe his friend was not getting old just yet.

'You know, it's a frightening thought,' Liam said, 'but I'm afraid I shall still be trying to kick pebbles into imaginary goals when I can barely walk.'

'Makes you wonder what sort of God would restrict your best footballing years to such an early part of life,' Docherty observed.

'Yes, it does,' the priest agreed. 'I'm sorry about your father,' he went on, as if the subject had not changed. 'Of course, I knew he was seriously ill . . . Is there no hope?'

'None. It's just a matter of time.'

'That's true for all of us.'

'It's a matter of weeks, then. Maybe even days.'

'Hmmm. It must be very painful for you.'

'Not as painful as it is for him.'

Liam gave him a reproachful glance. 'You know what I mean.'

'Aye. I'm sorry. And yes, it is painful. He's dying and I don't know how to deal with it. I don't know how to deal with *him*. I never have.'

'I know. But I have to say, and I've said it to you often enough in the past: I think he must carry more of the blame for this than you . . .'

Docherty scratched his ear and smiled ruefully. 'Maybe. Maybe. But . . .'

6

'Everybody loves him. Campbell Docherty, the man who'd do anything for anyone, who worked a twenty-hour day for the union, who'd give his last biscuit to a stray dog. One of our secular saints. He loves everybody and everybody loves him.'

'Except me.'

'There was no room for you, no time. Or maybe he just couldn't cope with another male in the family circle. It's common enough, Jamie. Glasgow's full of boys sleeping rough because their fathers can't cope with living with a younger version of themselves.'

'I know. I agree. But what do I *do*? It's nuts that I let myself get so wound up by this, I know it is . . .'

'I don't think so, Jamie. Fathers and sons have been trying to work each other out since the beginning of time. It's just something they do . . .'

Docherty shook his head. 'You know, every time I come back here I feel like I'm returning to the scene of the crime.'

'There's no crime. Only family.'

Docherty could not help laughing. 'Nice one, Liam.'

'Do you talk to him like you talk to me?' the priest asked.

'I try to. He even agrees with me, but nothing changes.'

'Maybe this time.'

'Maybe. There won't be many others.'

They walked in silence for a while. The dusk was settling over the park, reminding Docherty of all those evenings playing football as a kid, with the ball getting harder and harder to see in the gloom. 'Sometimes, these days, I feel like an old man,' he said. 'Not in body, but in soul.'

7

'Think yourself lucky it's only your soul, then,' Liam observed. 'It only needs one dark cloud coming in from the West, and every joint in me starts aching.'

'I'm serious,' Docherty insisted.

'So am I. But I know what you mean. You live too much in the past, Jamie . . .'

'I know. I can't seem to shake it, though. You know' – he stopped underneath a budding tree – 'there are two scenes which often come into my head when I'm not thinking – like they're always there, but most of the time they're overlaid by something more immediate. One is our parlour when I was a small kid. I must have been about six, because Rosie is still crawling around and Sylvia is helping Mum with the cooking, and Dad's sitting there at the table with a pile of work talking to one of the shop stewards, and I'm doing a jigsaw of the *Coronation Scot*. Remember, that blue streamliner? Nothing ever happens in this scene; it's just the way things are. It feels really peaceful. There's a kind of contentment which oozes out of it.'

'I remember that room,' the priest replied.

'The other scene is a style on a path up near Morar, for Christ's sake. I'm just reaching up to help Chrissie down, and she looks down at me with such a look of love I can hardly keep the tears in. Just that one moment. It's almost like a photograph, except for the changing expression on her face. It was only a couple of weeks later that she was killed.'

Liam said nothing – just put his hand on Docherty's arm.

'It's weird,' Docherty went on. 'I've seen some terrible things as a soldier. Oman was bad enough, but believe me, you won't find a crueller place than Belfast. I got used to it, I suppose. You have to if you're going to function. But sometimes I don't think I'll ever get over that room or that woman.' He turned to face the priest, smiling wryly. 'I couldn't tell this sort of thing to anyone but you,' he said.

'Most people couldn't tell it to anyone at all,' Liam said. 'You underestimate yourself. You always have. But I don't think you should put these two scenes of yours together. I think you will get over Chrissie, even if it takes another ten years. But that room of yours — it sounds almost too good to be true, you know what I mean? Like a picture of the world the way we want it to be, everyone in their proper place, living in perfect harmony . . .'

'Yeah. And what's even crazier: I know it wasn't really like that most of the time.'

'That doesn't matter. It can still be a good picture for someone to hold in their head. Particularly a soldier.'

'How did you get to be so wise?' Docherty asked him with a smile.

'Constant practice. And I still feel more ignorant every day.'

'Don't the Buddhists think that's a sign of wisdom?'

'Yes, but I have to beware the sin of pride where my ignorance is concerned.'

Docherty grinned. 'I think you're probably the most ignorant man I've ever met,' he said. 'And your time is up.'

The priest looked at his watch. 'So it is. I . . .'

'I'll drop by again tomorrow or the next day,' Docherty said. 'Maybe we can get to a game while I'm up here.'

9

They embraced in the gloom, and then Liam hurried back across the park. Docherty watched him go, thinking he detected a slowing of the priest's stride as he passed the kids playing football. But this time no ball came his way.

Docherty turned and began walking slowly in the direction of his parents' flat, thinking about the conversation he had just had, wondering how he could turn it into words for his father when the time came. Half the street lights seemed to be out in Bruce Street, and the blocks of flats had the air of prison buildings looming out of the rapidly darkening sky. Groups of youths seemed to cling to street corners, but there were no threatening movements, not even a verbal challenge. Either his walk was too purposeful to mistake, or here, on his home turf, they recognized Campbell Docherty's boy, 'the SAS man'.

His sister's face at the door told him more than he wanted to know. 'Where have you been?' she said through the tears. 'Dad died this afternoon.'

She was frightened for the first few minutes. The whole situation – sitting beside him in the back seat, her hands clasped together in her lap, watching the traffic over the driver's shoulder – seemed so reminiscent of those few hours that had devastated her life seven years before.

But this was London, not Buenos Aires, and the policeman beside her – if that was what he was – had treated her with what she had come to know as the British version of nominal respect. He had not leered at her in the knowledge that she was the next piece of meat on his slab.

That day it had been raining, great sheets of rain and puddles big as lakes on the Calle San Martín. And Francisco had been with her. For the very last time. She could see his defiant smile as they dragged him out of the car.

Stop it, she told herself. It serves no purpose. Live in the present.

She brought the crowded pavements back into focus. They were in Regent Street, going south. It was not long after three o'clock on a sunny spring afternoon. There was nothing to worry about. Her arrest – or, as they put it, 'request for an interview' – was doubtless the result of some bureaucratic over-reaction to the Junta's occupation of the Malvinas the previous Friday. Probably every Argentinian citizen in England was being offered an interview he or she could not refuse.

A vague memory of a film about the internment of Japanese living in America in 1941 flickered across her mind. Were all her fellow compatriots about to be locked up? It did not seem likely: the English were always complaining that their prisons were too full already.

Today was the day their fleet was supposed to sail. A faint smile crossed her face, partly at the ridiculousness of such a thing in 1982, partly because she knew how appalled the Junta would be at the prospect of any real opposition. The idiots must have thought the English would just shout and scream and do nothing, or they would never have dared to take the islands. Or they had not bothered to think at all, which seemed even more likely.

It was all a little hard to believe. The shoppers,

the late-lunching office workers, the tourists gathered round Eros – it looked much the same as any other day.

'We're almost there,' the man beside her said, as much to himself as to her. The car pulled through Admiralty Arch, took a left turn into Horse Guards Road, and eventually drew to a halt in one of the small streets between Victoria Street and Birdcage Walk. Her escort held the car door for her, and wordlessly ushered her up a short flight of steps and into a Victorian house. 'Straight on through,' he murmured. A corridor led through to a surprisingly large yard, across the far side of which were ranged a line of two-storey Portakabins.

'So this is where M hangs out,' she murmured to herself in Spanish.

Inside it was all gleaming white paintwork and ferns from Marks & Spencer. A secretary who looked nothing like Miss Moneypenny gestured her into a seat. She obliged, wondering why it was the English ever bothered to speak at all. It was one of the things she had most missed, right from the beginning: the constant rattle of conversation, the noise of life. Michael had put it all down to climate – lots of sunshine led to a street-café culture, which encouraged the art of conversation. Drizzle, on the other hand, was a friend of silence.

She preferred to think the English were just repressed.

A door slammed somewhere, and she saw a young man walking away across the yard. He looked familiar – a fellow exile, she guessed. In one door and out another, just in case the Argies had the temerity to talk to each other. She felt anger rising in her throat.

'Isabel Fuentes?' a male voice asked from the doorway leading into the next office.

'*Sí?*' she said coldly.

'This way, please.'

She walked through and took another offered seat, across the desk from the Englishman. He was not much older than her – early thirties, she guessed – with fair hair just beginning to thin around the temples, tired blue eyes and a rather fine jawline. He looked like he had been working for days.

The file in front of him had her name on it.

He opened it, examined the photograph and then her. Her black hair, cropped militantly short in the picture, was now past her shoulder, but she imagined the frown on her face was pretty much the same. 'It is me,' she said helpfully.

He actually smiled. 'Thank you for coming,' he said.

'I was not conscious of any choice in the matter.'

He scratched his head. 'It's a grey area,' he admitted, 'but . . .' He let the thought process die. 'I would like to just check some of the details we have here . . .' He looked up for acquiescence.

She nodded.

'You came to the UK in July 1975, and were granted political asylum in September of the same year . . . that was quick,' he interrupted himself, glancing up at her again.

'It didn't seem so,' she said, though she knew her father's money had somehow smoothed the path for her. She had friends and acquaintances who were still, seven years later, living in fear of being sent back to the torturers.

He grunted and moved on. 'Since your arrival you

have completed a further degree at the London School of Economics and had a succession of jobs, all of which you have left voluntarily.' He glanced up at her, as if in wonderment at someone who could happily throw jobs away in such difficult times. 'I presume you have a private source of income from your parents?'

'Not any more.' Her father had died four years ago, and her mother had cut all contact since marrying some high-ranking naval bureaucrat. 'I live within my means,' she said curtly.

He shrugged. 'Currently you have two part-time jobs, one with a travel agency specializing in Latin-American destinations, the other in an Italian restaurant in Islington.'

'Yes.'

'Before you left Argentina you were an active member of the ERP – the Popular Revolutionary Army, correct? – from October 1973 until the time of your departure from Argentina. You admitted being involved in two kidnappings and one bank robbery.'

'"Admitted" sounds like a confession of guilt. I did not feel guilty.'

'Of course . . .' he said patiently.

'It is a grey area, perhaps,' she said.

He smiled again. 'You are not on trial here,' he said. 'Now, am I correct in thinking that the ERP was a group with internationalist leanings, unlike those who regarded themselves as nationalist Peronistas?'

'You have done your homework well,' she said, wondering what all this could be leading to. 'I suppose it would do no good to ask who I am talking to?'

'I'm sorry,' he said, 'my name is Baldwin, Phillip Baldwin.'

'And you work for?'

'Oh, the Foreign Office, of course.'

'And what is this all about? Is the Foreign Office worried that the exile community is going to undertake a campaign of sabotage against the war effort?'

This time he did not smile. 'How do you view your government's invasion of the Falkland Islands, Ms Fuentes?'

'As just one more attempt to divert the attention of my country's people from their rulers' cruelty and incompetence.'

'Ah,' he said, twiddling his pen and looking out of the window. 'In that case, would you consider returning to your country to work for us?'

She was momentarily stunned. 'You mean as a . . . as a spy?'

'Yes, I suppose you could call it that.'

She half-laughed: the idea seemed so ludicrous.

Balwin seemed to take slight offence. 'Is it such a surprising request? You opposed that government once by force of arms. And it must have crossed your mind that defeat in this matter would probably finish the military as a political force for years.'

That at least was probably true. As was the reverse: victory would keep the beasts in power for the rest of the century. She looked across the desk at the Englishman, still idly twirling his pen. He was just going through the motions, she realized. He did not expect any Argentinian exile to agree to such a proposal, but someone somewhere in the bureaucratic labyrinth had decreed that they all had to be asked. As far as he was concerned, she would soon be walking away across the yard and another of her compatriots would be sitting in the chair answering the same questions.

'To spy on what?' she asked.

'That would depend,' Baldwin said slowly, stirring slightly in his chair. 'For the moment we are more interested in establishing a willingness in principle.'

'Are you offering anything in return for my services?' she asked.

His eyes narrowed. 'I think it would be hard to establish a real basis of mutual trust if remuneration was involved,' he said piously.

'Success would be its own reward,' she suggested sweetly.

'Something like that,' he agreed, with the faintest of grins.

'And if I wanted something other than money, like, for example, permanent residency visas for several friends?'

'That could probably be arranged.'

'I will consider it,' she said. The idea still seemed ludicrous, but . . .

Looking pleasantly surprised, Baldwin wrote down a number on his notepad, tore the sheet off and handed it to her. 'You can reach me on this number,' he said. 'Day or night.'

Isabel walked back to Piccadilly, phoned the travel agency with the news that she would not be back that day, and took a 19 bus to Highbury Corner. It was almost five o'clock. Her flatmate would probably not yet be home, but Isabel felt reluctant to risk having her thoughts interrupted by more instalments of the endless romantic soap opera which Rowan passed off as a life. She bought a cup of tea at the outdoor café in Highbury Fields and carried it across to one of the seats in the area barred to dogs.

For a while she just sat there and watched the world go by. Or rather, watched England go by. Since the meeting in Baldwin's office she had felt like she was living in an alien country. Which, of course, she was. It was just that most of the time the feeling was buried somewhere at the back of her mind.

'You must miss the heat,' people used to say to her when she first arrived. She had tried to explain that her birthplace in the far south of Argentina was just as cold and a lot windier than most of Scotland, let alone England, but nobody really listened. South America was jungle and gauchos and Pele and the carnival in Rio. It had to be hot.

She conjured up a picture of ice floes in the Beagle Channel, the wind like a knife, a beach full of penguins, the aurora australis shimmering in the southern sky. That was her home.

It was the one line, she realized, which had got to her. 'Would you consider returning to your country?' That simple question had somehow brought it all back. She had not been really unhappy in the prison of exile, not since the year or more of grieving for Francisco and of learning to live with what they had done to her. But she had not really been happy either, just endlessly marking time. The line from that Bob Dylan album of Michael's said it better than she ever could: 'And I've never gotten used to it, I've just learned to turn it off.'

That was her life — turned off. Friends, a lover, but no real comradeship, no real love. No purpose.

But could she really work for the English?

'My enemy's enemy is my friend,' she said softly to herself. 'Sometimes,' she added. Surely the Junta would lose this war anyway, without her putting her own life at risk?

'If no one else will fight, then all the more reason for us to.' She could hear Francisco saying it, in the candlelit lodgings in Córdoba. They had just made love, and as usual he had been lying on his back, blowing smoke rings at the ceiling, surveying the world situation.

They had tortured and killed him, and maybe this was fate's way of giving her the chance to even the score. Maybe the wretched Malvinas had finally found a use for themselves, as a grave for the military's prestige. Defeat would bring a new government in Buenos Aires, one with untainted hands, one that could admit to what had been done to all those tens of thousands. Such honesty might bring the hope of redemption for her country. And for her.

'Don't cry for me, Argentina,' she muttered ironically.

She got up and walked slowly across the park to the flat she shared. Rowan was not home yet, and for once Isabel felt the need of some alcohol. An opened bottle of burgundy supplied the necessary, and she sat nursing a glass in front of the six o'clock news. The fleet was sailing out of Portsmouth harbour, flags flying, men saluting, loved ones waving. She remembered what Michael had said the previous evening, that no matter how much he despised the patriotism and the flag-waving, no matter how clearly he could see through all the sanctimonious crap, he had been appalled to discover that there was still a small part of him that felt somehow connected, even proud, of all this.

She had understood exactly what he meant, because

she knew that a small part of her wanted the English to fail in this war, wanted the beasts of the Junta to triumph in Argentina's name. And more than anything else, or so she later came to believe, it was the need to silence that small voice which led her to call Baldwin the next morning.

The next few days seemed more than a little unreal. She called in sick to her two jobs, perhaps not really believing that her new career as a Mata Hari would amount to anything. The Englishmen who were supposedly preparing her for her new career certainly did not inspire much confidence.

For one thing, it rapidly became clear to Isabel that they knew next to nothing about her country, either in the general sense or in terms of the current situation. What information they did have seemed to come from either the Argentinian press or American signals intelligence. The latter source offered great wads of information, almost all of which was rendered useless by the lack of any accompanying indication of the enemy's intentions. The newspapers, needless to say, offered only lies and conceits. It was obvious that British Intelligence had no one on the ground in Argentina.

Now, faced with the prospect of having someone, the Intelligence people seemed initially incapable of deciding what to do with her. Isabel could imagine them discussing the possibility of her seducing General Galtieri and learning all the Junta's secrets. Still, she did not fool herself into believing that they thought any more highly of her than she did of them. She was, after all, an Argie, a woman and a communist – which had to be three strikes and out as far as the Foreign

Office was concerned. If it was not for the fact that she was the intelligence services' only proof that they were doing anything at all that was useful, she would probably have just been sent home in a taxi.

It was on Friday 9 April, the day the other Western European countries swung into line behind Britain's call for sanctions, that some semblance of a coherent mission was offered to her. Baldwin escorted her through a maze of Whitehall corridors and courtyards to a spacious top-floor office overlooking St James's Park, and into the presence of a cadaverous-looking Englishman with slicked-back black hair and a worried expression. His name was Colonel William Bartley, but he wore no uniform, unless the City gent's pinstripe suit counted as one.

'We have thought long and hard about where and how you could be most usefully deployed,' he said, after the exchange of introductions and Baldwin's departure. 'And . . .' He stopped suddenly, sighed, and leaned back in his chair. 'I've read your file, of course,' he continued, 'and you wouldn't expect me to sympathize with your politics . . .'

'No,' she said.

'But of course, if these weren't your politics then you would not be willing to betray your own country on our behalf, so I can hardly complain.' Bartley grunted, probably in appreciation of his own logic. 'But you're obviously intelligent, and you can doubtless see our problem.'

She could. 'You don't want to tell me anything which I might turn over to my beloved government. Well, what could I say to convince you?'

'Nothing. In any case we are not merely concerned at the possibility that you will pass on information willing. There is always the chance you will be captured. And of course . . .' Bartley left the unspoken 'tortured' hanging in the air.

'I understand. And you are right – there's no way I would endure torture to save your secrets.' As I once did for a lover, she thought. 'So,' she said, 'it's simply a matter of calculating risks, is it not? The risk of my being a double agent, or of getting caught, against the risk of not telling me enough to make using me worthwhile.'

'Exactly,' Bartley agreed.

She stared at him in silence.

'You are from the south,' he said, 'which is useful from our point of view. How difficult would it be for you to set up shop, so to speak, somewhere like Rio Gallegos? Are there people who would recognize you? What sort of cover story could you come up with?'

'I come from Ushuaia, which is a long way from Rio Gallegos. I might be recognized by someone – who knows? – but not by anyone who would question my presence in the area. I could say I was looking up an old college friend . . .'

'Who is not there?'

'I did not know she had moved, perhaps?'

'Perhaps. Since you know the country and the people I will leave it to you, but I will give you one other suggestion: you are researching a travel book, perhaps in association with an American equivalent of that agency you work for, checking out hotels, local transport, things to see. It's a good excuse for moving around.'

'Perhaps.' She admitted to herself that it sounded a good idea. 'And what is my real motive for being there? The airbase, I suppose. You want to know

which planes, what armaments, the pilots' morale.'
She paused. 'And you'd probably like to know each
time they take off. Am I going to have to carry a radio
set into Argentina?'

'I doubt it,' Bartley said, obviously taken by surprise. 'How did you work all that out?' he asked.

'By reading the *Observer*. The British fleet was
created to operate in the eastern Atlantic, within
the defensive cover provided by shore-based aircraft,
and the one thing that scares the Admirals is their
vulnerability to air attack without such cover.' She
looked at him. 'Is this the secret you were afraid I'd
tell the Junta?'

Bartley at least had the good grace to blush. 'We
think the Super Etendards may be based at Rio
Gallegos,' he added, 'and doubtless the *Observer*
pointed out how concerned we are about the Exocets
they carry.'

'It did. But if advance warning is what you need,
surely it has to be by radio?'

'Perhaps. We have several weeks to worry about
that, and if it becomes absolutely necessary then one
can be brought across the border from Chile when the
time comes. First, we need to get you bedded in.'

For the next few days she was given an in-depth
briefing on military matters, at the end of which
she could not only recognize a Super Etendard by its
silhouette but also identify a wide range of military
equipment which might conceivably be *en route* to
the Malvinas from the Rio Gallegos airbase.

In the meantime her journey to Santiago – via New
York and Los Angeles on three separate airlines – had
been booked, her share of the rent on her flat paid six

months in advance, and four fellow exiles had been given reason to wonder at the sudden beneficence of the Home Office in allowing them permanent residence status. Rowan and her other friends had been told that she had been given a three-month commission to update tourist information in Peru and Bolivia. They were all suitably jealous.

Michael was also angry. Why had she not consulted him? Did she think she could behave in a relationship as if she was a single person? Did she care about him at all?

The answer to the last was: not enough. She liked him, enjoyed talking with him, found sex with him occasionally pleasurable but mostly just harmless fun. It was not his fault, and she would have felt sorrier for him if she believed he really loved her, but as it was . . . The last night before her departure, as she watched her nipple harden in response to his brushing finger and kiss, the bizarre thought struck her that she was like a ship which had been struck below the waterline, and that her captain had ordered the sealing of all the internal bulkheads, the total compartmentalization of the vessel. The rooms were all still there but she could no longer move from one to another. There were no connections. In the torture chambers of the Naval Mechanical School she had lost the pattern of her being, which was probably just a fancy description of the soul.

Her plane landed in Santiago de Chile at five in the morning on 19 April. According to the newspapers, the Junta's response to US Secretary of State Haig's peace plan was being conveyed to London, but no one seemed too sanguine about the prospects. According to her own calculations, the British Task Force would be just over halfway to the Malvinas by this time. There was still between ten days and a fortnight before it came within range of the Argentinian Air Force.

The men in London had given her a new identity, albeit one very close to her own. She was now Isabel Rodríguez, a thirty-one-year-old Argentinian who had lived for several years in the United States, and who had never involved herself in the politics of her homeland. Later that evening, in her room at the Hotel San Miguel, she received the expected visitor from the British Embassy, a sallow, dark-haired man with wire-rimmed spectacles who looked distinctly un-English.

He introduced himself as Andrew Lawson. 'I am British,' he said apologetically, as if in the past doubts had been raised. 'I just look like a South American. Probably because my mother was Spanish. I have brought you the money' – he laid two piles of notes, one smaller Chilean, one larger Argentinian, on the bed – 'and the car is in the underground car park. A black Renault 5, AY1253S, in space B14. Have you got that?'

She nodded.

'I shall also be your contact in the south,' Lawson went on, taking a map from his pocket and unfolding it on the bed. 'See, this is Argentina . . .'

'I know. I was born there,' she said acidly. Maybe the Junta would win the war, after all.

'Ah, I'm sorry, of course. You know the south well?'

'I grew up in Ushuaia.'

'Ah, right. Do you know this road here, between Rio Gallegos and Punta Arenas?'

'I have travelled it many times, by car, by bus.'

'Good. What we need is a dead-letter drop – you understand? Somewhere where we can leave each other messages for collection. It should be on the Argentinian side, because the fewer times you have to cross the border the better. A stretch of empty road, a bridge over a stream, something like that.'

'It would be harder to find a stretch of road that isn't empty,' she said drily. 'Why must I cross the border at all?'

'A good question. And the simple answer is, I can't think of a safer way for you to let me know the location you've chosen. If you can . . .'

She thought about it. 'You can't come to me?'

'I could risk it, but let's face it, I'd have trouble passing as a local at the border. I may *look* like a Latin American, but my Spanish isn't good enough . . .' He shrugged.

'A go-between,' she suggested.

'The fewer people know who you are the better.'

That made sense. 'OK, so I come into Chile . . .'

'To Punta Arenas. Your cover is a tourist guide, right? So you have to check out the local museums. There are three in Punta Arenas: the Regional Magellanes, the Patagonian Institute and the Salesian College. I'll be at the Salesian each Thursday morning from the 29th on.'

She looked at him. The whole business suddenly seemed completely insane. 'Right,' she said.

The road across the Andes was full of wonder and memories. Isabel had last driven it with Francisco in the early spring of 1973, when they had visited Chilean friends in Santiago, both of whom had perished a month or so later in the military coup. Then as now the towering peak of Aconcagua had shone like a beacon, sunlit snow against a clear blue sky, but then the love of her life had been with her, and the darkest of futures still bore a gleam of hope.

This time too she stopped at the huge Christ of the Andes, bought a steaming cup of coffee from the restaurant and walked up past the statue and its admiring tourists to where she could see, far down the valley, the distant green fields of her native country.

She had over 1000 miles to drive, and she planned to take at least three days, acclimatizing herself to the country as she travelled. That evening she stayed in Mendoza and, after eating in a half-empty restaurant, sat in the city's main square and listened to the conversations going on around her. Most of them seemed to be about the Malvinas dispute, and she found the level of optimism being expressed hard to credit.

The purchase of a newspaper helped to explain the high spirits. According to the Government, the British were bluffing – there would be no war between the two countries. Britain would huff and puff, but eventually it would come to its senses. After all, what nation would really send a huge fleet 10,000 miles for the sake of 1800 people? Though, of course, the editorial was swift to mention that, if by some mischance it really did come to a fight, then the armed forces of the nation were more than ready to do what was necessary for the glory of, etc, etc.

'Wrong,' Isabel muttered to herself, staring across the square at the vast wall of the silhouetted mountains to the west. There was no hope of the British coming to their senses, and consequently no chance that they were bluffing.

Isabel's sense of a nation with its head buried deep in the sand did not fade as she travelled south over the next few days. Everywhere she went she heard the same refrain: there would be no war. How could the British fight one so far from home? Why would they do so even if they could? There was no antipathy towards distant England; if anything, the old connection between the two countries seemed almost stronger for their mutual travail. Isabel was half-amazed, half-amused, by how many of her countrymen and women felt vaguely sorry for the British. It was almost pathetic, people told each other, the way the old country clung on to these useless relics of their past imperial splendour.

Her own state of mind seemed to be fluctuating more wildly with each day back in her native country. It all seemed so familiar, and pleasantly so, and it took her a while to realize that what she was reliving was her childhood and youth in the countryside, that memories of the city years with Francisco would need different triggers – the smell of San Telmo streets on a summer evening, book-lined rooms on a college campus, young earnest faces, a gun laid out in pieces on an oilskin cloth.

Each mile to the south took her further from those years, closer to the innocence which they had destroyed. Driving down arrow-straight roads across the vast blue-grey steppes of Patagonia seemed almost like a trip into space, cold and cleansing, more than human.

* * *

It was four in the afternoon on Saturday 24 April when Isabel reached the outskirts of Rio Gallegos. The town seemed much changed from when she had last seen it some ten years before. The oil industry had brought prosperity and modernity, along with a refinery which peeked out over the mostly brick-built houses.

The Hotel Covadonga in Avenida Julio Roca seemed to avoid the opposite extremes of ostentation and a clientele composed entirely of sex-starved oil workers. It was also centrally located and spotlessly clean. The manager proudly announced himself as Manuel Menéndez, and was surprised but pleased to learn that she intended to make a lengthy stay. Rio Gallegos was not usually noted for its tourist potential.

After a brief but enjoyable bargaining session over a reduced long-stay rate, Isabel explained about the guide book she was researching, and how the town was ideally located as a centre of operations. But perhaps, she wondered out loud, the trouble with the British over the liberation of the Malvinas had led the military to place temporary restrictions on the ordinary citizen's freedom to travel?

Not as far as Menéndez knew. There was no longer any civilian traffic from the airbase, and Navy ships were more often seen in the estuary, but nothing much else had changed over the last few weeks. The border with Chile was still open. 'It is all over, is it not?' he said. 'We have the Malvinas back, and I suppose we must thank the Government for that.'

Isabel agreed and went up to her room. After unpacking her meagre travelling wardrobe, she felt tired enough to lie down for a short nap. But her mind was racing too fast for sleep, and she soon decided that she should not waste the last hour of light in her room. Wrapped up in an extra sweater and her Gore-tex windcheater, she strolled purposefully down the Calle Rawson towards the estuary shore. Here she found that a new and pleasant park had been created along the river front. Many families were in evidence, the children already sporting their winter woolly hats. Over by the balustrade a group of young men in Air Force uniforms were enjoying a boisterous conversation.

She walked the length of the park along by the water. Two coalers were anchored in the mile-wide estuary, and beyond them the northern shore offered only a vista of steppe extending into the grey distance. As she turned to retrace her steps a growing roar lifted her eyes to the sky. A Hercules C-130 transport plane was coming in to land at the airport south of the city.

Back at the Covadonga, Isabel lay in the bath, thinking that any delay was likely to weaken her resolve. Wearing the dress she had brought with such an eventuality in mind, she went downstairs to the desk and asked Menéndez's advice. 'Where could she have some fun on a Saturday night?'

It turned out there was a big dance that evening at a hall in Calle Pellegrini. After eating a less than exciting dinner at a restaurant off the main square, she made her way across to the hall. At the makeshift bar there were several single women, presumably prostitutes, so Isabel kept her distance and tried to look suitably lost. It was not long before a middle-aged businessman's wife gave her the chance to tell her story: a single woman in a strange town, wanting some company but ... She was soon adopted into their circle, a cross between a guest and a surrogate daughter.

She actually enjoyed the evening, and had almost despaired of it leading anywhere useful, when the party of Air Force pilots arrived. They were given a standing ovation, treated to free drinks and generally fêted as the nation's favourite sons. It did not take Isabel long to pick out her choice: he was tall and dark with a diffident manner and sad brown eyes. He looked as out of place as she felt.

His name was Raul Vergara, and fifteen minutes later they were dancing together, the rough serge of his uniform rubbing against her cheek. For one appalling moment she was back in the whitewashed room at the Naval Mechanical School, the lieutenant's swollen dick pushing against her obstinate lips, the smell of it mixed with the stink of fear that filled the building.

'You dance really well,' the shy young pilot whispered in her ear, breaking the dreadful spell.

2

The last slice of orange sun was disappearing into
the western sea as the eight SAS men made their way
across the deck of HMS *Hermes* toward the waiting
Wessex helicopter. For the first time in many days the
sky was clear and the ocean was not doing its best to
tip the ship over. Maybe it was a good omen. But it
was still bloody cold.

Each man was wearing camouflage gear from head
to toe, with the exposed areas of the face painted
to match. Somewhere in the bergen rucksacks slung
across their backs, among the 90 lb or so of weaponry,
communications equipment, medical kit and rations,
each man was carrying the tubes of 'cam' cream
he would need to freshen his make-up when the
need arose.

They had split into pairs to check each other's
cosmetic efforts before the final load-up. One of the
two patrol commanders, Major Jeremy Brookes, had
received five point eight for technical merit but only a
minus score for artistic impression. He smiled through
his mask at the thought.

Brookes's patrol, all of them members of G Squadron's Mountain Troop, were headed for the hills
overlooking Port Howard on West Falkland, and
none too pleased about it. 'But all the fucking

Argies are on East Falkland, boss,' Trooper Kenny Laurel had observed, with all the mildness of an articulated lorry.

'No, Hedge, they're not,' Brookes had explained, 'just most of them. And that's only as far as we know. The point of this exercise is to determine exactly where they are, every last one of them.'

'And where they're not,' Trooper Davey Matthews had observed.

'Thank you, Stanley. Besides which, someone had to draw the short straw, and it was us, OK?'

'Yes, boss.'

Admittedly, Brookes thought as he clambered aboard the Wessex, the straw no longer seemed quite so short. There might not be many Argies on West Falkland, but there was likely to be more than four of them. This was hardly a picnic they were embarking on. At the best it would probably consist of lying in a damp hole for days on end, bored out of their minds. He tried to remember who had said that a soldier's life was ninety-nine per cent boredom, one per cent pure terror. Was it Wellington? No, it was somebody else, but he could not remember who.

As they sat there waiting for the Wessex crew to appear – 'Fucking Navy were even late for the Armada,' someone observed – Brookes foolishly asked his seven co-travellers if any of them could remember.

'Genghis Khan?' a member of the other patrol offered.

'Nah, he said it was ninety-nine per cent terror,' someone corrected him.

'Bruce Forsyth,' Hedge suggested. 'What do you think, Mozza?'

32

Trooper David Moseley emerged from his reverie with a start. 'What?' he said.

'His mind's on other things,' Stanley said.

The little woman back home, I expect, Hedge thought. 'It drains your strength, Mozza, even thinking about them.'

'I was thinking about where we're going,' Mozza said, wondering guiltily whether not thinking about Lynsey at such a moment was something of a betrayal.

'We're all going to sunny West Falkland,' Hedge told him, 'where the beaches stretch golden into the distance and the hills are alive with the sound of sheep farting. We're all going on a summer holiday,' he sung, with a gusto Cliff Richard would have killed for.

So would their pilot, who had just arrived with the other two members of the crew. 'If you don't stop that horrible row Falkland Sound will be alive with your cries for help,' he said trenchantly.

'If you dropped him into Falkland Sound,' one of the other patrol noted, examining Hedge's undoubted bulk, 'it would probably drain it.'

'Then there'd only be one island to argue about,' someone else realized.

Major Brookes listened to the banter with half his mind, knowing it for what it was, a giddy chorus of nerves and apprehension. He still could not remember the author of his quote, and as he checked through his memory, another, less amenable one came to mind. He had first heard it from the lips of a dying IRA terrorist the previous year. Lying there, blood flowing freely from a neck wound into sodden leaves in an Armagh lane, the man had looked at him, smiled and recited: 'this is war, boys flung into a breach, like shovelled earth, and . . .'

He had died then, and it had taken Brookes many months to find the rest of the verse, and its source. Finally, the wife of an old friend had recognized it as a poem by the American Amy Lowell. He had looked it up and found the rest: 'and old men, broken, driving rapidly before crowds of people, in a glitter of silly decorations, behind the boys and the old men, life weeps and shreds her garments, to the blowing winds'.

These are the boys, Brookes thought, looking round at them: Mozza with his fresh-faced innocence, ginger-haired Stanley with his sleazy grin, the overwhelming Hedge.

At that moment the lights went out, the rotor blades reached a pitch which made conversation impossible, and the Wessex lifted up from the aircraft carrier's deck and started moving south-westwards, low across the South Atlantic swell.

Cecil Matheson poured himself a modest finger of malt whisky, took an appreciative sip and carried it across to the window. Through a gap between darkened buildings he could see light reflected on the Thames. In the street below he could see theatre and cinema-goers threading their way through the Saturday evening jam of taxis.

The buzzer sounded on his phone, and he took three quick strides across the room to his desk.

'Mr Lubanski is on the line,' his secretary told him.

'Mr Lubanski,' Matheson said jovially, wondering, not for the first time, why the American State

Department seemed to employ more Poles than the Polish Foreign Ministry. He had met this particular one on his last official visit to Washington, and been more impressed than enamoured of him. The fact that Lubanski was known to privately support a neutral American position *vis-à-vis* the current dispute only made the coming conversation more fraught with difficulty.

The lack of liking seemed to be mutual. 'Cecil,' Lubanski replied, with more familiarity but rather less enthusiasm. 'What can I do for you?'

'I'm sorry to take up your time at the weekend,' Matheson said with as much sincerity as he could muster at short notice. 'It's just a matter-of-clarification.'

'Uh-huh.'

'The President's speech on Friday . . .'

'The "ice cold bunch of land down there" speech?' Lubanski asked, a twist of malicious humour in his voice.

That was how Ronald Reagan had described the Falklands, and Matheson winced at the memory. 'Yes, that one,' he confirmed. 'Of course, we don't share the President's opinion in that respect, but we are . . .' He wanted to say 'glad that the US Government has at last realized its responsibilities to a NATO ally', but that would hardly be diplomatic.

'Pleased that we've finally fallen off the fence on your side?' Lubanski offered.

'That's certainly one way of putting it,' Matheson agreed, 'though I'd prefer to think you'd stepped down. In any case,' he continued hurriedly, 'we're obviously gratified by the sanctions announced by your Government, and by the President's promise of *matériel* aid. As regards the latter . . .'

'You'd like to know what's on offer.'

'Of course, but I'm sure that question can be handled through the normal channels. I have something more specific in mind.'

'Which is?' For the first time, Lubanski sounded vaguely interested.

Time to bite the bullet, Matheson told himself. 'AWACS,' he said. 'Airborne warning and control systems.'

'I know what AWACS are,' Lubanski said drily. 'And without putting too fine a point on it, I think I can safely say the answer will be sorry, but no.'

Like hell he was sorry, Matheson thought. 'Her Majesty's Government would like to formally request the loan of just two AWACS,' he pressed on.

'Like I . . .'

'If I could just continue,' Matheson said, rather more harshly than he intended, 'large British naval losses will hardly serve the interests of the United States. I'm sure I don't need to remind you that the Royal Navy's primary *raison d'être* is to safeguard the passage of American troops and armaments to Europe in the event of a major war . . .'

'No, you don't.'

'Then I fail to see the justification for a refusal of this request.'

'Bullshit, Cecil. You know damn well why we're refusing it. Put our own military into this little exercise of yours and twenty years of Latin-American policy goes down the tubes. You've already dragged us off the fence for the sake of 1800 sheep farmers, and now you want us to send AWACS planes? Are you sure you wouldn't like us to nuke Buenos Aires for you?'

Matheson took a deep breath, and swallowed the

temptation to tell Lubanski the best thing the State Department could do with its Latin-American policy was to tear it all up and start again. 'If we can't defend our ships against attacks from the mainland,' he said carefully, 'we may be forced to move against the source of the problem ourselves.'

'You mean bomb their bases? What with?'

'Vulcans from Ascension.'

For a few moments there was a silence at the other end. Then Lubanski, sounding more formal, replied: 'I think the British Government would be wise to examine the United Nations resolutions so far invoked, and particularly Article 51's definition of self-defence. I'm not at all sure that the United States would regard military action against mainland Argentina as falling within the scope of that definition. And, regardless of such legal niceties, I am completely certain that continued US support is contingent on a certain level of self-restraint in the British prosecution of the war.'

Another short silence ensued.

'You do realize how this looks from the British Government's point of view,' Matheson said eventually. 'You won't help us to protect our ships, and you won't allow us to protect them ourselves in the only way open to us. We've got young boys out there,' he went on, wondering whether sentiment would help, 'with next to no cover. And they're not fighting for sheep farmers – they're fighting against aggression, and for self-determination. I seem to remember,' he could not resist adding, 'that one of your presidents almost invented the phrase.'

'Before my time,' Lubanski said wearily. 'Look, Cecil, let me be as frank as I can about this. I personally

37

think your war is a crock of shit, and I wouldn't have risked alienating a single Hispanic voter or a single Latin-American government to support it. I have colleagues who disagree with me, and who'd love to support the old country, you know, all that Ivy League shit. But even *they* wouldn't loan you a single airplane. It's just too much to ask. This is not our war – it's yours. You fight the damn thing with what you've got.'

'We intend to,' Matheson said, struggling to keep his voice level. 'Thank you for your time,' he said coldly, and hung up. He could almost hear Lubanski 3000 miles away, smirking about some Brit in a snit.

He shook his head to clear it, and poured out a more generous shot of whisky. He had, after all, got exactly what he had expected from the call. Nothing. And it would do no harm to make the Americans aware, privately, of how angry the British were with them. A measure of guilt might increase their generosity in other matters.

The real problem lay not 3000 miles away, but less than one. Matheson was almost afraid to imagine what alternatives to the AWACS were brewing in the Prime Minister's restless mind.

The flight took slightly less than a hour, most of it over the sea. Darkness had fallen, but despite the lack of a moon the Wessex crew had no trouble identifying the northern coast of Pebble Island on such a clear night. The Passive Night Goggles, or PNGs, which they had recently received from American sources, only came into their own when they were contour-chasing across the north-central part of West Falkland proper.

They set the Wessex down in a wide stretch of

desolate grassland. The ground looked hard enough, but for an instant seemed to give alarmingly. It was, Brookes thought, as he leapt down onto it, like landing on a springy pine-forest floor.

The other three followed him out, and the door closed on the grinning, waving members of the other patrol, bound for a similar mission further down the island. As arranged, Hedge moved off ahead to take up a defensive position on the slight ridge 100 yards to the east. The words 'So where's the fucking hotel?' floated back across the din of the helicopter taking off.

The others grinned, and Brookes examined the map and illuminated compass as the silhouette of the Wessex faded with the sound of its rotors. An almost eerie silence descended. I'm a long way from home, Mozza thought suddenly. At least there's no fucking wind, Stanley was consoling himself.

Hedge inched his eyes over the ridge line and suddenly came face to face with a dark and menacing shape. 'Baa-aaa,' it said. 'Kebabs!' Hedge whispered viciously.

They had been deposited just over 14 miles, as the crow flew, from their chosen site for an OP, or observation point, overlooking the small Argentinian base at Port Howard. Of course, there were no crows in the Falklands, and it was, as one of the SAS planners on *Resource* had observed, a bloody sight further as the penguin flew. The same terrain in, say, Wales, would not have been considered particularly difficult, but here the general dampness and usual high winds made everything twice as difficult.

The spongy ground often seemed as sapping as the Wembley turf in extra time, but occasionally it would either turn hard enough to jar every bone in the body or soft enough to swallow each foot in a clinging, gelatinous muck. The hills were not exactly steep, but large expanses of the slopes were strewn with flat rock slippery with lichen. And no matter which way you turned the wind always seemed to be blowing right in your face.

Given that this particular stretch had to be covered in relative darkness and near-total silence, with 90lb on each back and a less than perfect map, Brookes fully expected the journey to take two whole nights.

He told himself to look on the bright side. At least it was a clear night – no one was likely to walk off a cliff or trip over a sheep. And what had he joined the SAS for if not to experience moments like this, dumped behind enemy lines in a hostile environment with only a few good mates and his own wits to keep him alive, the stars shining bright above? At his age there would not be many more of them. The Falklands might not be Tahiti, but they sure beat the hell out of south Armagh.

They were walking in a staggered version of the diamond formation generally favoured by SAS four-man patrols on open ground at night. Stanley was out front, the lead scout, picking out the required route, with Brookes himself some 20 yards back and to the left. He was the navigational backup, and responsible for the patrol's left flank. Further back still, out to the right, Mozza was taking care of that flank, while Hedge was 'Tail-end Charlie', occasionally spinning round to check their rear. He was about 50 yards behind Stanley.

As was true of any SAS four-man patrol, each man had one or more of the four specialized skills: Brookes had languages and demolition, Stanley demolition and signalling, Mozza signalling, and Hedge medicine and languages. All but Stanley had some knowledge of Spanish, but there was not likely to be much call for it on this trip, unless they took prisoners. Or were taken prisoner themselves.

As an officer, Brookes was enjoying his second term with the SAS; in fact, his military career had become a series of alternating periods spent with them and his own parent regiment, the Green Howards. His first tour of duty with the SAS had involved active service in Oman and training secondments in two other Arab states, while the current stint, now nearing its end, had found him dodging bullets and bombs in Armagh's 'bandit country' and dispensing advice to local defence forces in several newly independent West Indian countries. Hairy it might be, and often was, but service with the SAS had been a great deal more interesting than service with the Green Howards, whom fate had given a less than fascinating peacetime role. War games in West Germany were a lot less fun than he had at one time imagined.

His wife, Clare, had preferred life with the Green Howards, in the days when she had still cared. Now, with both the boys at Shrewsbury and her own small business taking off, Brookes did not believe she even noticed which unit he was attached to. She was too busy scouring the Welsh Marches for the antiques she flogged off to her fellow-countrymen across the Atlantic. Their Hereford house looked more like a museum every time he returned from active duty abroad. Even the Spanish villa they shared with friends of hers seemed like a little piece of Hay-on-Wye.

He found it all hard to think about, and wondered

why he was doing so on a starlit stroll through the Argentinian-held Falklands. Where better? he asked himself.

He was not getting any younger – that was half the problem. Sure, he still had most of his hair, although no one would know it from the grey stubble which protruded skinhead-style from his head. And he was just as fit as he had ever been. But he was not Peter Pan, and maybe the bergen on his back did feel a bit heavier than it should. You could make up in experience what you lost in suppleness of limb, but only up to a point.

He was thirty-eight. What was he going to do in seven years' time, when his active career ran out? Fight for one of the desk jobs? Not bloody likely. But what else? He had always vaguely imagined that Clare would be there to share their old age. He knew it had been completely unfair, not to mention stupid – after all, what possible reason could she have for putting her life on permanent hold while he had fun? – but he had somehow expected that she would. Now when she bothered to write letters they were full of Stephen, her semi-partner. He was queer, of course – 'He's *gay*, Jeremy, not queer! – but then again, what did it matter whether or not she jumped into bed with the bastard: the point was that she obviously found him more interesting than her husband.

And then there were the boys. Total strangers to him, and he really had no one to blame but himself.

This was his real family, he thought, this bunch of highly trained lunatics. Men who could mention Genghis Khan and Bruce Forsyth in the same breath. Unfortunately it was a family with a cut-off date.

* * *

Up ahead of Brookes, Stanley paused for a moment to check the map against the reading on his illuminated compass. Satisfied, he resumed his progress across the sodden heathland towards the distant silhouette of a low hill, the M16 with attached M203 grenade-launcher cradled in his arms.

How, he wondered, could a man's mouth feel so dry in such a place? Walking across this island was like walking along the back of an enormous wet dog. He could feel the damp creeping up his legs and thought about the next few days of endless fucking misery in a damp hole. Worse than a Saturday morning in the West Bromwich Shopping Centre with his ex-wife.

The thought of Sharon cheered him up. With any luck she was having a worse time than he was since Brett – what a fucking name! – had been sent down for armed robbery. Stanley nearly laughed out loud. The prat had rushed into a local sub post office, waved a gun around, escaped with about fifteen quid, and then run out of petrol on the slip road to the M6. Brilliant! And this was the man she had left him for, the Inspector Clouseau of the West Midlands underworld.

Still, he had to admit she had been wonderful in bed. That tongue of hers would win the Olympics if they ever introduced it as a sport. He sighed. So it went. There were plenty more tongues out there.

And come to think of it, the hill ahead looked just like a breast. That was the trouble with the SAS: the old winged dagger was certainly a come-on in the pubs around Hereford, but wearing it seemed to involve long stretches of time in places like this where women were particularly thin on the ground. According to one of the sailors on the old 'Herpes', the members of

Scott's Antarctic expedition were away from women so long that they had started sleeping with penguins. 'Not right away, of course,' the sailor had said, 'and only heavy petting to begin with. They just kind of slipped into the habit.'

Stanley had not believed a word of it, of course. But he could understand that sort of desperation, he really could.

About 30 yards behind him, Mozza was snatching glimpses at the night sky between watching the men ahead and the empty country on the patrol's southern flank. This was undoubtedly the clearest night since his arrival in the South Atlantic, but the book he had brought all the way from England was back on the *Hermes*, and he was having trouble matching up his memory with the constellations filling the heavens above him.

Not that he supposed it mattered which was which. Though he had always liked the idea of the constellations, and as a kid often wondered who had first connected the dots and made them all up. After all, the stars in Orion did not actually suggest a hunter; it was possible to connect them up that way, that was all. In reality it was chaos, which was just as wonderful, and maybe even more so.

He glanced round to check that Hedge was still in sight behind him, then turned his eyes right again. It was funny: he had been really nervous in the helicopter, but now they were down on the ground and alone and in real danger he felt fine. He did not even feel homesick any more, though maybe he would once they got back to the ship.

Did the others feel like that, he wondered. Both

Hedge and Stanley had several more years than his twenty-three, and of course the PC was almost middle-aged. It was not just the years, either: sometimes he felt like a real innocent in their company, although there was no real reason why he should. There were not many tougher places to grow up than Manchester's Hulme estates, so he knew how to use the two great weapons of self-defence: fists and a sense of humour, and not necessarily in that order.

Sex was another matter. Stanley and Hedge hardly ever seemed to talk about anything else, but Mozza could not help wondering whether they actually enjoyed the act as much as the endless anticipation. According to Stanley there was only one difference between sex and an SAS mission – the briefing and debriefing came in a different order. And that was funny, and Mozza had laughed as hard as the rest of them, but it had nothing to do with real life or real people. When he was with Lynsey ... well, it was magical. It was not a joke. And he would not dream of making it into one.

Maybe he was just lucky, he thought. He had often thought it. Maybe most people would not have wanted to grow up in Hulme but he would not have changed places with anyone. He supposed his family was poor by British standards, but only when it came to things, and even then, well, they had always had a TV. He had three sisters and two brothers, which had felt a bit too much at times, but they all got on, and being a bit cramped in the flat was probably what had started off the family tradition of spending each Sunday out in the country. That and the fact that his dad's job with British Rail got them a good discount on rail tickets.

And it had made him self-sufficient. It seemed strange maybe, but Mozza had thought a lot about this, about his ability to be alone in a crowd, to 'make his own space' as Lynsey put it, and he reckoned it was just something you had to learn as part of a big family in a small flat.

He thought about Lynsey. She was two years older than him, and had a kid already from her marriage to Jake. Mozza did not mind that at all: Hannah was a lovely kid and she seemed to like him. Jake had disappeared into thin air about two years ago, so it was hardly as if he was competing with anyone for the father role. And Lynsey ... well, she was just perfect. She was kind, she was bright, she was gorgeous. And, after almost three months of intermittent courtship, she seemed to love him. He was a lucky man, all right.

The fourth man in the patrol was feeling rather less fortunate. Hedge – a nickname grounded in both his surname and the unruly tangle of wiry hair which graced his scalp – was suffering from periodic stomach cramps, and wondering what he had done to deserve them. Eaten navy food, probably. He hoped they were a passing phenomenon, so to speak, because in thirty hours or so they would all be sharing a small hide, and if he was still farting like this the others would probably insist on him giving himself up to the Argies.

He grinned in the dark and turned a full circle, peering into the gloom. There was nothing out there but wet grass and sheep, he thought. Life in the fast lane.

Maybe his stomach was feeling better. Maybe it

was just nerves. Hedge had seen enough action in Northern Ireland not to feel like a combat virgin, but he supposed being behind enemy lines was a reasonable enough place to feel nervous no matter how often you visited. Crossmaglen was bad enough, although you knew help was in calling distance. But this felt like being out on a limb.

People said the Argies would be poor soldiers, but he had seen their football team play, and *they* took no fucking prisoners, so fuck only knew how their Army would behave. Hedge was not keen to find out, not just yet. A day or so of acclimatization, that was what he needed, and a digestive system more at peace with itself. *Then* they could start throwing the bastards his way.

As often at times like this, he thought about his father, killed in a steelworks accident when Hedge was only fourteen. Although he knew it was stupid, he always wished his father could see him in this sort of situation, all grown up, doing something necessary and doing it well. His father had been a Labour man through and through, but he had also been a real patriot, and Hedge knew he would have felt really proud of England these last few weeks. And of his son.

What his father would have felt about an army career, Hedge was less sure, though from what he could remember getting out of the house and away from his wife and two daughters had been one of his dad's main aims in life. Joining the army had achieved a similar result for Hedge, and once he was in he had quickly found more positive reasons for staying a soldier. There had always been new challenges to drive him forward, right up to the ultimate goal of making it into the SAS. It had been a close-run thing on the Brecon Beacons – he had damn near given up – but the voice inside his head whispering 'I'll be so proud of you' had somehow pulled him through.

They marched on through the night, making frequent short stops to check their position and a couple of long ones to evade what turned out to be imaginary enemy patrols. About two hours before dawn Brookes decided it was time to dig in for the day. They had covered over two-thirds of the distance required, but the final quarter would bring them close to known enemy positions and called for a much more cautious approach. There was certainly no chance of completing the journey that night.

As it was, they were almost too tired to dig out the lying-up positions for use through the coming day. Brookes chose the western slope of a gentle ridge for their camp, and each man had the duty of digging out a large enough 'scrape' for himself, and making a roof for it with wire and turf. The excavated earth, which would be clearly visible to Argentinian pilots, then had to be removed from sight. Fortunately, a shallow stream ran down beyond the next ridge, and the soil could simply be spread along its banks.

As the first hint of dawn began to appear in the eastern sky all four of them were entrenched under their own camouflage roof, too tired to worry about the damp seeping out through the earthen floor of the scrapes. Brookes's last thought was 'so far, so good', while Hedge was thinking about the explosive properties of methane and Stanley was remembering his first time with Sharon.

Mozza was using the patrol's telescope through a

hole in his netting to watch the stars fade away in the east, and wondering how the hell he was going to stay awake for his two-hour watch.

Bryan Weighell, or 'Wheelie' as he had been known in younger days, briskly made his way through the various checkpoints separating the car park from his destination in the bowels of Whitehall. It was a sharp spring Sunday, sunny but far from warm, and he was still wondering what the hell he was needed for. It could not be anything to do with the teams inserted into East and West Falkland the previous night; all that was being handled through the usual channels. Starting in the ladies' lavatory aboard *Resource*, he reminded himself with a grin. He could still imagine Mike Phillips's face when the Navy told him that this was the SAS's floating HQ for the duration.

He wished he was there in person. They also serve who sit around and drink Guinness, he told himself. But it did not feel the same, not at a time like this.

In Conference Room B only one empty seat remained. The Prime Minister, whom rumour claimed had been known to punish unpunctuality with exile to one of the caring ministries, actually greeted him with a smile. What does she want, Weighell wondered.

'Lieutenant-Colonel Weighell, Officer Commanding 22 SAS Regiment,' she introduced him.

He acknowledged the various nods and half-smiles.

'Perhaps I should go round the table,' the PM decided. 'Cecil Matheson,' she began, smiling at the tall, patrician-looking individual on her left, 'Deputy Head of the Foreign Office and Chairman of the Joint Intelligence Committee.' On his left was Reginald Copley, a thin, grey-haired man who was apparently head of the Foreign Office's Latin American Desk. Last in line was the moustached Air Marshal Sir George Railton, Deputy Chief of the Defence Staff.

At the end of the table an arrogant-looking young man in a plain dark suit represented MI6. His name, hard though Weighell found it to credit, was Anthony Sharp. On the PM's right, between her and Weighell, sat Brigadier Mark Harringham, representing Fleet HQ at Northwood, and the imposing bulk of Dennis Eckersley, the Number 2 at the Ministry of Defence.

Seven men and one woman, Weighell thought. Seven professionals and one politician. Seven smelling of Old Spice and one of gardenia. He remembered a particularly disgusting joke about Snow White and her favourite Seven-Up. He told himself to snap out of it.

'We have a problem,' the PM began. 'Cecil?'

Matheson recounted the gist of his telephone conversation with the American State Department the previous evening, and though he made no overt criticism of the American decision to deny the Task Force AWACS assistance, he left little doubt in the minds of his audience what he thought of it.

The Prime Minister's stony face suggested to Weighell that she shared Matheson's irritation but had had enough time to suppress her natural instinct to express it. Maybe there was an inflatable model of Reagan hidden away somewhere in Number 10, on which she launched occasional assaults with her handbag.

'Do you have comments, Brigadier?' she asked Harringham.

'It's not good news,' he said mildly. 'I don't want to sound alarmist, but the AWACS were our last chance of going into action with even half-decent air protection . . .'

'Perhaps you could spell out the details, Brigadier,' the PM suggested. 'I doubt everyone here is fully aware of them.'

'Certainly. But there's nothing complex involved. Our ships in the South Atlantic are simply under-protected, particularly against the Super Etendards and their Exocet missiles. The Sea Dart missile systems on the Type 42 destroyers have no defensive efficacy against low-level attack. The Sea Wolf system, which does, is only mounted on the two Type 22 frigates. For air defence we have only the Sea Harriers, and there are pitifully few of them. In fact, there are only thirty-two Harrier airframes in existence. Once they're gone . . .'

'What about radar?' the MI6 man asked.

'Shipborne radar is notoriously ineffective in heavy seas,' Harringham said, 'and we have no airborne radar. This is not,' he added with an air of understate-ment, 'the war we were designed to fight. But . . .'

'Thank you, Brigadier,' the PM interjected. 'Very well, gentlemen. This is the problem we are here to discuss. There appears no way in which the Task Force can be certain of protecting itself, and I need hardly spell out the consequences if, say, one of the carriers were to be put out of action. In such an instance I don't think we could countenance the recapture of the islands. We would have no choice but to return with our tails between our legs. Another Suez, gentlemen. Britain would be a laughing-stock.' She glared at the company, as if daring them to imagine such an outcome.

'But,' she continued, 'there are other options. Mr

Sharp, would you like to give us an update on the intelligence situation within Argentina?'

Sharp almost preened himself, Weighell thought sourly. He had never had much time for intelligence types. As one of his friends had memorably put it: these were the boys at public school who tried to wank in silence.

'We now have an agent in place,' Sharp was saying. 'And we're expecting some useful information about the location of particular units, and about the sort of stuff the Argies are airlifting into Port Stanley.' He surveyed the table in triumph.

The PM ignored him. 'Is that it?' she asked Matheson. 'We have one man in Argentina?'

Our man in Argentina, Weighell thought irreverently, and, as it turned out, wrongly.

'It's a woman,' Matheson said coldly. 'I need hardly remind everyone here,' he went on, 'that the budget for what is called "humint" – human intelligence – has been cut to the bone in recent years, with most of the available resources going to the procurement of "sigint" – signals intelligence, of course – either from GCHQ or the Americans. It's an unfortunate fact of life, but like the Navy' – he glanced across at Harringham – 'the Intelligence Services have been organized with Europe in mind, not South America.'

The PM looked less than mollified. Weighell found himself idly wondering who would come out of this particular imbroglio with more egg on their faces: the Foreign Office, the Navy or the Intelligence Services.

'As a matter of interest,' the Latin American Desk man was asking, 'where is this agent "in place"?'

Sharp hesitated, caught the look on the PM's face,

and blurted out: 'Rio Gallegos – it's one of the two airbases closest to the Falklands . . .'

'But unfortunately not, as we had thought, the one with the Super Etendards,' Matheson admitted. 'It seems they are based at Rio Grande on Tierra del Fuego.' He reached into his briefcase, extracted a clear plastic folder full of photocopies of a map, and passed them round.

Weighell examined it with interest. He had spent so much time poring over maps of the Falklands that the mainland 400 miles to the west had more or less escaped his attention.

'Brigadier,' the PM asked, 'I take it that the destruction of these airfields and the planes based there would drastically reduce the vulnerability of the Task Force?'

'Of course.'

'Does the Air Force have the capacity, Air Marshal?'

'I would like to say yes, Prime Minister, but frankly I doubt it.' He looked round the table. 'Most of you probably haven't heard the news, but early this morning one plane dropped a stick of bombs on the runway at Port Stanley . . .'

There were murmurs of appreciation all round the table.

'It was an epic flight,' Railton conceded, 'and the psychological impact on the occupying force may have been worth something, but I'm afraid the military efficacy of the operation was rather more doubtful. Only one bomb actually hit the runway, and bear in mind that Port Stanley, unlike the Argentine bases, is known territory. Even more to the point, the Vulcan needed seventeen in-flight refuellings *en route*. I doubt if we could send more than one plane at a time against these two mainland bases. They'd be sitting ducks.'

'Thank you, Air Marshal,' the PM said coolly. On her left, Weighell noticed, Matheson was having a hard job concealing his relief. But the Foreign Office man had been conned, Weighell decided: the PM could not have been expecting anything else from Railton. Where was all this leading?

'One question,' the Latin American Desk man said. 'Since the Super Etendards and Exocets pose the main threat, could we not just move our agent in Rio Gallegos to Rio Grande and set up some sort of communication link between her and the fleet?'

It was an intelligent question, Weighell thought.

'It might be possible,' Sharp agreed, 'but it would certainly place the agent at risk. She has a good cover where she is, and promises to provide invaluable intelligence on the airlift. Agents are always more vulnerable when moved, and there would be the extra risk involved in getting the radio to her.'

Weighell suddenly knew where it was all leading, and why he was there.

As if on cue, the PM turned her beady gaze in his direction. 'Lieutenant-Colonel Weighell, how would the SAS like to have a crack at these airfields?'

Weighell noticed Matheson's eyes roll in horror, and resisted the temptation to let her steamroller right over him. 'If it's a feasible option,' he said, 'then of course we'd like nothing better.'

'Does it look like one?' she persisted.

Weighell imagined he was being given a major insight into how cabinet government worked in the modern age. 'I'm sorry, Prime Minister,' he forced himself to say, 'but I'd need a lot more data than I have now, not to mention a clearer idea of the task required. Are we talking about observation or military action here?'

'Either or both,' she said decisively.

'Prime Minister . . .' Matheson interjected.

'Hold on a moment, Cecil,' she said, patting him on the arm in as patronizing a manner as Weighell could remember witnessing, 'let's find out what we're capable of before you start explaining why we shouldn't risk it.' She turned a smile on Weighell.

You could rob a bank with a smile like that, Weighell thought. 'We're talking about two totally different missions,' he said. 'An attack on either airfield would require up to a squadron of men – around sixty that is – inserted from the air at night. Probably a high-altitude low-opening parachute drop. From a C-130.' He paused, gathering his thoughts. 'That in itself would not present any great problems, unless of course they were dropped into the middle of an Argentinian military base we knew nothing about. But there are always unknown hazards – the mechanics of insertion are simple enough.' As the bishop said to the actress, he thought to himself.

'The obvious problem,' he continued, 'would come with the extraction. Particularly if we're planning to hit two bases simultaneously. I don't see any way of getting two squadrons out, by air or sea. You'd need either every submarine in the fleet or, at that sort of range, every helicopter. And I presume the thought of 120 SAS men crashing across the border into Chile is hardly desirable, even assuming they could get to it . . .'

'God forbid,' Matheson muttered.

'What if the C-130 drops the troops and they secure

the airfields?' the PM asked. 'Surely then the planes could land and take the troops off?'

'It's theoretically possible,' replied Weighell. He had to admit a part of him was thrilled by the idea. The rest of him urged caution, however. 'For such an operation to be anything more than a suicide mission,' he went on, 'we'd have to know a hell of a lot more about the airbases in question.'

'Prime Minister,' Matheson interjected again, and this time she let him have his say. 'Such action . . .' he began, before pausing, apparently lost for words.

'Such action would have Washington in uproar,' she said. 'I know. Obviously we have no desire to upset the United States. Nor would it serve us well to do so, at least in the long run. But we have to balance such concerns against the well-being of the Task Force. Whether we like it or not, Britain's standing in the world is in their hands, gentlemen. I am not prepared to risk defeat merely for the sake of not offending a few American politicians. So please, Lieutenant-Colonel, I would like some contingency planning done. Just in case.'

'Very well, Ma'am.'

'Now, for the second possibility you mentioned – observation.' The basilisk stare transfixed him one more.

Here at least, Weighell felt on much safer ground. What the four-man patrols were already doing on East and West Falkland could just as easily be done on the mainland. Or almost. 'We could put two four-man teams down close to the two airbases,' he said, 'probably by Sea King helicopter, though I'd have to check the range-to-weight ratios. I would guess it would have to be a one-way trip. The terrain hardly lends itself to staying unseen, but that's just as true of the Falklands, and we already have patrols ashore on both islands.'

'If the trip in was one-way,' Matheson observed, 'you still have the problem of how to get the men out again.'

'True,' Weighell conceded. 'But eight men is a very different proposition to 120. One or two submarines could probably take them off. At worst, as few men as that could seek asylum in Chile without causing a major row.'

'My objections remain the same,' Matheson said. 'Of course I agree with you, Prime Minister, that we may have to take diplomatic risks for the sake of a military victory. Or at least to avoid a military humiliation. But I cannot see that the military situation at present is such as to justify this sort of operation.'

'Brigadier?' the PM asked Harringham.

'I cannot comment on the diplomatic issue, Prime Minister. Any improvement in the fleet's AEW capability would obviously be beneficial, but I am yet to be convinced that the enemy air force poses much more than a theoretical threat to the Task Force.'

'Dennis?' she asked.

'I would have to agree with the Brigadier,' Eckersley said. It was the first time Weighell could remember him speaking.

'Very well,' the PM said. 'I cannot say I feel entirely happy about it, but for the moment we shall shelve the idea of mounting mainland operations.' She paused. 'However,' she continued, turning to Weighell, 'I want detailed contingency plans prepared for those operations we have discussed. And I expect' – this time

Harringham was her target – 'the SAS to receive the full cooperation of the fleet in this matter. If and when something happens to tip the balance – if the threat to the Task Force does become more than theoretical – then I shall expect both a different consensus of opinion and the possibility of immediate action.' She surveyed those around the table – making sure she remembered who had been present, Weighell decided – flashed one wide smile at them all, rose from her chair and swept out through the door.

Around the table there were several heartfelt sighs of relief. Weighell found himself wondering whether sending the Junta a video of the meeting might not encourage an early surrender.

That same Sunday Isabel Fuentes drove out of Rio Gallegos in the black Renault 5 and headed south across the almost undulating steppe towards the Chilean border some 40 miles away. There was almost no traffic on the road: in the first 10 miles she encountered two trucks, one bus and about a dozen cars.

It was one of those late autumn days she remembered from childhood, clear but cold enough to make you think of the winter to come. On the seat beside her she had a vacuum flask full of coffee and a couple of spicy *empanadas* wrapped in a paper bag. Under the seat, sealed in a plastic bag, were the facts she had so far managed to accumulate concerning the military situation at the Rio Gallegos airbase. There were not many of them, but she had had only two meetings with her sad-eyed pilot, and all he had wanted to talk about was the girlfriend he had left behind in the north.

Which she supposed was both good news and bad

news. She had been prepared to sleep with him, at least on that first evening with the alcohol running through her blood, but she had also known that to do so would have marked a new low, a new stage in what felt almost like a self-imposed programme of dehumanization. On the negative side, her new status as a friend and confidante, though easier to live with, did not promise quite the same degree of mutual intimacy or trust. She had the feeling she could get him into bed with her, but was far from sure that her state of mind would survive such a level of pretence.

She was approaching the bridge she had chosen for the dead-letter drop. It was one of about ten such bridges in a three-mile stretch two-thirds of the way to the border. All of them were simple girder affairs, slung across dried-up streams. Presumably when the snow melted in the distant Andes they sent a swift current down to the Magellan Straits a few miles to the south.

The bridge Isabel had chosen had nothing to recommend it but the faded letters ERP, which someone had painted in fiery red a decade before.

Just beyond the bridge, she stopped the car, pulling over onto the dry gravel of the steppe, reached over for her vacuum flask and at the same time conveyed the plastic bag from its place under the seat to its new hiding place, stuck into her belt beneath the thick sweater.

She got out of the car, poured herself a cup of coffee and surveyed the road. It was empty for as far as she could see, which was at least a mile in each direction. She clambered down into the streambed, lifted out the two rocks she had previously chosen, and wedged the bag into the space. Then she replaced them, covering one corner of plastic with gravel.

The bag would not be found by anyone who was not looking for it. As a last safeguard she took the small plastic bottle out of her pocket and emptied its contents onto the dry earth beneath the bridge. After all, where else would a woman stop to urinate on such a road?

'You're really getting into the spirit of things,' she told herself wryly.

After sleeping in shifts through the daylight hours, Brookes's patrol set out once more, this time in a cross between drizzle and fog, to complete their journey. They were only a few miles from the coast of Falkland Sound now, and the signs of civilization, if sheep farming qualified as such, were thicker on the ground.

So too was evidence of the occupation. On one frequently travelled piece of ground – 'track' seemed too grand a word, 'road' a ludicrous exaggeration – signs of wheeled traffic had recently been overlaid by the marks of a tracked vehicle, presumably military. Halting for a moment's rest at a gate in a wire fence, Mozza bent down to check his bootlaces and discovered a discarded cigarette end of decidedly alien appearance.

'At least it proves we're on the right island,' Hedge whispered above the wind. 'You're a regular little Sherlock Holmes, you are.'

It also proved that the Argentinians were in the habit of passing in this direction, which increased the patrol's caution and slowed their progress still further. But they found no other sign of the enemy before reaching their destination on a hill a mile and a half north of Port Howard. They thought they could detect the faintest of lights where the settlement should be, but, with the rain not so much falling as hanging like a sheet of mist, it was impossible to be certain.

There was still about three hours until dawn, and Brookes allowed himself the luxury of a fifteen-minute exploration of the immediate area. In such conditions, he decided, it was almost impossible to pick out the best site for their hide with any certainty, and he was reluctant to undertake major earthworks twice. It was not a matter of the effort involved, but the virtual doubling of the chances that their interference with nature's handiwork would be spotted from the air. He told the men as much. 'We'll have to spent another day in scrapes,' he said. 'Behind this ridge line, I think,' he added, looking upwards. 'As far above the water-table as we can manage without unduly advertising our presence.'

'I think we'll need stilts to get above this water-table,' Stanley observed.

A few minutes later, in a sheltered hollow on the northern slope, they had found what Hedge pronounced to be 'the shallow end of the pool'.

'Why is it we're always getting into scrapes?' Stanley wondered out loud as they started digging.

3

Shortly before ten a.m. on Tuesday 4 April 1982, in the operations room of the Type 42 destroyer *Sheffield*, a blip appeared on the radar screen. Whatever it was seemed headed their way, and fast. Less than three minutes later, on the ship's bridge, the officer of the watch and the ship's Lynx helicopter pilot made visual identification. 'My God, it's a missile,' they exclaimed simultaneously.

A few seconds later the Exocet ripped through the ship's side, starting fires that proved impossible to control, causing the deaths of twenty-one men, and ultimately dooming the vessel to a South Atlantic grave. For the Task Force as a whole, the war had suddenly become real.

News of the catastrophe reached the British people seven hours later, at nine p.m. Greenwich Mean Time. Even the Ministry of Defence spokesman, who always looked and sounded as if he had been preserved in a cryogenic chamber since 1945, could not flatten the emotional charge of such news.

All those refrains of 'Britannia rules the waves' which had accompanied the Task Force's departure now came back to haunt the cheerleaders. Plainly the Royal Navy was in less than complete control of this particular stretch of ocean. The mindless glorification of slaughter which had accompanied the sinking of the *General Belgrano* two days earlier took on an even hollower ring. Were tabloid typesetters in Buenos Aires now arranging the Spanish equivalent of 'Gotcha!' for the next morning's front page?

More insidious still, for the first time the dread possibility of failure seemed to hover in the British air.

James Docherty watched the announcement on a pub TV somewhere in the middle of Glasgow, and felt for a few minutes as if someone had thrown a bucket of cold water over him. When it was over, when the news had been given, the analysis offered – all the usual crap – Docherty sat at the bar, beer and chaser barely touched, head in hands.

For four weeks now he had been floating in a drunken ocean of self-pity, anger and hopelessness. He was 'heading on down' he had told any stranger who cared to listen, 'just like the Task Force', floating further and further away from all those problems which could not be resolved by the heady mixture of modern technology and judicious violence.

Now, three hours into another magical mystery tour of Glasgow's bars, he took the destruction of the *Sheffield* very personally. That fucking Exocet had hit him too, he realized, ridiculous as it seemed. But it wouldn't sink him, oh no. In fact, it would wake him up. Or something.

He gingerly eased himself off the stool, wondering if his body had been as sobered by the news as his mind. It had not, but after an endless piss, his head leaning against the tiled wall of the Gents, he felt ready to face the night.

A chill breeze was blowing down Sauchiehall Street

from the east. Docherty leant up against a shop window and let the cold blast revive him.

After the death of his father he had asked for extended compassionate leave. They did not want him for the war, so what was the point of hanging out in Hereford listening to all the others bellyaching? In any case, he was not at all sure he had any desire to go back. And if the bosses could see him now, he thought, the feeling would be mutual. A faint grin flickered across his unshaven face, the first for a while.

Two men walked past, talking about the *Sheffield*, and brought it all back. Enough, Docherty told himself. This is as far down as you're going. Anything more would be fucking self-indulgence. In fact it already was.

'Who knows?', he asked himself out loud, as he walked back towards the dump he had been staying in, 'if things get bad down there, then maybe they'll need more of us.' It was not exactly likely, but if the call did come he wanted to be in some state to receive it.

Four hundred miles to the south the Prime Minister arrived back at Number 10 from the House of Commons. In the chamber she had sat there looking stunned as John Nott announced the ship's loss, but earlier that day, in the relative privacy of Number 10, tears had been more in evidence. Now she was entering the third phase of her reaction – anger.

'I want someone from Northwood – preferably Harringham – and Cecil Matheson,' she told her private secretary.

'You have the full Cabinet in the morning, Prime Minister.'

'I'm aware of that, Richard. I want Harringham and Matheson here now.' She started up the stairs, throwing 'please tell me when they arrive' back over her shoulder.

Matheson was still working at the Foreign Office, but Brigadier Harringham had to be pulled out of his bath and shuttled across from Northwood by helicopter. By the time of his arrival he had conquered his irritation – he could guess what kind of a day the PM had endured.

Once the three of them were gathered around one end of the huge Cabinet table she lost no time in coming to the point. 'Two days ago, Brigadier, you said, and I quote, that you were "yet to be convinced that the enemy air force poses much more than a theoretical threat to the Task Force". I take it the events of the day have changed your mind?'

'Sadly, yes,' Harringham said quietly.

'If it had been one of the carriers instead of the *Sheffield* we would now be in severe difficulties, would we not?'

'Yes.'

'Prime Minister,' Matheson interjected, 'obviously I do not want to minimize the potential dangers here, but I feel I must point out that the best intelligence we have suggests that the enemy only possesses five more of these missiles, and has next to no hope of procuring any more.'

She looked at him coldly. 'As you well know, Cecil,' she said with barely controlled hostility, 'our so-called "best intelligence" couldn't even forecast the invasion. You heard that chinless idiot the other day – we have one agent in Argentina, and even she's in the wrong place! The intelligence you're talking about is just sophisticated guesswork, and it isn't half-sophisticated enough for me to risk this whole venture on. I want some people in there, on the ground, counting the damn things. Or at the very least providing some sort of early warning for the fleet.'

Matheson could not ever remember seeing her so incensed, and for the first and only time in his life he could see the truth of the expression 'you're beautiful when you're angry'. He decided that resistance at this point would just increase her momentum. 'I agree that the new situation warrants the dispatch of one or two reconnaissance teams,' he said.

'Good,' the PM replied, thumping the walnut tabletop with the flat of her hand. 'So I can count on both of you to back me in this regard if it should come before the War Cabinet.'

'Yes, Prime Minister,' they said in relative unison, Harringham offering a sleepy counterpoint to Matheson's plaintive lead.

As the two men emerged into Downing Street, Big Ben was striking midnight. A mile to the east, in the Aldwych studios of the BBC World Service, a newsreader was announcing the loss of the *Sheffield*. Ten thousand miles away to the south, and three time zones away to the west, Mozza was lying in the patrol hide above Port Howard, listening in through headphones to London's plummy tones.

He could hardly believe it, and listened all the way through the news broadcast just to make sure he had got it right. Stanley and Brookes were out on a recce, but Hedge was snoring gently in another arm of the cross-shaped hide, and Mozza decided to wake him. This was the sort of news he had to share.

Hedge couldn't believe it either. Or at least did not want to. 'It was actually *sunk* – you're sure?' he said, his voice strained by the need to remain in a whisper.

'No, not sunk,' Mozza whispered back. 'They didn't say that. But it was hit by a missile, and everyone was taken off. The ship was burning. So maybe it has sunk by now. They didn't say.'

'Christ!' Hedge muttered. He could think of nothing more appropriate to say. Both of them lay there, looking up at their turf and wire ceiling, thinking the same thing: if the ships of the Task Force were being sunk, then how the hell were they going to get back home?

Rio Gallegos, 400 miles to the west, was awash with sky blue and white flags. As she walked across the central plaza to the Rakosi Bar, Isabel found herself in a swirl of deliriously happy people. The *General Belgrano* was forgotten, or at the very least avenged. It was as if all the doubts the Argentinians had silently nursed within their hearts through the weeks of wondering and waiting had finally and explosively been laid to rest. Let the English ships come! Our Air Force will send them to the bottom of the sea, each and every one of them!

Isabel could imagine the reaction in Britain to the news: there would be a sort of stunned disbelief. One of their ships had been *sunk*, and by *foreigners*! She found herself, not for the first time, feeling contempt for everyone involved in the whole deadly farce – including, she had to admit, herself.

The atmosphere in the Rakosi mirrored that in the main square, only here the wine was offering additional lubrication to the festivities. She was greeted like an old and valued customer – something she was swiftly becoming – and invited to join in the toasts to the Air Force, the Navy, General Galtieri, Admiral Anaya, Mario Kempes, even Eva Perón.

She thought it unlikely that Raul would turn up that night – he was probably celebrating with his comrades out at the airbase – but resisted the temptation to return to her hotel just in case. Three glasses of wine worked their magic, and she was both celebrating with the best of them and watching herself from some hidden vantage point with barely restrained disgust.

Raul's arrival probably saved her from making a fool of herself, though how dangerous a fool she would luckily never know. He seemed to have had more than a few drinks himself, and insisted on taking her for a walk through the riverside park. His arm grew tighter around her shoulder, and when they turned at the end of the promenade to retrace their steps he pulled her to him and kissed her passionately, his beery breath almost turning her stomach, his right hand pressing at her left nipple as if it was a doorbell.

'Raul, no,' she said without thinking, and tried to disengage herself. She felt both nauseous and suddenly sober.

He leaned down to kiss her bare neck.

'Think about your Mariella,' she said softly.

'Ah, Mariella!' he said dramatically, and dropped his head on her shoulder. To her surprise he started shaking.

For a few minutes Isabel gently stroked his head as he clung to her. 'Come, let us sit down,' she said eventually.

He allowed himself to be led to one of the wrought-iron seats overlooking the darkened estuary.

'Tell me about it,' she said.

He gave her a half-laugh, half-sob, then wiped the tears away from his face with an angry sweep of the back of his hand. 'How can I tell you?' he asked. 'How can I tell anyone? You will just think I am a coward. I . . .' He looked at her imploringly. 'One of us sinks an English ship, and suddenly we are all heroes, but . . . we are . . . today Juan Morales was lost – I didn't really know him, but every day one of us is killed, every day . . .' He grabbed her arm. 'I am so afraid I will never see Mariella again,' he said.

'You will,' she replied. What else could she say?

Raul just shook his head. 'Another one of us dies and we are all celebrating because of the English ship,' he said. 'It's not just me,' he added, almost belligerently. 'Everyone is afraid.'

'Are the English so powerful?' she asked.

'No, it is we who are weak. We have so few missiles, and hardly any spares if the planes are damaged. There are so *few* of us. And the Army is sending boys to the Malvinas – I see them lining up to take the flight across each night and they are *boys*. We have experienced soldiers. Why are they not being sent to fight?'

'I don't know,' Isabel said, though she could make a good guess. They would be needed to protect the Junta from the people if and when it all went wrong.

The day after the sinking of the *Sheffield* dawned clear and cold, as if trying to make up for the gloom it had engendered in the SAS hides scattered across the two main islands. For the first time since their arrival eighty hours before, Brookes's patrol had a clear view of the landscape around them, and in particular the small settlement of Port Howard below. Similarly, this would be the enemy's first chance to see them.

Despite this threat, Mozza found himself more taken by the landscape than the apparently sleeping enemy garrison in the settlement below. The two night marches across endless swathes of peat, rock flats and wet tussock grass, had conjured up a rather boring picture of the islands, which the days of mist and fog had only served to reinforce. But here were the silver-blue waters of Falkland Sound beneath a pure blue sky, and the distant hills of East Falkland rising in subtle shades of green and brown between them. A flock of birds was drawing graceful patterns in the air above the water, and the randomly scattered handful of buildings which made up Port Howard seemed supremely insignificant, no match at all for the vastness which surrounded them.

It was weird, Mozza thought. This was what the war was all about, yet it seemed much further away here than it did among the Task Force. He reluctantly tore himself away from such thoughts, and back to the job in hand, jiggling the veil into position so as to prevent any tell-tale reflection, rearranging his legs within the cramped hide, and aiming the telescope at the settlement below.

It was strung out between the foot of the hill and a narrow inlet, which was itself separated from the Sound proper by a long peninsular no more than 200 yards wide. A couple of small boats were bobbing at anchor in the inlet, but there was nothing bigger – no fishing vessels and no enemy naval craft.

The settlement seemed to boast five actual houses, but there were three times as many buildings, including two large corrugated sheds, which Mozza assumed were normally used at some stage of the process whereby sheep were turned into either lamb chops, pullovers or both. To the south of these, and partly obscured by them, an acre or two of almost flat meadow had been adopted as a camp-site by the invaders.

Mozza counted the tents – there were just over 200. Reckoning four men to a tent, and taking into account that the officers had probably installed themselves in the available buildings, he thought the garrison must number about 1000 men. They had no artillery as far as he could see, and only two vehicles were visible: one jeep and a half-track armoured personnel carrier – probably the one whose trail they had come across on their second night's march.

He wrote down his observations, and was about to record the lack of air support when the drone of a distant helicopter insinuated its way into his consciousness. He watched it draw a lazy arc across the Sound, and then descend gingerly onto an area which had obviously been cleared with that purpose in mind, the grass waving wildly in the rotor's wind. Two figures climbed out, both in uniform. One was a lieutenant, the other, to Mozza's surprise, a general. They walked out from under the still swirling blades and paused, as if uncertain where to go next. Then they moved on across the grass towards the nearest clump of buildings.

On the near side of these, hidden from the new

arrivals, another couple of officers were hurrying in their direction. One was still apparently fastening his trousers.

'Morning crap took longer than expected,' Mozza murmured to himself. He looked at his watch. It was almost seven – time to wake Stanley. He wrote down the time of the arrival, the type of helicopter – a Huey UHIH – and the ranks of both the visiting officers and their reception committee. He took one more look through the telescope, and found the pilot standing up against his machine, having a piss. After a vigorous shake the Argentinian turned round and strolled a few yards away across the meadow, lighting up a cigarette and gazing around at the scenery with an obvious air of self-satisfaction.

'What's he thinking about?' Mozza muttered to himself. The wife back home? The wonders of nature? Or was the Argie a city boy, wondering what the fuck he was doing in the middle of nowhere? At that moment, as if he sensed the watching eyes, the man looked up towards the distant OP, stared for a moment, then turned away, taking another drag on his cigarette.

Mozza put down the telescope and used his unaided eyes for a quick panoramic sweep of the hillside. The four of them had decided, after a long, whispered discussion on their third night ashore, to plant themselves in this immense stretch of bare slope precisely because it gave them such a field of vision. In daylight at least there was no chance of their being surprised, and the freedom to talk without fear of being overheard was a priceless asset when it came to retaining one's sanity.

The downside of such an exposed OP was the lack

of any cover, or any other lines in the landscape which might draw the eye away from signs which the patrol had inadvertently left on the 'surface'. They had turned themselves into hostages of their own camouflaging skills, and only time would tell if they had occasioned some slight change in texture or colour only visible from the air.

At night, of course, none of the above applied. They were safe from the air, but the risk of an enemy patrol passing nearby was ever-present, so that strict silence had to be maintained at all times.

So far the only loud and inadvertent sound they had made was an enormous snort from the sleeping Hedge. That had been two nights before, and the rain had either covered the noise or deterred the Argentinians from venturing out on patrol. According to Stanley, the wind had been blowing the wrong way for the snort to be heard on the mainland 400 miles away.

Mozza remembered this as he worked his way back through the cramped space towards the gently snoring trooper. In response to his shake the ginger-haired Brummie's eyes opened with a start, only to wearily close once more when they saw who it was.

'Where's the luscious Conchita?' Stanley murmured.

'Which luscious Conchita is that?' Mozza asked.

'The one in my dream,' Stanley said sleepily. 'You're too young to hear the details. All I can say is that she brought her own Angels' Delight.'

It was raining in Hereford. It seemed to Lieutenant-Colonel Bryan Weighell to have been raining all day, the dark-grey skies adding their sombre voice to the general depression which the previous day's news had spread across the Stirling Lines HQ of 22 SAS Regiment. Even his tea was cold. He pressed his intercom to demand a fresh cup, and was informed that Major Neil Strachan had just arrived to see him. 'Make that two teas then,' he said. 'And a couple of rock cakes,' he added.

The red-haired, blue-eyed Neil Strachan came through the door with a smile on his face and a briefcase in one freckled hand. 'Rock cakes,' he echoed, in an accent straight out of the Great Glen. 'We *are* taking risks today.'

'I hope you've come to cheer me up,' Weighell observed.

Strachan sat down. 'That depends on what you find cheering. I've got the preliminary report you asked for. You've got a general map, I take it?'

Weighell lifted up *The Times Atlas* which had been leaning against one end of his desk, placed it between them and opened it where he had left the bookmark: Plate 121 – Argentina, Chile, Uruguay.

'That'll do for the wider picture,' Strachan said. He pulled a couple of smaller maps out of his briefcase. 'You wouldn't believe how hard it was to find more detailed maps. This one' – he was opening a 1:1,000,000 map of Argentina's Santa Cruz province – 'comes from the Bodleian Library, and I got this one' – it was a 1:500,000 map of Tierra del Fuego – 'from an outdoor activities bookshop in Covent Garden.'

'What are the Task Force using?' Weighell wondered out loud.

'God only knows. Probably old school atlases. Anyway . . .'

He was interrupted by the arrival of two steaming mugs and two ominous-looking rock cakes.

'I think I'll pass on the grenades,' Strachan said. 'I still haven't found the last filling they ripped out.'

'You don't know what you're missing,' Weighell said, taking a giant bite. 'Now what have you got?'

'Right. Let's start with the first idea, of dropping two squadrons onto their airbases to commit general mayhem. It's a non-starter, Bryan. I could tell you why in detail if you want, but it seems like a waste of time. It would just be a suicide mission to end all suicide missions. We'd probably lose less men using the Harriers in a kamikaze role.'

Weighell grunted. 'That's what I thought from the word go,' he said, 'and I think the PM thought so too . . .'

'I thought it was her idea . . .'

'It was. I think she just threw it into the pot so it would look like a concession when she plucked it back out again.'

'Makes sense,' Strachan agreed.

'But the other idea . . .'

'Is not so mad. In fact, it makes a lot of sense, if you ignore any diplomatic ramifications. Let's start with the job itself.' He placed his two maps side by side over Weighell's atlas. 'The terrain's far from perfect, mostly because there's no cover to speak of . . .'

'Like the Falklands.'

'Exactly. And since we already have patrols concealed above their bases on the islands there's no real reason why we shouldn't do the same on the mainland. Here and here' – he used the end of his pen to point out a particular spot on each map, one a few miles south of the Rio Gallegos airbase, one between the latter and the sea – 'seem like reasonable locations given the limits of the maps available to us. I would put in a request for American satellite photos, but that would rather give the game away and . . .'

'No, don't do that, not yet anyway.' Weighell was studying the two maps. 'And the idea would be to land them 20 miles or so away, as on the islands?'

'Maybe nearer. Maybe even farther away – I'll come to that in a moment. But one last word on the job itself: there's no technical problems I can see. They can send out the info in burst transmissions on a Clansman, which should minimize the chances of interception. Of course, if the Argies have any sense they'll be mounting patrols, but if they weren't then our lads could just sit there with their telescopes and have a picnic. There's bound to be some risk.'

'Ah, that reminds me,' Weighell interjected, the last chunk of rock cake poised perilously between plate and mouth. 'I've been trying to get some guidelines from Whitehall about our lads' status if they should be caught. Without any success; of course. There's been no declaration of war – there never is these days – so even if they're in uniform, and I'm still assuming they will be, then it's rather in the lap of the Argentinians.'

'Who don't exactly inspire confidence,' Strachan said soberly.

'No. And in any case the politicians are just as likely to insist the lads are not in uniform, so that they can wash their hands of them . . . I don't know . . .' He scowled. 'Let's leave it for the moment.'

'Right,' Strachan said. 'Getting them there. I don't have any cast-iron information, but from what I've gathered so far it seems that a one-way trip by a Sea King is the best bet.'

'It couldn't get back?'

'Not a chance. Which of course creates its own problem: what do we do with the Sea King once it has delivered its passengers, and even more to the point – what do we do with its crew?'

'What about the HALO option?'

'We don't think so. The consensus of opinion is that it would be much harder to get the men in unobserved that way. We think the Argentinian radar defences are too good for anything other than a low-level insertion. High-altitude, low-opening tactics won't do.'

'OK, so assuming you can render a Sea King and its crew invisible how do we get the patrols out again?'

'That shouldn't be a problem. One of the submarines will pick them up at two designated spots.'

Weighell took a gulp of his tea and found it had already gone cold. 'Under that cynical façade, do I detect a certain enthusiasm for this venture?' he asked.

Strachan took the question seriously. 'Yes, I think it could be done,' he answered. 'And should be,' he added almost as an afterthought. 'It *is* the sort of mission the regiment was designed for.'

'Well, the PM is certainly in favour,' Weighell said drily. 'Who do you have in mind for the magnificent eight?'

'Ah. Well, there's one obvious difference between the Falklands and Argentina . . .'

'One of them belongs to us?'

'In Argentina they speak Spanish. Of course, we hope the need for conversation doesn't actually arise, and that we can get in and out without a single "*buenos días*", but just in case something goes wrong it would be nice to send eight Spanish-speakers.'

'Are there that many in the Regiment?' Weighell asked incredulously.

'There are eight that we know of,' Strachan said. 'And would you believe that three of them are this moment sitting in an OP above Port Howard on West Falkland: Major Brookes and Troopers Laurel and Moseley?'

'Where are the other five?'

'Here in the UK. Two are from A Squadron, the other three from B. The B Squadron bunch have worked together before: an undercover mission in Guatemala during one of the Belize scares.'

'Sergeant Docherty,' Weighell remembered.

'Yes. His father died a month ago, and he's on compassionate leave, but the time's almost up.'

'He had all that time off when his wife died.'

'Yes, almost six months.'

'Why so long? I was in Oman at the time,' he added by way of explanation.

'Because they thought he was worth it,' Strachan replied. 'He's a damn good soldier.'

'This isn't just the Scots' Old Boys Network talking?'

'You must be joking – the bastard's a Celtic supporter.'

Weighell laughed. 'OK, you have him earmarked as PC. What about the others?'

'The other two Spanish-speakers in B Squadron are Wilkinson and Wacknadze. The two in A . . .'

'I would think six out of eight was good enough, Neil. If you've got two four-man patrols who know and work well with each other, then go with them.'

'Right.'

'Of course, it'll mean pulling Brookes's bunch out

of West Falkland,' Weighell added. 'All that bracing fresh air,' he mused. 'Have you called the others in?'

'Not yet.'

'Do it. By my reckoning they'll be sending the Marines ashore in less than three weeks from now. And by that time our job should have been done. We're on borrowed time, Neil.'

The mountain with which he shared a surname was wreathed in cloud, but Stewart Nevis – 'Ben' to his comrades in the SAS – had his eyes to the ground as he walked moodily up Fort William railway station's single platform. The conversation he had just had with his girlfriend was still going round and round in his head, and the temptation to go back for more was a strong one. But he would see her again the following day, and Morag would be none too pleased if he turned up again at the shop. The tourist season might be hardly started, but she took the division between work and play as seriously as she took everything else. They had wasted her lunch hour arguing, and that was the end of it until tomorrow.

He looked once more at the front page of the paper he was carrying, emblazoned with news of the catastrophe which had befallen the *Sheffield*. It was hardly the day to ask him to choose between the Army and her, Ben thought. But she had.

This should be an easy choice, he told himself, one eye on the Class 37 engine backing up the relief track, diesel fumes pumping into the grey sky. He loved Morag, and the SAS was just a job.

But it was more than that. Why could she not understand? Or maybe she did. Maybe she understood it better than him, which was why she was forcing him to choose.

'I won't marry a soldier,' she had said. It was as simple as that.

He had asked her what she expected him to do instead. His elder brother Gavin would take over the family farm, so there was no place for him there, at least not in the long run. And new jobs were not exactly thick on the ground around Fort William. So what did she expect him to do?

'Anything,' she had said. 'You could do anything. What's the good of what you're doing now?' she had asked, neatly changing the subject, he now realized. At the time he had been too busy defending himself.

'How often do we have a war?' she had asked. 'Once in a blue moon. And when we do have one half of you get left at home . . . oh, I know that's not your fault, you idiot, but don't go giving me all that nonsense about duty. You're in the army because you love it.'

Which was true enough, Ben admitted. The engine was being coupled up to the Mallaig train: it was time to get aboard.

He sat gazing out of the window as the train rattled through the junction and struck out for Banachie and the bridge across the Caledonian Canal. Outside his window Loch Linnhe stretched away to the south; on the other side of the train mountain slopes clambered towards the clouds.

His uncle had driven engines on this line from the beginning of the fifties through to his death from a heart attack in 1981. He had never really come to terms with diesels: the old steam engines, he had always said, were like women – you could always coax that little bit more out of them, particularly with a little tenderness. A few years later he had decided that women had changed as much as engines: these 'uppity-tight' modern women, as he called them, were just like diesels – one little problem and they just cut out altogether.

Morag was not like that, Ben thought. If anything she was a bit old-fashioned, even by Fort William standards. But then that was one of the things he loved about her.

She had said she was prepared to wait a year or so for Ben to make up his mind. There was no hurry. But in some strange way – as if the decision had nothing to do with him – he was impatient to know which way he would jump. He could not honestly imagine relinquishing either Morag or the SAS, but he seemed to have little choice.

At Arisaig he got down from the train and started down the lane towards the family farm. The sky was clearing in the west, and 10 miles away across the water Eigg was bathed in sunlight, but he still felt oppressed by his dilemma.

His mother was in the kitchen, rolling pastry for an apple pie. She glanced up as he came in, a worried look on her face. 'There's a message for you,' she said. 'It's by the phone.'

Ben went through into the living room, and read the note in his mother's neat writing. He had been ordered back to base.

'Is it the Falklands?' his mother asked from the door. Her voice was calm, her eyes full of anxiety.

'No idea,' he said.

Darren 'Razor' Wilkinson was also talking to his mother, though the view through their back-room window was somewhat different: a half-tamed garden and the backs of terraced houses in the next street. Out of sight between them, but distressingly loud all the same, trains on the Barking to Gospel Oak line ran through a brick-lined cutting.

'Who are you going out with tonight?' she asked from the armchair. She already had her uniform on for the night shift at Whipps Cross Hospital.

'Her name's Corinna – but then nobody's perfect.' He gave the sleeve one more stroke of the iron, and turned the shirt over.

'Where did you meet her?'

'You're not going to believe this,' he said, 'but in a vegetarian restaurant. A future one, that is.'

'You mean, that lot down the street who are doing up the place on the corner? I was thinking of offering them a hand, if I ever get a spare ten minutes.'

'Like mother, like son,' Razor said.

'You offered to help?' she asked disbelievingly.

'Not exactly. You remember Rick Manning? Well, he knows them from the Tap & Spile, and one of the women . . .' He grinned. 'He fancies her. So he volunteers both himself and me for a morning's hard labour.' He smiled at the memory. 'Nice people, though. For do-gooders, anyway,' he added slyly.

'And Corinna – is she a do-gooder?' his mother asked sweetly.

'I hope she'll do me good.' He leaned over and pulled the plug out of its socket. 'I'm going for a bath while you watch *Emmerdale*,' he said.

Upstairs, he tuned the radio to LBC in the hope of hearing some news of Spurs, did his best to extend his lanky frame in the short bath, and wondered how the evening would go. He hated first dates — it was always so hard to just be yourself.

He thought about Corinna. She was attractive enough — blonde, no more than verging on plump, a lovely smile — and she certainly seemed bright. Not that a degree usually impressed him, not in itself anyway. He thought most people would benefit from three years of freedom to read books and talk to each other without any irritating need to earn a living.

But if there was one thing he had learnt at school it was that the bright ones usually saw through everything a little too quickly for their own good. It was the plodders who went to university, them and the ones whose parents never considered any other possibility.

Fuck 'em all, he thought. He considered the possibility of fucking Corinna. She would be all cool and collected, he reckoned, the sort who neatly folded her clothes on the chair and lay there with the sheet up to her neck, waiting for you to pull it down.

Hmmm, he told himself. Down, boy.

It would be a fun way to spend a night, all right. But not, he suspected, much more.

It was a definite handicap, he decided, having a mother who was more interesting than his girlfriends. He could not understand why she had not found someone for herself — she was attractive, clever, had lots of interests, and was as nice as you could find. You would think there would be a queue of men stretching down the street.

He knew she had stayed single on purpose until he left home, but that was nearly six years ago, and she was not getting any younger. Maybe she was too interesting, and scared them off. He was convinced she wanted someone. It was such a lonely life when he was away, which was most of the time. And she worked so bloody hard for next to nothing. It made him angry just thinking about it. Fucking government.

He got out of the bath, dried himself and went downstairs in the Spurs dressing gown she had made him ten years before. The phone was ringing.

'Yes, he's here,' his mother said, handing him the receiver.

His orders were the same as Ben's. 'I'm afraid Corinna has missed her chance,' he said mildly.

Nick Wacknadze examined the prints on the walls of his host's home and sipped at the glass of wine Brendan had poured for him. It was not bad, and probably expensive: Brendan seemed like the sort who would enjoy demonstrating that he had a degree in yuppieology.

Not to mention modern art: none of the prints seemed to bear any relation to the world Wacknadze lived in, and they all seemed to be by men whose names began with M. Miró seemed to be a child, Munch someone who badly needed a good laugh, and Matisse was obviously colour-blind. Modigliani sounded like an ice-cream. Picasso, who at least had a name which began with another letter, must have felt pretty chuffed to make so much loot with such a bad squint. What a fucking con it all was.

'Are you interested in art?' Brendan asked, appearing at his shoulder like a wraith. He made the question sound like sympathy, as if it were impossible for someone like Wacknadze – a *soldier*, for God's sake – to appreciate any of civilization's finer points.

Wacknadze felt like hitting him, but that was not the

sort of response which would please his wife, Anne, busy chatting in the kitchen to Brendan's wife, Judy. The two women had met in pre-natal classes the year before, which was why he was enduring this particular 'dinner party'.

'I'm more into music,' he said.

'Oh. What kind?'

He's probably expecting me to say Abba, Wacknadze thought. Some kind of Celtic folk music was dribbling out of their hosts' expensive sound system, so he decided to take a chance. 'Early classical, Bach, medieval church music,' he said, and enjoyed watching Brendan's jaw drop a millimetre. And he really did have an interest in those kinds of music; he just never seemed to get the time to pursue it. The last time he had got an album of Gregorian chant from the library Anne had asked him whether it was playing at the right speed.

'Dinner's ready,' Judy said from the doorway, and the two men went through to the other half of the through lounge, where a walnut dining table occupied pride of place. Anne smiled up at him, but not as warmly, Wacknadze thought, as she smiled at Brendan. A glimmer of suspicion flickered across his mind.

He looked at Judy, wondering if she seemed aware of anything. She didn't. But she was not half as attractive as Anne, Wacknadze thought.

She was a better cook though, he thought, tucking into the meal. The other three were talking about the local housing market, a topic which proved easy to exhaust.

'As an Army man, how do you see this whole Falklands business?' Brendan asked after a long lull.

'In what way?' Wacknadze asked carefully.

'Well, don't you think the whole business seems a bit disproportionate? Sending an enormous fleet down there just to save a few hundred sheep farmers. It would be cheaper to pay them each a million pounds and hand the whole lot over to Argentina.' He laughed at his own acumen.

It would be cheaper, Wacknadze thought, but not in the way Brendan was using the word. 'I don't think you can put a price on principle,' he said shortly, hoping someone else would change the subject.

'Which principle do you mean?' Judy asked.

'That an aggressor shouldn't be allowed to get away with it.'

'OK,' Brendan agreed, 'but we're always letting them do just that. When the Russians invaded Afghanistan we didn't do anything.'

'There was no way we could do anything.'

'Exactly,' Brendan triumphantly. 'So this is not a matter of principle at all – we're only going to war with Argentina because we can.'

Did his host really believe this shit, Wacknadze asked himself. 'The way I see it,' he said, 'it's very simple. Those people want to be British – every last one of them – and if we *can* stop them being taken over by another country then we should.'

'You don't think Argentina has any case at all?'

'Nope. And even if it did, this is not the time to say so. We lost a ship yesterday, and a lot of men.'

'They lost a lot more men a couple of days ago.'

Wacknadze smiled. 'Well, they started it.'

'I don't . . .'

'Brendan, why don't you open another bottle,' Judy

said, 'and let's talk about something more cheerful, shall we?'

The rest of the evening passed smoothly enough, with Wacknadze leaving most of the talk to the other three, and trying to ignore both the sharp looks from Anne and the glow on her face when she listened to Brendan.

In the car on the way home she was first silent, then angry. 'Why were you so rude at dinner?' she wanted to know. 'There is more than one way to look at the world, you know.'

'You mean, I should learn to see both sides?' he asked sarcastically.

'It is generally considered a sign of maturity,' she said.

'Fuck maturity,' he said. 'Some of my mates are probably going to get killed out there, and you want me to feel sorry for Argentina? Jesus Christ, you can't send soldiers into a war and expect them to see both sides.'

'You mean, you have to wear blinkers before you can start killing people,' he said coldly.

He wanted to hit her, but she was driving. And by the time they got back home he just wanted to see the back of the whole fucking evening. He paid the babysitter her usual exorbitant fee and let her out the front door.

'Oh, by the way,' the girl said, just as she was about to shut the door, 'there's a phone message for you in the hall. Something about reporting in first thing in the morning.'

Another day would have helped, Docherty thought, examining himself in the toilet mirror. His eyes had lost their rusty edges, but his face still seemed almost preternaturally pale. He looked like a fucking ghost.

In fact, he thought, weaving his way back down the aisle to his seat, he looked even worse than he felt. Which was both good and bad, depending on which way you looked at it. Good because it meant it would not take that long to regain his usual fitness; bad because the bosses might think he was not up to whatever they had in mind for him.

He hoped to God it involved travelling a long way from Glasgow – the moon might just be far enough. Though wherever it was, as long as he had something to keep mind and body occupied it would be fine. The Falklands would be just dandy. Spitzbergen would be great. The only place he did not think he could stand was Belfast, and all those bloody hours sitting in cars both bored out of your skull and hyper-aware that someone might just walk up and blow your skull away.

If they ordered him there he would tell them to shove it, he thought, surprising himself with the vehemence of the feeling. Was he really ready to throw thirteen years of Army life out the window? Maybe he was.

And maybe not. He did not really know how he felt. He had held himself tight as a vice until his father's funeral, then taken to the drink with a vengeance. Neither form of existence had allowed for much in the way of feeling, which he supposed was why he had embraced them. Now, sober enough to feel the inside of his head shaking, he needed a third way of avoiding himself. Like playing cat-and-mouse with the Argentinian army on the Falklands.

The train was pulling into Preston. The old Ricky

Nelson hit ran through his head: 'I'm a travelling man, made a lot of stops, all over the world . . .' And he had. The Arabian desert, the mountains of Oman, Hong Kong, Belize and Mexico. 'And in every port I own the heart of at least one lovely girl . . .'

He had only ever owned the heart of one, and he had never been outside Britain with her. He was twenty-six, and Chrissie only eighteen, when they first met, at an exhibition of Islamic architecture in Edinburgh. Docherty fell in love with the graceful minarets and domes during his time in Oman, and he fell in love with her in front of a large photograph of Tamerlane's mausoleum in Samarkand. 'A soldier's tomb,' he said out loud, not realizing she was behind him.

'You must be one yourself,' she said with that simple directness she applied to everything and everyone.

'Is it that obvious?' he asked.

'My dad was one,' she said by way of explanation.

They had coffee together, then a walk in West Princes Street Gardens and a meal at an Italian restaurant on Castle Street, talking all the time. He admired her quickness and her knowledge, loved her sense of humour, felt almost intimidated by the loveliness of her face. He could hardly believe she could have any real interest in him. But at Waverly Station, where she came to see him off on the last train back to Glasgow, she returned and amplified his goodnight kiss, and agreed to meet him again the following weekend.

Three months later they were married. Another six months and she was dead, knocked down by a car on a zebra crossing less than 100 yards from their Hereford flat.

Docherty had not known what to do. For several

weeks he ranged the streets of Hereford and the surrounding countryside like a wounded dog, both pathetic and dangerous. Then one day he suddenly realized he had to get away – it did not matter where. He went into a library, opened an atlas at random, and found himself looking at a map of Mexico. He cleared his bank account and bought a return ticket – Mexico refused to admit travellers without one – and told his mates he was off. They managed to persuade him that compassionate leave would look better on his record than desertion, and for another twenty-four hours, while the formalities were gone through, he managed to hold himself together. The next day he was airborne, and that same evening he was strolling across Mexico City's central square, still in turmoil but somehow out of danger.

Over the next few months he travelled all over the country, staying in cheap hotels and eating in cheap cafés, falling in love with Spanish architecture as he had with Islamic. Chrissie was always with him, occupying a space in his heart and mind which nothing could apparently touch, but the rest of him slowly came back to life, reflecting the brightness of the Mexican light and landscape.

After five months he felt the country and the travelling way of life had done everything for him that they could. He began to hunger once more for his old, disciplined sense of purpose – that sense of service which he knew came from his father, but which he had offered to first the Black Watch and then the SAS. In any case he was running out of money.

He returned to Hereford and, somewhat to his surprise, was taken back into the regiment's fold. In the five years that had since passed neither he nor they had found any reason to regret the decision, but neither had Docherty learned to reopen Chrissie's mausoleum in his heart.

One day he would, Liam McCall had told him, but he was not so sure. He had always thought that one day he would come to terms with his father, but now he could only come to terms with not coming to terms. Or something like that. The bastards kept widening the goalposts. Jesus, he thought, I could do with a drink.

Fortunately the buffet bar was closed. The train was gliding through Warrington: in another twenty minutes it would be at Crewe, where he hoped there would be a connection for Shrewsbury and Hereford. Once the wait had only been ten minutes, but once it had been six hours.

This time they split the difference, and it was three. He watched the sun rising behind the Shropshire fields, silhouetting the mass of the Long Mynd, ate his breakfast of Mars bar, Pepsi and crisps between Ludlow and Leominster, and did his best to make himself look less dead than alive as the train rolled the last few miles into Hereford.

A cab took him to the Stirling Lines barracks in Redhill, where the orderly sergeant informed him that he was expected in the 'Kremlin' briefing room at 0900 hours. 'Christ, you look dreadful,' he added sympathetically.

It was only eight-forty: there was time for a proper breakfast. Docherty stowed his gear in his empty locker and made his way to the canteen, where three familiar faces already had their snouts buried in the trough.

'It's the boss,' 'Razor' Wilkinson announced.

'Welcome back, boss,' 'Wacko' Wacknadze said seriously.

'Ben' Stewart just smiled.

'And they promised me a new team of comics,' Docherty told the woman behind the servery, as he collected eggs, bacon and toast and a large mug of tea. 'A funny one, this time.'

She pursed her lips in sympathy.

'So where's the rest of B Squadron?' he asked the others as he sat down.

'All in the bosoms of their families,' Razor told him, 'except for Banjo – he's in detention for assaulting a parking meter in the High Street last night.'

'What did he assault it with?' Ben asked.

'The ultimate blunt instrument – his head. Some civilian wound him up about the war – about his not being down there – so Banjo charged him like a bull, and the other bloke just stepped out of the way . . .'

'Like a bullfighter,' Ben murmured.

'Exactly. And the bull head-butted a parking meter.'

Docherty could not help grinning.

'Anyway, boss,' Razor went on, 'to answer the unstated part of your question – we four are the only ones who've been called back. Which seems a bit weird. I mean, they're hardly likely to be chartering a C-130 just to send us down south, are they?'

'Maybe they'll stick us in with supplies or something,' Wacko observed.

'Oh great. Us four and a Hercules full of toilet rolls for G Squadron. But why just four of us? And why us four?'

'Spanish,' Ben suggested. 'You three all speak it, and they probably reckoned I was needed to make sure you didn't get lost.'

'With your map-reading skills we should take a sundial,' Razor said.

'All will be revealed in about five minutes,' Docherty said. He thought Ben was probably right about the Spanish, and that, coupled with the fact that only four of them had been summoned, suggested something very interesting indeed. 'Come on, let's get over to the Kremlin.'

They were the first to arrive, not counting the mounted water-buffalo's head which had surveyed the room since the regiment's Malayan days. It looked even more pissed off than usual, Docherty thought. Or maybe it was just him. He had probably needed more than the hour's sleep he had got.

'You look terrible, boss,' Razor told him.

'I know,' Docherty grunted. He closed his eyes, but only for a few seconds. Footsteps behind him announced the arrival of Lieutenant-Colonel Bryan Weighell and Major Neil Strachan.

'You look awful, Docherty,' was Weighell's first comment.

'Just a long train journey and no sleep, boss,' Docherty said brightly.

'If you say so. Anyway, good morning, gents. This is not a normal briefing – you'll be getting that on the *Resource* – but . . .'

'Does that mean the Task Force, boss?' Docherty asked.

'Yes, I'm sorry, I'm jumping the gun . . .' He noticed that all four men were grinning at him. 'I'm glad to see you're all eager to go,' he said, 'but don't get too carried away – this is a volunteers-only mission, and we want you to think seriously about what you're letting yourself in for before you volunteer.'

I was right, Docherty was thinking. It had to be the mainland.

'Neil here will give you the bare bones,' Weighell said.

Strachan got up to stand beside the map which had been hung in front of the blackboard. 'It's very simple,' he said. 'Even you lot should be able to understand it. Here are the Falklands' – he pointed them out – 'and here, more or less, is the Task Force. As you no doubt know, it has no air early warning system, and the perils of being taken unawares were demonstrated only too clearly the other day. The *Sheffield*,' he added unnecessarily. 'The Exocets are our major concern, but we're not even completely sure at which of these two airfields' – he pointed out Rio Grande on Tierra del Fuego and Rio Gallegos on the Argentinian mainland – 'they are stored. The Task Force needs advance warning of flights from both, and the plan is to put two four-man patrols ashore, one to monitor each airbase. They will report take-offs as they occur, thus giving the fleet about four times the warning they are getting at present.' He paused. 'It's hard to exaggerate how important such an increase in warning time could be. It could save one of the carriers, and that might mean the difference between victory and defeat, because if we lose one or both of them then we'll also have lost any chance of air cover for a landing operation in the islands. And such an operation is going to be difficult enough *with* air cover.' He paused again. 'Right, that is the why. Any questions there before we go on to the how?'

Jesus, Docherty thought. Was the Task Force that vulnerable? Apparently it was. In which case, the whole thing made sense and he had no questions.

'Right,' Strachan continued, 'the how. You will be flown to Ascension, and then flown on from there to the Task Force. A parachute drop, I'm afraid. You will receive the full briefing on the *Resource*, and it should be no more than a couple of days before you are flown in by helicopter. How long you remain will depend on the situation, but it should be no more than a fortnight – because by that time the bridgehead on the islands should be more than secure. Extraction will be by submarine, from a predetermined location at a set hour on a three-day pattern. Any questions?'

'Who are the other lucky bastards?' Razor asked.

Strachan looked at Weighell, who shrugged. 'I don't suppose there's any harm in your knowing. Assuming we can get them out of West Falkland in one piece, it'll be one of G Squadron's patrols: Major Brookes, plus Troopers Matthews, Laurel and Moseley.'

There were good-natured groans. 'And where are they going to find a helicopter large enough to carry us and Hedge?' Wacko wanted to know.

'If we're going in by helicopter, why can't we be taken out that way?' Docherty asked.

'It'll be a one-way trip going in,' Strachan admitted.

'So what happens to the crew?' Ben asked.

'That's still to be decided,' Weighell butted in. 'As is the question of uniform. How would you four feel about going in without uniforms, knowing there's a risk the Argentinians might treat you as spies?'

'I'll wear pyjamas,' Wacko said, 'if it gets us to do something other than sit around in England.'

'Why would we not be wearing uniforms?' Docherty asked. This was beginning to smell a little, he thought.

'Because the Government may want to disown you,' Weighell said bluntly. 'There's a lot of political ramifications to this, as you can guess. The Foreign Office is worried about losing friends if we look too aggressive . . .'

'Jesus Christ, boss, this is a *war*, isn't it?' Wacko wanted to know.

'To us it is,' Weighell said drily. 'The Foreign Office likes to think it's considering the long-term implications. Trade, that sort of thing . . .'

'Money,' Razor said disgustedly.

'Not just,' Weighell said. 'They have to keep our allies sweet, too, or the enemy will find it a lot easier to replace and upgrade its weaponry – particularly the Exocets.'

'The fucking French,' Razor said with feeling.

Great, Docherty was thinking. We put our lives on the line and the fucking Government is not prepared to even admit we're British soldiers. 'What are we supposed to be, if we get caught?' he asked. 'Albanians?'

'I don't know,' Weighell said, as honestly as he could.

'I guess the trick is not to get caught,' Ben offered.

'Right,' Wacko agreed.

Docherty looked at them. 'Razor?' he asked.

The Londoner shrugged. 'Let's worry about it when we have to. It sounds like an important job, boss,' he added quietly.

Docherty smiled inwardly. 'Aye, it does,' he agreed. And why the hell not, he told himself. He smiled at Weighell. 'Looks like we're your men, boss,' he said quietly.

'I thought you might be,' Weighell said.

'Your transport leaves for Brize Norton in a couple of hours,' Strachan added. 'I doubt if any of you have loved ones, but if you have you can use the Admin Office phone to give them the good news.' He stopped at the door. 'You lucky bastards,' he said affectionately, and disappeared.

Weighell wished them all good luck, then drew Docherty aside. 'Just wanted to make sure you know,' he said, 'that if the Government disowns you the Regiment won't.'

Docherty nodded. 'I'll tell the others,' he said.

When Weighell had gone the four of them stood there looking at each other. 'Just when I was getting used to the idea of a long and boring life,' Razor said. 'I'd better ring my mum.'

'I'm off home,' Wacko said. 'I'll be back in an hour.'

The other three trooped across to the Admin Office, and took turns using the phone and flirting with the secretaries. Razor woke his mum up, and spent ten minutes telling her not to worry. When he came off the phone there were tears in his eyes, which he tried, unsuccessfully as far as Docherty was concerned, to conceal. Ben spoke to his mother as well, though it seemed as if she did all the talking.

Docherty spoke to one of his sisters, who said she would pick a good time to tell his mother. He then decided, on the spur of the moment, to ring Liam McCall, but the phone rang and rang until a woman he did not know answered. 'Tell Liam that Jamie rang,' Docherty told her. 'Tell him I've gone to feed the penguins and exorcize a few demons.'

4

Staring into fog was almost hypnotic, Hedge thought. Since the onset of daylight banks of the stuff had drifted up Falkland Sound, as if taking over the night's job of rendering the world less visible. And if the experience of the last few days was anything to go by, it would hang around until night came back on shift.

'Another busy day dawns,' he murmured to Mozza, who was taking his time retreating to bed. 'At least we can all have a decent meal.'

There were compensations for the grey-out. Each man could spend time conceiving and preparing his own gourmet feast from the dried menu available, and cook it up on the tiny hexamine stove each carried. It tasted good, it warmed him up, and the whole process consumed time which might otherwise have been given over to boredom. On clear days and nights, by contrast, the fare was all cold: biscuits, chocolate and cheese. Or, for variety, cheese, chocolate and biscuits. The preparation time was what it took to remove the wrappers.

'I'd like my steak medium to well done,' Hedge whispered after the retreating Mozza. 'With chips and mushrooms and a pint of red plonk.'

This reminded Hedge of his full bladder. Another

of the advantages of fog, he thought, as he relieved himself on the open hillside a few yards away from the OP, was an honest-to-goodness natural piss. On cold, clear mornings you had to do it inside the hide, and let it out in dribs and drabs to minimize the tell-tale plume of steam. If the Argies were watching they would think they were encircled by men with prostate problems.

Hot meals, flowing piss – you're really grasping at straws, he told himself, as he eased his bulk back into the hide and double-checked that the camouflage netting was correctly in place. Let's face it, Hedge, he reminded himself, everything you're wearing is wet and likely to remain so for the foreseeable future, your feet are either numb with cold or feel like they're sharing your socks with a pair of dead fish, and you've no idea how much longer you're going to be stuck in this God-forsaken hillside on this God-forsaken island in this God-forsaken ocean. Your boat home is probably being sunk even as you think, and your PC has probably just woken up with the idea of checking out the enemy minefields tonight under cover of fog. Is this what you joined the fucking SAS for?

It probably was.

After all, what else would he be doing? If he was not in the Army he would be either unemployed or bored out of his mind. Or in prison like two of his schoolfriends, both of whom had hated their working lives so much that they had lost any idea of self-control at the weekends. They had half-killed some poor Paki just because he gave them the wrong sort of smile.

Hedge sighed to himself. He had never liked Pakis much himself, but since being in the Army, and particularly since being in the SAS, his feelings had changed, at least a bit. He supposed being in close contact with the Gurkhas in Hong Kong had made him think about such things, but he had the feeling that the more important changes were in how he felt about himself. People picked on others when they were scared or feeling hard done by, he reckoned, and he felt pretty satisfied with the way his life was going. He might not like sitting in a cold puddle for days on end but he had no doubts about what he was there for. And in his experience that was something really worth knowing.

At least this fog would clear, he thought to himself, staring out at the giant shroud. He remembered an Incredible Hulk story in which the hero found himself trapped in a parallel universe that was contained in a speck of dust on someone's knee, and idly wondered whether he had been miniaturized and dropped into the head of a dinosaur's Q-tip.

They had been the only passengers on the coach from Stirling Lines to the RAF base at Brize Norton, and they proved to be the only human cargo carried south by the Hercules C-130 to Ascension.

'I begin to understand why Ascension hasn't been developed for tourism,' Docherty said nine hours later. The fuel tanks which had been added to increase the C-130's flight range made the aircraft even more cramped than before, and the web seats had lost none of their capacity to torture each and every limb.

'That and the fact that there's fuck-all there,' Razor agreed.

'What do you mean?' Wacko wanted to know, 'the place is full of history.'

'I don't think G Squadron's Wankathon counts as real history,' Razor said.

'Napoleon was exiled here, you ignorant bastard.'

'What, the Man from Uncle?' Ben asked deadpan.

'No, you moron, the French guy. Napoleon Bonaparte.'

'Is he still around?' Razor wanted to know.

Docherty smiled to himself and refrained from pointing out that Napoleon had been exiled to St Helena, 800 miles away. Sometimes the three of them seemed so different, but at others they had an uncanny knack for following the same thread of absurdity. And usually in the same depraved direction. Their mothers probably loved them.

'Napoleon had one thing on you,' Wacko was saying, 'he could show a bit of restraint. When was the last time you said "not tonight" to yourself? Or to a woman, even?'

'No, no,' Razor insisted, 'you've got it all wrong. When he said "not tonight, Josephine" he meant no TV tonight, because he wanted to get her straight to bed.'

'They didn't have TV then, you idiot.'

'Yes, you idiot, it was the radio,' Ben said. 'Josephine was an *Archers* addict.'

And so it went on for most of the remaining hour of the flight. It took up the time, it stopped Wacko thinking about Anne and Brendan, stopped Razor worrying about his mum, and pushed Morag's ultimatum to the back of Ben's mind. It stopped them all from thinking about their aching limbs or the war awaiting them.

At Ascension's Wideawake Airfield the four of them stepped almost buoyantly onto the tarmac and surveyed the surrounding scenery. It was only just after dawn, but already they could feel the heat building, and there was no shortage of activity across the airfield. Supplies and aircraft seemed to be competing for space, and the one long runway looked more like a corridor than the usual road set on a large lawn. In one direction the remains of the volcano which had created the island rose up behind the various buildings ringing the airfield; in the other a multitude of naval vessels were rolling in the blue Atlantic.

'That way, chums,' the pilot told them with an airy wave of the hand, and they eventually managed to locate a less than enthusiastic welcoming committee in one of the temporary offices. He was not expecting any more SAS men, had nowhere to put them, and thought they must be joking if they thought a plane would take them on south. 'The whole fuckin' Army's leaving tomorrow, and some of them are having to use rowing boats.'

'No wonder Napoleon died here,' Razor muttered.

The sergeant eyed them all fondly. 'Why don't you go and find some breakfast in the Volcano Club while I get your gear out of the plane and try and sort something out,' he suggested.

It was not a bad idea: the steaks were thick and juicy, the fried eggs all unbroken, the chips elegantly poised between too crisp and too greasy. After demolishing their plates all four of them laid themselves out for sleep on rows of chairs, and Wacko at least was soon snoring with enough gusto to frighten the Navy.

Docherty found himself unable to doze, and sat back up, gazing out of the wide windows at the

Vulcans, Nimrods and Starlifters strewn across the airfield. For a moment he thought he was in one of those old war films, and that at any moment they would be trooping out to their planes, revving propellers, trundling up into the sky. But this was real, he thought, looking around at his comatose companions. All this effort to put right what a few moronic generals probably thought up over breakfast one morning. What a farce.

But at least it was their own farce, Docherty thought. And he had no problem with the idea of using force to show that walking into other people's countries was beyond the pale. It was just that somehow this all seemed a bit like overkill, and it worried him a little. Not a lot, but a little. Which was still too much.

Docherty had always thought the phrase 'yours not to reason why' was one of the dumbest things a soldier could ever tell himself. It made a lot more sense to spend some time working out why, because then it became a hell of lot easier 'to do or die'.

On Friday 7 May the day dawned on the hillside above Port Howard without any accompanying fog. There seemed to be a pattern, Brookes thought – one day with, one day without. He could think of no conceivable reason why this should be so, but then he did not understand how flicking a switch could fill a room with light either. Science was for the scientists to deal with.

It was by no means as bright as the day before yesterday had been, but he could see all he needed to of the settlement and camp below. Not much had happened since the visit of the inspection team – if that was what they were – two days previously. That day there had been a lot of standing in line, a lot of polishing weapons, a lot of salutes. In the hour before dusk there had even been a football tournament, with four teams playing three games on a sloping pitch beyond the camp. Brookes's knowledge of football was almost non-existent, but according to Stanley the level of technique had been high.

Which was hardly the sort of information the Task Force needed. Nor did Brookes feel that Stanley's masterplan – 'Let's go down and steal their ball' – would inspire much support in the ladies' toilet aboard the *Resource*.

The information they did need had mostly been gathered, and transmitted in code by short burst on the patrol's Clansman the previous night. It would have been a miracle if the Argentinians' Direction Finding (DF) equipment had picked up the transmission, let alone pinpointed its source, and as yet there were no signs in the camp below of any patrol activity.

Mozza's original guess-timate of the enemy's strength had been almost spot-on. There were between 920 and 950 men in the camp below, constituting, if the flag flying rather foolishly from one building had any validity, the 5th Regiment of the 3rd Brigade. The men were well armed, with rifles and SMGs comparable, if not superior, to those carried by the British, and they were energetically adding new trench positions and minefields around the settlement to those already dug out and laid.

A gun emplacement had appeared during the previous day's fog, complete with a 105mm artillery piece now pointing out into the Sound. It had presumably been stored in one of the outhouses, most likely with the aim of concealing it from satellite or other high-altitude surveillance. Now, with the prospect of a British landing drawing nearer, it was being made ready. Brookes thought that probably meant there were no others hidden away, but at some point he would have to decide whether the element of doubt necessitated a closer look.

He watched through the telescope as one of the enemy soldiers emerged from one of the sheds with a bucket and tipped what looked like vegetable peelings onto a growing pile. There was no doubt that their camp was growing dirtier and more untidy by the day, a fact which Brookes considered highly significant. On paper the Argentinians were numerous and well armed, but this unit at least was lacking in the sort of self-discipline which made for an efficient fighting force.

It was hard to put his finger on it exactly, but there was a general sloppiness about it all. They did not want to be here, that much was clear. Smiles were few and far between, scowls worn almost as part of the badly-kept uniforms. And the ordinary soldiers seemed incredibly young; hardly beyond the pimple stage. That was it, Brookes suddenly realized: this was an adolescent army, which might prove long on courage but would almost certainly prove woefully short on concentrated or prolonged effort.

This was one of two fatal weaknesses in the Argentinians' position. The other was the troops' lack of mobility. Maybe the enemy had 100 helicopters ready to transport this regiment to where it might be needed, but Brookes very much doubted it. When the Marines came ashore in a couple of weeks time, across the Sound 20 miles or so to the north and east, these troops would simply be stuck here in Port Howard, 1000 helpless and probably thankful spectators.

Brookes was smiling to himself at this prospect as he noticed the patrol leaving the camp below, obviously headed up into the hills. He watched for some fifteen minutes as the line of twenty-two men, sometimes visible, sometimes not, steadily climbed an invisible track which would take them a quarter of a mile or so to the east of the hide.

Then their line of march veered towards him.

He woke Hedge, and told the big man to wake Stanley and Mozza. When they were all assembled – as much as any four men could 'assemble' in a cross-shaped hide only 30 inches deep – he told them why they had been woken. 'There's an Argie patrol headed this way,' he said softly. 'Twenty-one of them. In another couple of minutes we'll have to go over to hand-signals, so . . .' He took a deep breath. 'It's just gone three o'clock,' he went on, 'so there's only about two more hours of light. If they spot the hide I'm for taking them on. With any luck we can get ourselves back over the ridge, and it'll be dark before they manage to get any reinforcements up here. What do you think?' he asked, in the democratic way the SAS took for granted.

'Sounds good to me, boss,' Hedge answered.

'Piece of cake,' Stanley agreed.

'What should we try and take with us?' Mozza asked, and wondered why his voice sounded so calm when the rest of him suddenly seemed anything but.

'The MP5s, the M203,' Brookes said. 'And we'll need the radio, of course. Sorry, Mozza, but you will have to take the extra weight. Get everything else out of your bergen now.' He turned back to the outside world. The enemy patrol was only about a quarter of a mile away, and seemed to be both spreading out and headed in their direction.

'We won't leave you behind,' Stanley was reassuring Mozza. 'We can't do without the radio.'

'He's young and fit,' Hedge observed. 'He hasn't spoiled himself with self-indulgence like some I could mention.'

'No more talk,' Brookes said curtly. 'Hand-signals only. If I yell then we're up and at 'em.'

The next ten minutes seemed more like ten hours, particularly to the three men who could see nothing, who could do nothing but wait and wonder and try to be ready when the time came. For Brookes the time may have gone faster, but at an even greater cost to his nerves. The Argentinian soldiers, each carrying an automatic rifle, were obviously intent on combing this particular hillside, though whether as part of a random sweep or because someone thought he had seen something suspicious Brookes had no idea. At any rate they were advancing across the slope in a long, sweeping line, each soldier walking a parallel path some 20 yards from his nearest compatriot.

Such a wide gap, Brookes reckoned, increased their chance of going undetected. But it also meant that if the hide was spotted, there was next to no chance of their killing many of the enemy, or of getting away.

The line drew slowly nearer. Brookes could see the face of the nearest soldier, a boy of not much more than seventeen, and prayed he had bad eyesight. On his present path he would come within a few feet of the hide, and could hardly fail to notice something. He was now about 50 yards away.

Brookes signalled '50' to the others in the hide.

They sat there stony-faced, wondering how their own breathing could sound so loud. Hedge felt his stomach silently rumble, and prayed that they would not be betrayed by one of his farts. Mozza was fighting a mad desire to shout out something, anything, to break the overwhelming silence.

The sound of boots swishing through wet grass grew louder. The boy was almost on top of them when his next in line further up the hill said something in Spanish, something about someone called Pérez which Brookes could not quite make out. It hardly mattered though, for whatever it was it made the boy laugh and look away at just the moment when a downward glance to his left might well have killed himself and all four men in the hide.

The swish of the boots began to fade, replaced by the sound of four Englishmen exhaling with relief. More minutes passed, rather less traumatically, until Brookes was able to report in a soft voice that the enemy patrol had passed out of sight around the far shoulder of the hill.

'I reckon this hide should get a perfect score for technical merit,' Stanley said proudly.

'Either that or the Argies were looking for a restaurant,' Hedge agreed.

Brookes thought he would tell them about the fortunate joke at some later date, preferably after the war was over.

On Ascension Island Docherty's patrol had eventually been found four empty bunks in a disused school, and nine hours' sleep had done wonders for their individual states of mind. They had then done exercises and gone for a much-interrupted run: on Ascension, it seemed, everyone was busy building personal empires and putting up fences around them. In the meantime the Falklands landing force was preparing for its departure the following day, and the small supply boats whizzed to and fro between the larger ships and shore as the fork-lift trucks drew patterns on the airfield tarmac.

The opportunities for entertainment were rather more limited. As Razor noted, the Navy boys could climb into their bunks together, but for real soldiers there was only the Volcano Club. Which was not saying much, Docherty thought to himself after the second pint. He was taking it more slowly than usual, aware that his body was still recovering from the previous weeks' abuse. The other three seemed to be taking their cue from him, or maybe they too were hyper-conscious of how important it was, in view of what lay ahead, not to risk their level of fitness.

The same could not be said for most of the other revellers. One group, on the far side of the room, seemed to be drinking like there was no tomorrow, and making enough noise to drown out the conversations of the remaining clientele. Every now and then they would burst into a new verse set to the melody of 'Summer Holiday': the most recent of which had featured the immortal line 'napalm sticks to spics'.

'Arseholes,' Razor muttered to no one in particular.

'They're just REMFs,' Ben said. 'Rear-echelon mother-fuckers,' he enunciated carefully. 'And you can bet your life they've never seen what napalm can do up close.'

'It's one of those things,' Docherty said. 'It's always the ones who know nothing who make all the fucking noise.' He had a strong desire to go over and make his feelings felt.

'It's like racism,' Wacko said. 'The places it's strongest in England are the places where there aren't any blacks. Like East Anglia.'

Razor glanced across at him, surprised. He had never exactly thought of Wacko as a racist, but the man was hardly famous for his liberal opinions. Then the connection hit him. With a foreign father, Wacko would have learnt the hard way.

The singing swelled once more. 'We won't cry for you Argentina, we'll just send you our Polaris . . .'

The four of them were saved by an Air Force officer, who told them that they would be leaving at 0700 hours the next morning. Suddenly all the noise and ugly jingoism seemed beside the point. Unlike the singers they were on their way to war.

They were in the helicopter: Francisco, herself and the two security men. Francisco was on the floor, smiling up at her, despite the wires which held his wrists and ankles in a knot behind his arched back, despite the burns and bruises visible on his face, despite the six bricks cemented together and attached by chains to the tangle of wires.

'Please, no,' she implored the security men. 'I'll do anything if you'll let him go.'

The one with the thin moustache smirked at her. 'You'll do anything anyway,' he said.

'She already has,' his partner said. 'Everyone at the School had her – she was such a nice piece of ass when she first arrived. And she was really eager to please.'

'No, no, that's not true,' she told Francisco desperately, and he seemed to believe her. His smile never wavered, even when they pulled him across the floor, said '*adiós*, pig', and pushed the block of bricks out into space. Then an expression of surprise seemed to suffuse his face, and he looked up once at her as his fingers grasped at the doorframe, before the foot smashed into his face and he was gone.

And then the face was slowly drifting down through the water, his hair waving, the smile fading into an open mouth, exhaling bubbles . . .

She woke with a start, shaking like a leaf. The church bells of Rio Gallegos were ringing for morning Mass.

If only Sharon could see him now, Stanley thought to himself. He was walking some five yards behind Brookes, closer when the mist thickened, further apart when it thinned. Generally though it seemed to be growing thicker the closer they got to Port Howard and sea level.

The previous night the patrol had received a coded radio message from the SAS operations centre on the *Resource*. They were being pulled out on the following night. No explanation was given, merely the coordinates of the pick-up zone some five miles away and their helicopter taxi's ETA.

It was hard to feel too sad about leaving their waterlogged home on a windy slope, but for Brookes the horrible suspicion arose that this might prove his last-ever mission for the SAS. If it had to be, then it had to be, but if so then it was going to be damn-near perfect. There was still one large gap in their knowledge which they needed to fill: the nature of whatever it was that the Argies had stored in the two large corrugated sheds close by the jetty on the inlet. They were probably full of corned beef or toilet paper or pictures of General Galtieri, but there was always the chance they might contain something posing more of a threat to the upcoming British landing. Surface-to-air missiles, for example.

There was only one way to find out, he had said, and that was to go and take a look. The others had agreed in principle, but disputed Brookes's proposed timing. He had intended to do the traditional thing, and go at once, under the cover of darkness. Stanley had disagreed, arguing that the early-morning fog would be just as concealing, and that the Argentinians would be unlikely to be using any thermal-imaging capacity they possessed at such an hour. The trooper's argument had convinced Brookes, which was why the two of them were now nearing a camp of 1000 enemy soldiers protected by little more than a curtain of water droplets and two silenced Heckler & Koch MP5 sub-machine-guns.

There was the sudden sound of laughter ahead and to their right, and Stanley noticed the hairs on his wrist were standing up on end.

Ahead of him he saw Brookes move his extended right arm slowly down and up, and accordingly slowed down. Then the PC moved his arm again, this time from the diagonal to the vertical, signalling a renewed advance.

What fun, Stanley told himself.

Brookes veered off to the left, as certain as he could be that the two of them were inside the protective ring of minefields. According to his map of the settlement, first drawn from sight and then transferred to memory, a house should soon be looming out of the fog slightly to their right.

A few more yards and it did. Brookes congratulated himself and signalled Stanley forward to join him. At that moment a loud voice echoed in the silence: 'Tea's made, Ted.'

It was almost shocking in both its ordinariness and its Englishness. The temptation to wander across and partake of a cup was almost overwhelming. Brookes and Stanley stared at each other, and both broke into the same stupid grin, white teeth gleaming in their blackened faces.

Brookes led off again, skirting what looked like rotting string beans on a line of canes and climbing over a low hedge and into a muddy lane. The simultaneous sound of feet and murmured Spanish sent him back the way he had come, and the two of them crouched down behind the foliage, MP5s at the ready.

Two uniformed figures slowly materialized out of the mist, carrying what looked like a packing case of ammunition. It was obviously heavy enough to absorb all their attention, because they passed by breathing heavily and dematerialized once more. Brookes and Stanley would have had no trouble coming up behind them and slitting each throat from ear to ear, but it had been agreed that this particular walk on the wild side should remain unknown to the enemy if at all possible. There was, after all, little chance of them slitting 1000 throats on the one trip.

They stood motionless for another minute, ears straining for sounds of any other activity. All they could hear was the murmur of voices way behind them, and the occasional squawk of a seabird somewhere out in front.

They resumed their progress, following the muddy

lane in what Brookes assumed was the direction of the
jetty. The sound of water lapping against the wooden
piers confirmed as much. The dark shape of the first
corrugated warehouse loomed out of the mist.

The two men inched along the side wall, and
Brookes put an eye round the corner. There was
no one in sight, but that was hardly surprising
when visibility was less than 10 yards. He signalled
Stanley to follow and started edging his way along
the front.

The main doors were shut, but the large, rusty
padlock – 'Made in Warrington' – had not been fastened. More sloppiness, Brookes thought to himself.
He listened up against the door, and heard no sounds
coming from inside. Signalling Stanley to cover him,
he pulled the sliding door to the left as silently as
he could.

Inside there was hardly any light, and it took their
eyes several seconds to adjust to the gloom. When
they did it was to an unexpected sight. The shed was
empty save for two tables and about twenty blank
road signs. Only one seemed to have been completed:
it stood proudly against the far wall, reading 'BAHIA
ZORRO 57 KILOMETROS'.

'Fox Bay,' Brookes translated for Stanley, and the
two men looked at each other with disbelieving faces.
The enemy was concentrating on getting the islands'
road signs right! There were not even any *roads*
worthy of the name. Brookes wondered what they
would discover in the other shed – copies of *Teach
Yourself Spanish For Sheep*?

It turned out to be empty, save for some shearing
equipment. The Argentinian garrison at Port Howard
was what it had seemed from the hide: a concentration

of force entirely lacking in mobility; no threat to anyone other than the dozen or so locals. And even the latter seemed to be still enjoying their breakfast cup of tea.

Brookes led off once more, back the way they had come. It might not be the safest route when it came to unexpected meetings with the enemy, but many hours of telescopic observation had seemed to indicate it was free of mines. And the fog, if anything, seemed to be thickening.

They passed down the lane, passed by the house where they had heard the English voices, and started up the hill away from the settlement. They were just passing the familiar landmark of an abandoned oil barrel when the shadows came out of the fog.

The three enemy soldiers saw Brookes at the same moment he saw them, but training and speed of reaction made all the difference. They were on their way back into base, not expecting trouble, their minds on breakfast or a warm bed. Two were carrying their automatic rifles by the barrel, one had his over the shoulder, and Brookes's cradled MP5 had killed the first two while they were still juggling. The third actually tripped in his shock, causing Brookes's second burst to miss him, but it seemed that Stanley, stepping swiftly out from behind the PC, had prevented the man from getting his finger to the trigger with an accurate burst through his chest.

Then, almost posthumously it seemed, the rifle fired once as the man crumpled, shattering the silence.

'Shit,' Brookes said with feeling. He thought for a second, half his mind listening for an alarm in the camp behind him. It came as a slowly swelling chorus of questioning voices and sporadic shouts.

'Let's at least get them off the track,' he whispered.

They lugged two of the men – boys, really, judging from their faces – some 10 yards into the fog, praying as they did so that they were not trespassing on a minefield. Stanley then dragged the third to join his comrades while Brookes waited on the track, listening to what sounded like a headless chickens' convention in the camp below.

'Let's make some speed,' he told the returning Stanley, and the two of them started up the hill at a half-run, the voices growing ever fainter behind them. For the moment they were safe, but only for the moment. To make matters worse, Brookes had the distinct impression that the fog was beginning to thin. If it evaporated entirely, he did not think much of their chances of escaping detection. Looking for a possible hide was one thing; looking for one you knew was there was another matter entirely. And with three of their comrades dead the Argentinians would hardly need motivating.

When he and Stanley got back to the hide, Brookes knew, there would have to be some swift decisions. He tried to get his own thoughts in order as Stanley navigated their way through the fog.

It took them an hour to reach 'home', where Hedge and Mozza were relieved to see them. They had spent the same hour nervously waiting to find out why the enemy had fired a shot, and whether he had hit anything valuable, like Brookes or Stanley.

'Decision time, lads,' Brookes insisted. He looked at his watch. 'We have sixteen and a half hours before the pick-up, at least seven of them in daylight. We can either head out now or stay put until dark. If we go, we risk being caught in the open if the fog clears. If we stay, we risk being found or so hemmed in that we can't make the pick-up at all.'

'Nice choice,' Stanley murmured.

'Isn't it? Preferences, gentlemen?'

'Yes,' Hedge offered. 'I'd feel better on the move. If the Argies don't find us during the day then they'll be out in strength tonight, and we were warned that they probably have thermal imagers. At least while the fog stays put their choppers can't fly, and we'll have no problem keeping ahead of the foot soldiers.'

'OK. Mozza?'

'Sounds right to me.' The thought of another long and tense vigil, cramped in the sopping hide, with no real chance of fighting their way out if they were discovered, held no appeal at all.

'Stanley?'

'Suits me. Though I'd feel happier if we had a couple of those hand-held surface-to-air missiles "Air Troop" got their grubby paws on.'

'I'd feel happier if we could find a greasy spoon,' Hedge said. 'Eggs, bacon, beans, sausage, mushroom, burger, onions and a double portion of chips. All of it hot.'

Brookes licked his lips despite himself. His wife was always going on about his cholesterol level. 'Let's get packed and out of here,' he said, 'before the Argies have us for breakfast.'

A little under ten minutes later they were ready to move. Stanley led the way, the others following in the accustomed order, though considerably closer together than usual because of the poor visibility. The hide's camouflage had been left in slight disarray, on the off-chance that the Argentinians would not only spot it, but waste valuable pursuit time by laying siege to an empty hole in the ground.

Since the most counter-productive thing they could do now was to get lost, the patrol's progress was slow, with Brookes and Stanley checking and double-checking each change of direction against their illuminated compasses and what little they could see of the terrain. Generally they were climbing, but the grain of the land ran against their chosen direction, so it was often a case of two steps upward, one step down. The only apparent witnesses to their march were sheep, most of whom expressed their resentment at the intrusion with a succession of indignant bleats.

All four soldiers continually examined the fog for signs of thinning, and were frequently convinced that they could detect as much. But the overall level of visibility somehow remained as restricted as ever. At around three they gathered beneath the lip of a convenient ridge for a ten-minute rest and a silent lunch of chocolates, biscuits and three-day-old rainwater. Mozza, looking around at the other three and the cocoon of mist they inhabited, found himself thinking about *Dr Who*, the favourite TV series of his childhood. The reason, he realized, was that the foreshortened horizon made it look like they were in a studio.

They strapped their bergens back on and resumed their march. Once more it seemed obvious that the fog was thinning. And this time it really was: slowly, but definitely.

After climbing up a small valley and crossing another ridge line, Brookes called a halt. Visibility was now about 100 yards and increasing rapidly. Somehow ahead of them to the west a pale wash of sunlight was trying to make itself seen.

'Scrapes,' Brookes said. The others groaned, but nevertheless took to the job with all the speed they could muster. The turf was carefully removed, the four shallow trenches dug, the excavated earth stuffed under a convenient slab of overhanging rock, and the hessian nets fixed for relaying the turf roofs. Less than fifteen minutes after Brookes's order the four of them were each lying on damp soil in relative darkness, listening to their own hearts beating.

It was hardly a moment too soon. Their last view of the outside world had been of mist peeling away from the land and rising into the sky in great swathes, like the smoke of gunfire escaping from a nineteenth-century battlefield. Now, through the gaps afforded by the clump of tussock grass above his head, Brookes could see patches of blue sky. What a life, he thought. He sincerely hoped any future wars the SAS got involved in offered a better climate and more amenable terrain.

'Action stations!' the RAF dispatcher shouted above the C-130 engines. 'Get your gear ready, lads!' He waved an imaginary wand, and the plane's tailgate started lowering itself, letting in the world with a roar and rush.

The four men began the tricky manœuvres necessary for inserting themselves in divers' dry suits. It would have been hard enough in the middle of the pitch at Parkhead, Docherty thought, let alone in this space between supply cases where there was barely room to swing a cat. But eventually they were all suitably encased, and zipping each other up like happy debutantes. Fins were stuffed into belts, and then each man hoisted himself into the parachute harness which had been adjusted to his measurements before their take-off from Ascension. Once the distress flares had been strapped to their wrists they could start worrying in earnest.

His three comrades were not especially nervous about jumping, but Razor had never taken to it. He knew his fears were no more sensible than those of anyone getting on a plane, but somehow the knowledge did not help. When all was said and done, the ground was a bloody long way down and bloody hard to boot. It was all very well them saying the odds of both parachutes failing were a million to one. If odds like that never came up then no one would do the football pools, would they? And as for jumping into the ocean: well, it might look all soft and welcoming but that water down there was hard as concrete if you hit it from this height. And even if it all went well those idiots in the Navy still had to find you before your balls froze and dropped off.

Look on the bright side, Razor told himself, at least there were no sharks. Or at least he hoped not. Jesus, what had brought that thought into his head? A picture of Corinna's face crossed his mind, and he visualized her up the ladder in the restaurant, painting the ceiling, the overalls tight around her bum. Now that was the type of thought he needed for a leap into oblivion.

'Five minutes,' the dispatcher in charge yelled at them. The pallets holding all their gear were already waiting on the tailgate ramp, and when the cargo-hold light turned green the team of dispatchers, all wearing full parachute gear in case of accidents, started rolling them off the end and out into space.

They were next. Docherty took the lead position,

knowing that most jumpers, no matter how experienced, still found that first look down a touch unnerving. He rather enjoyed it. Inverted vertigo, he thought to himself, looking down at the churning grey sea 1000 feet below. The only ships he could see were way to either side, but at that moment one slid almost directly beneath them. The pallets containing their bergens, weaponry, signalling equipment and personal kit were floating down gracefully.

The dispatcher slapped him on the back, and he launched himself out into the C-130's slipstream, into the first sensation of being hammered forward, then the relief of the harness tugging at the body, the open canopy filling the sky. The thought crossed his mind that it was like going down a slide as a kid: the series of familiar physical sensations, the excitement.

He jettisoned the reserve chute, pulled down on both steering toggles to reduce his forward motion and unclipped the reserve hooks from the main parachute as the ocean rushed up to meet him. A split second before impact he hit the harness release, eliminating the risk of drag and allowing the canopy to go with the wind.

The water was cold, even through the dry suit, but he felt exhilarated, as he always did after a jump. He managed to get the fins on, inflated his life-jacket, and trod water as he tried to get his head high enough for a look around. He could see nothing but waves for a moment, then one of the others became suddenly visible. Half a mile or so beyond the bobbing head a frigate was sailing blithely by across his line of sight.

How long could a man survive in water this cold, Docherty wondered. It would be rather an ironic end to his career – being transported halfway round the world just to be dropped from a great height into a watery grave. 'Where are you, you bastards,' he murmured to himself.

As if on cue, a rigid raider suddenly appeared not 20 yards away, headed his way. A hand reached down with a knife to puncture the life-jacket and make it easier to pull him aboard. Razor was already sitting there, a huge smile of relief on his face.

In his scrape Mozza was composing a letter to Lynsey, even though he knew he would forget most of it before he had the chance to write anything down. She would be worried, he guessed, and so he would not be telling her much of the truth – always assuming he would be allowed to. Nobody had said anything, but he supposed there would be some sort of restrictions.

He had not seen any penguins yet, so there was nothing much to report to three-year-old Hannah. When it came down to it he supposed the only thing he really wanted to say was that he loved them both and missed them. For a moment he had a picture in his head of Lynsey's face a few inches from his own in her candlelit bedroom and he almost felt choked with yearning.

A few feet away Hedge was not missing anyone half as much as a good meal. It was his only real grudge against the SAS: the way the bosses delighted in putting such a distance between the men and any half-decent canteen. There should be an SAS equivalent of meals-on-wheels, he decided, delivering hot meals to the various OPs. Either that or the Navy could run a take-away pizza service from one of the carriers. The OPs could order by radio.

He started working out the Morse code for extra pepperoni.

Stanley, for once, was not thinking about sex, Sharon, or sex with Sharon. Well, not directly, anyway. He was remembering the ten-point guide to the ideal woman which he and Barry Saunders had made up one night, sitting in a car outside the Divis Flats. It had been a good way to spend a few hours, but it all seemed a bit stupid now. Fuck knew why. His needs had not changed, or at least he hoped not. It was bloody Mozza's fault, Stanley thought, with all that crap about love and understanding and equality. Women were not equal, no matter which way you looked at it. If they were they would have them in the SAS, right?

OK, so that was crap reasoning, Stanley told himself ruefully. But the point was . . .

The drone of the helicopter forced its way into his consciousness. Number one – great breasts with great nipples, he silently mouthed as the drone grew louder. Number two – legs long enough for skiing on. It seemed almost on top of them now. Number three – a kiss you could splash around in. It was on top of them, a black shape against the sky, and the down-draught from its blades was tugging at the knot of grass which covered the head end of his scrape.

But had it seen them? There was no way of knowing.

Suddenly the grass was swept away, leaving Stanley looking straight up at the belly of a Puma helicopter. He reached for the M16, and at almost the same moment a pilot's face appeared round the edge of the machine, staring straight down at him.

The head jerked back, the helicopter reared up and to one side, and Stanley realized there was no longer any risk of bringing it down on top of them – all in less than a second. He threw himself out of the scrape, brought the rifle with its grenade-launcher attachment to his shoulder, aimed at the open cockpit door and fired.

With a dramatic whoosh the grenade exploded inside the cockpit, catapulting one pilot out and instantly killing the other. The chopper itself fell like a stone, bounced once on the ridge and toppled over and out of sight, before a loud explosion and a sharp plume of smoke announced its total demise.

The four SAS men climbed to the top of the ridge, and looked down at the burning wreckage below. 'Nice shot, Stanley,' Brookes said over his shoulder, as he walked back down to examine the pilot who had been blown clear. He was decidedly dead.

Brookes rejoined the others. 'There's another hour or so of light,' he said. 'I don't think either of them had time to radio in, but we'd better get moving.'

They resumed the march, and spent that hour of light waiting for the tell-tale sound of distant rotor blades. But none came, and a further two-hour journey in the dark brought them to the flat valley earmarked as the pick-up zone. They slept and watched in two-hour shifts until near the designated time, then set out the infrared lights to guide their taxi in.

It arrived on time, the pilot in his PNGs looking like a refugee from *Star Trek*. 'All aboard, chums,' he announced in a cheery whisper, 'and try not to dirty the seat-covers.'

Brookes asked how many of the other groups were being collected that night.

'Just you lot,' the pilot told him. 'Either you've been very naughty, or they've thought of somewhere worse to send you.'

5

At almost 23,000 tons the Royal Fleet Auxiliary *Resource* was one of the Task Force's larger ships. Surveying it from the helicopter which had brought them across from the *Hermes*, Docherty's patrol had expected a stateroom each, generous deck space for sunbathing and a personalized leisure centre. They had been given four bunks in the middle of a smoke-filled hold, and had needed to fight their way through G Squadron's clothes, equipment and bodies to stake even this claim.

They had swiftly been spotted.

'Oh, they're really scraping the barrel now,' someone observed. 'B' Squadron's arrived.'

'Looks like they've fallen overboard once already,' another voice noted.

Brookes's patrol returned to the *Resource* in the middle of the following night, but an unusually beneficent Navy found more amenable quarters for their first night back than the bunks in the hold. After glorious hot showers, they laid themselves out luxuriously on soft mattresses and dry sheets, and all but Brookes slept for ten hours straight. Even he managed nine.

They were allowed a copious brunch before business, and Hedge redeemed all the promises he had

126

made himself over the past week. After draining a second huge mug of tea he leaned back in his seat, belched his satisfaction and wondered out loud: 'What now?'

'We'll soon know,' Brookes said. 'I don't suppose they pulled us out to send us home.' At least he hoped not. He looked at his watch. 'Come on, it's time we moved. Mustn't keep the Green Slime waiting.'

Several corridors, ladders and hatchways later the four of them were rapping on the door of the ship's ladies' toilet and being bidden to enter. Things had improved since their last visit. The tables in the centre were overlain with files, tide charts and military reference books, a mass of radio equipment was neatly stacked on benches, and maps were pinned to the cubicle doors. In one open cubicle doorway a hot-drinks machine was humming quietly to itself. Through the two portholes the grey-green sea was seething.

The Green Slime – as SAS Intelligence was (sometimes) affectionately known – was represented by Major Bill Hemmings, a tangle-haired Welshman whom Brookes had known in Oman. They were about the same age, but intelligence work was taking its toll on Hemmings, adding a few inches to his waistline and the first glimmerings of a second chin. His brain, though, showed no signs of going to seed.

After almost an hour had been consumed in debriefing their completed mission on West Falkland, he told them to help themselves to drinks from the machine and disappeared.

'He's gone for our medals,' Stanley observed.

'He's gone for a crap,' Hedge said.

Mozza stared out at the sea while Brookes scanned

127

the littered tables for any clues to their next mission. He found none.

Hemmings returned, trailing in his wake Docherty, Razor, Wacko and Ben. Some introductions were not necessary: Docherty and Brookes, though hardly friends, had often served in the same operations together, while Razor and Stanley knew each from the regimental football team. Everyone knew Hedge.

'You gentlemen,' Hemmings told them once everyone was seated, 'are Operation Backyard. Now since only half of you have any idea what this is all about, I'd better fill you in.'

After he had finished he asked if there were any questions. Brookes was feeling almost too happy for rational thought: this was indeed a mission worthy of ending one's active career – he could have hardly have asked for anything better. The other members of his patrol were still busy absorbing the idea when Docherty raised his voice.

'I have a couple,' he said. 'At Hereford we were told there were still two issues outstanding – the helicopter crew and the business of uniform. Has anything been decided?'

'On the former, yes. The Navy have found us some heroes, gentlemen . . .'

There were groans of disbelief, and murmurs of 'Kiss me, Hardy.'

Hemmings smiled sweetly at them. 'Who have volunteered – *volunteered*, gentlemen – to drop you lads off in Argentina, get as far into Chile as they can with what fuel they have left, and then bring the chopper down somewhere uninhabited and hide out for at least a week before giving themselves up. They could hardly do more, now, could they?'

128

There were groans of grudging acceptance.

'As for the uniforms, we're still waiting for the politicos to make up their minds.'

Docherty nodded. He did not mind what happened to him, but he wanted to be damn sure the younger ones knew what they were getting into before he agreed to lead them onto the mainland.

Isabel kept the Renault at 60kph as she drove it down the dead-straight section of the road from the Chilean border, and only occasionally bothered to check the rear mirror. Her mind told her each trip had to be more dangerous than the last, but her heart told her the threat was minimal. The local military was busy with the war, and the police in this part of the world were only accustomed to the problems posed by drunken oil workers. The security apparatus's natural habitat was in the cities of the north, and in any case the threat to the ruling class's security had always come from the people they exploited, not the agents of foreign powers.

They had been well prepared to catch her as a revolutionary, Isabel thought, but were ill equipped to catch her as a foreign spy. The thought brought a bitter smile to her lips.

That morning she had awoken with the word 'traitor' echoing in her brain, and no matter how vehemently she denied the charge to herself, the word refused to go away. 'So what?' she said out loud in English, the way Michael used to say it. The way he no doubt still did, she reminded herself. Somehow it was hard to think of him as still alive. Francisco seemed more alive, and he was dead.

She was a traitor to her country, but only insofar as

her country could be identified with the Junta and its retinue – the rich families, the bought union bosses, the animals who did the dirty work for all of them. She was no traitor to her class, nor to humanity as a whole.

But she was a traitor to Raul. That was the problem. That was what was beginning to get to her. He had done nothing to her, nothing to humanity. He had joined the Air Force because he loved to fly, and because it was a career that offered good money and social prestige. And maybe because, like most young men, he liked his girl to admire him in his uniform.

There were nothing wrong with such ambitions, or such a life. And because he had pursued them the Junta was sending him out to die against superior forces, and she was milking him of information under the guise of friendship, and then sending it to the enemy, increasing the chances of his being blown out of the sky.

In the plastic bag she had left under the stone there had been a full report on morale at the Rio Gallegos airbase, information on the number of nightly flights to Port Stanley, and Raul's considered opinions of both his fellow pilots and the defensive tactics employed by the British ships. Thanks to Raul's male-obsessive interest in numbers and lists – what Michael had always called the 'trainspotter mentality' – there was also a complete breakdown of the planes stationed at Rio Gallegos.

If this little information package did not get him killed, she thought savagely, then nothing would.

But the die was cast, at least for her. Guilt over Raul might be consuming the last of her soul, but the reasons for doing what she was doing seemed stronger with each week back in her native land. Argentina was like a nation in thrall, a country under a spell. Reason, judgement, any sense of real collective interest – all had been jettisoned in this fit of chauvinistic madness. Something or someone had to puncture this bubble, break the evil spell, and from where she stood it could only be the British. To help them was to help her country, and all the Rauls would have to pay the price.

Hemmings had told them that 'Backyard' would probably be set in motion on the night of either Thursday 13 May or the following Friday. Docherty's patrol was eager to get moving, but realized that Brookes and the other three needed several days to make a full recovery from their week on West Falkland. Any longer, though, and there was a danger Hedge would completely strip the *Resource* of edible food.

There was in any case quite a lot to do, particularly for the two PCs. They were responsible for deciding on, acquiring and checking the equipment each patrol would need. All eight of them were expected to familiarize themselves with all the available knowledge concerning the terrain, and be able to recognize any item of Argentinian military equipment from, as Hemmings put it, an Exocet to a standard-issue General's jockstrap.

'Sky blue and white, right?' Razor said with a grin.

'On the button, son,' Hemmings replied. 'Now go and study these diagrams.'

'They're not of Gabriella Sabatini, are they?' Stanley wanted to know.

When they were not memorizing aircraft silhouettes, Argentinian rank insignia and inadequate maps, the eight of them were getting used to operating two new state-of-the-art PRC 319 radios. These could be used for normal voice, burst Morse or liquid-crystal keyboard transmission via satellite. They were, as their proud instructor pointed out, Direction Finder Unfriendly.

As the two signalling specialists, Wacko and Mozza took the keenest interest in this new technology, but all eight of them were expected to be familiar with its operation.

Many of their non-study hours were devoted to strenuous physical exercises, as each man sought to reach and maintain the level of physical fitness they all knew they would need in the days to come.

The remaining hours were spent in sleeping, eating, noisy games of Cheat and various solitary pursuits. Each man wrote home, albeit with varying degrees of willingness and sincerity. Brookes and Wacko wrote letters to their wives that said nothing of what was in their hearts, while Mozza found it impossible to write about anything else. Docherty tried writing to Liam McCall about what he was feeling, and found he did not really know.

By Wednesday all of them were eager to go, and hoping that the earlier date had been chosen. But Brookes, delegated to extract the latest news from Hemmings, found the Green Slime man more than a touch reticent on the subject. The early date was extremely unlikely, Brookes was told, but beyond that Hemmings could not say. He was waiting for clearance from Northwood, and preferred not to speculate on why it had not yet arrived.

Brookes reported this back to the others, and Stanley, reaching deep into his vocabulary, expressed what they were all thinking: 'Fucking politicians couldn't run a fucking war if their fucking lives fucking depended on it.'

Bryan Weighell turned off the TV in the middle of the weather forecast. He was more interested in conditions in the South Atlantic than Britain, he thought. Desk work for the SAS was like life after death: your soul was still out there where the action was but your body was rotting by a telephone.

He had just watched pictures of the QE2's departure from Southampton that morning, with 5th Brigade lining the decks, and probably the bars as well. The diplomats were still shuttling to and fro like pompous penguins, but as far as he could see the die was cast, and a forced landing on the islands just a matter of time.

So why could the regiment not get clearance for Operation Backyard? All that day he had been trying to get an answer out of somebody, but all to no avail. As far as he could tell the operation had not been called off, but neither did anyone seem inclined to admit it was still on. Basically, no one seemed to want to talk about it at all.

Weighell poured himself a generous slug of malt whisky and gently simmered. He was beginning to wish they had pushed for an immediate insertion, rather than allow Brookes's patrol such a generous recovery period. But the Intelligence assessment was that ten undiscovered days on the mainland were the most they could reasonably hope for, and the general consensus at Northwood was that advance warning of air attacks would be most valuable

during the actual landing operations on 21 and
22 May.

So they had agreed to insert the two patrols on the
14th. And now it was the evening of the 13th, and
Whitehall and Northwood had become deaf to all
enquiries. Weighell could imagine how the men on
the *Resource* felt: waiting for the signal to go was bad
enough when you knew it was definitely coming.

Who else could he ring? He could think of no
one. After all, if the Prime Minister was pointedly
not returning his calls, then who would?

He looked at the telephone, willing it to ring. And
it did. In his haste to pick it up Weighell spilt most
of his whisky across the table.

'Bryan?' a voice asked. It was Brigadier Mark
Harringham from Northwood.

'Mark. I tried to get hold of you today.'

'That's why I am calling. I can guess what you want
to know . . . I assume this is a secure line?'

'Yes.'

'Good. The answer is – we still don't know if
Backyard is a starter, and if so when. The 14th seems
unlikely . . .'

'Why, what's happened?'

'Politics, of course. The Foreign Minister threatened
to resign if our troops were put ashore on the mainland
before all the possibilities of the peace process – so
called – had been exhausted.'

'Why didn't she let him?' Weighell asked angrily.

'Well, it's hard to say, but I'd guess that since the
Belgrano she's been under a lot of pressure to at least
go through all the right motions – diplomatically, that
is. And of course he's on the other wing of the Party,

and she only appointed him a month ago . . . he's in a strong position.'

'Ok, OK. But what's he waiting for? As far as I can see, all the proposals are dead in the water.'

'Not quite. Apparently, Galtieri's done a back somersault today; he told the UN chap – Pérez de Cuellar – that sovereignty is not a pre-condition for more talks. Of course, he's probably just playing for time, but Henderson and Parsons have been called back here from New York for more meetings, and we've been told not to rock the boat for a couple of days. No more *Belgrano*s and certainly no SAS adventures on the mainland.'

A couple of days, Weighell repeated to himself. He swore under his breath. 'So what do you think the chances are?'

'About 50–50, I'd say. She's still all for it, but she needs some help . . . preferably a statement from the Junta saying all bets are off and inviting us to do our worst.'

'Which isn't very likely.'

'Oh, I don't know. From what I can gather there doesn't seem to be much coherent policy-making going on over there. They might invade Chile – just for the hell of it.'

Weighell laughed, but his heart was not in it.

Raul was almost an hour late getting to the Rakosi, and Isabel had already drunk more than was sensible for her. Which was nothing unusual, she reminded herself. It might be the winter closing in, or being back in a place where heavy drinking was the norm, but she suspected her increasing level of consumption was inspired by a more personal malaise. She was drinking to blur the edges of deception. As well as self-deception, she added to herself, as Raul finally came in through the door.

His face broke into a smile when he saw her, as it always did. The same smile twisted a knife in her heart. But at least he was not falling in love with her. That night by the river, when he had sobbed out his fears, had thankfully put paid to the chance of any such relationship. It had opened the way for others – the older mistress or the older sister – and she had managed without much difficulty to steer him in the latter direction.

'My guardian angel,' he greeted her gaily, and she winced internally.

He seemed in a good mood and for half an hour they swapped small talk, his attention often distracted by the football match on the TV behind the bar. She told him what she had done that day – which was to check all the Rio Gallegos bus companies for their routes and fares – and what she was planning to do the next day: travel down the coast to investigate the local accommodation possibilities for tourists visiting the penguin colony at Cabo Virgenes.

He said he wished he could come with her, but some bigwig from Military Intelligence was arriving from Buenos Aires. 'Some Colonel named Solanille . . .'

The combination of shock and alcohol loosened her tongue. 'Tomas Solanille?' she blurted out.

He seemed not to notice the emotional charge which edged her voice. 'Yes, I think so. Why, have you heard of him?' he asked offhandedly, his eyes on the TV, where Racing Club had just been awarded a penalty.

'I think my uncle knows him,' she said steadily,

136

as the goalkeeper went one way, the ball the other. Major Tomas Solanille had been one of the men who had questioned her after her arrest: a cold, arrogant man, the sort who commissioned genealogical charts to advertise his good breeding. He had done nothing to her, except hand her over to the animals at the Naval Mechanical School.

Which was more than enough.

'Are you OK?' Raul asked.

She looked up guiltily. The football match had ended. 'Just tired,' she said.

'Too tired for our walk?' he asked, with the air of a small boy whose promised treat seemed in danger of disappearing.

'No,' she said, smiling. 'Some fresh air would be nice.'

It was fresher than she had expected, and for once taking his arm and snuggling up to his shoulder needed no more justification than the temperature and the chill breeze blowing across the estuary.

'It will soon be winter,' he said. 'I have never seen a winter in the south.'

'Maybe some agreement will be reached,' she suggested. 'Or we will win a quick victory,' she added, remembering that optimism was still the official order of the day.

He grunted. 'There might be an agreement,' he said seriously, 'but I don't think we can win a war with the English. I think we must prepare ourselves for the worst.' He turned suddenly to face her. 'Of course we will do our duty,' he added hastily, 'you must not ever think otherwise.'

'I know you will,' she said. 'But maybe there is still hope. The English are a long way from home . . .'

He explained the situation to her as he saw it, then added something almost as an aside: 'of course, we are saving our best hope for the moment when it will most matter.'

'What is that?' she asked.

He looked at her, and for a moment she thought something in her voice or her face had given her away, but what she had taken for suspicion turned into a rueful smile. 'The missile that sank their ship *Sheffield*, we have very few of them. We must make them all count.'

How many, she wanted to ask, but that would be too much. 'Have you one for each English ship?' she asked, almost playfully.

'If only,' he replied, and asked her how much longer her work would keep her in Rio Gallegos.

'A few more weeks,' she answered, and started listing what she still had to do. There was no way now that she could get a precise figure for the Exocets.

When they parted outside the Covadonga Hotel half an hour later he hugged her and kissed her lightly on the cheek. 'Thank you.'

'Thank you,' she replied.

'No, not for the evening,' he said, 'thank you for being my guardian angel.'

She walked upstairs, tears welling up in her eyes, and angrily threw her coat down on the bed. Then for what seemed liked a long time she sat in the only chair staring at the empty wall. Images from a film she had seen on British TV came into her mind, though at first she could see no reason why her memory had dragged them up. Someone – she thought it was Michael Caine – had been strapped into a chair, and was being subjected to a *mélange* of futuristic lights and sounds that were intended to scramble his psyche. But Michael Caine had managed to get a piece of glass – no, a nail – and was gouging it into his own hand to take his mind off the weird light-show.

And it worked.

It would work for her, she realized. But she did not need a nail, only a pen. She would start writing down what had happened to her, to all of them, all those years ago. How could the life of one sad-eyed pilot compete with the ghostly hordes of the dead and disappeared?

She would start now. This moment.

Giuseppe had been first. Giuseppe with the dancing brown hair and blue eyes. He had been a medical student, a lover of football and blonde girls and the poetry of Neruda. Every Tuesday, come rain, shine or bank robbery, he had visited his mother in her small apartment in La Boca, and told her fictional tales of the college life he had abandoned for the ERP. And one Tuesday he had been on his way back to Avellaneda, walking on the high girder bridge across the oil-stained waters of the Riachuelo, when the black car had stopped and swallowed him.

They had found him the next morning, in the woods at Ezeiza near the international airport, though it was only the valueless ring he had worn on one finger which had enabled an identification. The body was a charred hulk, held together by half-melted wire embedded in the charcoal crust of what had once been wrists and ankles. He would never trouble the sleep of the Junta again.

And none of his comrades had ever slept soundly again. Fear had taken their hearts, but they had carried on. They had not known how to stop.

Isabel put the pen aside and walked across to the window. The street was empty, the town sleeping. She wanted to wake every one of them, to scream at them: 'Where were you when Giuseppe Trappatoni died?'

It had worked, she realized. Raul's life or death no longer seemed to weigh so heavily on the scales.

She went to bed and managed to sleep for a few hours. As dawn showed outside she went for a walk through the empty town, down to the riverside park. The sun was rising above the mouth of the estuary, throwing a line of reflected light along the centre of the wide river, between the anchored freighters. Behind her an oil tanker rumbled along Calle Orkeke.

Isabel remembered another tanker, another early morning. In Córdoba four of them had invaded a dairy depot, all wearing red masks, and hijacked a milk tanker. Then they had driven it to the Sarmiento shanty town, and dispensed milk by the bucketful to people who could not have afforded to fill a thimble. The looks on their faces had been worth a thousand theories.

They had mounted a similar operation a month later — only this time it had been a lumber company they had held up. Building materials had been stashed aboard lorries, and driven out to another shanty town, where families lived in homes made from packing cases. There too they were greeted as deliverers, if only from rain through the roof.

She had been telling that man in London the truth when she said she felt no guilt. On the contrary, she felt proud of everything they had tried to do, and sometimes done. Her comrades might all be dead, and the Junta still alive, but they had not died in vain. None of them. They had brought hope, no matter how short-lived; and they had demonstrated a simple humanity when such demonstrations invited a lonely and painful death.

And if she had any say in the matter, then one day they would get the recognition they deserved.

Please let this be good news, Weighell told himself as he climbed the last few stairs on his way to Conference Room B. The men gathered round the table were not quite the same as on the previous occasion. The FO's Latin-American expert was absent, as was Air-Marshal Railton. And this time Cecil Matheson was flanked by his superior, the grey-haired, weasel-faced Foreign Minister.

Weighell's first impression was that the latter looked thoroughly pissed off. Which probably did mean good news, he told himself.

The MI6 man, Anthony Sharp, looked full of the joys of spring, but that could just be congenital idiocy. Harringham appeared his usual cheerful self, while the MOD's Dennis Eckersley seemed more bored than anything. Weighell thought he could detect the faintest of knowing smirks on Cecil Matheson's lips.

There was no mistaking the Prime Minister's mood. The eyes had a definite glint to them, and the mouth showed about as much warmth as a Venus fly-trap. 'Good morning, gentlemen,' she said coldly. 'There is only one item of business to deal with – Operation Backyard.' She glanced at her Foreign Minister, and received a bleak stare in return.

She asked Weighell to explain the reasons why any further delay would severely reduce the value of the operation. He explained them. Harringham was asked to concur, and did so. The PM then outlined the Foreign Minister's objections, rather than let him do so himself. Such an operation might compromise the last chance of peace, she said, with about as much conviction as an English batsman facing the West Indian bowlers.

It was like watching a child tearing the limbs off a spider, Weighell thought, and for a fleeting moment felt almost sorry for the Foreign Minister.

Matheson provided the *coup de grâce* to his own boss, with some assistance from the beaming Sharp. Intelligence agents in New York – exactly whose agents was not specified – had managed to bug the Argentinian Consulate, and to record one end of a conversation between the Argentinian envoy to the UN and General Galtieri. This conversation – and other scraps recorded in the Consulate – clearly showed that the Argentinian Government had abandoned any hopes they might have had of reaching an agreement with the British which they could sell to their own people. The Junta's only remaining interest lay in putting off the evil day, in buying all the time that they possibly could in the forlorn hope that something somehow might provide the miracle needed for their own salvation.

'I believe this removes all the objections to proceeding with Operation Backyard,' the Prime Minister concluded. The Foreign Minister gave her a look which Weighell could only interpret as pure hatred, and muttered his acquiescence.

The silence in the newspapers was ominous, Isabel thought. The chance of peace was gone; now the Junta was just waiting for the blow to fall. She wondered if any of the uniformed idiots still thought they had any chance of victory, or if they were all just paralysed by the prospect of imminent defeat.

It was a raw, cold day, and the Patagonian steppe looked even more inhospitable than usual. Out in the distance, swirls of dust hovered in the wind like miniature tornadoes, while closer to the road the dry clumps of grass were being tugged this way and that with a violent intensity. Away to her left two small dark clouds had dropped out of the overall grey to mount guard over the blunt peak of Mount Aymond.

Maybe she would write a guidebook when this was all over, she thought. She was rapidly accumulating all the necessary information, and if such books needed their authors to have a feel for the area in question, then she thought she was well qualified. In Ushuaia there was a Museum of the End of the World, and it was not just a matter of geography. There was something about southern Patagonia and southern Chile that almost revelled in the idea of being a long way from anywhere else.

'Don't they know it's the end of the world – it ended when I lost your love,' she sang to herself. If she had anything to thank Michael for, then it was an education in English and American rock music.

No, that wasn't fair, she thought. He had tried to understand her.

The road went into a long curve around an outflung shoulder of the distant mountain. At the point where it straightened once more a car was parked off the road, and as she went past it pulled out onto the road behind her. She felt a sharp stab of anxiety, and a lightness in her stomach. In the rear mirror she saw the car accelerate to pass her.

She turned, heart in mouth, to glance at the driver and was relieved to find that it was Andrew Lawson, who she had last seen three weeks before in Punta Arenas. If he had come across the border in person, it had to be something important.

'We need to talk,' he shouted through the window. 'I'll pull up when we have a decent view in both directions.'

He pulled off the tarmac at a spot close to her bridge, where any approaching traffic would be visible at least a mile away. She left the road behind him and got out of the car. He was walking towards her with a gun in his hand.

Her heart sank.

'Have you got a spare tyre?' he asked.

'What? Well, yes . . .'

He took aim and squeezed the trigger. Her left front tyre exhaled noisily. 'So I've stopped to help a lady in distress,' he said with a smile. 'I take it you can play the helpless woman if you have to.'

'As well as you can play the moronic male,' she retorted. She felt really angry at him for scaring her like that. Only a man who had seen too many films and not enough reality could do something so stupid.

He was already retrieving her jack from the boot, oblivious to her anger. She decided to let it fade away. After all, how could an Englishman be expected to know anything about fear?

She looked up and down the highway. It was empty. 'Shall I put the stuff in your car?' she asked.

'Good idea,' he said, unfastening the second bolt. 'Just put it under the front seat.'

'Won't they check your car at the border?' she asked. It had occurred to her that if he got caught she probably would too. And he would probably have diplomatic immunity.

'It had occurred to me,' he said mildly, hearing the implied criticism.

'Yes, OK. I just . . .'

'I have a false compartment in the door,' he said. 'Real James Bond stuff.'

'What about the rear-mounted machine-guns?' she asked drily.

''Fraid not. Budget cutbacks, probably.'

'What do we need to talk about?' she asked pointedly.

'Ah, yes. The purpose of this little tête-à-tête in the Patagonian wastes. Some of our soldiers will be dropping in nearby in the not-too-distant future. In fact, they may well be here already – my boss hadn't been given the precise date when I last spoke to him. There's . . .'

'You mean here on the mainland?' she asked incredulously.

'Ummm, yes. Only a few men, I believe. They will be watching your airbase at Rio Gallegos for planes taking off, and so on. Under cover, of course.'

She found it hard to believe, though after a few moments' thought she could see no overwhelming arguments against such an operation. The next thing that occurred to her was how this might affect her own mission. 'You're not expecting me to take them breakfast each morning, are you?' she asked belligerently.

'No. But in the event of an emergency London thought it advisable that you should know of each other's existence.'

'What?'

'It makes sense, don't you think?'

'But what could they do for me? What could I do for them, come to that?'

'They could get you out of Argentina when they go. On a submarine, I presume, though I don't know. As for what you could do for them . . .' He shrugged.

'I could hardly hide them under my hotel bed,' she said sarcastically.

'You could perhaps help them get to the border,' he said reasonably. 'I don't know. Like I said: it just seemed sensible to give both you and them another possible option. That's all.'

'It also gives us both someone else to betray,' she said. 'What do they know about me?'

'Only your name and the hotel you're staying at. And they wouldn't betray you.'

'Why, because they're English gentlemen?'

'Because there'd be no reason for the Argentinian military to ask them.'

'You probably don't have many torturers who enjoy their work in England,' she said coldly. 'Are you going to give me the name of their hotel?'

'No, but I'm going to show you on the map the general area where they'll be holed up.'

She looked at him in amazement. 'And then what? You expect me to wander round the local countryside looking for a bunch of men in a hole reading the *Sun*?'

6

Aboard the *Resource* they had received word that the operation was to begin shortly before midnight on Saturday 15 May. The eleven men most concerned were told first thing the next morning, and a frantic day's preparations ensued. The supplies and signalling equipment were checked through once more; the weaponry given a final test fire from the ship's rails. Last-minute letters were composed, decisions on personal gear taken and retaken, nerves kept under control by the constant banter.

That morning the eight men of the two patrols – 'North' under Docherty, 'South' under Brookes – were introduced to the Sea King crewmen: Lieutenants Billings and Hatchard, and Petty-Officer Crabtree. This threesome seemed to be under the impression that they were going on a fortnight's camping holiday in Chile, and Hatchard asked the others what they thought about taking a hamper with them for the inevitable picnics. All three of them, the SAS men decided, were 'OK for the Navy'.

Docherty remembered the hamper as he stepped out onto the rolling deck shortly after ten-thirty that evening, and smiled to himself. The *Resource* was still making good headway into the west, and seemed to be showing fewer lights than usual. With all the modern detection equipment available, Docherty knew, it still counted for something to be hard to see in the dark. It was probably his imagination, but he felt he could feel the tension aboard the ship, accompanying this dark, silent voyage towards the enemy coast.

They might still be in the self-proclaimed exclusion zone, but they were a long way from help, and the moment the helicopter was airborne the *Resource* would be heading back towards the relative safety of the Task Force with all the speed its engines could muster.

The Sea King HC4 was waiting for them on the flight deck, its newly acquired extra fuel tanks adding to the ungainliness of its silhouette. Inside it had been stripped of all but the essentials, and maybe a few of those.

'It looks like a burglar's been in,' Razor observed.

'They've even taken the seats out,' Stanley complained.

'We have a normal range of 480 kilometres,' Lieutenant Billings announced, 'and we're probably travelling 700. I'm afraid we can't even carry your normal supply of bullshit.'

'They get testy when you complain,' Hedge noticed.

'Probably his time of the month,' Wacko murmured, and found himself thinking about Anne.

'It would have been more comfortable if they'd fired us at Argentina from a cannon,' Stanley said, grabbing a piece of fuselage floor to park himself on.

'They'll probably send us back that way,' Hedge said.

The nervous chatter continued until the door slid shut, whereupon a brief interlude of silence accompanied the helicopter's ascent from the moving deck.

According to the weather report the low-hanging bank of clouds above them extended all the way to the Argentinian coast, and would at least reduce the chances of their being spotted by the naked eye. There was also a stiff wind blowing out of the west, buffeting the helicopter and ensuring a far from easy ride.

Spread around the walls of the Sea King's belly the eight SAS men could see nothing of the outside world, and it seemed an eternity before Crabtree passed back the information that the coast was in sight. Docherty's North patrol began preparing themselves, stretching limbs, checking, for the umpteenth time, that all fastenings were secure, and running narrow-beam torches over each other's make-up.

'Try not to kiss each other too often in the first few hours,' Stanley advised them.

'He still thinks he's in West Bromwich,' Wacko said.

'One minute,' Crabtree told them, and almost before the words were out they were settling down onto Argentinian soil.

'Do you think they're still angry about Rattin and Alf Ramsey?' Razor asked.

'I would be,' Docherty said, as Brookes pulled back the door for them and let the wind in. A flat expanse stretched away into darkness.

The four men leapt down one by one, feeling the weight of their bergens as they landed.

'Good luck, lads,' Brookes shouted above the roar of the blades, gave them one last wave and slid the door shut. The Sea King lifted off into the cloudy sky, and flew off towards the south, leaving the patrol alone in a silence that was broken only by the wind and in almost total darkness.

Assuming that they had been put down in the right spot, they were about six miles in from the coast and roughly 25 south-west of the Rio Gallegos airbase. The countryside around them was virtually treeless steppe, which sloped gently up towards a line of low hills some 10 miles to the west. It was almost as empty of people as the Falklands, and almost as full of sheep.

For the moment, this was all hearsay, and the patrol was forced to rely for direction solely on its two illuminated compasses. Ben led off, followed in fairly close formation by fellow Scotsman Docherty, and Wacko and Razor. Each man carried a silenced MP5 sub-machine-gun cradled in his arms, a 9mm Browning High Power handgun and a favoured knife on his person.

Unlike Brookes's patrol, North had elected not to further burden themselves with more esoteric weapons. Docherty was a believer in sticking to basics unless there was a good reason not to, and since no members of his patrol shared Hedge's skill with a crossbow he had deemed it wiser to travel without one.

They were carrying more than enough, he thought, and increased mobility was usually worth a slight reduction in the range of fire-power at a patrol's disposal. But there was no set answer. Brookes had judged differently, and only time would tell who was right on this occasion. Maybe both of them. One thing was certain: it was too late for either of them to change his mind.

The thought of the woman crossed Docherty's mind. Hemmings had made a bad mistake in telling both patrols about her at the final briefing that morning – there had been no sense in giving her name and address to South, who would almost certainly never come within 100 miles of her. If one or all of Brookes's South patrol was captured and tortured – which was hardly out of the question given all they knew about the Junta – then she had been needlessly endangered.

Docherty had not said anything at the time – the younger men were wired up enough as it was – but he had been surprised by such an elementary error. Nor had he much liked the idea of her knowing of their existence: for all he knew she was incompetent enough to get herself caught and tortured. It had happened once. He thought about what Hemmings had told them about her: college student, urban guerrilla, tortured prisoner, exile. The only one the Intelligence Services had managed to persuade to work for them. She had to be special, he decided, one way or the other.

He would like to meet her. Since his time in Mexico he had come to realize that distance was a great aid in understanding one's own country, and he would have liked to hear what she had to say about Argentina since her exile and return.

He would like to meet her, but not on this trip. This time around he had no desire to talk Spanish with anyone but the sheep. And according to Razor many Patagonian sheep spoke only Welsh. Docherty smiled and checked his watch. They had been walking an hour.

Up ahead of him Ben was in his element. The wind, the smell of clean air, that sense of space which even near-zero visibility could not hide – it all seemed a far cry from the Hereford barracks or the crowded hold of the *Resource*, far more akin to the vast silence of Lochaber and the Great Glen. All the bustle and the restrictions and the pettiness were gone. All the artificiality. They were in the middle of nowhere, and at the centre of everything.

At the rear of the column Razor's thoughts were rather less cosmic. The Cup Final was only six days away, which seemed far too short a time to win the war and get Ossie Ardiles back to England. It would be the eighth time Spurs had been to Wembley since his birth, and the first visit he would miss seeing, though admittedly he had been a bit young to appreciate the Cup Finals in '61 and '62. His mother even claimed he had slept through the former, but that was hard to believe, even of a three-year-old supporter.

At least the coming Saturday's game would be on the World Service, and he would be able to listen in on earphones, provided they did not need the radio for anything trivial, like warning the Task Force of a massed Exocet attack.

Fifteen feet in front of Razor, and only just visible in the gloom, Wacko was still trying to drive thoughts of Anne and Brendan from his mind. The truly horrible part was that while the thought of her having sex with someone else, of her letting some other man slide his dick inside her, produced a sinking feeling in the pit of Wacko's stomach, he was simultaneously asking himself whether he was still in love with her. Alone of the four SAS men walking across the Patagonian steppe, Wacko would have almost welcomed some sort of impediment to their progress. Anything to take his mind off his beloved wife.

After dropping off North patrol the Sea King had

swung sharply south, crossing the Chilean border and continuing across the wide expanse of Lomas Bay, which separates the south-eastern corner of the South American mainland from the volcanic island of Tierra del Fuego.

Once over the island, the Sea King crew kept their craft some six miles to the neutral western side of the Chile–Argentine border, which bisects the island from north to south. Forty minutes later they turned abruptly east, back across the border into Argentina. Ten minutes more and they were putting the chopper down onto a stretch of meadowland some 18 miles to the west of Rio Grande.

Like the members of North before then, Brookes's men jumped down onto enemy soil, but from this point on their experiences began to diverge. An hour had passed, they were 100 miles further to the south, and the low cloud cover had begun to break up, revealing patches of starlit sky and vastly increasing ground-level visibility.

Like most things in life, Brookes thought, this was both a plus and a minus. But, remembering that dreadful first march through the mist on West Falkland, he was inclined to look on the sanguine side. At least it would make some sort of change, being able to see where they were going.

And the further they could see, the less paranoid they needed to be about making noise. 'Ready?' he asked. 'Then let's go.'

The land sloped down from north to south, and the four men set off on a south-easterly course, which was intended to take them slowly down to the Rio Moneta. Following this would bring them to a confluence with the Rio Grande, and five miles downstream from that

they should encounter the bridge which carried the
island's main road across the neck of the river's
estuary. A turn to the left would take them into the
town of Rio Grande; a turn to the right towards the
airbase.

All four men were enjoying themselves after the
cramped noisiness of the helicopter, mostly from
the pure sense of release, but also from the simple
satisfaction that came from confidence. Each man
was thinking that they had been through it all before:
the marches and the scrapes, the bored and cramped
hours in the OP. The wet, the cold, Hedge's farts.
What could Tierra del Fuego throw at them that West
Falkland had not? It even seemed drier, and anything
less than an inch of water in your boots had to count
as luxury.

The Sea King had reversed its aerial tracks, crossing
the border into Chilean Tierra del Fuego at almost the
same spot it had entered Argentina. The sky above and
to the west was now clear, a moon shining somewhere
behind them, and ahead to their left they could see
the forested slopes of the Pico Nose, the glow of it's
snow-capped peak shining in the moonlight.

'How are we doing for fuel?' Crabtree asked.

'Looks OK. We can make Dawson Island, at
any rate.'

The Sea King flew on, across grass-covered hills
and the black waters of the Whiteside Channel, which
separates Dawson Island from Tierra del Fuego.

'Doesn't look very inviting,' Lieutenant Hatchard
remarked, as they flew across the dark forested
island. 'I'd guess we have enough fuel to reach the
mainland.'

'How much of a guess is that?' his fellow lieutenant, Billings, wanted to know. 'The island looks a damn sight more inviting than the sea.'

'I'm pretty certain. And they wanted us as far away from the drop zones as possible.'

'So they did,' Billings agreed, only a hint of irony in his voice.

The Sea King ventured out over water once more, this time the famous Strait of Magellan. The three Navy men watched in silence as the fuel indicator stopped even bothering to flicker and the Chilean mainland inched steadily towards them. Ten minutes later they cleared the coastline and the coastal track, and Billings brought the helicopter down in a convenient clearing some 200 yards inland.

For most of a minute the three men sat in silence, savouring their safe arrival. It was 0220 hours on 17 May.

They removed their gear and, thinking to minimize the conflagration, tried to drain the remaining fuel from the tanks. There was none. Another half a mile and they would not have needed to destroy the helicopter.

As it was, they had to pile forest undergrowth into the Sea King to make sure of its destruction. As flames danced through the cab and hold, they turned away and started trekking up the hill, towards their intended camp-site.

None of them had noticed Juan Fonseca watching from the trees. He had been walking home along the coastal track from a friend's house after a long and particularly satisfying game of chess. It had been satisfying because he had beaten his friend for the first time in months, and it was perhaps the resultant sense of well-being which persuaded him to investigate the strange sight of a helicopter landing in the forest.

It was not something which became clearer as he drew near. He arrived to see the crew of three – Englishmen from the Falklands War, judging by their faces and the strange markings on the helicopter – setting fire to the craft they had just arrived in. They had then smiled at each other and taken off into the forest like backpackers.

Fonseca went to look at the helicopter, now burning rather desultorily, but could make no sense of the business. He walked back to the coastal track, and wondered what he should do.

Nothing, he decided. He could make the trip into Punta Arenas the next day and tell the authorities, but he could see no good reason why he should. Wednesday was his day for visiting the town, and the helicopter was going nowhere. The three Englishmen might be invading Chile, but somehow he doubted it. This had to be something to do with their war with Argentina, and where that was concerned he rather favoured the English. They, after all, were not always threatening Chile, the way Argentina was.

On board the *Resource* Bill Hemmings spent the night waiting nervously in the ship's radio room beside the brand new PRC319. Every now and then he would reach over and brush an imaginary speck of dust off one of the gleaming surfaces. Sod's Law being in force, the first signal arrived while he was out of the room collecting cups of tea for himself and the orderly, an anorexic-looking young chap from Liverpool.

It came as a written message on the screen: NORTH BEDDED DOWN FOR THE NIGHT . . .

OPERATION PROCEEDING AS PLANNED ...
OUT.

'Any reply, sir, or shall I just acknowledge receipt?'
the orderly asked Hemmings.

'Just acknowledge,' Hemmings said. It was the first
time he had seen the PRC319 in operation, and he was
impressed. Hemmings was also pleased that the sender
– either Docherty or Wacknadze – had not felt himself
constrained by past SAS practice to use the system's
burst-message Morse capability. The PRC319 evaded
transmission detection by picking out frequencies at
random from a wide range, and North's sender had
just demonstrated both an understanding of, and his
confidence in, the new technology.

Hemmings was still feeling pleased about this when
South reported in, using the burst-message Morse
facility. Either Brookes or Moseley obviously lacked
such confidence. It was most likely Brookes. Moseley
had seemed both intrigued and delighted by the new
system, but his PC was probably getting more cautious
and more set in his ways as he got older.

The message, when translated, was the same. South
was also bedded down.

A few minutes later the Sea King crew reported
their safe landing and their current location a few
miles further inland. They had taken the helicopter as
far from the SAS patrols as anyone could have hoped.
So far, so good, Hemmings told himself. The SAS
invasion of Argentina was going according to plan.

That morning dawned clear and cold over the Rio
Grande valley in Tierra del Fuego, cloudy and cold
over the grassy steppe south of Rio Gallegos on the
mainland. Both patrols were secure in their scrapes

half an hour before dawn, and the daylight hours passed without any great alarm. Better visibility had given South a safer location, high on a grassy slope beneath overhanging rocks in an empty valley. Dawn had been unkind enough to reveal a road not 200 yards from the North scrapes, but during the course of the day only four vehicles made use of it.

With darkness both patrols moved on. Each had a reasonably specific location in mind for their OP, but both were aware of the limitations of the maps they were carrying, and knew that their final decisions would have to await an inspection *in situ*.

Docherty's patrol had the longer journey that night, but also the easier one, and soon after 0200 they could see, with the aid of the telescope, the lights of Rio Gallegos three or four miles away to the north, and those of the airbase some two and a half miles away to the north-west. Within an hour they had picked out a likely spot for the OP and begun to excavate. If daylight showed a better or safer vantage point they would move house again the following night.

Brookes's patrol had a more difficult time. The area they needed to traverse was criss-crossed by tracks, contained several farms, and, according to the plethora of signs, was an area much frequented by anglers. They took it slowly and circuitously, aware that even one barking dog might pull the world down on top of them, and midnight had passed before they slipped across the main road and into the area of rough grassland north of the river estuary. The few lights of the town were visible away to the north-east, but the only visible evidence of the airbase came with a helicopter, which flew low and noisily over their heads before disappearing northwards.

It was almost 0430 before the patrol had worked its way round to a position between the airbase and the sea, and a provisional placement for the OP had to be swiftly agreed if the four men were to be safely out of sight by dawn.

More by luck than judgement, the location proved an ideal one. The area proved less flat than the map had suggested, more like a miniature landscape of hills and valleys, with the former rarely rising more than 10 feet and the latter seldom more than 10 feet wide. The OP was set on the eastern slope of a shallow dip on the edge of this strange countryside, and though it offered no direct view of the airbase a mile to the west, it did provide, as they soon discovered, a panoramic view of the sky above it. No planes would be taking off or landing without their knowledge.

Daylight on 18 May brought North rather less satisfactory news. Planes took off from Rio Gallegos airbase on a north-westerly course, and circled round behind the distant estuary before heading eastwards out to sea. The patrol was simply too far away from the airbase for precise observation. All through that day they filed as accurate a log of air-traffic movements as they could, but once darkness arrived they would have to move nearer and take up the digging tools once more.

Outside the Rio Grande airbase, Brookes had more adventurous plans. His patrol had also been monitoring traffic in and out, but so far they had seen neither Super Etendards nor Mirages, and Brookes decided a closer inspection of the airbase was in order. Shortly after midnight he and Stanley left a sleeping Hedge and an alert Mozza, and started working their way across the pocked grassland towards the airbase perimeter.

They moved slowly, frequently stopping for several minutes to listen for a possible patrol, but the only unnatural sounds came from motor vehicles, either around the airbase or on the road beyond it. Soon the yellow lights of the distant control tower were visible above the grassy knolls, and a further quarter of a mile brought them to where the land suddenly turned flatter, as if some enormous steamroller had been employed. Lying face down behind the final fold, the two men took turns examining the airbase through their image-intensifying night-sight.

About 50 yards ahead of them a tall wire fence, topped with razor wire but apparently not electrified, ran out of sight to both left and right. One hundred and fifty yards behind this fence, and parallel to it, a single runway stretched half a mile or more in each direction on a roughly east-west axis. Between fence and runway there was nothing but rough grass waving in the wind.

The only planes parked in the open were two Aeromacchi reconnaissance craft and a single Puma helicopter. All the others were presumably tucked up for the night in the long line of buildings on the far side, between the runway and the distant highway. Away to the left there were four identical long, one-storey buildings, which looked distinctly like barracks. Next in line to the west were a two-storey office building, several large cylindrical fuel tanks, what looked like a civilian terminal building, and three hangars of various sizes. The doors of the nearest one was open, revealing the front half of a Skyhawk.

Most interesting of all, almost directly opposite the SAS men's position, three concrete shelters in the shape of flat-roofed pyramids had been constructed, and foundations dug for three more. The doors of each were shut. Working on the theory that people gave the best protection to what they valued most, Brookes reckoned the shelters might well contain Super Etendards, Exocets or both. If they did . . .

Brookes took a deep breath. If they did, he could see very little in the way of their strolling over and blowing the planes into little pieces.

Getting away would not be so simple, of course.

Stanley's hand touched his arm, and he followed the Brummie's glance to the right. The night-sight showed a patrol of four Argentinian soldiers wandering lackadaisically along the outside of the perimeter fence, chatting.

They ambled slowly past, never even throwing so much as a glance in the SAS men's direction. As I was thinking, Brookes said to himself. It looked almost too easy.

In Rio Gallegos, on the following morning, Isabel Fuentes popped the last corner of the cinnamon pastry into her mouth and stared out of the wide front window of the Le Croissant patisserie at the rain sweeping across the intersection of Calles Estrada and Zapiola. On the opposite corner a Pinguino Company bus was slowly consuming a queue of waiting passengers, all of whom were attempting to shield themselves from the downpour with soggy newspapers held above their heads. As was usual in such situations, the driver, happily ensconced in his dry seat, seemed to be checking each ticket as if it was a forgery.

Isabel smiled, took a sip of the excellent coffee, and

went back to her newspaper's reporting of the Junta's final rejection of the British peace proposals. She could see that they had little choice in the matter – assuming that they wanted to save any face at all – but when all was said and done they were only prolonging the agony. And killing off the nation's young men in the process.

She folded the newspaper and stared out once more at the rain. This was not the day she should have chosen for a day off, she decided, but since the job itself was imaginary it hardly seemed worth worrying about. After almost a month's work the briefcase on the chair beside her was bulging with information for the discerning tourist, including a glowing write-up for the establishment she was currently patronizing – 'the best croissants south of Bahia Blanca', no less.

She smiled inwardly, and wondered how much longer this would go on. She had enough money for another six months – British Intelligence was either absurdly generous or had no idea of the Patagonian cost of living – although she felt she could not stand much more than another one in the Covadonga.

She would never have guessed it, but she missed cooking. Eating out all the time was not only boring; it became almost soul-destroying after a while. There were some things people needed to do for themselves, she decided, if they wanted to keep in touch with who they were. Maybe that was why the rich tended to lose touch, because they never did their own cooking.

There were compensations in all the free time offered by hotel life. Reading, for one: she seemed to be consuming novels at the rate of one a day, or one every two for the longer ones. She had a feeling that the small secondhand bookshop in

Calle Urquiza had not seen a better customer since TV arrived in town.

She took another sip of the strong dark coffee and wondered whether to have another pastry. There was no point in leaving until the rain abated.

A large limousine drew up at the kerb almost directly opposite her window-seat, splashing water from the swollen gutter onto the pavement. The rear door opened and two legs emerged, swiftly followed by the rest of Tomas Solanille. His hair was greyer than she remembered, but the aquiline nose and the bleak eyes were unmistakable. She almost cried out in her surprise.

Another man emerged from the driving seat on the far side, younger, with that lean, cadaverous look which she always associated with Colombian gangsters on American TV shows. The two of them hurried up the short flight of steps and into the patisserie. Sit at the back, she mentally urged them, but to no avail. They sat down at the only empty window table, just as the man occupying the table between her and them got up to leave. Only two other tables were occupied, both by pairs of women, and they were in the centre of the room.

Isabel felt exposed, frightened and close to panic. If he should recognize her . . .

At least he had sat down with his back to her. Keep calm, she told herself. Remember the old discipline.

Would he know her after all this time? She had recognized him, but that was different – she had been questioned by only one of him, whereas he had doubtless questioned hundreds like her. In a way she hoped he would recognize her . . .

Christ, she told herself, get a grip! This was not the

time or the place for restoring her faith in humanity. This was something to be got out of, as quickly as possible, as quietly as possible. As alive as possible.

It was a hell of a long way to the door. And first she had to pay the bill. Christ, she thought, that would have been a smart move – being chased into the street by the woman at the counter for not paying.

She got to her feet, took the briefcase in one hand and the newspaper in the other, and, turning in such a way that her face was never visible to the two men, went up to the counter and paid her bill. Then, taking a deep breath, she walked across the five yards separating her from the door, half-hiding her head with the newspaper, as if preparing to protect herslef from the rain outside.

The only problem with this was that it left no free hand to open the door. Solanille obliged, extending an arm to push it open, without even bothering to glance up at her face.

She emerged into the rain, shivering with the memory of fear.

Early on the morning of Wednesday 19 May Juan Fonseca started up his battered Dodge pick-up and drove the nine miles up the coastal track to the Chilean town of Punta Arenas. He had several things to pick up at the market, and it always paid to buy early, so it was not until nearly noon that he walked through the portals of the police station on the corner of Calles Errazuriz and Navarro. Once inside he had some trouble persuading the duty officer to take his story seriously, but the fortuitous arrival of an officer who knew Fonseca, and was ready to vouch for his reliability, saw the wheels of investigation grinding into motion. The local military base was informed, and a meeting of all parties arranged on the southern outskirts of town. From there a convoy of police and military vehicles followed the battered pick-up down the coastal track.

It was soon being shadowed by several other vehicles, each containing a journalist alerted by his or her informant in the ranks of the police and military. By the time the convoy reached that spot on the coast nearest to the burnt-out Sea King, it contained nine vehicles. A veritable swarm of people, uniformed and otherwise, poured up through the trees to examine the scene in the clearing.

Fonseca and various officers were exhaustively interviewed, photographs were taken, theories propounded. By mid-afternoon the more seasoned journalists were back in Punta Arenas, phone in hand, trying to sell the story to the nationals in Santiago and the international press associations. News of the helicopter's landing might have taken some 60 hours to cover the eight miles to Punta Arenas, but it only required a couple more to reach Buenos Aires and London.

From the latter it rebounded southwards, via Ascension, to the Task Force. Hemmings heard of the discovery as dusk was falling across the scattered ships of the fleet, and immediately signalled the two patrols on Argentinian soil.

For Docherty the news explained quite a lot. Half an hour earlier two lorryloads of army troops had arrived at the Rio Gallegos airbase, and in the meantime two helicopters had been flying obvious search patterns over the hills to their left. Despite the fact that the Sea

King had been discovered more than 100 miles away, someone in enemy intelligence had clearly put two and two together. If the helicopter had put down troops in Argentina, then the obvious place to look for them was outside the prime targets for reconnaissance – the two major airbases. Hence the arrival of the lorries.

At least it was getting dark. Docherty doubted whether an exhaustive search would begin before first light the next day, although the Argentinians might send out random patrols that night, particularly if they had access to thermal-imaging equipment.

He took another long look at the airbase through the telescope. Both helicopters had now landed, and the troops had mostly disappeared into one of the barracks buildings. The patrol was safe for the moment, but Docherty reckoned their chances of remaining undiscovered for another twenty-four hours were less than even. If they stayed where they were.

He turned to Ben. 'Wake the others,' he said.

When all four of them were gathered together, each lying in his own arm of the cross-shaped hide, faces only a foot or so apart in the central space, Docherty told the others of the Sea King's discovery, recounted developments in the airbase below, and asked for suggestions.

Razor came up with the same idea as Docherty himself. 'Why not move back to the other OP, at least for the day? We couldn't see what was happening from up there, even with a half-decent telescope, so with any luck they'll not bother extending their search that far out.'

'I agree,' Docherty said. He raised an eyebrow at the other two, who both nodded their acquiescence. 'Ok. I think we should move as soon as it's dark enough, or

even slightly sooner, before they start thinking about
trying out their image intensifiers. So you two start
clearing up here while Wacko calls home and tells
them what we're doing.'

'Right, boss.'

Docherty resumed his watch, and noted down
the return of an Aeromacchi reconnaissance plane.
Behind him Wacko was tapping lightly on the PRC
319's keypad, while Razor and Ben were gathering
up the patrol's gear. He had to admit it, Docherty
told himself: coping with life behind enemy lines was
a damn sight easier than coping with life at home.

A hundred miles to the south Brookes's patrol had
received the same news of the Sea King's discovery,
and drawn some of the same conclusions. They too
had witnessed an upsurge in helicopter activity over
the environs of the base, and although the siting
of their hide precluded any knowledge of arriving
troops, the prospect of such had entered their heads
before Docherty's info was relayed on to them by
Hemmings.

The major difference in their situation concerned
the surrounding terrain. From what they had been able
to gather, the area of pocked, lunar grassland seemed
to cover at least a dozen square miles. Searching it
thoroughly would require both a very large number
of men and an inordinate amount of time. The odds
against their being found seemed good to Brookes,
and the others concurred.

To pull back, as North was doing, seemed more
dangerous than staying put. There was nothing
behind them but more of the same and the sea.
To reach relative safety they would have to move

back inland, along the same difficult route through populated country they had used on their way in.

The clinching argument, though, was the existence of the concrete aircraft shelters. Brookes suspected they contained Super Etendards, and unless and until he discovered otherwise the PC could see no justification for removing the patrol from its observation duties. When those planes took to the skies the Task Force would have to be waiting for them, or who knew what fresh disaster might occur.

South would sit out any search.

7

The following day clouds filled the skies over both airbases. From North's original OP, Razor watched through the telescope as the Argentinian troops conducted a systematic sweep of the hills around the airbase. A long interval of rain did nothing to quicken their step, and after a while Razor began to feel almost sorry for the bedraggled lines in the distance.

The rain must also have helped mask the edges of their second OP, because the line of troops edged its way past the turfed-over roof of the empty hide without a second glance.

The whole scene reminded Razor of the hunt across the heather in the original film of *The Thirty-Nine Steps*. Even the countryside looked similar. He wondered if he might end up like Richard Hannay, handcuffed to a beautiful woman. Some hope, he thought. Some fucking hope.

A hundred miles to the south, Hedge was wondering whether there was a pizza delivery service in Rio Grande and coming up with much the same answer. The rain was falling on South as well, and with rather more venom.

As for the real enemy, the helicopters had been active overhead again that morning, but no Argentinian

169

troops had so far crossed the OP's line of vision. Which did not mean very much. In such country, and in such a noisy downpour, they could be 20 yards away and nobody would know the difference. Hedge was not fond of this particular site: he would have preferred one with a wider field of vision, even at the inevitable cost of greater visibility. It was just too nerve-racking, not being able to see anything.

Still, Brookes was a good bloke and a much more experienced soldier than he was, so . . .

'Penny for 'em,' Mozza whispered to his left. One advantage of the rain was that it made whispered conversation safe.

'I was just wondering what Johnny Gaucho's doing out there.'

'Probably drinking hot tea in front of the canteen TV,' Mozza said.

'Go on, rub it in.'

Soon after dusk, Brookes decided they needed a check on what was happening at the airbase. Stanley and Mozza were dispatched, travelling light, wearing PNGs and with only their Browning High Powers for armament.

Shortly after they had left, a message from Hemmings came through: the landing force would be hitting the Falklands beaches the following morning. 'Just thought you'd like to know,' Hemmings signed off, but Brookes, mulling over the message, wondered whether the Green Slime man was obliquely trying to say something else. Something like: 'if you're going to have a go at those Super Es, then tonight would be the night to do it.'

But if they had a go and failed, then who would be

there to give advanced warning of the planes' arrival over the Task Force?

And yet, and yet ... The Argentinian security looked pathetic, the chances of success good. He still had a couple of hours to make up his mind.

Mozza and Stanley, meanwhile, had reached that vantage point which Brookes and Stanley had occupied two nights before, and removed the PNGs. The scene looked much the same to Stanley, except for the fact that all three of the concrete shelters were now open. And inside each one, brilliantly illuminated in white fluorescent light, stood a gleaming Super Etendard jet. 'Geronimo,' he muttered under his breath.

'There's another two parked outside the far hangar,' Mozza whispered, handing him the night-sight.

Stanley saw them for himself. Four Skyhawks were lined up behind them. The two Aeromacchis were parked in the same place as they had been before. The helicopter had acquired a twin.

He gave Mozza the thumbs up, then jerked both thumbs in the direction of their OP. Both men slid back down the slope they had been lying on, put their PNGs back on, and started for home across the patchwork of hummocks and hollows, Mozza in the lead.

They had gone hardly 100 yards when a quietly spoken fragment of Spanish seemed to rise out of the silence, like a record fade-out in reverse. At almost the same instant a figure appeared above them, a blue silhouette against the night clouds, not more than 10 feet away.

Stanley's Browning made a sound like a stuttering cough and as the figure began to collapse another appeared, like the second in a line of ducks in a fairground booth. Mozza sent three bullets into the shadowy mass of the man's trunk, and he folded with a sickening groan.

Silence reasserted itself. The two SAS men stood motionless, eyes and ears straining for sight or sound of other enemy soldiers. For a moment there was none, but a slight scraping noise beyond the two corpses betrayed the third Argentinian.

He could have run off into the dark or started shouting, but he ran straight over the rise towards them like a lunatic, waving his gun around in search of a target. The combined power of the two Brownings threw him backwards in a tangled heap.

'Christ almighty,' Mozza murmured.

Stanley was already working out what to do with the bodies. The only digging tools they had were their hands, and it would take longer than they had to bury three men in such a manner. But just leaving them where they were would invite discovery. Once they failed to report in, a search would be mounted, and before too long helicopter searchlights would be beaming down on the corpses.

'We'll have to cover them somehow,' he decided. 'With grass.' He pulled the three bodies down into the hollow while Mozza tore out clumps of tussock grass. Somehow they managed to weave the long grass around and between the dead men in such a way that the first gust of wind would not blow it away.

'Good enough,' Stanley said. 'Let's go.'

They regained the OP without further mishap, but one look at the two men's faces told Brookes that something had happened.

'Trouble,' Stanley told him. 'We ran into three

Argies. Could have been a regular patrol or maybe not – there was no way of knowing. But they were armed. We took them out and covered them up, but they'll be missed sooner or later.'

Brookes looked at Mozza. 'You OK?' he asked.

'Yeah,' Mozza said, nodding. It had all been so quick. He was not sure how he was.

'The kid was brilliant,' Stanley said.

'What now, boss?' Hedge asked.

Brookes looked at his watch. It was 1913 hours. He told the other three about the message from Hemmings, and what he had read between the lines.

'I think you're wrong about that, boss,' Hedge said. 'Hemmings didn't strike me as the sort of guy who'd go in for hints – he'd just say it straight out. But . . .'

'You may . . .' Brookes started to interrupt.

'But having said that,' Hedge went on inexorably, 'I still think it's a fucking good idea, no matter who had it.'

'It's got my vote,' Stanley agreed. 'If we stay here they'll keep looking till they find us. So, if we've got to go, then we might as well take in all the sights on our way home. Like those concrete shelters.'

'The landing's tomorrow,' Brookes argued. 'The fleet will be at its most vulnerable. It's the one day they can't afford to be surprised by those Super Es.'

'They can't be surprised by planes that we've already blown up,' Stanley said emphatically.

'I know,' Brookes agreed. 'But it's a risk nevertheless. If we fail . . .'

'Who dares wins, boss,' Hedge said straight-faced.

'OK. We're all agreed? Right. Next question – do we seek approval from the Green Slime?'

'The way I see it, boss,' Stanley said, 'is that we're
the ones on the spot, and we're the ones who'll be
playing beat the clock with the Argies out there. We
know what's what. And we don't have time to fuck
around with politics.'

'Agreed,' Hedge said. 'At least, mostly. But why
not tell them what we're about to do, preferably just
before we do it? If they agree, great. If they don't,
we'll have to think up some reasons why we had to
go ahead and do it anyway.'

Brookes smiled. 'Very pragmatic,' he said.

'That's me, boss,' Hedge agreed.

'OK,' Brookes said decisively. 'I've been thinking
this over for a couple of days now, and there are
certain obvious problems. First off, the subs are busy
looking after the Task Force till the landing's over, so
they can't come for us before Sunday at the earliest.
Our only other escape route is across the Chilean
border, which, as you all know, is about 40 miles
the other side of the airbase. But we can't go rushing
round the airbase with 90lb bergens on our backs, so
we'll have to leave them somewhere for the duration.
If we leave them this side of the base we'll have to work
our way right round the place after all hell has broken
loose, so it seems better to move everything across to
the far side first. OK? Is that all clear?'

They all murmured assent, their faces deadly serious. Each of them was beginning to realize just how
difficult getting away with it was going to be.

'So,' Brookes continued, 'we'll pack everything up
and start off around nine, which will give us three
hours to get round the base with all our kit, stash it
somewhere, and be ready for a midnight start. Any
questions?'

There were none. Or at least none of the sort Brookes intended.

'We could set up in competition with Pickfords,' Wacko muttered, as the patrol prepared for yet another move, this time back to the forward OP. It was two hours after nightfall.

The shower promised them by the Task Force's meteorological experts had lasted about seven hours, and showed no sign of giving way to one of the promised bright periods. 'It's going to be more like a swimming pool than a home,' Ben complained.

'A man's castle is his swimming pool,' Razor added helpfully.

'Keep it down, lads,' Docherty admonished them. He was beginning to worry that the sheer incompetence of the enemy's search that day had engendered a dangerous overconfidence.

'Sorry, boss.'

And then again, Docherty thought, he was probably overreacting. They had seen the Argentinians wend their way back into the base, and in any case the rain and wind were more than loud enough to drown out the sound of lowered voices. Even so, bad habits were catching.

He considered the latest fruit of Razor's new preoccupation with mixing proverbs – 'Don't cross a bridge with a stitched chicken' – and smiled to himself.

'We're ready, boss,' Ben whispered.

They started off down the hill, and Docherty had a last look back at the OP site before putting on his PNGs. From 10 feet away there was no sign it had ever existed. And until someone or something had the misfortune to fall through the turf roof there would not be.

It took them a couple of cautious hours to cover the two miles to the forward OP, and another hour to bale it out sufficiently for any sort of even vaguely comfortable occupation. At least the rain had stopped by the time they finished, and over the next two hours a sky of broken clouds gave way to a cold and welcome clarity.

Docherty reported their move back to Hemmings, and had the following morning's landing on East Falkland confirmed. Tomorrow, he thought, as he lay back in the theoretical pursuit of sleep, tomorrow a lot of kids who had never seen real action would find out something about themselves they had never known before. That their instinct for survival was stronger than they had thought, or, more frighteningly, that it was a lot weaker. That a grown man's bladder really did have a will of its own. That time was as elastic as any dope-smoker knew it was. That nothing could be as ugly as death. Or as peaceful.

The smell of the damp earth walls was heavy in his nostrils. It was a good smell, he decided. The smell of life. As he drifted into sleep he saw one last picture in his mind: the myriad floating candles on the moonlit Lake of Patzcuaro, a fragile flame for each and every ancestor on the Mexican Day of the Dead.

Raul was again late arriving at the Rakosi, and this time the long wait wore more heavily on Isabel, who looked up each time the door opened, hoping for Raul, but half-expecting Tomas Solanille. When Raul did finally appear he was with several of his fellow pilots, and already the worse for drink. He greeted her with a kiss and the usual smile, but she could immediately see that he was in a bad state.

It did not take long to find out the reason: the next day the English were probably going to land, and the Air Force was supposed to stop them. The Rakosi was full of pilots who thought so and said so, loudly. The Army would do nothing, the Navy would do nothing. Fucking eunuchs, every last one of them. The Air Force had to do it all. If it was not for them the nation would have no honour.

One man who claimed to have a son in the Navy, and who objected to the pilots' blanket condemnation of all things naval, was hurled out into the street.

Isabel managed to get Raul away from his companions, and into one of the booths. His aggressiveness vanished, and he became desperately maudlin. 'This will be our last meeting,' he said. The next day he would be killed, and he wanted her to write to Mariella, but not to sign her real name, because Mariella might not understand his knowing another woman, so it would be better if she signed herself Pablo, or something like that.

Eventually she managed to persuade him that his chances of survival on the next day would not be improved by dulling his reflexes with an excess of alcohol, and that she was hungry, and that there was a nice restaurant in Calle San Martín where she could eat and he could drink coffee.

He sheepishly agreed, and an hour later was *compos mentis* enough to provide the information she most wanted. She had seen Solanille again, she said.

'The friend of your family,' he remembered.

'Is he based here?' she asked. 'I would like to pay my respects.'

He was based in Rio Gallegos, Raul thought. And in the town, not at the airbase. He was something to do with Intelligence, so he was probably based at their HQ on Calle Zapiola, opposite the police station.

They went for their usual walk through the park by the river, though the conversation seemed more stilted than usual. She was thinking that maybe he was right, and that this would be the last time she would see him. He now seemed preoccupied with the day to come, almost eager to be on his way.

'Thanks for looking after me,' he said when they parted, throwing her one more sad smile as his taxi sped off back towards the airbase.

She walked down Avenida Julio Roca, past her hotel, and for another couple of blocks before turning left down Calle Ameghino. From the next corner she could see across Calle Zapiola to where several lights blazed in an elegant three-storey building. Maybe Solanille was in there now, writing his memoirs.

She turned and started walking back to the hotel, telling herself she was being foolish. The man had not laid a finger on her, turned any electric switches, forced her to eat her own shit, or raped her on a rack.

He had just sent her to those who had.

Shortly before 2100 hours Mozza encoded Brookes's message — BELIEVE DISCOVERY IMMINENT STOP RELOCATING TO CHILE STOP FIVE SUPER ETENDARDS EYEBALLED STOP WILL ATTEMPT DEMOLITION EN ROUTE STOP OUT — transmitted it by 'burst', and then closed down the PRC319's reception capability.

A few minutes later the four fully loaded men were making their way in single file across the dark and broken landscape, wearing PNGs, silenced MP5s at the ready. There had been no audible outcry from the airbase during the last few hours, no sign whatsoever that the three men now wearing grass shrouds had been missed. So far fate seemed to be smiling on the SAS.

The weather too was lending a hand, in the form of a cold, persistent drizzle. Besides reducing visibility, such conditions were likely to reduce the enemy's enthusiasm for setting foot outdoors. If it stayed like this, Brookes mused hopefully, they might even get away.

But first things first, he told himself. First we get the planes, then we start worrying about saving our own skins. Even all four of their lives would be a cheap price to pay for saving a ship.

He wondered, not for the first time, if having such thoughts merely demonstrated a propensity for stupid heroics. He knew that was what his wife would think, and probably his sons would come to think so too, once they had had all sense of honour knocked out of them by either business or university. What the hell. It still seemed real to him, and where else on earth could he go for judgement other than to his own conscience?

Behind him Mozza's watchful countenance also hid a turbulent state of mind. The killing of the Argentinian – the first man he had ever fired on in combat – had left him . . . well, it was hard to say. His senses seemed heightened, but that might have more to do with the danger they were all in. He also felt a dull ache in his stomach, but Hedge would say that was just hunger. Mozza did not know. He wanted a chance to think it all through, but it looked as though that would have to wait.

They were skirting the western end of the runway now, the nearest airbase buildings half a mile distant. Somewhere ahead of them was the main highway, and just as that thought came to Mozza the lights of a car appeared, and began working their way across the patrol's line of march.

They crossed a rough fence which seemed to separate a sheep meadow from airbase property, and five minutes later reached the road. They crossed close to a stream bridge, and followed the stream up a shallow, rock-strewn valley for a few minutes more before Brookes called a halt and indicated a particular tumble of rocks. 'This will do,' he whispered.

The drizzle had stopped. They removed what they would need and stashed the bergens in convenient crevices. Each would carry a silenced MP5 and Browning, but only two men were carrying anything on their backs: in Stanley's case a canvas bag packed with explosive devices; in Hedge's a lethal crossbow.

They moved back down the valley, crossed the highway and traversed the long stretch of rough grassland. As they neared the end of the long runway cloud-reflected light from the airbase allowed them to dispense with the PNGs.

The previous night they had failed to find any sign of an alarm mechanism in the wire fence, but Brookes still had his heart in his mouth as he bent down to begin cutting. He could hardly believe their security could be this lax.

But it was. A minute later they were all through the flap, and Brookes was doing his best to render the break invisible with wire clips. The runway stretched towards the distant cluster of faint lights, and the four men began advancing alongside it in single file. It was ten minutes to midnight.

They had gone barely 100 yards when the lights on either side winked on. For a moment Brookes thought they had been seen, but the sound of an approaching plane provided a more reassuring reason for the sudden illumination. The four men spread themselves out flat on the grass and waited.

The plane – a Pucara – roared past, its wheels touching down alarmingly near them, sending spray into the air. Almost instantly the runway lights were extinguished. At least someone was awake in the control tower, Brookes decided. It was not exactly a comforting thought.

He wondered whether to wait until the airbase's sudden burst of activity had died down, and decided not to. For all he knew a whole squadron of planes was on its way to Rio Grande.

The patrol resumed its progress, and after a few minutes the blaze of something like a camp-fire became visible in the vicinity of the concrete shelters. On West Falkland the Argentinian sentries had often hunkered down around such fires, and Brookes thought that was probably the case here. He hoped there would not be too many of them.

The patrol moved away from the side of the runway and veered out onto open ground, so as to give themselves a line of approach to the rear of the concrete shelters. As they approached the built-up part of the airbase the ambient light grew slightly stronger, to the point where the PNGs again became as much of a hindrance as a help. Brookes found it hard to understand the overall level of illumination;

it was as if one person had demanded a blackout for security against air attack, another had demanded bright lights as protection against a ground incursion, and the two of them had been forced to compromise on the sort of dim lighting that would have graced a Victorian street.

Still, he was not complaining. The first of the half-built concrete shelters was only 100 yards ahead, and there seemed nothing to prevent them rendering at least three of the Super Etendards incapable of inflicting any damage.

They reached the rear of the first completed shelter, and Brookes hand-signalled Stanley and Hedge to reconnoitre around either side. While Brookes and Mozza waited for them to return, the PC gently ripped several clumps of grass from the sandy soil, smoothed out the surface with his hand and etched out a plan of the three shelters. When the other two returned five minutes later they were able to fill in the exact placing of the fire and four sentries.

The fire was more or less midway between the first and second shelters, and almost level with an imaginary line drawn through their front walls. Three men were sitting around it. Stanley raised one finger and then put his hands together behind one ear to show that one of them was asleep. The fourth man was slowly pacing to and fro along the line of the three huts.

Brookes thought for a moment then indicated on the diagram what he expected from the others. They all nodded.

Stanley went down the side of the shelter furthest from the fire, while Mozza took off on a long semi-circular walk which would take him down between the second and third shelters, where he would be able to intercept anyone running towards the centre of the airbase. Brookes and Hedge waited by the corner of the space between the first and second, taking turns to keep the men around the fire under observation.

Five long minutes passed, and it was beginning to seem as if the walking sentry had stopped walking when Hedge saw him emerge from the other side of the second shelter, exchange some undecipherable pleasantry with his two conscious comrades, and disappear behind the front of the first shelter.

Stanley, concealed behind the far corner, listened to the sound of the Argentinian's boots on the gravel growing slowly more distinct. Then he could hear breathing, the sharp intake of someone dragging on a cigarette, and the man was there, not four feet away from him, a black shape against the grey night. As he turned Stanley stepped forward, one hand reaching round to cover the mouth, the other drawing the sharp blade across the bare throat.

There was rush of blood, a slight, almost inaudible gurgle. Stanley lowered the body carefully to the ground, removed the man's peaked cap, and placed it over his woolly hat. Then he picked the cigarette up from where it had fallen and started walking back towards the fire some 40 yards away.

Something in his walk must have been wrong, because one of the men by the fire suddenly looked up suspiciously. 'Sal?' he asked.

'*Sí?*' Stanley said.

The man went for the rifle beside him, but his fingers were nowhere near the trigger when Stanley's Browning put a double tap through his upper torso.

His companion was quicker, ducking out of Stanley's

sight as he grabbed for his M16, but any sense of self-congratulation was laid to rest by the crossbow bolt which Hedge put through the back of his neck.

The third man, rudely awakened by the violent demise of the first, did not even bother to go for a weapon. He just launched himself out of his chair and into the possible salvation of the darkness. Stanley's Browning stopped him dead in his tracks.

The SAS men held their positions for a moment, ears straining for sounds of an enemy response.

There was none. Stanley and Hedge propped up the three Argentinians by the fire, and even added some broken packing cases to the flames. They did not exactly look real, but they would fool the eyes of any pilot coming in to land.

Brookes meanwhile was checking out the doors of the concrete shelter. His heart sank when he saw a state-of-the-art combination code plate beside it, but tried simply sliding the door anyway. It opened.

Inside his narrow-beam torch picked out the familiar nose-cone of the French-built jet. There was no sign of missiles, either Exocet or any other kind.

Stanley appeared beside him, the bag of explosives held loose in his right hand. 'How long, boss?' he asked softly, removing the time fuses and packets of C4 explosive.

'Say half an hour for this one. The same minus the time elapsed for the next, et cetera. OK? And keep it simple – just the nose-cones will do.'

He went back outside, hoping that half an hour would not be too long, or too short. They needed their presence to remain undetected at least long enough to find the other Super Etendards, and a few minutes extra for getting away would do no harm at all. On the other hand, if their presence was detected before the half hour was up then the enemy would have a chance to defuse the explosives.

There was no correct answer to this one   only the interplay of judgement and luck.

Stanley came out and they moved on to the second shelter, passing the three dead men around the fire. For some reason Brookes was reminded of the three trolls turned to stone in *The Hobbit*, a book he had often read to his boys when they were young. He had enjoyed them then, he thought, and maybe they had enjoyed it too.

Hedge had moved on up ahead, covering their front, while Mozza had been sent back to cover their rear. He took up station on the corner where Stanley had cut the guard's throat, his eyes drawn against his will to the pool of blood which had once sustained a life.

Stanley finished fixing the second plane, and Brookes waved Mozza up one shelter. Five minutes later all three fuses were burning, and the four men were gathered together in the shadow of the farthest shelter wall. Ahead of them a small parapet wall marked the perimeter of the large expanse of tarmac fronting the main hangars and, further on, the civilian airport building. There was precious little cover.

They had only twenty minutes before the explosives detonated, but there was always a chance no one would hear the small charges.

Two Aeromacchis were parked almost within spitting distance. 'Should we take them out?' Stanley asked.

'No,' Brookes said. 'At least not until we've made sure we've got all the Super Es.' There was no sign of any more guards, which did not mean there were none.

Once the four of them moved out of the shadows they might be visible from the control tower away to the left, but at least it was lit within, which would make it difficult for anyone inside to see out.

The fuses were burning away. 'OK,' Brookes decided, 'let's take the hangars one by one.'

He led off at a canter, swinging across the parapet wall, and the others followed. For the first time they were out in the light, and it felt like it.

They reached the first hangar door, and Hedge started sliding open a large enough gap for them to enter by. There was a harsh screeching sound of unoiled wheels, which seemed to hang in the damp night air. They all froze, but there was no indication anyone else had heard it.

The hangar contained several Pucaras, and Brookes shook his head to Stanley's gestured enquiry.

They moved on to the next, where Hedge took his time with the door, and managed to ease it sideways in virtual silence. Brookes was just squeezing through the crack when a voice rang out in the distance.

'Control tower,' Mozza whispered. 'He wants to know if we're "Díaz".'

'Díaz has changed shifts,' Brookes shouted back in Spanish. He could see a figure standing at the top of the control tower steps, a cigarette glowing as he took a drag.

'Who are you?' the man wanted to know.

'Gómez,' Brookes shouted back, raising his MP5. As the man backed through the doorway both he and Stanley opened fire with their silenced SMGs. The man seemed to leap from sight, and the sound of glass breaking carried across the intervening space.

Please be alone, Brookes pleaded, and for a few

seconds an unbroken stillness and silence seemed to answer his prayer. Then the light in the control tower abruptly went out, and the sound of a swelling air-raid siren filled the air.

For a few seconds they seemed paralysed by the sound.

'Any ideas, boss?' Hedge asked.

Brookes awoke from his momentary trance. 'Let's keep moving,' he said. 'Stanley, take the front. Mozza, Tail-end Charlie.' In the distance they could all hear motors revving.

They ran forward along the front of a third hangar, and Brookes looked inside as the others listened to the growing tumult of the enemy's awakening. Brookes was just re-emerging when a jeep loaded with men careered round the far corner of the building. Stanley and Hedge opened fire, sending the vehicle spinning out of control and into the corrugated hangar wall with a sound like a giant gong being struck.

No one emerged from the wreckage.

Stanley walked forward, and then ducked back quickly as someone opened up in his direction with an automatic rifle. He took cover behind a fork-lift truck loaded with empty pallets.

The PC looked at his watch, and turned to Hedge and Mozza. 'Hedge, get behind the parapet. Mozza, get back towards the shelters in case they try and outflank us. We'll be joining you shortly.'

He took cover himself behind the tailplane of a parked Aeromacchi, conscious of enemy movement on the tarmac ahead of them. 'We have to hold them for three minutes,' he shouted to Stanley.

'Piece of cake,' the Brummie shouted back. 'By the way,' he added almost conversationally, 'there's another couple of Super Es just round the corner there. I'd just seen 'em when the bastards opened fire.'

'I think they'll probably object if we walk over and plant some plastic on their noses,' Brookes observed. He fired a burst with his MP5, and there was a crash of someone diving, or falling, back behind cover.

'If I can get behind that truck,' Stanley shouted, indicating the fuelling tanker to his left, I can at least put a few holes in them.'

'Wait till we hear the others have gone up,' he ordered, and checked his watch. They should have blown by now.

He looked back just in time to see a flicker of light and to hear the first of the slight whooshing sounds he was waiting for. That was one Super Etendard which would not be launching an Exocet against a British ship. And that was another. And another.

Three down, two to go. He could see Argentinian troops moving up on the far side of the runway, and knew that there was no way they were going to get away from the airbase. They might as well do all the damage they possibly could.

'I'll cover you,' he shouted, knowing full well – and knowing that Stanley knew full well – that any covering fire he could provide in this situation was about as useful as a paper umbrella. Still, he began spraying three bursts in a random pattern across the entire front.

Stanley catapulted out from behind the fork-lift, took seven or eight running paces and launched himself into the roll which would take him behind the truck. As he disappeared from Brookes's sight the truck exploded in a huge sheet of flame, hit by Argentinian fire. Brookes bowed his head, blinding lights dancing on his retinas. Then, seduced by the sudden thought that everyone would be equally blinded, he launched himself in a slalom-like run across the tarmac, his MP5 waiting for its target.

Ten paces, twenty, and there was the nose-cone . . .

A violent pain in his chest seemed to come from nowhere, to well up and engulf him, and the lights went out.

Hedge saw him go down. He knew Brookes and Stanley must have had some good reason for doing impersonations of the Charge of the Light Brigade, but whether he would ever find out what it was seemed open to question. Still, he had to try.

He eased himself across the parapet with the intention of advancing in a crouching run. He had hardly gone two paces when the burst of fire hit him, and knocked him down like a skittle. With a supreme effort, and the good fortune of some poor enemy shooting, he managed to lever himself back across the wall.

Neither Brookes nor Stanley had moved out on the tarmac, and there seemed to be a lot of troops milling around beyond them. Hedge took as good a look at his wounds as he could manage in the dim light. It seemed like one bullet had shattered the shinbone, another had pierced the knee. He would not be going anywhere under his own steam for quite a while. It also hurt like hell.

He tried to lever himself up onto one leg, and sank back with a grimace of pain. He exhaled noisily and examined the darkness behind him, just in time to see Mozza materialize out of it. 'They haven't got round behind us yet,' Mozza said. 'Let's . . .' His voice trailed off as he saw the body of Brookes stretched out on the distant tarmac. And failed to locate the fourth member of the patrol. 'Where's Stanley?' he asked.

'Somewhere under that truck,' Hedge said brutally. 'And . . .'

'Is the boss dead?'

'Dunno. But it doesn't look like he's going any-where, and neither am I, so you get the fuck out of here, Mozza, while you still can.'

'I'm not deserting you,' Mozza insisted. He listened for sounds of pursuit but could hear none.

'The hell you aren't,' Hedge said, grabbing Mozza's sleeve. 'Listen to me, you numbskull,' he hissed. 'We've sent a few Argies to meet their maker here, and their mates are not going to be very pleased. Plus, we're not wearing uniforms and they're going to think they don't need any more excuse. And if they get all of us then there's no witnesses, right? They can do what they want, and when the time comes make up some cock-and-bull story about us all being killed in battle or lost at sea. But if you get away then the rest of us have got a chance of getting out of this alive. Got it?

'Yeah, I . . .'

'Then fucking go!'

Mozza went.

Ten rapid strides took him behind the hangar, and hopefully out of sight of the enemy. In the darkness he stopped to put on the PNGs, took a deep breath, and told his feet to be still while he spent ten precious seconds of running time in coherent thought.

There was no hope of retracing the patrol's entry route along the runway – that direction would take him back into the light, and back into the arms of the Argies. His best bet was to head in the general direction of the road, and hope he could find some way under, over or through the fence without any cutting equipment.

He moved off at a run, along the back of the hangar, and across an open stretch of darkened ground between a stagnant-looking lagoon and several lighted barracks. No shouts pursued him – only the distant sound of gunfire: Hedge must be still drawing fire and holding up the advance.

As the thought crossed his mind the gunfire stopped. Mozza hoped to God it had stopped because Hedge had surrendered.

He veered round the end of a darkened building and into another stretch of open ground. A hundred yards in front of him the airbase entry-exit road passed through a wide gateway in the fence and onto the highway beyond. One floodlight stood above the security checkpoint.

The idea of using stealth to escape flickered across his mind, but failed to take a hold. He was too wired up, too psyched out by the events of the last fifteen minutes, to even consider slowing down. Still running, he aimed himself at the open gateway like a torpedo, and for reasons he could not begin to understand, found himself wailing like a banshee as he did so.

A guard emerged from the doorway, more surprised than ready, and Mozza's MP5 took out both him and his companion before they could fire a shot. If he had not seen the two motorbikes leaning against the far wall he would probably have kept running straight across the highway and on towards the centre of the island.

But somehow the bikes registered in his consciousness, and brought him to a halt. He looked back –

no one was heading his way, not yet at least. The bikes were both 250cc Yamahas, and of a type he had ridden before, both in Hereford and Manchester. He got astride one, rolled it a few feet and then fired two treble-tap bursts into the tyres of the other, before throwing the MP5 into the darkness.

He rolled his machine out onto the highway, which sloped down towards the south, away from the direction he wanted to go. Or did he? He forced himself to spend time thinking it through. The way back to their kit was to the right, but what was there in his pack that he needed? There was no way anyone from the Task Force was going to come and collect him, so the radio would be no help.

What the hell – a silent exit was the best start of all, and the best thing he could do was get as far away from the airbase as fast as he could, in any direction. Once he was far enough away he could start heading west towards Chile. He eased the Yamaha onto the slope, and freewheeled away from the airbase gates. The hill went on and on, as if placed there by a friendly god, and he was almost a quarter of a mile from the gates before he needed to slip the bike into gear. The noise seemed deafening, but there was no sign of chasing lights on the road behind him.

He tried to picture the detailed map which Brookes had been carrying. Almost opposite the airbase, he seemed to remember, there was a turn-off which ran in a roughly westerly direction all the way to the border.

He had no sooner had the thought than a turn-off appeared. It had to be the one. Mozza swerved off the highway and onto the gravelled track, slowing down until he was more sure of the surface. It was OK, he decided. At a steady 30 miles per hour he could be at the border in an hour. But first . . .

He brought the bike to a halt, took out his Browning and used the butt to smash both front and rear lights. Then he replaced the PNGs and started off again. The track ran across the same sort of landscape they had first encountered after landing on the island: not exactly flat, but gently undulating grassland with little vegetation above knee height, just a few stunted trees in the stream bottoms. It was an easy ride, Mozza thought, but as the miles passed he began to get the distinct impression that the road was curving more and more to the south, and away from his intended direction.

The illuminated compass said he was going south-westwards, but compasses were notoriously unreliable this near to the poles. Meanwhile the sky was showing signs of clearing. It was not, he thought, as if he had any real choice but to follow this road wherever it went. Not when the alternative was a return to the airbase.

When the sky cleared he could get a proper fix from the stars. He resumed his journey across the dark and apparently empty landscape, and soon the road turned comfortingly towards the west. It held this direction for several miles, descending gentle rises to ford shallow streams and climbing gentle rises to begin descending again. It was like crossing a vast, wrinkled face.

Stars were becoming visible between the clouds as the road took another wide turn towards what he thought was the south. Another fifteen minutes and the clear sky to the south confirmed Mozza's worst fears. He was not on the road he wanted to be on.

He came to a halt and took off the PNGs. Almost directly ahead of him the four stars of the Southern Cross hung in the heavens. Extend the longer arm by four and half times its length, he told himself, and from that point draw a line vertically to the ground. That was the way to the South Pole. And he was heading directly towards it.

He let his mind wander for a moment, enjoying the unfolding majesty of the night sky: the inky depth of the Coal Sack hard by the Southern Cross, the yellow-white brilliance of Canopus low to the right, the almost devilish red glow of Antares above and to his left, like Sauron's eye in *Lord of the Rings*. The whole Milky Way seemed to float like a huge veil across space.

Faced with all that, the direction of the road seemed somehow less important. Unless and until it made a definitive turn to the east, Mozza decided, he would stay with it as long as he could. It was now approaching two o'clock, and in about four hours he would need to be under cover.

The road now seemed set in its ways, rarely deviating from its southward course. It was also climbing steadily, and the landscape was losing its openness, with stretches of grassland first alternating with swathes of trees, then giving way altogether to a rapidly thickening forest. It was in a rare break from the trees that Mozza noticed the first major signs of human occupancy he had seen since leaving the highway: a group of buildings clustered in the shelter of a valley away and down to his right. He wondered what they would make of the sound of his bike, and whether they would do anything about such an unexpected intrusion. There would be no telephone out here, but whoever it was might well be in radio contact with civilization.

There was nothing he could do about it if they were. He rode on, out of the forest and onto another stretch of high moorland, before the track came to an abrupt and unexpected end by the side of a rushing stream. The remains of a house, apparently long consumed by fire, sat on an adjacent rise.

Mozza concealed the Yamaha in a cluster of bushes that overhung the stream, took his bearings from the heavens, and headed out along the bank of the stream towards its source. Away to the west across the open heath, anything from 10 to 40 miles away, lay the Chilean border, but he now knew there was no chance of reaching it by dawn. Given that, he wanted tree cover by the time the sun came up, and memory told him the further south he went the more chance he had of finding it.

He knew he was physically tired, but adrenalin was still pumping life into his limbs, and he managed a steady four miles an hour across the often spongy surface. There was still an hour of darkness left when he found himself entering the fringe of a beech forest. Another half a mile brought him to what looked an ideal spot for a shelter. The earth-choked roots of a fallen tree offered a windbreak, and with some judicious scraping out and covering of gaps he had a relatively cosy, hard-to-detect place to sleep.

The thought of a cup of tea was almost irresistible, but he knew a fire would be too great a risk. Instead he breakfasted on water and a biscuit, and stretched himself out to sleep in the shelter he and nature had made together. Through the gaps in his roof he could see the fading stars, but now that he was motionless their stillness seemed almost depressing, like a reminder of his aloneness in the universe.

He remembered a psychological technique Lynsey had told him about – 'visualization' it was called, and that was what it was. You just had to visualize things you wanted as a way of making it more likely that they would come true. At least that was how he remembered her description of it.

He closed his eyes and tried to visualize his homecoming: Lynsey opening the door of the flat and the smile on her face as she opened her arms to take him in.

8

Soon after first light on that same morning a young Argentinian lieutenant was the first unfriendly witness to the British landing in San Carlos Water. He radioed his army superiors in Port Stanley that two landing craft were discharging troops. But since Argentinian experts had already declared San Carlos an impossible spot for the landing the lieutenant's superiors could only believe he must be imagining things.

The Argentinian Navy had intercepted the signal, however, and thought it worthwhile sending an Aeromacchi to check out the story. Its pilot flew blithely across the last ridge before San Carlos Water and was more than a little shocked to find what appeared to be the entire British fleet spread out before him. Less surprisingly, he beat a hasty retreat.

On the ships themselves, and in the defensive positions busily being constructed ashore, the British spent the next hour or so casting anxious eyes at the clear blue skies overhead. When would the enemy Air Force put in its first appearance *en masse*?

On the hill to the south of Rio Gallegos, Docherty and Ben watched the Mirages take to the air, arc away across the city and fade into the sky above the ocean. 'SEVEN MIRAGES DEPART RIO GALLEGOS 0842', Ben typed onto the keypad.

Ten minutes later four Skyhawks took to the air, and followed the same path out towards the Task Force, some 400 miles to the east in San Carlos Water and Falkland Sound. Ben's two typing fingers recorded the departure, and from the *Resource* it was relayed to the Task Force operational centre, and from there to the Sea Harriers hovering above the approaches to the islands.

On board the *Resource* Hemmings experienced a variety of emotions as the morning wore on. North was providing all the advanced warning that could have been expected, but the Mirages and Skyhawks were dropping to sea level before attacking, and there was still little the Sea Harriers could do to intercept them on their way in. At least the Task Force knew that no Super Etendards had left Rio Gallegos airbase that morning, and that there would be no surprise Exocet attack from that direction. North could have done no more.

As for South, there had been no news of any kind since the cryptic message the previous night, which Hemmings had received with a rare mixture of admiration and anger. The 'take-it-or-leave-it-but-we-know-best' style seemed to exemplify both the finest traditions of the SAS and irresponsibility on a grand scale. Where the hell were the four men now? Had they managed to put the Super Etendards out of action? There had been no reports of the plane that morning, which gave Hemmings grounds for hope, but there had been no radio contact from the patrol either, which gave him cause for anxiety.

And not just for the four men under Brookes's

command. If any of them had been captured, who knew what sort of treatment they were receiving from the enemy. The Argentinian military hardly inspired confidence, and the fact that the SAS men were out of uniform – thanks to the bloody politicians in London – would not exactly help their case. If things got nasty . . .

The SAS men were trained to withstand certain interrogation techniques, but not many men could hold out against the sort of brutality some regimes practised. And if any of them broke, then both Docherty's patrol and the woman in Rio Gallegos were in danger.

Hemmings cursed himself for giving her name to South, and wondered how long he could afford to wait before warning North. They could nothing before nightfall in any case. So why distract them from the important job they were doing? He wished he could send a submarine to pick North up, but all of them were needed to protect the Task Force from their Argentinian counterparts for as long as the landing operation required.

Hedge guessed it was sometime in the late morning, but he had no way of knowing for sure. The small room they had placed him in had no windows, and his watch had been removed by one of the soldiers. What was more, he seemed to have been slipping in and out of either sleep or unconsciousness ever since they had carried him in from where he had fallen.

They had not been gentle. Either the destruction of the three Super Es or the death of their comrades – maybe both – had enraged the Argie troops, and no effort had been made to spare him any pain as they manhandled him across the airbase towards his current lodgings in this anonymous room. Hedge reckoned he could not blame them: he knew how pissed off he would have been if the boot had been on the other foot.

Since then, however, he had mostly been left alone. On the only occasion he had been visited, by two officers in Air Force uniform, Hedge had feigned both an inability to understand Spanish and virtual unconsciousness, confining himself to an array of moans which he hoped would produce some medical attention. He had already reached his own diagnosis: the injury to his calf, while painful, was not serious, but the knee was in really bad shape. Such bad shape, in fact, that he was trying not to think about the possible implications for his future life. Always assuming he had one.

A man had eventually arrived with hot water and bandages, and, whether or not he was a doctor, had proved to possess remarkably gentle hands. Unfortunately he had not left any painkillers behind. Or any food.

Hedge would have liked to start banging on the door and demanding tortillas, or whatever it was they ate in Tierra del Fuego, but standard practice in such situations dictated a more restrained form of behaviour. He was supposed to pretend to be more tired and more badly injured than he was, just in case the Argies took it into their heads to start asking him questions with the gloves off. No torturer liked his victim to be continually slipping into unconsciousness.

Hedge shivered, and hoped he would be able to cope if and when the time came. He wondered where

Mozza was. For all he knew, the boy was in the room next door. Come to that, he was not even sure that Brookes and Stanley were dead.

There was the sound of a key in the lock. Hedge lay there with his eyes shut and feigned sleep.

'I think you are awake, Englishman. And I think you probably speak Spanish as well. My name is Segrera, Colonel Segrera of the Argentinian Air Force. I am here to inform you that Military Intelligence will soon be assuming responsibility for you. Before that happens – as one military man to another – would you like to ask me any questions?'

Hedge considered. The man sounded genuine. He opened his eyes and looked up at a thin-faced man with cropped, iron-grey hair. 'Are my companions dead?' he asked.

'Two of them are. The third escaped.'

Hedge's heart leapt, but his faced showed no sign of it.

'Will I be receiving any medical attention?' he asked.

'That will be up to Military Intelligence. There are no facilities here on the base.'

'And just exactly who are Military Intelligence?' Hedge asked, not really expecting an answer.

'My country's darker side,' the officer replied. 'If I were you, I would deal with them as carefully as you can.'

The sun was still high in the northern sky when Mozza woke. He did a 180-degree sweep of the surrounding countryside, and found only dappled forest in every direction. Feeling stiff, he scrambled out of the tree roots and tried some exercises. The pins and needles in his feet did not go away though, and removing his boots and socks he discovered a distinctly purple tinge to the skin, swelling and blisters. The trench foot which had threatened on West Falkland had finally come home to roost.

He felt a twinge of panic and let his mind settle back into reason. The only cure for trench foot was a combination of rest and warmth, and since he would have precious little of either until he reached Chile, there was not much point in getting himself in a state about it.

It was time to do some strategic thinking, he told himself sternly. First, he needed a good directional fix. Taking his knife he cut a three-foot length of straight branch from the nearest beech tree, and walked towards an area that looked light enough to be a clearing. Once in the sunlight, he pushed one end of the branch into the peaty ground and inserted a small twig where the shadow of the branch ended.

Back at the scrape he did an inventory of what he was carrying. He had two days' worth of high-calorie emergency rations in his escape belt, along with fish hooks and line, needle and cotton, and waterproof matches. The water bottle was still more than half full, and there was half a bar of chocolate in his jacket pocket. He was, he decided, unlikely to starve. And by the next morning, if he remained free, he should be far enough away to risk a fire and eat a decent hot meal.

In matters of clothing he was less well off. The Gore-tex jacket and trousers were warm enough for sea level, but from what he could remember the going would get higher before it got lower again. He was not really equipped for travelling in the snow, particularly at night.

He would worry about that when the time came. His only other serious problem – potentially, at least – was the state of his feet. And they would be warmer in motion than standing still. He gathered his stuff together and walked back to the sunlit clearing. Fifteen minutes had passed, and the shadow had moved significantly to the east. He placed another twig where it ended, removed the branch and used it to draw a line connecting the two twigs. He then checked his compass against this east-west axis, and found with much relief that it was hardly out at all. Now he could navigate with confidence at night whether or not the stars were visible.

Reckoning he had four hours before nightfall, Mozza started walking, keeping as close to a westerly direction as the configuration of the land would let him. At first the forest restricted his vision to not much more than 100 yards, but as the ground rose the trees became sparser, and a distant range of snow-capped mountains became increasingly visible. Eventually he emerged onto a small, bare plateau and found to his surprise that the range was a lot nearer than it looked: the snowy peaks had fooled him into thinking the mountains were bigger and further away. He was in fact confronting a range of snow-capped hills, and the snowline was only a few hundred yards above him.

For the next few miles the walking was ideal. He was on a north-facing slope – the warmer slope in the southern hemisphere – and out in the open, just above the tree line. Only once did the distant sound of a helicopter cause him to duck back beneath the cover of the trees, and that soon faded. It would not be the Argies who stopped him reaching Chile, Mozza decided. This was going to be a contest between himself and nature.

For the last hour of daylight he pushed against his own weariness, but it was only when he began to feel that his concentration was wandering that he decided to call a halt. The range of hills was behind him by this time, and he was back in the forest, working his way down a valley which seemed untouched by human presence. Animal tracks proliferated, particularly at stream-crossing points, and Mozza began to regret not bothering to enquire about the local predators before setting foot on Tierra del Fuego.

He made camp up against a north-facing, wind-sheltered cliff, and gathered wood for a fire as the dusk deepened. Not surprisingly, his feet were more swollen than before, and badly needed some real warmth. Without it, Mozza doubted if they would stand up to another whole day's walking. He had to risk a fire. The flames would only be visible from the south, and even if they were, there was nowhere for troops to be put down from a helicopter. He struck the match, applied it to the kindling, and warmed his feet by the growing flames as he ate two squares of chocolate.

The next requirement was a cooking utensil, and the only possible source was the forest. Mozza checked the trees around him, and settled on a species he did not recognize but which seemed close to birch in the texture of its bark. Using knife and fingers, he carefully stripped off a piece large enough for the cutting of a circle. Having laboriously removed the outer layer he folded the inner layer into four, fashioned a cone-shaped cup from it, and fastened it with several stitches of thick cotton.

Next he cut a long sapling and a forked twig, and balanced the former on the latter, so that one end could be weighted down by rocks and the other end used to suspend the cone cup over the fire. A sachet of dried soup was mixed with water and hung up to boil, with Mozza watching over the potentially combustible cone as his feet gently toasted. It all bought back memories of camping out with his brothers and sisters in the Peak District.

Once it was cooked he took his time drinking the soup, relishing each hot sip until it was all gone. He then boiled some water in the cone for tea, which he made with sachets of powdered tea, sugar and powdered milk. There were biscuits and another square of chocolate for dessert.

He had rarely tasted a better meal, Mozza thought. Only the special meal Lynsey had cooked him for his last birthday came to mind. He raised his cone of tea in a toast to her. 'I love her,' he told the forest. And I'm going to make it back to her, he told himself.

Four hundred miles or so to the east the British Army now had 4000 men ashore in the San Carlos beach head, and there was no sign of any significant response from those units of the Argentinian Army which were based in the islands. The same could not be said of the enemy air force, which had pressed home its attacks on the supporting fleet throughout the day with a great deal of skill and bravery. One frigate had been sunk, four others badly damaged, and it seemed mostly a matter of luck that the vital supply ships had emerged virtually unscathed.

The battle might be far from over, Hemmings thought to himself on the *Resource*, but the worst most probably was. The failure of the Super Etendards to put in an appearance might well have been crucial to the British success, and Hemmings hoped he knew the reason for their absence. But it was still proving impossible to raise South on the radio, and the patrol had not reported in. No matter what had gone right the night before, Hemmings had to assume something else had gone badly wrong in the meantime.

North should be told, that he was sure of. And Docherty's men should get themselves out of Argentina. Now that the troops were ashore, and now that they knew the Super Etendards were based at Rio Grande, any more information North could provide was hardly worth the risk, either to the men themselves or to Britain's diplomatic situation.

But what about the woman? Should he leave that to them? They were the ones who would be putting their lives at risk to warn her. Or was that unfair to her, leaving her fate in the hands of four men she had never met? Did she not deserve better of the British?

It was an impossible decision. The only comfort Hemmings could derive from the situation – and pretty cold comfort at that – lay in his inability to offer the SAS patrol any assistance in leaving Argentina. He would not order them to warn the woman, but he would suggest that she might be in a position to help them get away.

Docherty received the message with the sort of sinking feeling in his stomach he usually reserved for England-Scotland games at Hampden Park. Suddenly the lights of Rio Gallegos looked a lot further away than they had.

He showed the stored message to Ben, who rolled his

eyes heavenwards. 'Better wake the others,' Docherty whispered. He rubbed his eyes and tried to think the thing through. They were only about 30 miles from the Chilean border, the crossing of which was unlikely to present any problems. He could not imagine it was marked by more than a token fence, if that.

If they set out now there was at least an even chance they could make it before dawn.

Rio Gallegos, though, was in the opposite direction. If they wanted to warn the woman, then at least one of them could count on another fun-packed day in sunny Argentina.

'What's up, Doc?' Razor asked with a yawn.

Ben allowed him and Wacko to read the message for themselves.

'So we're on our way?' Wacko asked.

'That's what we have to decide,' Docherty said curtly.

'Which way?' Razor wanted to know.

'The quickest way out of this country is due south,' Docherty said. 'The border's about 30 miles away.'

'So what are we waiting for?' Wacko demanded. 'If we get a move on maybe we'll see some action on the Falklands.'

'If you'd read the message properly,' Docherty told him, 'you'd have seen that we're expected to camp out in Chile for as long as possible, so as not to embarrass anyone. And if the Chileans find us we'll probably be interned. Or at best flown back to England.'

Wacko shrugged. 'Still beats sleeping in a wet hole in Argentina.'

'The Cup Final's tomorrow,' Razor said wistfully.

'What about the woman?' Ben asked quietly.

'You're not serious!' Wacko exclaimed.

'She's fighting the same war, on the same side,' Ben argued. 'I think we should at least think about it.'

'OK,' Wacko said. 'This is what I think. She's an Argie communist. She's fighting her own war against her government and we just happen to be fighting them too. So she gets our help. She's just using us.'

Docherty tried to read Wacko's face in the gloom. There was some sense to what the man said, but there was a depth of anger accompanying the words which seemed out of all proportion to the subject. Did the mere *idea* of the woman make him angry?

'She's using us, we're using her,' Razor said. 'What's the difference? If she's on our side then we owe her.'

'Jesus Christ!' Wacko exploded.

'We don't all have to go into town,' Ben said. 'Maybe two of us, maybe only one. The others can start heading south. I'd volunteer to go in alone,' he said, 'but I'm the only one doesn't speak Spanish. But I'll go in with someone else.'

'I'll come along for the ride,' Razor said. 'Time waits for an old fool,' he added wisely.

They all started giggling, even Wacko. Somehow the knowledge that they were half-buried on a Patagonian hill doubled the absurdity of just about everything.

Docherty eventually brought them back to a semblance of order. 'I'm sorry to disappoint you, lads,' he said, 'but Ben here has the sort of ripe golden hair they don't often see in these parts, and Razor might as well have London tattooed on his forehead. I . . .'

'You, on the other hand, could be taken for Galtieri's father,' Razor said.

'Precisely,' replied Docherty. 'And I think it's a one-man job. You lot can head for Chile.'

'No way, boss,' Ben said. 'We'll wait for you here.'

'Yeah,' Wacko agreed, 'all for one and one for all and all that crap.'

'We'd be lost without you, boss,' Razor added. 'Where are we anyway?' he asked, looking round.

'I'm touched' Docherty said. 'But if I'm not back by morning . . .'

'We can assume she's beautiful, and you've decided to keep her all for yourself.'

'Something like that. Ben, let Hemmings know what's going on. I'm going to slip into something more comfortable, or at least less damp . . .'

'Not one of those Tartan condoms, boss?' Razor asked.

'Hey,' Ben said, 'that's not a bad idea. You could do them in all the various clan colours and sell them to the tourists.' He tried in vain to imagine Morag selling them in the shop. Still, the thought of her brought a pang to his heart, not to mention his loins. She had always had a wonderful way with her when it came to putting a condom on him.

Docherty re-emerged, if that was the right word for the squirming motion necessary to free him from the hide, and joined the three men squatting in the dark on the vast open hillside. He had exchanged the camouflage trousers for plain – the Green Slime had been unable to work out which would suit the colours of the steppe better – and was wearing them outside his boots, but otherwise his outfit was the same: Gore-tex jacket over thick sweater. The most striking change was to his face, which was free of 'cam' cream for the first time in five days.

He checked the action on the Browning High Power

and replaced it in his jacket pocket, then tied the cream's temporary replacement – a dark piece of cloth – around his face below the eyes.

'OK,' he whispered. 'I'll see you later. And keep down the noise,' he added over his shoulder.

'Good luck, boss,' Ben said softly.

'See if you can pick up any Spurs news, boss,' was Razor's parting shot.

It was slightly over four miles, Docherty reckoned, from the OP to the centre of Rio Gallegos. It would take about half an hour to reach the nearest road, then another hour into town, assuming he did not run into trouble on the way.

Somehow the prospect did not worry him. In fact, during his PNG-assisted passage across the dark and undulating landscape he felt an almost reckless sense of freedom. He was alone, in motion, imbued with purpose. Every sound seem magnified in the green world of the PNGs, and the feel of the breeze on his face seemed almost like a caress.

He reached the expected road, and started down a long slope. The lights of the airbase had disappeared from sight behind the hills to his left, but those of the town lay directly ahead.

Two cars passed him going in the opposite direction, and on both occasions he took care to dart out of sight as they approached. When one came up from behind him he considered hitching a lift, but swiftly dismissed the idea. His Spanish would pass muster, but he had no convincing cover story for being on this road.

The car swept past as he merged his shadow with that of a stunted tree by the roadside, and he watched its headlights illuminate the road into town. Another forty minutes of fast walking brought him to the outskirts, where new industrial developments were pushing untidily out into the grassy steppe. A wide avenue, which boasted the first happy-looking trees he had seen since Oxfordshire, led towards the town centre and the estuary. It seemed almost deserted of either traffic or pedestrians, but there were many lights on in the houses to either side.

He walked by some pedestrians: an arm-in-arm couple who did not even give him a first glance, let alone a second; then a youngish woman who did give him one swift look, but did not bother to repeat the experience. Docherty decided he could not look that unusual.

He walked down Calle Salta to the brightly lit Avenida Julio Roca, on which he knew the hotel was located. Here there was life: couples strolling along, cafés and restaurants doing business, groups of raucous young men hanging around on streets corners. He knew it should not, but somehow the normality of it all surprised him, maybe even upset him a little. This country was at war, but no one would have known it.

He supposed it was the same back home. The war would be on the news, and every evening the British people would be getting a vicarious dose of it. The rest of the time they would be going about their daily business, just like the people of Rio Gallegos. Tomorrow they would be watching the Cup Final and wondering whether it was Jimmy Hill's chin or beard which was that strange shape. And then going down the pub.

Docherty could see the neon sign for the Covadonga

Hotel not far ahead. He crossed over to the opposite pavement and bought a newspaper from a street vendor, thinking it might make him look marginally more like a member of the community. The vendor complained about the need to change a note, but seemed to find nothing surprising in Docherty's appearance.

He walked slowly on, studying the immediate vicinity of the hotel over the edge of the newspaper. There was no sign of police activity, no suspicious-looking characters leaning against walls or pretending to read newspapers. Other than himself, that was.

If she was at home, then he could tell her in person. But what if she was out? He supposed he could leave her a message – something she would understand but no one else would. But he would have to leave it with someone. Who would he say he was? What would fit in with her cover?

Isabel sat in the Renault, its window open to let in the breeze flowing over the estuary. Darkness had long since fallen, but she felt unable to drag herself away from the peace of the ruffled waters and star-strewn heavens.

All through the daylight hours her thoughts had been with the pilots contesting the skies over the Malvinas. Which, she had to admit, was pretty perverse. And not very helpful either, to them or herself.

The war could have been lost that morning, for all she knew. Certainly the Junta would be in no rush to publicize the end result of their own gross miscalculations. But even if it was still in full swing, the end could not be long delayed. She should be thinking about what to do when the time finally came.

Did she want to go back to England? It was a decent enough place to live, but ... She knew she could not just walk away from Argentina again. Here was where it had happened, and here was where it had to be exorcized, if such a thing was possible. She doubted that it was, but if she was ever to be truly alive again, then she had to try.

But how to begin? She could kill Solanille, she thought. It would not be difficult. If she did not care what happened to herself then she could do almost anything. But that would hardly be exorcism – just a potent cocktail of revenge and suicide.

She needed a drink, she decided, and there was a bottle of whisky in her hotel room. 'Fuck that for a game of soldiers,' she murmured in English. It had been one of Michael's favourite phrases, and only conceivable in a country where soldiers really did spend most of their time playing games.

No, she decided, she did not want to be alone. She turned the car round and drove across town to the Rakosi. It was almost empty, so she took a seat at the bar, where the barman-owner, Miguel, was catching up with his accounts. He looked depressed, but that was nothing unusual: his wife spent most evenings flirting with his customers.

He poured her a double whisky and said he thought he would have one himself. 'Problems?' she asked, almost eagerly. At least someone else's would be easier to cope with than her own.

'For all of us,' he said cryptically. 'I just got some news,' he added. 'The guy who delivers for the local brewery, well, he also does the airbase, and he'd just come from there.' He looked up and down the bar, as if anxious that no one else should hear. 'They lost seventeen planes today,' he said. '*Seventeen*,' he repeated, as if he could scarcely believe it himself.

'That's terrible,' she managed to say. Had Raul been one of them? She might never know. And what did it matter, she asked herself. If he was not, then someone else was.

Docherty walked confidently in through the front door of the Covadonga Hotel, and up to the reception desk, where Manuel Menéndez was poised over a crossword, chewing the end of his ballpoint pen.

'I would like to see Isabel Rodríguez,' Docherty told him.

Menéndez looked up at him hopefully. 'A cathedral town in France – eight letters?'

'Chartres,' Docherty told him. 'C-H-A-R-T-R-E-S.'

As Menéndez laboriously filled in the answer, Docherty took a good look round the spacious lobby. Over in the far corner an old man in a suit was watching a muted TV, but there were no other signs of human activity.

'Isabel Rodríguez?' he asked again.

Menéndez swung round reluctantly to check out the line of key-hooks. 'She is out,' he said.

Damn, Docherty said to himself. 'I would like to leave a message,' he said. 'It concerns tours in the mountains for tourists.'

The Argentinian managed to convey both indifference and acquiescence with the same shrug.

'Do you have any paper?' Docherty asked, thinking that it would have been more intelligent to have written the note out first.

As Menéndez rummaged around under his counter the street door swung open with a clatter, and Docherty swung round, slightly faster than he intended.

The woman's stride barely faltered. She was about the right age, and fitted the rough description Hemmings had given them: five foot eight inches tall, around nine and a half stone, shoulder-length black hair, dark-brown eyes, sallow skin, attractive. She was certainly the latter, Docherty thought. 'Isabel Rodríguez?' he asked for the third time, smiling as he did so.

Only her eyes betrayed any sense of alarm. 'Yes?'

'We talked on the telephone about the mountain tours,' he went on, moving his body between her and Menéndez, so that the latter would miss any confusion on her part. He need not have bothered.

'Oh, yes,' she said. 'Señor . . . I am sorry, I have forgotten your name.'

'Ramírez,' Docherty said, using the first name that came into his head. She was impressive, he thought.

'Well, would you like to go out for a drink? Or I have some in my room.' She did not bother to wait for his answer. 'Manuel, can I have my key.'

A minute later she was closing the door behind her and looking at him with a mixture of exasperation and anger. She did not need this, she thought, not today. Nor did she really want to know what he wanted from her.

'Can I pour us a drink?' Docherty asked, still speaking Spanish, and indicating the whisky on the bedside table. He felt he had earned it, after the last week or so.

'Just for yourself,' she said. 'What is your real name?' she asked, also in Spanish.

'Docherty. Jamie Docherty.'

Her lips creased in a faint smile, as if she was remembering something. She really was beautiful, he decided, but there seemed to be only sadness in her eyes.

'Miss Rodríguez,' he began, 'I have simply come to warn you. Our other patrol, outside Rio Grande – there has been no radio contact for almost twenty-four hours, and there is a good chance that they have been captured.'

She looked at him steadily.

'They have your name,' he said, 'as I think you know.'

'I was told.' She shrugged, and decided to pour herself a drink after all. 'Will they betray me?' she asked.

He started to say no, but stopped himself. If Wacko's feelings were reflected anywhere in Brookes's patrol, then maybe they would not be as careful as they should be. 'I don't know,' he said, looking straight at her. 'I doubt it, but I don't know.'

'Not even under torture,' she asked, almost aggressively.

'You probably know the answer to that better than I do,' he said simply. He put the empty glass down and got up. 'I just came to tell you what has happened. We are leaving tonight, for Chile. You can come with us if you want.'

Isabel studied his face, thinking that he might be a good man, without knowing why she thought so. 'No,' she said, 'I'll be all right.' The faint smile appeared again. 'Or maybe not,' she said, more to herself than to him. 'This is my home,' she added, realizing that some explanation was required.

'I understand,' he said. 'I'll be on my way.'

She started to move aside, but suddenly the thought of being left alone in that room was more than she could face. 'I can drive you out of town,' she said. 'It'll be safer.'

He hesitated. 'Are you sure?' he asked.

'Sure it will be safer? Yes.'

'Not for you.'

Maybe the SAS were English gentlemen after all, she thought. And maybe the Junta sent donations to Amnesty International. 'Let me worry about my safety,' she said brusquely. 'Do you have a map?'

He took it out, and showed her the spot where the road ran closest to the OP. 'I'll drop you there,' she said, as if they were popping into town together for a Saturday morning's shopping.

9

Once Docherty had disappeared into the darkness, Ben and Wacko had dozed off while Razor kept watch. Every few minutes he would diligently scan the distant airbase with the telescope, but the day's activity seemed over. Maybe they were simply licking their wounds, Razor thought. A lot more aircraft had flown out that day than had returned, and though it was possible that the missing planes had landed elsewhere, the messages from Hemmings suggested that most of them were headed for the ocean floor.

'There's no smoke without valour,' Razor murmured to himself, and smiled in the dark.

He thought about home and his mum and the house in Walthamstow. He wondered if she would like Corinna. Probably – his mum had a do-gooder streak in her about a mile wide, and she was getting pretty choosy about food these days. All those unsaturated poly-somethings. He sighed. It probably all made a lot of sense, but there was no doubt in his mind that beans on toast tasted better with white bread and proper butter.

He picked up the telescope again, just at the moment the noise of the helicopter became audible. The airbase still looked dead to the world, but the scrape of the chopper blades was growing louder.

And then he heard what sounded suspiciously like a cough somewhere out on the hillside.

It was too early for the boss to be back. Razor used his foot to wake Ben and Wacko. By the time they had joined him, their heads almost side by side to see through the observation slit, the helicopter was less than 200 yards away, trailing a spotlight beneath it, as if looking for the star performer on the huge stage of the Patagonian hillside.

It came to a hovering halt directly above them, flooding the roof of the hide with light.

But the voice, when it came, seemed to come from further down the slope. 'English soldiers,' it said, with a clarity of amplified sound which put Spurs' PA system to shame. 'You must leave your weapons and come out of your trench,' the voice went on. 'There are 100 soldiers all around you, so please do not try to be heroes.'

'Are there?' Razor muttered. 'Shall we try the back way out?' he asked the others.

'Yeah, let's be heroes,' Wacko said.

Ben nodded grimly.

'Ready?' Razor asked, as the amplifier began booming once more.

They were.

'One, two, three, go,' Razor barked, and all three men launched themselves through the turf roof and out onto the hillside, rolling free of the hide and springing to their feet in what seemed almost one continuous motion.

They were barely on their feet when one searchlight went on behind them, another burst into blinding light directly in their chosen path of escape, and someone opened fire with an SMG. Wacko went down like a sack of potatoes, two bullets in his chest and shoulder. The other two threw themselves down beside him to avoid a similar fate.

Two more searchlights burst into life on either side, and the helicopter seemed almost close enough above them to touch. When the Argies surround you, Razor thought, they do it with a vengeance.

Wacko was still conscious, but he seemed to be gritting his teeth with pain.

'Why spend the night out here when we have beds waiting for you?' the amplified voice boomed, just about audible above the helicopter.

'I'm going to stand up,' Razor told Ben. 'If the bastards shoot me, then try and take a few of them with you. If it comes to talking, don't let on we speak Spanish.' He took a deep breath and lifted himself slowly to his feet, hands held high, half-expecting any moment to feel the bullets cutting through him.

None came.

Ben stood up too, but still there was no gunfire. The helicopter was now moving away, its work apparently done.

'Our *amigo* is injured,' Razor shouted in English.

A couple of enemy troops rushed forward, SMGs at the ready, to cover them. The officer in charge, a paunchy colonel, followed at a more leisurely pace, growling orders at his subordinates, two of whom started tearing off the roof of the hide. He was accompanied by a cold-eyed man in plain clothes, and it was the latter who did the talking.

'You are so confident, you English,' Solanille told them in their own language. 'You think we are a Third World country, we cannot have thermal imaging, so you are quite safe in the dark.'

He walked over to look down on the exposed entrails of the hide. 'Impressive,' he said, and turned back to them. 'A cross has four arms, and there are four large bags here. But only three of you.'

'Our friend needs medical help,' Razor told him.

'Yes, he does,' Solanille said, looking down at Wacko without sympathy. He gestured to the colonel to do something, and turned back to Razor. 'He will receive help. Now where is the fourth man?'

'There is no fourth man,' Razor said. 'We have one bag each for our kit, and one for the radio.'

'And that is standard practice?' Solanille asked.

'It is standard practice,' Razor replied. SAS men were taught not to use simple yes or no replies, since these could be most easily used for the doctoring of tapes. Razor doubted whether this conversation on the hillside was being recorded, but he was not taking any chances. He did not want his mum listening to him apparently admitting to some atrocity or other on the BBC news. She was ambivalent enough about the SAS as it was.

'Ah. Then perhaps you can explain why the other patrol had four men?'

'Which other patrol?' Razor asked. He did not like the sound of all this one little bit, and he liked the look of this man even less. Still, he thought, at least they were lifting Wacko onto a stretcher rather than shooting him.

'The Rio Grande patrol,' Solanille said. 'One man is dead, two captured, one . . . we don't know. He is probably hiding in a hole like this one, wondering what to do next.'

'We have no knowledge of another patrol,' Razor said.

The Argentian smiled at him coldly. 'And I suppose your Queen Mother is a virgin,' he said contemptuously. He turned away. 'We shall continue this discussion in a nice warm room,' he said over his shoulder. 'Bring them.'

They drove slowly out of Rio Gallegos and onto the road signposted for Cabo Virgenes. Docherty found himself conscious of the movement of her thighs as she changed gears, and wondered whether she had had a boyfriend in England. If so, he guessed, then she must have left him without much explanation.

'Where are you from?' he asked

'Originally? Ushuaia, it's in Tierra . . .'

'I know where it is.'

'Have you ever been there?'

'No.'

'It's the end of the world,' she said, almost proudly.

'Oh, I've been to several of them,' he said, with a lightness which seemed to emphasize its opposite.

She found herself believing him. This was not the sort of man she had expected from the SAS. 'Did you serve in Northern Ireland?' she asked, switching to English.

'Aye,' Docherty said. It seemed churlish, not to say childish, to deny the truth to a woman who was driving him around behind enemy lines.

'Don't you think Ireland should be one country?' she asked, and immediately wondered why she was asking such a man such a question in such a situation. It was completely crazy.

He seemed not to mind. 'I understand the desire,' he said. 'I'm a Glasgow Catholic – how could I not?

But I guess ... I guess I've come to believe that fighting to get things changed often ends up causing more harm than just learning to live with things the way they are.'

Isabel thought about it.

'And I think people who blow up pubs should be locked up,' he added, almost as an afterthought, 'no matter what they kid themselves they're doing it for.'

'Sometimes the way things are ...' she began. 'Sometimes it's so bad that there's no choice but to fight.'

'That I can believe,' he agreed. 'I guess wisdom is knowing which is which.'

'A soldier-philosopher,' she said, only half-ironically.

He chose to take it straight. 'We are all many things,' he said. He could feel Liam McCall looking over his shoulder.

'We must be nearly there,' she said.

'About another half a mile,' he said. 'Over this ...'

He was silenced by the array of lights visible on the road ahead.

'They've seen us, so we have to go on,' she said calmly.

'OK,' he said, feeling for the Browning's grip in his pocket. The next few hundred yards seemed to take forever. Slowly the details behind the lights became clearer. There were several vehicles and a multitude of men in uniform.

A soldier stepped out to check them, but waved them on when he saw Isabel's worried face, and they drove slowly past the two armoured personnel carriers drawn up by the side of the road, and the two cars beyond them. Two men were being hustled aboard one of the former, and Docherty recognized Razor's unmistakable profile. In the light offered by one car's headlights Isabel saw Solanille standing talking to another officer.

'Your companions?' she asked, as the car crested the next shallow rise and began down another long slope.

'Aye,' Docherty said bitterly.

'I'm going to keep going for a mile or so,' she said. 'And then we'll have to sit for a while. I don't want to have to pass them again – it'll look too suspicious.'

'I can't believe they didn't stop us anyway,' Docherty said.

'In England they would have,' she said. 'Here they prefer to keep the ordinary citizen as far away as possible from such things. Once he saw I was a woman – and therefore nothing to do with anything military – he just wanted us out of there.'

A couple of minutes later she pulled the car over and switched off the lights. 'We can just keep going,' she said. 'I can get you to within a couple of miles of the border, and you can be across before first light.'

'No,' he said, almost absent-mindedly. Christ, what a cock-up, he thought. All their gear would have been taken, except for what he was carrying himself: one pair of PNGs, a telescopic night-sight, his knife, the Browning High Power, and the contents of his escape belt. 'Have you any idea where they'll be taken?' he asked Isabel.

'Maybe the airbase. Maybe the Intelligence HQ in town. You're not thinking of trying to rescue them?' she asked incredulously.

'I'm not leaving until I'm sure it's impossible,' he said.

She did not know what to say. Or do. Think, she told herself.

'Is there another way back into the town?' he asked.

'No. We'll have to wait. And I'm not at all sure I want to drive you back into town. Or myself, for that matter.'

'I can understand that,' he said. 'And I can walk if necessary. But I'll need some directions.'

'Let me think for a minute,' she said, wishing she had some alcohol in the car. She had a definite feeling that time was running out for her in Rio Gallegos, but where was the feeling coming from? Several directions. There was the possibility that the captured SAS men would give her away, the fact that her face had been seen driving past by the soldier, Docherty's visit to her hotel. When Menéndez heard the news the next day that English spies had been captured would he start putting two and two together? Probably not, but still . . .

And anyway, what was the point of her staying? At the rate the English were shooting down planes the war could not last much longer. And her primary source of information was probably dead. Unless she had a death-wish – a not inconceivable hypothesis, she admitted to herself – it was time for her to get out.

Would she have a better chance with this man or without him? That was hard to say. With him, probably – at least until they were clear of Rio Gallegos. Then alone

In the seat next to her Docherty was also wondering what he should do. As he saw it, he had three options:

to head for the border with this woman, to head back into town with her, or to send her on towards the border while he headed back into town on his own. The last option, while the least appealing from most points of view, unfortunately seemed the one demanded by his sense of duty.

'Look,' he said. 'If they catch me there's a good chance I'll be treated as a prisoner of war, or at the worst as some sort of hostage. If they catch you they'll probably hang you, or whatever they do to traitors in this country. So you should keep going, and try and get across the border. I know where the airbase is, so just tell me where to find this Intelligence HQ.'

This, she thought, was one of those rare moments when you got to choose. It was like a fork in the road of her life. If she went one way she would have one type of life, if she went the other it would all turn out completely differently. Crossing the border might mean safety, but it would also mean the end of any chance for her to resurrect her soul.

It was melodramatic as hell, she thought, but true all the same.

She turned to face Docherty. 'I'm not going to try and explain,' she said, 'because there isn't time and I don't think you'd understand in any case. But this is my war too, and I've been fighting it, either here or in my head in England, for ten years. Most of my friends are dead, and the thought of joining them lost its sting a long time ago. You see, I could cross ten borders and not leave this war behind, so let's just get on with it.'

In the gloom her face was decidedly madonna-like, he thought, all holiness and suffering and self-denial. He felt infinitely sorry for her, and, at the same time, drawn to her to more strongly than he wanted to be.

'I hear you,' he said. 'So which do we go for first – the airbase or town?'

'Town,' she said decisively. 'If we go cruising round the airbase at this time of night there's a ninety per cent chance we'll be stopped by someone or other. And I think it's more likely they'll be taken into town,' she added. With Solanille, she told herself. With Solanille.

She started the Renault, did a U-turn, and set off slowly back the way they had come, all lights off. At the top of the rise they could see that the APCs and cars had all gone, leaving just the open lorry. But there was no sign of human life.

'They must be waiting for you,' she said. 'You'd better get in the back seat, as far down as you can.'

Docherty packed as much of himself into the narrow gap as he could and waited, Browning at the ready, as they descended the slope.

'Nobody there,' she said a few moments later.

He climbed back into the front seat and watched the few remaining lights of Rio Gallegos draw steadily closer.

Razor and Ben had endured a long, jolting ride in the back of an armoured personnel carrier, surrounded by Argentinian soldiers who obviously felt they had accomplished the moral equivalent of kidnapping Mrs Thatcher. Still, they were obviously not a bad bunch of lads, Razor thought, listening to them chatting excitedly to each other. He would have liked to have thanked them for giving Ardiles and Villa to Spurs, but the need to conceal his knowledge of Spanish rendered a harmless conversation about football impossible.

He wondered how and where Wacko was. The head honcho in plain clothes had told them their comrade was being taken to the local hospital, but Razor and Ben had no way of knowing if he was speaking the truth. The only certainty was that Wacko was not with them.

After what seemed like half an hour, but was probably less, the APC slowed to a halt, and then reversed. The rear door opened onto a view of a wall with a door in it. The two SAS men, who had been handcuffed before getting aboard, were hustled out by two armed soldiers, and had time to glimpse a lighted street before the door closed behind them and their escort.

They were in a house, or at least an official building, not a barracks or military detention centre. A carpeted corridor led through to what looked like the lobby, where a uniformed man sat in front of several TV screens. They were guided past a room full of desks and office equipment and up a wide staircase, also richly carpeted. A chandelier hung in the stairwell.

Razor turned to Ben, whose face, like his own, was still covered with camouflage cream. 'Do you think they'll be able to lend us a couple of tuxedos?' he asked.

'*Silencio*,' said one of the guards with no great conviction.

They were prodded into an extremely spacious room on the first floor. A large polished table occupied the centre of the floor, but there were no accompanying chairs and it seemed to serve no purpose other than to support a large vase of flowers. Three ornate chairs sat beneath the three large windows, which were concealed by floor-length maroon velvet curtains with golden tassels. Razor remembered Spike Milligan's line: 'The curtains were drawn but the room was real.'

Solanille was sitting at a large desk in one corner of the room, talking on the telephone. A few feet away the flames of a coal fire were dancing happily in a Victorian-style grate. Above the mantlepiece was the portrait of a general with bright-blue eyes and a mouth like a man-trap.

'And the one who got away?' Solanille was asking in Spanish. Razor tried not to give any clue that he understood what was being said.

'Have you questioned the prisoner?' Solanille asked. His face betrayed frustration at the answer he was getting. 'Yes, yes, I understand,' he said, 'we have a similar problem here . . . yes, Luis, I will·talk to you in a couple of hours.' He put the phone down and looked at the two handcuffed SAS men.

Razor noticed for the first time that there were three Browning High Powers sitting on the desk, presumably his, Ben's and Wacko's. 'May I say something?' he asked.

Solanille grunted his acquiescence.

'What is your name and rank?' Razor asked.

Solanille frowned. 'Neither my name nor my position are of any concern to you,' he said.

'It is a courtesy usually accorded prisoners of war,' Razor said, sure he had heard the line before, probably in some crappy war film.

The Argentinian laughed. 'No uniform, no declaration of war – you will be treated as the terrorists you are,' he said. 'Your friends in Tierra del Fuego killed nine men,' he went on, 'and murder carries the death penalty in Argentina.'

Razor and Ben said nothing.

'We have checked out your equipment and clothes,' Solanille said, 'and it is obvious that there are four of you. Where is the fourth man?'

'There are only three of us,' Razor said.

Solanille shrugged. 'We shall see.'

'Ve have vays of making you talk, Englischer schwein,' Razor muttered under his breath. And they probably did. He felt more than a little uneasy. In fact, he admitted to himself, he felt bloody scared.

It was almost midnight now, but the streets of Rio Gallegos were far from deserted. 'Friday night,' Isabel explained, as a group of drunken oil workers lurched across the road in front of them.

'Just like Peterhead,' Docherty muttered.

She drove slowly down Avenida Julio Roca and came to a halt outside the hotel. 'I need to get something before we do anything else,' she said.

He opened his mouth to ask her whether whatever it was was really necessary, then closed it again.

She saw his hesitation. 'If by some miracle we can free your friends,' she explained, 'we can't just head for the border by the quickest route. We wouldn't get ten miles. So we're going to need money, and I don't suppose you're carrying many spare pesos.'

'No,' Docherty admitted. 'But I hear you're pretty good at robbing banks.'

She almost smiled, and reached for the door. 'If I'm more than ten minutes,' she said, 'take the car.'

Docherty sat watching the wide and mostly empty avenue. Pedestrians in pairs and groups wandered by, and an occasional car or taxi. The police were conspicuous by their absence. No one paid him any mind.

Isabel reappeared, carrying one small bag. 'I decided a change of clothing would be nice,' she said.

'I know what you mean,' Docherty said wryly.

She started the car. 'How far away should we park?' she asked.

'You know the place. How does around the nearest corner sound?'

'As good as anywhere.' She slipped the car into gear and pulled out in the wake of a cruising taxi. 'By the way,' she added, 'it's opposite the city police station.'

'Jesus,' Docherty murmured.

This time she did smile, and swung the Renault left down Calle Corrientes, across Calle Zapiola and right down Calle Libertad. In the middle of the second block she pulled up, and pointed at the house on her right. 'It's behind that, in the next street,' she said. The excitement of it all was beginning to get to her, as it had always done all those years ago.

They got out of the car, conscious of the emptiness of the street. 'I think it might be an idea if we tried to look like we're fond of each other,' Docherty said, putting his arm round her shoulder.

She hesitated for only a second before slipping an arm around his waist. 'Christ, when did you last have a wash?' she asked a few paces later.

'About a week ago.'

'As recently as that?'

They turned into Calle Ameghino and walked the block to Calle Zapiola. The police station on the far side of the road seemed dead to the world. 'This way,' she whispered, leading him to the right. 'Stop for a kiss in front of the second building.' Docherty did what he was told, kissing her lightly on the mouth before burying her head in his shoulder, and staring across the top of her head at the building as he ran his fingers through her hair.

'What can you see?' she whispered impatiently.

'A lot of curtains drawn across lighted windows,' he said. 'A uniform in the lobby watching screens. But there's no way of knowing if they're in there. Let's move.'

They resumed their progress, walking past a side entrance for vehicles. Docherty had a momentary glimpse of an illuminated yard, complete with surveillance camera above a lit doorway.

They turned right again. 'Any ideas?' he asked.

Isabel was remembering a very similar building in Córdoba, and a very similar problem, in the summer of 1974. 'There's only one way in,' she said. 'Through the front door.'

'We just go and knock?'

'Not quite. I go and look lost. Get the guard out here and . . . Or we could abseil in through the windows,' she added sarcastically.

'I prefer the first idea,' Docherty said. They discussed the details for a few moments, as they embraced on the pavement beside the car. 'Are you sure you can do this?' Docherty asked one more time.

Her face was expressionless. 'Like you said, it's the death penalty if I'm caught.'

'Then let's do it.'

Five minutes later she was standing in front of the glass doors of the Intelligence building, using mime to persuade the guard within that she needed help with some terrible problem.

Docherty watched from behind the porch, thinking how good she was, and wondering if her nerve would hold. He would have done it himself, but there was no way he could have got as close.

He could not see the guard, who was looking at her, then at the screens, and then at her again. She was gorgeous, the guard thought. Her coat was open and the swell of her breasts beneath the sweater almost brought a lump to his throat. And she looked so lost.

He came across to the door, and opened it a few inches.

She pulled Docherty's silenced Browning out of her coat pocket and shot him through the heart.

He went down with more noise than she had expected, but no other guards appeared to investigate. The two of them slipped inside, and she closed the doors behind her while Docherty dragged the guard's body back to the seat in front of the TV console, and propped it up as well as he could manage. The screens showed several views of the outside world, and two of the building's inner workings. Both these latter offered a fisheye-lens view of landings, which could only be those on the two floors above them. The top landing was empty, but the one immediately above them contained two seated guards, neither wearing uniform but both armed with SMGs.

From the screen it looked as though this landing was four-sided, like a balcony around a courtyard, and that the two guards were sitting in opposite corners, one facing the top of the stairs leading up from the lobby, the other out of sight to the rear.

Killing the first man would be easy enough, but getting to the second before he raised the alarm was going to be tricky.

Docherty thought for a moment, then outlined a plan.

'OK,' Isabel nodded.

He put his hand out for the Browning, and she reluctantly handed it back. Then it occurred to her to remove the dead guard's handgun from his leather police holster.

'Only as a last resort,' he told her.

She concealed it in her coat pocket and gave him a withering 'what kind of a fool do you take me for?' look. He shrugged an apology. They moved down a short corridor, and started up the long staircase, Isabel in the lead, hands grasped behind her back. Docherty brought up the rear, holding the gun on her.

They were about sixteen steps from the top when the first guard's head appeared in view. He stared first at her, and then at Docherty, with the same questioning look.

'She is an accomplice of the English spies,' Docherty told him abruptly, as if he was generously providing more explanation than the guard was due.

They were only ten steps from the top now, and the second guard would be coming into Docherty's possible line of fire.

'I have not . . .' the first guard started to say, and Docherty put a double tap through his forehead, whirling almost in the same instant in search of the other target.

The second guard was still standing open-mouthed when two bullets in the upper trunk punched him back into the chair he had just vacated.

A loud thump announced the first guard's meeting

with the floor. There were sounds in the room behind him, first of a voice, then of footsteps. Docherty and Isabel stepped swiftly forward, reaching either side of the door just as it opened.

A man stepped out, gun in hand. He had time for one surprised *qué*? before Docherty shot him through the head.

The SAS man stepped through the door, his Browning seeking out more targets. A man behind a desk sat perfectly still, another man's gun hit the floor as his hands reached up, and Docherty's two SAS partners grinned from ear to ear.

'What you been doing, boss – sightseeing?' Razor complained. He suddenly noticed Isabel standing behind Docherty. 'Don't answer that. We understand completely.'

'Where's Wacko?' Docherty asked. He noticed the two men were handcuffed. 'And where are the keys for those?'

'The keys are in his pocket,' Ben said, indicating the guard with his hands up. 'But we don't know where Wacko is. He took two bullets when we were captured. They say they took him off to hospital.'

'He was in bad shape, boss,' Razor said. 'There's no way he could travel.'

'He is being treated at the airbase you have been spying on,' Solanille told them, ingratiatingly. He became conscious that the woman was staring at him.

'Do you remember me, Señor Solanille?' she asked, walking slowly towards him.

'No,' he said. 'I do not have the habit of associating with traitors.'

She picked up one of the three silenced Brownings lying on the desk.

'What's going on, boss?' Razor asked Docherty.

The PC shook his head. 'It's her business,' he said. And unless she jeopardized their safety he had no intention of interfering.

'You sent me to the Naval Mechanical School,' Isabel was telling Solanille in a voice that sent a shiver down Docherty's spine.

The Argentinian's face expressed sudden recognition.

Isabel rammed the Browning's barrel into his genitals.

He cried out once in shock, and then looked up her with pleading eyes as her finger tightened on the trigger. 'No,' he whimpered. 'I never . . .'

'You never dirtied your own hands,' she said, held his eyes for what must been the longest seconds of his life, and then suddenly lifted the gun and whipped it fast and hard across his face, drawing a cascade of blood from his nose. She turned abruptly on her heel and told Docherty: 'Let's get out of here.'

'Take it easy,' he said gently, and watched her take a deep breath. 'We'll be gone as soon as we can.' He turned to Razor and Ben. 'Should we kill these two?'

The two troopers said nothing.

'If it was for the sake of the mission, I'd say yes,' Docherty said. 'But since we'd only be killing them to increase our chances of getting away . . .' He looked at the other two. 'I'd rather we just took our chances.'

'Sounds good to me,' Ben said.

Razor agreed.

'Tie them up, then. The curtain cords will do.' Docherty walked over to where Isabel was standing by the door. 'Any sign of life?'

'None,' she said.

'Which direction should we take?' he asked.

'If we get out of here without being seen, then south. We can be at the border in two hours.'

'Good. This Naval Mechanical School — what was it?' Docherty asked.

'It was a torture chamber,' she said.

'I thought it might . . .' he started to say, but Razor's warning shout had him stepping to the right and bringing up the Browning as his eyes sought the threat. He saw the automatic in Solanille's hand at the moment of detonation, and as the echoes of the crack merged into a cry of pain from Isabel he put a bullet through the Argentinian's left eye.

The surviving guard threw himself on the floor.

'No need to tie him up now,' Razor said, looking down at Solanille.

Docherty was examining Isabel's wound, and cursing himself for not being more careful. Her presence was not helping his concentration, he realized, and it was she who had paid the price. Why the fuck had he not thought to use the handcuffs?

'Just handcuff and gag the guard,' Docherty told Ben. Talk about locking the stable door after the horse has bolted.

'How is she, boss?' Razor asked, kneeling down beside them. He was the patrol's specialist medic, but Docherty had had almost as much medical training.

'I'll live,' she said, trying to prop herself up on one elbow. 'The moral of this story is don't threaten to shoot off a soldier's dick,' she said weakly.

'We are kind of attached to them,' Razor murmured. 'But you stay put for a moment,' he added, gently pushing her back down. He used his knife to cut away the blood-soaked section of her dress between breast and shoulder. The bullet had gone clean through, and he doubted whether there was any severe damage, but she was losing a lot of blood.

'Trouble, boss,' Ben said from the window. Docherty went across to join him. Two uniformed men were standing on the steps of the police station across the street, staring in the direction of the building they were in.

'They must have heard the shot,' Ben said. As he said it another man came out and the three of them started walking across the street.

'Shit,' Docherty said emphatically. 'Take the top of the stairs, Ben,' he said, and walked swiftly across to where the surviving guard was still lying face down, handcuffed, on the carpet. 'Is there a back way out of here?' Docherty asked him in Spanish.

The man looked up at him with an expression half-terrified, half-defiant.

'A bargain,' Docherty said, 'your life for a back way out.' He tried to look as if he did not much care what the answer was.

The man swallowed once. '*Sí,*' he said, 'I will show you.' Docherty pulled the man to his feet, and saw that Razor had got Isabel to hers. She looked deadly pale, and her face seemed pinched with the effort required to stay conscious.

'You'd better carry her,' Docherty told Razor. 'Let's go,' he said to the guard.

They emerged onto the landing just as Ben opened up with his silenced Browning. In the stairwell there was the sound of someone either jumping or falling back down the stairs, and a few choice Spanish epithets. Presumably the discovery of the dead guard at the console had already resulted in a general alarm.

Fools rush in, but you can't make them drink, Razor thought to himself, as the guard led them down a short corridor towards the rear of the building, and down a wrought-iron spiral staircase to a back door.

Ben opened it gingerly, and poked an eye round the corner. He could see and hear nothing.

They all emerged into a back yard. Across a six-foot wall two large houses were silhouetted against the night sky. It was topped by lines of razor wire, and Docherty was wondering how the fuck they were going to get Isabel across, when Ben announced the discovery of a gate.

'The escape gate,' the guard explained helpfully.

Ben had already shot away the padlock. The open gate revealed a narrow passage running between the two houses.

'Go!' Docherty told Ben and Razor. He turned to the guard, whose face seemed about to break up in fear. '*Muchas gracias, señor,*' Docherty told him, and closed the door in his face.

He ran down the passage in pursuit of the others, catching them at the opening onto the street. The Renault was still standing where they had left it, only 20 yards away.

'That's what I call planning, boss,' Razor said admiringly. He helped Isabel into the back seat and climbed in beside her. Docherty told Ben to drive. 'Just get us a few streets away,' he said.

Ben pulled away from the kerb, and Docherty turned to face Isabel. 'Which way?' he asked her.

She looked at him blankly for a moment, then her eyes came back into focus. 'Calafate,' she said.

'Where . . .'

'There's a map in the glove compartment,' she said.

'Where the hell's Calafate?' Ben asked.

'It's about 150 miles to the north-west,' Docherty said, examining the map. 'Not that far from the mountains and the Chilean border. And she's right – the whole Argentinian military will be looking for us in about half an hour's time. This border's a lot further away, but there'll be some cover. The road to the southern border is just flat and empty, like a target range. We'd never have made it.'

The other two absorbed this information. 'Join the SAS and see the world,' Ben murmured. 'So which way?' he asked, taking another turn to the right. He liked the idea of seeing some mountains again.

Behind him Isabel was remembering Calafate, which she had visited two weeks before as part of her cover job. It was a beautiful place, she thought, as she drifted into unconsciousness.

'Pull over for a minute,' Docherty told Ben. 'I want to know what we're doing before we hit the open road.' He squirmed round in his seat. 'How is she?' he asked Razor.

'Out like a light, but I think she'll be OK. There's not much I can do without any kit. I'd like to wash the wound though, first chance we get.'

Docherty looked at her. The face was still pale, but he had no reason to doubt Razor's diagnosis. Solanille's bullet had not killed her, but if his friends caught up with them then they probably would. And it did not look like she would be up to climbing any mountains for a while. Which meant . . .

'We need another car,' he said abruptly.

'What's wrong with this one?' Ben asked, surprised.

'Nothing. I meant an additional car. As in two.' He sorted out his thoughts. 'Look,' he told the two men, 'according to this map, four or five hours' drive should get us within a few hours hard hiking of the Chilean border. But there's no way she's going to be able to do any hiking at all, and we can't leave her behind. If it wasn't for her, you two would still be back there,' he added.

'OK, boss, but . . .'

'Just listen for once in your insubordinate life. If she and I can get to Calafate then there's a good chance we can pass ourselves off as a married couple or something. But if all four of us drive in then it'll look like an invasion. You two have camouflage trousers on, for Christ's sake . . .'

'You don't look that elegant yourself, boss . . .'

'Meanwhile you two can take this road,' Docherty insisted, showing it to them on the map, 'dump the car somewhere round here' – he pointed out a particular spot – 'and get the hell out of this fucking country.'

Ben and Razor said nothing.

'Well?' Docherty asked.

'Boss,' Razor began tentatively, 'you're not getting carried away by, well . . .' He nodded towards Isabel.

Docherty grinned at him. 'Who the fuck knows? The point is, can either of you clowns think of a better plan for giving all four of us a chance?'

They could not.

'Right, we've been here long enough. Let's find another car.'

They found an anonymous-looking black VW Beetle closer to the outskirts, parked on a convenient slope, its doors unlocked. Razor freewheeled it down the slope, and then hot-wired the engine. The sound seemed to carry alarmingly.

'The Renault's tank is almost full,' Ben said. 'What about yours?' he asked Razor.

'Better than half.'

'Follow us,' Docherty told him. 'I want to make some improvements, but let's get out of town first.'

He directed Ben down a wide, dusty street, looking for the large lagoon shown on the map. It appeared, black and still, reflecting a few dim yellow lights on its far shore. They came to a crossroads and followed the signs for Ruta 3 and the north, passing two cars and a full coach going in the opposite direction. The estuary appeared to their right, though it was hard to work out how wide it was. Clouds had driven in from the west and the stars had all been extinguished.

'If you see somewhere to turn off, take it,' Docherty told Ben.

They eventually found a turning, and less than a minute later found themselves in a car park for a picnic area by the side of the estuary. The three men got out.

'Have we really got time for a picnic, boss?' Razor asked in a concerned voice.

Docherty was looking back towards the city, where a light seemed to be bobbing in the dull black sky. It was a helicopter. 'Disconnect all the lighting in the Beetle,' he told Razor. 'I'll drive the Renault,' he explained to the two of them as Razor started work, 'with lights full on. You two should be able to follow the road by my lights. If we're spotted from the air, then, provided the night stays as dark as this, they should only see the front car. If they land on the road up ahead then you two hang back. If they believe it's me and the missus on our way to the mountains for a holiday, well and good. If they don't, then you two will have surprise on your side when it comes to rescuing us. Got it?'

'A masterplan, boss,' Razor murmured. 'The chopper's headed our way,' he added, almost as an afterthought. All three men watched it head up the highway they had driven out on, and pass low above the turning they had taken 200 yards away.

'We've got time for you to wash her wound,' Docherty told Razor.

'OK.' The Londoner found a way down to the river and soaked a piece of cloth in the near-freezing water. Back in the Renault, its application brought Isabel back to life, if only for a couple of minutes.

'*Qué pasa . . .?*'

'I'm just cleaning up the wound,' Razor said in Spanish.

She winced as he dragged dry blood away with the cloth. Still, at least that meant the bleeding had stopped. 'Where are we?' she asked.

'Just outside Rio Gallegos.'

'And going to Calafate?'

'So I'm told. You'd be better sleeping,' he told her. 'Let us worry about the travel arrangements.'

She managed a hint of a smile. To rely on the English SAS for escape from her own country – how many ironies could one situation contain? She closed her eyes.

Razor noticed the car clock, which said it was almost two. Add three hours for the time difference, he thought. The Cup Final was only ten hours away. He hoped Hoddle was having a better night's sleep than they were.

Outside the car Ben and Docherty were staring into space.

'All finished,' Razor said. 'We can go now,' he explained patiently.

'I was hoping to see that helicopter again before we moved,' Docherty said. 'But . . .'

Its light appeared in the western sky, and soon the accompanying drone of its engine seeped out of the silence. A minute later it was sweeping past them, still hugging the highway, this time heading back towards the town.

'Brilliant,' Docherty said to no one in particular. 'Let's go.' He climbed into the front seat of the Renault, took one look at the sleeping Isabel in the back seat, and started the engine. A minute later they were on Ruta 3 again, the Renault showing all its lights, the VW travelling just behind the limits of the other car's aura. It worked well: even knowing there was something to look for, Docherty could often see no sign of the VW in his rear mirror.

In the six miles to the Calafate turn-off they passed only two vehicles, both trucks, headed in the opposite direction, and once on the narrower Calafate road they seemed to be almost alone in the universe. To either side of the road the darkness stretched away, not yielding a single light for miles on end. They could have been traversing a desert, travelling through a tall forest or crossing an endless bridge. It felt more like a tunnel than anything else. For Ben, struggling without lights to keep the VW inside the tracks of the Renault, it sometimes seemed more like a video game than a real drive.

In the car ahead, Docherty was trying to calculate times and distances. It was one-fifteen when they left the Intelligence building, which meant that they could have been at the southern border around an hour later. How long would it take the Argentinians to realize that they were not on that road? Another couple of hours, perhaps. And then what would they do? Widen the search, and keep widening it? But they did not have an unlimited supply of helicopters or pilots. And they were supposed to be fighting a war.

The telephone, he thought. The poles ran alongside the road. Cutting the wire might be a giveaway, but it might be worth it. No, he finally decided. He and the woman would be stuck this side of the border for a couple of days at least, and he could not afford to leave any more trail for the enemy to follow than they already had.

It took him a while, but eventually Hemmings managed to get through to Bryan Weighell's home in the suburbs of Hereford. It was midnight, but Weighell was still awake. The events of the day had served as continuing shots of adrenalin, and even two large malt whiskies had failed to slow him down.

'What's the news?' he asked Hemmings, marvelling yet again at the clarity of the connection.

'Mostly good.' Hemmings briefly outlined what he knew of the situation ashore on the first night, and the current condition of the SAS units on the islands.

'What about North and South?' Weighell wanted to know.

'That's the bad news, and that's what I'm calling you for . . .'

'What's happened now?' Weighell asked, a sinking feeling in his stomach.

'We've lost radio contact with both groups. You know about Brookes's patrol. Well, they may have taken out some Super Etendards – we've no way of knowing. There's been no sign of them today – the Super Es, I mean – which looks good. If Brookes and the other lads have managed to nobble them then they deserve knighthoods. But there's no news of them. They could be dead, captured, or just lying low somewhere without a radio.'

'And North?'

'No idea. They radioed in that Docherty was going into Rio Gallegos to warn the MI6 woman, and that once he returned they'd be heading for the border. They may be on their way, but we tried to raise them again an hour ago and couldn't. So . . .' He let the implications speak for themselves.

'You think they may have been captured,' Weighell said.

'I think there's a good chance some of those eight men have been taken,' Hemmings admitted.

Weighell rubbed his eyes. 'OK,' he said. 'I'll get onto it. Thanks for calling, Bill.'

He hung up, took the whisky over to his desk and sat down with a pen and paper. He needed a list of people to call, a list of people to pressure. Somehow, through any and every channel available to him – and even a few that were not – he had to get word through to those Argentinian authorities who were holding his men. The message would be twofold: one, that he expected his men to be accorded all the privileges and rights due to prisoners of war; and two, that there would be no escape from retribution for anyone who treated them otherwise.

Ten miles short of Esperanza, Docherty flashed his brake lights twice to indicate he was stopping, pulled over to the side of the road, and got out of the car. A landscape of undulating hills was dimly visible: either dawn was coming a lot earlier than he had expected or the cloud cover was imperceptibly thinning. The latter, he decided, studying the sky.

The VW pulled up behind the Renault, and the other two got out. 'What's up, Doc?' Razor asked.

'Nothing. I've just been doing some calculations in my head, and I reckon that at some point in the next hour there's a good chance they'll be checking this road again from the air.'

'Can we afford to hang around, boss?' Ben asked. 'It'll start to get light in a couple of hours.'

'I don't know – it's a toss-up. But a fifteen-minute break wouldn't do me any harm, and I don't suppose driving that thing without any lights is exactly relaxing.'

'Not for the poor passenger, it isn't,' Razor complained. 'I just sit there expecting Jim Clark here to drive us off a cliff any moment.'

'You've spent most of the time sleeping,' Ben said trenchantly.

'Thinking. Not sleeping.'

'He snores when he thinks,' Ben told Docherty.

Docherty grinned.

'How's the invalid?' Razor asked.

'She's asleep. And she looks OK. I . . .' The sound of a helicopter insinuated itself into his consciousness.

'Boss, you're a genius,' Razor sighed.

Docherty said nothing, but felt absurdly pleased that his calculations had proved so accurate.

The helicopter swept towards them, flew straight over their heads and on up the road towards Esperanza. If Docherty had not pulled up, the Renault's lights would undoubtedly have been spotted before he heard the approaching helicopter above the car engine.

'Ten minutes to Esperanza and back,' he murmured.

'Unless they land,' Ben suggested.

'Let's pray they don't.'

The minutes passed slowly, and it was more than fifteen before the whirr of the blades re-emerged, and the single pinpoint of light brightened as the helicopter approached. The black shape loomed out of the black sky, clattered above them and was gone again.

Docherty gave it a couple of minutes, and then pulled the Renault back onto the road. In fifteen minutes they were entering the small town of Esperanza, where, until the appearance of the helicopter, he had been most afraid of their finding a welcoming committee. But it seemed as if the military authorities in Rio Gallegos were keeping matters exclusively in their own hands, presumably as a way of handling the whole business with the minimum damage to their own credibility. Whatever the reason, Esperanza was fast asleep, and blissfully oblivious of the passage of fugitive SAS.

Ten miles or so beyond the town the roads to Calafate and the border at El Turbio diverged. The three men got out of the cars once more, but there was nothing really to say, except good luck and goodbye for the moment. Docherty gave them a portion of

Isabel's money, just in case. Then the two troopers solemnly shook hands with their PC.

'We'll be staying at the Santiago Hilton,' was Razor's parting shot through the window, as the VW rolled away into the darkness. Docherty stood by the Renault for a few seconds, savouring the moment. He had good mates, there was a beautiful woman in the back of his car, and he was standing in the dark in the middle of nowhere, hunted by the forces of the enemy.

It sure as hell beat feeling sorry for himself in the Slug & Sporran.

10

It started to get light as the VW clambered up the last few miles of the long valley. Clouds still filled the view behind them, diffusing the dawn sunlight, but to the west the sky was clearing again. As they breasted the last in a series of slopes, a vista of snow-capped mountains appeared in the far distance.

'The Andes,' Ben murmured.

'And there I was hoping it was the Chilterns,' Razor replied. He was driving now, and enjoying it a lot more since he had been able to see where he was going. The hour he had driven without lights of any kind had been a nightmare. It would probably have been quicker to have just sat in a lay-by, if they could have found one in the dark.

Ben was still taking in the view. 'You've got no soul,' he complained. This was the reason he was not prepared to give up the SAS, he thought.

'A mountain range is a mountain range. It's just a lot of rock in one place, that's all.'

Ben looked at him pityingly.

'OK, it is sort of . . . majestic,' Razor agreed. Corinna would love somewhere like this, he thought.

'It's also Chile,' Ben said. 'Over there, it is.' He gestured in the general direction of the west.

'Would you like to be a bit more precise,' Razor

suggested. 'Like, how far from the border are we, and how far on the other side can we expect to find a suitable hostelry?'

'I think pubs are pretty thin on the ground in southern Chile,' Ben observed. 'In a couple of miles this road takes a bloody great turn to the left, and after another couple we're about five miles from the border. It looks like a downhill walk. Unfortunately, there seems to be something like a 40-mile walk on the other side.'

'Downhill?'

'Mostly. On the other hand,' he continued, 'if we keep going till we're a few miles outside El Turbio, then the border's still only about five miles away, and the main road to Puerto Natales is only a couple of miles on the other side.'

'But is it all downhill?'

'For you, it's all downhill.'

'That's the one then.'

'Wake me up when we get there,' Ben said.

Razor ignored him. 'I wonder how the boss is getting on,' he said.

'You mean, has he had her yet?'

'No, I don't. Well, yes I do. But not as crudely as that. It was all a bit weird, don't you think?'

Ben considered. 'I don't know. What else could he have done? She's one of ours and he couldn't . . . ah, Docherty's always been . . . you know, his wife getting killed and all that . . . he . . .'

'Thank you, Dr Freud. I think I'll just go back to wondering if he's had her yet.'

The first hint of light was still colouring the sky when Docherty pulled up the Renault on the outskirts of

Calafate. It was obviously not a big town, but the plethora of helpful signs for the tourists suggested it saw a lot of custom in season. Unfortunately the season had ended a month ago, which might mean all the hotels were closed for the winter.

At least there were no signs of a welcoming committee, he thought, watching the view gradually unfold with the growing light. Calafate seemed fast asleep beside its beautiful lake. It was almost seven – not the best time to be searching for a hotel room, but late enough not to be waking everyone up. And he did not want to be sitting here by the side of the road much longer.

In the back seat Isabel was, as far as he could judge, breathing more or less normally. It was time to wake her up. He took her hand and gently squeezed it. Her eyes opened, and her other hand went lazily up to brush her hair away from them. Then she saw him, and awareness came flooding back. Her shoulder began to ache. 'Where are we?' she asked.

'Calafate. Just outside. I want to get us off the street and out of sight, and I need to know if you can walk OK.'

'I don't see why not,' she said. 'I wasn't shot in the legs.'

He helped her out of the car, and she took a few unsteady steps. 'I do feel weak,' she admitted.

'Eat this,' he said, giving her a small piece of chocolate from his emergency rations. 'It may make you buzz a bit.'

It did, but she felt stronger. 'Where are the others?' she asked.

'On the road to Puerto Natales. They're going to get as close as they can, then walk across into Chile.'

'And you stayed behind for me.' It was not so much a question as an expression of surprise.

'We try not to leave men behind,' he said, 'let alone women.'

She gave him a strange look, and tried walking a few more paces. As long as she put no demands on her upper body there was no extra pain. 'I'll be all right,' she said, walking round and manœuvring herself slowly into the vacant front seat.

Docherty got in behind the wheel. 'Have you been here before?' he asked.

'Two weeks ago.'

'That's good. Where did you stay?'

'The Hospedaje del Glaciar. On the lake. I'll show you.'

He started the car, and she guided him through the empty streets of the town, and down the slight slope to the lake, where several hotels seemed to be fighting for the best view. One, slightly removed from the rest, was built on a small peninsula which jutted out into the lake. It was painted white, had two storeys, and boasted a wide verandah overlooking the still waters.

They left the Renault in the small car park behind the hotel, and rang the old-fashioned bell hanging by the front door. It all felt more than a little unreal to Docherty: less than twelve hours had passed since he had left the OP overlooking the Rio Gallegos airbase.

A plump woman with a huge mane of black hair opened the door, and her scowl-in-waiting changed instantly to a smile when she saw Isabel.

The two women hugged, and Docherty saw Isabel wince with pain, but she betrayed nothing. 'Do you have a room for us for the weekend?' she asked. 'My fiancé and I,' she added, introducing Docherty by the first name that came into her head – Franco. 'He has come to stay with me in Rio Gallegos for a couple of weeks.'

She took a deep breath, and Docherty was afraid she was in danger of collapsing. 'We have been driving most of the night,' he explained, 'and Isabel is very tired. Could she lie down, do you think?'

'Yes, I'm exhausted,' Isabel confirmed.

The woman, whose name was Rosa, showed them up to one of the rooms which led out onto the verandah overlooking the lake. It was sparsely furnished but scrupulously clean.

'Breakfast is at eight,' she said, and left them.

Isabel sat down unsteadily on the side of the bed with a heartfelt sigh of relief, and tried to bring her legs up so she could lie down. It was harder than she expected. 'Can you help me?' she asked Docherty.

'First, I want to look at your wound,' he said.

'It feels OK,' she said.

'No arguments.'

She relented and sat patient-like on the side of the bed.

'I'll need to take off the blouse,' he said.

'This is one of those highly ambivalent scenes, isn't it?' she said, as he started to peel off her blouse. 'You take off my clothes and I wonder if your motives are purely medical.'

Docherty smiled. 'There's nothing ambivalent about it at all,' he said. 'My motives for taking off your clothes on this occasion are purely medical. And if I start taking them off on some other occasion there won't be any ambivalence there either,' he added.

'I think you're an extraordinary woman. And very sexy too.'

He examined the entry and exit wounds carefully, trying to be true to his words and not to get distracted by the swell of her breasts beneath the brassière.

'You're not what I expected, either,' she said. He was not exactly good-looking, but there was something about the man that she responded to. Maybe she had finally cracked, she thought sourly.

'There doesn't seem to be any infection,' he said, 'but some hot water wouldn't be a bad idea. If there is any,' he added, looking round.

'There is,' she said. It was all in her never-to-be-published guide.

He soaked a convenient flannel and did as he had said, then helped her into a horizontal position and covered her with all the blankets he could find.

It was gone eight, and he felt ravenous. First, though, he badly needed a shower.

Ten minutes later he was reluctantly putting the same dirty clothes back on a clean body. He would have asked her whether she wanted him to bring her any breakfast, but she was asleep again, her hand across her face as if to ward off a blow.

Mozza woke himself with his watch alarm an hour before dawn, and spent it thawing himself out before a rekindled fire. His feet seemed no worse than the previous morning, which he supposed was the most he could have hoped for. After boiling water for tea he doused the fire, cleared up his camp-site, and sipped from the cone as the dawn lit the roof of the forest above him.

The first hour's walk had him following the lower

tree line round the upper slopes of a wide, moorland valley. The sky was not as clear as on the previous day, but there were still large patches of blue between the floating cumulus. The stream flowed into the valley from the west, and Mozza followed it back up into the forest, climbing alongside it for about three miles, until the trees suddenly cleared and he found himself confronting a large, silver-blue lake, surrounded on all sides by snow-capped hills. Two birds that looked suspiciously like eagles were drawing lazy circles in the sky above.

The lake stretched about six miles from east to west, between half a mile and a mile from north to south. It had an air of utter stillness, and working his way along its southern shore Mozza felt his mind settling into some sort of ease for the first time since the fire-fight at the airbase.

Every now and then he came across evidence of past human activity: a crumbling section of fence, a burnt-out fishing lodge, wooden piles that had once supported a jetty. The land had rejected them all, sent their creators scurrying back to the comfort of cities.

Almost halfway down the lake a narrow promontory leading out into the lake looked custom-made for fishing. Mozza cut himself a rod, attached his line, and impaled several berries from an overhanging tree on the hook. Then he cast the line and settled down to wait, keeping watchful eyes and ears on the world around him.

He did not have long to wait. Within a minute a medium-sized trout had taken the lure and been landed. Mozza cut it open and dutifully examined the contents of its stomach to check what bait he should be using, but it hardly seemed to matter. Another trout almost leapt out onto the shore to join him.

The temptation to cook them there and then was strong, but self-discipline prevailed. He walked on, allowing himself to dwell for the first time on the events of the night before last. He supposed Brookes and Stanley were dead, and though he could not say he had ever felt close to either of them, they had both been damn good soldiers.

Whatever that meant, an inner voice murmured.

He had always assumed that he could kill someone when the need arose, that when the moment came to turn the exercises and simulations and techniques into real combat he would find that switch which released him from moral inhibitions. Now he was not so sure. He had learnt silent killing techniques at Hereford like everyone else, and he was as technically adept as Stanley had been. But he was not sure whether he could have cut that guard's throat the way Stanley had.

And he was no longer sure he wanted to be able to do it. Shooting someone in self-defence was one thing; taking someone out in cold blood was another. But what did that mean? That he needed to look for another line of work? Maybe he did.

The road ran in alternating curves along the upper slope of a huge valley. To their right, at least 20 miles away, the far slopes were bathed in light, but the sun had yet to reach the depths in between. Almost directly ahead of them, and also far distant, a town nestled at the head of either a lake or an arm of the sea. 'Puerto Natales,' Ben said. 'We're about seven miles away from El Turbio,' he added, examining the map again. 'Sounds like a bandit who named himself after an engine. Anyway, I think we can start looking for somewhere to turn off.'

'Good idea,' Razor said dryly, 'but a bit on the late side.'

Ben looked up.

'About half a mile ahead,' Razor explained. 'You'll see it when we round the next curve.'

'Trouble?' Ben murmured. It was not really a question.

'A road block. A couple of vehicles and a few Johnny Gauchos.'

The next curve brought it back into view. A military lorry and a jeep had been arranged in an inverted V at a particularly favourable location. On one side of the road a solid rock wall prevented the block's circumvention; on the other was a precipitous grassy slope.

About a dozen troops seemed to be rapidly organizing themselves at the approach of their car.

'How wide do you think that gap is?' Razor asked conversationally, his foot pressing down on the accelerator.

Ben looked in disbelief at the fast-approaching roadblock. Two hundred yards, 150 ... 'About a foot,' he said, 'for Christ's sake ...'

'Not the one in the middle,' Razor said calmly, as the troops began raising their weapons, and his right hand eased down on the steering wheel.

Ben watched the valley loom towards them, hardly noticing the bullets which made two holes in the windscreen and passed between their heads, and felt his neck almost yanked from his body as the car surfed past the outer edge of the jeep, its right-side wheels scrambling for a hold and seeming to spend an eternity in finding one.

'That gap,' Razor said calmly.

'Jesus Christ,' Ben said.

The roadblock was shrinking in the rear mirror, but he did not slacken his speed. They went down one long, sweeping curve and then another.

'Trees,' Razor said.

A quarter of a mile ahead of them the road descended into the fringes of a coniferous forest. From their bird's-eye view they could see where logging operations had exposed a number of bald patches in the tree cover.

'Time to melt into them,' Ben said.

They were half a mile into the forest when Razor found what he was looking for – a tight curve over a steep and already logged slope. 'This'll do,' he said, slamming on the brakes, and reversing back up the hill.

'Out,' he told Ben, who dutifully obliged.

Razor accelerated forward. The VW was going about 20 miles per hour when he slammed the clutch into neutral and hurled himself out onto the road. He rolled over several times and scrambled to his feet, just in time to see the car disappear over the edge.

Ben was already running down the slope to his right, headed for the cover of the trees, and Razor raced after him, listening to the VW's passage, which sounded rather like a large animal breaking through underbrush. It ended suddenly with a satisfying explosion.

'I thought they were supposed to be indestructible,' Razor said breathlessly, as he caught up with Ben some 20 yards inside the trees.

'This is far enough,' Ben told him.

The two men put tree trunks between themselves and the road and waited for the pursuit to catch up. It was less than half a minute behind them. A jeep jammed with troops pulled up on the bend above, and voices floated down through the clear morning air. The word '*loco*' seemed much in evidence to Razor, but he might have been imagining it.

Whoever was in command showed no urgent inclination to send anyone down after the VW, let alone mount a proper search. Taking one curve on two wheels had obviously implanted the possibility of such an accident in the Argentinian commander's mind. As far as he was concerned, the SAS men were dead until proved otherwise.

The lorry arrived, picked up all but two of the men, and continued on its way.

The two SAS men breathed a sigh of relief. Though they were confident they could have outrun the opposition in rough country if necessary, a stroll in the sunshine was certainly more fun without armed pursuit.

Above them the pair of soldiers left behind with the jeep talked and smoked a leisurely cigarette before reluctantly clambering over the rim of the slope and disappearing from sight. Ben gave them a minute and then went up to check that there was no radio in the jeep.

'No,' he told Razor on his return. 'Chile, here we come,' he added, examining the map.

'More haste is a friend indeed,' Razor said wisely.

After eating breakfast Docherty stretched out on the bed beside Isabel, set the alarm on his watch and slept for four hours. He awoke feeling more tired than when he had gone to bed, and took another shower. Isabel was still asleep, but her face seemed more childlike, more at ease. She was about Chrissie's size, he thought, maybe an inch taller. He took the money from her shoulder bag and went out looking for new clothes for both of them.

Calafate looked like any tourist town out of season – half-asleep. Most of the few shops seem closed, either for the weekend or the off season, but on Calle 25 de Mayo he managed to find one selling clothes and camping equipment. The prices seemed extortionate, but he consoled himself with the thought that MI6 was paying. He bought a pair of jeans, two T-shirts, a sweater, spare socks and underwear for himself, and a couple of T-shirts and a sweater for Isabel. She already had a change of clothes, and if she wanted anything else one of them could always come back. He had only spent a quarter of the money.

He stopped off for a hamburger and coffee at an empty café, and watched the street through the window. He had not seen a policeman or soldier since leaving the hotel, and wondered how much longer they would be safe in Calafate. He guessed the Argentinians would be concentrating their search in the immediate area of Rio Gallegos, at least until they had reason to look elsewhere. Eventually though, they would connect the woman the guard had seen to the missing Isabel, and then the hunt for her car would begin. Luckily the car park of their hotel was out of sight from any road. They would have to be doing a rigorous check of all the hotels to find it.

He wondered how Razor and Ben were getting on and looked at his watch. It was midday – there was a good chance they would have reached the border by this time. The Cup Final was kicking off too, he realized, smiling to himself.

He finished the coffee and paid the cheque to a friendly young woman. He liked Latin America, he decided. Mexico had not been a one-off.

Back at the hotel he left the clothes and went out again. They needed an escape route, or preferably two – one to use in their own sweet time and one for emergencies. The tourist office was closed, but maps of the town and the province were displayed in its window. He spent ten minutes drawing rough copies and fending off offers of help from the locals.

Then he followed the town map to the Plaza San Martín, and walked uphill to the top of the long Calle Perito Moreno. From there he had a breathtaking view of the distant Andes, and the blue-green Lago Argentina stretching away from the town towards the mountains' feet.

It occurred to him for the first time that one way out of Calafate was by boat.

Isabel woke in the empty room of the Hospedaje del Glaciar and thought for one horrible moment that she was back in a cell. It was the light, she decided, or the lack of it. Her cell at the Naval Mechanical School had been dazzlingly bright with the fluorescent light on, perpetual twilight with it off. There had been no real night – only nightmares.

She climbed slowly off the bed, expecting a sharper pain than the one she received. It was healing well, she decided. There was nothing wrong with her body's recuperative powers. By the next day there would be little more than stiffness.

She pulled one of the curtains, and found the lake stretching away from her towards a distant line of blue hills. As she turned, the pile of bags by the door caught her attention, and she walked slowly across to investigate. He had been clothes-shopping! And for her, too. The thick sweater, a deep burgundy red, would suit her. She carried it across to the mirror and held it up in front of her.

Christ, she looked a wreck, she thought. Her eyes were like bruises in a ghost's face. She looked like someone who had just been shot, she thought, and laughed. It transformed her face. She was feeling good, she realized with surprise. Despite it all she was feeling good. Something somewhere had snapped. Some exorcism had taken place.

She wondered where the Englishman was now. Docherty, that was his name. She tried it out loud: 'Dokker-tee'. And he was a Scotsman, not an Englishman. They were touchy about such things. And she liked him.

Christ, what was she thinking? She had known him for less than twenty-four hours, and all she knew about the man was that he thought well on his feet, killed people efficiently and seemed to possess that streak of mad gallantry which often went with being one of the most unreconstructed macho bastards on the planet.

Just like Francisco, she thought, and she had for-given him everything because of his beauty and his politics and his ability to be tender. Well, Mr Docherty was not beautiful, his politics were likely to be conservative-verging-on-fascist, and she would prob-ably never know how tender he could be.

But she did like him. There was something about

him, some sadness maybe, which seemed incredibly human.

It was probably the snoring that had woken him, Wacko thought. He was in what looked like a hospital room, and directly in front of him, seated beside the door, a guard with an automatic rifle was dozing with his mouth wide open.

Wacko tried to move, almost cried out with pain, and seemed to lose consciousness again for just a few seconds. He felt really weird, he realized. Maybe some sort of drug had been pumped into him, or maybe it was just one of the consequences of being shot wherever it was he had been. The chest, he thought. He tried to examine his arm for needle marks but the room started to swim, and he had to close his eyes tight.

The next time he awoke – whether minutes or hours later was impossible to tell – it was to hear voices. There were two men, either standing in the doorway or just outside. Wacko kept his eyes closed and tried to concentrate on what they were saying. One voice was soft and one rasping, like two instruments alternating solos in a piece of chamber music. They were talking about someone or something named Solanille, about someone or other looking everywhere, about a woman – a 'mystery woman'.

'And what is to be done with this one?' the rasping voice asked. Wacko thought he could feel eyes glancing towards him.

'Nothing,' the soft voice said, causing Wacko to clench his fist in elation under the sheet. 'The war is probably lost,' the man said, his voice even softer than before, 'and who knows how the people will react . . .'

'But this is an Englishman. A terrorist. What do the people care about . . .'

'You are being naïve, Carlos. If the people turn on the Junta then it will be a lottery for those of us in the security services. But one thing is certain – the cleaner our hands appear to be the more chance we shall have of keeping our positions. I do not want my name on some list the English Ambassador to the UN reads out, just when a new government in Buenos Aires is looking for scapegoats in the security services.'

'I see what you mean,' Carlos agreed.

'Good.'

'So we wait for the war to be over, one way or another.'

'We hand him back to the Air Force, him and his friend from Rio Grande.' The soft-voiced one grunted, apparently with amusement. 'If by some miracle we win the war, then we can always ask for him back.'

The voices went on, but Wacko, unable to hold his concentration any longer, drifted back into unconsciousness. The next time he awoke Hedge was sitting beside him, apparently dressed in pyjamas.

'Welcome to St Gaucho's,' the big man said.

The sun was high in the clear blue sky when Razor and Ben emerged from the trees and saw, half a mile below them, a line of widely spaced white posts laid across the vast, wild slope, fading into the distance.

'It must be the border,' Ben said.

'Don't see what else it could be,' Razor agreed.

There was no sign of troops, nor of any other

humans. But for the line of white posts there was no sign that men had ever walked there before.

They moved down cautiously, looking for any signs of a minefield, without really expecting to find any. At a point directly between two of the posts Razor took a large symbolic step. 'One second you're a soldier at war, the next you're a tourist,' he proclaimed.

'Or an internee,' Ben corrected him.

'As long as there's a hot meal involved,' Razor said.

They walked on, their steps a little lighter for having crossed the border, but it was another four hours before they came upon a rough track. They followed it down into an idyllic little valley, where a stream danced happily over stones beneath lovely cypresses, and a real road wound out of sight to left and right.

Less than ten minutes had passed when a farmer responded to Razor's optimistic thumb, and stopped to give them a lift. He chatted merrily about nothing in particular, but seemed entirely devoid of curiosity as to who they were. He also failed to shed any light on the outcome of the Cup Final.

He drove them the five miles into Puerto Natales, a small town whose houses all seemed to be made of either wood or corrugated iron. At Razor's request they were dropped outside the Post Office, which happened to face the town's main square.

Ben sat in the latter while Razor entered the former, and stretched his Spanish to the utmost in a long but ultimately successful attempt to make a reversed-charge telephone call to the British Embassy in Santiago.

'Who shall I say is calling?' the Chilean official asked.

'Trooper Wilkinson of the SAS,' Razor told him. 'We're a sort of travelling show,' he added helpfully.

The Embassy answered immediately, as if they had been waiting for the call. Once Razor had explained his and Ben's geographical and pecuniary situations, he was told to wait in the square until a man named Lawson came to collect the two of them. It might be several hours before he could get there, and perhaps not before morning. In the meantime, somewhat unrealistically, they should try not to attract any attention to themselves.

Razor went back to Ben, and the two of them sat side by side on a bench, in their filthy Gore-tex jackets and camouflage trousers, staring at the statue of some Chilean general.

'Fuck this for a laugh,' Razor said after a few minutes. 'Let's try and change the Argie money, eat and drink ourselves into a stupor, find some nice girls and have a fucking ball.'

'As long as we don't attract any attention to ourselves,' Ben said.

'Goes without saying,' Razor agreed.

Docherty thought Isabel's face looked anxious when he let himself back into the room. 'There's no sign of the opposition,' he said quickly, and then noticed that she was wearing the sweater he had bought for her.

'It seems to fit,' he said. 'Is the colour OK?'

'It's lovely,' she said.

He felt pleased.

'But where have you been since?' she asked.

'Here and there. Exploring the town.'

'Don't . . . I mean, I'm not telling you what to do, but don't you think it would be better if we stayed out of sight.'

He took no offence. 'Yes and no,' he said. 'I wanted to make sure the car was as out of sight as possible, without actually pushing it into the lake. And I always like to know where the back door is, so to speak, just in case someone comes knocking at the front.' He grinned at her. 'Other than that, yes, we should stay out of sight.'

She sighed. 'Point taken.'

'Let me ask you a question,' he said. 'How long do you think it will be safe to stay here?'

She took time to think about her answer, which was the one of the things he most liked about her. 'Does anyone know we came this way?'

'Not that I know of, but . . .' He shrugged. 'You never know when someone's looking out through the lace curtains.'

'If they've lost us, then I'd guess several days,' she said, 'but there's no guarantee.'

'Of course not. Another question: have you ever done any mountain hiking?'

'Are you kidding?' I grew up in Ushuaia. I climbed every mountain in the National Park before I was sixteen.'

'Great. Well, this is the plan.' He brought out the map he had copied, and outlined their escape route. 'But you'll need all the strength you can muster,' he added. Somehow, going over it all with her had only emphasized how hard it might turn out to be.

'Don't worry about me,' she said, 'I've always been strong as an ox.'

268

'You don't look like one.'
She smiled. 'Just give me one more day.'

Mozza had spent the previous night camped in a convenient cave, just above the tree line on the northern slope of another range of miniature mountains. Puma tracks by the cave mouth had made him feel slightly ambivalent. While he would have loved to see one up close in the wild, he did not feel much like having to fight off an angry cat whose home he had stolen. Still, there were no recent droppings, and the two baked trout had been tasty enough to take his mind off everything else. He had slept like a child, perhaps in unconscious recognition of the rigours of the day to come.

The mountains were less than 3500 feet high, he reckoned, but the top three hundred were wreathed in permanent snow, and they looked just like the Alps through the wrong end of a telescope. More to the point, since the range ran almost north to south, he had no choice but to cross it.

Fortified at first light by another hot meal and drink, he was quickly on his way, climbing steadily up across the bare mountain towards the snowline. The temperature seemed to drop steadily despite the rising sun, and once he was into the snow his feet started to ache, and his eyes to blink. The going was not difficult, and he pressed on for the best part of another hour without ever seeming to be any nearer the summit, his vision assuming a pink hue which steadily darkened towards red.

He forced himself to stop, eyes closed, feeling his feet turning into blocks of ice, fighting off a rising sense of panic. 'Lynsey, Lynsey, Lynsey,' he said to himself. He visualized her face at the door, the smile, the embrace. He then tried walking with the PNGs on, keeping his eyes dangerously closed on stretches that seemed straightforward.

After what seemed an age he reached the top of the pass. Taking off the PNGs he could see, far in the distance and way down below, another large lake stretching away into the haze.

It was almost noon. He took another two biscuits and two more squares of chocolate, promised himself a cup of tea beneath the snowline, and started down. His feet were now sending out severe shooting pains, but somehow he knew the worst was over.

An hour later the snow gave way to alpine meadow, and he followed an icy stream down a steep, winding valley towards the occasionally visible lake. There was no wood for making a fire, but once out of the snow his feet had held their own, and he was confident he could reach the water before the sun disappeared behind him.

He was still some way from the lake when the noise started percolating into his consciousness. It grew steadily in volume as he approached, a sound somewhere between braying and squawking, like a football crowd full of angry donkeys.

It was only when he turned the last corner of the valley that he saw the source: hundreds upon hundreds of penguins were spread across the beach, walking up and down, apparently talking to each other.

They hardly seemed to notice his arrival. He turned the corner of the cliff, and found he had underestimated their numbers. There seemed to be thousands of them, spread as far as he could see up the lakeside beach, all honking up a storm.

Except that penguins only lived by the sea, he reminded himself. He had read it in Hannah's book of animals before he left. And if this was the sea then he was in Chile. He sniffed at the cold air to make sure, and smelt the salt. He was safe. He would be going home.

Docherty was woken by church bells the following morning, and decided that the chair he had slept in must have been engineered by a sadist. Every muscle in his body seemed stiff.

Isabel seemed much stronger for a good night's sleep, and the two of them had breakfast together in the almost empty hotel dining-room. Rosa continued to treat them as though they were favoured relatives, which perhaps had something to do with Isabel's fictional guidebook. In any case, her non-stop chatter about herself, the hotel and the town revealed no new cause for alarm.

Docherty spent most of the day spending MI6's money. He had been half afraid the camping shop would be closed, but as if engaged in a desperate effort to squeeze the last drop from the tourist trade, its doors were defiantly open. He purchased a tent, sleeping bags, footwear for Isabel, a pack for carrying it all – and everything else they would need for several days' hiking in subarctic conditions.

All day he kept an eye out for any sign of trouble, but the town seemed as becalmed as the waters of its lake. Newspaper headlines suggested great victories in the Malvinas, but to judge from the locals' faces they believed it as little as Docherty did.

Isabel stayed in the hotel, gathering her strength and letting her mind wander. If they got away, then where would she go? What would she do? What did she make of this man?

They ate dinner in the dining-room, and he talked about the months he had spent in Mexico. She found herself wondering more and more why this man did what he did, and then she remembered how and who he had been during that long night in Rio Gallegos. Some people, she thought, just do what they do because they know how good they are at doing it.

Back upstairs he did all but the last-minute packing, ramming more into the backpack than she would have thought possible. When he had finished, it seemed to weighed a ton, but was apparently half the weight he usually carried.

'We're ready,' he said, as much to himself as her. 'And the more sleep we get, the better,' he added.

'I think you should sleep in the bed tonight,' she said.

'OK,' he said.

'I mean with me,' she said.

'Yeah,' he said, making sure the door was locked. 'Don't worry, I'll keep my distance.'

She was silent for a moment. Then she stepped across to meet him, and put her two hands on his shoulder, and kissed him softly on the lips. 'I mean, I want us to make love,' she said. 'It doesn't have to be now. I just wanted to tell you.'

'Oh,' he said.

'If you want to,' she added.

'I've wanted to since the first moment I saw you in that hotel lobby,' he said. 'But you're not properly mended yet . . .'

'Oh, I can manage,' she said, easing her good arm around his neck. They kissed, first gently, then with a slowly growing passion that neither had known for many years.

'I shall need some help undressing,' she said.

'Look no further,' Docherty said mildly, caressing her hair. She carefully straightened her arms, allowing him to pull the sweater and T-shirt up over her head, and he managed to unfasten the bra with an ease which was unique in his experience.

He leaned down to kiss her breasts, noticing the faded scars of burns across them, and felt an intermingling of desire and pity which almost choked him.

She pulled him back up. 'They're old scars,' she said softly, and applied her fingers to his belt buckle.

After making love they lay talking in the large bed, half-conscious of the growing silence around them as hotel and town went to sleep.

'Tell me about you,' she said. 'You know all about me.'

'No I don't,' he said. 'I know you were a revolutionary, and you were captured and tortured, and your family managed to get you out of the country somehow. And that you agreed to work for MI6 because of your hatred for the Junta. But none of that prepared me for who you are.'

'So who am I?' she asked wryly.

'You're someone who couldn't shoot the man who sent you to the torturers . . .'

'I know. I could kill that man at the door, who I

273

had never seen in my life before, but I couldn't kill Solanille.'

'Your finger could have pulled the trigger. Your head knew how to give the order. Your heart just didn't want it done.' He smiled. 'In the films they always say that's what separates us from them.'

'In the films they still believe in good and evil.'

'And so do you.'

She smiled. 'Yes, I do. Outside myself I do.'

'And you make love like an angel,' he added, running his fingers through her hair and feeling himself beginning to stir once more.

'You're changing the subject,' she said. 'And you still haven't told me anything about yourself.'

'It's a sad story,' he said.

'It can't be that sad.'

'Why not? Do you think . . .'

'Because you make love like an angel too,' she interrupted him, running her hand down his stomach. 'You can tell me the sad story later,' she said.

An hour before dawn they left the hotel, walked swiftly down to the lake and along to the small motor boat Docherty had selected for their journey. A crescent moon hung in the sky, casting a thin light across the waters, but there were no witnesses to watch their departure. Docherty rowed them out into the lake and past the first headland, only engaging the outboard motor when they were about half a mile from the town.

The darkness began to dissipate, and then suddenly, or so it seemed, the snowy peaks of the mountains ahead were ignited by the still invisible sun, and seemed to burn with white fire.

Through the morning they passed down the blue-green lake, the wall of the southern Andes drawing ever nearer. They turned south where the lake divided, the shimmering wall of the Moreno Glacier visible in the distance, the cracking of its ice highly audible across the water. Just before noon Docherty grounded the boat in a shallow cove on the lake's south-western shore. He disembarked Isabel, himself and the pack, and then shoved the now-floating boat back out into the lake. For a moment it sat stationary on the water and then, as if called by its unfortunate owner in Calafate, started drifting back the way they had come.

Once Docherty had checked the map the two fugitives started slowly climbing the valley behind the cove, Isabel ahead, the laden SAS man behind. She looked strong, he thought, and he hoped to God she was.

That night they pitched their tent a good way above the lake, and discovered that Docherty had chosen the sleeping bags well – once unzipped they could be united to make a double.

The next day they resumed their climb, moving no faster than Isabel could easily manage, and stopping well before dark to set up camp as efficiently as the conditions warranted. Then they cooked, talked, made love and slept. The rest of the world had been left with the drifting boat below.

The following day was much the same. The sky stayed clear and the temperature dropped, but now they were more than halfway to their goal. And sure enough, soon after midday they crested what proved to be the final ridge, and found themselves looking down a long valley running into the west. They were standing on the border.

'Out of one fascist dictatorship and into another,' Isabel said cheerfully.

And out of one life and into another, she dared herself to hope.

Epilogue

The crew of the Sea King managed to sustain themselves for nine days in the Chilean wilderness, and only decided to hand themselves over to the authorities when a party of local trekkers blundered into their camp.

They were flown from Punta Arenas to Santiago, where they gave a press conference on Wednesday 26 May. 'We were on sea patrol when we experienced engine failure due to adverse weather conditions,' they explained. 'It was not possible to return to our ship in these conditions. We therefore took refuge in the nearest neutral country.'

The few people who believed this story did not include anyone in political or military service with the British or Argentinian governments.

By this time Razor and Ben were already on board a plane above the Atlantic, headed home to a discreet heroes' welcome and two weeks' immediate leave. Ben took the overnight train north with an anxious heart, not knowing how he was going to tell Morag that he had decided his future lay with the SAS. He did not want to lose her, but if she forced him to choose, then that would have to be his choice.

It was a beautiful morning in Fort William, and

she met him off the train with the news that she had
taken the afternoon off. This was surprising enough
in itself, but one look at her face and he knew that
she had missed him much more she had expected.
They took the local train to Glenfinnan and walked
up across the heather to a place above the viaduct,
the famous statue of Bonnie Prince Charlie a distant
spot far below, and made love beneath the blue sky,
the sun warm on their skin.

Afterwards, knowing what he had to say to her, Ben
felt almost guilty. But it was she who first broached
the subject of their future, announcing that she was
withdrawing her ultimatum. 'My father says you'd be
a fool to leave the Army at the moment,' she added,
'with unemployment rising so fast.'

He looked at her, wondering how he could get
across what he felt about it all. 'It what's I *do*,' he
said helplessly.

On arriving back at Heathrow, Razor had found to
his delight that the Cup Final replay was scheduled
for that evening. It was not exactly a good game,
and jet lag had added its contribution to his overall
exhaustion, but he managed to stay awake for the
sight of a Tottenham player holding up the Cup for the
second year running. And next season, with their two
Argies back in midfield, the sky would be the limit.

His mum was certainly pleased to see Razor back
– in fact she hardly seemed to stop fussing over him
from morning till night. Then he overheard her end of
a telephone conversation, and thought he understood
why. That evening he announced he was going out
with Corinna – which was true – and that it was
about time his mother found herself a man to look

after her. He was fed up feeling guilty for being away so much, he said.

And then she told him about the new man in her life, grinning like a schoolgirl.

Razor felt really happy for her, and could hardly stop smiling all evening, at least until Corinna found another use for his lips. Familiarity makes the heart grow fonder, he thought, as they wrestled each other into her bed.

In the third week of June, the week that followed the final Argentinian surrender in Port Stanley, there were memorial services for both Stanley and Brookes, in West Bromwich and Hereford respectively. Bryan Weighell and Bill Hemmings attended both of them, as did many of their regimental comrades.

At the end of the service for Brookes, Weighell asked Hemmings if the number of Super Etendards in service with the Argentinian Air Force had ever been finally established.

'Not with complete certainty,' the Welshman admitted. 'But every indication we have is that there were only five of them.'

'And they took out three,' Weighell murmured to himself.

'They did that. And the other two sank the *Atlantic Conveyor* and the *Coventry* four days later. God knows what damage they might have done with all five still available.'

'They'll get some recognition, of course,' Weighell said, 'but no one will know what it was for. Which always seems a pity, somehow.'

In the same week, in the northern Argentinian town of

Metán, a funeral Mass was held for the repose of Raul Vergara's soul. His body had never been recovered from the sea, but his spirit could be seen reflected in the upturned faces of his mother and father, brother and sisters, sweetheart and friends.

Later, back at the Vergara house, amid the expected protestations of sorrow and pride, the anger that now lay so close to the surface of Argentinian life was occasionally expressed. Bitter voices were heard asking how, after such a defeat and so many lost, the Generals could still cling to power.

A few days later Wacko and Hedge were dispatched for home via the Uruguayan capital, Montevideo. It was more than a month since their capture and Wacko felt good as new, but Hedge knew his knee would never be the same again.

Their treatment, first in Rio Gallegos and then in Buenos Aires, had improved as the Argentinian Army's fortunes had declined. Garbled reports of the negotiations for their release had reached them in the suburban villa where they were confined, but the government official's arrival that morning with the news of their imminent departure had come as a very pleasant surprise. A long drive to the docks had afforded them their first and last view of 'South America's Paris', and now they were leaning against the rail of a ferry across the River Plate, looking out on the scene of the famous battle.

Hedge had seen the film about five times as a kid, and had always secretly wanted the Germans to win. He supposed that that was because their captain seemed more English than the English. He stared out at the rolling waves and wondered if the film had been made here. He doubted it. In fact, they had probably shot most of it in one of those big tanks in the old film studios.

Despite the gammy knee, he had to admit to feeling pretty good. During the weeks in captivity, and particularly through those first uncertain hours and days, he knew he had held himself together well. He was glad to be going home, but he had no regrets about coming. He reckoned his father would have been proud of him.

Wacko was feeling much the same sense of achievement, and even looking forward to seeing Anne. The letters she had written since receiving news of his capture had seemed to come from a much more loving person than the one he remembered. Maybe there was still something there to build on, or maybe they would find it better to just go their separate ways. It seemed not to matter as much as it had.

Mozza did not arrive back in England until some time after Razor, Ben, Docherty and Isabel. His penguin colony had certainly been on Chilean soil, but a particularly remote part of it, and it took him the best part of forty-eight hours to find his first native. This fisherman gave him a lift to Dawson Island, and from there he got another to Punta Arenas, which was still discussing Razor and Ben's blow-out the weekend before. Mozza finally reached Heathrow on the first day of June.

Like Razor and Ben, he was given a fortnight's immediate leave, and the homecoming in Manchester proved everything he had hoped for. Lynsey's smile and open arms were exactly as he had visualized them in the forest on Tierra del Fuego, and every day for a week he had to tell Hannah the story of how he had met all the penguins on the beach.

His nights, though, were not so kind. For several in a row he had a dream of falling through a pool of blood, and each time he awoke in a cold sweat with Lynsey's worried face looking into his. Eventually he told her what had happened on the Rio Grande airfield, or at least enough of it to give her some understanding of what he was dreaming about.

She just held him tight until he fell asleep in her arms, but the next day, as they watched Hannah playing in the park sandpit, she said she had been thinking about it and wanted to say something. 'Maybe the dream is trying to tell you something,' she began, 'maybe you weren't meant to be a soldier, no matter how good you feel about being one.'

He turned his innocent eyes towards her. 'Why, what's wrong with me?'

'Nothing, nothing at all. Maybe it's what's right with you. People who wear their hearts on their sleeve can't cut themselves off from what they're doing. And you're like that. It's what makes you such a wonderful man.'

'I don't think I'm so wonderful,' he said. 'But maybe you're right about the rest.'

Isabel Fuentes and Liam McCall were sitting in his local, just round the corner from the church, waiting for Docherty to come back from visiting his mother.

'I've been thinking about who really won the war,' Isabel said.

'What do you mean?' the priest asked.

'I get the news from Argentina now,' she said, 'and it really looks like the military's days are numbered.

The elections will be held – everyone seems sure of it. My country will get a good government out of this war, or at least a better one. And at some point they will have to go back and look at what was done in the Dirty War. The Mothers of the Disappeared will accept nothing less, and now the people are behind them.'

She took a sip of her beer. 'Oh, I'm not saying that everything is perfect there, or that the torturers will all be punished. They won't be. But some will, and it will make it harder for the others to show their faces. Argentina is a better place for losing the war. Whereas England . . .' She sighed, and reached again for her glass.

'I know what you mean,' Liam said. 'The woman was on her way out, and now we've probably got her for the next ten years. And at the rate she's going there won't be much left of the country I used to love by the time she's finished.'

They both sat in silence for a moment.

'And what are you and Jamie intending to do?' he asked eventually. 'If you don't mind my asking.'

'We don't know,' she said simply. 'We were talking about it the other night, and we decided that there was only one thing we were both qualified for, and that was creating mayhem.'

Liam grinned. 'Is Jamie going to stay with the SAS?'

'I don't know,' Isabel replied. 'But you can ask him yourself,' she added, her dark eyes lighting up.

Docherty wended his way through the tables and sat down, taking her hand in his.

'We were just discussing your future,' Liam said.

'Oh aye, which future's that?'

'That's what we were trying to work out.'

Docherty opened a bag of crisps and handed it round. 'I've got two months left of a three-year term,' he said. 'When the time comes I'll decide whether I think this is a country worth serving. And if the answer is yes, I'll ask this woman here if she agrees with me. And if she does, then . . . who knows? Maybe we'll live in a bungalow outside Hereford and raise children.'

'Or maybe we'll go and create mayhem somewhere else,' Isabel said.

SOLDIER L: SAS

THE EMBASSY
SIEGE

Shaun Clarke

Prelude

Number 16 Princes Gate formed part of a mid-Victorian terrace overlooking Hyde Park and had been used as the Iranian Embassy in London for more than a decade. Until 1979, it had represented the Iran ruled by Shah Reza Pahlavi and his wife, the Empress Fara Diba.

Noted for its Italianate stucco façade and prominent frieze, it was a very large building spread over three main floors and an attic. The ground floor comprised an imposing entrance hall, a large, beautifully furnished reception room, toilets, an administration office, and an expansive library overlooking the rear terrace. The main stairs led up to the first floor and the rather grand ambassador's office, the more modest office of the chargé d'affaires, two administration offices and a storage room. The second floor contained two more administration offices, Rooms 9, 9A and 10, another toilet

1

and a telex room. The third floor was the busiest, containing the press counsellor's office, the press room, the commercial office, the xerox room, the switchboard, Room 19, the kitchen, a toilet, and two more administration rooms, one of which was empty. A well skylight with a glass roof, located between Room 19, the switchboard, the xerox room and the outer wall, overlooked the main stairs connecting the three floors. As the lift terminated on the second floor, the third floor could only be reached by the stairs.

When run by the Shah's young and eligible Ambassador, Parvis Radji, the Embassy had been noted for its lavish dinner parties and largesse when it came to supplying excellent caviar, French wines, cars, free hotels and first-class travel to British diplomats, journalists and other visitors whose goodwill and assistance were vital to Iran. However, while ostentatiously maintaining this front of gracious, civilized living, the Embassy had also been used as a base for SAVAK, the Shah's dreaded secret police, whose function was to spy on and intimidate London-based Iranians, mostly students. Many of these secret police were uneducated, unsophisticated and addicted to the Western 'decadence' they were supposed to despise: nightclubs, alcohol and bought women.

2

Such activities had, however, ended with the downfall of the Shah in January 1979. Six months after the revolution, the Ayatollahs replaced Parvis Radji with a new chargé d'affaires, Dr Ali Afrouz, a twenty-nine-year-old graduate in psychology and education. Once installed in the Embassy at Princes Gate, Ali weeded out the corrupt members of SAVAK, banned all alcohol from the premises, got rid of the more ostentatious luxuries of the previous regime, and in general ensured that Embassy business was conducted in a more modest, formal manner.

In the days of the Shah, the Embassy's front door had been guarded by the British security company Securicor. Unfortunately, when Dr Afrouz took over, he dropped the company and gave the job to an Iranian, Abbas Fallahi, who had been the Embassy's butler and knew precious little about security.

More knowledgeable in this area was Police Constable Trevor Lock, at that time a member of the Diplomatic Protection Group. This organization, being unable to give individual protection to each of London's 138 embassies and High Commissions, was based at several strategic points in West London, remained constantly on alert in case of emergency, and also provided individual armed guards as part of the British Government's token contribution to the embassies' security.

Though not due to serve at the Iranian Embassy that morning, PC Lock agreed to stand in for a colleague who required the day off for personal matters. So it was that at approximately 1100 on 30 April, the policeman strapped his holstered standard-police issue .38 Smith and Wesson revolver to his thigh, carefully buttoned his tunic over the holster, then set out for the Embassy.

One of the most loyal members of the Embassy staff was not an Iranian, but an Englishman, Ron Morris, who had joined as an office boy twenty-five years before, when he was only fourteen. Ron had graduated to the position of chauffeur, then, when the luxuries of the Shah's days were swept away, among them the ambassadorial Rolls-Royce Silver Ghost, he was made a caretaker and general maintenance man.

Just before nine o'clock on the morning of 30 April, Ron bid a routine farewell to his Italian wife Maria and cat Gingerella, left his basement flat in Chester Street, Belgravia, and drove on his moped to the Embassy, arriving there on the dot of nine. After parking his moped against the railings, he entered the building and began work as usual.

Two hours later, Simeon 'Sim' Harris, a thirty-three-year-old sound recordist, and Chris Cramer, a thirty-one-year-old news organizer, both with the BBC and widely experienced in the world's trouble spots, arrived at the Embassy to try yet again – they had tried and failed before – to obtain visas to visit Iran. They were met by the doorman, Abbas Fallahi, who led them to the reception room, located through the first door on the left in the entrance hall. While waiting there, they were joined by another visitor, Ali Tabatabai, an employee of Iran's Bank Markazi. In London for a fourteen-week course for international bankers run by the Midland Bank, Ali was visiting the Embassy to collect a film and map of Iran for a talk he was to give as part of his course. He sat beside the two BBC men and, like them, waited patiently.

These three visitors were soon joined by Majtaba Mehrnavard, an elderly, nervous man who bought and sold Persian carpets, but was there because he was worried about his health and wished to consult the Embassy's medical adviser, Ahmed Dagdar.

Ten minutes after the arrival of the BBC team, Mustafa Karkouti, a Syrian journalist who was the European correspondent for *As-Afir*, the leading Beirut newspaper, arrived to interview the Embassy's cultural attaché, Dr Abul Fazi Ezzatti. Shown into Ezzatti's office, Room 13 on the third floor, he was offered a cup of coffee and proceeded with his interview while drinking it.

Another newsman present was Muhammad Farughi, a fifty-year-old British national born in India. He was the editor of *Impact International*, a Muslim magazine based in Finsbury Park, north London. Farughi had come to the Embassy for an interview with the chargé d'affaires, Dr Ali Afrouz, for an article about the Islamic revolution in Iran, and was at once escorted to the latter's office, at the front of the building, on the first floor, overlooking Princes Gate.

On arriving at the Embassy for his day of duty on behalf of the Diplomatic Protection Group, PC Lock took up his usual position outside, by the steps leading up to the front door. On this particular morning, however, which was particularly cold, he was offered a warming cup of tea by the sympathetic doorman, Abbas Fallahi. As it would not have been proper to have been seen drinking outside the building, the frozen policeman decided to take his tea in the small ante-room between the outside door and the heavy security doors leading to the entrance hall. So he was not present outside – and, even worse, the main door was ajar – when the six armed men from Baghdad arrived at the doorstep.

Number 105 Lexham Gardens, Earls Court Road, was rather more modest than the Iranian Embassy. An end-of-terrace Victorian house with five steps leading up to the front door, it had simulated tiles on the steps and yellow awnings above the window to give the façade the appearance of a colourful Continental hotel. Inside, it was less grand. The foyer was papered with gold-flecked wallpaper, the carpet was blood-red, and an office desk served as reception.

Flat 3, on the second floor, contained three bedrooms, two sitting-rooms, two bathrooms and a kitchen. The rooms had the tired, slightly tatty appearance of all bedsits and flats in the city, with unmatching furniture, fading wallpaper, and a combination of bare floorboards and loose, well-worn carpets.

At 9.40 a.m. on Wednesday, 30 April 1980, the six Iranians who had shared the flat with another, Sami Muhammad Ali, left it one by one and gathered in the foyer. They were all wearing anoraks to keep out the cold and to conceal the weapons they would soon collect.

The leader of the group, Oan-Ali, real name Salim

Towfigh, had a frizzy Afro hairstyle, a bushy beard and sideburns. Twenty-seven years old, he was the only member of the group to speak English. His second in command was twenty-one-year-old Shakir Abdullah Fadhil, also known as Jasim or Feisal, a so-called Ministry of Industry official who favoured jeans and cowboy boots and claimed to have once been tortured by SAVAK. The others were Fowzi Badavi Nejad, known as Ali, at nineteen the youngest and smallest member of the group; the short, heavily-built Shakir Sultan Said, or Shai, twenty-three and a former mechanic whose almost blond hair fell down over his ears; Makki Hounoun Ali, twenty-five, another Baghdad mechanic who now acted as the group's humble housekeeper; and a slim young man named Ali Abdullah, known as Nejad.

Though not as obviously dominant as Oan, Ali Abdullah was greatly respected by the others because his older brother Fa'ad was one of the most important leaders of the Democratic Revolutionary Front for the Liberation of Arabistan. Fa'ad Abdullah operated in exile in Iraq and broadcast regularly for the Arabic and Farsi sections of Radio Baghdad, exhorting the Iranians to rise up against the regime of the Ayatollahs.

Ali was a serious young man. More ebullient was

Makki, who informed one of the other residents that the group was heading for France. In the foyer, Ali informed the Egyptian caretaker, Ahmed, that their nine bags, weighing a total of 203lb, would be collected by David Arafat, the property agent who had rented them the flat through his Tehar Service Agency in Earls Court Road. It would then be air-freighted back to Baghdad by him. After depositing the bags with Ahmed, the group left the building.

Makki waved goodbye to those watching through the glass doors of the foyer, then blew a handful of kisses and followed the others along the pavement.

For the next hour and a half, in the steel-grey morning light, the group moved from one safe house to another, collecting an arsenal of weapons that included two deadly Skorpion W263 Polish sub-machine-guns, three Browning self-loading pistols, one .38 Astra revolver, five Soviet-made RGD5 hand-grenades, and enough ammunition for a lengthy siege. By eleven-twenty the six men were assembled in Hyde Park, near the Albert Memorial, their weapons hidden under their coats, engaged in a last-minute discussion of their plans. Just before eleven-thirty, they left the park, crossed the road, and arrived outside 16 Princes Gate. The front door of the Embassy was ajar.

After covering their faces with the loose flap of

their *keffias*, the traditional patterned Arab head-dress, so that only their eyes and noses were visible, the men removed their weapons and stormed through the open front door of the Embassy, into the entrance hall. Hearing the commotion at the outer door, PC Lock darted out of the small ante-room and was practically bowled over by the terrorists rushing in. The deafening roar of automatic fire close to his ear was followed by the sound of smashing glass. A large slice of flying glass from the inner-door panel slashed PC Lock's cheek. Before he could remove his pistol, and as he was in the throes of sending an unfinished warning to Scotland Yard, one of the Arabs wrested the portable radio from him and another prodded his head with the barrel of a Maitraillette Vigneron M2 machine pistol. Putting up his hands, the policeman was prodded at gunpoint across the entrance hall, towards the door of reception.

Waiting there were Sim Harris, Chris Cramer, Ali Tabatabai and the highly strung Majtaba Mehrnavard, who all heard the roaring of the machine pistols, the smashing of glass and the thudding of bullets piercing the ceiling of the entrance hall. There followed frantic shouting in Arabic, then a voice bawling in Farsi: 'Don't move!' Understanding the words, Ali Tabatabai wanted to go out and see what was happening, but Cramer, an experienced newsman, stopped him with a curt 'No!' When he and the other BBC man, Sim Harris, turned to face the wall with their hands over their heads, Ali did the same.

A few seconds later PC Lock entered the room, his hands clutching his head, his face bloody. Following him were two women who also worked in the Embassy, and following them, prodding them along with semi-automatic weapons, were more terrorists with their faces veiled in *keffias*.

One of the veiled terrorists, speaking in English, warned the hostages that they would be killed if they moved, then he and the other terrorists led them at gunpoint across the entrance hall and up the stairs to the second floor.

On the third floor, the journalist Mustafa Karkouti was still deeply involved in his interview with Dr Ezzatti when he heard the machine-gun fire from below. Rushing from the office, both men saw other Embassy staff rushing past, heading down the stairs. Assuming that they were heading for a fire exit, Karkouti and Ezzatti followed them, but soon found themselves in another room that had no exit at all. There were about nine people in the room, including three or four women.

To protect all those gathered in the room, the

door was locked from inside. Five minutes later, however, it was kicked open and one of the terrorists entered, looking like a bandit with his *keffia* around his face and a pistol in one hand and a grenade in the other. After firing an intimidating shot into the ceiling, he ordered everyone to place their hands on their head and face the wall. When they had done so, another man masked with a *keffia* entered the room and, with the help of the first man, guided the hostages at gunpoint down the stairs to the second floor, where other Embassy staff were standing with their hands on their heads, guarded by two other masked, armed terrorists.

Ron Morris, the caretaker, was still in his office on the fourth floor. Hearing the muffled sounds of gunfire, his first thought was that a student demonstration was under way, with the police firing blank cartridges. He ran down to the first floor, where he saw PC Lock and Abbas Fallahi with their hands on their heads, being guarded by an armed Arab. Morris instantly turned around and went back up to the second floor, where he passed an accountant, Mr Moheb. On asking the accountant what was happening, he received only a blank, dazed look. The caretaker hurried up to his office on the fourth floor, planning to phone the police, but just as he was dialling 999, he heard shouting and running feet on the stairs. Not wanting to be caught with the phone in his hand, he put it down and sat behind his desk until an armed terrorist entered. Speaking in English, the terrorist ordered him to leave the room, then prodded him at gunpoint down the stairs to Room 9A on the second floor, normally occupied by the Embassy's medical adviser, Dr Dadgar, but now filled with many hostages, all with their hands either against the wall or on their heads.

One of the gunmen searched the hostages. After frisking Morris, finding his spectacle case and throwing it to the floor, the gunman searched PC Lock, but in a manner so inept that he failed to find the policeman's holstered pistol.

While this search was going on, other members of the Embassy staff were managing to flee the building. Zari Afkhami, who was in charge of the medical section, had her office at the rear of the ground floor. Hearing the gunshots and shouting, she opened the door, stepped into the hall, and saw a gunman prodding PC Lock in the chest with a gun. Running back into her office and closing the door behind her, she alerted an elderly clerk who had a weak heart. Afkhami opened the window and climbed out, followed by the clerk. Catching sight of two workmen at the rear of the building, she asked them to call the police.

Another official escaped by boldly climbing out onto the first-floor balcony and making his way across a parapet to the Ethiopian Embassy next door.

One who attempted to escape, but failed, was the chargé d'affaires, Dr Afrouz, who was still being interviewed by the Muslim journalist Muhammad Farughi in his office on the first floor when the attack began. Hearing gunfire and shouting, both men went to the office door, where Farughi was instantly seized by a terrorist. Afrouz managed to make it back across to the rear of his office, where he clambered out through the window. Unfortunately, in his haste he fell, spraining his wrist and bruising his face badly. Hauled back in by the terrorists, he was prodded at gunpoint into a room where there were no other prisoners. There, one of the gunmen fired a shot into the ceiling, possibly to intimidate Afrouz. He then led the limping diplomat out of the room up the stairs to the second floor, where he was placed in Room 9A with the other prisoners.

Shocked by the appearance of the injured diplomat, and assuming that he had been beaten up by one of the terrorists, Ron Morris asked one of the terrorists for some water. He bathed Afrouz's face, then examined his jaw and confirmed that it was not broken. The chargé d'affaires, still shocked and in pain, fell asleep soon afterwards.

Informed of the attack on the Embassy, the police were already gathering outside. An officer entered the back garden, where he saw an armed Arab looking down at him from an upstairs window. Aiming his pistol at the terrorist, the police officer asked what the group wanted.

'If you take one more step you'll be shot,' the Arab replied in English.

By eleven-forty-five Scotland Yard knew that one of its men, PC Lock, was one of the hostages, that he belonged to the Diplomatic Protection Group, and that he had been armed. This last fact, combined with the information that gunshots had been heard, gave them further cause for concern.

By midday, the Embassy was surrounded by police cars and vans, ambulances, reporters, press photographers, and armed policemen wearing bulletproof vests. Other police officers were on the roof of the building, clearing spectators from the balconies of the adjoining buildings. More police were across the road, opposite the Embassy, clearing people out of the park and sealing off the area.

The siege had commenced.

1

The wind was howling over the Brecon Beacons as Staff-Sergeant Bill Harrison, huddled behind a rock for protection, surveyed the vast slopes of the Pen-y-Fan to find his four-man CRW (Counter Revolutionary Warfare) team. The men, he knew, would be feeling disgruntled because the tab he was making them undergo they had all endured before, during Initial Selection and Training, with all the horrors of Sickeners One and Two. The four men now climbing the steep, rocky slope were experienced SAS troopers who had fought in Aden, Oman or Belfast, and none required a second dose of the 'Long Drag' or 'Fan Dance' across this most inhospitable of mountain ranges – or, at least, would not have done so had they been asked to do it while carrying an Ingram 9mm sub-machine-gun and a 55lb bergen rucksack.

This time, however, there was a slight but

diabolical turning of the screw: they were making the same arduous tab while wearing heavy CRW body armour, including ceramic plates front and back, and while breathing through a respirator mask fixed to a ballistic helmet. In short, they were being forced to endure hell on earth.

That was only part of it. Staff-Sergeant Harrison had not only ordered them to climb to the summit of the mountain, but had then informed them that he would be giving them a thirty-minute head start, then following them to simulate pursuit by a real enemy. Thus, even as they would be fighting against exhaustion caused by the heavy body armour and murderous climb, as well as possible claustrophobia or disorientation caused by the cumbersome helmet and respirator mask, they would be compelled to concentrate on keeping out of Harrison's sub-machine-gun sight. This would place an even greater strain on them.

In fact, they had already failed in their task. Even though wearing his own body armour and head gear to ensure that his men would not feel he was asking them to do what he could not, the tough-as-nails staff-sergeant had taken another route up the mountain – to ensure that he was unseen by his men while they were always in his sight – and circled around them to take up this position above

them, just below the rocky, wind-blown summit.
The men would be broken up when they found him
blocking their path, emulating an enemy sniper; but
that, also, was part of this lesson in endurance.

Harrison had been a member of the 'Keeni Meeni'
assassination squads in Aden in 1966, survived the
incredible SAS hike up the mighty Jebel Dhofar
in Oman in 1971 and, in 1976, spent days on
end in freezing observation posts in the 'bandit
country' of south Armagh, sweating it out, waiting
to ambush IRA terrorists. For this reason he knew
all about endurance and insisted that his men be
prepared for it.

They had already lost this one, but they were
still good men. Hiding behind his rock, one hand
resting lightly on his PRC 319 radio, the other on his
Ingram 9mm sub-machine-gun, which was loaded
with live ammunition, Harrison watched the men
advancing arduously up the slope and recalled how
their work in Northern Ireland and led to their
induction into the CRW.

All four men – Lance-Corporal Philip McArthur
and Troopers Danny 'Baby Face' Porter, Alan Pyle
and Ken Passmore – had been shipped in civilian
clothing to Belfast immediately after being 'badged'
in 1976. There they had specialized in intelligence
gathering and ambush operations, working both

in unmarked 'Q' cars in the streets and in OPs on the green hills of Armagh. By the end of their tour of duty in Northern Ireland, they were widely experienced in intelligence operations and therefore ideal material for special training in the 'killing house' in Hereford and subsequent transfer from their individual squadrons – B and D – to the Counter Revolutionary Warfare Wing.

Once in the CRW Wing, they were given more Close Quarters Battle (CQB) training in the 'killing house', then sent for various periods to train even more intensively with West Germany's CSG-9 border police and France's Groupement d'Inter-vention de la Gendarmerie Nationale (GIGN) paramilitary counter-terrorist units, the Bizondere Bystand Eenheid (BBE) counter-terrorist arm of the Royal Netherlands Marine Corps, Italy's Nucleo Operativo di Sicurezza (NOCS), Spain's Grupo Especial de Operaciones (GEO), and the US 1st Special Forces Operational Detachment, created specially for CRW operations.

The overseas postings had been designed to place a special emphasis on physical training and marksmanship. These included advanced, highly dangerous practice at indoor firing with live ammu-nition in other kinds of 'killing houses', such as mock-up aircraft, ships and public streets; abseiling and parachuting onto rooftops, parked aircraft and boats; hostage rescue in a variety of circumstances (which had the cross-over element of training in skiing, mountaineering and scuba diving); and the handling of CS gas canisters, and stun, fire and smoke grenades. Finally, they were taught how to deal with the hostages, physically and psychologically, once they had been rescued.

So, Harrison thought, those four hiking up the last yards to the summit of this mountain are going to be bitterly surprised at having lost – but they're still good men.

By now the four men were only about 20 yards below him, fifty from the summit, and obviously thinking they had managed to make it to the top without being caught. Wearing their all-black CRW overalls, respirator masks and NBC hoods, they looked frightening, but that did not deter Harrison. Smiling grimly, he raised his Ingram 9mm sub-machine-gun with its thirty-two-round magazine, pressed the extended stock into his shoulder, aimed at the marching men through his sight, then fired a short burst.

The noise broke the silence brutally. Harrison moved the gun steadily from left to right, tearing up soil and stones in an arc that curved mere inches in front of the marching men. Knowing that the bullets were real, they scuttled off the track in opposite directions, hurling themselves to the ground behind the shelter of rocks and screaming for Harrison to stop firing. Grinning more broadly, the staff-sergeant lowered his Ingram, put the safety-catch back on, then used the PRC 319 radio to call the leader of the four-man team, Lance-Corporal Philip McArthur.

'You dumb bastards. You're all dead meat,' the message said.

Lying behind the rocks lower down the windswept slope, the four men received the message with incredulity, then, almost instinctively, turned their surprised gaze to the exploded soil that had cut an arc just a short distance in front of where they had been walking, practically up to their feet.

'I don't believe it!' Trooper Alan Pyle exclaimed, removing his respirator mask from his face as the others did the same, all relieved to be breathing pure, freezing air. 'That daft bastard was using live ammo and nearly shot our fucking toes off.'

'He's too good for that,' Trooper Danny 'Baby Face' Porter said. 'If he'd wanted to shoot your toes off, you can be sure he'd have done it.'

'Just like you, eh?' said the third trooper, Ken Passmore, grinning admiringly. 'A real crack shot.'

'Yeah,' Baby Face replied with modest pride. 'I suppose you could say that.'

'All right, all right,' snapped Lance-Corporal Phil McArthur. 'Stop the backslapping. We've nothing to be proud of. After all, we *were* as good as dead. Now let's pick up our gear and go and face the great man.'

Breathing more easily without the masks, but crushed by being 'killed' by Harrison, the men picked up their weapons and other kit and advanced up the hill until they reached the staff-sergeant. Squatting behind the rock with a big grin on his face, Harrison was strapping the PRC 319 to his shoulders and picking up his Ingram.

'Nice try, men,' he said, 'but if this had been a real operation you'd all be belly up by now. Are you SAS men or not?'

'Fucking 'ell, Sarge,' Phil McArthur protested as he glanced back down the mountain at the broad sweep of the Brecon Beacons far below. 'We could hardly breathe in these bloody masks. And that hike was a killer.'

'Piece of piss,' Harrison replied. 'I got this far without taking a deep breath. I think you need some more exercise.'

The men stared warily at him. All of them were breathing heavily and still bathed in sweat, even though the wind was howling across the mountain, slapping icily at them.

'No more exercise, please,' Ken Passmore said, already drained. 'I can't move another inch.'

Harrison grinned with sly malice. 'What were your instructions, Trooper?'

'To get to the summit of the mountain,' Ken replied, 'without being shot or captured by you.'

'Which you were.'

'Right.'

'Which doesn't mean it's over, you daft prat. You've still got to get to the summit, so get up and go, all of you.'

In disbelief the breathless men glanced up to the summit, which was 50 yards higher up, though the distance seemed far greater and the steepness of the climb was horrendous.

'Jesus, Sarge,' Alan complained. 'After the climb we've just made, that last leg is going to be impossible.'

'Right,' Ken said. 'That slope is a killer.'

'Either you make that climb,' Harrison told them, 'or I have you RTU'd and standing by dusk on Platform 4, Hereford Station, outward bound. Get the message?'

'Yes, Sarge.'

'Come on,' Baby Face shouted. 'Let's get up and go.'

Though still trying to get their breath back, the weary men covered their heads and faces again with the respirator masks and ballistic helmets, humped their bergens onto their backs, picked up their Ingrams and reluctantly began the steep climb to the summit.

Within a few yards they were already gasping for breath, their feet slipping on smooth rocks, bodies tensed against the wind, the sweat soon dripping from their foreheads into their eyes. Twenty yards on, where the wind was even more fierce, the slope rose at an angle so steep it was almost vertical. Holding their sub-machine-guns in one hand and clinging to rocks with the other, they laboriously hauled themselves up until, about 20 yards from the summit, all of them except Baby Face decided to give in. Falling behind, they just leaned against high rocks, fighting to regain their breath, about to call it a day.

Harrison's Ingram roared into life as he fired a short burst in an arc that tore up earth and pieces of splintered rock mere inches from the feet of the men who had given up. Shocked, they lurched away from the spitting soil and scrambled with a strength they had felt had been drained out of them up the last, cruel section of the slope. Each time they fell back, another roar from the Ingram, ripping up the soil and rocks just behind the men, forced them to move hastily higher, finally following Baby Face off the sheer slope and onto the more even summit.

When the last of them had clambered onto the highest point, gasping but still surprised at their hitherto untapped stamina, Harrison followed them up and told them to remove the masks and breathe proper air. When the men had done so, they were able to look down on the fabulous panorama of the Brecon Beacons, spread out all around them, wreathed in mist, streaked with sunshine, thousands of feet below. Lying there, now completely exhausted, they gulped the fresh, freezing air, grateful that they would at last be able to take a good break.

Just as they were about to have a brew-up, a message came through on the radio. Harrison listened intently, then said: 'Got it, boss. Over and out.' Replacing the microphone on its hook, he turned to his weary men. 'Sorry, lads, no brew-up yet. We've got to return straight away. The Iranian Embassy in London has been seized and we're being put on stand-by. This isn't a mock exercise. It's the real thing. So pack your kit and let's hike back to the RV.'

Recharged by the prospect of real action, the men hurriedly packed up and began the hazardous descent.

2

By three p.m. on the first day, in a basement office in Whitehall a top-level crisis management team known as COBR, representing the Cabinet Office Briefing Room, was having a tense discussion about the raid on the Iranian Embassy. Presiding over the meeting was a man of some eminence, addressed as the 'Secretary', Junior Defence and Foreign Affairs ministers, representatives of MI5 and the Metropolitan Police, including the Police Commissioner, and the overall commander of the SAS CBQ team, addressed as the 'Controller', though in fact he was much more than that when it came to issues involving international politics and the defence of the realm.

'The function of this meeting,' the surprisingly genial and unruffled Secretary said, 'is to lay down guidelines for the police and, if necessary, the Army. First, however, the Commissioner of the

Metropolitan Police will fill us in on the general situation.'

The Commissioner cleared his throat and sized up his audience before speaking. 'The Embassy is being held by a six-man team of Iranians who were trained in Iraq, issued with Iraqi passports, and supplied with weapons brought in by diplomatic bag from Baghdad. We now know that they all visited the British Embassy in Baghdad last February to pick up individual visas to visit the UK. When asked how they would live in the UK, they each produced the same amount of cash: £275. In each case the purpose of the visit was recorded as being for medical treatment. Once in London, they were placed under the command of an Iraqi army officer, Sami Muhammad Ali, who flew home the day the siege began.'

'Who's leading them now?' the Secretary asked.

The Commissioner showed them a picture of a well-built Arab with frizzy hair, a bushy beard and long sideburns. 'The ringleader, Oan-Ali,' he said. 'Real name Salim Towfigh. Twenty-seven years old. Records show that he comes from Al Muhammara in the Khuzistan province of Iran, just across the Shatt-al-Arab river border with Iraq. Studied languages and law at Tehran University, where he became politically active and eventually militant. Fluent in four languages: Farsi, Arabic, German and English. He's believed to be one of those who took part in the riots that occurred there on 29 May last year, when 220 men and women in the crowd were reported killed and approximately 600 wounded. Certainly he was imprisoned and tortured by SAVAK, which only made him more militant. On 31 March this year he turned up with four other Arabs in Earls Court Road, where they took two flats at 20 Nevern Place. One of the flats was on the second floor, the other in the basement. Only three of the men signed the register: Oan-Ali, Makki Hounoun Ali, and Shakir Abdullah Fadhil. The caretaker was an Iraqi student studying computer engineering. He says he didn't examine their passports thoroughly, though he noted that they were issued in Iraq. The men told him they had just flown in from Baghdad. Apart from that, the caretaker learnt little about them. They claimed to have met each other by chance on the plane to London. One said he was a farmer, the other a student, the third a mechanic. The group is particularly remembered by the caretaker and other members of the household because, though Muslims, they came in late at night, invariably drunk and often with local prostitutes. Eventually, when they became embroiled in an argument over prices with one of the ladies in the basement flat, the caretaker, a devout Muslim, threw them out of the house.'

'Sounds like they weren't particularly sophisticated,' the Secretary said. 'Muslims seduced instantly by Western ways: alcohol and sex. Certainly not very disciplined.'

'That's worth bearing in mind,' the Controller said. 'A lack of discipline in a siege situation could go either way: either helping us to succeed or leading to mayhem and slaughter.'

Deliberately pausing to let the Controller's words sink in, the Commissioner then continued reading from his notes: 'After being thrown out of the house in Nevern Place, the terrorists dropped into the Tehar Service Agency, an accommodation agency run by a Jordanian named David Arafat and specializing in Arab clients with plenty of money and often dubious intentions. Arafat rarely asked questions of his clients, but claims that Oan-Ali told him he had left his previous accommodation because his group had been joined by two other friends and they needed larger accommodation. Subsequently, Arafat fixed them up with Flat 3, 105 Lexham Gardens, just a few hundred yards north of his Earls Court Road office.'

'And *were* there more men at this point?' the Controller asked.

'No,' the Commissioner replied. 'It was the same five who had been in Nevern Place who took over the flat in Lexham Gardens. However, the flat has three bedrooms, two sitting-rooms, two bathrooms and a kitchen, and according to the Egyptian caretaker, the five-man group grew to seven over the next few days. After that, there were times when as many as a dozen men would be there at the same time.'

'Do we know who the others were?' the Controller asked.

'No. We *do* know, however, that some of the others in his group are former members of the Democratic Revolutionary Front for the Liberation of Arabistan and that one of them, Fa'ad, broadcasts for the Arabic and Farsi sections of Radio Baghdad, exhorting the people of Iran to rise up against the regime of the Ayatollahs.'

As the Controller nodded and wrote in his notebook, the Commissioner concentrated once more on the file opened on the table before him. 'Intelligence has reason to believe that though Oan-Ali led the raid, he didn't actually plan it himself. One of those who moved into 105 Lexham Gardens was Sami Muhammad Ali, an Iraqi army officer described in his passport as an official of the Iraqi Ministry of Industry. Other meetings which Ali was known to have attended took place at 55 and 24 Queens Gate, the latter only two doors up from the office of the Iraqi military attaché.'

'How ironic!' the Secretary purred, smiling like a Cheshire cat.

'Finally,' the Commissioner continued reading, 'on 29 April, the day before the seizure of the Embassy, it was Oan-Ali who visited David Arafat, the property agent, to tell him that his friends were leaving Lexham Gardens – supposedly going to Bristol for a week, then returning to Iraq. He asked Arafat to crate their baggage and air-freight it back to Baghdad. The address he gave was a post-box number. By the following morning, when the rest of the group seized the Embassy, Oan-Ali had disappeared.'

'How many hostages?' the Controller asked.

'Twenty-two in all. Fifteen Iranians, the British caretaker, one Diplomatic Protection Group police constable, and five visitors, four of whom are journalists. The DPG constable, PC Lock, had a pistol concealed on his person and may still possess it.'

'That could be helpful,' the Secretary said with a hopeful smile.

'Or dangerous,' the Controller reminded him,

32

then turned back to the Commissioner. 'Do we know more about the hostages?'

'One is Mustafa Karkouti, the European correspondent for *As-Afir*, the leading Beirut newspaper. Thirty-seven years old, he's Syrian by birth, but educated in Damascus and Beirut. He was known to be pursuing the story of the hostages held by Iranian students at the American Embassy in Tehran. We also know that a month ago he attended an Islamic conference in London, to hear a speech by the Iranian Embassy's cultural attaché, Dr Abul Fazi Ezzatti. He then fixed up a meeting with Dr Ezzatti at the Embassy for Wednesday, 30 April, at eleven a.m. He was there when the terrorists seized the building.'

'Any use to us?' the Secretary asked.

'Could be. He speaks fluent English and Arabic, as well as a fair bit of Farsi.'

'That could come in handy.'

'Exactly. Also useful is the fact that Karkouti works out of Fleet Street and lives with his wife and child in Ealing. He therefore knows the English mentality, as well as the Iranian, which could be helpful to my negotiators.'

'Who else?'

'Ron Morris, a forty-seven-year-old Englishman, born in Battersea, London. Son of the

station-master at Waterloo. Left school at fourteen, spent six months in a factory in Battersea,
then obtained a job as an office boy for the
Iranian Embassy. That was in 1947 and, apart
from his two years' National Service, he's worked
for the Iranians ever since – first as an office
boy, then as a chauffeur, and finally as caretaker
and general maintenance man. In 1970, when
he'd been with them for twenty-five years, he
was given a long-service bonus of a ten-day trip
to Iran.'

'Is he political?'

'No, Mr Secretary. He's a regular, down-to-earth
type, not easily ruffled. Reportedly, he views himself as being above politics. Lives with an Italian
wife and a cat in a basement flat in Chester Street,
Belgravia. Collects replica guns. His work for the
Iranians is certainly not political.'

'So he could be useful.'

'Yes and no. As the maintenance man, he knows
every nook and cranny in the building. That knowledge could encourage him to try to escape.'

'And the others?'

'The Diplomatic Protection Group's Police Constable Trevor Lock. Known as a good man. He
had a standard police-issue .38 Smith and Wesson
revolver holstered on the thigh and so far there's no

report that the terrorists have found it. According to a recent report, however, Lock was slightly hurt and is bleeding from the face.'

'Have the hostages made contact yet?'

'Yes, Mr Secretary. Ninety minutes after the seizure of the Embassy, the terrorists asked for a woman doctor to be sent in. At first we assumed this was for PC Lock, but in fact it was for the Embassy Press Officer, Mrs Frieda Mozafarian, who's had a series of fainting fits combined with muscular spasms. Lock is apparently OK – just a little bruised and bloody.'

'So how do we handle this?' the Secretary asked.

The Commissioner coughed into his fist. 'First, the police will negotiate with the terrorists. Undoubtedly the terrorists will want media coverage of their demands, so we'll use this as a bargaining chip. As their demands won't be directed at the British Government, but at the Iranians, we can afford to cede this to them.'

He paused, waiting for their reaction.

'Go on,' the Secretary said, clasping his hands under his chin and looking disingenuously benign.

'Having met them halfway with media exposure for their demands,' the Commissioner continued, 'we try to talk them out, letting the affair stretch

on for as long as necessary. During that period, we'll
attempt to soften them up with food, medical attention, communications, more access to the media,
and the involvement of their own ambassadors
and those of other friendly Middle Eastern states.
We'll also ask for the release of certain hostages,
particularly those ill or wounded. This will not
only reduce the number of hostages to be dealt
with, but encourage the terrorists to feel that
they're contributing to a real, on-going dialogue.
In fact, what we'll be doing is buying enough time
for the police and MI5 to plant miniature listening
devices inside the building and also scan it with
parabolic directional microphones and thermal
imagers. Between these, they should at least show
us just where the hostages are being held.'

'And what happens when the terrorists' patience
runs out?'

'Should negotiations fail and, particularly, if the
terrorists kill a hostage, or hostages, clearance will
be given for the SAS to attack the building.'

The Home Secretary turned his attention to the
Controller, who looked handsome in his beret with
winged-dagger badge. 'Are you prepared for this?'

'Yes, sir. The operation will be codenamed
"Pagoda". We'll use the entire counter-terrorist
squadron: a command group of four officers plus

a fully equipped support team consisting of one officer and twenty-five other ranks, ready to move at thirty minutes' notice. A second team, replicating the first, will remain on a three-hour stand-by until the first team has left the base. A third team, if required, can be composed from experienced SAS soldiers. The close-quarters support teams are backed up by sniper groups who will pick off targets from outside the Embassy and specially trained medical teams to rescue and resuscitate the hostages.'

'You are, of course, aware of the importance of police primacy in this matter?'

The Controller nodded. 'Yes, Mr Secretary. Coincidentally, we've just been preparing for a joint exercise with the Northumbria Police Force, so the men and equipment are all in place at Hereford. That's only 150 miles, or less than three hours' drive, away. We're ready to roll, sir.'

'Excellent.' The Secretary turned to the Metropolitan Police Commissioner. 'Do you have any problems with this scenario?'

'No,' the Commissioner replied. 'My views today are those of Sir Robert Mark regarding the Spaghetti House siege of 1975. Those terrorists will either come out to enter a prison cell or end up in a mortuary. They'll have no other option.'

Some of the men smiled. The Home Secretary, looking satisfied, spread his hands out on the table. 'To summarize, gentlemen ... There will be no surrender to the terrorists. No safe conduct for the terrorists out of the country. Either this affair ends peacefully, with the surrender of the terrorists, or the SAS go in and bring them out, dead or alive. Agreed?'

The men of COBR were in total agreement.

3

As the team on the Pen-y-Fan were contending with the arduous return hike to the four-ton Bedford lorry that would take them back to Bradbury Lines, the SAS base in Hereford, another team, consisting of Staff-Sergeant 'Jock' Thompson, Corporal George 'GG' Gerrard, Lance-Corporal Dan 'Danny Boy' Reynolds and Trooper Robert 'Bobs-boy' Quayle were dressing up in heavy CRW Bristol body armour with high-velocity ceramic plates, S6 respirator masks to protect them from CS gas, black ballistic helmets and skin-tight aviator's gloves in the 'spider', their eight-legged dormitory area, in the same base in Hereford. They did not take too much pleasure in doing so.

'I hate this fucking gear,' Corporal 'GG' Gerrard complained, slipping on his black flying gloves. 'I feel like a bloody deep-sea diver, but I'm walking on dry land.'

'I agree,' Lance-Corporal 'Danny Boy' Reynolds said, adjusting the ballistic helmet on his head and reluctantly picking up his respirator. 'This shit makes me feel seasick.'

'I *hate* the sea,' the relatively new man, Trooper 'Bobs-boy' Quayle, said grimly, 'so these suits give me nightmares.'

'Excuse me?' Staff-Sergeant 'Jock' Thompson asked.

'What, Sarge?' Bobs-boy replied.

'Did I hear you say that suit gives you nightmares?'

'That's right, Sarge, you heard me right.'

'So what the fuck are you doing in this CT team?' Thompson asked.

Bobs-boy shrugged. 'I'm pretty good with the Ingram,' he explained, 'close quarters battle.'

'But you suffer from nightmares.'

The trooper started to look uncomfortable. 'Well . . . I didn't mean it *literally*. I just meant . . .'

Danny Boy laughed. 'Literally? What kind of word is that? Is that some kind of new SAS jargon?'

'He's an intellectual,' GG explained.

'Who gets nightmares,' Danny Boy added.

'A nightmare-sufferer and an intellectual prat to boot,' Jock clarified. 'And we've got him on *our* team!'

'I didn't mean . . .' Bobs-boy began.

'Then you shouldn't have said it,' the staff-sergeant interjected. 'If you get nightmares over CRW gear, we don't want you around here, kid.'

'Dreams,' Bobs-boy said quickly. 'I meant *dreams*. Really nice ones as well, Sarge. Not nightmares at all. I dream a lot about scuba diving and things like that, so this gear suits me nicely, thanks.'

'You can see how he got badged,' GG told the others with a wink. 'It's his talent for knowing which way the winds blows and always saying the right thing.'

'The only sound that pleases me is his silence,' Jock said, 'and I'd like that right now. Put those respirators on your ugly mugs and let's get to the killing house.'

'Yes, boss,' they all chimed, then covered their faces with the respirator masks. Though this kept them from talking casually, they could still communicate, albeit with eerie distortion, through their Davies Communications CT100E headset and microphone. However, once the respirators were attached to the black ballistic helmets, they looked like goggle-eyed deep-sea monsters with enormously bulky, black-and-brown, heavily armoured bodies – inhuman and frightening.

'Can you all hear me?' Jock asked, checking his communications system.

'Check, Corporal Gerrard.'

'Check, Lance-Corporal Reynolds.'

'Check, Trooper Quayle.'

All the men gave the thumbs-up sign as they responded. When the last of them – Bobs-boy – stuck his thumb up, Jock did the same, then used a hand signal to indicate that they should follow him out of the spider.

After cocking the action of their weapons, they introduced live rounds to the chamber, applied the safety-catch, then proceeded to the first of six different 'killing rooms' in the CQB House for a long day's practice. Here they fired 'double taps' from the Browning 9mm High Power handgun, known as the '9-milly', and short bursts from their Ingram 9mm sub-machine-guns, at various pop-up 'figure eleven' targets. They were also armed with real Brocks Pyrotechnics MX5 stun grenades.

The 'killing house' had been constructed to train SAS troopers in the skills required to shoot assassins or kidnappers in the close confines of a building without hitting the hostage. As he led his men into the building, Jock felt a definite underlying resentment about what he was doing.

The Regiment's first real experience in urban

terrorism had been in Palestine, where SAS veteran Major Roy Farran had conceived the idea of having men infiltrate the urban population by dressing up as natives and then assassinating known enemies at close quarters, usually with a couple of shots from a handgun. Though Jock had never worked with Farran, he had been a very young man in Aden in 1964 when Farran's basic theories had been used as the basis for the highly dangerous work of the Keeni Meeni squads operating in the souks and bazaars. There, teams of men, including Jock, all specially trained in CQB and disguised as Arabs, had mingled with the locals to gun down known Yemeni guerrillas.

Loving his work, dangerous though it had been, Jock had been shocked by the extent of his boredom when, back in Britain, he had been RTU'd to his original unit, the 2nd Battalion, Scots Guards, for a long bout of post-Suez inactivity. Though he subsequently married and had children – Tom, Susan, then Ralph, now all in their teens – he had never managed completely to settle down into the routine of peacetime army life.

For that reason he had applied for a transfer to the SAS, endured the horrors of Initial Selection and Training, followed by Continuation Training and parachute jumping in Borneo. Badged, he had fought with the Regiment in Oman in the early 1970s. Unfortunately, he returned from Oman to more years of relative boredom until 1976, when he was posted to Northern Ireland, where, in Belfast and south Armagh, he learnt just about all there was to know about close-quarters counter-terrorist warfare.

Posted back from Northern Ireland, Jock was again suffering the blues of boredom when, luckily for him, the Commanding Officer of 22 SAS decided to keep his CQB specialists busy by having them train bodyguards for overseas heads of state supportive of British interests. One of those chosen for this dangerous, though oddly glamorous, task was Jock, who, bored with his perfectly good marriage, was delighted to be able to travel the world with diplomatic immunity and a Browning 9mm High Power handgun hidden in the cross-draw position under his well-cut grey suit.

During those years, when most routine close protection of UK diplomats in political hotspots was handled by the Royal Military Police, the SAS were still being called in when the situation was particularly dangerous. For this reason, the need for men specially trained in close-quarters work led to the formation of the Counter Revolutionary Warfare Wing.

In Munich in September 1972, the Palestinian terrorist group Black September took over an Olympic
Games village dormitory and held Israeli athletes
hostage, leading to a bloody battle with West
German security forces in which all the hostages,
five terrorists and one police officer were killed. The
shocked West German and French governments
responded by forming their own anti-terrorist
squads. In Britain, this led to the formation of
a special SAS Counter-Terrorist (CT) team that
would always be available at short notice to deal
with hijacks and sieges anywhere in the United
Kingdom. Those men, like their predecessors in
Aden and in the CRW, had been trained in the
'killing house'. Jock Thompson was one of them.

The CQB House is dubbed the 'killing house' for
two good reasons. The first is that its purpose is to
train men to kill at close quarters. The second is
that real ammunition is used and that at least one
SAS man has been killed accidentally while training
with it.

Jock was mindful of this chilling fact as he led his
four-man CT team into the building and along the
first corridor, toward rooms specially constructed
to simulate most of the situations an SAS man
would encounter during a real hostage-rescue
operation. The men had already been trained to

45

enter captured buildings by a variety of means, including abseiling with ropes from the roof, sometimes firing a Browning 9mm High Power handgun with one hand as they clung to the rope with the other. This particular exercise, however, was to make them particularly skilled at distinguishing instantly between terrorist and hostage. It was done with the aid of pictures on the walls and dummies that were moved from place to place, or that popped out suddenly from behind artificial walls or up from the lower frame of windows.

This began happening as Jock and his men moved along the first corridor. Dummy figures bearing painted weapons popped out from behind opening doors or window frames to be peppered by a fusillade of bullets from the real weapons of the training team. Once the targets had looked like Russians; now they were men in anoraks and balaclava helmets.

The major accomplishment lay not in hitting the 'terrorists' but in *not* hitting a 'hostage' instead. This proved particularly difficult when they had less than a second to distinguish between a dummy that was armed and one that was not. To hit the latter too many times was to invite a humiliating rejection by the SAS and the ignominy of being RTU'd.

The exercise could have been mistaken for a childish game, except for one thing – like the weapons, the bullets were real.

Completing a successful advance along the first couple of corridors, Jock's team then had to burst into various rooms, selected from drawings of the reconstructed killing house, shown to them during their briefing.

The CT team is divided into two specialist groups: the assault group, who enter the building, and the 'perimeter containment' group, consisting of snipers who provide a cordon sanitaire around the scene. In this instance, Jock and his men were acting as an assault group. This meant that they had to burst into a room in pairs and instantly fire two pistol rounds or short, controlled bursts of automatic fire – the famed SAS 'double tap' – into each terrorist, aiming for the head, without causing injury to either fellow team members or the hostages.

Reaching their selected rooms, the four-man team divided into two pairs, each with its own room to clear. Leading Red Team, with Danny Boy as his back-up, Jock blasted the metal lock off with a burst from his Remington 870 pump-action shotgun, dropped to one knee as the lock blew apart, with pieces of wood and metal flying out in all directions, then cocked the Browning pistol in his free hand and bawled for Danny Boy to go in.

The lance-corporal burst in ahead of Thompson, hurling an instantaneous safety electric fuse before him as he went. The thunderous flash of the ISFE exploded around both men as they rushed in and made their choice between a number of targets – the terrorists standing, the hostages sitting in chairs. They took out the former without hitting the latter, delivering accurate double taps to the head in each case.

Each man had his own preselected arc of fire, which prevented him hitting one of his own men. In this instance, the two men could easily have done this when they burst from a 'rescued' room back into the corridor to come face to face with either another dummy or with the other team, Corporal 'GG' Gerrard and Trooper Robert Quayle. Likewise, when Blue Team burst out of their own 'rescued' room, they often did so just as a dummy popped out from behind a swinging door, or up from behind a window frame, very close to them. The chilling possibility of an 'own goal' was always present.

Even so, while the men had found this form of training exciting, or frightening, in the early days, by now it had become too familiar to present any novelty. To make their frustration more acute, once the figures had been 'stitched' with bullets, or the room 'cleared' of terrorists, the men then had to paste paper patches over the holes in the figures, using a paste-brush and brown paper, in order that the targets could be used again by those following them. Because they had to do this mundane task themselves – even though they were firing real weapons, exploding ISFE, and hurling stun grenades – they became increasingly bored as they made their way through the various rooms of the killing house.

Their irritation was made all the worse by the fact that a day of such training led not only to sweaty exhaustion, but to raging headaches from the acrid pall of smoke and lead fumes which filled the killing house. So, when finally they had completed their 'rescue' and could stumble out into the fresh air, they were immensely relieved.

'I'll tell you something,' Danny Boy said later, as they were showering in the ablutions of the spider. 'If I don't get killed accidentally by one of you bastards during those exercises, I'll be killed by the fucking boredom of doing them over and over again.'

'They don't bore *me*,' Bobs-boy said. 'I just hate

the CRW suits and body armour and helmet and mask. I feel buried alive in them.'

'You feel buried alive because you're like the walking dead,' GG taunted him. 'You're as limp as your dick, kid.'

'Nightmares!' Danny Boy exclaimed.

'Dreams,' Bobs-boy corrected him.

'All I know,' GG said, 'is that we haven't done a real job since Northern Ireland and we've now had four years of bullshit. One more run through that bloody killing house and I'm all set for the knacker's yard.'

'Or Ward 11 of the British Army Psychiatric Unit,' Danny Boy said, 'like Sergeant "Ten Pints and a Knuckle Sandwich" Inman.'

'Sergeant Inman was in a psychiatric ward?' the relatively new Bobs-boy asked incredulously.

'Correct,' GG replied. 'Oman, Belfast, Hong Kong and then straight into the horrors of Ward 11, where – I have it on the best authority – he made the insane look sane.'

'But Sergeant Inman's supposed to be one of the best soldiers in the Regiment,' Bobs-boy said, looking even more puzzled.

'He is,' Danny Boy replied. 'He just happens to have a couple of little problems that have to be sorted out.'

'And they let him stay on with the Regiment?' Bobs-boy asked, stupefied.

'Right,' GG said. 'He likes a pint – or twenty – followed up by a dust-up. He's only unhappy when he's not fighting.'

'Not giving knuckle sandwiches, you understand,' Danny Boy added. 'By fighting, we mean doing our job, which isn't scrapping in pubs.'

'And the fact that we haven't done that since Northern Ireland,' GG said, 'which is all of four years ago, is what's driving us – and Sergeant Inman – mad.'

'He's with the Commandos at the moment,' Bobs-boy said. 'That should keep him happy.'

'It doesn't keep *me* happy,' Danny Boy said. 'One more run around that fucking killing house and I'm going to kill myself.'

'Hey, you lot!' Jock bellowed as he entered the ablutions and looked in disgust at the naked men under the steaming showers.

'The Head Shed,' the staff-sergeant told them, referring to their Commanding Officer, 'has just received a message from the Kremlin – the intelligence section at Regimental HQ, in case you new boys don't remember. They told him, through the Metropolitan Police, that a group of armed terrorists has taken over the Iranian Embassy. The

Bedfords will get us there in three hours, so get your bare arses out of those showers and cover them up and get ready. We leave in one hour.'

Dripping wet and naked as the day they were born, the three men cheered and clapped at the news.

4

In the Royal Marines Commando Training Centre in Devon, SAS Sergeant Inman, formerly with the Royal Engineers, now thirty-eight years of age, was frog-marched between two NCO Military Policemen into an office where the Commanding Officer of the base, Lieutenant-Colonel William Fairworth, was seated behind his desk, studying the notes before him and sardonically raising his eyebrows at the SAS sergeant sitting in a wooden chair beside him. When Sergeant Inman had snapped to attention between the two MPs and saluted the CO, the latter stared steadily at him before saying: 'At ease, Sergeant.'

Inman stood at ease. Lieutenant-Colonel Fairworth glanced at the notes, then looked up and said: 'Drunk and disorderly again, Sergeant. This is no laughing matter.'

'Beg to differ, sir, but the other man threw

the first punch, so I'd no choice in the matter.'

'You're being disingenuous, Sergeant. What matters is not who threw the first punch, but who started the argument.'

'He insulted the Regiment, boss.'

'Sir!' SAS Sergeant Shannon snapped. 'You are talking to the Commando CO – not the SAS. We don't use the word "boss" here.'

'Sorry, Sergeant. Keep forgetting.'

'You forget a bit too much for my liking,' Fairworth said, glancing down at the report again. 'Such as respect for the traditions of other regiments, which is why you get into trouble in pubs.'

'I can't help myself, sir.'

That much was true. Sergeant Inman had been on the sniper course for only a fortnight, but during that time he had been brought back by the MPs three or four times, either for plain drunkenness or for fighting in some pub or other. In fact, he was bored out of his mind and had had enough of the Commandos. He wanted to go back to Hereford with the men and routines he knew and loved.

'You have an interesting track record, Sergeant Inman. Royal Engineers, then with the SAS in Oman, Belfast and Hong Kong, always with commendable results. Unfortunately, you appear to be unable to get anything right once you're in a non-fighting environment. This has led to psychiatric problems that were treated – supposedly successfully.

Sergeant Inman winced, having hoped that the Royal Marine Commando CO would not have been informed of his little experience in the psychiatric unit of the British Army.

Well, fuck it, he thought. He should never have been sent there in the first place. Or, perhaps he should have been, since the psychiatrists were even madder than the patients, though with much less reason.

He had his reasons, after all. He had been suffering from the exhaustion of a long run of ugly business: first the assault on the Jebel Massif in Oman, then Operation Jaguar, also in Oman, then the now legendary Battle of Mirbat, which even to this day gave him bad dreams and soaked his sheets in sweat.

Some good men had died there. Their deaths had been gruesome. To make matters worse, the survivors had been returned to a Britain that did not know they existed – neither them nor the battle.

Of course, that was the SAS way. Anonymity was everything. Nevertheless, Inman had found it pretty odd to have fought such a mighty battle, such a bloody affair, only to return home to an official silence that had made him feel worthless.

Exhaustion – certainly. But also something much more than that: the emptiness of not being recognized, of being cast aside, combined with the terminal boredom of having nothing to do in a non-combatant environment.

True enough, Inman was already feeling depleted when they sent him to Northern Ireland and the Q cars and covert observation. A right nasty job, that one. By the time he returned again to the SAS Sports and Social Club in Redhill, Hereford, he had killed too many in CQB and was feeling sick to his soul.

Of course by that time, also, he needed it and could not live without it . . . Which is why he had taken up drinking and getting into the odd fight. This, in its turn, was why he had ended up in Ward 11 with all those barmy shrinks.

So how did he deal with this matter when facing a Royal Marines Commando CO who did not know about his traumas and probably resented the SAS anyway?

Be bold. Who dares wins.

'Not supposedly, sir,' Inman replied boldly. 'The treatment was one hundred per cent successful.'

'That may be the case, but I have to warn

you, Sergeant, that your habit of drunken fights, table-smashing and insubordination is not being applauded. The fact that you're a particularly good soldier in battle conditions is not going to save you if, as I think is happening, you start being seen as an over-the-hill, alcoholic troublemaker.'

'I'm not alcoholic, sir,' Inman said, as bold as brass. 'I only drink too much when I'm not fighting – overseas with the Regiment, that is.'

'Is that supposed to be a joke?' Sergeant Shannon asked.

'No, Sarge. The plain, unvarnished truth. No amount of training or retraining will keep me satisfied. I need a real operation.'

Though both men were sergeants, Shannon was in this case acting as second in command to the CO.

'We can't create operations just for you, Sergeant. You're thirty-eight and experienced enough to know that at this stage of your career most of your time will be taken up with training, retraining and guard duties. You should count yourself lucky that, given your age, not to mention your psychiatric history, you were still chosen for this Commando sniper course rather than cross-graining the bukits for the nth time on the Pen-y-Fan.'

Why the fuck don't you just stop yapping, Inman

thought, and send me back to the Regiment, where I belong? I won't beat up any of your bloody Commandos, then. I'll be a good little boy.

'I do appreciate that, sir, but I just can't get my act together here. I feel all out of sorts.'

'You've always felt out of sorts,' Shannon snorted. 'That's why you had psychiatric treatment. You can't adjust to anything but war. I'd call that unhealthy.'

'Quite so,' Lieutenant-Colonel Fairworth said, glancing again at the report lying open on his desk. 'The evidence certainly indicates that you're totally unsuitable to a peacetime Army, whether it be in the Royal Engineers, the SAS or here. I'm thinking of recommending that you be RTU'd back to the Royal Engineers and there put up for summary discharge from the service.'

'Please don't do that, sir.' Now Inman was seriously worried that he might have overstepped the mark. This was a Commando officer – not a member of the SAS. In the latter Regiment, a tolerance for individual eccentricities was customary and Inman had survived many an episode for that very reason. Though aware of his own explosive tensions, his tendency to become rapidly bored, and his irresistible need to release his frustrations with bouts of heavy drinking and fighting, he was unable to control these impulses and knew that they would get him into serious trouble sooner or later. That time might have come. The very thought of being thrown out of the Regiment filled him with panic. 'I promise to control myself in the future and concentrate on the training,' he mumbled.

'I'll personally guarantee that he does that,' Shannon said. Having served with Inman in Oman and Belfast, he admired him as a soldier and felt a great deal of loyalty towards him. He and Inman had been through a lot together and that counted for something. Also, regardless of his many faults, Inman was a damned good soldier who deserved to stay with the Regiment. 'I'll do it if I have to work him into the ground. He won't get time to make a fool of himself again. Put him under my wing, sir.'

Fairworth studied Inman's report, shook his head wearily, then gently closed the manila folder. Turning to Shannon, he said: 'That's an admirable offer, Sergeant, but I'm afraid I have to reject it. Sergeant Inman has done this once too often for my liking and is, I believe, now too old to mend his ways.' He looked directly at Inman. 'It's my intention to terminate your four weeks here and send you back to Hereford with the recommendation that you be RTU'd with a view to discharge. I'm sorry, but I . . .'

The CO was cut off in mid-sentence by the telephone. Picking it up, he listened intently for some time, then slammed it down again.

'The Iranian Embassy in London has just been seized by terrorists,' he said. 'Your Regiment is on stand-by. You're both to leave immediately for Hereford.' He closed the folder and handed it to Shannon when the latter stood smartly and approached the desk. Lieutenant-Colonel Fairworth smiled tightly at Inman.

'Lucky you,' he said softly.

'Thank you, sir!' Inman responded, snapping off a crisp salute, then gratefully turning away and following the excited Shannon out of the office. Once outside, the latter turned to his old mate and gave him a wicked grin.

'Fairworth wasn't kidding,' he said. 'You really *are* one lucky bastard.'

'Don't I know it,' Inman replied. 'So what's the story, Paddy?'

'As I'm already an expert sniper,' Shannon replied, 'which is why I was teaching a prat like you, I'm bound to be in the perimeter containment group. As for you, since you've just been swilled out of the Commando sniper course, you'll almost certainly be back with one of the assault groups, which places you in the front line of fire. Just where you belong, you fucking lunatic.'

'Trust a Paddy to recognize a soul mate. So when do we leave?'

'The Bedfords are being prepared right now. We pack up and move out within the hour.'

'Sounds like heaven,' Inman said as both men walked away from the HQ, revitalized by the thought of packing up and going back to their own world.

'As you all know by now,' the Controller said to his men in a briefing room in the Kremlin, the intelligence wing of the SAS HQ in Hereford, 'the Iranian Embassy was occupied this morning by six Iranian terrorists trained and armed in Baghdad. They're armed with two Skorpion W263 Polish sub-machine-guns, three Browning self-loading pistols, one .38 Astra revolver and five Russian RGD5 hand-grenades. As far as we know, they have a lot of ammunition.'

'We've got a lot of ammunition as well,' the CRW Red Team leader, Staff-Sergeant Bill Harrison, said. 'That's not our major anxiety, boss.'

'So what is?'

'Their motive.'

'Why?'

'Because the motive tells us how they might react.'

'Very good, Staff-Sergeant.' The Controller smiled in his quietly understated public-school manner. 'The stated purpose of their mission is to publicize the plight of Arabs in Iran and to demand the freedom of 92 political prisoners held in that country.'

'Is that generally believed?' asked the head of the Blue Team, Staff-Sergeant 'Jock' Thompson.

The Controller shook his head. 'No. It's our belief that Saddam Hussein, a gangster of a politician, wants back the eastern half of the Shatt-al-Arab boundary with Iran, ceded to that country in 1975. It's also our belief that following the successful Iranian seizure of the American Embassy in Tehran, Saddam is using the seizure of the Iranian Embassy in London as his own display of strength to the Arab world.'

'Who's in charge of negotiations with the terrorists?' Blue Team's Sergeant Inman asked, always keen to smell the meat of the matter.

'As this is a political matter, the operation is in the hands of the Cabinet Office Briefing Room, COBR – pronounced like the snake. This top-level committee also includes representatives of the police, MI5 and, of course, this Regiment. In other words, we have a direct channel to the top of the decision-making pyramid and operational links with the police at the location of the siege.'

'So *they* decide when we go in – not us,' the contentious sergeant said.

'Correct.'

Nothing about Inman bothered the Controller, even if it bothered a lot of others in the Regiment. In fact, the Controller's considerable respect for Inman's talents had compelled him to drag him back for special training in CRW skills. Though Inman had made no bones about hating the necessarily repetitive training in the 'killing house', the Controller had not been disappointed.

Inman, with his special brand of sharp-edged aggressiveness, had proved himself as a CRW natural. Now, though he was grinning in a challenging manner at the Controller, the latter was merely amused and responded with the simple, albeit deadly, facts.

'This being a political matter,' he said, 'we have to remain neutral and use force only when no other options are left. We'll be informed when that time comes. Meanwhile, it's the police who'll negotiate with the terrorists. Initially we remain on the sidelines.'

'We're supposed to be an anonymous Regiment, boss,' Staff-Sergeant Harrison said. 'Seems to me that if we go into that Embassy we'll be doing so right in front of TV cameras, radio commentators and the international news media. That puts us in the spotlight.'

'Again, we've no choice,' said the Controller with a shrug. 'Besides, the days when the Regiment only operated overseas are already over. For the past few years London has become a battleground for numerous Middle East terrorist groups, so we've no choice but to tackle them on home ground. If they wear civilian clothing, so will we; it's a new form of warfare.'

'Do you think the terrorists can be talked out of the Embassy by the police?' The question, surprisingly, came from Red Team's Lance-Corporal Phil McArthur, not normally noted for putting himself forward. Sitting beside his closest Red Team friends, Troopers Alan Pyle, Ken Passmore and Danny 'Baby Face' Porter, he was visibly embarrassed even as he asked the question. Danny, nick named 'Baby Face' because he looked like the cowboy hero Audie Murphy and was just as deadly, was embarrassed by nothing.

'Personally, I doubt it,' the Controller said. 'Those terrorists were making their plans in London when uncensored television reports of the Desert One disaster, in which the US Delta Force – widely viewed as our cousin – left eight dead in burning helicopters in their failed attempt to rescue American hostages from Tehran. The terrorists would almost certainly have seen those televised reports. To them, the American disaster would have been a good omen. So, no, I don't think they'll be talked out of there.'

'What weapons will we have?' Jock Thompson asked.

'The Ingram?' Blue Team's Lance-Corporal 'Danny Boy' Reynolds asked, referring to the American 9mm sub-machine-gun normally favoured by the SAS CT teams.

'No,' the Controller replied. 'Since the joint SAS/GSG assault on the hijacked Lufthansa airliner at Mogadishu, we've been looking for a weapon that fires rapidly and precisely, but at low velocity, so that the bullets will hit the intended target without penetrating it and striking another. As excessive fire-power will result in a propaganda victory for the terrorists, we want this operation over as quickly as possible. We've therefore settled on the Heckler & Koch MP5.

'Untried,' Blue Team's special sniper, Sergeant Pat 'Paddy' Shannon said bluntly.

'Untrue. It's been tried and proven excellent.'

'In what way?' Staff-Sergeant Harrison asked.

'Like the Ingram, it's small and compact – 5½ lb when empty; 27 inches in length. Unlike the Ingram, however, it fires from a closed bolt, which reduces the shift in balance when it's fired, thus giving it uncommon accuracy. For this reason, also, it rarely jams. Calibre, 9mm. Rate of fire, 800 rounds per minute. It offers a choice of single-shot, fully automatic or three-round burst fire, with an effective range of 200 yards. Fifteen- or twenty-round box magazine.'

'I read somewhere that this weapon *does* jam,' Harrison objected.

'Earlier models did. The latest model doesn't.'

'Ho, ho,' Inman said in his usual mocking manner.

The Controller just grinned. 'The weapon was made in West Germany. We know how bright the Germans are. They soon discovered that another, foreign-made bullet could yield unparalleled accuracy. Those bullets, however, were the culprits that caused the old-style magazine to jam. The problem was solved simply by making the magazine curved instead. It doesn't jam any more.'

'Let's hope not,' Inman said.

'What else will we be using?' Blue Team's Trooper 'Bobs-boy' Quayle asked.

'The Browning 9mm High Power handgun . . .'

'The good old 9-milly!' Bobs-boy crowed, referring to the thirteen-round weapon beloved of
the SAS ever since its use in the famous Keeni
Meeni assassination operations in Aden during the
early 1960s.

'. . . and the Remington 870 pump-action shotgun, which we'll need to blast the locks from the
doors of locked rooms. Also, plastic explosives and
flash-bangs, the latter for their shock effect on the
terrorists during the first few seconds of the siege,
and CS gas grenades. To prevent you from wasting
time donning gas masks during the attack, you'll
put them on before the attack commences and wear
them throughout the whole operation.'

'The flash-bangs and CS gas grenades could cause
a fire inside the building,' Harrison pointed out.

'That's a chance we'll have to take,' the Controller replied. 'Apart from the sub-machine-guns, we
have nothing more effective in such a confined space
– particularly if we're masked against the gas and
the terrorists aren't.'

'So what's the plan of action?' asked the baby-
faced killer, Danny Porter.

'The police are negotiating with the terrorists at
this moment,' the Controller said, 'and have so far
succeeded in having a few of the hostages released.
They are already being debriefed and will provide

invaluable information about the state of mind of the terrorists, what weapons they have, and where they're holding the other hostages. The negotiations are also distracting the terrorists, and buying the police time, enabling the latter to bug the building and scan it with thermal imagers.'

'So what do we do while they're scanning the building?' Jock asked.

'You're in two teams: Red and Blue. The Red Team will be insinuated into the Royal College of Medical Practitioners, located right next door to the Embassy. This team will be headed by Captain Williams, your CRW instructor, and consist of twenty-four men. To avoid the press, you'll be transported from here by hired vans to the Regent's Park Barracks of the Household Cavalry, in Albany Street, where you will stay when not on alert. You will, however, when called out on alert or for daily training, be smuggled into the grounds of the college in the same Avis vans. From there you will make your way to the Forward Holding Area in the college by clambering unseen over the walls and rear gardens.'

'And once in the FHA?' Harrison asked.

'Your team's task is twofold. First, you have to be ready for an assault on the Embassy at ten minutes' notice, if the terrorists start killing. To be known as the "Immediate Action Plan", this will involve breaking in through the upper windows to clear the building room by room with CS gas and firearms, trusting that you can reach the hostages before the terrorists slaughter them. Your second task is to prepare for the "Deliberate Assault Plan", which is to be put into motion at a time chosen by us if and when the terrorists are exhausted and the location of the hostages is known.'

'Do we have much info on the Embassy?' Inman asked.

'Quite a lot, in fact. For a start, hostages are already being released and debriefed, which should produce a good deal of intelligence over the next few hours. Also, we have complete drawings which you'll be shown when the training commences.'

'And in the meantime?'

'Basically, what we're dealing with is a fortress situation. The Embassy is a very large, mid-terrace building on six floors, four of which are above ground. There are fifty rooms in all. It's to the advantage of the terrorists that the building can easily be defended front and rear because of the open spaces to either side of it. We're therefore considering a frontal charge, as well as abseiling from the roof onto the balconies along the front of the building. Before any final plan for that is made, however, and while more information about the inside of the Embassy is being received, our own Intelligence cell, aided by a member of the Embassy staff, is fabricating a model of the building. Based on this information, a full-scale hessian model of the Embassy's main rooms is already being constructed at Regent's Park Barracks, where an Embassy caretaker will describe the layout for us.'

'Any questions?'

'No.'

'Then let's go.'

Excited to be back in business, the men hurried out of the briefing room.

6

Because this was the first SAS operation to take place on British soil and, worse still, in full view of the media, the usual arming of the men and donning of the required dress prior to the operation was avoided. Instead, the men of Red Team were transported from Hereford to London in hired vans, all wearing civilian clothing like factory workers and none of them armed. Their weapons and equipment were transported separately in crates stacked high in furniture vans.

'I like travelling in style,' Alan Pyle said sardonically as he sauntered with the others up to the van parked in the holding area. 'It makes me feel right at home.'

'He's a Londoner,' his fellow trooper, Ken Passmore, explained to those with ears. He was a clear-headed, unprejudiced Geordie. 'I think that says it all.'

'Right,' his mate, Danny Boy, agreed, being from Bridlington, Humberside, which he often recalled with the deepest loathing. 'People from the South, as we all know, are born and bred rich. They *all* travel in Avis vans.'

'I've never been in one,' Bobs-boy said. He was from Rickmansworth, Hertfordshire, and had seen the odd Avis van, though no one thought it was really that unusual that he had never been in one. 'This will be my first time.'

'You're so sophisticated,' Alan told him.

'You think so?' Bobs-boy asked. 'I have to confess that I like the old 4 x 4 Bedford, so I might like the Avis.'

'What a fucking prat!' Corporal George 'GG' Gerrard whispered to his mate, Lance-Corporal Phil McArthur, as he swung the rear door of the van open. 'Straight off the farm!'

'Just get in the fucking van,' Phil replied, 'and let's go and find some action.'

'I trust we do,' grunted GG.

Strangely enough, as the van was carrying them along the M40 to London, the men broke with tradition by avoiding the customary 'bullshit' and speaking only when necessary. Perhaps this was due to the fact that this was not a long journey, that they were wearing civilian clothing and that they all had the feeling that they were already in action. By the time they had left the motorway, the men were absolutely silent. When the van eventually turned in through the guarded gates of Regent's Park Barracks, in Albany Street, they piled out and quickly made their way into the bleak, dusty barracks. Shocked by what they found on entering the dormitory chosen for them, they returned to the bullshit.

'I don't believe it,' GG groaned, taking in at a glance the dust on the brick window ledges and floor, between the rusty, steel-framed Army camp-beds with their battered, stained mattresses. 'It looks like a cowshed.'

'The Household Cavalry!' Phil snorted. 'I thought we'd be living like lords, but just look at this doss-house!'

'I bet *they* live like lords.'

'Who?'

'The Household Cavalry. They're probably in another part of the barracks, walking on thick carpets, sleeping in silk sheets, getting hand-jobs from maids in nothing but white aprons.'

'We have to basha down *here*?' Danny Boy could not believe it either. He had lived in many a hole in Humberside in his time, but this was the pits.

'I lived better in Notting Hill Gate,' Alan

informed them, 'when I shared a flat with half-a-dozen kids who didn't know what a vacuum cleaner was and were too stoned to take a bath.'

'These toilets stink,' Baby Face announced from where he stood at the end of the dormitory. 'The water's come right up to the top and it's covered in brown slime.'

'Jesus Christ!' Bobs-boy said.

'God have mercy!' GG added.

'Are you men complaining?' Staff-Sergeant Jock Thompson asked, his shadow stretching out from his feet where he stood in the doorway, his thick arms folded across his broad chest, his face flushed and unsmiling.

'Not me!' GG said.

'I'm happy as Larry,' Bobs-boy said.

'These toilets stink,' Baby Face repeated, 'so they must need unblocking.'

'Then unblock them,' Jock said, 'and clean up this place. When you've done that, make up your bashas, unpack your kit, then go back out to the parking area to wait for the vans. If you're not out there in thirty minutes sharp, you'll all face a fine.'

'Yes, boss!' the men barked simultaneously, feeling blessed when Jock nodded grimly and departed once more.

'Phew!' Phil said softly. 'Well, lads, let's get to it.'

They made up their bashas on the rusty steel-framed beds, quickly dusted down the floors and windows – though the dust returned almost immediately – managed with much cursing to unblock the toilets, then went back out to the parking area, where Jock was waiting for them, just in time to greet the arrival of the furniture vans. When the vans braked to a halt, the men unloaded the crates of weapons and equipment, then carried them inside with much huffing and puffing.

'If we were in any other regiment,' GG complained, 'we'd have crap-hats to hump this stuff in for us. Trust the bloody SAS!'

'I blame it all on the Household Cavalry,' Phil said. 'Those bastards are probably watching us right now from their more luxurious quarters.'

'Having a good laugh,' Bobs-boy said.

'Spoilt bastards,' added Danny Boy.

'Stop whining!' Jock bawled, appearing out of nowhere and casting his enormous shadow over them as they humped the gear in. 'If I hear one more complaint from you lot, I'm going to start throwing fines around.'

'No complaints from me,' Bobs-boy said, struggling backwards with the crate being shared with Alan. 'I love unpacking things.'

'He's gone already,' Alan said, lowering his end of the crate, 'so you can put the crate down. When you've done so, wipe the brown from your nose. It's beginning to smell.'

'What?'

'Never mind.'

After opening the crates, the men stripped off their civvies and put on their CRW gear. This consisted of black CRW assault suits with felt pads in knees and elbows; flame-resistant underwear; GPV 25 wrap-around soft body armour with hard ceramic composite plates front and back; NBC hoods for protection against heat, dust and smoke (the men would not be wearing helmets); and the 800gm S6 respirator with nosecup filter for protection against gases, aerosols and smoke; scratch-resistant, polycarbonate eyepieces, also resistant to chemical or solvent attack; tinted lenses for protection against the flash from stun grenades; and microphones mounted in front of the mouthpiece, to be linked by means of a communication harness to the assault team's radio transmitter.

'This is the part I hate most,' Bobs-boy said as

he adjusted the CRW vest in the hope of being a little more comfortable. 'It always makes me feel a bit weird.'

'I agree,' Danny Boy said, slipping on his black, skin-tight aviator's gloves. 'This gear makes me feel evil.'

'You pair of ponces talked that way in the killing house,' GG said, ignoring the fact that he had said much the same thing at the same time, 'and got a rocket from that bastard Thompson. I'd keep quiet if I was you.'

'Hey, you lot!' Jock suddenly bawled, having just materialized in the doorway. 'Are you ready or not?'

'Yes, boss!'

'Then let's move it!'

Leaving the spider, the men proceeded to the lecture hall, where they were divided into three teams – Red, Blue and the perimeter containment group, otherwise known as snipers, to be condenamed Zero Delta. They were then allocated their weapons, the armaments they received depending on which particular role they had been assigned in the forthcoming operation. While most of them were armed with the new Heckler & Koch MP5 sub-machine-gun and the standard-issue Browning 9mm High Power handgun, those in the perimeter containment teams led by Sergeant Shannon were given the L42A1 .303-inch bolt-action sniper rifle with tripod. A few members of the assault teams, tasked with breaking into the locked rooms of the Embassy, were given the Remington 870 pump-action shotgun. Some were put in charge of a variety of explosive devices, including frame charges and explosive door cutters. All of the men were also issued with spare magazines, ISFE, CS gas and MX5 stun grenades.

Finally, the equipment was distributed according to each man's assigned role in the operation. This included W.J. Crow lightweight aluminium assault ladders; sledgehammers, axes, wrecking bars, glass-cutters and grappling hooks.

Once dressed and armed, the men were officially on stand-by and ready to go.

The Controller gave them a briefing in the barracks, where diagrams of the Embassy, including the layout of the individual rooms, were pinned on blackboards. The Controller indicated the drawing under discussion with a wooden pointer and the men listened intently while sitting on the edge of their beds, wearing their complete CRW gear. To an outsider, the gathering would have made a bizarre, menacing sight.

'I believe the planning team has covered every

possible angle,' the Controller told them, 'though naturally, in a highly volatile situation like this, we can't be too sure, so you'll have to be prepared for the unexpected.' He paused to let these words sink in. 'The attack will focus on a single objective: to rescue the hostages from the Iranian Embassy, if necessary. In order to do this, Red Team will clear the top half of the building, from the second to the fourth floor. Blue Team will tackle the lower half from the basement and garden, upwards to the first floor. Blue Team will also handle evacuation procedures.'

'How do we enter?' Staff-Sergeant Harrison asked.

'Red Team will drop two abseil teams, each of four men, in separate waves from the roof, down to the second-floor balcony at the back of the building.' The Controller tapped a photographic enlargement of the balcony with his pointer. 'Once on the balcony, Red Team will break in through those three big windows.' He indicated the windows with his pointer. 'While this first group is thus engaged, another group will be tasked with attacking the third floor, descending from the roof by ladder onto a sub-roof at the rear, known as the lighting area.' He indicated the area as shown on one of the drawings of the Embassy. 'At the same time, at fourth-floor level, a third group will blast a way in through the skylight, direct from the roof.'

'And Blue Team?' asked Jock, that team's leader.

'Blue Team will be in charge of the garden-level basement, along with the ground floor and first floor. As far as we can ascertain from the layouts, what will be required is an explosive charge to be put in the french windows overlooking the ground-floor terrace at the back. A similar bit of surgery will be required on the front, first-floor balcony window leading to the Minister's office. Access to that balcony isn't a problem since it adjoins the balcony of the Royal College of Medical Practitioners, already being prepared for a take-over by us.'

'What might be a problem,' Harrison pointed out, 'is finding the explosive power needed to demolish those windows. They are, as I recall, made of specially reinforced glass installed originally on SAS advice.'

The wisecrack copped a few laughs and sardonic comments from the men. When they had settled down again, the Controller said: 'It didn't escape our attention that the windows had been installed on our advice and are particularly tough to crack. However, we believe that a special frame explosive, matching that of the window frame to be demolished, will do the job. At the critical moment, the explosive will be carried from balcony to balcony and lifted on to the target – like a jacket fitted onto a tailor's dummy, as it were. I'm sure you can manage it.'

'What else is Blue Team responsible for?' Jock wanted to know.

'For the firing of CS gas canisters into the rear second-floor windows at the beginning of the attack. At the end of the attack, it's Blue Team that will hold an undiplomatic reception party in the garden.'

'A *what*?' Bobs-boy asked.

'An *un*diplomatic reception,' the Controller repeated with a grin. 'That means you will manhandle everyone found in the Embassy – terrorists and hostages alike – out into the back garden and there search them, bind their hands and feet, lay them face down on the grass, and proceed to question them until you've ascertained who's a terrorist and who a hostage. You will do so with dispatch, tolerating no protest and being a little rough if necessary. That's why it's called an undiplomatic reception.'

'Neat,' the trooper said.

'Who's orchestrating the operation?' asked Jock.

'A command group led by myself and a controller, operating from a sixth-floor flat overlooking the rear of the Embassy, out of sight of the journalists.'

'How long do you think the siege will last, boss?'

'I've no idea. I only know that those men are determined, so it could last for a long time.'

'What do we do while we wait?'

'Immediately after this briefing you'll pack your kit and prepare to be insinuated into the Forward Holding Area in the Royal College of Medical Practitioners, located next door to the Embassy. While you wait on stand-by, you'll familiarize yourselves with both the Immediate Action Plan and the Deliberate Assault Plan, training with full kit and studying every photograph, drawing, report we've got on the terrorists and their unfortunate hostages. Another hostage has been released since our arrival here and that means even more information on the terrorists and their arms and state of mind. Also, a replica of the Embassy has been constructed in the Forward Holding Area and you'll use that to familiarize yourselves with the building and your own place in both the Deliberate Assault Plan and the Immediate Action Plan. As the former becomes more defined, its most important elements will be fed into the latter: the scheme to storm the building as a prompt response to any murders. The learning process will therefore be non-stop – at least until you're either stood down for good or called to implement the attack plan. Rest assured, you'll be busy. Any more questions?'

When his question was followed by the silent shaking of heads, the Controller said: 'All right, men, let's go.'

Heavily burdened with weapons, sledgehammers, ladders, abseiling ropes and other equipment, the men in the sinister black CRW outfits marched out of the dormitory and clambered into the vans parked outside. The convoy eventually rolled out of Regent's Park Barracks and headed south-westwards for Princes Gate.

7

Once in the Royal College of Medical Practitioners, at 14 Princes Gate, the men of Red Team clambered up onto the gently sloping roof in full CRW gear, then made their way stealthily across to the adjoining roof of the Embassy, where they quietly tied the required number of abseiling ropes to the chimneys, then left the rest coiled up beside each chimney.

When this was done, they crossed back to the college and made their way back down to the rooms designated as their Forward Holding Area. There, the learning process for Red Team did indeed become non-stop in the frustrating periods between false alerts and being stood down again. This happened many times during their first twenty-three hours in the college.

When on stand-by, the men of Red Team were allowed to strip off their heavy CRW outfits to wear casual clothing. But as each new terrorist deadline approached, they had to get into their fighting equipment and out onto the roof to prepare to go into action, on a radio message, 'London Bridge', at four minutes' notice. They were, however, stood down repeatedly, which caused much frustration.

'This is driving me crazy,' grumbled Phil McArthur as he divested himself of his CRW gear for the fourth time. 'Why the hell don't they let us cross that roof and get on with the job?'

'It's because they're trying to talk the terrorists out instead of sending us in,' Staff-Sergeant Harrison informed him.

'Damned Met!' Trooper Alan Pyle said in his oddly distracted drawl, showing no real irritation. 'They're only good for directing the traffic and they're not good at that. What *are* they good at?'

In fact, he was recalling how, from the roof of the college, he had been able to look all the way along to the metal scaffolding and canvas marquee of the press enclosure hastily constructed in Hyde Park, as well as the numerous vans, cars and trailers of the police and media, with TV and communications cables snaking across the road. Down on the street, directly in front of the adjoining Embassy, inside an area cordoned off with coloured tape, a plain-clothes policeman had been negotiating with the terrorists, speaking English when conveying his message via the hostages Sim Harris and PC Lock, or through an interpreter when speaking directly to a terrorist. It had looked like a circus down there, but nothing seemed to be happening.

'All they do,' Alan continued, 'is talk, talk, talk, while those bloody terrorists create one deadline after another, just stringing the bloody coppers along. They should send us in right now.'

'They can't make up their minds because the terrorists' demands keep changing,' Jock explained.

'That's exactly what Alan meant,' Baby Face said. 'Those terrorists are calling all the shots, so we should go in right now.'

'I agree,' Sergeant Inman said. 'The more we wait, the more hysterical they'll get and the more dangerous that makes them. Also, the more we wait, the more they'll expect us, which loses us the element of surprise.'

'Right,' Baby Face said. 'They're thinking it's early days yet and we should move while they're thinking that. We could take them before they blink.'

'You're a pair of fucking warmongers, you two,' Jock broke in. 'You're only interest is in having a little mix and tasting their blood. Your interest stops right there.'

'And you?' Inman asked.

'What about me?' Jock replied.

'Whose interest do you have at heart, since you're sounding so noble?'

'Don't be insolent, Sergeant. I'm still the senior NCO. You try to cut me with that sharp tongue and I'll tear it out of your throat.'

'That's pulling rank, Staff-Sergeant.'

'I treat a mad dog like a mad dog.'

'I'm just saying that the element of surprise is all we've got here – and we're losing it fast.'

Jock nodded, showing no animosity. 'Maybe you're right, pal. Who knows? You just might be.'

The first message about the occupation had been received by phone at the *Guardian* newspaper. Conveyed from the terrorist leader, by now known by all as Salim, his real name, via the hostage journalist Mustafa Karkouti, it stated that the terrorists had occupied the Embassy for their 'human and legitimate rights', which were 'freedom, autonomy and recognition of the Arabistan people'. The second phone message, conveyed by Karkouti to a Senior Deputy Editor of the BBC's External Services, was a clarification that the terrorists were from Iran – not Iraq as had been widely believed – and a demand for the release of 91 prisoners being held in Arabistan.

At four-thirty p.m. on the first day the terrorists had released a female Iranian hostage, wrongly thinking, because she had fainted, that she was pregnant. Shortly after the woman's release, police activity outside the Embassy was intensified, with cordons completely ringing the area, the nearby main road, Kensington Gore, barred to traffic between the Albert Hall and Knightsbridge Barracks, and a carefully guarded press enclosure created near Exhibition Road.

A Police Forward Operations Room, Alpha Control, was set up in the Royal School of Needlework at 25 Princes Gate, from where all police and military activity was controlled.

By six o'clock all the buildings around the Embassy had been evacuated and the Metropolitan Police had begun speaking directly to the terrorists, either by phone or through the Embassy windows, in English and Arabic.

During the first of those conversations, Salim stated that if his demand for the release of the prisoners in Arabistan was not met by noon the following day, he would blow up the Embassy and all inside it.

At eleven-thirty that same night, another hostage, Dr Afrouz, the Embassy's chargé d'affaires, telephoned the Foreign Ministry in Tehran, to explain that the terrorists were all Iranian citizens, Muslim brothers, and that they would end the siege when the Iranian government agreed to a degree of autonomy for Arabistan.

Nothing had happened during the first night, but in the early hours of Day Two, Thursday, 1 May, another message from Oan-Ali informed a BBC News Desk deputy editor that the British hostages and other non-Iranian hostages would not be harmed, though the deadline for the safety of the others was still valid.

'Meanwhile,' Staff-Sergeant Harrison told his frustrated Red Team as they crouched in full CRW battle gear, surrounded by weapons, abseiling equipment and sledgehammers, on the windy roof of the college, 'thermal imagers and bugging devices planted in the walls of the Embassy have revealed that the hostages, men and women alike, are presently being held in Room 9A on the second floor.'

Shortly after this revelation, the audio-surveillance devices picked up the sound of a terrorist firing a threatening burst into the ceiling of Room 9A, causing some of the women to scream. This was followed by a phone call from one of the hostages, BBC sound recordist Sim Harris, explaining that his fellow hostage, BBC news organizer Chris Cramer, was writhing in increasing pain from the symptoms of a virulent dysentery he had picked up in Rhodesia, and needed a doctor.

The police refused the request.

A second request met with the same response, though this time the police cleverly suggested that Harris should try persuading the terrorists to release his friend. Harris did so, and at eleven-fifteen that morning the Embassy door was opened to enable Cramer to stagger to a waiting ambulance.

'Those two hostages,' Harrison explained, 'when questioned by the police, revealed a great deal about what's going on inside the Embassy.'

'So?' Baby Face asked.

Harrison sighed at the trooper's ignorance. 'With each new scrap of information from a hostage, our assault plans are changing. That's why we never start rehearsing – and why each one is different. As for Cramer, he's told us a lot. So you lot are now in for lots of work.'

'What kind of work?'

'More rehearsals of revised situations. They should keep you busy.'

'Gee, thanks,' GG said.

Ten minutes after the noon deadline, Salim phoned to say, in his poor English, that he was giving the Iranian Government until two that afternoon to meet his demands. When that deadline also passed with no response from the Iranian Government, there was no sound of an explosion inside the Embassy.

'It seems that Salim has changed his mind,' Staff-Sergeant Harrison told them after speaking on the radio phone to the Controller, who was based for the time being in Alpha Control at 25 Princes Gate. 'He's holding out for more than they're offering and they're going to call his bluff.'

'Calling his bluff could get a hostage killed,' Inman responded. 'Those fucking Arabs aren't playing games.'

'Nor are we, Sarge. We're just engaged in a bit of the old in-and-out: a little cry of protest here, a sigh of gratitude there; first cold, then hot; now advancing, now retreating; giving a little, then taking some away; stepping forward, then back again, maybe turning in circles. It's what's known as a protracted negotiation and the Met are good at it.'

'I'm glad they're good at something,' Alan chipped in. 'I was giving up hope.'

'Oh, they're good,' Harrison insisted. 'The police negotiators are very good indeed and have, I believe, managed to cool things down a little. All is calm for the moment.'

But things were hotting up outside. There,

beyond the police cordons, nearly 400 Khomeini loyalists demonstrated and were met by abuse from hordes of British louts howling derision and shaking their fists. Many were arrested.

That afternoon, the terrorists again insisted that if the Iranian Government acceded to their modest demands, the siege would end peacefully. Again the Government did not respond. This encouraged Salim to ask for three Arab ambassadors – from Jordan, Iraq and Algeria – to arrange for a plane to take him and his fellow terrorists out of Britain, when they were ready to go.

Shortly after eight p.m., when the police were drilling holes in the walls of the Embassy to insert more audio-surveillance probes, two of the hostages, Mustafa Karkouti and PC Lock, appeared at a first-floor window, both covered by a terrorist gunman, to ask what the noises were. The police denied that they were responsible and another night passed peacefully.

Throughout that tense first twenty-three hours, the SAS's Red Team had been repeatedly put on alert, each time having to don their full CRW outfits, collect their weapons and equipment, including abseiling ropes and harness, then go out onto the roof of the college, ready to clamber over onto the roof of the Embassy. Each time, to their immense frustration, they were made to stand down again.

They were, however, given no rest. Instead, they studied every photograph, drawing, report and other scrap of information fed to them about the people next door. Also, with the helpful narration of a former Embassy caretaker, they repeatedly studied a plywood scale model of the Embassy, working out just how they would enter, what routes they would take once inside, and what specific targets, or rooms, each team would be responsible for clearing. Their positions and routes were demonstrated with the aid of toy soldiers placed at various points outside and in the corridors and rooms of the scale model.

'I feel like a right dick doing this,' Alan said.

'You *are* a right dick,' Phil told him, 'so you've nothing to lose.'

'Toy soldiers and doll's houses,' Trooper Ken Passmore said. 'It takes me back to my school days.'

'You played with *doll's houses*?' Phil asked him.

'And wore skirts,' Ken replied. 'I managed to get into the SAS by flashing my knickers at the drill instructors. It's a common girl's trick.'

'Do we go left or right at the end of that corridor?'

Baby Face asked, pointing at the model of the Embassy and looking as sombre as always.

'Left,' Harrison said, then offered a loud sigh. 'It's nice to know I've got *one* trooper with concentration. Any more questions, lads?'

'Yes,' Phil said. 'Who do I have to fuck to get off this job?'

'Ken Passmore!' they all cried out in chorus, being desperate for light relief.

This they did not get, however. After twenty-three hours of being called out onto the roof of the college, fully armed and dressed, and with abseiling equipment, ladders and explosives to hand, only to be stood down again and returned to yet more planning around the scale model, the men of Red Team were not only immensely exhausted, but fast running out of patience.

They returned to the Regent's Park Barracks to catch up on their sleep.

Blue Team arrived at the FHA at three-thirty a.m. on Day Three. Like Red Team, they had been transported from Bradbury Lines to the Regent's Park Barracks by van, then moved on to the college in furniture vans. While Red Team caught up with a little sleep, the twenty-four-man Blue Team, headed by an SAS captain, took over the responsibility for the Immediate Action Plan and, like Red Team, were compelled to spend hours studying the scale model of the Embassy next door. They, too, were called out more than once, then stood down again.

'It's driving me bonkers,' Danny Boy said after the third alert and stand-down. 'Up on that fucking roof, all set to roll, then called back down again. What the hell are they playing at?'

'The terrorists keep changing their demands,' Jock informed him. 'Oan-Ali threatens to blow up the building, so we're called out on alert. Then instead of blowing the building up, he releases a hostage, so we're stood down again. It's a form of psychological warfare and it's very effective.'

'It's certainly affecting *me*,' GG complained. 'If we're stood down once more, I'll throw myself off this fucking roof.'

'Goodbye,' Danny Boy said.

'Fuck you,' GG shot back.

'I don't mind,' Trooper 'Bobs-boy' Quayle said. 'At least they're keeping us busy.'

'I'd rather keep myself busy with a pint of bitter,' GG said. 'All this stop-go's no good for me.'

'Stop whining, you lot,' Jock told them. 'I'm fed up with the sound of your voices. Now let's go back down.'

'Yes, boss!' they all sang in unison, picking up their weapons and equipment and following their leader back down the stairs to the FHA below.

By this time, confirmation had been received from the audio-surveillance team that the hostages were indeed in Room 9A on the second floor.

Shortly after this information was conveyed to the police and SAS, Salim appeared at the window, pointing a pistol at the head of a terrified hostage, the Embassy's cultural attaché, Dr Abul Fazi Ezzatti, whom he threatened to kill unless he was allowed to talk to the media by telephone or telex.

'I'm sorry, Salim,' the police negotiator told the terrorist leader, 'but we can't do that just yet. We need time to set it up.'

'Liars!' the Iranian screamed.

Nevertheless, instead of killing the visibly distressed hostage, he merely pushed him roughly aside, out of sight behind the window frame. Intelligence later discovered that the terrified Ezzatti had then collapsed, foaming at the mouth.

'The terrorist leader is clearly reaching the end of his tether,' the Controller told the exasperated men of the Blue Team shortly after they had been called down yet again. 'My personal belief is that the killing will start soon and we'll have to go in there.'

'I certainly hope so,' the action-hungry Sergeant Inman said. 'I'm brain-dead from sitting here.'

Another deadline was set for a few hours later. This time the terrorists demanded a talk with someone from the BBC, which they would conduct through their hostage Sim Harris. Though the police at first refused, more death threats from the terrorists finally made them relent.

That afternoon a managing editor of BBC TV news was produced to stand outside the Embassy and conduct a conversation with the sound record-ist, who was standing at a first-floor window with Oan-Ali aiming a gun at his head from behind the curtain.

'This time,' the Controller told his gathered Red and Blue Teams, 'Salim has demanded a coach to take his fellow gunmen, the hostages, and at least one unnamed Arab ambassador to Heathrow. The non-Iranian hostages, he claims, will be released there. The aircraft will then take the terrorists, their hostages and the unnamed ambassador to an unspecified Middle East country. Once there, the hostages and ambassador will be released. Salim also wants a communiqué about his aims and grievances to be broadcast in Britain this evening.'

'He'll be bloody lucky,' Jock said.

He was right. That evening the BBC gave Salim's demands only the briefest of mentions. Though expressing his outrage through Sim Harris, the terrorist leader again took no action against his hostages.

'I know you men are getting more frustrated at all these false alarms,' the Controller said at another meeting in the FHA, 'but I have at least obtained the promise that if there's no peaceful outcome – and I doubt that there will be – then, when we're finally committed, there'll be no last-minute change of mind. Once we start, we don't stop.'

'Any increase in intelligence,' Red Team's experienced Sergeant Inman asked, 'since our briefing back in Bradbury Lines?'

'Yes. Most important was the evacuation of the BBC Television News organizer, Chris Cramer, with severe stomach cramps, at eleven-twenty a.m. yesterday. Cramer was able to confirm that PC Lock still has his pistol; that there are six terrorists – not five as initially believed; and that each terrorist carries two hand-grenades as well as small arms.'

'Is it true, as rumour has it, that the terrorists have wired the building for a doomsday explosion?'

'The terrorists certainly made that claim. Unfortunately, neither of the two released hostages could either confirm or deny that they actually did it. The hostages spent most of their time locked in Room 9, on the second floor, while the terrorists wandered freely about the building – so it could indeed have been so wired without the hostages' knowledge.'

'Does Salim still want the release of those 92 prisoners in Iran.'

'No. He phoned the negotiators yesterday evening to say he just wanted a bus with curtained windows to carry his men and the hostages to an airport, and an aircraft to fly the rest of the party, including the Iranian hostages, to the Middle East. However, as he also wanted the ambassadors of Iraq, Algeria and Jordan, as well as a Red Cross representative, to be present during the transfer, that's not likely to happen.'

'Which is why we're now examining alternatives to a fortress attack,' Jock said shrewdly.

'Correct, Jock,' said the Controller. 'Salim's increasingly jittery and indecisive, which means he could start killing soon. If he does, we'll be called in. Meanwhile, we're continuing to install audio-surveillance probes and 8mm high-grain microphone probes in the walls of the Embassy.'

'They must be able to hear the sound of the drilling,' Inman said.

The Controller shrugged and grinned. 'The first time we drilled, the terrorists sent PC Lock and a

Syrian journalist to the window to ask the police if they were making the noise. According to the released hostage, Chris Cramer, when the police denied the charge but the noise continued, the quick-witted PC Lock told the terrorists it was the sound of a London mouse.'

This provoked a few snorts of mirth.

'Good man,' GG said.

'What's Whitehall's attitude at the moment?' Harrison asked. 'Are they the ones holding us back?'

'Yes,' the Controller replied. 'Reportedly, the Home Secretary, Foreign Office representative Douglas Hurd, and Metropolitan Police Commissioner Sir David McNee have between them opted for a policy of maximum patience. While this excludes capitulation to the terrorists' demands, it also rules out any pre-emptive assault by us, unless a hostage is murdered.'

'That strikes me as leaving the initiative to the terrorists,' Inman said, sounding disgruntled.

'Maybe. But it can also be viewed as a policy of psychological attrition under the guise of negotiation. Short of sending us in on an assault, there's not much else they can do.'

'But I *want* to go in,' Inman insisted.

'Too bad,' Harrison said.

Inman looked directly at the Controller. 'So do you think, boss, that the terrorists will surrender peacefully?'

The Controller shook his head. 'No. It's not in their culture. Sooner or later they'll do some serious damage, then you'll get your chance, Sergeant.'

At that moment a message from the FHA below came through on the Controller's VHF/UHF hand-held transceiver. When it ended, he turned to his men and said tersely: 'Another hostage is being released right now. Let's have a look.'

Hurrying to the edge of the roof, the men all looked obliquely at the cordoned-off area directly in front of the adjoining Embassy. It was eight-fifteen. Darkness was falling. Across the road, in Hyde Park, the canvas marquee of the press enclosure was bathed in floodlight. Picking their way through the tangle of cables and clambering boldly up the metal scaffolding around the marquee were many press photographers eager for a good shot of the emerging hostage. Closer to the Embassy, on the road at both sides of the area cordoned off by police barricades strung with coloured tapes, two 100-foot mobile gantries towered over the clutter of police vans, squad cars, trailers and ambulances. The restricted area itself, directly in front of the Embassy, was ringed with police. Isolated in the middle of the ring, but close to the front door of the Embassy, was a plain-clothes police negotiator with his civilian interpreter.

From the roof of the college, the Controller and his men were unable to see the front door of the Embassy, but they saw a lot of heads turning in that direction as a beam of light fell over the police negotiator and his colleague, indicating that the front door had just opened. A long, tense silence followed.

The Controller and his men leaned farther forward over the parapet of the college roof, straining to see who was emerging from the adjoining front door. The sound of shouting could be heard. The negotiator shouted something back and this was translated into Arabic by his interpreter.

Eventually, after what seemed like a long time, a woman came into view, walking from the hidden front door of the Embassy to the waiting negotiator. She spoke to him. A couple of police medics then rushed up to her, took hold of her by the arms and led her back to one of the parked ambulances. After being taken to hospital for a check-up, she would be passed on to the Metropolitan Police for debriefing and interrogation regarding what was happening inside the Embassy.

No sooner had the woman been rushed away

than the sound of a door slamming was heard. Simultaneously, the light beaming onto the road from the front door of the Embassy blinked out. The police negotiator then hurried back to the senior officers grouped outside an HQ trailer parked at the far side of the road. When the negotiator passed on the message given to him by the released female hostage, the officers hurried away in different directions.

The Controller instantly called the HQ trailer on his hand-held transceiver, asking what was happening down below. He was informed that the woman was an Embassy secretary, Mrs Hiyech Sanei Kanji, who had been released solely in order to pass on another message from the terrorist leader. After hearing the message, the Controller passed it on to his own men.

'If the terrorist demands aren't broadcast,' he told them, 'they'll kill a hostage.'

All the men stiffened slightly, as if galvanized, then Inman, the most enthusiastic of all, asked: 'Does that mean we go in?'

The Controller dashed his hopes by shaking his head gravely. 'No,' he said. 'Mrs Thatcher has just endorsed the agreed strategy of maximum patience. That means we stand down again.'

'Shit!' the sergeant exploded, glancing down

in disgust at the floodlit road in front of the Embassy.

Wearily, the men picked up their weapons and equipment, then made their way down from the college roof and to the FHA, from where they would be driven back to the Regent's Park Barracks for sleep, then more training.

8

The barracks were bleak, draughty and dusty, with frequently blocked toilets and no hot water. When not sleeping on their steel-framed camp-beds, the men were subjected to a seemingly endless succession of intelligence briefings from the 'green slime', repeated lessons about the assault plans with the scale model of the Embassy, and further anti-terrorist training. Some of the latter was being done in other locations in London, notably abseiling from the roof of Pearl House, a police residence in Pimlico.

Frustrating though all of this retraining was, it was made even more so by the fact that, since it was being conducted in the heart of the city, most of it, apart from the abseil training, had to be confined to boring lectures, rather than the physical skills. The men suffered such lectures in the freezing cold of a large, draughty room in the barracks, most of them muttering their resentment, when not actually shivering with cold.

'Bear in mind,' the Royal Army Medical Corps psychologist informed them, 'that a siege situation will always produce what is known as transference, which begins with mutual terror or revulsion and ends in mutual dependence, even friendship. Though the hostages may at first fear the gunmen, eventually they will come to feel that they are all in this thing together. Should negotiations be protracted, the hostages will come to resent the authorities outside the building and blame them for the lack of progress. From this will spring empathy, even sympathy for the terrorists, and eventually a friendship based on total dependence.

'When this transference occurs, the behaviour of hostage and terrorist alike will become even more unpredictable and dangerous. For this reason, when you forcibly enter a building under siege, you will be compelled to treat both in exactly the same way, making no attempt to distinguish between them. For this reason, also, when you clear the building, those rescued, hostage and terrorist alike, will *not* be driven directly away to prison, police station or hospital, but will be subjected immediately to an appropriate reception outside the building. This means being bound hand and foot, laid face down on the ground, then interrogated until adequate proof of identity or loyalties has been received. The hostages will then be separated from the terrorists and removed for debriefing, which will include psychiatric treatment to ensure that their emotional links to the terrorists are completely broken. This is not always easy.'

'Easier than attacking a building under siege,' Baby Face muttered. 'Those psychos have got jam on it.'

Baby Face was a natural soldier, a quiet, shy young man who had been born with the instincts of a killer and lived for the Regiment. Born and raised in Kingswinford, in the West Midlands, where he had led a life of almost total anonymity until reaching the age to enter the Army, he had joined up as soon as he could. Once in, he knew just what he wanted to do, which was apply for the legendary SAS. Naturally, he passed the notoriously tough Selection and Training stages with flying colours and soon found himself in Northern Ireland, where he was involved in surveillance from OPs in south Armagh and in highly dangerous CRW operations in the Catholic ghettos, using a Q car. Danny had made his first killings there, sometimes with the renowned 'double tap', at which he was an expert, other times in full-scale assaults with other SAS soldiers against IRA supporters in well-defended blocks of flats. Either way he had learned to shoot to kill without thinking twice.

Now, sitting in this draughty hall and compelled to listen to boring lectures, he distracted himself with thoughts of previous SAS engagements – a fire-fight with PIRA terrorists in rural Armagh; his lone killing of a Republican gunman on the roof of a housing estate in the Falls – or with thoughts of his family and friends. But the hard truth was that for him the former always took precedence over the latter.

'Communications,' said the lecturer from Royal Signals, Catterick, interrupting Baby Face's reverie, 'is possibly the most important aspect of any CRW operation. The nature of communications, or the lack thereof, can subtly sway the terrorists' thinking and behaviour. As for the men on the ground, full and adequate communications are of vital strategic importance and therefore cannot be ignored. For this purpose we have now developed a wide range of communications equipment suitable for short-range contact in siege situations. These would include everything from the standard-issue microprocessor-based tactical radio, the PRC 319, to the Davies Communications CT100 communications harness. The latter comprises an electronic ear-defender headset with earphone for the team radio – the CT100E – and a socket for connection to the CT100L body-worn microphone. It is therefore ideal for hostage-rescue work.

'Though the ear-defender is so designed as to restrict high-pressure sound from gunfire and grenade explosions, it allows normal speech to pass, including reception at all times from the assault team radio. It is, of course, a body-worn microphone with a front-mounted press-to-talk button which is disabled when the microphone is attached to the S6 respirator.

'Other items of similar CRW importance might be the Davies Communications M135b covert microphone and covert ear-worn receiver; various hand-held transceivers operating in the VHF/UHF frequency range and with built-in encryption facilities, such as the Landmaster III range from Pace Communications; and the Hagen Morfax Covert SKH, or surveillance communications harness, comprising a miniature microphone and earphone. In addition we have . . .'

'Dogshit,' Inman whispered into Baby Face's right ear. 'That's all any of this means to me. I'm already done in by that bastard droning on and on. What the hell are we doing sitting here when we could be on the roof of the Embassy, at least listening in? I've been through all this crap before and don't need reminding.'

'Yeah,' Baby Face replied in his soft manner. 'I know what you mean, Sarge.'

'Right. I know you do. You and me, kid, we know what we want – and what we *don't* want is this shit.'

'That's right, Sarge, we don't. What we want is to get off our backsides and abseil down those walls. We want to get inside.'

'Dead right, we do. We're forced to sit here and swallow this lot when we could be out there solving the problem. Abseil down the walls, blast the windows out, chuck in a couple of good old flash-bangs, fill the rooms with a cloud of CS gas and then go in after the bastards. We'd have them lying face down on the rear lawn before they knew what was happening.'

'I think you're right, Sarge.'

Baby Face revered Inman as one of the best soldiers in the Regiment, despite the fact that he was also known as a troublemaker. Although he hardly looked it, Inman was two years short of forty and had put in more hard experience with the SAS than anyone apart from Staff-Sergeant Richard 'Dead-eye' Parker, who was now with D Squadron. He was a hard man with a low boredom threshold, which made him volatile and unpredictable when not in action. Nevertheless, he loved the Regiment, respected its best soldiers, irrespective of rank, and had a particular fondness for young Danny for that very reason. He knew that, like himself, Baby Face could not stand inactivity and wanted to get the hell out of the barracks and back to the Embassy.

Let the kid loose in that building and you just couldn't lose, he thought to himself as he looked at the cherubic young trooper.

'Intelligence is, of course, one of the most important aspects of a siege situation,' the Kremlin-based green slime instructor informed them as they sagged in their hard wooden chairs in the draughty, dusty dormitory being used as a lecture hall, 'and it is, of course, based largely on surveillance. As I'm sure you can imagine, the nature of surveillance in a siege situation is very different from that undertaken in an OP or from a Q car. As the prime difficulty in a siege situation is the building under siege, the major concern is to find out, before any assault is launched, what's being said and done inside. Electronic surveillance is therefore the order of the day and for that we have a variety of highly advanced listening and viewing instruments for which brick walls and closed windows are no problem.

'First and foremost is the Surveillance Technology Group range of systems, including an audio-surveillance lens and high-grain microphone probe, only 8mm in diameter, that can be coupled to any combination of tape recorder, 35mm camera or closed-circuit TV system and will monitor conversations through walls and other partitions, including reinforced windows. Even better is the same company's laser surveillance system, which consists of a tripod-mounted transmitter that directs an invisible beam onto the window of the target house, collecting the modulated vibrations created on the glass by the conversation going on inside. The modulated beam then bounces back to an optical receiver which converts it into audio signals. Those in turn are filtered, amplified and converted into clear conversations which can be monitored through headphones and recorded for subsequent examination. Thermal imaging is, of course, another viable option when darkness falls and it can be . . .'

'Jesus!' Trooper Alan Pyle hissed melodramatically. 'Will this torment never end?'

Unlike Baby Face, who spent more time thinking about fighting with the SAS than anything else, most of the younger SAS men banished the boredom of the lectures with predictably idealized thoughts of sex with wives, girlfriends, busty tabloid beauties and film and TV actresses. The more experienced hands, such as Phil and GG, tried gamely to forget sex and concentrate on their training, but the lectures were a soporific that rendered even them drowsy and so all the more prone to lustful fantasies.

'I wouldn't mind if we could leave these barracks at night,' Danny Boy said, relaxing on his camp-bed, 'to go out and pick up a bird in Camden Town. But being stuck here, night after night, is like being in prison.'

'Or a monastery,' Bobs-boy said.

'There speaks the man of God,' said Alan in his sardonic drawl, 'from the depths of experience.'

'An experienced wanker, more like,' said Ken derisively.

'Check your own mattress,' Bobs-boy retorted.

'My mattress, which was stained, is now soaked night and day,' the unembarrassed Ken came back without hesitation. 'I'm overloaded with tip-top sperm.'

'Have you noticed,' Alan asked, 'how the more those bloody instructors drone on, the more you start falling asleep and the more your head fills with horny thoughts?'

'Boredom breeds lust,' said Bobs-boy mock gravely.

'I just want to get back to Princes Gate,' Baby Face solemnly informed them, 'and into that Embassy. That's what we're here for.'

'We should be so lucky,' Inman said, stretched out on the adjacent camp-bed. It's not going to happen.'

'I think we will,' Baby Face insisted. 'In the next day or two. I'm sure of it.'

'Let us pray,' GG said lugubriously.

'Explosives,' the Royal Army Ordnance Corps demolition expert informed them at the next lecture, 'are almost certainly the most vital tools in any assault on a building being held by terrorists. Because that building also contains civilian hostages, the need for a precise knowledge of explosives is paramount. Obvious points of entry to such a building are doors, windows, and skylights, most of which will have to be forced with tools, weapons or, in the case of reinforced windows and skylights, with carefully calibrated quantities of explosive. As you all know by now – or *should* know by now – there are two types of explosive: low explosives, such as gunpowder, where the detonation is by burning; and high explosives, which the RAOC favours, where the charge is set off by an initiator. One reason we favour high explosives is that contrary to popular belief they're relatively insensitive – which prevents premature detonation – and resistant to heat and humidity. Among the best in current use are plastic explosives such as PETN, RDX, Semtex, Amatol and TNT. For the particular purposes of the kind of siege in which you are presently involved, we have developed what is known as a frame charge. This is an explosive in strip form that can be used for blowing precision holes through doors and brickwork, though it's infinitely more useful as an explosive shaped to a window frame for blowing out heavily reinforced windows. With regard to the way in which such a rapid-entry device is used . . .'

'Did he say premature detonation or premature ejaculation?' Alan asked when they were back in their temporary spider. 'Or am I just going mad?'

'I'd call it just finding your true self,' Ken replied.

'It's the boredom,' Phil explained. 'It's so bad, we're hallucinating. When that RAOC prat was droning on up there, I kept fantasizing about that Debbie Harry being up on stage instead. I've always fancied her.'

'Sexy,' groaned Alan.

'A good singer,' Phil agreed.

'I like her latest single,' Bobs-boy put in. 'I think it's "Call me". Otherwise, I'm not wild about her.'

'Well, she makes me detonate prematurely,' GG informed them. 'It's those lips.'

'The only detonation I'm looking forward to right now,' Inman said, 'is the one that's going to blow in the windows of that bleedin' Embassy. I want to get in there.'

'You just want to kill some terrorists,' said Jock, the Blue Team's staff-sergeant, who had just that moment entered the barracks to call the men out for more abseil training at Pearl House. 'Though I doubt if you'd mind if they were hostages, knowing you, Inman.'

'You wrong me,' Inman replied.

'*I* want to kill some terrorists,' Baby Face informed them all in his deceptively innocent, schoolboyish manner. 'I thought that's why we're here.'

'You're here to do as you're told,' said Sergeant Harrison, like Jock having just returned to barracks. He now stood beside his fellow team leader and said: 'And we're here to tell you to get off your backs and pack your kit for some abseiling. We move out in ten minutes.'

'It's better than nothing,' Inman said, swinging his legs off his camp-bed. 'Come on, men, let's go.'

In fact, if the demolition lectures were as boring as all the others, they did at least offer a slight respite. For the men, though not permitted to practice with real explosives within the confines of the Regent's Park Barracks, could at least tinker with defused explosive charges and detonators. This gave them something to do, other than listen to the droning voices of the green slime or instructors from the Royal Signals, Royal Engineers, REME, RAMC, RAOC, and even the Hereford and Army School of Languages, whose representative had come to teach them some basic Arabic in case they needed to talk to the terrorists.

'I need to talk to a terrorist like I need a hole in the head,' Phil said in the back of the Avis van that was carrying them to Pimlico for another few hours of abseil training. 'If I hear any bastard talking in Arabic, I'll make sure it's his last words.'

'Most of the hostages speak Arabic,' Baby Face said in his quiet, solemn way, 'so that gives you a problem.'

'Not me, Trooper. I've no problem with that at all. My only interest is in saving the British hostages. To hell with the rest of them. So if any bastard speaks Arabic to me, he won't talk for much longer.'

'I second that,' Ken said firmly. 'Once we get in there, we won't have time to decide who's a terrorist and who's a hostage, so I say they either get down on the floor or they get their wings clipped. You tell them to shut up and lie down or you blow them to Kingdom Come. No two ways about it. If they insist on talking and the chat is in Arabic, I'm taking no chances. A short burst from the MP5 or a double tap; they'll get one or the other.'

'There's women in there as well,' Baby Face reminded them.

'Women terrorists?' Bobs-boy asked.

'No, hostages. Female hostages. I think all of them work in the Embassy and were there when the terrorists took it over. We can't shoot women, can we?'

'Why not?' Inman asked gruffly. 'Most married men want to shoot their wives, so we might be doing someone a favour if we stitch a few in the Embassy.'

'That's out of order,' Danny Boy said. 'Worse than picking on your dog instead of having it out with your neighbours.'

'How did neighbours and dogs get into this conversation?' Bobs-boy wanted to know.

'Never mind,' Danny Boy said.

In fact, he hated his neighbours. His home was on a grim Humberside council estate with his wife and two children, a boy and a girl, and he had been fighting with his neighbours for the past couple of years about his backyard fence, which they claimed clipped three inches off their own yard. Danny Boy did not give a damn about his fence – he just could not stand the fat bastard, a butcher, who lived next door, so he continued the fight just for sport. While this amused him during his rare visits home, his wife Belinda, who let the kids run wild, was highly embarrassed, having once been best friends with her neighbour, Florence, the fat slob's wife. In truth, this knowledge only encouraged Danny Boy to keep up the aggro; it was his way of paying his slovenly wife back for letting the kids run wild, encouraged by that other slattern, Florence.

Yes, Danny Boy, who passionately loved his cat, Oscar, hated both his neighbours and had dreams of finding them cowering in the Embassy when finally he crashed in.

Not to stitch them, he thought. No, I wouldn't go that far. Just a couple of flash-bangs, followed by a dose of CS gas and an undiplomatic reception on the back lawn, face down in the grass and trussed up like chickens. That should teach them a lesson.

'I've got good neighbours,' said Ken, the Geordie. 'Where I come from, people are friendly and helpful, and so are the folks next door. We like to share a pint, get in some darts, have a night in the amusement arcade – all husbands and wives, like. It's a pretty good life.'

This was true enough. The only thing Ken missed when with the SAS was his life back in Newcastle-upon-Tyne, where the people – at least those still with a job – believed in working hard and playing hard without being too fancy.

Ken had had a job in a brickworks until he was eighteen, then he had met a girl from Keele, sweet-faced Beryl Williams, and discovered that she was as sweet as she looked, which is why she ended up pregnant, luckily by Ken. Doing the decent thing, he had married her and set up house in Keele, near his new wife's parents. They were as nice as she was, solid working-class, and had made terrific grandparents when the first child, Audrey, came along and was followed ten months later by Mel. By that time, Ken's wage from the brickworks was inadequate and he decided, in a spontaneous bid to better himself, to join the Army.

After his initial training, he was posted to the Staffordshire Regiment. Surprised to discover how much he enjoyed being away from home, but bored by life in the infantry, he had decided to try his luck with the SAS, which had already developed a glamorous reputation. Surprised again to get in, he had soon found himself in Oman, which was exactly the kind of exotic location he had joined the Regiment for. Unfortunately, he was only sent there in July 1976, and in September the SAS were pulled out of the country for good. By December that same year, he had found himself in Northern Ireland, which was considerably less exotic, though it certainly taught him a lot about CRW. Now, ironically, here he was again, about to fight a battle on British soil. You just couldn't credit it.

'The only good life you're going to find is right here with the Regiment,' his good friend and fellow trooper, Alan Pyle, told him. 'You'd be worthless without it. Working in a brickworks, for God's sakes. Who wants to know about *that*?'

'Oh, I had a good time,' Ken replied distractedly, thinking about his many good times. 'It wasn't that bad, really.'

'Sounds bloody boring to me, but one man's meat . . .'

Alan had his own idea of a good time, which was going to the dogs, spending a few bob in the bookies, having a night out with the boys, or shagging his arse off. Born to decent, middle-class parents, both teachers, in Swiss Cottage, north London, and educated in private schools, including the London School of Economics, Alan had rebelled at seventeen. Having taken to drink and drugs, he dropped out of the LSE and slipped into a dreamy kind of non-existence in a sordid shared flat in Notting Hill Gate. In just such a state, he had attended an army recruiting drive for a laugh. To his amazement, when his mind was straight again, he found that he had been accepted and was in for the full term.

No longer on drugs, though with an abiding fondness for drink, he had relished the singular disciplines of life in the 2nd Battalion, Queen's Regiment, but often found himself yearning for something more. Desperate to get away when he got a WRAC corporal pregnant during a night of sin after a drink-sodden party, he had been persuaded by a close and similarly compromised friend to apply for the SAS.

Accepted and badged, Alan had been posted straight to Northern Ireland and found, once again to his amazement, that he loved it because it was dangerous. Still single and not desperate to be married, he had thrown himself wholeheartedly into the disciplines of the Regiment, as well as into its unique social world. Since much of that world was centred around the Sports and Social Club in Hereford, he became firm friends not only with his fellow troopers, but with NCOs such as Lance-Corporal Phil McArthur and Corporal George Gerrard, both veterans of Oman and Northern Ireland, both bachelors and both good fun. Though Alan was still basically an educated, middle-class Londoner slightly removed from the other troopers, he felt at ease with men older and more experienced than himself – veterans like Phil and GG. Such men were amused by Alan's drawled, sardonic comments and treated him kindly. They were also pleased that he genuinely respected them and did not try to put them down.

'I joined the army to see the world,' Ken said, 'and here I am in the back of an Avis van, seeing only the West End.'

'But you'll soon be high above it all,' Alan reminded him, 'so appreciate what you've got.'

'What I've got is a sore arse from sitting on those hard chairs in that freezing lecture hall. I can't pretend it's a hoot.'

'You'll come to life when you get up on that roof and do some abseiling,' Inman assured him. 'We'll all wake up then.'

'At least it's something to do,' said Baby Face.

He was right, for although the lessons in demolition gave them a reason to use at least their hands, tinkering with explosive charges and detonators, they failed to offer a way of letting off steam or getting rid of excess energy. Abseiling, on the other hand, was as near as they would get to adventurous physical activity while in the holding area of the Regent's Park Barracks. Originating in Malaya as an SAS Standard Operating Procedure (SOP) used to let a soldier make a quick descent from a helicopter with the aid of a rope and harness, it was being practised rigorously by each man. It provided a means of gaining access to the various balconies of the 80-foot-high Embassy, by lowering themselves down the sides and rear of the building. For this reason, nylon abseiling ropes had secretly been tied to the chimneys of the Embassy during the first day of the siege and were still coiled up there on the roof, ready for the arrival of the SAS abseilers.

At Pearl House, which was almost as high as the Iranian Embassy, the men spent nearly all day on the windswept roof, taking apart and reassembling the abseiling equipment, then lowering themselves as rapidly as possible down the back wall, using a system considered too dangerous by even skilled mountaineers because there are many ways in which it can go wrong.

The abseiling equipment consisted of a strong nylon rope, a harness and a metal device, the descendeur, which was clipped to the harness and through which the rope was then threaded. Manipulation of the descendeur against the rope as the abseiler drops creates a 'friction break', enabling the wearer to control his rate of descent: slow, medium or rapid.

Though favoured by the SAS because of its convenience and speed during an assault, abseiling is in fact a highly dangerous activity that has caused many deaths among climbers, novices and veterans alike, even in non-combat situations.

Nevertheless, abseil training remained one of the few activities that allowed the men to let off excess energy when they were stood down yet again and returned from the FHA at the Royal College of Medical Practitioners to the holding area in Regent's Park Barracks. Besides, abseiling was dangerous and most of the men had joined the SAS partly because they got a kick out of taking risks.

Unfortunately, the abseil training was usually followed either by another 'Hyde Park' signal calling them out on stand-by and another frustrating stand-down, or by more hours of mind-numbing lectures about subjects they had already covered time and time again.

This particular day, Day Three of the siege, after the men had repeatedly gone over the edge of the roof of Pearl House and dropped down the side of the building – sometimes all the way to the ground; at other times stopping and entering the building via balcony windows; all the time observed and applauded by admiring police constables and officers – they were driven back to their temporary barracks and allowed to get the only good night's sleep they would have for a long time.

They were called out of bed first thing in the morning by yet another 'Hyde Park' alert.

9

Day Four began with a conversation between Salim and the police on the field telephone, during which the former poured out his frustrations at the lack of progress in negotiations and insisted that because of 'British deceit' the British hostages would now be the last to be freed. Again he insisted on speaking once more to the BBC and when again this was refused, he said that a hostage would have to die.

The police knew that inside the Embassy, as one terrorist stood guard over the hostages, trying to stay awake, the others, distracted by the sound of drilling as more probes and bugs were inserted in the walls, were prowling restlessly, guns lifted, expecting an attack through wall or ceiling at any time.

On the roof, the members of the SAS's Red Team were quietly checking that their ropes were still in position. Satisfied, they tiptoed away, clambered onto the adjoining college's roof, then made their way back down to the FHA, where the mood was increasingly tense.

'He's run his string out to the limit,' Sergeant Inman said, 'and it's going to break any minute now.'

'Then his kite flies away,' Baby Face said with a faint but deadly smile. 'We won't have too long to wait.'

'Dead right,' Inman said.

The demands and offers were repeated throughout the day as the police played a cat-and-mouse game with the terrorists. Because they knew that the terrorists would be listening to the news on the radio, they called a press conference at which they avoided the word 'terrorist' and referred instead to 'hostage takers'. Eventually, however, Salim's threat to kill a hostage compelled them to bring a BBC news desk deputy editor, Tony Crabb, to the Embassy to talk to the terrorist leader.

Speaking from an upstairs window on behalf of the latter, one of the BBC hostages, Sim Harris, asked Crabb why he had not broadcast Salim's statements. When Crabb blandly replied that there had been a 'misunderstanding', Harris replied: 'You must put out the right statement; otherwise everyone here could be killed.'

Before Crabb could reply, two other hostages, PC Lock and the Syrian journalist, Mustafa Karkouti, appeared at the window to tell Crabb and the police negotiator that Salim was in deadly earnest about his threat to start the killing.

'All right,' the negotiator finally said. 'I'll personally take down Salim's statement and make sure it's correct.'

When the negotiator had taken out his notebook and pen and was ready to take down what Salim said, the latter, standing behind Mustafa Karkouti and aiming a pistol at his head, relayed his statement through the Syrian. Talking from the shadows behind Karkouti, he repeated his personal details, then made his statement, which the police officer carefully wrote down, word for word.

'One: We swear to God and to the British people and Government that no danger whatsoever will be inflicted on the British and non-Iranian hostages if the British Government and the British police don't kid the group and don't subject the life of the hostages and the group to any danger, and if things work to the contradictory direction everyone in the building will be harmed.

'Two: We demand the three ambassadors – Algerian, Jordanian and Iraqi – and a representative of the Red Cross to start their jobs in negotiating between us and the British Government to secure the safety of the hostages as well as the group's members and to terminate the whole operation peacefully. If any of the three ambassadors is not available he could be substituted by first the Libyan, or the Syrian or the Kuwait ambassador.

'Three: The reason for us to come to Britain to carry out this operation is because of the pressure and oppression which is being practised by the Iranian Government in Arabistan and to convey our voice to the outside world through your country. Once again, we apologize to the people and the Government for this inconvenience.'

Salim stepped out of the shadows to peer over Karkouti's shoulder and check that the negotiator was writing everything down. When the officer stopped writing and glanced up from his notebook, Salim added, through Karkouti: 'And I demand a guarantee that this time my statement will be broadcast accurately and as soon as possible.'

'OK,' the negotiator replied. 'But what do we get in return?'

Salim thought about this for a moment, then replied: 'What do you want?'

'The release of some hostages.'

'One,' Salim said.

'More than one,' the negotiator said. 'How about three?'

'Two,' Salim said.

The police officer nodded. 'Agreed.' There was silence for a long time, then the negotiator asked: 'Who will be released.'

'One moment. We must decide,' Salim said, then both men disappeared from the window. A considerable period of time passed before the two men returned, with Salim still aiming his pistol at Karkouti's head.

'Two,' he said. 'Haideh Kanji and Ali-Ghola Ghanzanfar.'

Another police officer, who had come up to stand beside the negotiator, now flipped through his notebook, studied a list of names, then said: 'Kanji's the twenty-three-year-old secretary to the Embassy's two accountants. Being three months pregnant, she's an obvious choice.'

'And Ghanzanfar?'

'A Pakistani educationalist. According to the statement of a previously released hostage, he snores dreadfully at night – so loud that he even annoyed the terrorists. They're probably glad to get rid of him.'

The negotiator grinned. 'I suppose so. Well, it's better than nothing.' Again using the radio phone, he asked Salim if the hostages were to be released before or after the promised BBC broadcast.

'After,' Salim said.

'We want them before.'

'No. They are my safeguard that the broadcast will be made and done correctly – on the nine o'clock news.'

'Release one before and one after,' the negotiator suggested patiently.

'No. Both hostages will be released immediately after the broadcast.'

'Then *we* have no guarantee. We could make the broadcast and you could then break your word and keep the hostages.'

Salim exploded with fury behind Karkouti. 'I do not break my word!' he screamed.

'What if we refuse to make the broadcast unless the two hostages are released first?' the negotiator asked calmly when Salim had calmed down.

'If my statement is not read at nine tonight,' Salim replied, 'I'll kill a hostage and send out the body.'

Hearing that statement, Karkouti sank to his knees in full view of everyone, obviously pleading with Salim not to do anything rash. PC Lock appeared just behind him, framed by the window, to lean down and whisper comforting words to him.

Surprisingly, Salim then screamed in frustration at PC Lock, his words carrying clearly to the police officers in the middle of the road. 'What can we do? We treat you well, we like you, we agree with what you say, but the police do not keep their word!' He then grabbed Karkouti by the shoulder, jerked him upright, and pushed him and PC Lock out of sight.

'Well, do we make the broadcast or not?' Crabb, the BBC news desk deputy editor, asked the police officers. The one standing beside the negotiator nodded. 'Yes.' He held his hand out to the negotiator. The latter tore Salim's statement from his notebook and passed it over. 'Let's go back to my trailer,' the senior police officer said, 'and I'll give you a photocopy of this statement. Then you can take yourself off to Broadcasting House and arrange for it to be read out on the nine o'clock news, unless you receive a message stating otherwise. You stay here,' he said to the negotiator, 'and keep him engaged.'

'Will do,' the negotiator said, glancing up at the window as the other two departed. There was no one at the window. Indeed, no one returned for a long time, which enabled the negotiator to leave for lunch. When he returned, there was still no one at the window. He kept leaving and returning until, when he was in one of the police trailers, sharing a cup of tea with some fellow officers, another message came through on the field telephone, informing him that Salim wished to speak to him. Hurrying to the front of the Embassy, the negotiator waited patiently and eventually, at just before six p.m., Salim appeared at the window, standing as usual behind the now frightened Karkouti.

. 'On the advice of my friends,' Salim said through the Syrian, 'I have decided to show good faith by releasing the woman hostage before the broadcast is made tonight. She is coming out now.'

While Salim was speaking, the front door of the Embassy opened and the face of a terrorist wearing a *keffia* peered around it. Satisfied that no one was attempting to charge the building, he opened the door and stepped aside to let the pregnant woman, Haideh Kanji, leave the building. She did so slowly, carefully, as if not quite believing what was happening, then walked more quickly once she had stepped off the pavement and was on the road. The terrorist slammed the door shut just before the hostage reached the negotiator. The woman was weeping for joy. Up on the scaffolding of the press enclosure, photographers with telephoto lenses were frantically taking pictures.

The negotiator took Haideh Kanji by the arm and

started leading her towards the police barricades, but before they had reached them two medics hurried from the throng to help her the rest of the way. When all three had disappeared back into the crowd packed along the barricade, the negotiator turned back to face the Embassy window. Using his field telephone, he thanked Salim for releasing the woman and assured him that his statement would be broadcast that evening.

Three hours later, on the nine o'clock news, Deputy Assistant Commissioner Peter Neivens, the head of information at Scotland Yard, meticulously read out Salim's statement.

Within minutes of that broadcast, the second hostage, Ali-Ghola Ghanzanfar, was released from the Embassy.

10

'According to the released hostage, Ali-Ghola,' the Controller of the SAS CQB team said to the other members of COBR at a meeting in the evening of Day Five, 'everyone in the Embassy, including the hostages, was overjoyed at hearing Salim's statement broadcast. They cried, hugged and kissed each other. Even the terrorists cried – at least, all except Salim. They were also jubilant when the two hostages were released. Indeed, as Ghanzanfar was being led away from the other hostages, to leave the building for good, the remaining terrorists joined the hostages in their room, sitting with them, their guns in their laps, all laughing and joking together. By way of celebration, and as a conciliatory gesture, the police then sent in a dinner ordered from Pars, a nearby Persian restaurant. So a good time, as best we know, was had by terrorists and hostages alike.'

'I think the celebratory meal was a touch of genius,' the Secretary said. 'It must have lowered the temperature considerably and brought the terrorists and hostages closer together, at least temporarily.'

'Naturally, I agree,' the Police Commissioner said.

'You would,' the Controller said with a grin, before glancing down at his notes and growing serious again. 'Anyway, to get back to the real business, we have a problem with this demand linking the release of hostages to some sort of intervention by the ambassadors. In my view, there's no serious hope that the negotiators can deliver a deal on that hypothesis.'

'You're correct in that assessment,' the genial Secretary said. 'The Foreign Office has already been on the phone to the Kuwaiti Ambassador, Sheik Saud Nasir Al-Sabah, and the Jordanian chargé d'affaires, Kasim Ghazzawi. So far, while both men expressed their willingness to discuss the matter at a later date, neither has showed willingness to help or involve themselves in the matter unless we offer safe conduct for the terrorists. As that's something we simply cannot do, the talks ended in deadlock.'

'What about the International Committee of the Red Cross?' the Commissioner asked.

'Earlier this afternoon they announced that,

provided all parties were agreeable, they would send their delegates into the Embassy to give first-aid treatment, if necessary, and to assist communications between all parties concerned. While their motives are no doubt humane, their mention of first-aid treatment and material and moral comfort has merely added to the increasingly doom-laden atmosphere.'

'Does Salim know about this?'

'Not exactly – though he must surely suspect it. Certainly, just before this meeting convened, he reduced his demands again. Now he wants only one ambassador to mediate, and a guarantee of safe passage for him and his comrades.'

'He is, however, close to the edge,' the Controller reminded them. 'Which means he's unpredictable.'

'Nevertheless,' the Commissioner insisted, 'we have to keep talking at all costs in the hope of averting an attack on the Embassy in which the hostages might be killed along with the terrorists.'

'I'm not trying to push for my men,' the Controller said. 'I'm just not sure that all this talking is getting us anywhere.'

'I should point out to you,' the Commissioner countered, 'that our record for handling siege situations has so far been impeccable. There have been two similar sieges in recent times. The first was at the Spaghetti House restaurant in Knightsbridge in October 1975, when three gunmen barricaded themselves in a basement with six waiters. In the second, two months later, four IRA terrorists seized a married couple in their council flat in Balcombe Street, Marylebone, holding them hostage for six days and nights. Both situations presented the Metropolitan Police with highly sensitive issues on the ground, as well as possible international repercussions depending upon the outcome. In both cases our tactics brought the siege to a successful conclusion, with the hostages released unharmed and the gunmen surrendering.'

'I'm not arguing with your tactics,' insisted the Controller. 'I'm only worried that the constant talking and general indecision is placing a strain on my men – as, indeed, it's already doing with the police.'

'If you're referring to the fact that the strain has led to one of my men being replaced, I should point out that so far he's the only one, which is really not that high a price to pay.'

'It's not its effect on our own men,' the Controller said. 'We also have to take into account the effect it may be having on the terrorists. It is my belief, for instance, that their leader, Salim, is getting close to the edge. As we all know, thanks to the audio-surveillance devices implanted in the walls of the building, the tension did explode earlier this morning over something quite trivial. That row led to yet another false alert for my two assault teams.'

The SAS man was referring to a row that erupted when some of the terrorists sprayed subversive slogans on the walls of a room where the hostages were kept. The chargé d'affaires, Dr Afrouz, had been incensed by the slogans and strongly voiced his opinion to the terrorists involved. Even more incensed, however, was another hostage, Abbas Lavasani. Being the most devout member of the Embassy staff, Lavasani was furious at the written insults against Ayatollah Khomeini and engaged in an argument with those responsible. One of the terrorists angrily pulled out his gun and was only prevented from shooting Lavasani by the diplomatic intervention of the Muslim journalist Muhammad Farughi. PC Lock and Karkouti then hurried Lavasani out of the room where, out of ear-shot of the angry terrorists, Karkouti reprimanded him for letting his temper spoil all the gains of the past two days. When the Syrian also told Lavasani that he, as a man of God, should not let himself be responsible for the deaths of the other hostages, Lavasani burst into tears.

'That row,' the Controller said, 'was an indication that both terrorists and hostages are becoming more volatile. A lot could develop out of that – and none of it good.'

'Nevertheless,' the Commissioner said, 'I insist that we keep playing for time. The longer the siege can be maintained, the greater the chances of getting the hostages out alive. A lengthy siege also presents the distinct possibility of psychological transference, in which the individuals, terrorist and hostage alike, develop sympathy for one another and even, in certain cases, become friends. If such a situation develops – and it certainly has in the past – the terrorists will be more likely to release their hostages. Failing that, we can at least reach a situation where we can convince the terrorists that they cannot get away and it would be in their own interests to come out peacefully. It is my belief that as Salim has already decided against blowing up the building, and has since reduced his demands, there is a chance that he will indeed decide that he has gained what he most wanted – publicity for his cause – and therefore needs to take it no further. In other words, he might yet come out without a fight.'

'He won't come out peacefully if we deny him safe passage out of the country – and we all know that's something we cannot agree to. Sooner or later that knowledge will sink in . . . then what will he do?'

Mercifully the ensuing silence was broken by the shrill ringing of the red telephone on the Secretary's desk. Picking it up, he listened thoughtfully. Then he smiled and put the receiver down again.

'Some good news at last,' he said. 'Apparently the Syrian journalist, Mustafa Kàrkouti, has been suffering from severe diarrhoea and fever. For that reason Salim has just released him. He's presently being debriefed in a Metropolitan Police HQ trailer outside the Embassy, so I suggest you both take yourselves over there and hear what he has to say.'

'Damned right,' the Controller said.

Leaving the basement room, they took the lift up to the ground floor and left the building by the guarded front doors. A chauffeur-driven limousine was waiting for them outside in the lamplit darkness of Whitehall. Once in the car, they were driven quickly to Kensington, making small talk about the siege until they arrived at the police barricades in Princes Gate. As he clambered out of the limousine, the Controller glanced up to see the great canvas marquee of the press enclosure in Hyde Park. There, high up on the floodlit scaffolding, dozens of photographers were perched like black birds, cameras at the ready. 'At least they've got a head for heights,' the Controller said as he hurried beside the Commissioner to the trailer being used as the police HQ, pushing his way through milling ambulance men. Identified by the constable on guard outside the trailer, he let the Commissioner enter first, then followed him up the three steps and through the open door.

Inside, an exhausted, ill-looking Mustafa Karkouti was sitting in a hard wooden chair, virtually surrounded by men from the Metropolitan Police intelligence department, as well as one white-smocked medic. The latter had just removed a thermometer from Karkouti's mouth and was thoughtfully studying it. As the Police Commissioner introduced the SAS Controller to those who did not know him, the medic grinned at Karkouti and said: 'Those tablets are working. Your temperature's dropped to normal already and your blood pressure's OK. When these men have finished with you, we'll take you to the hospital for no more than a good rest and observation. After that, you'll be all right.'

'Thank you,' Karkouti said with a slight smile of relief, as the medic packed up his little bag and left the long, packed trailer.

'Has he given you much so far?' the Commissioner whispered to one of his senior police officers.

'A windfall,' came the whispered reply. 'We know everything that's going on inside: the names, the weapons, the whereabouts of the hostages, the psychological state of the terrorists. He sent out the wrong hostage.'

'Wrong for him, right for us,' the Commissioner noted.

'Correct.'

'Has he finished talking?'

'No. He's just about to tell us what's happened since Ghanzanfar was released. He believes that Salim's authority over the rest of the team – uneducated men in their twenties – is fading because the siege is going on too long. They were told it would last no longer than twenty-four hours, so now they're pretty unhappy.'

The Commissioner nodded and glanced at the Controller, then both of them sat at the back of the trailer, in the shadows well away from Karkouti and those talking to him.

'So the last time you saw them in good mood was when Ali-Ghola Ghanzanfar was released?' the police interrogator asked.

'Yes,' the journalist replied. 'We all had such a

good time together when Ghanzanfar was released, sharing that Persian meal sent in by the police – rice, kebabs and Bandit biscuits, washed down with Tango orange and Pepsi. Ron Morris used an orange crate as a table. He even put paper napkins on it. PC Lock and Morris had a cheerful conversation, the latter swearing that once released, he would never go back to working in the Embassy, the former insisting that he would return because he liked the work so much.'

'I know PC Lock,' the interrogator said, trying to make the conversation as casual as possible. 'He's a constable who loves his work, so he'll go back to work.'

Karkouti smiled. 'I suppose we *all* will.'

'So for a time there, when you were having that meal, you were almost like friends.'

'Yes. In fact, the atmosphere was so euphoric, Salim even gave me an interview. I'd been trying to get one since the start of the siege and he finally relented. He just sat there with his rifle across his lap, smiling – as he normally never did – and talking his head off.'

'You took notes?'

'Of course.' Karkouti handed over his notebook. The interrogator scanned it quickly. 'It's lengthy and detailed,' he said, 'so I'll only summarize it. When we're done here, I'll have the notes photocopied and give you all copies.' He paused as he went back to the start of the notes, then he said: 'It confirms that Salim is twenty-seven years old, comes from a middle-class family, studied at Tehran University, graduated from the Linguistics Faculty, participated in the Iranian students' struggle, and was indeed imprisoned and tortured by SAVAK. His occupation of the Embassy he views as self-defence, meaning resistance to what he calls the Ayatollah's cruel Farsi-ization of the Arabistan province and his relentless exploitation of Iranian Arabs. His aim is to help gain autonomy for his people in Arabistan and regain the name 'Arabistan' instead of its present name, 'Khuzistan'. The purpose of the Embassy take-over is to gain publicity for his cause and place pressure on the Iranian Government through world public opinion. He hopes that the take-over will end peacefully, though this depends entirely on the British authorities and the Arab ambassadors whom he'd asked to be brought here.' Lowering the notebook to his lap, the interrogator said to Karkouti: 'This information will be invaluable in shedding light on their behaviour and possible actions.'

'Good,' Karkouti said.

'So what happened after the meal?'

'We were taken down to the Ambassador's room on the first floor, where we had the best sleep we'd had since the siege commenced. I think we all slept soundly because we took the broadcast and release of the other hostages as hopeful signs.'

'What about the following morning? This morning.'

'The mood was still euphoric. The terrorists heard the early news bulletins claiming that the Arab ambassadors were willing to help.'

'Which was wrong,' the interrogator said.

'None of us were to know that,' Karkouti said. 'We all thought they were true.'

'Sorry. Please continue.'

'The untrue stories about the Arab ambassadors, combined with the news that the Red Cross were standing by, naturally filled Salim and his fellow gunmen with optimism. Being in good mood, they ran a bath and offered to let us use it first. PC Lock and I were the first to receive invitations. I said, quite rightly, that it would be discourteous to bathe in front of the woman, but PC Lock said he wanted to keep his uniform on to preserve his image.'

'His *image*?'

Karkouti smiled tiredly. 'That's what he said. His real purpose was to ensure that the terrorists did not find the pistol strapped to his thigh.'

'A clever man, PC Lock.'

Karkouti nodded. 'Yes. Anyway, as the deadline passed, boredom set in again and the terrorists – who were now also complaining about how long they had been in the Embassy – tried to distract themselves by scrawling subversive slogans on the walls of our room with magic marker pens.'

'Exactly what did the slogans say?'

'"Long live the Arabistani people." "We demand fundamental changes." "Death to Khomeini"' . . . and so on. Salim had to ask the Muslim journalist Muhammad Farughi how to spell "fundamental".'

'From what we picked up from our audio-surveillance devices, Farughi kept a low profile regarding this.'

'Yes. He was taking down notes for an article he hoped to write some day. He copied down the slogans on the wall even as the gunmen were writing them.'

'Then the row began with Dr Afrouz and Abbas Lavasani.'

'You heard all that through your bugging devices?' Karkouti asked.

'Yes.'

Karkouti shook his head in wonderment. 'That is truly amazing.'

'What about after the row was over? Do you

think it had an effect on the relationship between the terrorists and the hostages?'

'Yes. Definitely. We had been growing closer together, more considerate of each other, but all that ended with the row over the slogans. Now, they were distant to us again. Also, it was clear that they'd had enough and just wanted out. They complained to Salim about it. They said the police would not take them seriously unless they killed someone. That's when Salim reduced his demands again by settling for one Arab ambassador and asking only for a guarantee of safe passage for him and his men. Salim was now very tired and, I think, disillusioned. Like his men, he just wanted out, but he had his pride to protect.'

'And, shortly after reducing his demand, he decided to let you go?'

'Yes. By now, my diarrhoea and fever had been followed by a numbness in the arms and legs and I found it painful to urinate. Even so, when he made the offer, I asked him to let one of the women go instead of me. He refused, insisting that I needed medical attention. Then he walked me downstairs to the front door and once there, let me out.'

'Did you have any final words together?'

'Yes. He confessed that he was depressed because the operation had been planned to last for about twenty-four hours and now it had gone on for nearly a week.'

'Anything else?'

Karkouti took a deep breath, then let it out slowly. 'He said I was to tell you that if you didn't get in touch with the Arab ambassadors something bad would happen.'

'Those were his exact words?'

'Yes. He said . . . "something bad".'

Hearing these words, the SAS Controller stood up and hurried out of the trailer, determined to talk to his men and prepare them for action.

11

The sixth day found the Red and Blue Teams still practising their abseiling techniques in Pimlico. Recalled to the FHA at the Royal College of Medical Practitioners, they were informed by the Controller that the Home Secretary had turned the screws on the terrorists again by letting them know that the 'ambassadorial' phase had passed and that the only concession they would get was a visit from an imam from the Regent's Park Mosque.

'The Home Secretary's hoping that the Iman will act as a mediator,' the Controller said, 'but whether he does or not, I think the killing will start eventually. If it does, the Deliberate Assault Plan will require two hours' notice to succeed. This plan's the one that gives the maximum chance of surprise and best hope of hostage survival. The not-so-good news is that even if all goes as intended, the best chance of saving hostage life is no more than sixty per cent of the total.'

'So what if we have more time, boss?' Red Team's Lance-Corporal Phil McArthur asked. 'What, for instance, if we get another full day's preparation and training?'

'I'd estimate that by then both plans – Immediate Action and Deliberate Assault – would merge into a response time of a few minutes.'

'Then maybe we should all say our prayers that the talking's continuing,' Blue Team's Corporal George Gerrard said.

'Maybe,' the Controller said. 'The only problem with that is that suddenly time seems to be running out. According to a message from PC Lock, Salim's self-control finally snapped this morning. First, he told Lock that he thought the police were drilling through the walls to try to get into the building. In fact, they were drilling holes for the insertion of fibre-optic and spike cameras. This led to the plaster on the first-floor landing bulging out.'

'Dumb bastards,' Sergeant Inman said.

'Salim saw the bulging wall and went mad. Luckily, PC Lock managed to convince him that even if the police *were* intending to break through the walls and storm the building, they would certainly not do it during the day, but only at night.'

'Lock's response was clever,' Danny Boy said. 'He bought some more time.'

'Unfortunately, it didn't end there,' the Controller continued.

'I don't think I can listen to any more of this,' Bobs-boy whispered to his fellow trooper, Baby Face.

'Given the sparseness of sockets for their bugs, the police simply lowered them from the roof down the chimneys. As they should have known would happen, bits of debris were dislodged by the bugs and made a lot of noise when they fell. Salim went mad again.'

'I don't bloody believe it!' Jock Thompson spluttered. 'It's us, not the police, who should be planting the surveillance devices. If we did, at least the job would be done properly and not cocked up every inch of the way. What a bloody waste!'

'Even worse,' the Controller continued remorselessly, 'Iran's Foreign Minister sent the *hostages* a telegram, praising them for their forbearance in the face of the quote, "criminal actions", unquote, of Ba'athist Iraq. He also informed the hostages that Iran would spare no effort for their release and that thousands of Iranians were ready to enter the Embassy to bring punishment to the mercenaries, meaning the terrorists. Naturally, Salim read the telegram and was further incensed.'

'Poor boy!' Staff-Sergeant Harrison exclaimed sardonically. 'Nobody loves him.'

'Finally, finding all this too much to take, Salim exploded and told Lock to inform the police that unless there was a prompt answer to his demand for the ambassadors to come into the negotiations, a hostage would be shot in half an hour. He then moved the male hostages out of the large second-floor room where they've been for days and took them down the hall to the telex room – Room 10 – overlooking Princes Gate.

'And the women?' Trooper Ken Passmore asked.

'They're still where they were, in Room 9A, overlooking the rear gardens.'

'Any other changes in atmosphere since that move?' Sergeant Inman asked.

'Well, both PC Lock and Sim Harris have made it clear by phone and, after that, through a conversation between them and Police Superintendent Fred Luff – conducted on the part of Lock and Harris from the first-floor front balcony – that they're alarmed at the changed atmosphere. So much so, in fact, that they warned Luff that they feel they're in danger. They started sensing this when the terrorists put on their anoraks and wound their *keffias* tightly around their heads. That means they're ready to fight or kill.'

'Were Lock and Harris given any message to take back to the terrorists?' Harrison asked.

'Yes. They were told to tell Salim that the Foreign Office was still holding discussions with the designated ambassadors and that if he listened to the BBC World Service's midday news bulletin, he would hear confirmation of that fact.'

'*I* listened to that news bulletin,' Inman said, 'and I heard sweet FA.'

'Exactly,' the Controller responded. 'That's why the trouble will start soon. In fact, Salim has given us forty-five minutes before he kills the first hostage.'

That turned out to be the case. Abbas Lavasani, a deeply devout, unmarried twenty-eight-year-old, had arrived only two weeks before to take up his position as the Embassy's chief press officer. A phone call that afternoon from PC Lock to the police negotiator revealed that Lavasani had volunteered to be a martyr after the bitter row with Salim about the terrorist leader's anti-Khomeini graffiti.

Subsequently, at one-thirty, only a few hours after the SAS Controller's briefing with his men, when Lavasani indicated that he wished to visit the lavatory, Salim led him out of the telex room where the male hostages were held and down to the ground floor. There, after letting Lavasani use the lavatory, Salim had argued with the police over the radio telephone. He then handed the phone to PC Lock, who was present with Sim Harris, and told him to inform the police negotiators that he had a man whom he was going to shoot. While Lock was doing so, Salim ordered two of the other terrorists to truss Lavasani's hands behind his back and then tie him to the bottom of the banisters. He made Lock inform the negotiators of this fact also.

When Lock had described the chilling details of this scene, the negotiators, still playing for time, said the ambassadors would meet at five p.m. When Lock had passed this message on to Salim, he and Sim Harris were conducted back upstairs to rejoin the other hostages in the telex room.

Shortly afterwards, they heard Lavasani talking on the telephone, identifying himself to the police negotiators outside. Even as he uttered his own name, he was cut off by Salim's: 'No names! No names!' Then there were three shots in quick succession. Some hostages thought they heard groaning, others a choking sound. Silence followed.

Salim finally broke that silence by speaking

himself to the negotiators on the phone, telling them that he had just killed a man.

According to PC Lock's subsequent phone conversation with the negotiators, Salim, looking pale, then entered the telex room to tell the hostages that he had shot Lavasani.

'If you've killed a hostage then your cause is finished,' Ron Morris told him. You can kill all of us now. One or twenty makes no difference. Your cause is lost.'

'I am prepared to die,' Salim told him, then walked out of the telex room.

12

Most of those outside the Embassy could not believe that the killing had started. There was no sign of a body and the possibility remained that Salim was bluffing.

One of the few who contradicted this view, however, was the Controller, who insisted that the time was right for such an event and that a hostage had almost certainly been killed.

An hour after Salim's announcement, COBR was again in session in its basement room in Whitehall. There, while glancing at the television set flickering in one corner, waiting for the news, the Secretary, no longer quite so amiable, said: 'I *do* believe that until we receive proof that a hostage is dead it would be disastrous to react as if we believe it actually happened.'

'It happened,' the Controller insisted.

'Shots were heard,' the Police Commissioner said.

'Salim said he had killed a hostage. That doesn't constitute proof. Salim *could* be bluffing.'

'Whether he's bluffing or not,' the Secretary said, 'he's accepted the five o'clock deadline for a meeting with the Arab ambassadors, none of whom are likely to show up without the promise of safe conduct for the terrorists. If that happens, we'll have to pass control of the situation from the police to the SAS.'

'I can't argue with that,' the Commissioner said. 'We have no other option.'

'My thanks,' the Controller said.

'Not at all,' the Commissioner replied. 'No point in playing brinkmanship in a situation like this.'

'Very sporting,' the Controller said.

'We're a nation that loves sport.'

'So what happens,' the Secretary said, not amused by their banter, but turning his attention to the Controller, 'when that deadline arrives without sight of the ambassadors? Or, heaven forbid, when the terrorists produce proof of murder?'

'Our preparations for a Deliberate Attack will be completed by that time. From five p.m. onwards the assault can be launched with minimum delay. I should point out, however, that my men will have a better chance of success if they're given the go-ahead before nightfall – at eight-thirty.'

'Agreed,' the Commissioner said.

'What's vital, even imperative, is that between the time proof of murder is produced and the start of our assault, the terrorists should be fed a cover story to keep them happy and off guard.'

'I think you can depend on my negotiators to do that,' the Commissioner replied. 'They've been doing it for six days, after all, and made no mistakes so far.'

'I have one other point to make,' the Controller said. 'It's that the soldiers, once committed, should be left to get on with their job. If the Deliberate Assault is approved then halted at the last moment, it would be a disaster for morale.'

This did not sit too well with the Secretary who, in the manner of such men, wished to steer a careful middle course.

'I would,' he said, 'like to keep the emergency cover in place. This still allows the police to pass control to the SAS at short notice if multiple murders start inside the Embassy.'

'And if they don't?' the Controller asked testily.

'I'm not sure about that yet. Before making a decision, I'd like to take further counsel with the Police Commissioner here. I would also wish to inform both the Prime Minister and the Defence Minister at what might be termed the moment of decision. For now, other imponderables remain, such as: Is there a body?'

'I say no,' the Commissioner said.

'I say yes,' the Controller said.

'Why can't we just demand proof of Salim's claim by asking to see the corpse?'

'Because if we did,' the Commissioner said, 'and he hasn't yet actually killed someone, he might do so just to furnish us with proof.'

'Ah!' the Secretary said, still easily surprised, even in his mature years, by the slippery nature of politics.

'So what about the Arab ambassadors, due to show up at the Embassy at five?'

'I don't believe they'll show up,' the Controller said. 'According to my intelligence, they're gathered together right now at the offices of the Arab League in Green Street, Mayfair, trying to resolve their confusion over their supposed role in the whole business. They're particularly aggrieved because they believe that the Foreign Office has deliberately spread the notion that the initiative in all dealings with the terrorists has been taken by the Arabs, not by the FO.'

'Are they right?' the Commissioner asked.

'Of course,' the Secretary said with a bland smile. 'But don't say I told you so.'

'Anyway, there's little doubt,' the Controller continued, 'that the Arab ambassadors, while expressing their overriding concern to save life, will avoid all involvement by insisting on a safe passage out. They know we can't give them that.'

'But what if they do decide to take part?' the cautious Secretary asked. 'Whose terms do we play by? Ours or theirs?'

'Ours,' the Commissioner said. 'This is happening on the streets of London. I want them to turn up in good time or, failing that, I want clear guarantees that they *will* be coming. I don't want any failed promises based on our supposed guarantee of safe passage for the terrorists. They either come on our terms or not at all.'

'I think not at all,' the Controller said sardonically, 'because they won't want involvement unless they can arrange that safe passage. That would protect them from criticism. Those men have their own motives.'

'Why don't we avoid the ambassadors altogether,' the Secretary asked, 'by simply calling Salim's bluff and letting the deadline pass?'

'Because if no one has been killed so far,' the Commissioner replied, 'and I do not believe they have, then calling Salim's bluff could actually lead to the first killing. The blame would then fall squarely on us.'

The Secretary sighed and glanced at his watch. 'Four-forty-five,' he said. 'Fifteen minutes to go. Let's have a drink, gentlemen, and see if the Arab ambassadors show up.'

'Not a hope,' the Controller said.

Fifteen minutes later, at exactly five p.m., with the television news showing no new developments outside the Embassy, the Commissioner phoned his on-the-ground trailer HQ to enquire if anything had happened. Putting the phone down again, he glanced at the Controller, then turned reluctantly to the Secretary. 'My friend here was right,' he said graciously. 'None of the ambassadors showed up.'

The Secretary spread his hands on the table and lightly drummed his fingers. After pursing his lips, as if tasting a vintage wine, he asked: 'And what about the terrorists? Have they responded at all?'

'Not so far,' the Commissioner replied.

The Secretary glanced at his watch again. 'One minute past the deadline,' he said. 'Let's give them time to think about it and see what transpires. Another drink, gentlemen?'

The response came thirty minutes later. The men of COBR were just finishing their second drink when the Secretary's red telephone rang.

Instead of reaching for it, he merely nodded at the Police Commissioner, who picked it up, listened thoughtfully, then put it down again.

'That was our negotiator,' he said. 'Salim has just phoned to say that he still wants to see the ambassadors. If they're not there in thirty minutes, another hostage will be killed and his or her body thrown onto the street.'

The Secretary sighed again. 'Can your negotiators keep him talking?'

'Probably not much longer.'

'Do you think he'd speak to the Iranian Consul-General by telephone?'

'I doubt it. I think it's too late for that.'

'What about the Imam of London's Central Mosque, as was suggested before?'

'Dr Sayyed Darsh,' the Commissioner said. 'A good man. His friend, the Libyan broadcaster Muhammad Mustafa Ramadan, who regularly attended prayers at the mosque, was gunned down on its steps only a few weeks ago. That incident deeply affected Darsh. For that reason, when Superintendent Bernard Hodgets of the Anti-Terrorist Squad contacted him, he initially had doubts about whether or not he should go.'

'Why?' the Secretary asked.

'He believes strongly that the mosque exists to

serve Muslims in London, whatever their national-
ity, and that it can only do so if the Imam remains
neutral regarding Arab politics. However, the death
of his friend, shot down on the steps of the mosque,
changed that line of thinking.'

'So he's going to talk to the terrorists?'

'Yes. Hodgets personally collected him from the
mosque and took him to Hyde Park Police Station
for what turned out to be a very long wait. An hour
and a half later, at five o'clock precisely, he was
taken from there, escorted through the barricades
surrounding the Embassy, and plunked down in
the back of a police van, which is where he is
now. When the time is ripe, he'll be taken from
the police van into the police negotiating room of
Alpha Control, now located in the nursery school,
where he can talk to Salim by radio phone.'

'Can he say what he wants or has he been
briefed?'

'He's been briefed to remind the terrorists of his
eminence as an Islamic cleric, then emphasize the
immorality of what they're doing in the name of
Islam. He is also to reassure them that if they end
their resistance and come out peacefully, no harm
will come to them and that he will be present at
the surrender to ensure that this is so.'

'In other words,' the Secretary said, 'you're not

asking him to negotiate or bargain at all. His function is really to convey your terms for surrender.'

'I suppose so,' the Commissioner said.

'And if the Imam also fails to persuade them?'

'Then the SAS Deliberate Assault Plan will commence immediately.'

The Secretary pursed his lips and drummed his fingers once more, then sighed and stood up behind his desk. 'Excuse me, gentlemen, but I have to make a private call.' He walked out of the room. They could hear him murmuring into a phone at the other side of the door. Eventually, the door opened and he returned to take his seat at the other side of the long desk. 'I've just spoken to Mrs Thatcher,' he said, 'and she's approved of our plans for an assault should the forty-five-minute deadline bring us to a negative situation. However, she wishes to remind all concerned that we cannot afford a repeat of Desert One. This operation must be successful.'

'It will be,' the Controller said.

The Secretary nodded. 'May I suggest, then, that we take a short break and meet back here just before six? Personally, I'll spend the time having a light snooze, which should settle the whisky in my stomach and enhance my thought processes.'

'I'll get in touch with my Blue and Red Team

leaders,' the Controller said, 'and check that they're prepared.'

'I'll stay here by the telephone and TV,' the Commissioner said, 'and keep in touch with events. If anything happens, I'll call you.'

'You do that,' the Secretary said, then stood up and left the room with the Controller.

Forty-five minutes later, just before six o'clock, the three men, along with representatives of the Foreign Office and the Ministry of Defence, met around the same long table in the same basement room in Whitehall. Learning that the latest deadline had just passed, that no Arab ambassadors had materialized, and that so far there had been no response from the terrorists, every man in the room sensed that the time for negotiation was over.

'If he produces unambiguous evidence that a hostage had been murdered,' the Secretary finally announced, 'the Deliberate Assault Plan will be put into effect. Please prepare for it.'

Instantly, the Controller phoned the SAS FHA, right next door to the Embassy, to put his Blue and Red Teams onto a ten-minute stand-by.

Before that time was up, however, a phone call from the assistant to Commander Peter Duffy, head of the Anti-Terrorist Squad, informed them that at that very moment the Imam was in the police negotiating room on the second floor of Alpha Control and had just finished speaking to Salim on the radio phone.

Unfortunately, the conversation had been heated and not remotely successful, with the Imam begging Salim to wait until the ambassadors had finished their meeting in the Arab League office in Mayfair and Salim responding that if the ambassadors did not turn up in thirty minutes, he would kill not one but two hostages. When the Imam tried pleading for Salim to think again, the latter slammed his phone down.

Even as the Imam was telling the police that he was 'very disturbed' by Salim's tone of voice, the radio telephone rang again. When one of the negotiators picked it up, he was told by Salim that he had changed his mind and was not going to wait for another thirty minutes. Instead, he would kill a hostage in two minutes.

The Imam rang Salim back to quote the Prophet Muhammad to him, but Salim slammed the receiver down again.

A few seconds later, when the Imam's phone rang again and he picked it up, at first he heard nothing but heavy breathing.

Then he heard the sound of three shots and the line went dead for the last time.

*　　*　　*

When the Secretary, who had taken the call from Commander Duffy's assistant, put the phone down, he relayed the story to the rest of the COBR team. Shocked, they hardly knew what to say and instead turned to the television set in the corner. A newsflash had just begun. The screen showed the Iranian Embassy for what seemed like an awfully long time. Eventually, the front door was opened and the eyes of a terrorist appeared above a tightly wound *keffia*, peering out cautiously. When the door opened further, two other men could be seen inside, tugging at something heavy, trailing it laboriously across the broken glass on the lobby floor until they reached the entrance. There they turned back into the building, pushed the heavy object out onto the street, then slammed the door.

A corpse lay like a sack of rubbish on the pavement. It was Abbas Lavasani.

13

A small group of nervous policemen dashed to where the murdered press officer lay and hoisted him onto a stretcher. After carrying him back to one of the waiting ambulances, they were able to identify the corpse. The police pathologist, while not yet able to ascertain the exact time of death, was able to establish immediately from the coldness of the body that Lavasani had been dead for hours. He had therefore not been killed by the shots heard just a few minutes ago.

'Either there's another dead body inside,' the pathologist said, 'or Salim has just killed one man and fired those second shots as part of a bluff.'

'It makes no difference now,' the superintendent replied. 'Just a few minutes ago Sir David McNee, our guvnor, telephoned to say he was committing the SAS to action. It's out of our hands now.'

This was true. At seven minutes past seven,

171

the Controller formally took control and hurried back to the SAS FHA at the Royal College of Medical Practitioners, next door to the Embassy. There he found his men already getting into their flame-resistant underwear. The Controller took a seat at the far end of the dormitory while the men continued dressing by putting on their black CRW assault suits with flame-barrier knee and elbow pads; GPV wrap-around soft body armour with hard ceramic composite plates front and back; and specially reinforced, flame-resistant boots. Though the CRW assault suits each had an integral S6 respirator with nose-cap filter, anti-flash hood and goggles, the men would leave these hanging loose until the operation began.

When they finished dressing and were look-ing, as the Controller thought, suitably sinister, they opened their lockers and withdrew their per-sonal weapons. Sitting on the end of his bed, each man thoroughly cleaned his new Heckler & Koch MP5 sub-machine-gun by removing the magazine, cocking the action and ejecting the 9mm round. He then stripped the weapon and cleaned the working parts by threading the metal beads of the pull-through down the barrel and then oiling the breech-block. This task completed, he reas-sembled the weapon, replaced the thirty-round magazine, snapped home the cocking handle and set the safety-catch. Much the same process was used for the Browning 9mm High Power hand-gun, the Remington 870 pump-action shotgun and, in the case of the sniper team led by Sergeant 'Paddy' Shannon, the L42A1 .303-inch bolt-action sniper rifle.

Even as the members of the sniper team were checking and snapping shut their steel bipods, the Red and Blue Teams were checking their webbing, spare ammunition, ISFE, CS gas and MX5 stun grenades. The Heckler & Koch magazines were worn on the left hip, the Brownings on the right, and the spare High Power magazines worn on the left thigh and right wrist, the latter for rapid magazine changes.

As each man finished his preliminary tasks, he sat on the edge of the bed and waited for the others. When the last of the men was done, the Controller stood up to give the final briefing. First he checked his watch and asked all his men to do the same.

'It is now exactly 1915 hours,' he said, 'so please ensure that you all have the same time.' As the men checked their watches, the Controller said: 'The operation commences in five minutes. While we prepare ourselves on the roof, a police negotiator will be keeping the terrorists distracted with promises of a bus to the airport and PC Lock as his driver. You all know your tasks, but let me just summarize again.'

He paused to let those adjusting their watches do so before putting on their black, skin-tight aviator gloves, then continued.

'Red Team is to clear the top half of the building, from second to fourth floors. Blue Team will tackle the lower half from the basement and garden upwards to the first floor, and handle evacuation procedures and the undiplomatic reception on the rear lawn.'

Glancing at Red Team's Staff-Sergeant Harrison and Blue Team's Staff-Sergeant Jock Thompson, he received a nod of acknowledgement from both.

'Once on the roof of Number 16, Red Team's Call Sign Two will lower a frame explosive down the skylight well, lay it as accurately as possible on the window frame, and blow out the skylight at fourth-floor level. Red Team's two groups, Call Sign One and Call Sign Two, each of four men, will then abseil in separate waves from the roof. Two men from Call Sign One will continue down to the ground floor terrace to hack through the back doors and enter with flash-bangs. Call Sign Two will drop to the first-floor balcony and break in through the window with the use of explosives

174

and, if necessary, sledgehammers. To attack the third floor, the remaining two men from Call Sign Two will descend from the roof onto a sub-roof at the rear, known as the lighting area. As all of you men have been allocated your individual tasks, I give this information solely for the benefit of Blue Team, who should know what you're up to.'

'I'm still worried about those windows,' Harrison said. 'I mean, anything we personally recommend has to be tough to get through.'

The Controller waited until the men had stopped laughing.

'The only uncertainty about that concerns the explosive power needed. Each team is therefore being equipped with a special frame charge, approximately the same size as the windows, and packed with a carefully calibrated quantity of plastic explosive. If you plant the frames against the window surround and then explode them, I think they'll do the job.'

He paused to let all of this sink in and to let them ask questions. There were no more questions.

'Blue Team is in charge of the basement at garden level,' the Controller continued, 'along with the ground floor and first floor. Theoretically, all that should be required to get in is an explosive charge to put in the french windows overlooking the ground-floor terrace at the back and a similar bit of surgery on the first-floor front balcony window leading to the Minister's office. As that balcony adjoins this building, access to it shouldn't be a problem. Blue Team, supported by the Zero Delta sniper team facing the building, will also be responsible for firing CS gas canisters into the second-floor rear windows, where we believe the hostages are being held, though they might have been moved by now. The same team is responsible for evacuation of those found inside and will supervise the reception party in the garden afterwards. Any questions?'

There were still no questions, so the Controller looked directly at Sergeant Shannon, leader of the sniper team.

'The sniper teams led by Sergeant Shannon will be divided into two groups and located in a block of flats at the rear of the Embassy and at a camouflaged position in Hyde Park, at the front. When the attack commences they will pump CS gas through the broken windows and also give the assault groups covering fire if and when terrorists emerge from inside the building, either onto the balconies or through the doors. Any questions so far?'

Again there were no questions.

'Once inside the building, you will proceed to your separate tasks as outlined in the merged

Immediate Action Plan and Deliberate Assault Plan and rehearsed with the scale model of the building in the Regent's Park Barracks. Resistance is to be met with force and you will shoot to kill. You will not attempt to distinguish between terrorist and hostage. Anyone found inside the building will be manhandled out onto the back lawn, where Blue Team will supervise their reception. This briefing is now at an end, so are there any last questions?'

'Yes,' Sergeant Inman said. 'Who's directing the operation? And from where?'

'The whole operation will be orchestrated by a command group, led by me, operating from a sixth-floor flat overlooking the rear of the Embassy.'

'Out of sight of the journalists,' Jock said.

The Controller grinned. 'I think you've got the picture. Any *more* last questions?' There were none, so he checked his watch, then looked up and said: 'Let's go.'

Even as the negotiator at ground level kept talking to Salim, PC Lock and Sim Harris, keeping them distracted, the twelve-man assault team stood up and marched awkwardly out of the large room, heavily burdened with their weapons, ammunition, break-in tools, abseiling equipment and explosive frames. After making their way up the stairs, the eight members of the Red Team's two groups emerged, via a skylight, in the fading light of evening, onto the roof of the college adjoining the Embassy. The men of the Blue Team took another route, emerging quietly onto the balcony that led from that building to Number 16. There they stopped and waited.

The time was exactly seven-twenty p.m.

Once on the gently sloping roof, the men of the Red Team made their way carefully and silently to the adjoining roof of the Embassy, codenamed 'Hyde Park', and spread out to go about their separate tasks. The four men of Call Sign Two, led by Lance-Corporal Phil McArthur, went immediately to kneel down by the well around the fourth-floor skylight and prepare the explosive frame to be lowered by rope. As they were doing so, the men of Call Sign One went to the rear of the building, overlooking the lawns 80 feet below. There they found the ropes still tied to the chimneys and coiled beneath them, as they had been from the first day of the siege. Slinging their sub-machine-guns over their shoulders, they proceeded to put together the three components of the abseiling equipment by clipping the metal descendeur to the harness, then slipping the recently purchased nylon rope through the descendeur. Standing on the edge of the roof, each man of the abseiling team covered his face with his respirator, hood and goggles, checked that the integral microphones and radio receivers were working, and prepared himself, psychologically and physically, to go over the side.

The abseilers looked like black-clad deep-sea divers.

By now, the four men of Call Sign Two had fixed ropes to the four sides of the large frame explosive and were lowering it down the well to the fourth-floor skylight. When the frame was dangling just above the skylight, they manoeuvred it into position by tugging gently on the ropes, then dropped it carefully over the frame of the skylight so that both frames were more or less matching. When this had been done, the men lay the ends of the four ropes gently on the roof, set the explosive charge with a timer and electronic detonator, then covered their faces with their respirators and joined the other abseilers on the edge of the roof overlooking the rear of the building.

Meanwhile, on the balcony behind protective walls at ground-floor and garden level, the Blue Team, who had already covered their faces with their respirators and goggles, waited with explos-ives and ladders, each man tuned into the radio fre-quency that would enable him to strike the moment the attack signal, 'London Bridge', was given.

At that very moment, the attention of Salim and his fellow terrorists was being distracted by the promises being made by the police negotiators. Each time the negotiators called, which they were now doing constantly, first making a promise, then trying to wriggle out of it, Salim would become more agitated and distracted.

The male hostages in the telex room, Room 10, overlooking Princes Gate, and the female hostages in Room 9, on the second floor, were becoming increasingly fearful as the protracted negotiations continued and Salim came close to the end of his tether.

Finally, at the request of the now very disturbed Salim, PC Lock phoned the negotiators again, asking them to get the bus to the Embassy as soon as possible because the terrorists were expecting an attack any minute. When the negotiators smoothly denied that such an attack was on the agenda, Salim wrenched the phone from PC Lock to personally complain that he could hear suspicious noises all around the building.

'No strange noises, Salim,' the police negotiator replied smoothly, glancing at his watch.

At that precise moment, an explosive charge blew away the reinforced skylight roof.

The attack had begun.

14

From the first day of the siege the police had made it perfectly clear that reporters and cameramen, while permitted to view the front of the Embassy, would not be given entry to any area or building affording a view of the rear, where most of the SAS assault would take place.

That evening, an ITN news director, determined not to be obstructed in this way, smooth-talked his way past the police guarding the barricade and was permitted to take a brief stroll along Exhibition Road. Halfway along the road, he stopped to have what appeared to be a casual conversation with the night porter of a block of flats which looked onto Princes Gate. One top-floor flat in particular, he learned, had a good view of the rear of the Embassy and its gardens.

Returning along Exhibition Road, the ITN man thanked the police for their courtesy, then made his way back to the immense press enclosure in Hyde Park, opposite the Embassy.

The following morning, the owner of the top-floor flat in Exhibition Road gave permission to ITN for a TV camera to be installed in his apartment, in the room that overlooked the rear of the Embassy. The problem was getting it in there.

Later that morning, shortly before noon, two men dressed in business suits and carrying suitcases covered in stickers indicating that they had travelled a lot clambered out of a black cab that had stopped at the police barricade at Exhibition Road. The businessmen explained to the police that they had just been abroad and were about to stay with a friend who lived along Exhibition Road.

The police guard kindly informed the cab driver as to how he could enter Exhibition Road by another route. The cabby thanked him and drove off, taking the businessmen with him.

About ten minutes later, the two well-travelled businessman got out of the cab, paid the driver, and carried their suitcases across the pavement to the building that overlooked the rear of the Embassy.

Like all of the blocks of flats in Exhibition Road at that time, this one was guarded by a policeman. However, when the owner of the top-floor flat told the policeman on duty that he was expecting the callers, they were allowed to enter the building with their well-travelled suitcases.

Once in the top-floor flat, the two 'businessmen' opened the suitcases and withdrew a lightweight ITN TV camera, micro-link equipment and a radio telephone. They set up the camera at the window, then sat behind it and waited patiently.

At seven-twenty p.m. on Day Six of the siege, the ITN news director was back in the press compound, watching his monitor. While most of the other TV cameras were focused on the front of the Embassy, he was receiving a view of the back, from a high vantage point.

As he studied the monitor, he was stunned to see what appeared to be a group of eight sinister, black-clad figures, all wearing respirator masks and carrying weapons and other equipment, emerging via a skylight on the gently sloping roof of the Royal College of Medical Practitioners and making their way stealthily across to the roof of the besieged Embassy.

The formerly secret SAS were about to appear on television all around the world.

15

At the radio signal 'London Bridge' Staff-Sergeant Harrison slipped on the harness and bravely stepped backwards off the Embassy roof to begin his dangerous descent down the 80-foot wall. Hanging out from the wall did not make for a comforting sensation, but Harrison gamely lowered himself down, using the descendeur to control the speed of his drop.

'First man over,' a voice said in his electronic headset. 'Second man over.'

Glancing up, Harrison saw the second Red Team abseiler, Trooper Ken Passmore, about five feet above him, stepping backwards off the edge of the roof, using his booted feet for leverage as his body arched out over the fearsome drop to begin the descent. Satisfied, Harrison glanced down and saw the third-floor window about ten feet below him. Growing more optimistic and excited, he continued his descent, first passing the attic floor, then approaching the balcony window below it.

He had travelled no more than 15 feet when his rope snagged, leaving him dangling just below the attic floor, above the third-floor window.

'Damn!' he exclaimed into his throat mike. 'The bloody thing's seized up!'

'Oh, no!' Ken replied, his voice eerily distorted in Harrison's earphones.

Frustrated, Harrison attempted to unsnag the harness. When he touched it, he almost burned his fingers, and cursed softly.

'What's happened?' Trooper Passmore asked, now dangling a few feet above him, unwilling to drop any further until Harrison moved.

'This new rope,' Harrison said. 'Bloody awful rubbish! It's overheated because of the friction caused by my weight and then ravelled into a knot. Damn!' he muttered, wriggling frantically 65 feet above the rear terrace and lawns, turning this way and that, his feet pressed to the wall, as he tried to disentangle himself. 'I can't unravel the bloody thing!'

Inching lower in his own harness to stop right above him, Ken tried to set him free. For a moment he felt dizzy, looking down at that dreadful drop, but he managed to get a grip on himself and endeavoured again to set Harrison free. Suddenly, by jerking too hard, he made his harness go into a spin and instinctively swung his feet out to prevent himself from crashing into the wall. To his horror, he heard the sound of breaking glass.

'Shit!' he hissed.

Glancing down, he saw that his booted foot had gone through the third-floor window, smashing the pane. The glass broke noisily, some shards raining into the room, others falling all the way down to the terrace, where they were smashed to smithereens, making even more noise.

'Christ!' Harrison groaned in frustration and mounting anger. 'We're compromised already.' Knowing that this was true, and shocked that it had happened so quickly, he snapped into his throat mike: 'Go! Go! Go!'

At that moment, the frame placed over the well skylight exploded with a mighty roar, smashing the glass, shaking the whole building, and causing part of the roof to collapse, the debris raining down on the stairs joining the front and rear second floor.

Simultaneously, Sergeant Shannon's sniper team, Zero Delta, located behind a high wall at the front of the building, began firing CS gas canisters through the broken windows.

From ground positions in front of the Embassy,

other members of Zero Delta fired CS gas canisters into the second floor, smashing the windows.

While Harrison and Ken Passmore struggled in their harnesses just above the broken third-floor window, the second pair of abseilers, Inman and Baby Face, dropped down past them, not stopping until they reached the ground-floor terrace. Another pair, Phil and Alan, dropped rapidly to the first-floor balcony window.

Once on the terrace, Inman and Baby Face released themselves from their harnesses. With a swift, expert movement, the staff-sergeant swung his pump-action shotgun into the firing position and blasted the lock off the doors, causing wood splinters and dust to stream out in all directions. Kicking the doors open as Inman dropped to one knee, holding the Remington in one hand and withdrawing his Browning with the other, Baby Face hurled a couple of MX5 stun grenades into the library and rushed in even as they were exploding. Inman followed him, turning left and right, preparing to fire a double tap if he saw any movement.

Though their eyes were protected from the blinding flash by the tinted lenses in their respirators, a combination of condensation on the lenses, natural adjustment to the half-light, and the swirling smoke from the flash-bang made them view the thousands of books on the walls through what seemed like fog.

'Not a soul here,' Inman said as the condensation on his lenses cleared but the smoke continued swirling about them, 'so let's get down the stairs.'

When Inman had slung the Remington over his left shoulder and removed his sub-machine-gun from his right, they hurried out of the library and went straight to the stairs to the cellar. There they were joined by a couple of other Red Team soldiers, emerging from a cloud of swirling smoke like bizarre insect-men from another planet.

'We have to clear the rooms downstairs,' Inman said into his throat mike. 'Was that your brief, too?'

'Yes.'

'Then let's go.'

Though aware that terrorists might be hiding in the cellar and that the entrance could be booby-trapped, they wrenched away the ladders covering the door, tugged the door open, and made their way carefully down the stairs, into the gloom below. Though there was a commotion in the Embassy above them, the cellar was deadly quiet.

'Careful,' Baby Face warned Inman as he took

the lead going down, prepared to fire his Browning. 'We can't see a bloody thing down there.'

Agreeing with Baby Face, Inman, when only half-way down, hurled a stun grenade, which exploded with a thunderous crack that ricocheted eerily around the basement. Getting a brief look at the cellar in the brilliant, fluctuating illumination of the flash-bang, he saw no sign of movement and decided that it was safe to descend all the way.

Reaching the corridor at the bottom, he carefully tried the door of the first room but could not open it.

'Locked,' he said. 'They're probably all locked. Well, let's unlock 'em.'

Taking aim with his Browning, he 'drilled' the lock with a couple of 9mm bullets, causing more wood splinters and dust to fly away. When the lock had been blown off, he dropped again to one knee and gave cover as Baby Face threw in a flash-bang and rushed in with the others, aiming left and right, as the grenade exploded and illuminated the room with its brilliant, phosphorescent light.

The room was empty.

'OK,' Inman said, still kneeling by the door, holding his Browning in the firing position, 'let's try the next one.'

They applied the same procedure to the next

189

room, found it empty, and so tried the next one along, which also was empty. They repeated the SOP all the way along the corridor, clearing one room after another, but finding all of them empty.

On entering the last room, however, Inman thought he saw something moving. Instantly, he let off a burst of twenty rounds from his sub-machine-gun. This produced a catastrophic, metallic drumming sound. When the bullets stopped hitting the rolling target, he saw what it was.

'A bloody dustbin!' Baby Face cried out from behind him. 'You've got a quick trigger finger, Sarge!'

'Go screw yourself,' Inman said.

Heading back up the cellar stairs and into reception, they crossed a hallway filled with the smoke from stun grenades and burning curtains. It was also filled with the noise of other members of the assault teams who, having burst into the building from the front and rear, were now clearing the rooms on all floors with a combination of flash-bangs, CS gas grenades, and all the skills they had picked up in CQB training in the 'killing house' in Hereford. The walls and carpets in the hallway and along the landings were singed black and shredded by a combination of grenade explosions and bullets. The smoke was darkening and spreading.

'Christ, what a mess!' Inman said.

He and Baby Face headed for the smoke-wreathed stairs, where they could hear the hysterical voices of female hostages. When they reached the source of the bedlam, they found soldiers forming a line and passing the women down with a speed that left little time for kindness. Most of the women seemed to be in shock, and their eyes were streaming from the CS gas. They were guided down the stairs and through the library, then out onto the lawn. Some were weeping with joy.

Though the Embassy seemed crowded with soldiers, some were still outside. Indeed, on the first-floor balcony, the plan to blast a way through the rear french windows had to be abandoned because of the risk of injuring or killing Staff-Sergeant Harrison, still struggling with Ken Passmore to break free of his harness and now in danger of being burned alive by the flames pouring out through the third-floor window.

'Damn it, Passmore, do something!' Harrison was bawling as both of them twisted in their harnesses, swinging in and out, scorched by the flames and choking in the smoke, vainly trying to release the jammed descendeur. 'This bloody thing is going to be over before we get in there. 'Come on, Passmore! *Do something!*'

'It won't budge!' Ken shouted.

Denied the use of explosive, Alan and Phil, now on the first-floor balcony, smashed through the windows with sledge hammers and threw in flash-bangs. They were releasing themselves from their harnesses and clambering into the office of the chargé d'affaires even as the brilliant flashing from the stun grenades was lighting up the room.

At the front of the Embassy, the Blue Team, caught in the golden light of the early evening and in full view of the stunned reporters and TV cameras in Hyde Park, clambered from the adjoining balcony and along the ornate ledge until they reached the heavily reinforced windows of the Minister's office.

Glancing sideways as he made his way along the ledge, Jock saw the police cordon in the street below and the press enclosure across the road, where a lot of TV cameras raised on gantries were focused on the Embassy and, it seemed, on him. Startled, he looked away and continued his careful advance until he came up behind the first two men.

Danny Boy and Bobs-boy, being the first at the window, saw Sim Harris staring at them in disbelief from the other side of the glass.

'Get down!' Danny Boy bawled through his respirator. 'Stand back and get down!'

Though clearly stunned, the sound recordist did as he was told, standing away from the window to let Danny Boy and Bobs-boy, who were being covered by Jock and GG, place the frame charge over the window.

While they were still putting their plastic strip charges in place, a terrorist armed with a Polish-made Skorpion W263 sub-machine-gun appeared at the second-floor window of the telex room immediately above them. The man flung the window open and hurled something down.

'Grenade!' Jock bawled.

However, clearly the terrorist had forgotten to draw the detonating pin and the grenade bounced harmlessly away. That was his first mistake. His second was to expose himself at the window long enough to become a target for the SAS sniper, Sergeant Shannon, hiding across the road in Hyde Park. Aiming along the telescopic sight of his bipod-mounted L42A1 .303-inch bolt-action sniper rifle, Paddy hit the man with a single round. The terrorist staggered back, dropping his gun, then disappeared from view.

As the frame charge blew in the first-floor window, filling the air with flying glass, Jock hurled in a stun grenade. The exploding flash-bang ignited the curtains and filled the room with smoke.

Suddenly, Sim Harris reappeared, emerging ghost-like from the smoke and looking gaunt. Carefully approaching the window, he leaned out to stare disbelievingly at the SAS men in their black CRW suits, body armour, respirators and balaclava helmets.

'What . . .?'

'Get the hell out of there,' Jock said. Ignoring the flames, he and Danny Boy grabbed Harris by the shoulders and roughly hauled him out through the smashed window, onto the balcony, where they pressed him down onto his hands and knees. 'Stay here and keep your head down,' Jock told him, 'until you're told to do otherwise. Wait till someone comes for you.'

As Jock and the other three Blue Team members scrambled through the window, a revitalized Harris sat up on his haunches and shouted excitedly after them: 'Go on, lads! Get the bastards!'

By now, Phil and Alan, of the Red Team, had made their way across the smoke-wreathed stairs of the first floor. There they heard shouts from an adjoining office – that of the Minister's secretary.

Rushing in, they found the police hostage, PC

Lock, struggling violently with a bearded terrorist who was holding an RGD5 hand-grenade in one hand and a Skorpion W263 Polish sub-machine-gun in the other. Though clearly in pain, PC Lock was wrestling gamely with the bearded terrorist, holding his right wrist to prevent him from hurling the grenade and falling with him over the furniture in a noisy mêlée. Lock had drawn his own .38 Smith & Wesson revolver and was trying to put it to the terrorist's head with his free hand, but either he just could not manage it or he was reluctant to kill at close quarters.

As the two men wrestled furiously, Phil grabbed Lock with his free hand and jerked him away from the terrorist, whom he recognized instantly from photographs as the leader, Salim.

'Trevor, leave off!' he bawled.

As Phil turned away from Lock, Salim, who had almost fallen over, was trying to regain his balance. Before he could do so, the lance-corporal fired a burst of automatic fire at his head and chest and his fellow SAS man, Alan, did the same, both using their MP5 sub-machine-guns. Hit by fifteen bullets, Salim was thrown backwards like an epileptic having a fit and smashed down through the furniture to lie face up in the rubble on the floor.

He died instantly, becoming the martyr he had long dreamed of being.

Heading across the first-floor landing towards the rear of the building, past burning curtains, through pockets of smoke, and brushing against other hurrying, bawling SAS soldiers, Phil and Alan tried the door to the Ambassador's office.

'Locked!' Phil said into his throat mike.

He was raising his MP5 to blow the door open when it was opened from within and he found himself face to face with a youthful terrorist armed with a Browning.

Before Phil could fire again, Alan, just behind him and to the right, fired a short, savage burst from his MP5. The terrorist screamed and staggered back into the room, then Phil threw a stun grenade after him. The combined blast and flash threw the terrorist even further back and made him stumble blindly. Alan fired a second time, making the terrorist scream out again, but instead of falling he gained the strength of the desperate and staggered deeper into the smoke-filled room, eventually disappearing.

'Shit!' Alan cried, squinting to see through the condensation on his respirator lenses, as well as through the smoke.

'He's still alive, he's wounded and he's desperate,' Phil said to his mate. 'And he's got a weapon.'

'We can't see a damned thing in there,' Alan said.

'We can't let that bastard get away.'

'So let's go in after him.'

They advanced into the room, but as they entered the smoke, Phil felt himself choking.

'Shit!' he spluttered. 'It's CS gas and it's penetrated my respirator. I'm choking to death. I've got to get out of here.'

Coughing harshly, he staggered outside, ripped his respirator off, breathed the air, which was filled with the less noxious smoke from burning curtains, then placed his respirator back over his face and took deep, even breaths.

'Anybody got a light?' Alan shouted into his throat mike, now trapped in the dense smoke in the room and not able to see a thing.

Jock, on his way up from the ground floor, heard Alan's cry for help. Hurrying up the stairs, he found Phil about to re-enter the smoke-filled room.

'Let me go first,' Jock said. 'I've got a torch bolted to my MP5.'

Turning on the torch and holding the MP5 as if about to fire from the hip, he advanced into the room with Phil beside him. When he moved the sub-machine-gun left and right, up and down, the thin beam of light from the torch illuminated the darkness and, eventually, Alan.

Not wishing to speak, Alan used a hand signal to indicate that he thought the terrorist was hiding in the far left corner of the room. Nodding, Jock moved towards the trooper, waited until he had fallen in beside him and Phil, then led them carefully through the dense smoke, aiming the barrel of the MP5 left and right, up and down, lighting up the darkness and, more dangerously, pinpointing his own position to the hidden enemy.

No shots were fired at him and eventually, in that thin beam of light, Jock, Phil and Alan saw a hand, then a face . . . and then a Browning.

The wounded terrorist was sprawled on a large sofa near the bay window overlooking the garden. He was covered in blood. When he weakly took aim with the pistol, his hand shook and wavered uncertainly from left to right.

The three SAS men all fired their Heckler & Koch MP5 sub-machine-guns simultaneously, stitching the terrorist repeatedly, throwing him into convulsions, making him writhe dementedly and shake like a rag doll in the hands of an angry child. Pieces of torn upholstery, foam-filling and feathers exploded from what had been a luxurious sofa, only to drift back down like snow on his bloody remains.

This time, hit by twenty-one bullets, the terrorist did not survive.

At the rear of the building, on the third floor, some Red Team members were still in serious trouble. On the outside wall, just below Ken Passmore, Staff-Sergeant Harrison remained trapped in his abseiling harness, dangling and kicking ever more frantically 75 feet above the rear terrace. To make matters worse, flames from the fire were now roaring out of the general office window and starting to burn up his legs. To avoid being burnt even worse, and also to avoid choking in the billowing smoke, he had been kicking himself away from the wall, as if on a swing. However, this helped very little, for each time he swung back to the wall, he found himself in the smoke and flames again.

'Cut me loose!' he finally bellowed in desperation.

'Jesus, boss, I . . .'

'Just do it!'

Aware that if he cut the nylon rope, Harrison could plunge to a brutal death, Ken was reluctant to do so. Nevertheless, with the fire in the third-floor room growing stronger and the flames licking out through the window to coil up on the wind and attack the staff-sergeant, Ken saw that he had no choice. He therefore withdrew his Fairburn-Sykes commando knife from its sheath and, with a great deal of effort, being himself trapped in mid-air and scorched by the flames, hacked through the nylon cord snagged in the descendeur.

'Any second now!' he bellowed as the last threads were shredded.

Harrison fell through the flames onto the balcony. Burnt and blistered, but free at last, he smashed the third-floor window with his small, belt-held sledgehammer, hurled in some stun grenades, and swung himself into the smoke-filled interior of the large general office, where, according to their briefing, most of the hostages were held.

The room was empty. It was also locked, barricaded and piled high with inflammable material that had just been ignited by the flash-bangs.

Nevertheless, when Ken had followed him into the room, Harrison advanced blindly with his trooper through the dense smoke and flames until he reached the locked door, which he recognized only after tracing it with his fingertips. Already in a temper because of his bad start, he blew the locks apart with a couple of shots from his Browning. The locks gave way in a hail of dust and wood splinters, but the doors, barricaded from the other side, remained firmly locked.

'I'm going to try another route,' Ken said.

Retreating to the balcony, he clambered across to an adjoining window ledge. From there he could see inside the room, where a terrorist was striking matches to set fire to paper piled up against the wall. Before the terrorist could look up and see him perched on the ledge, Ken smashed the window and hurled a stun grenade. The explosion shook the terrorist and temporarily blinded him; so, although he managed to raise his pistol to fire, he fled from the room instead.

Still perched on the window ledge, Ken aimed his MP5 and fired from the hip.

The weapon jammed.

Cursing, Ken drew his Browning, clambered off the ledge, dropped into the room, and went after the terrorist, the former mechanic Shakir Sultan Said. He lost the terrorist temporarily in the smoke, but then saw him racing into what Ken knew, from his frequent rehearsals with the plywood model of the Embassy, was the telex room, where most of the male hostages were held. It was off to the right across the landing, which was covered in smoke.

Unseen by Ken, another terrorist, Shakir Abdullah Fadhil, the group's second in command, had just run into the room with Badavi Nejad and Makki Hounoun Ali, when Said, fleeing the trooper, also reached it. Seeing the unarmed male hostages huddling fearfully together in the corner of the room, Fadhil swept them with a burst of automatic fire from his Skorpion W263 sub-machine-gun, causing them to turn into a shuddering mass of blood-stained protoplasm in which, for the moment, it was impossible to tell who had been hit and who spared.

Inspired by this gross act, Badavi Nejad emptied his .38 Astra revolver into them as well.

The Embassy doorman, Abbas Fallahi, at least knew that he had been hit – and saved. Checking for wounds as he crouched with the other frightened hostages, some of whom were now covered in blood, he discovered that he had only been saved from death because a 50-pence coin in the right pocket of his jacket had deflected the bullet. Fallahi was just uttering profound thanks for his salvation when a canister of smoke, fired from the other side of Princes Gate, smashed through the window of the telex room, hitting him and knocking him to the ground as the room filled with smoke.

Having helped in the attack, Badavi Nejad dropped his pistol in panic and wriggled his way in amongst the surviving hostages. As he was doing so, Fadhil was throwing his sub-machine-gun through the window and emptying his pockets of ammunition. Said, being the last to enter, could think of nothing to do other than stand in the smoke-filled room with his finger crooked inside the pin of a grenade.

Ken, now being followed by Harrison, heard the shots and screams of the victims as he charged towards the telex room. Even as he was rushing towards that sound, some of the surviving hostages were wriggling away from the group on the floor, grabbing the discarded weapons and ammunition of the terrorists and throwing them out of the window into the street below.

With his MP5 in his left hand and his Browning in his right, Ken reached the telex room, kicked the door open and immediately turned the corner, crouching, gun raised in a classic CQB stance. When he saw the figure to his left, grenade in hand, he quickly fired a single round at the head. Entering Said's skull just below the left ear, the 9mm bullet exited through his right temple, blowing out blood, bone and brains, and killing him instantly.

Emerging from the general office and following the sound of shooting, Harrison, still in a raging temper, soon reached the telex room, where he found one dead terrorist, one dead hostage and two badly wounded men.

'Who's a terrorist?' he heard himself bawling

angrily before he could stop himself. 'Who's a terrorist?'

Receiving no reply, he grabbed the first English-looking person he could find and jerked him roughly to his feet.

'I'm not a terrorist. I'm Ron . . .'

Before the caretaker could say anything, Harrison, despite the dreadful pain of his burns, threw him roughly across the room towards the door where, he knew, other SAS men would manhandle him, none too gently, down the stairs, through the library and out onto the rear lawn where, like all the others, terrorist and hostage alike, he would be laid face down on the ground and trussed up like a chicken.

'Who's a terrorist?' Harrison shouted again, hardly recognizing the sound of his own voice. 'Who's a damned terrorist?' An Iranian face looked up from the smoke-wreathed, blood-soaked group on the floor. 'You!' Harrison bawled. 'Who are you?'

'The cultural . . .'

'Who are the terrorists?'

Jock and GG burst into the telex room as the Iranian on the floor pointed tentatively at two men sitting with their backs to the room and their hands on the wall. Before Harrison or anyone else could say anything, Jock and GG fired a sustained burst at the two men, hitting one in the head and the other in the neck and pelvis, punching both of them forward face first into the wall, where they slid shuddering down to the floor, leaving a trail of blood.

'Stay there!' Harrison bawled at the others. 'Don't move unless instructed!' He turned to Jock and GG. 'Let's check them quickly for weapons, then get them out of here. Keep your eyes peeled for terrorists.'

The first thing they did was separate the wounded and the dead from those still untouched. Among the hostages attacked by the terrorists, Dr Afrouz, the chargé d'affaires, had been hit by two bullets, one of which passed through his right thigh; Ahmed Dagdar, the medical adviser, had been savagely wounded by six bullets; and another member of staff, Ali Samad-Zadeh, had been killed outright.

As nothing could be done for the last-named – or indeed for the dead terrorist already identified as Shakir Sultan Said – GG, as a medical specialist, temporarily staunched the wounds of the two wounded hostages with field dressings. Satisfied that he had done all he could here, he left the room with Jock to take part in the evacuation of the building and the 'undiplomatic reception' outside on the back lawn.

16

Even before the survivors were moved out of the choking atmosphere of the telex room, Harrison, now cooled down, and Ken, still level-headed, tried to identify the 'worms' who had wriggled their way into the huddled mass on the floor.

The hostages, some with eyes streaming from CS gas, others covered in the blood of those killed or wounded, all dishevelled, most in shock, were bundled out one by one, then passed by the chain of Red Team soldiers along the corridor with its smouldering curtains, bullet-peppered walls and blackened carpets, down the smoke-filled stairs, across a hallway reeking of stinging CS gas, all the way out through the relatively untouched library and onto the rear lawn, where darkness was falling.

The first 'worms' were easily identified because they had forgotten to remove their green combat jackets. Others, however, had had the sense to do so and were marched with the genuine hostages down the stairs to the lawn, where the female hostages were already face down on the grass, their hands and feet tethered.

One of them did not make it that far. As the last of the hostages was being taken from the telex room, the Red Team searched the suspects and were put on their guard by two who seemed too wary and alert to be hostages.

'If they're hostages I'm Donald Duck,' Ken said.

'And I'm Mickey Mouse,' Harrison replied, increasingly impressed by the trooper. 'Let's have a talk with them.'

Leaving both men to the last, they waited until the other hostages had left, then spoke first to the smaller, more nervous of the two suspects.

'Lie down,' Harrison told him.

The man did so, stretching his arms above his head without being asked, like someone used to the experience.

'Who are you?' Harrison asked, standing over him and aiming him MP5 at his spine.

'Student. I am student.'

'I'll bet you are,' Harrison murmured. Stepping away, but keeping the suspect covered, he nodded to Ken. 'Search him,' he said.

The trooper did so, running his hands over the

suspect's body, then pushing his legs open and inspecting his crutch. There he saw the glint of metal – something that resembled a pistol magazine – and then a holster tangled up in the trousers.

'Well, well,' Ken said dryly, 'what have we here, then?'

Suddenly drawing his arms in towards his body, the suspect started rolling over onto his back. Before he could do so, Harrison fired a short burst into his back, killing him instantly, and punching him belly down again, onto the floor.

When Ken turned the body over, he found a hand-grenade as well as the magazine for a .38 Astra revolver. 'Little bastard,' he said. Quickly frisking the body, he came up with an Iraqi identity card, the details of which he read aloud to Harrison. 'Makki Hounoun Ali, twenty-five, a Baghdad mechanic.'

'A mechanic who carries a .38 revolver,' Harrison replied. 'Pull the other one, darling.'

Harrison turned to grin at Ken, but when he did so, he saw the trooper and his double, standing almost side by side, though one was slightly overlapping the other, slightly transparent, like a ghost.

At first Harrison was shocked, thinking he was hallucinating. Then he realized that his burns on his legs were hurting dreadfully and that the pain was causing him double vision. Though the pain remained agonizing, he heaved a sigh of relief.

'I'm not feeling too good,' he confessed. 'I think I'd better go out and see the medics. Can you handle the rest of this?'

'Sure, boss.'

'Good man,' Harrison said.

He turned away to leave the room, felt nauseous, saw two of everything, then fell down through a spinning, light-flecked darkness into oblivion.

Shocked, Ken leaned over him, checked that he was still breathing and realized that he had passed out from a combination of pain and exhaustion. Using the throat mike on his respirator, he called up the special medical team, asking for a stretcher.

While the normally sharp-eyed trooper was thus engaged, the second suspect, Fadhil, the second in command, slipped away into the smoke and gathering darkness, where he mingled with the last of the freed hostages on their way down the stairs.

The members of the Blue Team who had cleared the basement and ground floor had met up with the other members of the Blue and Red Teams from the upper storeys to form the chain along which the hostages were now passed or – as some would later have it – thrown from hand to hand down the stairs and out through the library, then onto the lawn to be trussed up for more intensive body searches and interrogation. Brutal though this would have appeared to the uninitiated, it sprang from the soldiers' fear that the terrorists might have hidden an explosive charge on one of their own people or on a hostage, as their final response to this attack.

Formerly of the Blue Team, now part of the Red, Sergeant Inman was standing in the chain, next to Baby Face, about halfway down the main staircase linking the first floor to the ground, when he heard the sounds of what he thought was a scuffle above him and shouted a warning to the Red Team members up on the landing.

To his relief, it was only the last of the hostages stumbling down the stairs, most of them looking frightened and dishevelled, their eyes streaming from CS gas. Then Inman, with eighteen years of hard experience behind him, saw a face that was calculating rather than scared. That was all he needed to see.

'That one's a terrorist!' he bawled.

The sound of his voice cut through the fearful atmosphere like a knife as those dark eyes under an Afro hairstyle stared down in panic. Instantly recognized as a terrorist by his green combat jacket

210

— Inman's outburst had merely confirmed it for the doubtful — the man was struck on the back of the head by the butt of Phil's MP5. After crying out and stumbling forward a few steps, he advanced down the broad stairs almost at the crouch, his hands over his head as he was punched and kicked down by the chain of soldiers.

When he drew level with Inman, the latter saw a Russian fragmentation grenade with the detonator cap protruding from his hand. Without thinking twice, the sergeant removed the MP5 from his shoulder and slipped the safety-catch to automatic. Unfortunately, his own mates were in the line of fire and prevented him from shooting at the terrorist. Frustrated, he raised the weapon above his head and brought the stock down on the back of the Arab's neck, hitting him as hard as he could. The terrorist's head snapped backward.

At that moment, the four Red Team members at the top of the rubble-strewn stairs opened fire simultaneously, emptying their magazines into the terrorist as he fell. First convulsing wildly in the murderous hail of bullets, then rolling down the stairs and coming to rest on the floor, the terrorist spasmed and vomited blood. He then opened his hand to release the RGD5 grenade, which rolled a short distance across the floor and then came to a stop, making a light drumming noise on the tiles.

Luckily its pin was still in its housing.

After hurrying down the stairs to frisk the dead man, Inman withdrew a wallet containing an identity card and some other papers.

'Shakir Abdullah Fadhil,' he pronounced after studying the items in his hands. 'Also known as Feisal. Aged twenty-one, born in Baghdad, and another Ministry of Industry official. I'll bet he was.' Pocketing the identify card and papers, which he would pass on to Military Intelligence, Inman leaned over the body to make a rough count of the bloody wounds. Straightening up again, he said to the soldiers still on the stairs: 'There are almost forty bullet holes in that bastard and he deserves every one of them.' Grinning, he added a few last words: 'And the pubs haven't closed yet.' Then the sergeant sauntered through the library and out onto the rear lawn.

For some time after that incident, more shots echoed throughout the building as the SAS men blasted away locks to check other rooms. The fires that started with the burning curtains had now engulfed the top of the building and the smoke was forming black clouds that drifted all the way down.

The integral UHF radio headsets in the men's respirators crackled into life as the Controller informed them that the building was ablaze and must be abandoned.

'The Embassy is clear. I repeat: the Embassy is clear.'

Outside on the lawn, most of the hostages were lying face down on the grass, their feet and hands bound. Those remaining were being processed the same way.

Sim Harris, also bound hand and foot, but grateful to have escaped with his life, was asked to identify any surviving terrorists. There was only one left. Identified by PC Lock and Harris, as well as the other survivors, he was Badavi Nejad, also known as Ali Abdullah. Dragged roughly to his feet by Inman and Baby Face, he was handed over to the police and driven away without delay.

Sim Harris, as he lay on the rear lawn, listening to the complaints of another trussed-up hostage, said: 'Think yourself lucky.'

Inman heard the remark. Grinning, he turned to Baby Face and said: 'Now doesn't that make it all worth while?'

'Go screw yourself, Sarge,' Baby Face said with a grin. Then he walked away, heading back to the FHA next door to meet up with his mates.

17

The SAS assault on the Iranian Embassy at 16 Princes Gate, London, ended approximately fifty minutes after it began.

Fifteen minutes later, back in the Forward Holding Area in the Royal College of Medical Practitioners, next door to the Embassy, those who had taken part in the operation stripped off their CRW assault kit, packed it into their civilian holdalls, and wrapped their Heckler & Koch MP5 sub-machine-guns in plastic bags to be taken away for examination, this being the first time they had been used by the Regiment.

'The shortest battle I ever fought,' Jock said. 'It must be some kind of record.'

'Right,' Harrison replied. 'Fifteen minutes to clear the building, thirty-five minutes to check the premises and conduct an undiplomatic reception for the poor sods we rescued – won't they love use? – then another fifteen minutes to pack up our gear and move out of the FHA. Sixty-five minutes from start to finish, then back to Hereford. Not bad at all, mate.'

'We'll be in the *Guinness Book of Records*,' Jock said. 'Take my word for it.'

'No, we won't,' Harrison replied, being more of a realist than his Scottish friend, 'because we don't exist. At least, not officially.'

'We *didn't* exist,' Jock emphasized, 'but we certainly do now. We're all TV stars.'

'Then God help us, Jock.'

Just before leaving the college to enter the Avis vans that would take them back to their temporary bashas in Regent's Park Barracks, the SAS men received a visit from the Home Secretary, William Whitelaw, who, with tears in his eyes, thanked them for all they had done.

Approximately two and a half hours after the siege had ended, the Commanding Officer of 22 SAS handed back control of the cleared, though badly damaged Embassy to the Deputy Assistant Commissioner of the Metropolitan Police, thus officially ending SAS involvement.

Out of a total of twenty-six hostages taken in the Embassy, five had been released before the assault, nineteen had been rescued, and only two had died, neither killed by the SAS.

The survivors included the caretaker, Ron Morris, and PC Lock, who was awarded the George Medal.

There were no SAS casualties at all.

Five of the SAS men were personally decorated by the Queen. Four received the Queen's Gallantry Medal, and one received the George Medal.

Those facts reflected great credit on the SAS and, combined with the fact that most of the operation had been viewed by television viewers worldwide, made theirs, virtually overnight, the most renowned regiment in modern military history.

The sight of those sinister, hooded, well-armed, black-clad figures entering a smoke-filled building in the middle of London captured the public imagination and turned the SAS, formerly anonymous, into the focus of relentless public and media scrutiny, for good or for ill.

The deterrent effect of Operation Pagoda was evident from the fact that no similar event occurred in the United Kingdom for more than a decade afterwards. That single SAS operation had, in effect, protected London from a particularly odious brand of international terrorism.

Ironically, after the inquest and the trial of the surviving terrorist, there was media criticism of the force used by the SAS. The official response from Hereford was that the object of the operation was to rescue hostages and that to do so in a burning building reported to have been wired for a 'Doomsday' explosion did not leave the assault force any other option.

Though the Regiment then tried to sink back into its former anonymity, concentrating on intelligence gathering and security in the absence of a major military task, it never fully regained its former, generally preferred anonymity.

Indeed, twelve months later, at a private bar in Hereford, some of those who had taken part in the Embassy siege could still be heard excitedly discussing it while drinking their beer and Scotch.

'My first time on TV,' Jock Thompson said. 'When I clambered across that first-floor balcony, I almost found myself posing.'

'You should have blown the press a kiss,' Phil McArthur told him. 'They would have loved you for that.'

'A disaster,' someone else said out of the blue, having just arrived, unexpected, at the bar. 'They should have kept the press out of there altogether. That's *my* opinion.'

All those in the small group stared in surprise at the quietly spoken Baby Face, who looked like an innocent schoolboy but was known to be deadly.

'A disaster?' Alan Pyle repeated, as if not hearing right. 'Are you kidding us, Baby Face?'

'This Regiment's supposed to work in secrecy,' Baby Face informed him, 'and that means we should never be seen on TV, discussed on the radio, or even read about in the papers. All that's gone since the Princes Gate siege and I think it's a bad thing.'

'Aren't you proud of what you did there?' Corporal George Gerrard asked. 'I mean, what we all did there was something pretty special, so you shouldn't resent the world knowing about it.'

'I just mean . . .' But Danny could not explain it. Even back home, in Kingswinford, where he was willing to admit that he had fought in Northern Ireland, he refused to let anyone know that he had been one of the sinister, black-clad figures on the roof of that Embassy. He was certainly proud of what he had done, but he disliked the way the operation had been blown up by the papers. The SAS had always taken pride in staying in the background, but the Iranian Embassy affair had destroyed its anonymity and even made it notorious. Baby Face hated the thought of that.

'I loved it,' Sergeant Inman confessed. 'It made me feel like a star. I used to feel like a dick-head, just another faceless soldier, but now everywhere I go, when I say I'm in the SAS, women cream at the sight of me, men burn up with envy, and everyone wants to know what we get up to. I think I'm going to write a bestseller about it.'

'Better be quick,' Jock said. 'You might have left it too late. That Trooper Andrew Winston – the big black bastard from D Squadron – has already had some of his bloody awful poems published and now thinks he's Tolstoy.'

'Who's Tolstoy?' Ken asked.

'I know him,' Bobs-boy Quayle said. 'Not Tolstoy – Andrew Winston. He fought in Defa and Shershitti, in Oman, in the mid-1970s. He's a fucking good bloke.'

'Good man or not, he's getting his poems published,' Jock said, 'and he claims he's going to write about the Regiment and make his name overnight.'

'It just goes to show what this Regiment's becoming,' Inman muttered, licking his moist lips. 'There was a time when no one knew we existed, but Princes Gate changed all that.'

'Not for the best,' Baby Face said. 'I'm certain of that. As for you, Sarge' – he looked straight at Inman – 'you wouldn't be thinking of wasting your time writing if you had another decent war to fight.'

'I think you're right,' Inman replied, 'but alas,

there won't be another war. Those days are gone
for good.'

'God help us,' Jock said.

That conversation took place during a celebratory drink in the Paludrine Club at the SAS base,
Bradbury Lines, Hereford, on 5 May 1981, precisely one year after the Princes Gate siege. Eleven
months later, on 2 April 1982, a garrison of British
Royal Marines guarding Port Stanley, capital of
the Falkland Islands, was forced to surrender to
Argentinian forces. Three days later, a Royal Navy
Task Force sailed for the Falklands. The very same
day, but in secret, D Squadron, 22 SAS, flew out
of England on a C-130 Hercules transport plane,
bound for Ascension Island and another war.

SOLDIER M: SAS

INVISIBLE ENEMY
IN KAZAKHSTAN

Peter Cave

1

Moscow – March 1945

General Sergei Oropov sucked deeply on a thin, knobbly cheroot of black Balkan tobacco, inhaling the acrid smoke and attempting to savour it. Failing, he sprayed it out from between his clenched teeth, sending it jetting on its way with a convulsive, chesty cough. The faintly blue smoke rose towards the high ceiling of the large, overheated and airless office, blending into a murky pall made thicker by the steam escaping from a leaking radiator. The heating system, along with the ventilation fans, had been faulty for over three months now, and it was still impossible to find labour sufficiently skilled to fix it.

'Thank God this damned war will soon be over,' Oropov muttered testily, knowing that it could be merely a matter of weeks before Germany was finally forced to capitulate. Russian troops had almost reached the Oder, the Western Allies had established a firm bridgehead east of the Rhine and troopers of Britain's already legendary 1 and 2 Squadron SAS ranged throughout Europe, organizing and arming local resistance fighters and carrying out long-range reconnaissance and sabotage attacks as far north as Hamburg and Lübeck.

The remark was not really intended as dialogue,

1

more as a private thought expressed aloud. Nevertheless, Oropov's companion took it up, seizing on the opportunity for a mild rebuke to be administered, a propaganda point to be gained.

Tovan Leveski's thin lips parted slightly in a mirthless smile. 'One does not thank God any more – one thanks Stalin. It was the strength of the Russian bear which crushed the German jackal to death. But of course, comrade, I agree with your sentiments, at least. It will be good to have our brave young men back from the German front – to finish our necessary business in Poland.'

It was Oropov's turn to smile, but with faintly malicious humour.

'That too, of course. Although, personally, I was more looking forward to buying some decent Cuban cigars.'

Oropov's grey eyes twinkled briefly as Leveski twitched, reacting uncomfortably to the obvious jibe. It felt good to score a point over the man, whom Oropov both disliked and distrusted. It was not just the fact that he was, basically, a civilian; it went a lot deeper than that, with potentially more sinister implications.

Leveski represented a new and unknown quantity. The exact nature of his sudden new post was ill-defined, as if deliberately vague. There were mutterings and rumours in the corridors of the Kremlin. No longer obsessed with matters of war, Stalin was stirring politically again. There was talk of new purges to come, of heads rolling and personnel once again disappearing at short notice and in suspicious circumstances. Stalin's feared secret police, previously concerned with purely internal matters, were now extending their awesome powers. Now the newly formed KGB, with people like Leveski at its head, were moving in to take an active interest in military, European and overseas matters. It impinged directly on Oropov's authority as head of wartime intelligence, and it was extremely disquieting. It was definitely a time for staying on top, and being clearly seen to be on top. A time to know exactly what was happening all around oneself – and, even more important, who was making it happen and why.

With these thoughts in mind, Oropov decided it was politic to adopt a more conciliatory attitude towards his companion.

'Speaking of Poland, Tovan Leveski, what news from Warsaw?'

Leveski shrugged, a gesture of vague irritation. 'Mixed, as ever. Confused and conflicting reports, rumours, snatches of Allied propaganda. The usual wartime rubbish. The very thing my new department was set up to rationalize.' He broke off to nod deferentially towards Oropov. 'With your cooperation, of course, comrade.'

'Of course,' Oropov said, nodding, his face suddenly more serious. 'I was merely a soldier, doing a soldier's job in a time of war. Now we must all work together in the cause of peace, and for the good of the Motherland.'

The brief speech presumed a response. Predictably, Leveski obliged.

'A toast, comrade?' he suggested.

'A toast indeed.'

Oropov slid open a drawer in his desk and drew out

a quarter-full bottle of Stolichnaya and two conical, stemless glasses. He handed one to Leveski, filled it, then splashed a generous measure into his own.

'*Rodina*,' Oropov grunted, waving the glass briefly in the air before placing it to his lips and draining the fiery vodka at a single gulp.

'*Rodina*,' Leveski responded with suitable fervour in his voice. The word translated simply as 'The Motherland', but it carried the patriotic zeal of an entire national anthem to anyone with a drop of Russian blood in their veins. In a society which had largely turned its back on the Church, it was the litany of a new and potent religion.

The time for pleasantries was over, Oropov decided. It was obvious that Leveski had not entered his office on a purely social visit. He returned the bottle of vodka to his desk, smiling up at the man politely. 'Well, Tovan Leveski, what can I do for you?'

The little man cleared his throat, managing to make the apparently innocent gesture a censure of Oropov's smoking habit.

'We are a little concerned about the lack of information currently on file regarding Allied armaments projects.'

Oropov ignored yet another implied rebuke. He raised one shaggy eyebrow the faintest fraction of an inch. '*We*, comrade?'

'I,' Leveski corrected himself hastily, uncomfortably aware that he had just let something slip, without fully understanding its relevance. Just like General Oropov, he had yet to adjust fully to the scope of his position and powers. 'I find myself slightly worried about the gaps in our intelligence. I was briefed to acquaint myself fully with current military research, but I find some of your dossiers and files rather sparse, to say the least.'

Oropov made a steeple of his fingers, pressing them gently against his lips. He eyed Leveski stonily. 'Specifically?'

'Specifically, this "Manhattan Project". As a military man, you must surely appreciate the momentous implications of a nuclear fission bomb. Yet we appear to have no idea at all just how advanced the Americans are in its development. Cause for worry, would you not agree, General?'

'Indeed,' Oropov agreed. 'And, equally, a matter for the tightest and most efficient security screen we have ever encountered. The potential power of atomic weaponry is not lost on the Americans, either. Our files represent our finest efforts and the deaths of two top agents. I assume you have followed up on the cross-reference file relating to the German research facility at Telemark?'

Leveski nodded. 'Of course. Again, a woefully thin report and a disgusting fiasco. The damned Norwegians and the Allies made fools of us. It should have been Russian troops who stormed that laboratory. Then the secret of heavy-water production would be in Soviet hands, not at the bottom of some damned fiord.'

'Our troops were otherwise engaged at the time,' Oropov pointed out rather icily. 'But a tragic loss to Soviet science, I agree. However, I understand our own atomic research facility is now well established.'

Leveski's lips curled into a sneer. 'Oh yes, two or

three years behind the blasted Allies, at a conservative estimate.'

He hunched his shoulders, as if to subdue a shiver of rage, finally releasing only a faint shrug. 'However, that is past news. What matters now is the future. Do we have any active personnel inside the Manhattan Project?'

Oropov shook his head. 'No one with scientific knowledge, I'm afraid. There is a woman – a minor clerical worker – who is able to send us copies of purchasing invoices, interdepartmental memos, that sort of thing. We are able to glean a little theoretical knowledge, but not much else.'

Leveski digested all this information for a while, assimilating it into the dossier in his brain.

'Have we made any attempts to get to the man Oppenheimer direct?' he asked finally. 'Our records suggest that in his postgraduate days, at least, he had certain . . . sympathies?'

Oropov spread his hands in a gesture of resignation. 'A fact also realized by the Americans. Oppenheimer is a very important man, and a deeply mistrusted one. His every move is closely monitored. It is impossible to get an agent within shouting distance of him.'

'So we have nothing? No one? No chance of further information. Is that what you are telling me?'

Oropov was beginning to wilt under the mounting attack. 'It's not as bad as that,' he countered, somewhat lamely.

'No? Then please tell me how bad it actually is, comrade.'

Leveski knew that he had his man on the run

now. There was little point in any further pretence at friendliness.

'There *is* one man – in England. Klaus Fuchs. We have him as a sleeper. He is not attached to the Manhattan Project, but his work involves him in a closely related field. In a year or two, perhaps, he may be of great use to us.'

'A year or two?' Leveski said dismissively. He rose from his high-backed chair, his mouth twitching angrily with barely repressed frustration. 'In a year or two, comrade Oropov, Russian science will be left behind like a sick, abandoned animal. Out in the cold, waiting to die.'

There was a slight tremor in Oropov's voice when he finally spoke again. He was acutely aware that Leveski had only just started to show his claws, and the Kremlin rumours were beginning to assume a chilling reality.

'What is expected of me, comrade Leveski?'

'You don't know? Then I had better spell it out for you,' Leveski sneered. 'The demands of this war, and sheer Nazi fervour, have resulted in one of the greatest explosions of science and technology this world has ever known. Those scientific breakthroughs are the key to the future – the richest and most precious spoils of war. At this very minute the Allies are picking their way across Europe like scavengers, snatching up the juiciest morsels. Physicists, rocket experts, engineers, designers, the finest brains of Germany – all falling into capitalist hands. Any day now the Western powers may have the secret of the atomic bomb. In a matter of a few years, the power to deliver it across oceans and continents. In a decade, world domination in their pockets. And if that happens, comrade, we might as well sell our bodies and souls back to the Tsars, because we will have lost everything this great nation has struggled and bled for. Something the Russian people would never forgive, General. And perhaps more important to you, personally, something that *I* would never forgive.'

The gauntlet was down. Oropov struggled to control a nervous shiver, and failed. His voice was little more than a croak.

'What do you want me to do, comrade Leveski?'

The man was now regarding him with undisguised contempt. 'I'm glad that you finally realize how high the stakes are, General. And, no doubt, the penalties for failure. I want a short-term plan. A definite and positive strategy to ensure that Russia snatches some worthwhile prize from this war. Give me a phoenix from the ashes, General – that is all.'

Leveski turned on his heel and moved towards the door. He delivered his parting shot over his shoulder, without turning round. 'You have forty-eight hours, General. I expect to see a detailed report on my desk by Thursday.'

He closed the door quietly, almost gently behind him. Strangely, this seemed to reinforce the aura of menace he left behind him rather than lessen it.

Alone now, Oropov gave up the uneven struggle to stop his hands from shaking. He delved into his desk, pulled out the vodka bottle and uncorked it with his teeth. Holding the bottle directly to his lips, he gulped down the harsh spirit. It did little to thaw out the icy chill he felt in the pit of his belly.

He stared blankly across his office at the closed door

through which Leveski had exited, racking his brain for a single optimistic thought. There was nothing. One realization swamped everything else. War, or at least *his* kind of war, was coming to an end, and a completely new kind of war was about to begin. With a terrible sense of resignation, he knew that he had little if any part to play in the waging of it.*

* In August 1945, three days after the second atomic bomb fell on Nagasaki, General Sergei Oropov was arrested by the KGB, found guilty of treasonous activities against the State, and executed by firing squad. All files relating to his last assignment, which he had code-named Project Phoenix and put into operation some two months previously, were removed from Military Intelligence and taken to KGB headquarters.

2

Berlin – June 1945

The two jeeps zigzagged through the rubble-strewn streets on the outskirts of what had once been the thriving city of Berlin. Another brilliant innovation from David Stirling, who had created the concept of the SAS in 1941, the small, nippy and versatile American vehicles were ideal for the war-torn terrain. Gutted, smashed and burned-out buildings formed an almost surrealist landscape which could have come straight from the tortured imagination of Hieronymus Bosch.

Corporal Arnold Baker, known affectionately to his comrades as 'Pig-sticker', or usually just 'Piggy', in tribute to his prowess with a knife, surveyed the dead city from the passenger seat of the leading jeep.

'Jesus, this was some savage fucking war,' he said gravely, shaking his head as though he still could not quite believe the evidence of his own eyes.

His driver, Trooper Andy Wellerby, sniffed dismissively. 'Save your bleeding pity, Corp. When was the last time you saw London? Or Coventry, for that matter.'

'Yeah.' Piggy took the point, tearing his eyes away from the desolation and concentrating once more on the road in front of him. 'What's that up ahead?'

Wellerby waved his arm over the side of the battered Willys jeep, signalling for the vehicle behind him to slow down. He tapped lightly on the brake and squinted into the distance. Just over a quarter of a mile further up the long, straight road towards Brandenburg, a line of military vehicles sealed it off. Wellerby could make out a line of about a dozen uniformed figures standing guard beside the vehicles. He groaned aloud.

'Not another bleeding roadblock? Bloody Yanks again, I'll bet. It's about time somebody told those bastards that it was us Brits who invented red tape.'

Piggy was also concentrating on the grey-uniformed soldiers. He shook his head slowly. 'No, they're not GIs, that's for sure. Uniform looks all wrong.'

Wellerby let out a slightly nervous giggle. 'Maybe it's a bunch of fucking jerries who don't know the war's over yet.'

It was meant to be a joke, but one hand was already off the steering wheel and unclipping the soft holster of his Webley .38 dangling from his webbing. At the same time Piggy was checking the drums on the twin Vickers K aircraft machine-guns welded to the top of the jeep's bonnet. In the utter chaos of postwar Germany, just about anything was possible. All sorts of armed groups were out on the streets, both official and unofficial, from half a dozen nations which had been caught up in the conflict. Quite apart from regular soldiers and covert operations groups, there were resistance fighters with old scores to settle and ordinary citizens with murder in their hearts. Even a shambling line of what appeared to be civilian refugees or released concentration camp prisoners might conceal one or two still dedicated and still fanatical Waffen SS officers who would kill rather than surrender.

'Damn me. They're bloody Russkies,' Piggy blurted out, as he finally recognized the uniforms. He sounded indignant rather than surprised.

'What the hell are the Russians doing setting up roadblocks?' Wellerby wanted to know.

Piggy shrugged. 'Christ knows. Everyone's getting in on the act. And I thought we had enough problems with the Yanks, the Anzacs and our own bloody mob.'

It was the light-hearted complaint of a fighting soldier increasingly bogged down in the problems of peace. The war might be over, but Berlin was still a battleground of bureaucracy, with checkpoints and roadblocks everywhere and dozens of garrisons of different military groups still waiting for Supreme Allied Command to work out a concerted policy of occupation. For the time being, it was still largely a policy of 'grab something and hold on to it'. Or just follow the orders one had, and muddle through.

But even so, it did not pay to take chances. The intensive training, both physical and mental, which any potential SAS trooper had to undergo did more than just produce a soldier whose reflexes and abilities were honed to near-perfection. It developed a sixth sense, an instinct for trouble. And Piggy Baker had that instinct now. There was something not quite right about the situation – he could feel it in his bones.

'Pull up,' he muttered to Wellerby out of the corner of his mouth. As the jeep stopped, he turned to the second vehicle as it, too, came to a halt some six yards behind.

Behind the wheel, Trooper Mike 'Mad Dog' Mardon looked up with a thoughtful smile on his face. 'Trouble, boss?'

Piggy shrugged uneasily. 'I don't know,' he admitted. 'But something smells.'

Mad Dog grinned. 'Probably just our passenger. The little bastard's been shitting himself ever since we picked him up.'

Piggy glanced at the small, bespectacled civilian sitting stiffly and uncomfortably in the rear of the vehicle. Stripped of its usual spare jerrycans and other equipment, the jeep was just about capable of carrying two passengers on its fold-down dicky seat. Just as he had throughout the journey, the German looked blankly straight ahead, ignoring Trooper Pat O'Neill, who guarded him with his drawn Webley held across his lap.

'Pat, I need you up at the front,' Piggy said. He nodded at the jeep's own pair of Vickers guns. 'On the bacon slicer, just in case.'

O'Neill glanced sideways at his prisoner. 'And what about Florence Nightingale here? Little bastard might decide to do a runner.'

'Improvise,' Piggy told him.

'Right.' O'Neill cast his eyes quickly around the jeep, finding a length of cord used to lash down fuel cans and fashioning it into a makeshift slip-noose. Dropping it over the German's neck, he pulled it tight and secured the loose end to the mounting of the spare wheel. Satisfied with his work, he crawled into the passenger seat and primed both the Vickers for action.

13

Piggy felt a little easier now, but there was just one last little precaution to take. He reached to the floor of the jeep and hefted up his heavy M1 Thompson sub-machine-gun. Slamming a fresh magazine into place, he slipped off the safety-catch and leaned out over the side of the jeep, jamming the weapon into a makeshift holster formed by the elasticated webbing round the spare water cans. The weapon was now concealed on the blind side of the Russian troops, and ready for action if it became necessary.

There was not much more he could do, Piggy thought. He glanced sideways at Wellerby. 'Right, take us in – nice and slow.'

The two jeeps approached the Russian roadblock at a crawl. Despite Winston Churchill's eventual conviction that Stalin was one of the good guys after all, there was still a deep-seated mistrust between the two armies.

As Wellerby brought the leading vehicle to a halt, Baker studied the line of twelve Russian soldiers some ten yards in front of him. They stood, stonily, each cradling a PPS-41 sub-machine-gun equipped with an old Thompson-like circular drum magazine. If it had not been for the uniforms, they would have looked exactly like a bunch of desperadoes from a Hollywood gangster film.

There was something about their stance which made Baker feel even more uneasy. In the heady aftermath of victory, most Allied soldiers had tended to let discipline relax, and embrace a general feeling of camaraderie. These Russians looked as though they were fresh out of intensive training and ready to ship out to the front line.

He stood up in the jeep, scanning the line for any sign of an officer. There was none. 'Who is in charge here? Does anyone speak English?' he asked in a calm, authoritative tone.

There was no response. The Russian soldiers continued to stare straight through him, virtually unblinking. Several seconds passed in strained silence.

Inside the cab of one of the covered Russian personnel carriers, Tovan Leveski examined the occupants of the two jeeps thoughtfully. He too had been a little confused about their uniforms from a distance, having been briefed to expect a standard British Army patrol. Now, at close hand, he could see that these were no ordinary British soldiers. Clad in dispatch rider's breeches, motorcycle boots and camouflaged 'Denison' smocks, they could have been anything. But it was their headgear which finally gave the clue. The beige berets, sporting the unique winged-dagger badge, clearly identified them as members of that small, élite force which had already started to become almost legendary. Clearly, even four SAS men were not to be taken lightly.

Quietly, Leveski murmured his orders to the eight more armed soldiers concealed in the truck behind him. Satisfied, he opened the passenger door and dropped down to the ground.

Piggy regarded him cautiously. Although the man ostensibly sported the uniform and badging of a full major in the Red Army, he seemed to lack a military bearing. However, the 7.62mm Tokarev TT-33 self-loading pistol in his hand certainly looked official enough.

'I am in charge of this detachment, Corporal,' Leveski said in flawless English.

It was a sticky stand-off situation, Piggy thought to himself. Even with the incredibly destructive firepower of the Vickers to hand, he and his men were hopelessly outnumbered – and there was no way of knowing how many other armed troops were inside the vehicles which made up the roadblock. Besides, military bearing or not, the officer still outranked him. For the moment there was nothing to do except play it by ear. They were no longer in a war situation, after all. Apart from the Germans and Italians, everyone was supposed to be on the same side now.

'Do you mind telling me the purpose of this road-block?' Piggy demanded.

Leveski smiled thinly. 'Certainly. My orders are to monitor all military movement on this road, Corporal. Perhaps you in turn would be so good as to tell me the exact nature and purpose of your convoy.'

Piggy considered the matter for a few seconds, unsure of what to do. His orders had been specific, but were not, as far as he was aware, secret. He could think of no valid reason to withhold information, yet something rankled.

'With respect, Major, I fail to see what business that is of the Russian Army.'

Leveski shrugged faintly. 'Your failure to understand is of absolutely no concern to me, Corporal. 'What does concern me, however, is your apparent lack of respect for a superior officer and your refusal to cooperate.'

Piggy conceded the point, grudgingly and despite the dubious circumstances. 'All right, Major. I am

16

leading a four-man patrol to escort a German prisoner of war to the railway marshalling yards at
Brandenburg. And, since I have a strict schedule to
adhere to, I would appreciate it if you would order
your men to clear the road so that we can continue.'

'I'm afraid I can't do that,' the Russian said in a flat,
emotionless tone. 'You and your men are in breach
of the Geneva Convention, and I cannot allow you to
continue.'

Piggy stared at the Russian in disbelief, starting to
lose his temper.

'Since when has it been against the rules of the
Convention to transport prisoners of war?'

'Military prisoners are one thing, Corporal. Civilians are another matter,' Leveski informed him
calmly. 'You do have a civilian in your custody,
do you not? One Klaus Mencken – Dr Mencken?'

'Doctor?' Piggy spat out the word, in a mixture
of loathing and ridicule. 'My men and I have
come directly from Buchenwald concentration camp,
Major. This "doctor" was in charge of horrific,
inhuman experiments on Jewish internees there. His
speciality, I understand, was removing five-month
foetuses from the womb for dissection. The man
is a war criminal, Major, and is on his way to an
international trial to answer for those crimes against
humanity. So don't quote the Geneva Convention
to me.'

The impassioned speech seemed to have had no
effect on the Russian, who continued to speak in a
calm, emotionless voice. 'I must insist that you hand
Dr Mencken over to me.'

'By what damned authority?' snapped Piggy, openly

17

angry now, having had more than a bellyful of the Russians.

'By the authority of superior strength.'

The new voice came from a few yards away.

Baker's eyes strayed to his right, where a Russian captain had just jumped down from the back of one of the personnel carriers. The man walked unhurriedly towards the leading jeep, being very careful to stay out of the line of fire of the Vickers.

'I am Captain Zhann,' he announced. 'You and your men are in the direct line of fire of no less than eighteen automatic weapons. Now please, Corporal, I must ask you to move back from that machine-gun and order your men to step calmly out and away from your vehicles. If you do not comply, my men have orders to open fire. You would be cut to ribbons, I can assure you.'

It was a threat that Piggy found easy to believe. Assuming that the remainder of the concealed troops also carried the thirty-five-round PPSh-41 sub-machine-guns which were on display, the Russian captain had the cards fully stacked in his favour. Each individual weapon had an automatic firing rate of 105 rounds a minute, and in a full burst, a cyclic firing rate approaching 900 rounds a minute. And the 7.62mm slugs were real body-rippers. At that range, they would all be dead in the first five seconds. Still, there remained time for at least a token show of defiance.

'And if I refuse?' Piggy asked.

Zhann shrugged. 'Then you and your men will be slaughtered needlessly. A pointless gesture, wouldn't you say?'

Piggy could only stare at the Russian in disbelief.

The whole thing was crazy. It was peacetime, for Chrissake. They had all just fought the most bitter and savage war in human history. It was unthinkable that anyone would want to carry on the killing.

'You're bluffing,' he blurted out at last, suddenly convinced that it was the only explanation. 'Apart from which, you'd never get away with it.'

Leveski stepped forward again. 'I can assure you that Captain Zhann is conducting himself according to my specific orders,' he muttered chillingly. 'And what would there be to "get away with", as you put it? A simple mistake, in the confusion of a postwar city. A tragic accident. The authorities would have no choice but to accept that verdict.'

Piggy's fingers tightened around the firing mechanism of the Vickers. He moved the twin barrels a fraction of an inch from side to side – mainly to show Leveski that he had control.

'Aren't you and your captain forgetting something, Major?' he pointed out. 'If it comes to a shoot-out, it'll be far from one-sided. I can virtually cut your vehicles in half with one of these babies.'

The Russian gave one of his chilling smiles. 'What I believe the Americans call a Mexican stand-off,' he observed. 'However, we would still appear to have the advantage. As you see, I have four covered lorries. Only one of them contains armed troops. Your problem, Corporal, would be in knowing which one to fire on first. You must surely appreciate that you wouldn't get time for a second guess.'

It was becoming like a game of poker, Piggy thought. But what made the stakes so high? It made no sense at all. Unless, of course, the Russian *was* bluffing. No stranger to a deck of cards, Piggy decided to call Leveski's hand.

'You must understand that my men and I cannot be expected to surrender our weapons,' he said in a flat, businesslike tone. 'And I cannot believe that you would push this insanity to its logical conclusion.'

As if understanding his corporal's reticence to surrender without a fight, Trooper Wellerby spoke up.

'We ain't got a choice, have we, Corp? What's a piece of rubbish like Mencken to us, anyway? If the Russkies want him that bad, you can bet your sweet fucking life they ain't planning to take him to no birthday party.'

Piggy could not repress a thin smile. In attempting to make light of the situation, Wellerby had hit the nail on the head. He was right: what were the lives of three brave troopers measured against the Butcher of Buchenwald? If only a tenth of the stories about him were true, he deserved not an ounce of human consideration. Whether Mencken died from a British noose or a Russian bullet, it made no difference at all. On the other hand, Piggy knew that he had no moral right to condemn his men to almost certain death. He returned his attention to Leveski.

'All right, Major,' he said, 'in the interests of avoiding conflict, I will allow you to take the prisoner. But I must point out that I regard this as an act of hijacking and I will be reporting it to higher authorities as soon as we reach Brandenburg.'

Leveski allowed the faintest trace of satisfaction to cross his face. 'Your objections are noted, Corporal.' He began to walk towards the second jeep. Releasing the hastily made noose, he gestured for Mencken to alight and led the German towards the waiting Russian convoy.

Even now, the Nazi was arrogant. He still felt justified. He had just been obeying orders, he had done no wrong. He glared at Leveski defiantly. 'I suppose you Russian dogs intend to shoot me. Then do it, and get it over with. I would not expect the luxury of a trial from Bolshevik lackeys.'

Leveski ignored the insults, switching on his chilling smile. 'Shoot you, Herr Doktor?' he murmured in a low voice. 'Oh no. On the contrary, we are going to treat you like a VIP. You are going to Russia to join some of your colleagues. You will soon be working for us, Doctor — doing what you appear to enjoy doing most.'

He took Mencken by the arm, escorting him towards the nearest truck and bundling him up into the cab. Jumping in behind him, Leveski barked instructions to the driver, who fired the vehicle up into life and prepared to move off with a crunch of gears.

As the truck started to move, Leveski stuck his head out of the open window, nodding towards Captain Zhann. 'You have your orders, Captain,' he said in a low voice. 'We cannot afford any survivors to tell the tale.'

Zhann nodded curtly in acknowledgement, but his face was as grim as his heart was heavy. He was a good soldier, a professional soldier. And the job of the soldier was to kill the enemy, not murder what amounted to an ally. But an order was an order, and much as he detested the increasing power and influence of the KGB in military matters, to defy a command was to place his own life on the line.

He glanced at Piggy. It was a mistake which was to cost him his life. For in that fleeting look, Piggy saw something beyond the expression of respect for a fellow soldier. He saw regret, and he saw pity. Even as Zhann's hand twitched at his side in a prearranged signal, Piggy's highly tuned senses were already primed. That very special instinct was alerted, and his body tensed to respond.

Ninety-nine soldiers out of 100 would have missed the faint, muted click of a dozen PPSh sub-machine-guns being cocked simultaneously. Piggy did not. More importantly, he pinpointed the exact source of the sound immediately: third lorry, fifteen degrees to his right.

'Shake out,' he screamed at the top of his voice. Even as he yelled, the Vickers in his hands was pumping out its devastating 500 rounds a minute – a lethal cocktail of tracer, armour-piercing shells, incendiary and ball. Beside him, Wellerby had already dived over the side of the jeep, retrieved the Thompson and rolled back under the vehicle, from where he began raking the legs of the Russian soldiers who had been standing in line.

Piggy swung the spitting machine-gun along the side of the third lorry from the cab to the tailgate, concentrating his fire at the level where the side panel met the canvas cover. The fabric of the canopy shredded away like mist evaporating in the sunshine, whole sections of it bursting into flame and drifting into the air on its own convection currents. The side panel disintegrated into splinters of wood and metal, finally revealing the inside of the truck like the stage of some monstrous puppet theatre on which life-sized marionettes jerked and twitched in an obscene dance of death.

Caught on the hop, the rest of the Russian troops had reacted with commendable speed. Leaving their unfortunate colleagues who had caught Wellerby's raking ground-level burst from under the jeep writhing on the ground with shattered legs and kneecaps, those who could still move threw themselves down and rolled for what cover they could find.

The second set of Vickers never had a chance to open up. Pat O'Neill took a chest full of rib-splintering 7.62mm slugs which lifted him out of the jeep and threw him several feet behind it. He was dead before he hit the ground. Seconds later, Mad Dog caught it in the gut and slid lifelessly down in his seat, his head bowed forward like a man in prayer. Beyond the arc of the sub-machine-guns, two surviving Russian soldiers had rolled into a position from which they had a clear line of fire to the underside of the lead jeep. Andy Wellerby did not stand a chance as a deadly cone of fire from the two guns converged on his trapped and prone form.

Piggy had only the satisfaction of seeing Colonel Zhann's upper torso dissolve into a massive bloody stump before the Russian fire came up over the side of the jeep and caught him in the thighs and groin. He fell sideways, landing half in and half out of the jeep as the clatter of gunfire finally ceased.

Pain swamped his senses, but his eyes were still open and his brain could still register what they saw. Just before the blackness came down, Piggy saw the lorry containing Leveski and Mencken dwindling into the distance.

'We owe you one, you bastards,' he grunted from between clenched teeth just before he collapsed into unconsciousness.

Miraculously, Piggy survived. But he was to hobble for the rest of his life on a pair of crutches and one tin leg. Just one year after leaving the military hospital, he joined the Operations Planning and Intelligence Unit at Stirling Lines – ironically enough, nicknamed 'The Kremlin' – and had a distinguished career until his retirement in 1986. Throughout his service years, his colleagues would come to know him for one particular conviction, which became almost a catch-phrase.

'Never trust a fucking Russian,' Piggy would say. 'Never trust a fucking Russian.'

3

Puerto Gaiba, Bolivia – May 1951

The man who called himself Conrad Weiss watched the two strangers walking along the shabby riverside and knew that the day he had feared and dreaded for six years had finally arrived.

They were coming for him; of that Weiss had absolutely no doubt. The two men were smartly dressed and obviously Europeans – both extreme rarities in a little Bolivian backwater town on the River Paraguay. He assumed that they had been to his house and extracted directions to the boat from his wife. He hoped that they had not tortured or hurt her. Although he had originally taken Conceptua in bigamous marriage purely for reasons of political expediency, Weiss had grown genuinely fond of her and the two olive-skinned sons she had borne him.

The two men strolled unhurriedly towards the luxury motor cruiser, which stood out like a sore thumb among the jumble of dilapidated river fishing craft. Weiss thought, momentarily, of the loaded Luger he kept in his cabin locker, quickly dismissing it. If the men were coming for him they would be trained agents, armed and alert. Besides, even if he did manage to kill them both, others would follow. They knew where he was now.

It seemed best to play innocent, attempt to bluff it out. There was at least a reasonable chance of getting away with it, Weiss reasoned. His false Swiss identity papers were the flawless work of a master forger, and his assumed identity was rock solid. And, even if that failed to impress his investigators, he had distributed vast sums in bribes to corrupt Bolivian officials in high places. That should protect him against an official attempts at extradition. Of course, they might have plans to smuggle him out of South America forcibly. Or simply to kill him where he was. In which case, his six-year run of good luck would have finally run out.

Weiss had developed a philosophical attitude to what had basically been a second life for him. He had been incredibly lucky, and more than a little cunning. When the Allies had liberated Auschwitz, he had managed to slip through the net disguised as one of the Jewish prisoners. Undetected even after six weeks in a temporary transit camp, he had finally managed to buy his ticket to freedom from an American sergeant for a handful of gold nuggets. Whether that sergeant had ever known that those nuggets came from the dental fillings of murdered Jews, Weiss had never known, or cared. He had evaded everybody – even the British SAS units on special duty to round up and arrest known and suspected war criminals. At the time, that was all that had mattered.

For the gold itself, Weiss had cared even less, for it had represented but a small fraction of the fortune in stolen jewelry and valuables he had amassed during his four years in the death camp. It was that fortune which had bought him the identity of

Conrad Weiss, a retired Swiss watchmaker, and his passage to Bolivia.

But luck was at best a temporary phenomenon. The two men now mounting the gangplank of his boat both testified to that.

Bluff it out, then. Play the cards you held and hope for the best, Weiss decided. Propping himself up against the stern rail, he tried to look innocently surprised.

The first man aboard had a smile on his face, but his eyes were cold.

'Herr Weiss?'

The reply was non-committal. 'Who wants to know?'

'Ah, you are worried, cautious. As of course you should be,' Tovan Leveski murmured in good German. His hand dropped slowly and gently towards the front of his well-cut jacket, slipping open the buttons. He studied Weiss's eyes, following every move.

'Let me assure you, Herr Weiss, that we mean you no harm. We are not what you probably think we are. For a start, both of us are completely unarmed.' Leveski pulled his jacket aside carefully, to show that he was not wearing a waist or shoulder holster. He half-turned to his companion, motioning for him to do the same.

Weiss's surprise was genuine now. 'Who are you? What is it you want with me?'

'Just to talk. We have a little proposition to put to you. One that I think you will find extremely fascinating, my dear Doctor.'

The German's sharply honed survival instinct cut in automatically, despite Leveski's disarming manner.

'Doctor? Why do you call me doctor? I was a simple watchmaker in Switzerland until my retirement.'

The cold smile dropped from Leveski's face. 'Please do me the courtesy of crediting me with intelligence, Doctor. I have not come all this way to be insulted. You are Dr Franz Steiner. You were in charge of the medical research facility at Auschwitz from 1941 to 1945. Your highly specialized work concerned the grafting and transplantation of amputated limbs in human subjects. You were several years ahead of your time in recognizing the problems of spontaneous rejection – a problem which, I might add, has since been much more widely studied.'

Something told Steiner that, armed or not, Leveski was not a man to antagonize. His bluff had been called, yet no threats had been offered – only a tantalizing reference to his work. Steiner found himself increasingly fascinated.

'You have overcome the rejection problem? Isolated the antibodies which cause it?'

Leveski shook his head. 'Not yet, Doctor. But we will – or rather, you will. With our help, of course.'

Steiner suddenly realized that his first question remained unanswered. He repeated it. 'Who are you? What do you want with me?'

Leveski dipped his hand carefully into the inside pocket of his jacket and drew out his identity card, which he flashed under Steiner's nose. 'My name is Tovan Leveski. My companion is Viktor Yaleta. As you see, we are both official representatives of the government of the USSR.'

Leveski saw the look of uncertainty which flickered across the German's ice-blue eyes. 'You are surprised,

Doctor. You should not be. The fact that we may have been enemies in the past has no relevance to our business here today. It is something which transcends accidents of birth, mere geographical boundaries. We are talking about science, Doctor – pure science. Medical reasearch – the very future of the human race. Does that not interest you?'

Steiner shrugged off the pointless question. 'Of course. Who could fail to be interested?'

Leveski nodded towards the hatch which led down to the boat's cabin. 'Then perhaps we can discuss this in greater comfort?'

Nodding thoughtfully, Steiner turned, leading the two Russians to the short companionway.

'So, how did you find me?' Steiner asked, more relaxed now that the danger seemed to have passed, and mellowed by a large glass of local brandy.

Leveski smiled. 'Find you, Doctor?' He inclined one shaggy eyebrow. 'We never lost you. We have known your exact whereabouts since 1946. We simply had no use for your particular talents until now. Your work was well ahead of its time, as you probably realize.'

Steiner sipped at his brandy. 'And what exactly are you offering me?'

Leveski spread his hands in an expansive gesture. 'Virtually anything, my dear Doctor. The resources of the finest and most comprehensive research facility in the world. Unlimited funds, an inexhaustible supply of human subjects for experimentation. And, probably most important to you, Doctor, total freedom to conduct biological experiments without any ethical or moral restraints. The chance to play God, in fact.'

Even if Steiner had not already been hooked, this last phrase would have clinched it. His eyes had a dreamy, faraway glaze to them. 'This research establishment you spoke of. What is its actual purpose?'

'To push the boundaries of medicine, surgery and biochemistry to their ultimate limits – and then beyond,' Leveski said grandly. 'To dream impossible dreams, and then to make those dreams come true. To travel on unknown roads – and to make new maps for others to follow in the future.'

Steiner's heart surged. It seemed that he had heard such dreams outlined before, not so long ago. But those dreams had gone sour, decried and finally smashed to dust by a world which did not understand. Now, suddenly, it was as if he were being given a second chance.

'And my colleagues? Who would I be working with?' he wanted to know.

'Others like yourself. Scientists who have dared to work in areas avoided by the squeamish and faint-hearted. We scoured Europe for them – the concentration camps, the germ-warfare establishments, the genetic study centres set up by your late Führer in his dream of a pure master race. All supplemented with the cream of our own scientists, of course.'

'The human subjects? You would use your own people for such experiments?'

Leveski shrugged carelessly. 'Some. Dissidents, activists, criminals, lunatics – the scum of our society. Polish Jews, prisoners of war, Mongolian peasants – the world is seething with displaced and expendable people, Doctor. As I told you, our supply of subjects is virtually inexhaustible.'

There was only one, comparatively minor question left to ask.

'What about my wife and sons?' Steiner wanted to know.

Leveski shook his head firmly. 'I am afraid that our offer is for you alone, Dr Steiner. You must simply disappear without trace. They would be well provided for, of course. Your own needs would also be well catered for. There will be no shortage of available women where you are going.'

Steiner considered the matter unemotionally. There was just one last point to be cleared up.

'Suppose I turn down this proposition?' he asked.

'Ah.' Leveski looked apologetic. 'Unfortunately, you now know too much to be left alive. Perhaps you are aware that at this moment several Israeli assassination teams are highly active throughout South America. We would simply pass on our information about your whereabouts to one of them. It would then be just a matter of time.'

The Russian broke off, to turn to his compatriot. 'Viktor, why don't you tell the good doctor how the Israelis' victims die?'

The other man spoke for the first time, in a deep, guttural voice. His thick lips cracked open in a bestial, malicious grin. 'Choked to death on their own genitals,' he grunted, with obvious relish. 'Hacked off and stuffed down their throats.'

Leveski stared Steiner coldly in the eyes, letting the image sink in. 'Mind you, they might have something a bit more special for someone who used to perform surgical amputations without anaesthetic,' he volunteered.

Steiner held the Russian's gaze, the ghost of a smile playing over his lips. 'When do we leave?' he asked.

4

London – January 1993

Lieutenant-Colonel Barney Davies glanced around the Foreign Office conference room with a slight sense of surprise. He had not been expecting such a high-powered meeting. Nothing in the message he had received had given any indication that this was to be any more than a briefing session. Now, noting the sheer number of personnel already assembled, and the prominence of some of them, Davies could tell that this was to be no mere briefing. It looked more like a full-blown security conference.

He reviewed the cluster of faces hovering around the large, oval-shaped table. Nobody seemed prepared to sit down yet; they were all still waiting for the guest of honour to arrive. It had to be pretty high brass, Davies figured to himself, for he recognized at least two Foreign Office ministers, either of whom could quite comfortably head up any meeting up to and perhaps including Cabinet level. He teased his brain, trying to put names to the faces.

He identified Clive Murchison almost immediately. He had had some dealings with the man during the Gulf War, the successful conclusion of which probably had something to do with Murchison's obvious and rapid climb up the bureaucratic ladder.

Tending towards the curt, but irritatingly efficient, Murchison was of the old school, the 'send a gunboat' brigade. His presence alone reinforced Davies's feeling that this meeting was serious stuff.

Naming Murchison's colleague proved a little trickier. Windley? Windsor? Neither name seemed quite right. It fell into place, eventually. A double-barrelled name. Wynne-Tilsley, that was it. Michael Wynne-Tilsley. Still technically a junior minister but well connected, tipped for higher things. Word was that he had the PM's ear, or maybe knew a few things he should not. In political circles, Davies reflected, that was the equivalent of a ticket to the front of the queue.

There were half a dozen other people who meant nothing whatsoever to Davies. Whether they were civil servants or civilian advisers, he had no idea, although there was probably the odd man from MI6 or the 'green slime' in there somewhere.

There was, however, one more face that he definitely did recognize. Davies's face broke into a friendly grin as he strolled across to the slightly hunched figure in the electric wheelchair. Reaching down, he gave the man's shoulder an affectionate squeeze.

'Well, you old bastard, what are you doing here? Thought you'd retired.'

Piggy Baker looked up, grinning back. 'I had . . . have. They dug me up again to bring me in as a special adviser on this one.' The man extended his hand. 'Barney, good to see you.'

The two men shook hands warmly. Finally, Davies drew back slightly, appraising his old comrade. He noted that Piggy no longer bothered to wear his artificial leg.

'So what happened to the pogo stick? Thought they would have rebuilt you as the six billion dollar man by now. All this new technology, prosthetics and stuff.'

Piggy shrugged carelessly. 'They did offer, a couple of years back. But what the hell? I'm too old to go around all tarted up like Robocop.' He broke off, nodding down at the wheelchair. 'These days, I'm happy enough to ponce around in this most of the time.'

Davies nodded, his face suddenly becoming serious. 'So, what's all this about? Looks like high-powered stuff.'

Baker's face was apologetic. 'Sorry, Barney, but I can't tell you a thing until the briefing. OSA and all that, you know.'

'Yes, of course.' Davies had not really expected much else. He knew all about the Official Secrets Act, and official protocol. He had come up against it himself enough times.

There was a sudden stir of movement in the room. The babble of voices hushed abruptly. Glancing towards the large double doors, Davies was not really surprised to see the Foreign Secretary enter the room. He had not been expecting anyone less.

The Foreign Secretary headed straight for one end of the oval table and sat down. 'Well, gentlemen, shall we get down to business?' he said crisply. He glanced across at Wynne-Tilsley as everyone took their chairs. 'Perhaps you would be so good as to introduce everybody before we begin the briefing.'

Wynne-Tilsley went round the table in an anti-clockwise direction. Just as Davies had supposed, most of the personnel were civilian advisers or from the green slime, the Intelligence Corps.

The introductions over, the Foreign Secretary took over once more. 'Gentlemen, we have a problem,' he announced flatly. 'The purpose of this meeting is to determine what we do about it. Let me say at this juncture that it is not so much a question of should we get involved as *can* we get involved. Which is why I have invited Lieutenant-Colonel Davies, of 22 SAS, here today.' He paused briefly to nod towards Davies in acknowledgement, before turning to Murchison. 'Perhaps you would outline the situation for us.'

Murchison rose to his feet, riffling through the sheaf of papers and notes in front of him. He spoke in a clear, confident tone – the voice of a man well used to public speaking and being listened to.

'Essentially, we've been asked by the Chinese to infiltrate former Soviet territory,' he announced, pausing for a few moments to let the shock sink in. He waited until the brief buzz of startled exclamations and hastily exchanged words were over. 'Which, as you might gather, gentlemen, makes this a very sticky problem indeed.' Murchison then turned to face Davies directly. 'The general feeling was that this is an operation which could only be tackled by the SAS if it could be tackled at all – although the complexities and nature of the specific problem could prove even beyond their capabilities.'

It seemed like a challenge which demanded a response. Davies rose to his feet slowly, addressing the Foreign Secretary directly.

'You used the word "infiltrate",' he said thoughtfully. 'An ambiguous word at the best of times. Some clarification would be appreciated.'

The Foreign Secretary nodded. 'I appreciate your concern, Lieutenant-Colonel, and I understand your reserve. Just let me assure you that we are not talking about an invasion force here, nor would we go in with any hostile intent. However, it is possible that your men would encounter hostile forces.'

Not much wiser, Davies sank back into his chair. 'Perhaps I'd better hear the rest of the briefing,' he muttered.

Murchison rose to his feet again. 'I think the background to the problem will be best explained by Captain Baker,' he said. I know Lieutenant-Colonel Davies is well aware of his colleague's position, but for the rest of you I had better explain that Captain Baker was for many years with SAS Operations Planning and Intelligence. He has been called here today because he has been close to this particular story for a long time.'

With a curt nod in Piggy's direction, he yielded the table and sat down again.

'You'll excuse me if I don't stand, gentlemen,' Piggy began, a wry grin on his face. He paused for a while, marshalling his thoughts. Finally, he took a deep breath and launched into his rehearsed brief.

'Just after the Second World War, it became apparent that the Russians were gathering together scientists, doctors and medical staff from all over Europe for some sort of secret project,' he announced. Turning towards Davies, he added a piece of more personal and intimate information. 'As it happens, I

37

had a personal encounter at the time, and there are three plaques mounted outside the Regimental Chapel at Stirling Lines because of it. So you might say that I have always had a deep and personal interest in the ongoing story.'

So, Davies thought, it was personal – to them both. Family business. An old score that needed settling. But why now? Why the Chinese involvement? He listened intently as his old friend went on, now with a deeper sense of commitment.

'Suffice it to say that when I moved to OPI I initiated a monitoring operation on this project, which has been kept up to the present day,' Piggy continued. 'And although there has been no official liaison with our own Intelligence Corps, I believe that they too have been keeping an eye open, as, indeed, have our American counterparts.'

Davies broke off briefly to cast a questioning glance towards Grieves, the officer from the green slime. The man nodded his head wordlessly, confirming Piggy's suspicions.

'We know that the original project was code-named Phoenix by the Russians,' Piggy went on. 'Everything suggests that it was never officially embraced by the Soviet government, but placed largely under the control of the KGB, and kept under tight security wraps. For that reason, our intelligence is patchy, to say the least, and we have had to surmise quite a lot of what we were unable to know for fact. What we *do* know, however, is that in 1947 a secret research facility was set up in a fairly remote and mountainous region of Kazakhstan, fairly close to the Mongolian border. While we still do not know the exact purpose of this original facility, we have always assumed it to be a biological research project of some kind. It is also logical to assume that the underlying concept of this research facility was in military application, although there may have been some spin-offs into mainstream science. It is more than possible, for instance, that the dominance of Soviet and Eastern Bloc athletes during the fifties and sixties was directly due to steroids and other performance-enhancing drugs which were developed in the Kazakhstan facility.'

The Foreign Secretary had been busy making notes. He looked up now, tapping his pen on the table to draw Piggy's attention.

'So what you are saying, in effect, is that this project has never actually offered any direct, or perceived, threat to the Western powers, or us in particular? At worst, in fact, it might have cost us a few gold medals in the Olympics?'

Piggy nodded, conceding the point. 'Up to now, yes. But recent developments have given us cause to think again.'

The Foreign Secretary chewed his bottom lip thoughtfully. 'And what are these new developments?'

'With respect, sir, I believe I can best answer that,' Grieves said, rising to his feet and waving a buff-coloured dossier in one hand. Satisfied that he had the floor, he cleared his throat with a slight cough and carried on. 'About three months ago, GCHQ monitored what appeared to be some kind of distress signal sent out from the Kazakhstan facility to the old KGB HQ in Moscow. From this, we must deduce two things – A, that some sort of accident or emergency situation had occurred within the complex, and B, the personnel inside are seemingly unaware that the KGB has been virtually broken up and disbanded over the past year or so. This further suggests that they might be completely out of touch with what has been going on inside the Soviet Union and the world at large.'

'But how can that be?' the Foreign Secretary wanted to know. 'Surely they must have regular contact with the outside world – supplies, that sort of thing.'

Grieves shook his head. 'Not necessarily, sir. Our intelligence has always suggested that the facility was designed to be virtually self-sustaining. As long ago as 1969 an American spy satellite carrying out routine surveillance of the Soviet nuclear weapons testing facility at Semipalatinsk happened to overfly the base and monitor an internal nuclear power source. This suggests that it has its own closed power source, and it is probable that they also have their own hydroponic food-production facility along with a pretty sophisticated recycling system. The very nature of the complex has always been secretive, even autonomous. It is more than likely that it even has its own security system – a private army, in effect.'

'Just what are we actually talking about here?' Lieutenant-Colonel Davies interrupted. 'A scientific research facility or a bloody garrison? Just how big is this damned place, anyway?'

If the Foreign Secretary found Davies's language at all offensive, he gave no sign. 'A good question,' he muttered, glancing questioningly at Grieves.

The Intelligence officer shrugged faintly. 'Again, inconclusive evidence,' he said. 'Satellite observation suggests that much of the complex is built

underground, but we don't know how many subterranean levels there might be. Basically, we have
no way of knowing the actual size and personnel strength of the establishment. It might house
a few dozen scientists and support staff. Or it
could be an autonomous, full-scale community, of
several hundred people living in a miniature city.
Don't forget that this place has been established
for nearly fifty years now. There's no guessing
how it has developed.'

Grieves fell silent for several seconds. When he
spoke again, his face was grim and his tone sombre.
'Of course, personnel numbers could well be a purely
academic point. They may, in fact, all be dead
anyway. Which, incidentally, is where the Chinese
come in. They're afraid that some sort of chemical
or biological contamination may have escaped from
within the complex, and may already have crossed
the Mongolian border.' He paused again, longer this
time, to allow the full significance of his words to
register.

Finally, Davies attempted a brief recap. 'So what
you're suggesting is that this place may have been
engaged in chemical or bacteriological warfare research,
and something nasty might have got loose?'

Grieves nodded. 'In essence, yes.'

'Have the Chinese any direct evidence for this?'
Davies asked. 'Have there been any actual deaths?'

Grieves consulted his notes briefly. 'It's difficult
to be absolutely sure,' he replied. 'You have to
understand the unique background and make-up
of Kazakhstan itself. It's vast — almost unbelievably
so. You could fit Britain, France, Germany, Spain,

Finland and Sweden into it quite comfortably. Yet it only has a total population of some seventeen million — an improbable mix of races and cultures including native Kazakhs, Tartars, Uzbeks and Uigurs along with emigrant Russians, Germans and others. In Stalin's heyday, Kazakhstan was Gulag territory. When the concentration camps were disbanded, many of the inmates settled in the area. Stalin also used the region as a dumping ground for vast numbers of people he considered 'political undesirables' — Volga Germans, Meskhetian Turks, Crimean Tartars and Karachais to name but a few. So we're talking about millions of square miles still sparsely populated by people of widely differing religions, cultures and languages. And we are also dealing with a particularly remote region, in mountainous terrain not far from Mount Belushka. Because of the nature of this terrain, and the scattered, semi-nomadic distribution of the peasant population, there is no direct communications network. Any information which comes out of the area is essentially rumour, or word-of-mouth reports which might have been passed through several dozen very simple people before reaching the ears of the authorities. However, there are enough reports of dead and missing goatherds, peasant farmers and the like filtering through to give these Chinese fears some credibility.'

'So why can't they go in and sort it out for themselves?' Davies asked. 'After all, they're right there on the spot.'

Grieves did not attempt to answer. Instead, he glanced towards the Foreign Secretary.

'With respect, Lieutenant-Colonel,' said the latter,

addressing Davies directly, 'you're looking at this through the eyes of a military man, without taking into account the highly complex and sensitive political issues involved here. This whole region is a territorial minefield. There have been border clashes between the Chinese and Russians for the last three decades, and stability balances on a knife-edge. The Chinese don't dare to make a serious incursion into Russian territory for fear of sparking off a major incident.'

'Then it's up to the Russians to sort it out for themselves, surely?' Davies suggested.

The Foreign Secretary smiled thinly. 'Perhaps you're forgetting that there is virtually no longer any centralized decision-making inside former Soviet territory,' he pointed out. 'Every region, every state is in turmoil – fragmented and politically unstable if not actively in the throes of civil war. The Kazakhstan region is no exception. There are perhaps up to half a dozen different guerrilla groups and political and religious factions already fighting for territory virtually on a village by village, valley by valley basis. You only have to look to Georgia, just across the Caspian, to get an idea of what's going on there.'

Davies nodded thoughtfully. Grieves coughed faintly again, drawing attention back to himself.

'Actually, to answer Lieutenant-Colonel Davies's last question, I ought to point out that we believe the Russians *did* manage to send in at least one military team to investigate,' he volunteered. 'Our intelligence suggests that they disappeared without trace, with absolutely no clues as to what happened to them. We have no way of knowing if they even managed to get anywhere near the research facility.'

'But I still fail to understand how the Chinese reckon to get us involved in all this,' Davies said, becoming increasingly bogged down in the political intricacy of the entire affair.

The Foreign Secretary treated him to another thin, almost cynical smile. 'Politics sometimes makes for strange bedfellows,' he said. 'The Chinese are desperate for Western acceptance after the Tiananmen Square massacre. They are equally desperate for access to European trade markets, and, rightly or wrongly, they seem to believe that Britain could be holding the top cards in the Euro-deck right now. And, as we are already involved in close association over the Hong Kong business, they feel they have an ace of their own to play.'

Davies started to understand at last. 'So it's a threat, basically?' he said. 'Unless we play ball with them, they'll make the Hong Kong negotiations more difficult?'

The Foreign Secretary smiled openly now. 'I see you're beginning to get a grasp of modern-day diplomacy,' he murmured, without obvious sarcasm. He paused to take a slow, deep breath. 'So, Lieutenant-Colonel Davies, that's it, in a nutshell. We appear to be stuck with the problem, and the SAS would appear to be our only hope.'

'To do what, exactly?' Davies demanded. He was still not quite sure what was actually being asked of him.

The Foreign Secretary stared him directly in the eye. 'To get in there, monitor the situation and neutralize it if possible. Of course, you understand that we are talking about some of the most difficult and inhospitable terrain in the world, under the most extreme climatic conditions. As I understand it, the difference between daytime and night-time temperatures can be as much as 20°C. Once you're up into the mountains, you can expect extremes as low as minus thirty – plus fierce and bitter northerly winds straight down from Siberia.'

Davies nodded thoughtfully. 'Not exactly the Brecon Beacons,' he muttered. The reference to the SAS testing and training grounds went over the top of the Foreign Secretary's head.

'You would, of course, be given the full support of the Intelligence Corps and access to all the relevant files,' the latter went on. 'You would be expected to liaise with Captain Baker about the finer points of the operation, including more detailed briefing about the geography of the region. All I require from you at this stage is a gut assessment as to the feasibility of the operation. In short, could your men get a small team of scientists into that complex with a reasonable hope of success?'

The last sentence was a sudden and totally unexpected sting in the tail. Davies jumped to his feet angrily, quite forgetting the company he was in as he banged his fist down on the table. 'No bloody way,' he shouted, vehemently.

The Foreign Secretary kept his cool admirably, merely raising one eyebrow quizzically.

'Come now, Lieutenant-Colonel. I would have thought this was right up your street.'

'No bloody civilians, no bloody way,' Davies repeated, virtually ignoring him. 'The SAS isn't a babysitting service for a bunch of boffins who probably couldn't even step over a puddle without getting their feet wet. If we go in at all, we go in alone. And if we need any specialist know-how, we'll take it in our heads.'

The Foreign Secretary seemed unperturbed. 'Yes, Captain Baker more or less warned me that that would be your reaction,' he observed philosophically. He thought for a few moments. 'Well, as I can't order you, we shall have to resort to Plan B. Your men will secure the area and neutralize any obvious threat to an Anglo-Chinese team of scientific experts who will be airlifted in behind you. Can you do that much?'

Davies simmered down. 'We can have a damned good try,' he said emphatically. 'What about insertion into the area?'

'That's one of the matters we're going to have to discuss,' Piggy put in. 'But basically you'd probably have to assemble somewhere neutral like Hong Kong. You'd go in as civilians, of course – either as tourists or visiting businessmen. From there you would be contacted by the Chinese and transferred to a military base on the mainland. We would expect the Chinese to put you over the border somewhere just inside Sinkiang Province, probably 100 miles north-east of Tacheng. You would then be facing a foot trek of around 350 miles. It's going to give you supply problems, but there's a possibility the Chinks would be willing to risk a brief air incursion into Soviet territory to drop you one advance cache. Certainly no more, since the official Kazakhstan government is extremely well armed with the latest high-tech kit. The republic has even managed to retain nearly fifteen per cent of the former Soviet total nuclear arsenal, much to the Kremlin's annoyance.'

'In that sort of mountainous terrain?' Davies shook his head. 'No, we'd probably never find it. And if we put it in with a homing beacon there's every chance someone else would get to it before we did. No, we'd have to go in on a self-sustaining basis. What's the local wildlife situation?'

Piggy shrugged. 'Sparse – particularly at this time of year. Probably a few rabbits or even wild deer in the foothills, but not much else. Your best bet would probably be airborne. Carrion crow, the odd golden eagle – probably not much different to turkey if you eat 'em with your eyes shut.'

'Sorry, but you two gentlemen seem to have lost me,' the Foreign Secretary put in. 'I thought we were discussing a military operation, not a gourmet's picnic.'

The politician went up an immediate notch in Davies's estimation. The man had a sense of humour.

'It's a question of weight and distance ratio,' Davies hastened to explain. 'With a round trip of 700 miles, my men are going to be limited in the amount of food and supplies they can carry in their bergens. They're already going to have to be wearing heavy thermal protection gear and, from the sound of it, Noddy suits as well.'

'Noddy suits?' the Foreign Secretary queried.

The SAS man smiled. 'Sorry, sir. I mean nuclear, chemical and biological warfare protection. Cumbersome, uncomfortable, and all additional weight. Quite simply, it's going to be physically impossible to carry all the gear they will need for an operation of this size and complexity. So we cut non-essential supplies such as food. Troopers are trained to live off the land where necessary.'

'They could, of course, take in a couple of goats with them,' Piggy suggested. It was not intended to be a facetious remark, but Davies glared at him all the same.

'I'm concerned about keeping them alive – not their bloody sex lives,' he said dismissively. 'And in that respect, where do we get kitted up, if we're going in as civvies?'

'No problem,' Piggy assured him. 'We can arrange for anything you ask for to be ready and waiting for you when you arrive at your Chinese base.'

The Foreign Secretary was standing up and gathering his papers together. 'So I can leave you two to sort out the details?' he asked, beginning to feel slightly uncomfortable and superfluous. 'How soon do you think you might be able to come up with a reasonable plan of operations?'

Davies shrugged. 'Six, seven weeks maybe. There's a lot of groundwork to be done.'

'Ah.' The Foreign Secretary frowned. 'I'm afraid we don't have the luxury of that sort of timescale,' he said. 'There is another problem.'

'Which is?' Davies wanted to know.

Murchison answered for the Foreign Secretary. 'It's a question of climate and temperature,' he explained. 'If there *has* been a biological leak, our experts seem to think that the extreme cold might well keep any widespread contagion in check for a while at least. Come the spring, and warmer weather, it could be a different picture altogether. We had been thinking in terms of getting something off the ground in three weeks maximum.'

Davies sucked in a deep breath and blew it out slowly over his bottom lip. It was a tall order, even for the SAS. He looked at the Foreign Secretary with a faint shrug. 'I'll see what I can do,' he said quietly, unwilling to make any firmer promise at that stage.

The Foreign Secretary nodded understandingly. 'I'm sure you will do everything you can, Lieutenant-Colonel.' He glanced almost nervously around the table before directing his attention back to Davies. 'You understand, of course, that if anything goes wrong, this meeting never took place?'

Davies grinned. It was a story he had often heard before. 'Of course,' he muttered. 'They never do, do they?'

The two men exchanged a last brief, knowing glance which established that they were both fully aware of the rules of the game. Then the Foreign Secretary picked up his papers, nodded to his two ministers and led the way out of the conference room.

Left alone, Davies crossed over to Piggy and slapped him on the back. 'Well, I think you and I need to go and sink a few jars somewhere,' he suggested.

5

'So, what's your gut feeling on this one?' Davies asked Piggy after he had helped install his electric wheelchair in the lift down to the high-security underground car park.

Piggy let out a short, explosive sound halfway between a grunt and a cynical laugh. 'You know my views on anything to do with the fucking Russians,' he replied. 'And I'm not too sure about the bloody Chinks, either. Personally, I'm inclined to the view that every takeaway in London is part of a plot to poison us all with monosodium glutamate.'

Davies grinned. 'You're a bloody xenophobe.'

Piggy shook his head, a mock expression of indignation on his face. 'That's a vicious rumour put about by those jealous bastards at Stirling Lines. I take my sex straight.' He paused to flash Davies a rueful grin. 'At least, I do when Pam hasn't got a bloody headache these days.'

Davies smiled back. 'Christ, are you two still at it? You dirty old man.'

'*Lucky* old man,' Piggy corrected him. 'Actually, I think it's just the delayed effect of all those hormones I was taking for forty years.'

Davies's eyes strayed briefy to the wheelchair, and

Piggy's truncated torso. 'You never had any problems, then?' he asked, a little awkwardly.

Piggy grinned again. 'No, the old Spitfire still flies. They may have shot the undercarriage to hell, but there was nothing wrong with the fuselage. The hormone treatment did the rest.' His face suddenly became serious again, almost sad. 'No kids, of course – that's the only part that still hurts.'

Children were a sore point with Davies as well. 'Count yourself lucky,' he muttered. 'Mine hardly ever bother to even talk to me these days. Now they've got a new dad and a new baby-sister, I'm just a relic from the past.'

'You never bothered to remarry, then?'

Davies laughed ironically. 'Like the old cliché – I married the job,' he said. 'And the SAS can be a jealous bitch. Besides, there aren't that many understanding women like your Pam around these days.'

They had reached the car park level. Piggy looked up into Davies's eyes as the lift doors hissed open, a wry smile on his face. 'We're still doing it, aren't we?' he murmured.

'Doing what?' Davies didn't quite understand.

'The bullshit,' Piggy said, referring to the casual banter which virtually all SAS men exchanged before operations.

Davies gave no reply. He helped steer the wheelchair through the doors into the underground car park. Instinctively, he began to walk towards his own BMW, suddenly pausing in mid-stride and looking back at Piggy somewhat awkwardly.

'Look, I've only just realized that my car isn't

equipped to take that chariot of yours,' he muttered in embarrassment.

Piggy smiled easily. 'No problem, I do have my own transport, you know.'

'Yes, of course.' Davies relaxed, feeling a bit better about his near-gaffe. 'So, where would you like to go for a drink? I'm afraid I'm not really up on London pubs these days.'

Piggy looked at him with a faint look of surprise. 'Who said anything about a London pub? There's only one place for a pair of old troopers like us to have a drink – and we both know exactly where that is.'

It was Davies's turn to look a little bemused. 'The Paludrine Club?' he said, referring to the Regiment's exclusive little watering-hole back at Stirling Lines in Hereford.

'And why not?' Piggy prompted. 'We can do it in just over two hours, given a following wind. Besides, we're going to have to do some serious planning, and where better than the Kremlin?'

Davies glanced at his BMW again, the sense of embarrassment returning. 'Two hours flat out is some hard driving – even for me,' he pointed out awkwardly.

Piggy followed the direction of his gaze and then broke out into an open laugh. 'Christ Almighty, Barney, do you think I'm driving a fucking three-wheeler or something?' He fingered the controls on the arm of his electric wheelchair, steering it over towards a black and silver Mitsubishi Shogun. Pulling a small remote control panel from his pocket, he activated the door lock and automatic winching gear. As the lifting plate sighed down to ground level, Piggy rolled the wheelchair onto it, locked the wheels in position and set the controls again. Effortlessly, the powerful motor hoisted wheelchair and occupant up into the driving cab.

Davies looked up at him, impressed. 'Last one there buys the drinks,' he said, grinning. 'I assume you're planning to stay at my place for a couple of days?'

Piggy smiled down as the wheelchair started to slide into the driving position. 'You assume correctly, my old friend. Everything's already packed in the back.'

He pulled the door closed behind him. Seconds later the Shogun roared into life and lurched away towards the exit with a squeal of rubber on concrete.

Laughing like a schoolboy, Davies broke into a run towards his own car. They were off. But he could already feel the surge of adrenalin in his system which told him he was setting out on something far more challenging than a race up the M4. And something potentially far more dangerous, he reminded himself as he slipped in the ignition key and gunned the powerful BMW into life.

Davies walked away from the bar after paying for the drinks – a small brandy for himself and a double gin and tonic for Piggy. He had not deliberately let Piggy win, he told himself. Perhaps it was just that he was a little more cautious these days, with a little more respect for things like speed limits. Or perhaps it was simply that Piggy still had that extra something to prove to himself. Either way, he actually felt quite good about buying the drinks. Reaching the table, he set them down and sat eyeing Piggy over the rim of his balloon glass, waiting for him to open the conversation.

Piggy picked up his cue. 'First thoughts?' he queried.

Davies sipped at his brandy. 'Two four-man patrols, over the same route but spaced about two hours apart.'

His companion nodded thoughtfully. 'Sweep and clean. And back-up if necessary. Makes good sense. Any thoughts on personnel yet?'

'Mike Hailsham springs to mind.'

Again, Piggy seemed in general agreement. 'Yeah, Major Hailsham's a good CO. Any special reasons?'

'Two main ones. Firstly he has intensive experience of anti-bacteriological equipment and techniques from the Gulf War. He skippered the frontline undercover raids on the Scud bases when we still thought Saddam was going to start dumping anthrax on the Israelis.'

'And second?' Piggy wanted to know.

'And he has fluent Russian,' Davies said. 'Although how much use that's likely to be, I'm not too sure at this point.' He broke off to look questioningly at Piggy. 'You've studied the region. What's likely to be the most common language?'

'Russian's probably as good as anything,' Piggy said. 'The native Kazakhs do have their own tongue, basically derived from Turkish, but most of the younger ones have probably been taught Russian as a second language by now. You can forget the older generation. Before 1917 they didn't have a written language at all – no books, no schools, no permanent records of any kind. It was just a very simple nomadic culture, and basic storytelling or folk song were about the only ways of communicating information.' He tailed off, realizing that he was starting to ramble a bit. 'Anyone else in mind?'

'Andrew Winston would be a good bet, I think,' Davies said. 'Again for the basic reason that he was with Hailsham in Iraq and knows the score. 'And he's a tough bastard. If anyone can nip up a mountain with a full bergen on his back, that big black sonofabitch can. In fact, he'd probably beat everybody else just so he could have ten minutes on his own to sit on the top and write a couple of poems.'

Piggy listened to his friend's eulogy without really understanding it, not knowing the mild-mannered but combat-lethal Barbadian sergeant. Soldiers like Winston were the members of a new breed of SAS men – thinkers and idealists rather than the hardened death-or-glory boys of his own early years.

'And Cyclops, of course,' Davies was going on. 'If you're right and we're going to have shoot down bloody eagles to stay alive, then I want the best sniper in the Regiment.'

Again, Piggy was not personally familiar with the man, but his shooting prowess was legendary. Already five times Army sharpshooting champion, Corporal Billy Clements was the undisputed king of the L96A1, otherwise known as the Accuracy International PM. In his hands the 7.62mm calibre weapon was as accurate and as lethal at 800 yards as a stiletto is at six inches. It was a skill born of almost fanatical practice on the firing range, and one which had given Clements his odd nickname since he appeared to be almost constantly squinting down the eyepiece of a telescopic sight. However, stories that he was incapable of reading even the largest print at less than arm's length remained unproven, since no one had ever actually seen Cyclops trying to read anything.

'Well, that's three names to conjure with for a start,' Davies said as he turned his attention back to his brandy. 'I'll issue recalls this evening and we'll set up a prelim briefing in the Kremlin for 09.00 hours the day after tomorrow.'

He drained his glass after swilling the last few droplets around the bowl and inhaling the fumes with genuine appreciation. Placing it back on the table, he pushed it in Piggy's direction.

'Your round, I think. If we're going to get religiously pissed, we'd better get a move on.'

6

To an outsider, it would have been inconceivable that the apparently ill-assorted bunch of men assembled in the briefing room in the 'Kremlin' could function as the most cohesive and effective fighting unit in the world. But *they* knew, and that was what counted. They knew themselves as few men ever do; and they knew each other, and each other's capabilities.

Major Mike Hailsham glanced around the room at the small gathering with almost paternal affection. Not that any of them really needed fathering, he reflected. Used strictly as a term of endearment, the word 'bastards' fitted them all rather neatly as individuals. But collectively, that was a different matter entirely, and it was from this standpoint that Hailsham's sense of pride emanated.

Considering the short notice, he had done rather well, Hailsham told himself. Davies's brief had been nothing if not explicit. 'Imagine the shittiest, toughest assignment you can and get me two teams by the day after tomorrow.' The names of Sergeant Andrew Winston and Corporal Billy Clements had already been dropped into the hat. The rest were his own personal choice, only arrived at after a great deal of thought. Given a brief like that, a man picked his companions very carefully indeed.

Piggy sat directly beneath the large stuffed water-buffalo head which decorated one wall of the briefing room. A memento of the Regiment's days in Malaya, it was also a symbol of unity, of exclusivity – the totem of a closed and quasi-secret brotherhood. For the SAS was indeed a brotherhood, and Stirling Lines was their highly exclusive lodge.

Piggy also reviewed the assembled men, but from a slightly different perspective. Most were strangers to him, and yet he felt that he knew them all as intimately as he knew his own family. Personal acquaintance did not really enter the equation, and time meant nothing. There were blood ties. These unfamiliar faces were direct descendants, the inheritors of a strict line of succession which stretched unbroken from the summer of 1941 to the present day. A quietly spoken Scots Guards lieutenant named David Stirling had conceived a crazy idea, and the idea had spawned a legend.

Yes, they were all brothers under the skin, Piggy thought – and it helped to fill the void of knowing that his own direct family line would end with his death.

Davies respected them all, but he envied them too. They would go, and he would stay behind. Ahead of them, these men faced danger, incredible hardship and conditions that a man would not want to inflict on his worst enemy. But to them it was life, Davies knew. A life that they had chosen to live, sucking out every precious moment and savouring it until it ran dry of juice and the clock stopped ticking. With his own safe, desk-bound job and retirement looming up, Davies might be seen by others to be one of the lucky ones, a man who had survived the odds and finally beaten the clock. Yet he feared the day as it drew inexorably closer. The end of his service career might not be a death, Davies thought bitterly, but it would be an amputation. His eyes strayed briefly to Piggy's mutilated body in the wheelchair, and he drew uncomfortable comparisons. With a conscious effort, he pushed away his thoughts and tried to concentrate on the job in hand.

Cyclops was bemoaning to Andrew Winston the fact that he had been recalled from leave.

'The trouble with this bloody job is that you never know where you are,' he complained bitterly. 'One minute I'm romping around in a king-sized waterbed with a pair of nympho sisters and the next I'm kipping down in the spider with a bunch of smelly bastards with tattooed arses.'

Andrew's black face broke open into a dismissive grin, revealing a double keyboard of gleaming white teeth. 'You'd never manage to fuck two sisters, you lying bastard,' he teased. 'Everyone in the Regiment knows you've got a prick like a rifle. Too long, too thin, and only one shot up the spout before you have to reload.'

Cyclops was not going to be put down so easily. 'Try a Franchi SPAS pump shotgun and you're a bit nearer the mark,' he countered. 'Fat, fast and ferocious, and enough charge to spray an entire room with one shot.'

'Dream on, man,' Andrew said, laughing. He turned away, moving across the room to talk to Troopers McVitie and Naughton, both only twenty-one but chosen by Major Hailsham on Andrew's personal recommendation. Neither seemed particularly grateful for this singular honour.

'Well, what have you got us into this time, you black bastard?' Jimmy McVitie demanded in his gruff Glasgow accent.

'Whatever it is, I hope we can knock it out in a couple of days,' Barry Naughton added optimistically. 'I'm due for leave in just over a week's time.'

Andrew grinned benignly. 'In answer to your two kind enquiries, A, we're going on a nice little trip to China, and B, you could both have grey hairs on your goolies before we get home again.'

Barry chose to see the bright side. His eyes flashed with eager anticipation.

'Great, I've always wanted to screw a Chinese bird,' he said, enthusiastically.

Jimmy regarded him with a serious expression on his face. 'Ye ken a Chinese woman's cunt runs the other way, do ye not?' he said. 'Straight across, like a little yellow letterbox.'

His companion's face creased into a sceptical smile. 'That's bullshit,' he muttered, but there was just the faintest suggestion of doubt in his voice. He looked up at Andrew, seeking a second opinion. 'It's not true, is it, boss?'

The sergeant's face was grave. 'Oh, it's true enough,' he confirmed. 'That's why you never see Chinese women sliding down banisters.'

Barry looked at them both blankly, now totally confused. As if at some secret signal, Andrew and Jimmy both raised their forefingers to their mouths at the same time, rubbing them rapidly up and down over their lips. Blubba-dubba-dubba-dubba-dubba-dubba.

They both collapsed into silent laughter as Barry's face told them that he had been well and truly suckered. The young trooper glared at them both without malice. 'You pair of prats,' he spluttered, then fell silent as a faint flush of embarrassment began to spread over his face. He slunk away, looking for someone to take his revenge on.

Finding himself heading in the general direction of Corporal Max Epps, Barry paused for a moment. The tall, burly Mancunian was not known for his sense of humour, nor for his ability to engage in witty repartee. The man was essentially a loner – a trait which had given birth to his nickname, 'the Thinker'. Under normal circumstances, he was quite happy with his own company, and those who knew him respected that as they respected the man himself. What counted was his contribution to the team when circumstances were not normal. For under fire, or when the going got tough, Epps's character was a mirror-image of his physical presence. Sturdy, dependable, rock-solid. With twenty-six years of intensive soldiering under his belt, he was a comforting man to have around.

But he was definitely not a man to wind up, Barry decided. He veered away across the briefing room, homing in on Tweedledum and Tweedledee, who were, as ever, looking like a pair of Siamese twins who had been separated against their will.

Terry Marks and Tony Tofield had got used to the smutty, but basically good-natured jokes about the closeness of their friendship. Both young, both Londoners and both only recently badged, they accepted the ribaldry of their fellow SAS men because they knew that no one seriously thought that there was anything unnatural about their liking for each other's company, or had any doubts about their sexual orientation. So Terry and Tony had become a natural pair, soon shortened to 'T One' and 'T Two' because it rolled off the tongue better, and finally Tweedledum and Tweedledee.

The pair exchanged a knowing glance as Barry sauntered towards them. Even to a couple of comparative newcomers, the young trooper's gullibility was well known. Baiting him was already a regimental sport.

Innocent as ever, Barry walked right into the trap. 'Hey, you guys. Have you heard? We're going to China,' he announced briskly. 'I suppose you've heard the story about Chinese women's fannies?' He paused expectantly, waiting for a feed-in line. None came. Instead, Tweedledee just nodded knowingly. 'What, about them being so small?' he asked.

Barry was thrown. 'How do you mean?' he asked uncertainly.

Tweedledee held his thumb and forefinger an inch or so apart. 'They're only about this big – about an inch long,' he said in a matter-of-fact way.

He was not going to get caught again, Barry decided. But it was already too late. The trap had been sprung.

'In fact, they're hardly what you'd call a crack at all,' Tweedledee continued, then glanced aside at his companion with a big grin on his face.

'No, more of a little chink, really,' Tweedledum

finished for him. It was a pretty pathetic joke, but they both laughed uproariously.

'Bastards!' Barry exploded. More irritable than ever, he turned away and went to sulk in a corner.

It was time to cut the bullshit and get down to business, Davies decided. Picking up a wall pointer, he rapped it a couple of times on the table. 'Gentlemen, can I have your attention,' he demanded loudly.

All at once the buzz of conversation ceased and smiles faded from faces. The atmosphere of casual conviviality in the room was instantly replaced by an air of earnest anticipation.

'Thank you,' Davies said. He gestured over to Piggy, who had taken up position under the wall display and large-scale maps of the Kazakhstan region. 'For those of you who don't know, this is Captain Baker, ex-SAS and ex-OPI. He will give you an initial briefing on our theatre of operations and a rough idea of what you can expect. Afterwards, I shall hand over to Major Hailsham and we'll be holding a Chinese parliament, so you can all have your say.'

The 'Chinese parliament' represented the essence of SAS philosophy, in minimizing the importance of mere rank in favour of military experience. It was an informal discussion held by the CO of an operation at which each man, regardless of rank, was free to offer advice and criticism and suggest his own alternatives. Valuable in its own right, the system also reinforced the Regiment's classless and truly democratic outlook and the belief that every man had his own valued and important contribution to make.

There was a long silence after Piggy finished his

briefing on the geography and climatic conditions of the target area. News that they might also be facing a threat from unknown chemical or bacteriological agents merely extended it.

It was inevitable that the silence would be broken with a joke. Both Davies and Major Hailsham had been fully expecting the typical response of men facing up to a life or death challenge. It was a mantra against the terrors of the unknown.

Surprisingly, it came from a totally unexpected source.

'Well, I'll be all right,' the Thinker intoned in a rich, deep baritone. 'My old dad kept his Mickey Mouse gas mask from the Second World War in the garage for years. I'll just nip home and get it.'

'You're not talking about one of those things with two flaps of rubber over the nose-piece and a flexible tube on the mouth, are you?' Cyclops jeered. 'That wasn't a gas mask, you plonker. Everybody knows those things were standard Army-issue condoms. The idea was to make sex so fucking boring that all the men couldn't wait to get back to barracks.'

'Yeah, only they didn't work too well,' Jimmy put in. 'That's probably why you were born, Thinker. We've often wondered.'

A loud chorus of cathartic laughter rippled around the briefing room. Major Hailsham let it die away naturally before addressing the men.

'On a more serious note, gentlemen, you will all, of course, have to report for a three-day refresher course in anti-chemical warfare protection. After that, we'll all be taking a nice week's holiday in the country.'

'A bit of mountain scenery, perhaps?' Jimmy asked, sensing what was coming.

Hailsham smiled. 'Good guess, Trooper. Yes, we'll all be tripping off to the Brecon Beacons for some climbing practice. Two or three runs up Pen-y-Fan with a bergen full of bricks on our backs should soon have us all leaping about like a bunch of mountain goats.'

This news was greeted by a loud chorus of groans, none of them louder than those from the younger troopers like Tweedledum and Tweedledee, for whom the harsh basic training in the Welsh mountains was still a comparatively recent ordeal. Yet they all realized its importance and value. Even the biting gale-force winds and icy blizzards of a Welsh winter would seem benign compared with the conditions they could expect on the mission.

'So, your suggestions, gentlemen,' Hailsham said, throwing the briefing open. 'And if anyone says, "Let's go to Majorca instead", I'll personally kick his arse round the Clock Tower.'

'What's the latest intelligence on guerrilla activity in the region, boss?' Andrew asked.

'Good question,' Davies commented, taking over. He consulted the notes which Major Grieves had handed him the previous evening. 'Basically, our latest information is that things are hotting up fast. The Uzbek Popular Front, the Birlik, appears to be gaining a lot of ground recently, and the principal Muslim brotherhoods are beginning to splinter into different Sunni and Shiite factions. Without putting too fine a point on it, Kazakhstan is rapidly shaping up as another Yugoslavia. What's more important from our point of view is that any one of these guerrilla groups is likely to regard us as a strictly hostile presence. And you can forget any notions of a bunch of simple peasant farmers armed with pitchforks and the odd shotgun. Many of these groups are exceedingly well armed with Kalashnikovs, mortars and grenade-launchers. And what they might lack in training is compensated for by the fact that this is their home patch. As a result, they know how to use the terrain to their advantage. They know instinctively where to hide, where to launch an ambush and how to disappear after they've hit. It's a formidable technique, gentlemen, and one which the Russians found out to their cost in Afghanistan.'

'And what's our brief if we get bumped by one of these outfits?' Cyclops asked. 'Shoot 'em in the legs and let 'em limp away?'

Davies looked at them all gravely. 'I don't need to remind you that this is not our war,' he said simply. 'Obviously you will be expected to avoid direct confrontation if at all possible. If not, your lives, and the integrity of this mission, become your number one priorities. You'll have to make up your own minds if and when the occasion arises.' He paused, looking around the room. 'Now, are there any more questions?'

There was a long pause, broken by a few odd mutterings but nothing spoken publicly. Hailsham looked round one more time before finally nodding. 'Then go out and have a good time tonight, lads. As of tomorrow you'll all be confined to barracks until this mission is completed. We expect to go in two weeks.'

Davies walked over to Piggy as Hailsham followed his men out of the briefing room. 'Do you think they have any real idea what could be in store for them?' he asked.

Piggy shrugged. 'I doubt it,' he said, honestly.

7

High in the Sailyukem Mountains, in the south-western fringes of the Western Sayan range, the building seemed to be nothing more than a low, flat expanse of grey concrete which seemed to melt into the rocky hills surrounding it. Snow-covered and desolate, it was merely a vaguely geometric shape which looked oddly out of keeping with the peaks and contours of the enclosing terrain. Other than the dozen or so frozen human bodies which had not yet been completely covered by the swirling snow, or the burnt-out shell of the Russian MIL Mi-6 'Hook' helicopter 100 yards away, there was nothing to suggest the Phoenix Project was anything but abandoned.

But deep inside there was life, even though here too, there was also much evidence of death. Silent and locked laboratories, sealed corridors and entire closed-off wings of the upper levels were littered with corpses, some human, some animal, some hideously indefinable. Hermetically sealed, and with all heating and power sources isolated, the building was a cryo-genic mausoleum, preserving the bodies in much the same condition as when they had dropped, some four months previously.

On the fifth subterranean level, Tovan Leveski paced his small air-conditioned office and wondered if and when a second attack would come. He did not fully understand the first, any more than he could understand why his KGB paymasters had ceased all communication over a year earlier.

But then there was much that he could not comprehend any more. Although his body was over eighty in strict chronological age, he had the outward physique and appearance of a fit and healthy man of less that half that age – the direct result of one of the first of the project's long-term experiments into arresting the ageing process, an initial step towards the dream of human immortality. Like so many of those early, hopeful experiments, it had been long abandoned. Too late, the scientists had realized that the drugs worked well enough on the physical body but could not arrest the insidious decay of the brain which comes with ageing. In fact, they even accelerated it. So Leveski survived, but with the mind of a centenarian trapped inside a middle-aged body. A mind which even at the height of its powers had fringed on the psychotic.

There were still a few brief moments of clarity left to the Russian, although they were becoming increasingly infrequent. When the epidemic had first become apparent, he had still retained the mental power to order the lower levels to be sealed off, condemning the healthy and uninfected to die along with their sick companions. And when the Army assault helicopter had arrived, in response to an unauthorized distress signal, it had been Leveski who had masterminded its destruction and the slaughter of those few soldiers who managed to escape from the burning wreck.

Now he waited, wondering if they would try again, and failing to understand why the once-prestigious Phoenix Project seemed to have been so abruptly and utterly abandoned by those who had so enthusiastically supported and nurtured it for so long.

But though slow and feeble, Leveski's mind was still capable of sporadic cunning. He had taken precautions. If they did come again, Phoenix was ready for them. He still had control over eighty to ninety per cent of his original security force. The outer perimeter of the complex had been electronically mined and the wrecked helicopter and several of the Russian corpses booby-trapped. Any new intruders would die as the first ones had. This thought afforded Leveski a degree of satisfaction, despite his prevailing depression and sense of abandonment. Outsiders were unwelcome, and must be killed. In his confused state, he was incapable of conceiving that the assault force had been on a mission of mercy and rescue. To Leveski, they had been simply invaders, coming to unveil the secrets of the Phoenix Project.

And many of those secrets were too dark, too guilty, to ever be revealed to the outside world. For nearly fifty years, Phoenix had been inviolate, a law unto itself. Funded by secretive agencies without reserve and staffed by experimental scientists without principles, Phoenix had carried out a range of experimentation which was without precedent and almost beyond the imagination of a normal mind. Using the unfortunate inmates of Soviet labour camps and asylums as basic stock, the Phoenix scientists simply bred their next subjects in much the same way as a battery farm would produce new chickens. By the mid-1950s they were able to incorporate new discoveries in the field of hormone research to force male and female children into sexual maturity at a much younger age, thus saving a few extra years on each new generation. A decade later a generation had been reduced to just ten years, and *in vitro* fertilization techniques and the use of fertility drugs to create multiple births were increasing both the breeding stock and the available gene pool.

But with the 1980s came the new climate of *détente* and *glasnost*. Official Kremlin interest in the Phoenix Project, which had never really been acknowledged in any case, began to wane. Soviet scientists in the mainstream of research became convinced that they had more than made good any technology gap with the West, in all branches of science. Phoenix, although it continued to be well funded by the KGB, became something of an embarrassment, and best forgotten.

Increasingly cut off from the outside world, the Kazakhstan complex rapidly became fanatically and fiercely independent – a secretive and self-sufficient community which closed ranks around itself and its short but terrible history.

Cyclops motioned the nearest air hostess over with a wave of his finger and ordered two more cans of beer, ignoring the faint look of disapproval on her face. Reaching down into the webbed pocket on the back of the seat in front of him, he retrieved the four previous mangled cans and placed them on her tray.

Jimmy McVitie accepted one of the offered beers

with a wry grin. 'Well, I'm bloody glad I don't have any shares in British Airways,' he said. 'You'll have drunk 'em into bankruptcy before we reach Hong Kong.'

Cyclops opened his can expertly and held it to his lips, taking a deep draught before answering. 'Make the most of it while you can. You'll find it pretty difficult sinking a pint with a bloody respirator over your face.'

Jimmy shuddered just thinking about it. 'God I hate those bloody things,' he said with distaste. 'That's going to be the worst part of this little jaunt.'

Cyclops grinned. 'You could always take the new Irish version,' he suggested. 'You carry two rats in a little cage – like miners used to take live canaries down the pits. When they keel over, you know it's time to close your mouth and stop breathing. It's not only foolproof – it actually serves a dual purpose.'

Jimmy bought into the gag. 'Oh aye, and what's that?'

Cyclops eyed his companion over the rim of his can. 'When you get hungry, you can eat the fucking rats.'

The Glaswegian was not amused. 'Don't even joke about it,' he warned his mate. 'With the sort of scran we're likely to be getting our teeth into, rats might be a bloody delicacy.'

It was a sobering thought. 'Mind you,' Jimmy went on philosophically, 'I did a four-day survival course on Dartmoor once and the boss had us eating worms. You sort of stir-fry the wriggly little bastards into a goo. A bit like grey porridge, really.'

'Aw, Christ,' Cyclops groaned, wrinkling up his

nose in disgust. 'What do they taste like, for God's sake?'

Jimmy shrugged. 'Not too bad, funnily enough. Fucking gritty, though. The trick is to suck it down without chewing too much.' Having imparted this nauseating piece of culinary information, he returned to his beer with no apparent damage to his appetite.

Food and drink were not high on Major Hailsham's list of priorities at that precise moment. With six hours still to go before their own Cathay Pacific flight to Hong Kong, and a fast car waiting to whisk them directly to Heathrow airport, he sat in the ops room at Stirling Lines with Sergeant Andrew Winston, running a final check on the list of arms and equipment they would need on the mission.

'So we're decided on bullpups, are we?' Hailsham asked, referring to the somewhat controversial Enfield L85A1 SA-80 assault rifles which had been made available to the Regiment just before the Gulf War. The weapon had suffered from several teething problems, including vital bits such as magazines falling off under combat conditions. These early design faults had now been largely corrected, but the gun retained a somewhat dubious reputation.

Andrew nodded. 'I think so. Weight has got to be one of our primary considerations, and the SA-80 offers an appreciable saving over a conventional SLR or an M16.'

It was not a point which Hailsham was prepared to argue with. The chunky 5.56mm weapon might not be popular, but it was ideally suited to the operation, being easy to wield and possessing high accuracy up to a range of 300 yards. The fact that its design incorporated a plastic stock and foregrip made it markedly lighter than any other assault rifle with similar fire-power, weighing less than 11lb when fully loaded with a thirty-round box magazine. In addition, each man would be wearing the back-up of a standard Browning High Power 9mm handgun on his hip – a valuable addition to his personal armoury.

Cyclops's L96A1 sniper rifle was another priority. Hailsham and Winston had considered the possibility of including a second and heavier 12.7mm Barret as back-up and rejected it. If Cyclops went down, any one of them could still handle the L96A1 creditably, if not with the same uncanny skill. And the weapon itself was by now proven reliable. Short of actual combat damage, it was rugged enough to survive most conditions.

A pair of general-purpose machine-guns, or GPMGs, were equally essential. The SAS had always made extensive use of this weapon, and it was rare for any four-man patrol to venture out without at least one. Although heavy, weighing in at nearly 24lb without ammunition, its belt-fed, devastating and accurate fire-power at ranges of up to 1500 yards had demonstrated it to be a life-saver in any situation where heavy cover was required. As was often the practice, the 200-round spare ammunition belts would be shared out and carried by all the other members of the team.

'There is one minor blessing,' Andrew pointed out. 'At least up in the mountains we're unlikely to come up against anything really heavy. So we can safely do without any anti-armour capability.'

Hailsham thought this over for a few seconds, before finally nodding thoughtfully. 'Our main weakness is going to be attack from the air,' he then said. 'If we're anywhere near rebel activity, it's a sure bet that the official Kazakhstan Army is going to be monitoring the area with regular helicopter patrols. It would be nice to justify carting along a Stinger, but I think it's going to be out of the question. What do you think?'

Andrew shook his head slowly and doubtfully. 'I agree that it probably wouldn't be feasible to take it all the way,' he agreed. 'But you're right — being without any SAM cover at all leaves us extremely vulnerable. How about a compromise? We take a Stinger and say four missiles in with us as far as the lower foothills and then cache it at our first RV point for retrieval later? That way we would at least have some protection while we were still out in open country.'

It was a good suggestion, and Hailsham considered it carefully. The American Stinger system was a very effective hand-held surface-to-air missile, ideal for protecting small, isolated units from enemy air attack. It had certainly proved its worth in the Falklands, in similar terrain to the miles of steppe that they would have to cross before reaching the foothills of the Western Sayan. The weapon's main drawback, from the point of view of this, or any other SAS patrol, was that the launcher alone carried a 33lb penalty and its individual missiles were each a similar weight. It was a lot of extra baggage for a threat which might not even materialize. Hailsham was in two minds about it.

'I'll volunteer to carry it, if it makes any difference to your decision,' Andrew put in, noting Hailsham's continued hesitation. 'And that's not sheer masochism – I'd feel happier.'

The major thought for a couple more seconds, then said: 'All right, you've got it. But we dump it as soon as we start any serious climbing. Hopefully the mountains themselves will give us reasonably adequate air cover.'

Andrew grinned with relief. 'Understood, boss. Now, what about mortars?'

This did not need as much thinking about. 'We've only got one choice, haven't we?' Hailsham asked. 'It'll have to be a couple of 51mm. Anything heavier is out of the question. I'll take one; the Thinker can carry the other. Ammo?'

'Mixed bag,' Andrew said without hesitation. 'Frags and smoke for daytime use; flares for night.'

Hailsham ticked off the last two items on the personal list he had scribbled out earlier. 'Add a Claymore for each team and six fragmentation and four stun grenades apiece and that should take care of the hardware. We won't be exactly travelling light, but it's a step up from water pistols and a big stick.'

It was intended as a joke, but it reinforced what they both knew – the two patrols were cutting armaments to a bare minimum, perhaps even below adequate protection levels.

'Mind you,' Hailsham added, trying to put things in a better perspective. 'We should keep in mind that we're not actually supposed to be fighting anybody.'

Andrew smiled thinly. 'Yeah, but has anyone told those bastards that?'

It was not a question that Hailsham wanted to answer. He scooped up his little pile of notes from the table. 'Well, we've done our shopping list. Let's just hope the delivery service is making house calls to China this week.'

'In plain brown envelopes, of course,' Andrew joked.

Hailsham laughed. 'More like a couple of wooden crates labelled "agricultural machinery". Or maybe "atomic warheads for Iraq" – that should guarantee priority service,' he added wryly.

Tweedledum and Tweedledee were already in Hong Kong, having flown in to Kai Tak airport on a charter flight the previous day. Not surprisingly, they had forgone a sightseeing trip of the city they called the 'New York of Asia' in favour of a round of its myriad bars and brothels. They sat now in the opulent, over-ornate vestibule of a particularly up-market whorehouse in downtown Kowloon, eyeing the dozen or so beautiful young Chinese girls who were parading coquettishly about in their colourful *cheong-sams*, giggling and winking as they competed for the two troopers' custom.

It was a difficult choice. Tweedledee's face was rapturous as he ran his eyes over the feast of ripe young bodies, assessing each one like a choice cut of meat in a butcher's window. A ten-hour diet of beer and wine had put him in an expansive mood.

'Not a bad life, this SAS lark,' he observed to his soul-mate. 'Lots of good healthy exercise, foreign travel and the chance to fuck exotic women.'

Tweedledum grinned drunkenly. He pulled one of

his standard-issue condoms from his pocket, ripped open the foil and dangled the limp latex tube under Tweedledee's nose. 'And they look after us like a mother hen,' he said, giggling. 'We might get shot, blown to fuck, gassed, poisoned or fried, but at least we'll die with clean dicks.'

The irony of the statement eluded Tweedledee's drink-befuddled brain. He merely grinned vacantly and pointed to a pair of girls dressed in identical yellow *cheong-sams*. They looked like twins.

'How about those two?'

Tweedledum nodded enthusiastically. 'I'll ask the *mama-san* if she's got a double room,' he said, licking his lips in anticipation.

Tweedledee looked at his companion slightly dubiously, but said nothing. There were times, he felt, when doing things together could be taken a bit too far.

Across the city, Trooper Barry Naughton was just returning to the room in the Royal Pacific Hotel which he was sharing with Corporal Max Epps. He floated several inches above the floor, for it had been an unbelievably magical evening, and he was in seventh heaven.

Sung Lu, the girl had said her name was. And she was not a whore, Barry reminded himself – even though she had demanded money after they had made love in her sordid little hotel room. It was, as she had explained in her tiny sing-song voice, merely to convince her sick and elderly mother that she had been a good girl and stayed at her job in the bar on Wing Sing Street, where he had met her.

78

And she had told him that no man had ever made love to her so wonderfully before. She had even told him that she loved him. 'I love you, soldier-boy,' she had murmured frequently during their brief but frantic embrace. Somehow, it did not seem to matter that she could not actually remember his name, or that she dressed with almost indecent haste after it was all over.

Barry had made love to a beautiful young Chinese girl, and she had told him that she loved him. He was almost bursting with pride and happiness as he let himself into the hotel room. He had to tell someone, even if it was only the Thinker.

'I'm in love,' he announced dreamily as he walked in through the door.

His room-mate looked up from his bed, where he had spent the evening writing a long and thoughtful letter to his wife.

'Ya daft prat,' the Thinker muttered dismissively, bursting the bubble.

8

The rendezvous point on the Chinese mainland was the White Swan Hotel in Canton. Major Hailsham and Andrew had flown in direct, having changed planes without ever leaving the confines of Kai Tak airport. Tweedledum and Tweedledee had tagged themselves on to a party of British and German package tourists making a 'Chinese Highlights' sightseeing tour, and Cyclops, Jimmy and Barry had taken the train from Hong Kong. The Thinker, different as ever, had opted for a fairly leisurely boat trip up the Pearl River.

Now, all finally assembled in one of the hotel's small conference rooms, they waited for their promised Chinese contact. The atmosphere was unusually subdued, even slightly tense. The transition from Hong Kong to 'foreign' territory was subtle, but tangible. Although they were still dressed as civilians, there was no longer any doubt that they were really soldiers, or that the mission was for real. Even Tweedledum and Tweedledee, who might normally have been expected to regale the group with lurid and wildly exaggerated accounts of their night in a Hong Kong whorehouse, sat uncharacteristically apart, saying nothing.

They all sipped weak green tea from delicate porcelain cups, mostly under sufferance. Alcohol was banned now, for the duration of the mission. The next real drink to touch their lips would be consumed in the Paludrine Club either as a celebratory toast to all those who had made it back, or as a homage to the ones who had failed to beat the clock. Even in a regiment which made its own rules and ignored much of the more formal military discipline, there were still unspoken routines, and customs to be observed.

Hailsham consulted his watch. There were still two minutes to go before the appointed time, and their Chinese contact would be punctual to the second, he knew. As with many Eastern cultures, courtesy and politeness were highly important, even stylized, and it was considered as much of an insult to arrive early as to be late for an appointment.

At precisely three-fifteen, the conference room door opened and a bellboy ushered in the Chinese delegation. There were three of them: two men and, surprisingly, a woman carrying what appeared to be a medical bag. They were all dressed in civilian clothes.

Hailsham nodded politely to the obvious leader. He was tall for a Chinese, and with an unusually dark complexion which betrayed an ancestry stretching back to the days when the Mongol-Tartar hordes swept through central and eastern Asia. He reminded the major of pictures he had seen of North American Indians.

He acknowledged Hailsham's nod with a polite smile, although he made no attempt at a formal greeting. 'I am General Chang,' he announced in flawless English. 'This is Captain Leng Pui and Dr Su.' He glanced around the room. 'Are you all taking part in this mission?'

Hailsham nodded. 'What you see is what you get.'

'Good.'

General Chang motioned to the woman, who stepped forward, laid her bag on the desk and opened it. She withdrew a small membrane-sealed bottle containing a colourless liquid and several disposable syringes.

'Perhaps you and your men would be so good as to roll up your sleeves,' Chang suggested, looking at Hailsham again. 'Dr Su will administer a small injection to each of you.'

A slight frown clouded Hailsham's features. 'Injection?' he queried. 'We weren't briefed on this. What is it?'

Dr Su was carefully loading each syringe and laying them down in a neat row along the table. 'It is nothing,' she murmured soothingly. 'Just a little booster vaccine, that is all. We have no specific knowledge of what biological contaminants you might be exposed to. This will give you some measure of protection against some of the possible viral strains.'

Hailsham was still not sure. 'What about after-effects?' he asked. 'My men will need to be in peak condition. We can't afford anything which might impair their performance in any way.'

The doctor smiled. 'There will be none, I assure you. Now, if you would be so good as to line up, I will administer the injections.'

Hailsham considered the matter for several more seconds. Finally, he shrugged, slipped off his jacket and began to roll up his shirt sleeve, volunteering himself as the guinea pig. A muted babble of conversation broke out as the rest of the men fell into a ragged line behind him.

'Jesus Christ, Thinker, you've gone as white as a bloody sheet,' Jimmy observed.

The burly Mancunian tried hard to raise a scornful grin, but failed miserably. He chewed at his bottom lip nervously, fighting to control the irrational phobia which had haunted him since childhood and was still one of the few things which could reduce him to a quivering jelly. As someone so self-contained, it bothered him greatly that he had a weakness, something he could not control. Some men feared being trapped in confined spaces, others had a morbid fear of snakes, or spiders. The Thinker was terrified of hypodermic needles.

Jimmy could see the big man's hands trembling, but he found it hard to accept the evidence of his own eyes. This was the man he had watched single-handedly charge up a rocky hill towards an Argentinian machine-gun nest at Goose Green, the M16 in his hands spitting furiously as a fusillade of 9mm slugs chewed up the ground around his feet. This was the man who could slog on through the roughest, toughest route march, his step sure and solid when others around him were beginning to turn to jelly at the knees. And now here was that same man reduced to a nervous wreck at the sight of a tiny silver needle.

The Glaswegian was about to turn to the rest of the men and make a joke at the Thinker's expense, but something stopped him. It was not just the warning, baleful glare in the corporal's eyes. It was the sudden, somewhat frightening realization that they were all, in one way or another, vulnerable.

Instead, he nudged the Mancunian gently in the ribs, winking at him. 'Don't worry, Thinker,' he muttered quietly. 'It's only a little prick, after all. A bit like Trooper Naughton, really.'

The Thinker flashed him a sheepish grin, which bore more than a trace of gratitude. 'I just hate bloody injections,' he murmured, getting back a little of his self-assurance from the shared joke. Nevertheless, he averted his eyes when it came to his turn, still unable to actually watch the needle sliding into his flesh.

Typically, Tweedledum found a source of ribald humour in the situation, grinning up at Dr Su with brazen familiarity as she dabbed his arm with an antiseptic wipe. 'Hope this is good for the clap as well, darlin'. I've never been too sure about those standard-issue condoms.'

The woman's face was a flat mask of oriental inscrutability as she inserted the needle. Nevertheless, it seemed to Tweedledum that she gave it a quite pronounced and unnecessary jerk as she pulled it out again. He was not grinning quite so broadly when he walked away from the table to rejoin his companions.

The unexpected medical treatment dispensed with, Dr Su packed her bag again and left the room. General Chang turned to Major Hailsham.

'The first thing I have to tell you is that the mission will be going ahead virtually as we have planned,' he announced. 'Transport has been arranged and is waiting outside the hotel to take you all directly to a

Chinese Air Force base just outside Wuchow. From there you will be airlifted to Tacheng, where you will pick up your arms and equipment.'

The man's delivery was bland, but Hailsham had already picked up on that one little word – 'virtually'.

'Do I take it there has been a change of plan?' he asked.

Chang smiled thinly. 'You are very astute, Major. I compliment you. Yes, as you so rightly assume, we have had to modify our original plans slightly in the light of some recent developments.'

Hailsham's face was grave. He looked at the tall Chinaman darkly, making no attempt to disguise his annoyance. The very essence of all SAS operations was meticulous planning and preparation. Last-minute changes were not only unwelcome – they were dangerous. Nevertheless, he tried to be as polite as possible. 'Perhaps you would care to explain, General,' he suggested.

'Our latest intelligence reports tell us that guerrilla activity in the area has increased far more than expected in recent weeks,' Chang informed him. 'As a result, official Republican forces have also built up considerably. My superiors now feel that our original plan of inserting you and your men over the border by helicopter is unwise, both from your point of view and from ours. We think it much safer to parachute you in at night, from a transport plane flying at commercial altitude. HALO, I believe you call it, if our understanding of your procedures is correct.'

'You've done your homework, General,' Hailsham

muttered, returning the man's earlier compliment. 'In which case you should be aware that we use modified parachutes, work with our own RAF Special Forces Flight and drop from an open rear ramp on a Hercules C-130. I take it you have none of these things.'

General Chang seemed to take this observation as a personal affront. His body stiffened, his Mongoloid eyes narrowing even further. 'The Chinese People's Air Force is also highly trained, Major. We have modified Iluyshin bombers with a side-opening door which your men would find more than adequate. Our own special forces seem to have little trouble in utilizing similar techniques to those of your own.'

Hailsham met the man's eyes directly, facing the challenge. His gut reaction was to rise to the bait, but he resisted, shaking his head slowly. 'I'm sorry. General, but I'm not prepared to make that decision without consulting my men. In private, if you don't mind.'

Chang's expression had hardened to obvious rage now, mixed with the faintest trace of incredulity. 'Consult your men?' he demanded angrily. 'Do you not just give them orders? May I remind you, Major Hailsham, that this joint mission was requested and planned at government level?'

Hailsham remained calm and polite in the face of the implied threat. 'I'm afraid we do things a little differently in the SAS, General. We call it democracy. Now, if you would be so good as to give me a couple of minutes alone with my men.'

For a moment, the Chinaman held his ground, muscles working nervously beneath the flattened contours of his face. Then, clenching his fists into tight knots, he turned stiffly and strode towards the door, nodding curtly towards Captain Leng Pui to follow him.

Hailsham waited until the door had closed behind them before addressing the men. 'Well, I suppose you all heard that. So, what do we think about it?'

Andrew threw it straight back at him. 'What's your opinion, boss?'

Hailsham thought for a second. 'My instinctive reaction is to say scrub the mission,' he admitted. 'But perhaps I'm overreacting.'

'It'd certainly scrub your chances of getting on this year's honours list, boss,' Cyclops put in. 'I reckon they'd have you cleaning out the latrines with a toothbrush a week after we got back.'

'Aye, and it'd be your own fucking toothbrush as well,' Jimmy added, for emphasis.

Hailsham let the ripple of nervous laughter die away. 'Seriously, though, we're not in the business of taking uncalculated risks. And that's exactly what we're being asked to do. A night drop, over unknown territory, from an unfamiliar aircraft and with chutes of dubious performance. That's a lot of rogue equations all in one go.'

'On the other hand, we've all done side exits,' Andrew cut in. 'And we could raise our canopy height a few hundred feet to give us all that extra margin of safety.'

'And we could show that Chinky bastard a thing or two about the finest regiment in the world,' the Thinker muttered, gingerly rubbing the bruise on his arm, which was still smarting. He was not at all happy about the thought of having gone through his ordeal for nothing.

Hailsham looked at them all with a sense of pride. 'So the general concensus is that we go for it?' he asked, although he already knew the answer.

Andrew nodded, his ebony face splitting into a grin. 'Who dares wins, eh, boss?'

The matter was closed, the decision made. With a final nod of approval, Hailsham strode to the door and opened it to let the two Chinese officers back into the room.

'We've decided to go along with your change of plan,' he announced stiffly. 'But with one proviso. We do a dummy run over neutral territory to familiarize ourselves with your procedures and equipment.'

General Chang looked relieved. Perhaps *too* relieved, Hailsham thought. 'That can be arranged,' the Chinaman said, once again stony-faced. 'Now, if you are ready, I will escort you and your men to the transport.'

Hailsham fell back slightly, closing in on Andrew as the men filed out of the room and through the hotel lobby towards the twelve-seater minibus which was parked outside.

'What's up, boss?' Andrew asked Hailsham. It was obvious that the major had something on his mind, and wanted to talk.

Hailsham shook his head uncertainly. 'I don't know. Maybe it's nothing,' he replied. 'It's just that I can't help wondering if these slitty-eyed little bastards have any more surprises up their sleeves.'

88

9

Major Hailsham sat in the training seat of the Shenyang F-9 fighter plane, gazing out through the perspex canopy at the sheer grandeur of the panorama spread out some 20,000 feet below him.

To his left, the soaring, jagged and snow-capped peaks of the Tien Shan range competed for his attention with the twisted gullies and canyons of the Turfan Depression almost immediately below. Tearing his eyes away to look to the right, he could see the flat, featureless expanse of the Mongolian Plateau and the vast reaches of the Gobi Desert beyond.

It all looked so barren, so utterly hostile, he thought. Yet the desolate and virtually worthless terrain had been the prize in a history of bloodshed and battle which stretched back over 400 years, the most recent change of ownership coming at the turn of the nineteenth century when the Soviet Union had managed to annex some fifty million square miles of territory from their Chinese neighbours. Right up to the present day, it had remained the scene of countless secret wars and border skirmishes between the two communist giants. No one in the West had the faintest notion of how many lives had been claimed over the years, and it was more than probable that no one really cared, either.

The plane was safely inside Chinese territory, flying north-eastwards along the line of the Sinkiang-Kazakhstan border towards the roughly triangular confluence with Mongolia. Hailsham had insisted on the reconnaissance flight, even though the practice drop over the lower foothills of the Tien Shan mountains earlier that morning had been an unqualified success. Retrieved almost immediately by helicopter, he and his men had been safely back at the Tacheng airbase in good time for lunch. Despite his earlier misgivings, Hailsham had no complaints so far about Chinese efficiency or their good intentions to make the mission a success.

But there was not much to be seen from inside the belly of a modified Iluyshin 28 bomber, and not much chance to study the scenery below when one was free-falling from 38,000 feet and concentrating on getting one's canopy timing right. So Hailsham had requested a personal inspection flight closer to the actual target area and, surprisingly, General Chang had agreed without the slightest hesitation.

They were clear of the Tien Shan range now, flying along the line of the long valley plain between the Tarbagaty range to port and the Altai Mountains to starboard. Ahead in the distance, Hailsham could just make out the towering 15,000-foot peak of Mount Belukha beyond the Kazakhstan border, and knew that they were rapidly running out of airspace which could be considered fully 'safe' in broad daylight. It took just one overzealous rebel with a SAM-7 at his disposal to make a slight miscalculation of distance, and there would be two more statistics on the list of secret casualties. Hailsham leaned forward, tapping the Chinese pilot lightly on the shoulder and making a circular motion in the air with his forefinger. Nodding, the pilot banked the Shenyang into a long, raking curve and settled the fighter into a straight course which would take them back to Tacheng.

So everything appeared to check out, Hailsham mused to himself. There seemed to be no point in hanging on any longer than necessary. They would go in tonight, an hour or two before dawn. That would give them time to establish a hide and observation post for the following day. Such an OP would give them a vantage point from which they could recce the immediate area and perhaps establish enemy positions from the glow of camp-fires by night. In the early morning light, Hailsham planned to send out the first patrol, led by Sergeant Winston, to set up the first RV point before moving on into the lower foothills. It was normal practice for SAS patrols to move only by night, but they had a lot of ground to cover and they were not officially in a combat situation. Hailsham was counting on any guerrilla groups conducting a basically unsophisticated technique of ambush and sneak attack on their already known enemies. They would already have those established positions, and would hardly be expecting a new force to be literally dropping into their laps. In addition, the small size of the operation, and the high degree of natural cover they could expect once they got into the mountains, gave them an excellent chance of making daylight progress without being spotted. There was also one other factor in their favour. Their main brief was to evade other forces, not to stalk them. And although it was not a normal SAS tactic, running and hiding was an easier option than going in on the attack. As in chess, the defensive player tends to control the play – at least until the endgame.

It was not, perhaps, the most satisfying of strategies, but Hailsham felt confident that it would foot the bill. It had to, since there was no longer any time to come up with any better plan of action.

Just let it be clean, he thought to himself. They were good men who had all risked their lives fighting against their country's real enemies. They most certainly did not deserve to die in a hastily conceived and half-baked operation such as this one. Hailsham's silent plea was something just short of an actual prayer. He had been a professional soldier for too long to retain much belief in a wise and benevolent God.

In Hereford, it was eight-thirty in the morning as Barney Davies tapped out the Foreign Secretary's private, 'hot' number. The call went directly through, bypassing the ears of the whole entourage of personal assistants and secretarial staff, although it was probably monitored by one or other of the British security services.

Davies's message was brief and to the point. 'They're going in tonight,' he said simply. 'At 03.00 hours, local time.'

'Thank you, Lieutenant-Colonel Davies,' the Foreign Secretary said quietly. 'You will of course keep me informed as to developments.' He hung up without waiting for an answer.

* * *

'Correct me if I'm wrong, but haven't we already done this once today?' Cyclops asked as they filed into the converted bomb bay of the Iluyshin 28.

'Nah, you must have been having one of your recurring wet dreams,' Tweedledee told him. Turning to the rest of the men, he warmed to his theme. 'Did Cyclops ever tell you he gets a hard-on from heights? That's why he can't go up ladders. Every time he gets near the top, his old man pops out and pushes him off again.'

'He'd have to be fucking close to the wall,' Jimmy threw in. 'What he's got's only good enough for diddling sparrows.'

'Should suit you down to the ground, then,' Tweedledum ventured. 'We all know that the Scots have notoriously tight arses.'

The big Glaswegian growled, shaking a ham-like fist in the younger man's direction. 'I'll see you, Jimmy,' he threatened good-naturedly, parodying his own stereotype.

A high-pitched bleeping cut through the bullshit, indicating that the side hatch was about to close. With a faint metallic squeal, the heavy steel door swung into position, then drew in and locked tight. The aircraft began to throb as the Chinese pilot throttled up the twin Soloviev D-30KP engines, which had previously been purring at idling speed.

'Well, looks like we're off on our hols, lads,' the Thinker said drily. The observation met with a less than rapturous reception.

Hailsham, sitting alone on the far side on the bomb bay, consulted his watch, squinting slightly in the dull-yellowish light from the plane's rudimentary lighting system. It was 01.00 hours. Two hours to the drop zone and teatime at home. He found himself wondering what his ex-wife had given the kids for their evening meal as the Iluyshin began to lumber up the runway, gathering speed as the engines roared ever louder.

It was at times like these that Andrew liked to compose poetry in his head, or at least draft out the bones of an idea which could be fine-tuned and committed to paper at a later stage. It was something to do with body chemistry, he had always vaguely understood – this in-between time, this hiatus just before a mission when every nerve and fibre was tingling with adrenalin yet the brain was somehow idling, numbed with the delay between thought and deed.

Yet not one original thought would come clear in his head. Instead, snatches and phrases from other poets buzzed around, with varying degrees of relevance or meaning. The opening lines from one of Walt Whitman's poems – one of Andrew's personal heroes – seemed particularly apt, given the circumstances.

Come my tan-faced children,
Follow well in order, get your weapons ready,
Have you your pistols, have you your sharp-edged
    axes?
Pioneers! O pioneers!

With these words running around in his brain, Andrew found himself covertly studying the faces of the men around him, analysing and trying to understand what their expressions betrayed. He caught the Thinker's eyes directly, and it was like suddenly coming across a mirror in a darkened room. He felt inexplicably embarrassed, almost guilty, and smiled sheepishly.

The big Mancunian smiled back, but it was a gesture of reassurance, of a secret shared and understood. Andrew felt relieved, instinctively sensing what the man was communicating to him. A man's thoughts were private, personal – and precious. Especially at a time like this.

They were off the runway now, and climbing steadily. Barry Naughton felt the familiar tingle running through his body. Born partly of a fear of flying and partly of personal pride at having largely conquered it, it was like a little power surge from which he could draw inner reserves. This, and the knowledge that he was about to go into a battle situation, recharged and changed him. He was an equal among equals now. As valued, and as valuable, as any one of his peers.

That was the young trooper's secret – the factor which had led him to seek the Army as a career in the first place, and had steered him towards the SAS in particular. And, in no small measure, it had also been the one thing which had got him through the harsh basic training which had beaten many tougher men.

Out in Civvy Street, even in the barracks, Barry knew that his fellow troopers often saw him as the natural butt of a joke, of a bit of piss-taking. A regular Clark Kent, in fact. But the SAS was his secret telephone box. A set of olive-greens became his Superman costume. It was a good feeling, even if psychologically dubious. It sustained him.

'Well, I reckon it's time to open the beauty parlour,' Jimmy said, pulling out his pair of camouflage sticks. He rolled spittle and phlegm around in his mouth, spat it into the palm of his hand and began to work his base foundation into a sticky, creamy consistency before smearing it over his face and neck with the other hand.

Taking his lead, the rest of the men set about applying the 'cam' cream, taking care to cover all exposed areas, such as ears, chin, throats and the backs of their hands and wrists. With the base coat dulling down the natural sheen of their skin and contours of their faces, they proceeded to compound the effect by stroking wide, diagonal smears of black stick to their faces and foreheads to break up the broad outline of their features. Finally, they each smeared the black make-up thickly over more prominent features such as noses, chins and cheekbones, leaving the natural hollows a much lighter shade.

For Andrew, of course, the procedure was slightly different. Jimmy grinned at him as he drew a white make-up stick across his ebony skin.

'Jesus Christ, Sarge. You look like a fucking zebra,' he pointed out.

Suddenly they all had a target.

'Come on, boss, give us a chorus of *Swannee Ribber*,' Tweedledum suggested.

Not to be outdone, Tweedledee joined in the banter. 'Or how about an impression of Larry Parkes?' He waggled his hands in the air while opening and closing his mouth silently.

Andrew grinned good-naturedly. He had heard it all a hundred times before. 'When are you honky bastards going to come up with something original?' he said wearily. 'Anyway, now all you ladies have your warpaint on, how about getting ready to rig up? Or are you planning to float down on your petticoats like a bunch of overweight fairies?'

It was a good point. Watched by their sergeant and Major Hailsham, the men moved naturally into a practice routine, forming themselves into two lines, facing each other. From the carefully stacked bundles of bergens and equipment at one end of the Iluyshin's belly, the primary and reserve chutes were retrieved, then passed carefully from hand to hand along the two rows. Each man chose the partner immediately facing him, watching each other as they slipped into their thermal suits, zipped them up to the neck and then began to shrug on their chutes. With everything in position, it became a question of checking each other's rig, checking straps for tension and making sure every buckle and ringclip was firmly locked in position.

Finally, it was time for each partner to help the other pull on his heavy bergen, and tuck them up just below the small of the back beneath the main parachute packs.

Andrew finished putting the final touches to his make-up and inspected all six men, making his own final check. Then, turning to Major Hailsham, they set about rigging each other up.

'Now we're ready to party,' Andrew finally

announced. With Hailsham's assistance, he busied himself checking the chutes for the Controlled Air Delivery System (CADS) which would take down the heavier equipment, guided by radio-control devices in the hands of himself and Hailsham.

The whole make-ready procedure had taken just over an hour. Hailsham checked his watch again, satisfied that they were well ahead of schedule. The converted bomber was still well inside safe airspace, the pilot keeping it in steady and level flight at 15,000 feet. Another half an hour and he would start to climb as they approached the Mongolian border area. Then it would be time for them all to hook into the onboard oxygen supply, before switching to their personal canisters for the actual drop. But for now, there was nothing more to do except wait and try to relax.

In fact, the aircraft began to climb almost immediately, much to Hailsham's surprise. He cast a questioning, sideways glance at Andrew, whose face bore a similar puzzled expression. The sergeant shrugged, having no answer.

The interior temperature began to cool quite markedly. The Thinker flexed his body, stretching his muscles as best he could under the restriction of the enclosing parachute harness and the weight of his equipment. What the hell was going on? he wondered to himself. He had caught the brief and silent exchange between Andrew and Hailsham, and it had been enough to tell him that something was not quite as it should be. None of the others seemed to have noticed, and he figured it was not his place to point it out. He trusted Hailsham implicitly, as they all did. No doubt the CO would keep them all fully informed as and when he saw fit.

The rest of the men had begun to react to the drop in temperature now, despite their thermal suits. As with any ordeal of shared discomfort, it triggered off another little exchange of bullshit.

'Christ, it's colder than a witch's tit,' Barry said, shivering.

Cyclops grinned at him. 'You just wait until you get outside,' he answered. 'Just imagine being bare-arsed naked on a glacier and you'll get a rough idea.'

Barry shivered again. 'I hope for your sake that you remembered to wear a fur-lined jockstrap,' Jimmy told him. 'I've heard of guys on these night drops whose cocks got so stiff with cold on the way down that they just broke off with the shock of landing.'

But Barry was not taking the bait. 'Fuck off!' he said simply, grinning at the big Scot.

'Anyway, you could be in a bit of trouble yourself, Jimmy,' Tweedledum pointed out. 'You didn't have your porridge this morning, did you?'

'Talking of that, what do badgers have for breakfast?' Cyclops asked. He waited for a few seconds of expectant silence before answering his own question. 'Ready-brock.'

It was a lousy joke, but they all smiled anyway.

A sudden loud and insistent bleeping cut through the mood, snapping them all back into alertness. Simultaneously a red warning light began to flash from the ceiling of the bomb bay. They all knew exactly what it signified. The pilot was about to depressurize the interior of the plane.

'What the fuck?' Hailsham blurted out, his face

now registering something more serious than mere surprise. He checked his watch again quickly, his mind racing. There was no way that he could be that much out on his calculations. Even allowing for an unexpected tail-wind, they could not possibly have reached the drop zone so long ahead of schedule. There were only two real possibilities: either the Chinese pilot had made a serious miscalculation or he was deliberately planning to drop them short of the DZ. But either one was purely academic now. The temperature was already plummeting as the thin, freezing air outside the plane began to rush in to replace that which was being evacuated. Hailsham could feel a tightness in his chest. They needed oxygen, and they needed it fast.

'Get your masks on – now,' he barked. Adjusting his own, he moved into the centre of the converted bomb bay and connected its flexible plastic hose to the central oxygen supply console on the ceiling.

The flashing red light and warning bleeper went off together as the plane became fully depressurized. In the sudden silence that followed, there was only the faintest residual hiss as the side exit door's hermetic seals were released. Then, with a brief metallic squeal, the heavy door began to pull out and away, revealing the star-spangled blackness of the night sky.

There was no longer any time to worry about what might or what might not have gone wrong with the Chinese planning of the operation. It was all automatic now, Hailsham reflected. Training and instinct took over. As if in some ancient and time-honoured tribal ritual, he moved forward with Andrew, the pair of them dragging the CADS into place between them. Behind that, the rest of the men formed themselves into two short rows in preparation for the jump – one to the left, one to the right.

'Switch to personal oxygen,' Hailsham snapped.

Moving together like the parts of a well-oiled machine, each man disconnected his mask nozzle from the on-board supply and snapped it into position on the bottle he carried on the side webbing of his parachute harness. All eyes lifted to the small red light which glowed like a malevolent eye above the hatch door, which was now fully open. Time seemed to freeze. The men fidgeted nervously as they waited for the red light to wink out. It eventually did, accompanied by a loud buzzing noise. Seconds later, it was replaced by a green one, flashing on and off in a slow, regular cycle.

Hailsham made a final adjustment to his face mask, pressing it more firmly into position. He pulled his passive night goggles down over his eyes – a gesture immediately copied by the rest of the men. The rhythm of the flashing green light was increasing now, building up until it was a constant pulse. Finally, it ceased flickering altogether and remained on. It was time to go.

Hailsham and Andrew dragged the CADS chutes to the lip of the open hatch. Then, with a brief nod at each other, they pulled the heavy equipment container with a concerted effort and launched themselves into space.

Behind them, the six troopers followed their lead at spaced intervals, throwing themselves out into the icy blackness in the classic free-fall position. Spread-eagled like featherless birds, they began to plummet towards the ground below, the bitter, rushing air tearing at their bodies like an Arctic blizzard.

It was that moment, Hailsham's brain screamed, that breathless, deathless moment of utter commitment. Falling irrevocably, yet strangely suspended between heaven and earth as if in some drug-induced fantasy in which the spaces between time itself had become distorted.

They were going down.

But where? Hailsham needed to know. For Christ's sake, where?

10

It was a desert, Hailsham thought. He was standing in the middle of a bloody desert! With a conscious effort, he pushed aside his initial sense of rage at the Chinese, trying to concentrate on the more immediate and practical problems.

First things first. He busied himself hauling in his chute, gathering the billowing folds of material around his feet. Luckily there was only a faint breeze, which made the job comparatively easy. Stamping the gathered parachute into a lumpy ball, he held it between his feet and released his harness straps. He moved his head slowly from side to side, taking in his surroundings and attempting to locate the rest of his men.

In the eerie, greenish glow of the passive night goggles the surrounding terrain was like a schoolboy's impression of a lunar landscape. OK, so it was not exactly desert, Hailsham told himself as he started to make out a little detail and some sense of his surroundings. It was open steppe country – a vast, flattish area of thin grasses and stunted bush and scrub. In the far distance, virtually making up the horizon, the foothills of the mountain terrain which should have marked the outer perimeter of their original drop zone showed up as a jagged, darker green line.

It was difficult to make an accurate assessment of distance with the PNGs, but Hailsham estimated that the first line of hills was at least eight miles as the crow flies. With first light probably less than two hours away, the immediate problem was obvious. Even if they started out immediately, they would be dangerously exposed long before they could reach cover. What was even more worrying were the half-dozen or so pinpricks of light which he could make out between them and the foothills. Obviously camp-fires, but whether they were of nomadic Kazakh tribesmen or guerrilla forces, there was no way of knowing.

Something moved in Hailsham's peripheral vision — a dark, lumpy shape, bouncing or rolling towards him. As his head whirled to confront the sudden menace, his hand was already flying to his hip, clawing at the holstered Browning.

The tension in his body, and the adrenalin rush which had triggered it, seeped away in relief as the wispy, vaguely spherical object brushed against his legs and stopped. Hailsham reached out to touch its dry and brittle fragility. It was a clump of sage brush, torn loose from its tenuous roots in the dry and dusty steppe soil and bowled along on the breeze. He flicked it away again, and watched it continue its erratic course across the arid plain.

Other dark shapes were approaching him now, but these were identifiable and comfortingly familiar. Andrew loomed up out of the darkness first, like a shadow within a shadow. Behind him, Hailsham could pick out the reassuring bulk of the Thinker and the slightly shorter figure of Jimmy.

Andrew glanced at the Browning, which Hailsham still held in his hand. 'Expecting trouble, boss? Or were you planning to fire off a salute to greet us?'

Hailsham holstered the pistol. 'Where are the others? Did everyone make it down safely?'

The sergeant nodded. 'No problems. They're waiting over by the CADS, about 300 yards that way.' He jerked his thumb back over his shoulder. 'I reckon you must have caught a last-minute updraft or something.'

'It sure as hell wasn't a thermal,' Hailsham muttered, shivering. He reached down to pick up his chute, anxious to start moving. 'I suppose you've already noticed that we have company?' he asked, jerking his head towards the foothills.

'We've also got a few problems,' the Thinker confirmed. 'Cyclops seems to think they'll probably have dogs, and we just happen to be directly downwind right now.'

'Shit!' Hailsham hissed. It was something he had not considered, and the last thing they needed at that particular moment was further complications. He fell into step behind Andrew as he began to lead the way back to the main force.

Barry had already opened the CADS container and broken out a couple of folding shovels. He and Tweedledum were busy digging a trench in which to bury the parachutes. Hailsham tossed his own into the pile.

'So, what's the plan, boss?' Tweedledee asked. 'Do we bed in or are we going to get moving?'

'Damned good question,' Hailsham answered. Under normal circumstances, it would have been standard practice to seek out somewhere to dig a trench hide for the morning. Exposed as they were, they might just as well erect a bloody great flagpole instead. 'Short of us all doing about a dozen four-minute miles in succession, I'd say our choice of options was strictly limited.' He broke off, staring out across the open ground towards the foothills once again. The cluster of camp-fires seemed to be concentrated in one small area. Probably a sheltered gully between two ridges of hills, he guessed. Which meant that the campers, whoever they were, probably had a clear forward view over the plain but restricted vision on either side of them. There seemed only one possibility that offered a fair chance of making progress without being spotted.

'We'll split into our two patrols now,' Hailsham announced. 'It'll mean a pretty lengthy detour, but if we fan out we stand a reasonable chance of getting far enough before daybreak to dig in somewhere that offers at least partial cover from any OP in those hills. With a bit of luck, they'll be shipping out at first light anyway – in which case they'll either have their backs to us or they'll cut straight through between us.'

'And if they don't?' Andrew asked.

Hailsham shrugged. 'Then we'll have them caught in a pincer between us. If they prove to be hostile, we'll at least have a fighting edge. We can hit them from two sides.'

Andrew nodded. It was as good a plan as any, given the circumstances. 'Of course, the good news is that it could just turn out to be a bunch of nomads,' he pointed out. 'In which case, if we're lucky, we'll all get to eat goat stew for breakfast.'

'I liked the sound of baked eagle better,' Cyclops observed. 'Smelly bastards, goats.'

'You ain't gonna reek of violets yourself by the time you've humped all your gear over to those hills,' Andrew pointed out. 'It might be bloody cold, but you'll still work up a sweat under those layers of Gore-tex.'

'It's not as bad as I expected,' Jimmy said brightly. 'I've been in colder places. My old lady's bedroom, for a start.'

'You wait until we get up in those mountains,' Tweedledum warned him. 'Your old lady's bedroom will seem like a Moroccan whorehouse.'

'His old lady's bedroom *is* a Moroccan whorehouse,' Tweedledee put in, raising a good-natured laugh.

Hailsham let the merriment die away. 'Right, we'd better get going,' he said finally. 'And once we *do* get moving, we cut the bullshit, is that understood? All communication will be on a strictly business-only basis. Sound travels a long way in open country like this.'

'I suppose that rules out a nice stirring marching song?' Cyclops ventured.

Hailsham glared at him. 'Trooper, I'll kick your arse if you so much as break wind,' he promised. 'Right, let's do it.'

The men broke naturally into the two agreed patrols – Tweedledee, Tweedledum and Cyclops staying with Hailsham; Jimmy, Barry and the Thinker with Andrew. They busied themselves sharing out the supplies and spare ammunition. Andrew slung the heavy Stinger launcher over his shoulder, forcing a grin in Hailsham's direction as he felt the full weight of his extra burden. 'And, yes, I'm still glad I insisted on bringing it,' he said out loud, in answer to an unspoken question.

Fully laden, the two patrols lined up, facing their objective. Hailsham scanned the far ridge of hills through his PNGs, seeking out a primary RV to meet at if they both managed to evade the encampment successfully. Just above and behind the site of the camp-fires, he could make out a long, flat ridge broken by a single high, rocky outcrop. As a landmark, it was good enough. He pointed it out to Andrew.

'If we make it to the hills safely, we RV there at 10.00 hours tomorrow,' he instructed.

The sergeant nodded. 'We'll be waiting for you,' he promised. 'Any prefences for lunch?'

Hailsham smiled, clapping him on the shoulder. 'Just be there,' he said.

The patrols moved out at a tangent from each other, the laden bergen on each man's back making them look like a small caravan of strange, two-legged dromedaries. There were no farewells. To say goodbye admitted the possibility that you might not see one another again. Fanning apart in a wide 'V', they were soon out of sight of each other, even with the aid of the PNGs.

No, he did not regret bringing the Stinger along, Andrew reminded himself, although the extra 65lb of the launcher and the single missile he carried made him feel like a pack-mule. Even so, he still hoped he would not have to use it in anger. For there was no real enemy. If they were forced to kill, it would be for all the wrong reasons, and there would be no pride, no glory, in that.

The thought depressed him. It was a shit mission, and had been from the start. The only enemy, if there was one at all, was what was lurking in wait for them up at that research complex. An invisible enemy, an unknown threat. And the SAS were soldiers, not bloody Ghostbusters. Andrew sighed, thinking about it. Yes, it was a shit mission all right. And he and his men were being used like pieces of toilet paper.

They had covered no more than about seven miles, and it was already becoming noticeably lighter. To his right, away from the hills, Andrew could see a misty band of lighter green creating a thin stripe between the darkness of the terrain and the sky. He raised his hand to the PNGs, lifting them away from his eyes. The stripe was a faint ochre glow now, sandwiched between two slabs of blackness. In a short time it would begin to glow red, then golden, as the early morning sun pushed its umbra ahead of it.

Andrew's gaze travelled to his left, picking out the twinkling of the camp-fires once again. They were closer now, but they seemed higher than they had appeared from their original position. He snapped the goggles back into place and stopped, raising his hand in the air.

The Thinker closed up on Andrew's right shoulder, lowering his mouth to his ear. 'What's up, boss?' he whispered.

Andrew pointed ahead, slightly over to his right.

'Am I imagining it, or is the terrain sloping down ahead of us?' he asked.

The corporal strained his eyes into the gloom. It was difficult to define contour or elevation, but there did appear to be a shallow but sustained incline ahead of them. 'Yeah, I think you're right,' he agreed. 'But we should be going up, not down, if we're heading towards the hills. What do you reckon?'

Andrew sucked at his teeth. He was not sure, but it was a strong hunch. 'I reckon we might have just found ourselves a little bonus,' he said quietly.

Barry had moved up to join them. Behind him, Jimmy kept his distance, remaining in the Tail-end Charlie position. Andrew waved him forward.

'Listen, I want you to skirt out to the right,' he told the Scot as he finally came near. 'Sweep around in an arc and then rejoin us about 200 yards ahead. Thinker and I reckon there's some sort of depression over there. Check it out, will you?'

'You got it, boss,' Jimmy said, slipping away as Andrew shrugged the heavy Stinger into a more comfortable carrying position and began to move off again.

By the time Jimmy had finished his sweep and moved back to rejoin them again, Andrew could see him coming from a good 200 yards away. It was definitely getting lighter – and rapidly. He hoped that Jimmy was going to confirm his suspicions. He was in luck.

'You were right, boss,' Jimmy whispered. 'It's like a very shallow gully, but it gets steeper as you move down. My guess is that it's a dried-up wadi that's

110

been scoured out by the spring snow-melt coming down from the mountains.'

Andrew could not repress a wry grin. 'I'm impressed, Trooper,' he said. 'Nobody told me that you'd graduated in geology.' Serious again, he added: 'How deep do you reckon it gets? Enough to give us cover?'

But Jimmy was way ahead of him. 'Let's put it this way, boss. I couldn't even see you, let alone that ridge of hills over yonder. Looks like we've just found ourselves a place to hole up for a few hours.'

It was all the confirmation Andrew needed. 'Right, let's go for it,' he hissed, breaking away to the right. 'If we can't see our friends up in the hills, it's a pretty safe bet they won't be able to see us, either. The sooner we get dug in, the better.'

Following his lead, the patrol began to move slowly back down the path taken by the Glaswegian. A few minutes later, the last of the camp-fire lights winked out of view as they dropped down below the lip of the shallow ridge and continued their descent.

Major Hailsham had also been acutely aware of the imminent approach of dawn and the urgent need to find some sort of cover. He scanned the bleak terrain ahead with increasing frustration. There was nothing that could be turned to their favour, not even a shallow dip in the ground. It was beginning to look as though they would have to do it the hard away.

He slipped off his PNGs and turned to face the rising sun. A broad band of reddish-gold light was now visible over the horizon. He estimated that they probably had less than three-quarters of an hour before they would be illuminated against the barren background of the steppe like flies on fly-paper.

Time, then, was of the essence – and location seemed not to make much difference. Hailsham brought the patrol to a halt, summoning in Cyclops from 'Charlie' position. 'Looks like we're going to have to dig in here,' he told the men flatly. 'It's not exactly summer camp, but it's going to have to do.'

They all knew what to do. Tweedledum and Tweedledee took a pair of shovels and began to dig out a long, narrow trench. In true SAS tradition, Hailsham dropped his bergen and knelt down to help, scratching at the earth with his bare hands. Cyclops, showing the sort of initiative which had earned him more than one official accolade in the past, sat down on his behind and began to scrape away soil with the heels of his boots.

It was a tough and laborious job. The red, dry and crumbly earth was more like coarse sand, sliding back down the sides of the trench almost as fast as they could scoop it out. Eventually, however, they had managed to gouge out a rough V-shaped slit in the ground, about six feet deep at its lowest point and about five feet wide. It was not much, but for the next few hours, at least, it would be home. Now all they needed was something to cover the top once they were inside. Hailsham remembered his alarming encounter with the rolling clump of sage brush. Where there was one, there could be others, he rationalized. Leaving the three troopers to finish off the slit-trench as best they could, he went in search of further roving herbage.

He returned some ten minutes later, dragging four wispy balls behind him. With the laces from his boots, he lashed them loosely together and held them down with one foot as he rummaged through his bergen for a coil of climbing rope. Finally, after weighing the balls down with his bergen, he ushered the men into the hastily improvised hide and waited for them to settle down as comfortably as was possible. The three men chose to arrange themselves like a rowing team, each sitting behind the other's back with his knees pulled up.

Hailsham found himself thinking of the games of 'Sardines' he had played as a child, and it made him smile. Scrambling down into the single space left, he pulled his bergen in on top of him and arranged the sage brush above his head until it virtually covered the top of the trench. With luck, from the outside it would just look like a clump of drifting grasses which had bunched themselves together. As long as no one decided to take a closer look, it should suffice.

Hailsham tapped Tweedledee lightly on the shoulder. 'You and Tweedledum try and grab an hour's kip,' he hissed in the trooper's ear. 'Cyclops and I will keep watch until daybreak, and if our friends don't move on, we'll have to think again.'

Tweedledee nodded silently, and passed the message on to his mate. The two troopers lolled sideways against the side of the trench hopefully, although the chances of getting any real sleep were minimal. They both fully realized how exposed they all really were. The situation was hardly conducive to relaxation. At best, the next few hours would be a tense and tedious waiting game.

11

It was the sort of morning that had inspired countless writers and poets over the centuries, Andrew Winston among them. In other circumstances, he would have seen it as the start to a beautiful day. Lines from one of his own early efforts ran through his head as he surveyed the blood-red orb of the dawn sun beginning to lift away from the knife-edge of the horizon.

> Morning
> And the blood-streaked labour pains of light
> Striate
> Across the swollen belly of the dawn.

He smiled ruefully. One day he would finish that particular poem, equating the sunrise to a new birth. Right now, more urgent problems occupied his thoughts.

He slithered out of the hollow which he and his men had scooped out of the side of the gully and began to crawl up its sloping side on his belly. Reaching the top, he peered cautiously over the lip, bringing a pair of powerful non-reflective binoculars up to his eyes.

Despite the earliness of the hour, the encampment

was already a hive of bustling activity. The camp-fires had been doused, and Andrew could make out individual figures scurrying about, packing up their blankets and equipment. He nodded to himself, smiling. It looked as though Hailsham had been right: they were preparing to move out.

They were a motley bunch, perhaps forty to fifty strong. Some wore vaguely military-style uniforms or camouflaged fatigues, while others were clearly dressed as civilians, swathed in brightly striped *khalats*, topped by turbans or embroidered skull-caps. With a slight sense of shock, Andrew noticed that there were also several women and children in the party.

The Thinker had slithered up the side of the ridge to join him. 'Friend or foe, boss?' he whispered in the sergeant's ear.

Andrew handed him the binoculars. 'Take a look for yourself,' he murmured, waiting silently while the other man scanned the encampment.

Finally lowering them again, the Thinker glanced sideways with a faint shrug. 'At a guess, I'd say they were a bunch of refugees with an armed escort,' he volunteered.

'That's what I thought,' said Andrew, nodding. 'But not very well armed, from the look of things. All I saw were a few old breech-loading rifles. No heavy guns, no mortars, as far as I could see.' He took back the binoculars, raising them to his eyes once again. 'From the way they're gathering their stuff together, I'd say they were getting ready to move up further into the hills.'

'Damn,' the Thinker hissed under his breath. 'That

means they're going to stay ahead of us. That'll give them the advantage of the high ground and all the cover they need to spring an ambush if they feel like it.'

Andrew nodded morosely. Those had been his thoughts exactly.

'So, what do you reckon?' the Thinker asked.

'About the only thing we can do is to give them enough headstart so we stay outside the range of those rifles,' Andrew replied with a sigh. 'But if they do decide to set an ambush, we're not going to know about it until the shooting starts. And even if they have only got a few rifles, that gives them one hell of an edge.'

'In short, a bit of a bastard,' the corporal observed. 'Looks like we got hold of the shitty end of the stick, boss.'

It was an understatement. 'And those fucking Chinks handed it to use,' Andrew said bitterly. 'What the fuck were they playing at?'

The Thinker was silent for a few seconds, pondering. Finally, he said: 'Maybe they knew something we don't.'

Andrew grunted. 'Yeah, and something they maybe didn't want us to know, either.' He stiffened suddenly, raising one hand for silence. Holding his breath, he looked up, his eyes scanning the sky. 'Can you hear what I hear?'

The other soldier strained his ears. Sure enough, echoing down from the hills, he could hear a distant, faint, but unmistakable sound. Both men waited with bated breath as the muted *pocka-pocka-pocka* of a helicopter became gradually louder.

The chopper appeared from nowhere. One moment it was just a distant sound, and the next it was in clear view, rising from behind a high ridge of hills to the far right of the refugee encampment. Andrew snatched up his binoculars again, training them on the black shape silhouetted against the golden sky.

'Soviet-built Mil Mi-24 Hind-A,' he muttered, identifying the craft almost at once.

'Christ,' the Thinker spat out, realizing the implications at once. The Hind-A was strictly an assault helicopter, invariably armed with a large-calibre machine-gun in the nose, three other guns on each of the auxiliary wings and four underwing pods equipped with up to thirty-two 57mm rockets. The Soviets had used them extensively during the Afghanistan conflict, to devastating effect. Their destructive capability and sheer fire-power were awesome. One thing was certain, the Thinker realized: it sure as hell was not on a reconnaissance mission.

The noise from the helicopter's engines was overpowering now, wiping out the need to whisper. Andrew whistled loudly through his teeth. 'Christ Almighty – so *that's* what the fucking Chinks wanted to keep quiet about,' he exploded. 'It looks like Republican forces are gunning these bloody hills as a matter of course.'

The noise of the helicopter had brought Jimmy and Barry scrambling up the side of the gully.

'Heard we had company, boss,' Jimmy said. 'Want us to break out a gimpy, just in case?'

Andrew shook his head. 'We've got to remember – this isn't our bloody war,' he reminded them. 'You heard the orders – we stay out of trouble unless it comes looking for us.'

The other trooper looked up at the Hind-A as it began to curve round on a banking sweep, losing height rapidly. 'Well that bastard's not looking for a couple of pals to play with, I can tell you that for nothing,' he said sardonically. 'And if one of them's not trouble, I don't know what is.'

'Yeah, you're probably right,' Andrew agreed, keeping a wary eye on the flight path of the chopper as he spoke. It was completing its turn now, and beginning to drop straight down into the narrow pass between the two ridges of hills where the refugees were. 'And I've got a nasty feeling that it's just found exactly what it's looking for.'

Even as he spoke, they all saw the flashes of flame spit out from the nose and the wings of the helicopter. A split second later, the staccato crackle of heavy gunfire echoed out across the steppe, rolling off the sides of the hills like thunder.

'Jesus wept,' Andrew blurted out, snatching up the binoculars and training them on the tiny camp. 'Those poor bastards don't stand a chance.'

Andrew watched panicking figures running everywhere, desperately trying to seek some sort of cover as the helicopter's blanket fire-power chewed up the dusty soil all around them, creating what looked like a small-scale sandstorm. He saw several of the fleeing figures tossed aside like rag dolls as heavy-calibre slugs from the chopper's nose-gun tore into their bodies. Others just dropped where they stood, as armour-piercing bullets passed straight through them.

There was no attempt to return fire. It was a strictly one-way massacre.

Perhaps half the victims of the attack died in the first few blistering seconds of the aerial assault. Through the binoculars, Andrew could see at least three women among the dead. Then, suddenly, the bodies were all there was to be seen, as the survivors disappeared behind rocks and found fissures in the hillside to hide in.

The sounds of heavy gunfire ceased abruptly and the Hind-A climbed away from the gully, circling round until its pilot had a side view of what had been the encampment. As the helicopter hovered like a malevolent insect, Andrew watched the nose drop and the tail section come up until it resembled a scorpion about to strike.

And strike it did. Four bursts of flame and streaking smoke trails presaged the rapid descent of rockets into the rocky foothills, where they exploded like short, sharp thunderclaps.

'Fuck this for a game of soldiers,' Andrew screamed suddenly. He threw himself back down the gully into the dug-out, emerging a moment later with the Stinger launcher and two missiles tucked under his arm. Grunting with exertion, he hauled them back up to the lip of the ridge and began to make the launcher ready for combat.

'I thought you said this wasn't our war?' the Thinker said laconically, as Andrew slipped a missile canister into the rear end of the launcher and hefted it into position over his shoulder.

The sergeant clapped his eyes to the optical sight. 'This isn't war, it's sheer fucking slaughter,' he grunted, his fingers tightening around the stock and trigger. Bypassing the optional IFF 'friend or foe' identification transponder, he lined up the Hind-A in the sights straight away and locked on.

The launcher bucked in his hands as he squeezed the firing mechanism, launching the infrared missile. As if in slow motion, the warhead streaked unerringly towards its target, homing in on the hot exhaust gases from the twin Isotov turboshaft engines mounted above the helicopter's cabin.

The Hind-A exploded in a red and orange ball of fire, spewing down shattered and smoking pieces of scrap metal in a deadly rain. Then it was gone, with only a few oily black streamers of smoke to mark the fact that there had ever been an aircraft in that particular patch of the sky.

Andrew lowered the launcher to the ground, glancing sideways at Jimmy, Barry and the Thinker with an unspoken question in his eyes. The satisfied smiles on their faces answered him more than adequately. They were all equally glad that the phoney, invisible war was over at last. Now they had a real fight on their hands, with a real and clearly identifiable enemy. They were soldiers again, doing what they were trained to do, and what they did best.

The sergeant grinned broadly at all of them, sharing their relief. 'I think you might say we just chose sides,' he said. 'Let's just hope we chose the right one.'

Two miles away, Major Hailsham watched the last smoking fragments of the Hind-A snaking to the ground and felt a similar sense of elation. He could not fault Sergeant Winston's decision to shoot down the helicopter. Under the circumstances he would have done exactly the same – on purely tactical if not humanitarian grounds. Sooner or later, the pilot would have tired of shooting fish in a barrel and gone looking for other targets. The war would have come to them anyway – Winston had merely pre-empted the fact.

Hailsham reviewed his next move in light of the development. It was extremely unlikely that the pilot or crew had had time to send any sort of message to base. From the moment their on-board sensors had registered a missile locked on to them to the moment of impact had been less than five seconds. Allowing for at least three seconds of surprise and confusion at the completely unexpected attack, the helicopter crew would have been dead before any of them could push the panic button, let alone relay any information.

Hailsham's thoughts turned to the people in the hills, whoever they were. The fact that there had been no attempt to return fire during the attack suggested that they were only lightly armed, if at all. And Hailsham guessed that by now they would either be retreating higher into the hills or digging into cover to tend their wounded. They might be confused, even worried about the source and nature of the sudden new players in the game, although such considerations would not be foremost in their thoughts. Tactically then, Hailsham reckoned, it was as good a time as any to make a forward move, and he automatically made the assumption that his sergeant would think exactly the same way. All things being equal, they would simply RV earlier than planned.

He stretched himself luxuriously, throwing back the

crude sage-brush roof of the hide. 'Well, gentlemen, I think it's time to bug out and head for the hills,' he announced breezily.

Tweedledum, Tweedledee and Cyclops scrambled to their feet gratefully, relieved to be able to stretch their cramped bodies. 'Reckon there are any more of those things about, boss?' Cyclops asked.

Hailsham shrugged, although personally he doubted it. All the intelligence information he had received at the secondary briefing indicated that the official Kazakh Republican forces were stretched pretty thinly, trying to cover a vast area in which multiple and sporadic outbreaks of guerrilla activity and ethnic clashes kept them constantly on the hop. It seemed more than likely that the Hind-A had been a lone bird on a simple search-and-destroy mission, probably from a safe base well inside the border, such as Leninogorsk or Blisk. If that assumption was correct, then the helicopter would not be due back at base for at least an hour and a half, so it would be a minimum of two hours before anything else could be sent to the area to find out what had happened to it.

But this was pure speculation, and Hailsham was not going to swear to it under oath. 'Let's just put it this way,' he said. 'The easiest way to find out would be to hang around here waiting.'

It was a good point. Cyclops set about helping Tweedledum and Tweedledee unload their equipment from the trench hide, after which they hastily filled it in again and covered all traces of its existence as best they could. There was no point in giving the enemy an obvious point from which to track them.

Finally packed up and ready to march, they

assembled behind Hailsham as he scanned the lowest foothills, searching for the best route to their destination. The obvious, and the easiest, path was the most direct – straight across the steppe towards the gully where the refugees had made camp. Such a route had clear advantages. First, it represented the shortest possible distance between them and the cover of the hills, and secondly it would save a considerable amount of climbing through difficult terrain.

But the obvious solution to a problem is not necessarily the best, and the SAS had never been noted for taking the easy option. The attractions of the route were balanced by the potential dangers, Hailsham realized. He was only assuming that the group already in the hills had limited weaponry. They may have deliberately chosen not to return fire upon the helicopter to conceal their true strength, he reflected. Equally, they may simply not have had enough time to prepare an adequate defence against the attack. So they remained a largely unknown quantity.

With all these factors in mind, Hailsham struck out on a path which would take them well to the left of the encampment and into a stair-like series of rising hills towards the mountains proper. It was a circuitous route, but he reckoned that, with the initial climbing done, it should be possible to cut across what appeared to be a fairly easy plateau towards the RV. He could only hope that his sergeant was making a similar decision.

12

In fact, Andrew's decision was much more straight-forward and easy to make. Daylight had revealed that the shallow gully which had afforded them protection would also offer a straight and easy route directly into the mountains.

It appeared that Jimmy's initial assessment of the geological oddity had been correct. The gully was a natural channel scoured out of the plain by the annual spring floods of melt water which had poured down out of the mountains over thousands, perhaps millions of years. Now down into its deepest part, Andrew gazed along the floor of the depression to where it began to incline into the foothills with a smile of satisfaction on his black face.

'Looks like Mother Nature's given us our own private motorway,' he said to the Thinker.

'Pity she didn't think to put in a couple of rest stops,' the big Mancunian muttered. 'I'm bloody starving.'

'Stop worrying about your belly,' Jimmy grunted, humping his heavy bergen up on to his broad back. 'Let's just get the hell out of here before the fucking Russkies come to find out what's happened to their nice whirlybird.'

'Bloody good idea,' Barry Naughton agreed. 'We

can worry about scran when we're off this fucking plain. Anyway, there's bound to be a McDonald's sooner or later. There always is.'

The Thinker did not appreciate the humour. He glowered at the trooper. 'Yeah, bloody dream on,' he growled, but set about loading up his own equipment with a new sense of urgency. He held back as the others began to move out, taking his turn as Tail-end Charlie.

They had covered less than a mile, but Hailsham was sweating profusely under his multiple layers of thermal clothing. The sun was still low in the sky, but the wide difference between daytime and night-time temperatures was already apparent. The major stopped, holding up his hand to bring the patrol to a halt.

'I think we ought to strip off a couple of layers,' he suggested, dropping his bergen to the ground.

The suggestion was gratefully received by everyone, as was the chance of a brief rest while they were complying with it. And, of course, it provided a natural break for another bout of the inevitable bullshit.

'I reckon we'll all have a bloody good dose of crotch-rot before we get out of this weird fucking country,' Tweedledum complained. 'One minute it's trying to freeze your bollocks off, next minute it's trying to cook 'em.'

Cyclops grinned at him. 'You're not supposed to still have any. Somebody back at Training Wing must have fucked up.' He glanced over at Hailsham. 'Ain't that right, boss?'

Hailsham finished packing the garments he had taken off back into his bergen. After glancing at

Tweedledum and Tweedledee, he smiled at Cyclops. 'Well, I was promised a pair of bollockless bastards,' he agreed. 'And so far I've had no cause to complain.'

Caught in a trap of his own making, Tweedledum was uncharacteristically silent, temporarily stumped for a suitable rejoinder. Grinning sheepishly, he shrugged on his heavy pack once again and turned to face the foothills.

The four-man patrol set out again to trudge the last two miles across the steppe.

In the Chinese operations room back in Tacheng, General Chang had a satisfied smile on his face as he replaced the telephone receiver. He glanced across at Leng Pui, who was eyeing him quizzically.

'Yes, that was the British authorities,' he confirmed with a nod. 'They were requesting an update on the operation.'

'And what did you tell them?' Leng Pui asked.

Chang shrugged. 'What should I tell them? That everything is proceeding according to plan.' He broke off, to leer at his fellow officer. 'But our plan, of course – not theirs. No point in mentioning that.'

'No point at all,' Leng Pui agreed, echoing Chang's devious smile. 'I think perhaps they might not be too pleased if they knew we were using their precious SAS as pawns in our own game. I must commend you, General. This scheme of yours seems to be working remarkably well.'

Chang preened himself. He was not one for false modesty. 'As I knew it would,' he said. 'This business with the Russian research facility was an unexpected gift from the gods. I could not let it pass without turning it to our advantage. We have everything to gain, and nothing to lose.'

'And if the SAS soldiers survive?' Leng Pui asked.

Chang affected a careless shrug. 'Unlikely,' he said quietly. 'But even if they do, what will they know, and what can they prove?' He shook his head, smiling even more confidently. 'No, the cards are firmly stacked in our favour, my dear Captain. The British SAS are merely playing out the game to my rules. The outcome does not really matter one way or the other. We shall have achieved our objective.'

Leng Pui regarded his superior with a look of frank admiration. 'You should have been a diplomat, not a soldier,' he ventured.

'In these changing times, it is perhaps most prudent to be both,' Chang observed, nodding thoughtfully.

Andrew's reference to the wadi as a motorway was proving to be strangely accurate, for the further they progressed along the dried-out watercourse the clearer it became that it had served as a major route for others in the past. The patrol had already passed several long-abandoned camp-sites, and caches of dumped waste and discarded equipment. They had also noted at least two sites in which loosely piled mounds of rocks and stones suggested makeshift graves. Andrew had assumed them to be civilian, probably marking the passage of nomadic tribesmen or goatherds down to the sparse grazing of the plain during the summer months.

The latest find, however, looked considerably more recent, and was definitely more military in nature.

Andrew pulled up the patrol, gazing around at the obvious signs of a recent battleground. One side of the gully bore unmistakable signs of entrenched positions, and there were several patches of scorched and blackened earth where it was clear that mortars had been positioned. The surface of the ground was littered with spent cartridge and shell cases. This had been no band of refugees with a few rifles, Andrew thought. The site betrayed the fairly recent presence of a very well-armed and well-trained fighting unit.

The Thinker had broken away from the patrol to do a little private investigation of the discarded hardware. In the back of his mind, there was the faintest hope of finding the odd tin of rations which had been overlooked. He dropped to his knees beside the shattered remains of a mortar which had been fired just once too often. Beside it, the reddish soil was still stained a dark brown with the blood of its unfortunate operator.

The Thinker looked up and gestured to Andrew. 'Here, boss, I think you ought to come and take a look at this,' he called out. There was something in his tone which put the sergeant on his guard. He moved across cautiously, finally kneeling beside the man.

'What is it?'

The Thinker held up part of the mortar base plate and two shell cases for his inspection. 'Notice anything unusual about these?' he asked.

Andrew was not sure what he was supposed to be looking for. He weighed the objects in his hands for a few seconds, peering at them closely without noticing anything amiss. Then, suddenly, he realized that the armaments were all of Chinese manufacture.

He whistled through his teeth and said: 'You reckon this could have been a Chinese force? This far inside the border?'

The Thinker shrugged. 'Either that or the Chinks are deliberately arming rebel guerrilla groups against the official Republican forces. Whichever way you look at it, our slit-eyed friends appear to be playing a double game here. Which rather makes me wonder about our position in the scheme of things.'

Andrew nodded. The man had a good point, and one worth thinking about. 'Maybe that's why they dropped us short of the original target zone,' he mused, eventually. 'It could be this was something they were trying to hide.' He paused, racking his brains for a more simple and understandable explanation, before finally finding one. 'Of course, it could be that a rebel group just happened to get hold of some Chinese ammunition. These guerrilla factions aren't usually too fussy who and where they get their arms from.'

The Thinker looked doubtful. 'Yeah, you could be right – but I reckon something smells,' he muttered firmly. 'There's been something fishy about this whole operation right from the start, if you ask me. I reckon we're the bloody patsies in this little set-up.'

Andrew was not convinced, but he decided it was something to keep in the back of his mind. Certainly he shared at least some of his companion's misgivings. Their situation was complicated enough as it was, without any further unknown quantities. It was not a comforting feeling. He dropped the two shell cases to the ground and straightened up. 'Well, there's not much we can do about it now, anyway,' he said resignedly. 'We've got a rendezvous to keep.' As an afterthought, he bent down again and scooped up one of the shell cases.

'Souvenir?' the Thinker asked. 'Or are you thinking of going into the recycled brass business?'

Andrew grinned, tucking the case into his already overladen bergen. 'I suppose the old man ought to take a look at this,' he murmured thoughtfully. 'Maybe he can make a bit more sense out of what's going on.'

They turned their backs on the scene of battle and began to make their way up the steepening incline of the wadi once again. Another half an hour of steady marching brought them to the first line of real hills, which rose in a series of rocky waves above them.

'Well, so much for the after-dinner stroll,' Andrew grunted. 'Now we all start really working for a living.'

Major Hailsham and his group had also left the steppe behind them and begun their ascent into the mountains. He reviewed the route ahead with a sense of satisfaction, knowing that his choice had been a good one. The foothills rose ahead of them in an irregular, stair-like progression of crags and clefts and, although initially presenting a sharp and fairly steep climb, soon gave way to the jagged line of a natural fissure which would provide good footholds and a relatively easy way to gain height quickly.

'Nice one, boss,' Cyclops complimented him, following Hailsham's eyes up towards the soaring, snowcapped peaks which were their final destination. 'Now all we've got to do is make like mountain goats and we're home and dry.'

Hailsham raised his eyes to the rapidly darkening sky above them. Thick, black clouds of cumulus were beginning to build up, sweeping in from the north over the top of the mountain range. What had been clearly defined snowlines on the higher peaks only an hour before were now misty and out of focus as high-altitude winds whipped up the loose snow and carried it out from the sides of the mountains in thin, airborne drifts. Even down here in the shelter of the lower hills, Hailsham could feel the break-up of the fairly still air pattern which had been a feature of the plains. At the moment, it registered merely as faint, swirling gusts of cooler air. But once they got a few hundred feet higher, it would be a different matter, Hailsham knew. All in all, the imminent change in the weather suggested that Cyclops was being more than a little optimistic in his predictions.

'I wouldn't count on the "dry" bit, if I were you,' Hailsham warned him. 'In fact, given this sort of terrain, I wouldn't count on anything at all.'

The corporal belittled the warning with a carefree grin. 'Listen, boss, I'm prepared for anything,' he said with mock confidence. 'It can't be any worse than the Lake District.'

Hailsham laughed out loud. 'If you found a pile of shit in your Christmas stocking, you'd think Santa Claus had brought you a racehorse,' he said.

Marvelling yet again at the sheer good humour and resilience of the men he had had the privilege of commanding for most of his career, Hailsham strode briskly forward to begin the arduous climb.

13

Just as Hailsham had figured, just under two hours of hard climbing brought them to a long, flattish ridge of bare rock forming a narrow plateau between the central massif of the mountain range and its band of lower foothills. Dragging himself on to the shelf, which was at this point about as wide as a three-lane motorway, he sought the temporary shelter of a low, rocky overhang, grateful for the chance to take some relief from the biting wind – and to rest.

The cold air scoured his lungs as he drew in long, shuddering gasps of breath. Age was beginning to show its hoary head, Hailsham thought, ruefully. Or perhaps he was just getting soft. He drew himself closer into the rock face, making room for the others to bunch up beside him, huddling together for extra warmth. Slowly, his breathing returned almost to normal, and he began to shiver.

The threat of a storm seemed to have passed – at least for the time being. Throughout their climb the wind had increased steadily, sweeping away the black clouds but adding a considerable chill factor to the air temperature. The temporary break would give them all a chance to replace their previously discarded thermal clothing – a move which was well overdue,

Hailsham realized. And, if temperatures were likely to fall much lower, it would soon be time to start thinking about stripping down their weapons and removing all excess oil and grease from everywhere except the camming surface of the bolt mechanisms. The techniques of keeping weapons in working order in such extreme cold had been learned by bitter experience. In unusually cold conditions, all lubricants tended to thicken, heightening the chances of sluggish action or even jams. Even spare ammunition had to be wiped regularly, to prevent any build-up of oil, ice or condensation. But conditions were not yet that extreme, Hailsham decided. The operation could safely wait until they reached their rendezvous point. First things first: cold-weather protection for the outside and a quick calorie boost for the inside.

Stripping off his heavy bergen, Hailsham clawed at it with stiff fingers, pulling out the two extra layers of Gore-tex body-suiting and a bar of chocolate. Shrugging on the extra clothing again, he bit into the chocolate and crunched it between his teeth before swallowing it greedily. A couple of swigs from his water canteen completed the hurried snack, after which he scrambled to his feet again.

The others were still nibbling at their chocolate bars in an almost leisurely fashion. Hailsham scowled down at them. 'Come on, you lazy load of buggers. What do you think this is – a bloody Sunday school picnic? We need to get off this exposed ridge before this wind gets any higher.'

Cyclops looked up at him with a pained expression. 'Christ, boss, I thought we were going to spend a bit of time enjoying the view,' he muttered. He popped the last chunk of chocolate into his mouth and scrambled to his feet, checking his watch. 'At this rate, we're going to be early for our date,' he said. 'I do hope Andrew isn't going to stand us up.'

'He'll be there,' Hailsham replied confidently. 'And if I know the stubborn bugger at all, he'll still have the Stinger with him.'

Waiting a few more moments until Tweedledum and Tweedledee deigned to join the party again, Hailsham set out across the flat expanse of the plateau at a stiff pace. There was another, equally good reason for getting off the ridge as soon as possible, he thought. They were exposed not only to the elements, but also to an aerial observer – and it could not be long now before someone came looking for a chopper which had failed to return to base.

In fact, the subject was at that very moment being discussed at top level back in the Kazakh Republican State department in Alma-Ata. Premier Andrei Kuloschow was a worried man. For months now, the reports of civil unrest and ethnic violence in rural areas had been increasing almost daily. Both militarily and in diplomatic circles, the Birlik, as the Usbek Popular Front was popularly known, were seen to be gaining in power and prestige. Though they were not yet strong enough to pose an open challenge to the official Republican Party of Kazakhstan, such reports of gathering strength were enough to embolden Birlik members, and other dissenters, into ever more frequent shows of defiance which had now spread into major urban areas. In Alma-Ata itself, there had been three food riots and half a dozen demonstrations in the past week alone. The problems were getting too close to home for comfort, and what had started as merely sporadic outbreaks of guerrilla activity was rapidly escalating into civil war.

And now, it seemed, another heavily armed military helicopter had been wiped out of the sky while on what should have been a routine mission. The first, of course, could have been simply down to bad weather. At least two of his military advisers had warned him against the mission to the unknown research facility in the Sailyukem Mountains, but Kuloschow had overridden them for reasons of his own. In his parlous political state, he considered it more than prudent to curry favour with the Communist Old Guard, who still wielded considerable power behind the scenes back in Moscow if not actually in the Kremlin. So he had complied with the discreet request to send a surveillance helicopter to the remote complex, despite the adverse weather reports at the time. It had not returned, and there had been no further communication. Perhaps, when the weather cleared, he would send another to find out what had happened.

But that was another matter. The loss of the second helicopter, reported only a few minutes ago, was a lot more worrying. Quite apart from the loss to the increasingly stretched and cash-starved military, the propaganda value of this latest development was potentially devastating. If news, or even a rumour, got out that a rag-tag band of guerrillas had managed to get hold of sophisticated anti-aircraft weapons, it would raise the stakes dramatically and demoralize his own troops.

Kuloschow looked up at Major Osipov, who had just brought him the news.

'So there's no doubt that it was shot down? No other explanation?'

Osipov shook his head gravely. 'None, comrade. Air control definitely monitored an automatic distress call from the helicopter's computers seconds before it disappeared off the screens. A missile was locked on and closing.'

Kuloschow frowned, placing his elbows on his desk and locking his hands together in a tight knot. Forming a steeple with his two forefingers, he tapped them against his chin thoughtfully.

'Your recommendations, Major?'

Osipov regarded the Premier with barely disguised contempt. The man was weak, with the impressionable, vacillating mind of a politician. And these were times for strength, for making military, not diplomatic decisions.

'I think you know my recommendations,' he replied. 'Although you choose to largely ignore them.' Osipov's tone was both mocking and censorious. He had not forgiven the other man for the loss of the first helicopter.

Kuloschow felt the waves of antagonism emanating from his chief military adviser and let them wash over him. The last thing he could afford was to offer open defiance; his hold on power was too tenuous. He desperately needed the support of the military, if not its respect. The threat of a military coup against his shaky government was real enough as it was, without provoking it further.

As ever, the best the Premier could do was offer the man a sop, a vague promise.

'Your views are, as you say, quite clear to me, Major,' he said. 'But so are mine to you. I regard your solution as the final option, to be resorted to only when all others have been exhausted. I will not sanction genocide while the eyes of the world are upon us.'

Osipov shrugged dismissively. He had heard the objection a dozen times before, and had his own answer to it. 'Then we make the world look away,' he said simply. 'We turn their eyes elsewhere. The Western powers need a new common enemy now that the Iron Curtain is down. Give them one. Give them the Chinese.'

Kuloschow felt himself shrink inside, a tightening knot of insecurity and fear deep in his belly. Such talk was above and beyond his abilities and comprehension, he knew. Before the formation of the Republican Party in 1991, and the decision to secede from the Russian Federation, he had been a simple Party official, a regional administrator – nothing more. Fate had thrust power upon him, but had neglected to prepare him for it. He was used to local decision-making, the politics of internal and strictly local power. To even consider becoming involved in national, let alone international, politics made him terrifyingly aware of his limitations.

Struggling to keep such fears from Osipov, he tried to bring the discussion back to a level that he felt reasonably comfortable with.

'But right now, this minute. What do you suggest we do about this missile threat?'

Osipov allowed himself to smile contemptuously, having the measure of the man and wanting to show it. 'There's not much we can do, for a few hours at least. Those guerrillas will have scattered back into the mountains and the weather is closing in. Until it clears again, we can't safely send in another helicopter. And an air strike would be both expensive and largely futile. Basically, we have to wait until they come out again – and then be ready for them.'

Kuloschow nodded, feeling oddly relieved. To have no choice at all took away the burden of decision. It was at least a respite from pressures, albeit a temporary one.

'Then we wait,' he said.

Having reached the rendezvous point, Hailsham and his team also had nothing to do except wait. His prediction that Andrew and the others would be there waiting for them had proved to be unduly optimistic. He could only assume that they had not been quite so fortunate in finding a reasonably direct route up through the hills.

'Well, you were wrong about the black man, boss,' Cyclops observed, somewhat superfluously. 'Maybe I should have taken a bet.'

'Except I wasn't offering one,' Hailsham retorted. He fished out his high-powered binoculars, handing them to Cyclops and nodding up to the craggy pinnacle of rock above them. 'Instead you've won the chance to shin up there and take a look-see.'

'Thanks a lot, boss,' the corporal groaned sarcastically as he slung the binoculars over his neck and scrambled off with good grace.

Hailsham watched him clamber up the steep rock face until he reached a deep fissure which ran around to the far side of the outcrop. Traversing it as easily as if he were on a child's climbing frame, Cyclops disappeared from view.

'Time to grab some scran, boss?' Tweedledee asked.

Hailsham nodded. 'Be my guest,' he said, generously. 'Have yourselves a full-scale banquet if you like.' He grinned wickedly, knowing that all any of them had were the meagre but sustaining high-calorie ration packs they carried in their escape belts.

The major likewise thought about eating, then rejected the idea. Taking a swig of water from his canteen instead, he looked up again just as Cyclops swung into view again round the side of the crag. Coming down only marginally faster than he had gone up, the man dropped back on to the ledge and grinned triumphantly. 'Back in time for tea, I notice,' he said brightly.

'Well?' Hailsham grunted.

Cyclops paused only to take a couple of deep breaths. 'They're coming,' he announced happily. 'I reckon they're still about 400 feet below us, but they seem to have found some sort of path. From the look of it, I'd say it links up the site of that camp we saw earlier and another little gully over the far side of this ridge. Could be a goat track or something.'

Hailsham thought about this before asking: 'Any sign of the natives?'

Cyclops shook his head. 'If they're there, then they're well hidden – but then you'd expect them to be. Anyway, I didn't hang around for too long, just in case.' He paused, drawing in a few more breaths and allowing his body to relax. 'Mind if I make a suggestion, boss?' he said eventually.

'I'm listening.'

'Just something else I noticed from up there,' the corporal went on. 'The path that Winston's on forks off about a quarter of a mile away. It could provide the best route forward, for all of us.'

Hailsham digested this information. 'So you reckon we ought to go down and intercept them?' he asked.

'It might save time,' Cyclops confirmed with a nod. 'If we wait until they get here, we'll have to make a choice whether to go through the gully or to back-track. And if there *are* any guerrillas in there . . .'

He did not bother to finish, for Hailsham had clearly got the message. The man was right, the major reflected. If they chose to go through the gully, it would be ideal terrain for an ambush. And eight troopers together stood a better chance than four. There was also another consideration. The biting wind sliced along the exposed ridge like an icy razor. Being on the other side of the crag might offer a little more protection – and at least being on the move would help to keep their body temperatures up. Staying still and waiting would only weaken them.

It was this last factor which made up Hailsham's mind. He clapped Cyclops on the shoulder with one hand. 'Yes, good thinking, Corporal,' he said. He looked over at Tweedledum and Tweedledee, who had already consumed their scant meal. 'Well, if you gentlemen have finished washing up the silverware, we'll press on,' he announced.

In truth, both men were grateful for the chance

to get moving again, but it would have been out of character to accept the news without a token protest.

'Aw, boss, I need time to let my dinner go down,' Tweedledum complained. 'I've got a real delicate digestion, you know?'

'Yeah, and he'll fart all the way up the bloody mountain just to prove it,' Tweedledee put in. 'Just make sure you're not the poor bastard behind him.'

Hailsham grinned. 'That won't be my problem. It'll be yours. It's your turn to be Charlie.' He turned to Cyclops, nodding up at the climb ahead. 'Is it worth roping up?'

Cyclops shook his head dismissively. 'Nah – piece of piss, even for an old man like you, boss.'

'Cheeky bastard,' Hailsham grunted, but he was smiling. Nevertheless, he was quite content to let the younger man lead the way. No point in pushing it, he thought. Age and rank still brought some degree of privilege – even in the SAS.

He reached the fissure easily enough, feeling a nice, comforting pressure against both sides of his boot as he jabbed his toes into the crevice and began to edge his way around to the blind side of the crag behind Cyclops. Then, suddenly, he felt a cold knot in his guts as he saw the one little feature of the traverse which Cyclops had neglected to mention. Just ahead of them, a rocky outcrop jutted out from the main body of the pinnacle, forming a two- or three-foot overhang.

'Shit,' Hailsham hissed. He braced himself against the almost inevitable feeling of weakness in his legs as he prepared to face his own personal nightmare.

Cyclops still appeared totally confident. Reaching out, he hooked his fingers over the rim of the outcrop and tensed his arms before swinging his body out into space. Rocking himself from side to side, he let himself sway like a pendulum until he could kick out and lock his boot into a firm toehold. Having inched his fingers along the remainder of the overhang until he could shift his body weight into balance, Cyclops pushed himself away and locked both hands over a knobbly, potato-sized projection, pressing himself against the rock face like a gecko. Changing his foothold from right to left, he completed the tricky manoeuvre and began to climb steadily again.

Hailsham let him get well clear before setting out himself. Sucking in a deep, slow breath, he fought to calm his fears. It was stupid to allow himself ever to get into this state, he told himself. It was just a lump of rock, nothing more. He had negotiated worse obstacles than this a hundred times before, and would probably cope with a few more before he finally hung up his boots. Besides, he could not afford to let Tweedledum see his fear. Reaching up to the rim, he dug his fingers into the cold rock and tensed himself to spring clear from the fissure.

As ever, the terrifying certainty that he was going to fall tore at Hailsham's mind and body for a few seconds. Then he was hanging out over the 200-foot drop below him, his body being buffeted from side to side like a rag doll by the swirling winds. Just one step this side of panic, he kicked out wildly at the main body of the rock face, the toe of his boot scraping against it ineffectually as he tried to locate a firm hold. The weight of his body on his fingers seemed impossible to bear. Every fibre of his being screamed that he was trapped now, and would hang suspended above certain death until those fingers gave up the struggle.

'Up a bit, boss,' came Tweedledum's voice from behind him. 'You're reaching too low. Bring your foot up about another nine inches.'

Hailsham did as he was told, making what felt to him like his last desperate kick out for salvation. His boot scraped against smooth rock for a few more seconds, then caught on something. Feeling like sobbing with relief, he turned his foot, digging his toe deep into the welcome crevice and taking the strain off his arms.

Weak but triumphant, he followed Cyclops up the remaining hundred feet of the rock face and finally collapsed beside him on another small plateau.

'All right, boss?' Cyclops asked, grinning.

It took a lot of doing, but Hailsham managed to fix an idiotic grin on his face as he looked up. 'Piece of piss,' he said breathlessly, not quite sure whether Cyclops believed him or not.

As Tweedledum and Tweedledee finally joined them, Hailsham scrambled to his feet and brought his binoculars up to his eyes. Cyclops pointed to the other patrol's position with his finger.

Hailsham had to concur with the corporal's initial assessment. The path they were following certainly seemed to be a regular passageway through the lower hills of the mountain range, probably following a fault line. But there were definite areas where it was clear that natural features had been modified or adapted for the passage of human feet. Places where piles of small boulders had been rolled or dragged aside and the natural line of the path widened were dead giveaways.

Having identified Andrew's patrol, who were making good progress up a particularly steep and winding section of the path, Hailsham swung the binoculars slowly to the left, picking up the fork which Cyclops had mentioned. Again, he could not fault the man's reading of the situation. It definitely appeared to be a secondary track which carved a circuitous but accessible route around the side of another small peak. The general direction was certainly right. It would appear to be their best route forward, just as Cyclops had surmised.

Hailsham lowered the binoculars, nodding thoughtfully. 'We'll intercept them at the fork,' he announced. 'Anyone have a better idea?'

The others shook their heads. 'We're with you, boss,' Tweedledee said. 'You're the sherpa.'

It sounded like a good, democratic decision. Hailsham took the lead, stepping out on a downward course which would take them into the other patrol's line of vision within a few minutes. Although he trusted his men implicitly, Hailsham firmly believed in a modicum of caution. With potentially hostile forces known to be somewhere in the surrounding hills, the sooner they were seen and identified the better, just in case anyone below them was feeling a bit jumpy. As an extra precaution, he unstrapped his SA-80 and held it out in both arms across his chest to signal non-hostile intent.

'We got company, boss,' the Thinker announced, as

Hailsham and his patrol came into view over the top of a ridge. The big Mancunian was already dropping to his belly even as he spoke, his hands swinging the Enfield into a businesslike position.

Andrew hit the ground a split second behind him, bringing his binoculars up and training them on the advancing quartet. He began to scramble to his feet again. 'Relax, fellers,' he called out softly. 'It looks like the old man's coming down to meet us.'

'Maybe he wants to offer one of us a piggyback,' Jimmy suggested hopefully. 'Or perhaps he's just pissed off with the whole thing and has decided it's time to pack up and go home.'

'I keep telling you, Trooper — you're too much of a bloody optimist for this game,' Andrew said, grinning.

Jimmy shrugged. 'I'm just a naturally lucky bastard. It started the day me mam decided to breast-feed me.'

The sudden, sharp crack of a rifle shot echoed around the sides of the enclosing hills. His instincts honed by the finest and most intensive combat training in the world, Andrew dropped back to the ground like a stone, his head whipping sideways to check his men.

'Anybody hit?' he screamed.

With equally fast reactions, Jimmy, the Thinker and Barry all barked out a denial. Andrew swung his binoculars back to his eyes, training them on the other patrol's position.

Hailsham, Tweedledee and Cyclops were already down on the ground in defensive positions, having rolled into whatever scant cover they could find.

Only Tweedledum remained on his feet, his face twisted into a mask of pain and shock and his left hand clasped tightly around his throat from where blood spurted out through his fingers. For perhaps three full seconds, he continued to stand stock-still until he lurched slightly sideways like a drunken man, his legs seeming to buckle under him. Almost as if in slow motion, he dropped to his knees and then toppled sideways. His body rolled down the rocky side of the hill for several yards before finally coming to a stop against a large boulder.

Andrew's teeth were clenched tightly together as he slowly lowered the binoculars to the ground.

'Oh, shit!' he groaned. 'Holy fucking shit!'

14

With his face pressed close against the rocky ground, Hailsham watched Tweedledum's body roll away down the slope in front of him. Raising his head slightly, he tried to pinpoint the source of the single shot, but there was nothing to give any sort of a clue. He could only assume that it had come from somewhere higher in the hills to the left of them.

He glanced to either side of him, locating the other men and making a candid assessment of their position. It was not good. Only Tweedledee had found anything which could be described as cover, having rolled into a shallow depression in which a few stalky tufts of grass had found a tenuous foothold. Both he and Cyclops were laying on bare and open ground, with no more than a few fist-sized rocks scattered between them and the foot of the hill.

Hailsham's heart was pounding in his chest as the seconds seemed to tick away a slow eternity. Why was there no more fire? he wondered. Even a lone sniper, or a rear-guard lookout must see that they were totally exposed. So why was he not even now just casually picking them off like fish in a barrel?

The question immediately begged another. If his guess as to the gunman's position was anywhere near correct, then he must also have had the other patrol in clear view for some considerable time. Why then had he not shot at them? It made no sense. Unless . . .

A wild thought came into Hailsham's head; wild – but in this bizarre situation the only one which provided a rational explanation. Could it possibly be that the sniper had been protecting Winston and his men? That he had perceived the approach of Hailsham's patrol as an attack, and only now had started to doubt that judgement? Hailsham looked down the hill again, to where Tweedledum's body lay huddled against the boulder.

He glanced over his shoulder at Cyclops. 'Listen – I'm going down,' he announced curtly. 'Be ready to give me covering fire if you have to, but don't open fire unless you're fired at first. Got that?'

'You got it, boss,' Cyclops hissed back. 'But what the fuck's going on?'

Hailsham did not bother to try to answer him at that point. He was not even sure if he *had* an answer, although the next few minutes might conceivably provide one. Rolling on to his back, he slipped the catch of his SA-80 into the safe position and cradled the weapon tightly against his belly and chest. Then, taking a deep breath, he threw himself down the hill towards Tweedledum's position. Rocks and stones tore at his body as he rolled over and over down the slope with increasing speed, but Hailsham hardly noticed. His brain was more concerned with the sudden and sharper agony of a bullet tearing into his flesh. Compared with that, a few bruises were nothing. Finally, miraculously, he was lying beside the stricken man in the welcome cover of the large boulder.

Tweedledum was unconscious, but still breathing. Judging from the position of his head against the boulder, Hailsham reckoned, he had probably knocked himself out on impact. The first task was to ensure that the airway was open and clear. Hailsham slipped his fingers cautiously around the sides of Tweedledum's head, probing gently for any tell-tale signs of sponginess which might indicate a skull fracture. The cranium seemed solid enough, Hailsham thought with a sense of relief, and there were no signs of fluid or blood seeping from his nose or ears to suggest internal brain damage. He could only hope that there was no damage to the neck or spine. Not that it really mattered, he reflected on noticing the amount of blood which had already soaked into the ground. If he could not manage to get to the wound and staunch the bleeding, then Tweedledum's clock would run out soon enough anyway. Gently, Hailsham turned the wounded man's face to the side in the normal recovery position and pulled an emergency field dressing pack from his escape belt.

Once exposed, the wound looked better than he could have dared to hope. The bullet appeared to have entered the side of the throat, just under the jaw. Miraculously, it had missed the jugular by centimetres, ploughing on in a downward path until it encountered the firmer tissue of the shoulder muscles. There was no sign of an exit wound, so it was probably still lodged there.

Hailsham wiped away as much blood as he could and pressed the dressing into position over the wound, wedging it in place with a couple of handy stones. It was all he could do for the moment. From now on,

Hailsham reflected, Tweedledum's life depended on their all surviving the next few minutes.

Edging his way around the boulder, he called down to Andrew: 'Listen, Winston – I got a theory that these guys think they're on your team.'

Andrew's voice came back immediately. 'Yeah, I'd thought of that myself, boss. They could have taken a pop at us anytime for the last five minutes or so. So what do you reckon?'

'Feel like putting it to the test?'

This time there was just a momentary hesitation before Andrew replied. 'I'm willing if you are, boss. So far it's been looking like a good week for me,' he called back.

'Then let's do it,' Hailsham shouted. He began to rise slowly to his feet, stepping out from behind the safety of the boulder. His heart in his mouth, he started to walk slowly down the rest of the hill as Andrew likewise left his cover and stood waiting to meet him.

The 300 yards which still separated them seemed like as many miles. Hailsham continued to walk down the hill at a steady, apparently casual pace, even though every instinct in his highly trained mind told him it was against all the rules of survival. Oddly, he found himself thinking of an old black and white film he had once seen, called *The Long Walk*. That particular walk had been the route of a condemned man from his cell to the gallows. Or had it been the electric chair? Hailsham could not exactly remember which, but his present situation was chillingly similar.

Seconds dragged into minutes, and still no sound

came down from the high ground above him other than the roaring of the wind through the gullies between the hills. Then suddenly it was over and Hailsham was standing at Andrew's side, once more daring to hope that he had been right.

The sergeant's face betrayed his own tension, but he managed to raise a faint smile. 'Looks like we might have guessed this one right, boss. Either that, or our chummy up there is taking a fucking long time to reload.'

Hailsham let out a nervous, tension-relieving laugh – almost a giggle. 'The only problem is I didn't work out the next move yet. What do we do now – stand here like a couple of bloody lemons until the Seventh Cavalry gets here?'

'I got news for you. They ain't coming,' Andrew said gravely. 'Seems like they had a previous engagement or something. What say we show these guys what a friendly pair of bastards we are?'

As he spoke, the sergeant was unhitching his SA-80 very gingerly. Bending down extremely slowly, he laid the weapon out on the ground in front of him and stepped back a couple of paces. It seemed like a sensible gesture, Hailsham thought, following suit.

The two men stood together in silence for several moments, both scanning the hills above them for the faintest sign of movement. Finally, Andrew had to voice the question which had been struggling to surface for the past five minutes.

'What about Tweedledum, boss?'

Hailsham bit at his lower lip and sighed. 'He could make it,' he said quietly. 'But he needs better medical attention than we can give him out here in the open.'

'Bandit,' Andrew hissed suddenly. 'Top of the second ridge, about two o'clock.'

Hailsham's eyes had been scanning the left side of the hills above them. They flicked quickly to the right.

'Yeah, got him,' he confirmed, quickly picking out the turbaned head which had just become visible above a small outcrop of rocks. Even as he looked, two or three more figures appeared out of nowhere.

'These guys are good,' Andrew muttered in grudging admiration.

Hailsham shrugged faintly. 'Well it *is* their turf,' he said almost defensively, although he too was quite impressed. From the top of the hill he had just come down, he would have sworn that the area was clear.

Eventually, some half a dozen people were in plain view, staring down expectantly at the two men. It seemed that they too were unsure of the next move. There was only one way to end the stand-off, Hailsham decided.

'I'm going up,' he announced quietly. 'Let's hope my Russian is up to the local dialect. Otherwise it's sign language.'

'Want me to come with you, boss?' Andrew asked.

Hailsham shook his head. 'No sense in both of us putting our heads in the noose. They've seen that we're friends now. Let's hope that's enough to convince them.'

'Hearts and minds, boss?'

Hailsham grinned. 'This one's more like balls and arses. Ours,' he said as he moved forwards, beginning the steep climb up to the rebel position. Andrew's eyes were on him every step of the way, until he reached the first of the waiting figures, paused briefly and then melted out of vision.

Nearly a quarter of an hour passed before Hailsham reappeared again at the top of the escarpment. He was alone. He picked his way down the slope until he was in prominent view and paused. Raising both hands in the air, he made clear signs for everybody to join him.

Andrew allowed himself a sigh of relief and then turned back to his men, still deep in cover, and said: 'Looks like it's party time, fellers.' He glanced up the hill to his left, noting that Tweedledee and Cyclops had already risen to their feet and were scrambling down towards Tweedledum. Nodding in their direction, he said to the Thinker, who had just reached his side: 'Go and give them a hand – they could probably use it.'

'You got it, boss,' the Thinker shot back before striking off at a tangent up the hill to help pick up and transport the wounded trooper.

Looking more like a bunch of battle-worn stragglers than an élite fighting troop, they all started to make their way up the hill to where Hailsham was waiting for them.

'So, what's the deal?' Andrew asked, when he had got his breath back.

Hailsham smiled at him and said: 'Looks like you're the flavour of the month. Shooting down that chopper had made you a national hero.' He paused for a moment. 'They're Usbek, mostly refugees from a Kazakh massacre about five days ago. They find it almost impossible to believe that anyone would want to help them. The fact is, they're almost universally feared and despised by both the native Kazakhs and the immigrant White Russians. It seems they have a reputation for overbreeding. The men are supposed to be super-potent and the women oversexed.'

Andrew nodded knowingly. 'Yeah, and I bet they all like loud music and have a natural sense of rhythm,' he said sarcastically. Somehow, it was a story he seemed to have heard before.

Hailsham let the comment pass. 'Anyway, they want to do whatever they can to help us in return. If nothing else, they can probably give us the best route through the higher mountains and provide some valuable intelligence on known rebel positions.'

'What about Tweedledum?' Andrew asked. 'Anyone up there with any medical skills?'

Hailsham shrugged. 'Probably not much above the witch-doctor level,' he admitted. 'Folk medicine, a few herbal remedies, that sort of thing. But at least it will give us a chance to dig that bullet out and patch him up as best we can. This way he's got a fighting chance, at least.'

The major turned back up the hill and began to lead the way to the temporary camp. Some twenty or thirty swarthy, beaming faces greeted them as they climbed over the top of the escarpment and started to descend into the gully below it.

Andrew looked around, whistling faintly through his teeth. 'Not bad for a bunch of refugees,' he said.

The set-up was impressive, considering the nature of the terrain and the people who had created it. In less than a couple of hours the Uzbeks had managed to build a small-scale mountain fortress out of bare rock and earth which would have done credit to a trained military outfit. Apparently using their bare hands, men and women alike had scooped out miniature caverns beneath the larger rock formations and established four protected lookout positions built of rocks, stones and piled earth which gave them panoramic views over the full 180 degrees of the surrounding hills and the valley below. One natural rock fissure had been cleared of loose stones and shale and built up into a fireplace fully protected from the biting wind. Although there was no sign of even the most stunted scrub or brush in the immediate area, they had somehow managed to gather enough wood to create a more than adequate supply of fuel, and a small but welcoming fire was already crackling away merrily.

'Looks like these guys could teach us a thing or two,' Andrew conceded.

Several of the Uzbek women scurried to help the Thinker, Tweedledee and Cyclops as they carried the wounded Tweedledum into the camp. With frantic hand signals and a great deal of fuss, they managed to guide the impromptu stretcher party to a sheltered area near the fire and hastily created a makeshift bed with blankets and animal skins. It was probably not the most hygienic of places to lay a wounded man, but at least it looked comfortable.

Hailsham glanced aside at Andrew as an elderly Uzbek approached them, with a clearly worried younger man trailing miserably in his wake.

'Oh, perhaps I ought to explain something,' Hailsham whispered quickly. 'Rank and uniform don't appear to mean too much to these people. So as far as they're concerned, you're the boss because you're the one with the weapon which can knock helicopters out of the sky. I'm just the interpreter.'

Andrew regarded his superior warily. 'Why do I get this feeling that you're trying to prepare me for something?' he asked. 'Who are these two guys coming over, anyway?'

Hailsham smiled thinly. 'The old fellow is called Mukhtar. He's sort of the head man around here,' he explained. 'As for the younger chap – well, you'll find out about him in a second. Basically, I think you're going to have an executive decision to make.'

There was no time for further explanation, even if it had been forthcoming. Hailsham turned to face the older man, muttering a greeting in Russian. The Uzbek nodded in Andrew's direction, then pointed to his companion before rattling off what seemed to be an impassioned speech.

'What's he saying?' Andrew hissed.

Hailsham translated for him. 'He says you are a good friend,' he explained. 'And he bitterly regrets that one of your men has been shot. However, he is quite prepared to make reparation.'

'What sort of reparation?' Andrew asked.

Hailsham grinned. 'That's the decision you're going to have to make. The young man is Safar. He's the one who opened fire. Without putting too fine a point on it, Mukhtar wants to know if you would like him shot.'

'Christ Almighty, boss,' Andrew exploded. 'What the fuck am I supposed to say?'

Hailsham continued to grin infuriatingly. 'Yes or no, basically.'

Andrew looked relieved. 'Then tell him no, for Christ's sake. Tell him I forgive him ... it was an accident. Tell him anything.'

Hailsham turned back to the old man and spoke rapidly. Finally, Mukhtar nodded sagely, and Safar looked relieved. With curt, almost formal nods, both men walked away again.

'You bastard,' Andrew growled, though now grinning at last. 'You knew that was coming, didn't you?'

'Just thought I'd let you glory in the power of command for once,' Hailsham said over his shoulder as he strode towards Tweedledum.

The young trooper had regained consciousness and was looking weakly up at Tweedledee, who hovered anxiously over him, looking almost embarrassed at his concern. Hailsham dropped to his knees beside the improvised bed and examined the man's wound more carefully. Most of the bleeding had stopped, and the amount of caked and dried gore on Tweedledum's throat and clothing did not seem quite as much as Hailsham had initially feared.

Tweedledum's eyelids fluttered weakly as he recognized the major. An apologetic smile formed on his pale lips. 'Sorry about this, boss,' he managed to whisper. 'I guess I should have ducked.' The smile faded, to be replaced by a plea in Tweedledum's watery blue eyes. 'How bad is it, boss?' he asked anxiously.

'Don't try to talk,' Hailsham urged him. 'Just try to relax. You're going to be all right.'

Tweedledum's eyes flickered uncertainly. He wanted to believe, but he knew the form. 'You ain't bullshitting me, boss?'

Hailsham forced what he thought to be a suitably reassuring smile. 'I'm not bullshitting you, Trooper,' he promised. 'Once we get that slug out of you, you're going to be as right as rain.'

Suddenly, feeling an insistent nudging in his ribs, Hailsham glanced up and saw a young Uzbek woman standing over him, a small cooking pot filled with boiling water swinging from one hand. With the other, she was doing the nudging, while babbling away in a dialect which Hailsham did not recognize. However, it did not require a great deal of translation to realize that she was telling him to get out of the way. He moved aside and the woman knelt down and began to attend to Tweedledum, washing away the dried blood around the wound with a piece of surprisingly clean-looking fabric. She knew what she was doing, Hailsham thought, noticing her gentle and careful strokes. Clearly these people were more than used to dealing with bullet wounds. Rising to his feet, he strode away in search of Mukhtar to elicit more information.

The woman, it seemed, had been a nurse before the troubles started. Forced by ethnic hatred out of the city hospital where she had worked, she had returned to her native village. There, circumstances had quickly elevated her to the position of doctor, anaesthetist and chief surgeon all rolled into one. Only there was no anaesthetic left, Mukhtar explained apologetically. There had been no drugs at all for some months now.

It was certainly one step up from the witch-doctor he had predicted, Hailsham reflected. At least the woman had some clinical skill, and an understanding of basic hygiene. Even as he returned to watch, she had produced an old but still serviceable scalpel and was attempting to sterilize it with a burning brand from the camp-fire. When the steel blade was glowing a dull red, she immersed it in a fresh pot of boiling water and set it aside on a flat stone to cool. Producing another piece of clean cloth, she rolled it into a thick sausage and thrust it between Tweedledum's teeth, gesturing for Tweedledee to hold it in place.

Hailsham did not stay around for the actual operation – not because he was squeamish, but because there were more important matters to attend to. He sought out Andrew, who was being fêted by a small group of younger Usbek freedom fighters, including Safar, who seemed to have adopted him as a father figure.

'So, how's the national hero business?' Hailsham asked, jokingly.

Andrew looked embarrassed. 'How do you say "no thanks" in this lingo?' he asked. 'These guys have virtually nothing, yet they keep on trying to give me presents. Blankets, bullets, all sorts of stuff.'

Hailsham taught the big Barbadian a polite refusal and waited patiently until he had repeated it to his assembled group of admirers. He began to walk away slowly as Andrew finally got himself free and fell into step beside him, with Safar trotting happily on his heels.

'You're very honoured,' Hailsham said, impressed.

'What they're offering you is their most precious possessions. Life or death, in fact.'

Andrew nodded. 'Yeah, I sort of got that idea myself.' He paused thoughtfully. 'I suppose there's nothing else we can really do for them, is there, boss?'

Hailsham stopped in his tracks, eyeing Andrew warily. The sergeant was thinking about leaving the Stinger with them, he could tell. He shook his head, firmly yet with a trace of regret. 'We've already interfered enough,' he pointed out. 'Our orders were not to get involved, remember?'

'Yeah,' Andrew sighed, nodding faintly. 'Just like Captain Kirk and the crew of the *Enterprise*. Prime Directive and all that.'

'Something like that,' Hailsham confirmed, smiling. 'I didn't know you were a Trekkie.'

Andrew grinned. 'There's a lot you don't know about me, boss.'

'There's a lot I don't know about a lot of things,' Hailsham said. 'That's what makes life interesting.' He led the way over to the rest of the men, who were huddled near the fire, guarding the equipment.

'Looks like we're going to get some hot scran,' the Thinker said hopefully, nodding towards two Usbek women who were busy cooking something up in a couple of large pots.

'There you are – I told you we'd find a McDonald's,' Barry put in. 'Anybody fancy a Big Mac?'

'More likely a Big Rat,' Jimmy snorted, bringing them all down to earth.

There was a sudden silence as Tweedledee slowly walked over to join them. He sat down moodily, ignoring them all, obeying the conventions. It was not done to talk about either the dead or the wounded. Nevertheless, Hailsham was aware of the man's eyes on him, a mute plea underlying the sadness in them. He understood. Although they were all comrades, the two Tweedles shared a special relationship. Saying nothing, Hailsham climbed to his feet and went to speak to the nurse to get some sort of prognosis.

They were definitely guests of honour, Hailsham realized, noting that the food had been prepared for them alone. He felt slightly guilty as the Usbek women served them small bowls of a thick, pungent stew, for he was aware that it probably represented half their meagre rations for the week. But it would have been churlish to refuse their hospitality, and he and his men had their own food supply problems to worry about.

Following their example, Hailsham tucked into the meal gratefully, ignoring the strong smell and rather unusual taste. He scooped up the thick stew with pieces of dry, biscuit-like bread, and when that ran out, he used his fingers. Regardless of the taste, it was hot and nourishing, with plentiful lumps of a chewy, whitish and unidentifiable meat, along with roots and brown rice to give it body, and the flavouring of various steppe herbs, which lent a strong and aromatic bouquet. The meal finished, Hailsham was not sure if it was considered good form to belch, as in some Arabic cultures, so he restrained himself. As it happened, the Thinker did it for him, albeit from a natural tendency rather than ethnic etiquette. Two of the Usbek women smiled proudly, Hailsham noticed, so the gesture was obviously appreciated.

Having put down his bowl, Hailsham sidled over to Tweedledee, who was still picking somewhat half-heartedly at his own portion.

'He's going to be all right,' he assured the trooper. It was more than just optimism, for Hailsham had been greatly impressed by the young Uzbek nurse's handiwork, and she had seemed in no doubt that her patient would make a rapid recovery.

Tweedledee's face brightened, momentarily, before falling again. 'We're going to have to leave him behind, aren't we, boss?' he asked.

Hailsham nodded. 'But we'll be leaving him in good hands,' he pointed out. 'As soon as he's fit enough to move on his own, Mukhtar assures me, they'll show him the way to the Mongolian border, where he should be treated fairly. So far, the Mongolians have refused to get involved in any of this. Once we get home, we can initiate diplomatic moves to get him out safely. There shouldn't be a problem.'

Hailsham was not absolutely sure about the latter part of this information, but managed to sound convincing. Tweedledee brightened up again, returning to his stew with renewed enthusiasm. Hailsham rose and tapped Andrew on the shoulder, urging him to his feet. He led the way across the camp to where Mukhtar and several of the younger Uzbeks were holding some sort of parley. As ever, Safar stuck to Andrew like a shadow, loping along at his heels.

They were warmly welcomed into the group. Hailsham and Andrew squatted down on two blankets which were laid out for them. From underneath

the folds of his *khalat*, Mukhtar produced a bottle
of vodka, which he offered proudly to Andrew. After
taking a swig of the fiery liquid, the sergeant passed
the bottle around the group as Hailsham engaged in
a conversation in which there was much pointing
up into the mountains and much worried shaking
of heads. Even though the language went above his
head, Andrew was left in do doubt that the Usbeks
did not approve of their final destination.

He nudged Hailsham in the ribs as discreetly as he
could. 'What are they saying, boss?' he whispered.

'They know of the region we're headed for,'
Hailsham said quietly. 'They say it's a bad place.
Animals, and men, die up there. There is a curse,
they believe.'

Andrew pondered this information. It all tied in
with their own intelligence. Sudden and inexplicable
death would certainly seem like a curse to simple
and uneducated minds. They would know nothing
of chemical or biological poisons, radiation sickness
or any of the other possible dangers which might be
lurking in the high mountains.

'So basically they're warning us not to go on?'
Andrew said.

'In a nutshell, yes,' Hailsham replied. 'But if we are
really determined, then Safar will go with us part of
the way as a guide. Mukhtar says we will never make
it without help to find safe routes and passes through
the mountains.'

Hailsham returned to the negotiations, which were
shortly brought to a conclusion by the draining of the
vodka bottle and a round of handshakes.

'I take it we've accepted their offer?' Andrew said.

Hailsham shrugged. 'There didn't seem to be much choice,' he said wearily. 'Mukhtar painted a pretty bleak picture of the terrain ahead of us, although how much of it was a chance to boast about their own prowess and bravery, I don't know.'

Andrew glanced over his shoulder at Safar, hovering behind him. 'They don't need to boast about their bravery,' he pointed out. 'That poor bastard is probably scared shitless, yet he's willing to go with us.'

Hailsham shrugged. 'Like us, I don't think he has a great deal of choice in the matter. He owes you his life. Tribal ethics mean he's more or less committed to you until he repays that debt. To refuse would be to invite being totally ostracized by his fellow tribesmen. The Uzbeks clearly set great store by honour.'

'Probably another reason why they're feared by many of the other groups,' Andrew said. 'People seem to find it hard to accept any culture which stays true to itself, retaining its own values. In the thirties it was the Jews. Now it's the Asians and blacks.'

Hailsham smiled gently. 'Philosopher as well as poet. You continue to surprise me, Andrew.'

'Fuck it, I surprise myself sometimes, boss,' Andrew blurted out, struggling to assert a more macho image and failing.

Hailsham stared up into the high mountains above them, noting the plumes of snow which were being whipped off the higher peaks by the swirling winds. 'Weather's getting worse up there,' he announced. 'Time to get moving.'

Andrew understood the man's reasoning well enough. Making ground into really bad weather minimized the chances of any unwelcome helicopter surveillance. It would also put them in country where any airborne drop of pursuit troops would be virtually impossible. Even so, it was a far from pleasant prospect. He nodded his assent, adding: 'I'll go and tell the men we're ready to move out. I'm sure they'll be thrilled.'

'Positively ecstatic,' Hailsham agreed, with a cynical smile. He turned to look over at Tweedledum. 'I suppose I'd better go and explain the position. Tell the men they're welcome to come and say goodbye to him if they want to.' He began to walk over towards the stricken trooper.

Despite obvious pain and trauma from his recent surgery, Tweedledum had managed to stay conscious and even forced a weak smile as Hailsham stood over him. The major felt even more confident about the young nurse's prediction that he would pull through safely.

'Hi, boss,' Tweedledum said weakly. 'I don't suppose you've come to offer me a piggyback.'

Hailsham smiled back, realizing that Tweedledum was well aware of the score. 'You've got some sick leave coming, Trooper. Won't it be nice to spend it with such friendly people?' He explained briefly the arrangements for getting him over the Mongolian border. 'You're going to be OK,' he said firmly.

Forgetting his wound for a moment, Tweedledum tried to nod, wincing with the sudden pain. He gritted his teeth, fighting to keep the brave smile on his face. 'Have a drink waiting for me in the Paludrine Club, will you?'

Hailsham nodded. 'You got it. Mind you, you might not want to come home at all. Mukhtar, the head man, tells me he's going to lend you one of his wives to keep you warm at night. And for anything else you might need, once you get your strength back.'

'And here's the even better news,' came Tweedledee's voice from behind him. 'The rest of the boys have agreed to leave you their entire condom ration as a going-away present.'

Hailsham turned, to see the men all hovering behind him, waiting to say their goodbyes. It was time to make a discreet exit, he decided.

Just as Cyclops had originally suggested, the best way forward was the fork off the pathway which Andrew's patrol had followed. Safar pointed to it as they all heaved on their bergens once again and prepared to move out.

Mukhtar and a small delegation of the Uzbek men and women had come to see them off.

'*Shchisliva*,' said the head man. 'Good luck to you.' There was no attempt at a formal handshake.

Hailsham bowed his head ceremoniously. '*Daragoy drook*,' he replied. 'Dear friend.'

One of the women stepped forward, holding out a stick on which were impaled several small skinned and fire-seared animal carcasses. It was obviously a parting gift of food, Hailsham thought, accepting it with a suitable look of gratitude. Turning away, he followed Safar down the hill away from the camp.

The Thinker looked at the distinctly unappetizing string of charred bodies with a look of distaste on his face. 'What the bloody hell are those?'

'Probably marmots,' Hailsham told him.

The corporal looked even more disgusted. 'Bloody hell,' he repeated.

Cyclops grinned at him. 'Don't turn your nose up, Thinker. What the hell do you think was in that stew you enjoyed so much?'

'Aw, Christ,' the Thinker exploded. 'Do you mean I've been eating bloody monkeys?'

Cyclops shot him a pitying look. 'You daft prat,' he said witheringly. 'You're thinking of marmosets. Marmots are burrowing rodents – sort of a cross between a squirrel and a rabbit.'

The pained look on the Thinker's face told Cyclops that he found the fine distinction no more appetizing. 'Well all I can say is I'm bloody looking forward to that fucking eagle,' the Thinker muttered thickly.

Cyclops grinned again. 'I've got to shoot the bastard first.'

They all fell silent, concentrating on keeping their balance as they started to descend the steepest part of the hill.

15

General Chang was in a rare complimentary mood. Used as he was to almost total subservience and efficiency, he habitually took excellence for the norm and questioned the slightest deviation from perfection. There might be some areas in which the great communist system occasionally broke down, but the military machine ran with smooth and well-oiled precision.

He regarded San Hung with a benevolent smile. 'You have done well,' he said generously, studying the report which the young lieutenant from military intelligence had just brought to his attention. 'I shall make it my business to see that a commendation goes on your record.'

San Hung did not linger to bask in this uncharacteristic warmth. Past experience had taught him that General Chang's moods could change as rapidly as a pattern of fallen leaves in the wind. With an obsequious bow, he excused himself and backed out of the room.

Chang thumbed the intercom on his desk, summoning Leng Pui, who appeared from one of the interconnecting offices as though he had been primed and waiting for the call. He, too, could not help but notice the rather smug and self-satisfied smile on his superior's face.

'You look pleased, General. Your plans continue to go well?'

Chang allowed himself a patronizing nod. 'With a bit of help from our SAS friends,' he conceded. 'They seem to be playing the game even more enthusiastically than I had hoped.' He picked up the typewritten intelligence report and handed it to the other man.

Leng Pui read the document carefully. It seemed almost trivial – merely an intercepted emergency distress call sent to the Kazakh military base in Alma-Ata some hours earlier. Under normal circumstances it might well have been filed away with dozens of other monitored messages and scraps of intelligence, but it was clear from Chang's attitude that this particular message had some special significance.

His failure to grasp that significance straight away placed Leng Pui in a somewhat awkward and vulnerable situation. Chang was obviously in a mood for praise and self-congratulation. To disappoint him by showing ignorance would not be wise.

Improvising with the sort of devious cunning he had learned from his superior, Leng Pui assumed an approving smile. 'This is excellent news,' he said, with forced enthusiasm. 'And you think the SAS are responsible?'

Chang shrugged. 'Who else could it be? Nothing we have learned has ever suggested that these mountain guerrilla groups possess a SAM capability – and we certainly have not supplied them with such. Mortars, shells and guns, yes – but nothing on this scale. Yet this distress call definitely establishes that a Kazakh military helicopter was brought down by a missile strike. Quite obviously, the SAS have chosen sides, as I fully expected them to do sooner or later.'

'But sooner being better?' Leng Pui said slyly, beginning to catch on at last.

Chang beamed at him. 'Exactly.'

'And now?' Leng Pui asked.

'And now we initiate the next move in the game,' Chang answered. 'We make sure that this information gets leaked to the appropriate Kazakh authorities. Knowing that they have a new enemy to contend with will confuse and disorientate them. Whatever moves they make to deal with it will inevitably split their already overtaxed military capabilities and weaken them.'

'Making it that much easier for our own troops to continue fomenting trouble in the border areas,' Leng Pui said, now fully appraising the situation. 'And we gain a bonus, of course. Giving them the British as a scapegoat will provide a possible explanation of why the rebel factions have been able to arm themselves so well in recent months – and, indeed, to inflict such damage.'

'You miss the most subtle, but perhaps the most important factor,' Chang pointed out, annoyed that Leng Pui had not picked it up and congratulated him. 'Creating bad relations with the British will have severe diplomatic, as well as military, repercussions. It will almost certainly affect any Russian attemps to gain economic aid and trade agreements with the European Community. So they will continue to be weak on two fronts – at the very time when our own economy is going from strength to strength. The face of war has changed, Leng Pui. Today the banknote is as formidable a weapon as the bomb.'

'But if the British should find out . . .' Leng Pui left the awful thought unspoken.

'We must ensure that they don't,' Chang said with a chilling smile. 'Whatever happens, we must appear to be completely innocent in all this. Which is why the SAS must never return from this mission alive.'

'And if they do?'

'Then we shall have to kill them ourselves,' said Chang with a shrug. 'A helicopter or transport-aircraft crash on the way back to the Tacheng base. A tragic accident – or even better, some suggestion of a Kazakh attack – might suit our purpose best.'

Chang looked directly into Leng Pui's eyes, seeking admiration and finding it. His expansive mood bordered on euphoria. 'I shall entrust you with the task of leaking this disinformation to Kazakh sources,' he said, as though he were offering the man some rare and precious gift. 'But you must be discreet, and extremely subtle. I have no wish to see my plans fail now because of clumsiness.'

Leng Pui nodded deferentially. 'You can count on me, General,' he promised.

Chang allowed himself a thin smile. 'Yes, I'm sure I can,' he murmured, knowing that his second-in-command had also walked into his intricately spun web of deceit. Now, even if the unthinkable happened and things went wrong, he had an underling to blame. It was another comforting safety-net to have beneath him now that he was walking such a high and dangerous tightrope on the world stage.

* * *

What had started out as an open mountain path had now closed in to form a tight and narrow ravine as Safar led the SAS team up into the higher mountains. Although steep, with a fairly steady incline of about thirty-five degrees, the floor of the ravine continued to be reasonably even and obstacle-free, suggesting that they were still following a regular route which was well trodden during the spring and summer months. The directness and comparative accessibility of the path had allowed them to make good and steady progress, gaining considerable distance and height in the past three hours.

But this bonus was more than balanced by a single disadvantage. The narrow ravine faced almost directly north, and acted as a natural funnel for the savage winds tearing down from the wastes of the Siberian plains. It was like trying to climb along a wind-tunnel, but with the added problem that this wind carried a body- and mind-numbing chill factor which reduced the ambient temperature to well below zero. It tore through every square inch of their protective clothing, sucking out the precious body heat created by their physical exertion.

Every yard gained was a triumph over physical torture, and there was a mental penalty to be paid as well. Like the rest, Hailsham was fully and constantly aware that it could only get progressively worse the higher they went. This knowledge clawed constantly at a man's bodily strength and mental resolve, sapping both.

With savage humour, Hailsham made a mental note to mention the place to a couple of the guys in Training Wing when they got back to Stirling Lines. It might appeal to their more sadistic inclinations. Certainly it made the 'Fan Dance' – the 40-mile endurance march up Pen-y-Fan which marked the final phase of SAS recruitment selection – seem like a summer afternoon stroll. And in terms of a 'sickener', or testing ordeal, climbing up an icy wind-tunnel was one innovation which had yet to occur to someone's nasty little mind.

It was certainly God-forsaken terrain, Hailsham thought, staring ahead of him up the seemingly endless climb towards the snowcapped mountains. He could only admire the sheer tenacity of the rugged semi-nomadic tribespeople who called this country home and found it worth fighting, even dying, for. This admiration focused on the figure of Safar 20 yards ahead of him, trudging steadily onwards with hardly a break in his step and never a backward glance. Clad in a goatskin jacket and a few tattered blankets and with only a small skull-cap to cover his head, he seemed oblivious to the cold which chilled Hailsham to the bone even through the protection of his high-tech thermal gear. Perhaps it was simply a matter of growing acclimatized, Hailsham reflected. Or maybe it was a genetic thing – generations of survival in such extreme conditions producing a thickening of the blood, or some bodily capacity to produce extra heat.

The thought depressed Hailsham, sapping his resolve to go on. They should not be here, a silent voice screamed in his brain. They did not belong in these mountains, in this country, in this stupid, logic-defying situation. He tore his eyes away from the little Uzbek guide, staring down instead at his next step, and the step after that. How many had he already taken, he wondered. How many more would he take before they reached their objective? How much longer could his body continue to dredge up new reserves of strength?

It came as almost a shock to Hailsham to suddenly realize that his mind had locked into a cyclic chain of depression and defeat. 'Stupid bastard,' he cursed himself under his breath. It was not physical strength he needed most now – it was mental stamina. He was forgetting the most basic rules of endurance survival. More importantly, he was forgetting his men, and their psychological needs. They must be suffering the same mental and physical anguish, and indeed it was probably worse for the youngsters like Barry and Tweedledee. He fought to clear all negative thoughts from his head, concentrating on the positive aspects of what they had achieved so far. Positive reinforcement – that was the key phrase that the psychology boys liked to use a lot when they were discussing continuation and cross-training exercises.

Hailsham broke step, coming to an abrupt halt and turning to look back down the steep incline behind him. The steppe was far below and behind them now, their original drop point an invisible spot beyond the horizon. His men were strung out at irregular intervals back along the ravine, looking isolated, fatigued and every bit as dispirited as he himself had been. It was time, he decided, to give the men an opportunity to recharge their mental and physical batteries with a short rest and the chance of some comradeship and shared humour. He held his ground as Cyclops, the

Thinker and Tweedledee trudged wearily to join him. Barry and Jimmy were still a good 50 yards behind them, with Andrew the straggling backmarker, still encumbered by the crippling weight of the Stinger on top of his formidable personal burden.

The major waited until they were all clustered around him again, and then faced forwards to check on Safar. The Usbek guide had got the message now, and had come to a halt about 60 yards ahead of them. Realizing that a rest had been called, he started to backtrack slowly to join them.

'Tea break, boss?' Cyclops asked. 'I could do with a nice hot cuppa. Hope somebody remembered to bring the fucking kettle.'

'Dunno about the kettle, but the poor old sarge looks like he's carrying the bleeding kitchen sink,' Jimmy observed as Andrew finally staggered in to join them.

It was Hailsham's cue to tap the heavy missile launcher slung across Andrew's broad back. 'Time to ditch it, Andrew,' he murmured. 'We said the lower foothills, remember?'

Andrew put on a brave face. 'It's all right, boss. I can manage it for a while longer,' he insisted.

'We could take turns,' the Thinker suggested. 'It's been a pretty handy little tool to have along, so far.'

Hailsham gave the idea only fleeting consideration, finally shaking his head. The climb ahead of them could only get more demanding, the weather conditions worse. It was important for the men's morale that they perceive the task ahead of them as getting easier, not ever harder. Shedding excess weight now would help to give them all that much-needed boost.

The decision made, Hailsham was adamant. 'The Stinger stays here,' he said firmly. 'We'll cache it, along with all the spare missiles the rest of you are carrying and any other non-essentials.'

'Christ, boss, we're travelling bloody light as it is,' the Thinker pointed out. 'There ain't much else we can ditch, is there?'

Hailsham shrugged, conceding that the corporal had a point. 'Maybe not,' he agreed. 'But shed what you can. We're going to need to be as light-footed as mountain goats in another day or so. The less energy we waste now, the easier it will be when the going really gets tough.'

To start the ball rolling, Hailsham stripped off his own bergen and rummaged through his basic equipment, discarding what few bits and pieces he considered reasonably expendable. The others followed suit, and in a few minutes there was a small pile at the side of the ravine.

'Wonder what the bye-laws round here are like for littering?' Jimmy said. 'We don't want to upset the locals, do we?'

'I expect they're already pissed off, what with all those bits of junk from the helicopter scattered all over their nice clean mountains,' answered Barry, raising a smile. 'And talking of dumping stuff, how do we have a crap without freezing our arses off?'

'Do it in your pants,' Jimmy suggested. 'It might help to keep your balls warm. Only stay downwind from me, that's all.'

'Wouldn't have thought it would bother you,' Barry retorted. 'You're full of crap already.'

Hailsham smiled to himself as the lavatorial humour

served its traditional purpose of lightening the men's spirits. The rest break was obviously having its intended effect. He busied himself dragging all the bergens into a pile across the width of the narrow footpath. Heaped one on top of the other, they made a partially effective windbreak. Hailsham squatted down behind it, grateful for its shelter.

'Why don't we all sit down and have a cosy little cuddle?' he said with a leer. 'And if you're all really good boys I'll tell you the story about the whore and the donkey in Kuwait City.'

'Which one did you fancy then, boss?' Jimmy shot back. But he took Hailsham's suggestion at face value, sitting down and pressing himself up against his superior officer in the lee of the makeshift windbreak. The idea caught on quickly. Tweedledee, Andrew, Barry, Cyclops and the Thinker joined them gratefully, squatting down in a tight little circle and huddling together to pool their precious body warmth.

Nobody thought of inviting Safar, who seemed content to sit on his own in the teeth of the wind, studying them with a faintly pitying smile.

16

It was with mixed feelings that Major Osipov studied the latest piece of intelligence intercepted by the Alma-Ata military base. While on the surface it appeared to offer him a perfect chance to act on his own initiative, he was all too aware of the possible dangers of sticking his neck out. Premier Kuloschow might be weak as a politician, and lacking any vestige of respect within the military, but he still had strong Party connections, some of whom still wielded considerable power behind the scenes. The time and circumstances for a military coup were rapidly ripening, but had yet to reach their best season for plucking. To bite too deeply, too soon, could be to taste the hard sourness of unripened fruit instead of the soft succulence of sweet flesh.

Osipov made a mental effort to control the impetuosity which fuelled his boundless ambition. For once, it would do no harm to err on the side of caution, bide his time until he had more pieces of the strange jigsaw puzzle which had been thrown down in front of him. For if, as the coded message suggested, the British SAS had now become involved, then he would need to be very sure of his ground before making any move at all. It was not even certain that the information was genuine. Perhaps it was nothing more than a deliberately leaked piece of disinformation put out by the Chinese for reasons of their own. Certainly that would not be a new trick, or a ruse which had not succeeded in the past. Much as Osipov despised the Chinese, he had a healthy respect for their cunning. In truth, they were a worthy enemy, which only sweetened the game.

Osipov considered the matter objectively. It was clear that he needed more answers, which, paradoxically, meant that he first needed more questions. But who to ask? Where to start looking? His whole body tensed with the sheer frustration of it all. For Kuloschow was probably nearer to the essential information than anyone, even though he was probably still unaware of it. And to give the politician the slightest hint that the mysterious research facility in the Sailyukem Mountains might be the key to something of international importance would be to show his own hand prematurely, and lose the initiative which he had now gained.

That the research station *was* the key to the mystery, Osipov no longer had any doubts. Whether the Chinese message was genuine or not made little difference. The fact remained that a military assault helicopter had been destroyed while on a routine surveillance mission – and that made it a military matter demanding a military response. And in that response lay the means to achieve his own ends – simple, direct and myopically brutal. For given a credible pretext, Osipov felt sure that he could justify an all-out genocidal war against the Birlik and any of the other rebel factions which threatened the fragile status quo. It would be a move which would at once restore the morale and the ambition of the military hierarchy who even now were poised for a return to the power and the glories of the old regime. And Major Yuri Osipov would be at the head of that power, the triumphant returning warrior in whose face all that glory was reflected.

That, in essence, was the crux of Osipov's grandiose but essentially simple plan. It also incorporated his essential weakness, his own personal blind spot. For his thinking was strictly conditioned by the limitations of his military training and background. There had never been anything else. He saw everything in direct and simplistic terms. The roots of power lay in strength and control, and the only reference point was the strength of the old and familiar past. His conditioning, both by his military upbringing and his political convictions, left little room for any understanding of diplomacy, certainly not any acceptance of its possible role in the scheme of things. The major was ill-equipped to deal with even the basic politics of a simple and authoritarian regime, let alone the increasingly complex, fragmented and subtle influences now at work within an embryonic democracy. So he simply ignored them. It was a philosophy which, up till now, had always worked well enough.

Osipov returned his full attention to the business of the intelligence report and how he was going to use it to his best advantage. It was decided, then, that he would keep the information from Premier Kuloschow, at least for the time being. With that as a starting point, his primary task seemed clear enough.

Somehow he had to find out more about the suddenly important Phoenix Project and what might possibly lie behind the wall of secrecy which surrounded it. Until he had some answers on that score, any questions as to the reasons behind the involvement of the British SAS were superfluous.

Which brought him back to his original problem: where to start looking. Someone must have access to the information he needed. His own military intelligence seemed to be the most logical place to initiate the search. It was, after all, inconceivable that the secretive structure of his own system could work against him. Surely the slave could never be turned against the master — even in these turbulent times. Secure in this conviction, Osipov applied himself to the task in hand.

The storm seemed to fall down from the overhanging mountains with the sudden ferocity of a surprise mortar attack. One moment Hailsham and his men were huddled together against the icy blast of a strong but steady wind. The next they were engulfed by elemental forces of unbelievable fury. The wind no longer seemed to have a definite direction. It wheeled and whirled above them like a demonic, crazed, living thing — out of control and seemingly hell-bent on destroying any other form of life which dared to defy it. Swirling, cyclonic gusts approaching eighty miles an hour ripped first along the length of the narrow ravine and then quartered to roar across its width, creating within the trench a temporary vacuum which sucked the very breath out of their mouths and lungs as it scoured the ravine floor and drew up grit and small rocks with the force of missiles.

Rolling waves of thick black cloud gathered from nowhere to hang like a blanket over their heads. Day was suddenly night, but a night which was pierced every few seconds by the blinding glare of sheet and streak lightning raging both above and between the higher mountains. Each flash was almost immediately followed by the deafening clap of thunder and the rolling echoes which followed it, confirming that they were in the very eye of the storm.

Hailsham's limited knowledge of meteorology told him that the storm was caused by a sudden and severe temperature inversion and not uncommon to mountainous regions. This piece of information led inevitably to two further conclusions – one good, one bad. Although among the most violent and destructive of all weather extremes, such storms were essentially short-lived, sometimes lasting only a few minutes. But they were almost certain to lead to a further temperature inversion, bringing savage cold and the strong likelihood of blizzard conditions in their wake. With the reasonable expectancy that the fierce winds would persist for several hours after the actual storm had subsided, the wind-chill factor would be horrendous, and heavy snow and drifting could soon turn the mountain path which had been their friend into a new and terrible enemy. Already the bucketing mix of hail, sleet and freezing rain was beginning to churn up the floor of the ravine, threatening to turn the steep incline ahead of them into one vast mud-slide.

To stand up and remain upright for more than a

few seconds would have been virtually impossible, so Hailsham did not even try. With considerable effort, he managed to drag himself towards Safar on his hands and knees, his body rocked from side to side by the buffeting winds. The little Uzbek had dropped from his exposed position on a large flat rock at the first sight of the looming clouds, and was now curled, foetus-like, beneath its scant shelter.

Hailsham curled up beside him. Normal conversation, even shouting, was out of the question above the roar of the wind and the now almost continuous thunder. Cupping his hands around the man's ear, Hailsham used them as a megaphone.

'We've got to get out of here,' he shouted in Russian. 'Can we make it to anywhere more sheltered?'

Safar appeared to think for a few moments, finally nodding his head. Mutely, he pointed further up along the ravine in the direction they had been travelling and then closed and opened both hands, extending all his fingers stiffly. It was a gesture which was obviously meant to convey the number ten, Hailsham realized. But whether the man meant ten kilometres, ten miles or ten minutes' travelling time was unclear. He shouted again into Safar's ear: 'I don't understand.'

The young man uncurled himself, copying Hailsham's improvised ear-trumpet technique. 'There is a cave. Perhaps ten minutes from here. But we will have to climb to it. It will not be easy.'

Whipping hailstones stung Hailsham's face like shotgun pellets. He could almost feel the air temperature dropping again, as the expected inversion started to take place. Soon the hail and sleet would start to give way to driving snow and they would all be trapped in a total white-out. There was really no choice: they had to make a move and they had to make it now. He jabbed one finger up the ravine, nodding his head. Turning, he began to scramble back towards the huddled knot of his men as Safar attempted to push himself to his feet.

Heads bowed, the tight circle of troopers looked for all the world like a bunch of Buddhist monks crouched in prayer. Only Jimmy dared to look up as Hailsham slithered into the group. Teeth gritted against the rasping wind and the sting of hail, the Scot tried to contort his face into a grin.

'Fucking hell, boss – and I thought the weather in the Highlands was changeable,' he screamed out at the top of his voice, but the words were snatched away on the teeth of the wind.

Hailsham made no attempt to shout, merely signalling the intention to move out with a complicated series of hand gestures which would have put a mime artist to shame. They served their purpose well enough. With a series of shoves and nudges, the message was passed around the huddled circle and the men started to struggle to their feet and retrieve their stacked bergens.

Picking up the heavy and unwieldy backpacks was one thing; trying to put them on again was something else. The men might just as well have been attempting to light cigarettes under water. As fast as a man managed to hook his bergen over one shoulder, a blast of wind would catch against it and either sweep it over his head or throw man and backpack to the ground together. It might have been funny in a silent film; here it was merely a useless and painful waste of energy. As was so often the case in times of shared difficulty, the only answer lay in teamwork. Sorting themselves into twos and threes, the men helped each other to shrug on their backpacks and equipment until they were all fully laden again and ready to move out.

Hailsham had hoped that the additional weight of the bergens would give them all a little more stability. Instead they created a larger area of wind resistance, and the two opposing forces more or less cancelled each other out. Crouched over like a small band of misshapen dwarves, the men fell into a ragged line behind Hailsham and began to shamble up the increasingly treacherous floor of the ravine path. Virtually no one managed to remain on both feet for more than a few moments at a time. Before they had covered a quarter of a mile, all were caked in thick mud, soaked through and bruised from frequent and painful contact with the ground, the rocky sides of the ravine, or each other. Their senses numbed by the ear-splitting crashes of thunder and the roaring wind, and physically exhausted by the uphill struggle and the constant battle for a decent lungful of air, they had only the harshness of their survival training to drive them on in conditions where lesser men might have given up any hopes of survival.

Not that similar thoughts did not occur to them, training or no training. Perhaps for the third time in as many minutes, Hailsham considered calling a halt to the agonizingly slow forward march and huddling down again in the hopes of sitting out the storm. But common sense and a dogged determination to survive prevailed each time, and he forced his unwilling feet to shuffle on, one leaden step at a time. Apart from the physical difficulty of forward movement, the element of mental frustration was itself challenging. He might take ten or so forward steps before one foot slipped on a patch of icy mud, or a savage gust of wind from an unexpected quarter knocked him sideways. Then it would be a question of scrabbling with hands and fingernails against the slippery floor of the ravine, trying to arrest the downhill and backward slide which would rob him of the few precious feet he had gained. But slowly progress was made, and the small party dragged itself on towards its unknown goal as the storm continued to rage about them.

The mountain path began to widen out, the enclosing walls of the ravine becoming less high. With this diminishing protection came a new challenge which seemed wildly out of proportion to the comparatively minor change in the surrounding terrain. The wind assaulted them now with renewed fury, forming an invisible wall across their path. Ahead of him, Hailsham could see the slight figure of Safar pressed forward at a seemingly impossible angle, as though he were a puppet suspended on wires. Straining into the teeth of the gale, his feet scrabbling along the slimy floor of the path, he looked like a mime artist telling the tale of a man suddenly confronted with a huge but imaginary plate-glass window. Only when the fierce wind abruptly dropped, or veered off in another direction for a split second, was it possible for the little Uzbek to make any forward movement at all – and that would only be in clumsy, lurching steps which might take him all of three or four feet before the invisible obstacle returned to block his progress once again.

It was obvious that Safar was finding the task beyond him. Crouching down even lower and pushing his broad shoulders into the wall of wind like a rugby player scrumming down, Hailsham threw himself forward with dredged-up reserves of energy, gradually closing the gap between them. Motioning over his back with one arm, Hailsham urged the rest of the men to close ranks behind him, tightening up from a strung-out, ragged line into a physically connected knot of brawn, muscle and sinew. Their combined weight and force seemed to make quite a difference. Rather like a tug-of-war team in reverse, they began to make steady forward progress once again, pushing the blanket-clad Safar out in front of them like a colourful standard.

Another seven or eight minutes of struggling along in this concerted fashion brought them to a place where the path opened out even wider, dipping down to form a shallow bowl at the base of a massive and towering pinnacle of rock. Grateful for the limited amount of shelter it provided, the entire party collapsed weakly in the lee of the cliff-like rock to regain some strength.

The raging eye of the storm seemed to have passed over them now. Hailsham found himself counting off the seconds between lightning flashes and the thunderclaps which followed, applying the old formula of five seconds to a mile. The interval between light and sound was clearly noticeable now, and extending rapidly. Hailsham estimated that the centre of the storm was now at least three-quarters of a mile behind them, and moving away at a speed of around forty miles an hour. Conversation was now possible again, provided it was conducted at fairly close range in short, shouted bursts.

'Where now?' he yelled to Safar.

The man's swarthy face cracked into the semblance of a grin. Glancing upwards, he jabbed one finger vertically into the air along the line of the almost sheer rock face towering over their heads.

'Jesus Christ!'

Hailsham's explosive curse was delivered for his own benefit, but for some reason it seemed to increase Safar's sense of amusement. Grinning like a monkey, he shook his head from side to side as if to offer Hailsham some welcome reassurance.

'Easy,' the Uzbek blurted out. 'I show you easy way.' He pressed his back against the rocky wall behind him and began to push himself to his feet again. Beckoning for Hailsham to follow him, he started to edge along the base of the pinnacle to where it disappeared behind a couple of huge, weather-worn boulders.

The base of the rock face began to curve to the right. Following Safar around it, Hailsham finally saw the reason for the guide's enthusiasm: a giant jagged cleft in the main structure of the massif which cleaved almost vertically upwards. The effect was to create a vast chimney which was more than generously provided with craggy outcrops forming a crude but negotiable stairway. Looking up it, Hailsham tried to estimate its height – a calculation somewhat complicated by the fact that the cleft tapered towards the top, distorting the natural sense of perspective which would have allowed a true assessment. He guessed that the main fissure rose a good three hundred feet before narrowing into little more than a split in the rock. Seen from this level, the last thirty feet or so looked like being a rather tight squeeze for an average-sized man. Hailsham could not help feeling slightly dubious, particularly when he considered the Thinker's bulky frame.

He gestured up towards the top, shouting to Safar. 'How wide?' he asked, moving his outspread hands in from arm's length to just over a foot apart.

Safar held out his hands about eighteen inches apart. 'Is easy,' he insisted again. 'Even for big man.'

The Usbek seemed to be confident enough, Hailsham decided. No doubt he had used the chimney before, either as an emergency escape route or a temporary bolt-hole. Assuming he was right, even the Thinker or Andrew should have no trouble in squeezing through the narrow gap, although they would all have to take off their bergens and equipment before starting the climb.

Jimmy had slithered up to join them. He looked up, following Hailsham's point of view to the top of the cleft and smiling happily. 'Stairway to Heaven,' he shouted almost exultantly.

Hailsham failed to understand the Scot's obvious enthusiasm for a moment, finally remembering that rock climbing and mountaineering were his favourite forms of leisure pursuit. On his periods of leave, he did this sort of thing for fun. There was no accounting for taste.

'You crazy bastard,' Hailsham yelled at him. 'You're actually going to enjoy this, aren't you?'

Jimmy nodded, his eyes gleaming. 'Want me to lead?' It was a request rather than an offer.

'Too bloody right,' Hailsham screamed back. 'Only let Safar up first. He will be at the top by the time we get our bergens roped up. Each man will have to pull them through behind him, but it shouldn't be too much of a problem.'

'I'll go back and get the others organized,' Jimmy shouted, turning and beginning to edge back round the rock face. Hailsham turned his attention to Safar, jerking his head upwards in a clear gesture for him to start climbing. Stepping into the wide base of the fissure, the little Usbek jumped onto the first flat ledge of protruding outcrop and began to clamber up the chimney. Hailsham watched him progress steadily with almost primate-like agility, marvelling yet again at the man's apparent ability to tap new reserves of energy.

The major began stripping off his assault rifle and bergen, opening it to take out a coil of thin but tough nylon cord. He secured the SA-80 butt upwards and then slung the heavy bergen beneath it. The rope was only two hundred feet long, but each man carried his own coil. Any two of them tied together should be more than enough for the job, Hailsham figured. By working on the chain principle, adding a new length every time someone retrieved their equipment, they would be able to hoist all the equipment up without facing the problem of how to lower a flaccid rope back down through the convoluted and craggy sides of the chimney.

Jimmy reappeared round the curve of the rock face, leading the rest of the men. He lashed his own rope to the end of Hailsham's, then secured the free end tightly around his waist. Waiting only for a curt nod of approval from the major, he followed Safar's lead and started the ascent.

Although physically demanding, the climb was not technically difficult. Even the final stage, which required a certain amount of bodily contortion to get through the narrowest of the crevices, was not beyond the ability of a reasonably fit man with a head for heights. To the SAS troopers, their bodies hardened to peak fitness, it was little more than a routine exercise.

Cyclops, the last man to come up, hauled up his gun and bergen and untied them both, deftly coiling his rope again and returning it to its allotted place. Hailsham considered their new situation. Somewhere on the way up, what had looked like a single and isolated pinnacle of rock at the bottom had merged into the next ridge of mountain behind it. The top of the chimney had opened out onto a wide, flat ledge, which in turn gave way to a narrow pass which seemed to have been slashed out of the mountain with a horizontal, scythe-like sweep. It was an odd-looking formation, and Hailsham could not even guess at the geological forces which could have created it.

Now that they were clear of the chimney, they were all fully exposed to the full force of the elements once again, whose fury showed no signs of diminishing. Although the thunder and lightning had all but ceased, the winds were as savage as ever, and the ambient temperature had dropped dramatically. Obviously the secondary temperature inversion was well under way. All of a sudden the downpour of sleet and rain ceased, to be replaced by a swirling white blanket of fat, sticky snowflakes. Within seconds, it was virtually impossible to pick out any feature more than a few feet away. Hailsham could only hope that Safar knew the terrain intimately, for any further progress now would be almost blind.

The men all pressed themselves in to the deepest part of the ledge, uncomfortably and acutely aware that any one of the violent and unpredictable gusts of wind which constantly clawed along the ledge could suck them from it at any moment and toss them back down the express route of the three-hundred-foot climb they had just negotiated. With knowledge like that, having his back to a solid wall of rock gave a man some degree of consolation.

In view of the dangers, Hailsham thought about ordering the men to rope themselves together, then decided that would be equally risky. Any safety factor was likely to be outweighed by the fact that they were all physically weak from the exertion of the recent climb and their senses dulled by the constant onslaught of the weather. If one man went off the edge, it was more than possible that the next one in line would simply have neither the strength to absorb the sudden strain nor the speed of reaction to do the right thing in the first vital second. In that case, there was every chance that they would all plunge to their deaths without a prayer. All in all, it was probably better that every man took his own chances, Hailsham decided. He had sufficient faith in each one of them to know that they were as much aware of the potential dangers as he was.

Wet snow plastered Hailsham's face mask and

goggles, obscuring his vision completely. He clawed at the tinted plastic covering his eyes, managing to improve his immediate field of vision to a misty yellowish blur in which he could just about see nearby shapes. Safar's blanket-swathed form appeared as a vaguely ovoid patch of brighter colour against the general dull ochre. Very gingerly, Hailsham picked his way past two other figures, which he took to be Andrew and Jimmy, and pressed his mouth to the side of Safar's face as it finally came into rough focus.

'How far to this cave?' he yelled.

'Very near,' came the shouted reply. 'Perhaps thirty yards, no more. I will lead the way.'

Hailsham shook his head violently. 'No,' he shouted, emphatically. Reaching up, he pressed Safar's head with his fingers, turning it in the direction of Jimmy, standing next to them. 'You follow him, as close as you can.'

Meekly, Safar nodded his head in assent, without understanding Hailsham's reasoning, which was essentially simple. The Usbek guide, being the smallest and lightest of any of them, was the most vulnerable, Hailsham figured. And Jimmy was the most experienced mountaineer in the party. It seemed only logical that he should lead.

The Scot, having overheard the shouted exchange, slipped neatly into his role. Keeping his back still firmly pressed against the rock face, he began to move along the ledge, testing each step with a cautious probe of his left foot before transferring his weight to it. Safar, followed by Andrew and then Hailsham, moved in his wake, their arms outstretched against the rock behind them so that their fingertips were almost touching. Only the sheer size of the blurry figure next to him told Hailsham that the Thinker was the next man on his immediate right. He had no idea of the order of the rest of the men following, although it was really of no importance. Perhaps exercising more caution than was strictly necessary, the windswept party made slow but steady progress along the ledge.

A sudden yell from Jimmy came out of the swirling white fog for a brief second before the sound was snatched away on the wind: 'I think I see something.'

Even as Hailsham turned sideways, a sudden and particularly fierce gust struck him full in the face as the wind changed direction again and blew directly against the main rock face. The immediate after-effect was to cause a strong back-draught which temporarily sucked the blinding snow away from the ledge like a giant vacuum cleaner. In a few moments of comparatively clear vision, Hailsham was able to see the mouth of the cave as a dark gash against the overall greyish-white of the mountain. He could even make out the look of triumph on Jimmy's face as he stepped in front of the cave's mouth and began to turn towards it.

Above the howl of the roaring winds, the staccato burst of gunfire from a Russian AK-47 hit them all with almost physical shock. For the merest fraction of a second before the blizzard closed back again, Hailsham saw Jimmy's body lifted clear off its feet by the force of the dozen or so slugs which chewed into his upper torso and threw him backwards over the lip of the ledge. The screaming wind drowned out the faint sounds of the trooper's body bouncing off a series of rocky outcrops on its way to the ground below.

Shock might well have frozen another man in his tracks. For Hailsham, it merely triggered off the lightning responses which had been programmed and reinforced by a lifetime of training. He reacted instantly. No longer concerned with caution, he threw himself past the still figures of Andrew and Safar, rolling his body along the rock face until he was a matter of inches from the mouth of the cave. His fingers were already clawing at his webbing, deftly unhooking a stun grenade and transferring it to his right hand, where he pulled the pin. Counting off the vital seconds, he jumped momentarily into the entrance of the cave and tossed the 'flash-bang' in, rolling back against the shelter of the solid rock face again in one smooth, fluid movement.

Even in such a moment of sudden and terrible crisis, Hailsham's mind was still making rational decisions. He could have chosen a fragmentation grenade, or he could have simply unhooked the nearest one, not knowing or caring which type it was. But the stun grenade was a deliberate choice. Jimmy's death was something which was over and done with. It was not an act which immediately cried for vengeance. One trooper was dead – but six remained alive. Hailsham's responsibility was to them now. Whoever was in the cave, he needed them alive, not dead, for it was impossible to get information from a corpse.

The grenade exploded with an echoing roar. The mouth of the cave belched light and smoke, the force of the explosion clearing a dark vortex in the blizzard. Hailsham swung his SA-80 into position and threw himself into the cave, his keen eyes sweeping the interior. The dull, greenish glow of a chemical light aided him as he made a lightning assessment. Even as Andrew jumped in behind him ready to provide covering fire, he had identified the position and harmlessness of the two occupants and was moving towards them, his finger on the trigger.

The two men, both natives, lay sprawled and motionless on the floor of the cave, temporarily concussed by the effects of the grenade. Hailsham jumped forward, kicking away the AK-47 and the much older PPS-43 which lay beside their bodies.

He waved the business end of the SA-80 menacingly as the first man groaned faintly and began to stir. His finger positively itched against the cold metal of the trigger. Now that the moment of crisis had passed, and his cold logic had been followed through, a wave of pure emotion swept through his body: anger, and sorrow, at the sheer tragedy and futility of Jimmy's death tore at his guts and brain. An eye for an eye, a tooth for a tooth. The compulsion to pull the trigger and rip both men to bloody shreds of flesh and bone was so strong that it threatened to overwhelm him completely.

Strangely, it was the sound of the rest of the troopers pouring into the cave behind him and the massed click of cocked weapons which helped him to remain calm.

'Hold your fire,' Hailsham heard himself bark. His finger eased off on the trigger as the second man began to revive and pull himself up into a sitting position, staring up at the sudden invaders with a look of sheer terror in his eyes.

'Who the hell are they?' Andrew asked, the question tailing off into a faint sigh of despair.

'Kazakh,' Safar spat out, total hatred and venom in his voice. He rattled off a short and highly impassioned speech in Russian which caught Hailsham unawares. Long before he had managed an effective translation, the little Usbek had thrown himself forward and was reaching under the folds of his blankets.

Too late, Hailsham realized his intention. In a matter of seconds Safar had produced a wicked-looking knife and had dropped to his knees in front of the two captives. With two savage, sweeping strokes, he had slit both their throats.

The Uzbek climbed to his feet again, turning towards Hailsham and Andrew with a happy smile on his face. It was an expression which begged gratitude and admiration, much like a young puppy who has just taken his first crap outside the house. His sparkling eyes clouded with confusion at the major's look of hopeless anger.

With a heavy sigh, Hailsham let his weapon droop towards the ground. He turned to glance at Andrew, his teeth gritted in a gesture of utter frustration.

'Goddammit – I wanted them alive,' he muttered helplessly. 'They could have given us valuable intelligence about whatever other guerrilla forces are out there.'

Andrew glanced down dispassionately at the two bloody corpses. 'It appears our little Usbek friend knew something about them,' he observed.

Hailsham nodded, remembering Safar's brief speech before dispatching the two Kazakhs. 'He seems to think they were part of the raiding party which carried out the massacre in their village recently. This ethnic hatred thing obviously cuts both ways.'

'So what do you think they were doing here on their own?' Andrew mused. 'An advanced scouting party, do you reckon?'

Hailsham grunted. 'Bloody good question. Wish I had the answer. If there are any more of these bastards about, I was hoping to know about it. They obviously shoot first and ask questions afterwards.'

Cyclops was bending over the two bodies, admiring Safar's knifework. He was obviously impressed. 'Sweeney Todd couldn't have done a neater job,' he murmured, turning to the Uzbek. 'Nice one, Safar. If I ever do get to shoot that bloody eagle, you can chop its fucking head off.'

Although he did not understand the words, Safar was quick to pick up the suggestion of praise he had been seeking earlier. He grinned again, for the first time in the last few minutes.

'What shall we do with the bodies, boss?' Cyclops asked. 'They ain't going to be much company if we're staying around for a while.'

Hailsham nodded towards the mouth of the cave. 'Just drag 'em out and drop 'em over the edge,' he replied. 'There's not much else we can do.'

The Thinker stepped forward to help carry the two dead Kazakhs to the edge of the ledge and dispose of them. Afterwards he walked back to the thick pool of blood on the floor and made a vain attempt to cover the gory patch up with dirt with the sole of his boot. Failing, he unzipped himself and pissed over the floor.

Tweedledee let out a low groan of disgust. 'You dirty bastard,' he complained. 'We've probably got to kip in here tonight.'

The Thinker was unrepentant. 'More hygienic,' he muttered, justifying his action. 'One of the bastards might have had AIDS or something.'

Tweedledee was not impressed with this dubious logic. 'So we settle for a dose of the bloody clap instead, do we?' he demanded sarcastically. 'Well I know where *you're* dossing down, that's for bloody sure.'

Normally Hailsham would have let the harmless banter go. This time, however, he responded with unaccustomed edginess. 'All right you two, knock it on the head,' he snapped. He walked quickly to the mouth of the cave and peered out. Even through the white-out of the blizzard, it was clear that the daylight was fading. They had made it to the shelter of the cave just in time. 'OK, so we basha down here for the night,' he announced curtly. 'We'll grab some scran now and then get a decent night's kip. We'll need to be on our toes tomorrow.'

Andrew rummaged through his bergen and fished out the stick of preserved marmot. Only partially cooked, unflavoured and stone cold, it was chewy and barely palatable, but no one complained. Jimmy's death, and Hailsham's sombre mood, had subdued them all. They ate in strained silence. The Scot's name was never mentioned. It was the unspoken law. He would not even exist again for any of them until his name appeared on a clock-tower plaque back in Hereford.

17

Major Osipov had not been as discreet as he imagined. More importantly he had overlooked one small thing, in what was to prove a fatal error of judgement. In his contempt for Premier Kuloschow he had failed to grasp the essential nature of the man himself. For while he might be militarily, even diplomatically naïve, Kuloschow was not a fool. And he was at heart a politician, naturally endowed with the devious cunning of that breed.

At best, politics was an exposed and vulnerable profession. Even in the most stable and well established of systems, sudden and dramatic change could sweep up through the levels of power without warning, and with lightning speed. What might begin as a small pebble dropped into a seemingly calm pond had created a huge ripple by the time it reached the shore. And in the chaotic fragility which had followed the break-up of the former Soviet Union, such ripples could easily grow into huge waves which smashed down everything in their path. There could be no defence – only some sort of early-warning system which would detect that first tiny disturbance.

The other fundamental rule of politics was that the man at the top could easily become the most vulnerable – unless he did something to protect himself. The astute politician was aware of that fact and made preparations accordingly. Kuloschow was no exception to this rule. Although raw in actual experience, he was well versed in the theory of political power.

'The buck stops here,' as the Americans liked to say. It was not strictly true, of course, since it presupposed a man being careless or stupid enough to let the buck get that far in the first place. Or lacking the foresight to put in place a series of measures which could deflect that buck from its path.

Major Osipov had failed to grasp any of this. His 'discreet' enquiries through military intelligence into the buried secrets of the Phoenix Project had been the original pebble in the pond. Premier Kuloschow's strategically placed chain of spies and informers had detected the first ripple and passed on a warning. This in turn had set in motion an inexorable series of events which could end only one way.

There was a perfect phrase to describe this phenomenon. The Russian peoples dearly liked to believe that it had originated in the roots of their own colourful language. Roughly translated, that phrase was: the shit's about to hit the fan.

Kuloschow had few illusions about the precise nature of his own position. He was little more than a figurehead, and probably only a temporary one at that. He was premier in name only – a purely titular office in which he danced, puppet-like, to another's hand on the strings. And it was to that hand that Kuloschow now had to turn.

It was ironic, even slightly insane. For all the cataclysmic upheaval which continued to sweep through Eastern Europe, very little had actually changed. Economic reforms, political moves and counter-moves, optimistic talk of democracy and Western treaties aside, one thing remained constant. The old ideas still ruled, the former regime was still in place and poised to resume its control of power at any time. The old guard had not been dismantled or swept away. They had merely gone undercover, biding their time until the moment was right to re-emerge and assume their former power once again.

Kuloschow was aware of all this, and the knowledge both limited and channelled his possible courses of action. Osipov had unwittingly opened a can of worms, and that action had caused the ripples which had alerted Kuloschow. Now he, in turn, had felt forced to pursue the same delicate matter at a higher level. In this process of escalation, the ripples had become the very waves which Kuloschow recognized and feared. Hidden powers and men with dark secrets foresaw the threat and took steps to pull its teeth. Power put trust in power; strength relied on strength. The hidden men appealed to their oldest ally – the military. Through Major Osipov.

Thus, in a bizarre twist of fate, the snake had taken its own tail between its fangs and bitten it. The circle was closed.

Andrew awoke to the first grey fingers of light creeping into the gloom of the cave. He rose quietly, careful not to disturb any of the other sleepers around him. Stepping gingerly over the bodies huddled closely together for warmth, he walked to the mouth of the cave to survey the new morning.

Although it was still bitterly cold, the storm had completely abated and the winds had dropped to little more than an erratic stiff breeze. A few flakes of snow fluttered down from the leaden sky, but otherwise it promised to be a calm, if not pleasant, day. Andrew luxuriated in a few precious and rare moments of privacy and peace before looking up into the mountains and their final objective, seeing with the eyes of a soldier but the soul of a poet. The soldier saw a forbidding landscape of ravines, crevasses and treacherous, icy gradients which muttered danger and death. The poet saw the grandeur of snow-covered mountains which sang of challenge and human triumph.

Lost in such thoughts, the sergeant was completely unaware of Hailsham stepping up behind him.

'Morning, Andrew. Enjoying the view?'

Andrew turned, with a slight start of surprise. He forced a smile to his lips, masking his sense of disappointment that his private moment was over. 'Something like that,' he replied with a nod. He paused for a while as Hailsham's eyes took in the same panorama. 'What do *you* see out there, boss?'

Hailsham did not even think about the question. 'My job,' he answered simply, but it said more about him than he could possibly have realized. He walked back to his bergen and returned with his binoculars and map. Taking up the binoculars he trained them on the distant mountains again, scanning in a wide sweep until he found the two reference points he was searching for.

'How far now?' Andrew asked. 'Or perhaps more to the point, how long?'

Hailsham shrugged. 'In actual distance, probably no more than fifteen or twenty miles, as the crow flies. Trouble is, we're not crows.'

Andrew grinned weakly, still studying the same snowcapped mountains. 'Maybe just as well,' he observed. 'This is more like penguin country.' He was suddenly serious again. 'Can we make it in the next forty-eight hours, do you reckon? We're starting to get bloody close to our sell-by date.'

Hailsham sighed deeply. He did not really need reminding that they were now a full day behind their planned schedule. Even though he had incorporated some leeway into his original plans, things were getting uncomfortably tight. Much more delay, and it would become impossible to complete the mission and get back to the rendezvous point with the Chinese in time for safe retrieval. Which would leave him with a difficult decision to make: whether to scrub the mission and beat a hasty retreat, or complete the job they had come to do and risk being stranded. Neither response would be very satisfactory – from either a personal or a professional point of view.

Safar had now woken up and come over to join them. It was perhaps bad timing on his part as Hailsham turned the burning question of the moment on him: 'How much longer?'

At least he was optimistic, Hailsham thought with a slight sense of relief. With his usual irrepressible good humour, the Usbek could not even see a problem. 'I will take you to the next mountain plateau by evening,' he promised with an easy smile. 'From there you will be able to see the place you seek.'

'And Kazakh guerrilla forces?' Hailsham asked. 'Are we likely to encounter any hostility?'

Safar shrugged. 'If we see them, you will kill them,' he said firmly.

Hailsham was grateful for the young man's blind faith, at least. If nothing else, it went some way to alleviating some of his own doubts. For the moment, he preferred not to even think about the secondary problem of the official Kazakhstan Republican forces. Now that the storm has passed, it was surely only a matter of hours before helicopter patrols would be out looking for them. And Safar's reference to a mountain plateau had been rather disconcerting, suggesting an ideal site from which to launch a search-and-sweep operation. It would not take much military planning to set up a landing and refuelling base in a dangerously short space of time. Just two choppers and a small support team of maintenance engineers would give them the capacity to scour an area of up to fifty square miles within the next two days. The next two *vital* days, a little voice inside his head reminded him, in case he had not already realized.

Hailsham mentioned nothing of these fears to Andrew. Keeping some problems to oneself was one of the responsibilities of command. But his consideration was largely wasted, for the black sergeant had already identified and thought about the problem for himself. He had seen enough of the new morning to know that the weather was lifting fast, the heavy and low cloud cover already beginning to break up and melt away. In an hour or two it would be ideal flying weather.

A reconnaissance mission was probably well under way at that very moment, with planes or helicopters already warming up on the tarmac at Alma-Ata. They might even be in the air already.

It was not a pleasant thought to dwell on, Andrew realized suddenly, pulling himself up with a mental jolt. He glanced across at Hailsham. 'So, what's Safar's verdict?' he asked.

The question snapped Hailsham out of his own gloomy thoughts. 'Sorry, I keep forgetting that you don't follow the lingo,' he apologized, quickly passing on a rough précis of Safar's information.

Andrew assimilated it with a curt nod. 'I guess the sooner we get going the better. Someone's going to be coming looking for us – and somehow I don't think they'll be bringing us morning coffee.'

Despite himself, Hailsham smiled. 'You could be right,' he conceded. 'They sure as hell won't be wanting to wish us a nice day, either.'

In fact, if they had seen the sealed and coded orders which Major Osipov was at that very moment opening, they would have been as surprised and confused as he was.

Osipov read the orders carefully for the second time, just in case there was some room for misunderstanding. There was none. They were as clear and as unambiguous as they were baffling. No matter how he tried to find some hidden rationale, he failed miserably.

In fact, the instructions were so completely bizarre that Osipov might well have suspected some sort of trick. But they carried a top security coding and had come through the correct channels. Only one thing was certain: they had not passed through Premier Kuloschow's hands on the way.

18

For breakfast the troopers finished off the remainder of their high-calorie ration packs. It might be the last meal any of them got for some time. From now on they were on a strict survival regime, and would have to live off the barren terrain – a prospect which was not exactly promising. Thinking about it, Hailsham realized that none of them had actually noticed any signs of animal life since landing. Not that they had been specifically looking for it, of course, but it was somewhat disquieting, all the same.

At least water was no problem, Hailsham thought. He supervised the operation of packing freshly fallen snow from the ledge outside into their canteens, replenishing their dwindling reserves. Although several of the men had urinated out through the mouth of the cave before bedding down the previous night, they had all shown the foresight and consideration to aim sideways and piss with the wind behind them. Apart from which, all were sufficiently versed in mountain survival techniques to scoop up only snow which was pristine white. Rule number one, Hailsham thought to himself, recalling the phrase often echoed by ski instructors: Never eat yellow snow.

Finally, they were all packed and ready to move out.

The men gathered in a knot at the entrance to the cave, obviously expecting some sort of rallying call from the boss. Hailsham did not disappoint them. He looked at them calmly but firmly.

'All right, let's get ready to move out,' he announced. 'I'm not going to call a full battle order at this point, but I want you all to be ready for a shake-out at any time. Just in case the thought hasn't already occurred to you, our two friends last night were obviously part of a guerrilla combat unit – and these particular natives are far from friendly. Whether they were a scouting unit or just a couple of stragglers, we have no way of knowing. But the strong likelihood is that there will be others in the vicinity, so keep your eyes skinned and your ears open.' Hailsham paused for a second. 'Is that clear?'

'Clear as a virgin's piss,' the Thinker murmured, with a nod. It was a comment which evoked an immediate guffaw of derisive laughter from the rest of the men.

'When the fuck did you ever meet a virgin?' Tweedledee demanded. The Mancunian grinned at him benevolently.

'A bloody sight more times than you,' he countered. 'The difference being that I didn't leave 'em in the same state.'

It was an effective put-down. Tweedledee lapsed into silence, having the good grace to know when he had been bested. He followed the others' lead in shrugging on his bergen and running a final check on his SA-80. All weapons had already been cleaned and wiped free of overnight condensation as a matter of routine.

'OK, let's hit the road,' Hailsham said. 'And watch your steps out on that ledge. I probably don't need to remind you that we had a little bit of snow last night.'

As understatements went, it was a little bit like the guy in the lounge bar of the *Titanic*: 'I know I asked for more ice in my drink, but this is ridiculous.' The previous night's blizzard had brought down well over fifteen inches of thickly packed snow. Although the high winds had blasted most of it over the side of the ledge, there were several places where an outcrop of rock, or a fissure, had provided somewhere for it to stick fast. Once started, heavy drifts had quickly built up, some of them as tall as a man and spread across the full width of the ledge. In fact, looking along the narrow route which they had to negotiate, Hailsham thought the irregular series of white mounds looked like a spaced-out sentry line of headless snowmen performing guard duty on the mountain path.

He pushed such fanciful thoughts from his head, considering the series of snowdrifts as the obstacles they actually were. Although clearing them out of the way should not be too much of a problem, it would be time-consuming and not without risk. The ledge was totally exposed, and well within rifle range of many of the surrounding peaks, and someone equipped with a half-decent telescopic sight would be able to pick them off like ducks in a shooting gallery. If there *were* any more guerrillas in the immediate vicinity, Hailsham could only hope and pray that they did not have a Cyclops among their ranks. Or indeed that their armaments did not extend to the latest laser-sighted hardware.

He was slightly surprised when Safar stepped outside the cave and turned back in the direction they had come from the previous night. Although there was no real reason for it, he had somehow expected that their route would be in the opposite direction. Double-checking, Hailsham reluctantly questioned the Usbek guide's sense of direction.

'Why are we backtracking?'

Safar pointed along the ledge in the opposite direction and shook his head violently. 'No way on,' he explained. 'That way leads only to a sheer rock face. Impossible to climb. We must go back.'

He seemed pretty certain, Hailsham thought. With a faintly resigned shrug, he fell into step behind the guide and began to pick his way carefully over the more obvious patches of ice and snow which glistened in the diffused light of the pale morning sun. Even though the ledge was well over two feet wide at this point, it was still hazardous and nerve-racking going. Some of the frozen patches were not apparent until the men actually trod on them. Two or three times in the first twenty yards, Hailsham felt one of his feet slide out on an invisible section of black ice, or skid on some loose shale beneath the snow which had been blown down from the main face by the savage winds. At such times, he could only recover himself, shrink back into the inner part of the ledge and marvel at the fact that they had ever made it through the full fury of the storm.

Finally they reached the widest section of the ledge at the top of the chimney. Hailsham relaxed slightly, tensing again only when he glanced down the plunging fissure which they had previously climbed. In the cold light of morning, and in the aftermath of the blizzard, it was no longer a negotiable stairway between the two levels of this part of the mountain. Overnight, driven and packed snow had completely filled in the open section, turning it into a gleaming white chute in which all footholds had been totally obscured. It reminded Hailsham of a near-vertical bob-sleigh run. He glanced uncertainly at Safar, who was hovering uncomfortably around the mouth of the chimney.

'I hope you're not going to tell me that we have to go back down again,' he muttered thickly.

Much to Hailsham's relief, the little Usbek shook his head and pointed upwards. Following the line of his finger, Hailsham's eyes took in a short, stiff but negotiable climb towards a long, ridged hog's back which stretched, he estimated, about two miles to the left. Assuming that Safar intended to lead them around it, the route then gave way to a section of rugged and broken hillocks and cols of snow-covered rock and beyond that what appeared to be a sheer rock face. It was this eventual obstacle which gave Hailsham the most cause for concern. It was difficult to judge from this distance and with the naked eye, but at a rough estimate the vertical cliff was anything from seventy to a hundred and twenty feet high and looked treacherously glassy.

Hailsham unslung his binoculars and lifted them to his eyes to take a more detailed look. It was not immediately encouraging. Seen in greater detail, the vertical rock face was indeed well over a hundred feet high, and as smooth as if it had been cleaved out with a single blow of some mighty axe. Apparently devoid of suitable hand or footholds, it looked impassable.

Hailsham scanned along the wall of rock and ice to the east, eventually identifying another one of the odd, slashed-out ledges which seemed to be a fairly common feature of this stretch of mountain. It ran horizontally for perhaps half a mile or so, then started to slope up at an increasingly steep gradient, eventually forming a small pass which led around the end of a blind ridge. Beyond that, it was impossible to even guess what lay ahead, but Safar had spoken of a plateau and Hailsham could only assume that it lay immediately above the sheer rock face. Sudden, cataclysmic subsidence millions of years ago would account for both the cliff-like drop and the broken and rugged crags below it. Satisfied with his schoolboy geology and comforted with the probability of a safe and easily negotiable route, Hailsham lowered the binoculars and glanced across at Safar once again, nodding his agreement.

'It looks OK,' he conceded.

The young man treated him to one of his cheerful grins. 'No fuckin' problem. Piece piss,' he said proudly.

Hailsham smiled to himself. The Usbek was learning fast, he thought. By the time he got back to his own people, he would probably be able to cuss as fluently as a regular squaddie. Which might well come in useful in the future, since Tweedledum was probably at that very minute teaching the Uzbek women a few choice phrases of his own with which to enrich their native language.

Andrew and Cyclops had moved over to join them. Cyclops jerked his thumb towards the little Uzbek guide. 'Does Sherpa Tenzing here know where we're going?' he asked.

Hailsham was still smiling. 'No fuckin' problem,' he said, mimicking Safar's broken accent.

Cyclops regarded him blankly, failing to understand the humour. 'Ask a bloody silly question,' he muttered to himself moodily, sloping away to rejoin the others.

Andrew looked slightly worried, Hailsham noticed. There was obviously something on his mind. 'Care to share it with me, Andrew?' he said.

The Barbadian looked uncertain for a few moments, finally shrugging. 'I suppose I'm just a bit worried about our little reception committee last night,' he admitted finally. 'If the other direction from the cave is impassable, they can only have come down the route we're about to take up.' He broke off to nod up at the higher mountains. 'And it can't have escaped your attention that there are at least three places in that terrain up ahead which would make damned good positions for an ambush.'

Hailsham's face was suddenly serious again. 'The thought had occurred,' he said candidly. 'But your concern is noted and appreciated. However, I don't see that we have much choice in the matter. Do you? I'm always open to suggestions.'

Andrew's thick lips curled into a rueful smile. 'We could always hop on the first bus home,' he murmured. 'Failing that, I'm afraid I don't have much to offer.'

Having been reminded of the problem, Hailsham was busy thinking it all through again. He was silent for a long time, running as many permutations as he could think of through his head. Finally he spelled out what few conclusions he had come to.

'Everything rather depends on who those two were, where they came from and where they were going,' he announced. 'If they were scouts, then it's a pretty sure bet that there's a larger force somewhere up ahead of us. In which case, the chances of an ambush or an attack will depend on the strength and intentions of that force. And how they perceive us, of course. They might well consider it prudent to go into hiding and let us pass, rather than attack.' Hailsham paused. 'Right so far?'

Andrew nodded. 'Pretty well, I should think. But there's a lot of "ifs" in there, boss.'

Hailsham sucked at his teeth. 'On the other hand, they could have been two stragglers trying to reach a rendezvous point when the storm broke. If so, then the question is: were they going up – or coming down?'

'There is one other possibility,' Andrew put in, just in case Hailsham had overlooked it. 'They could have been loners – either survivors from a group which had been attacked, or a couple of deserters who'd had enough and were going home to their families.'

Hailsham let out a little snort. 'Now who's creating a lot of "ifs" he replied, a faintly sardonic smile playing about the corners of his mouth.

The entire discussion was basically pointless, Andrew suddenly realized, grinning ruefully. Hailsham was right, of course. In the final analysis, they simply had no choice. No matter what lay ahead of them, or what might possibly happen, there was only one way forward and they had to take it.

The two men looked at each other with sheepish

grins on their faces, both suddenly aware of the futility of their conversation.

'You realize that we've just wasted a good five minutes,' Andrew pointed out, rather superfluously.

Hailsham nodded. 'The thought had occurred,' he said, falling back on the phrase which had triggered the discussion in the first place.

They had made good time, covering a good three miles in just over a couple of hours. The men were in good spirits, encouraged by the reasonable ease of the climb and the weather, which could only be described as benign compared with what they had experienced previously. The temperature remained comfortably above zero, keeping the thick blanket of snow on the ground soft and light. Even where it had piled up into drifts which came up to their knees, they had little trouble ploughing through it, the leading man creating a path for the others to follow. Just to spread the strain even more, Hailsham had ordered a change in the marching order every half a mile or so. The last of the heavy cloud cover had melted away now, leaving a high and light mist of cirrus which occasionally allowed the pale, watery sun to shine through for several minutes at a time. Despite the fact that the wind had freshened slightly again, and was blowing against them along the side of the hog's back, it was a pleasant enough day for healthy outdoor activity, and the trek was bracing without being too strenuous. In another time and place, Hailsham might have considered it a jaunt rather than a mission.

Viewed at close quarters, the cliff-like rock face looked even more formidable than Hailsham had supposed. Viewed through the binoculars, which had a slightly foreshortening effect, it had appeared to be vertical, but he saw now that this was not the case. In fact, it actually cantilevered at an angle of about 110 degrees for the first twenty or thirty feet, before returning to the vertical. Great sheets and rivulets of ice festooned various parts of the face, glistening in the weak sunlight. Even the most experienced climber, armed with specialist equipment, would have found it challenging in the extreme. On the plus side, the ledge he had noticed was considerably wider than he had assumed, quickly becoming an open pathway which curved around the side of the mountain.

Hailsham focused his eyes on the spot where the pass disappeared from his line of vision, then scanned the surrounding area. The fears of an ambush he had shared with Andrew now resurfaced. If one was to come at all, that would be the place, he realized, for that particular spot was in a direct line of fire from any one of a dozen locations higher up the surrounding peaks. He found the prospect sufficiently worrying to bring the party to a halt. Outlining the situation in a few well-chosen words, he prepared the men for a heightened state of alert.

'Until we reach the plateau, you're all to consider yourselves under full battle order,' he told them. 'And that means aggressive fire, by the way. These jokers have already shown us how trigger-happy they are, so I don't want anyone playing Mr Nice Guy. If you see anything, shoot first and worry about evasive action afterwards. Is that understood?'

The question was largely rhetorical, but a rattle of cocked and primed weapons gave Hailsham any answer he might have needed. He turned his attention to Safar, who was standing immediately behind him. 'This might be a good place for you to turn back,' he murmured in a gentle but oddly insistent tone. 'You have done more than enough, and we all thank you for it. But now it might be advisable for you to return to your people.'

Hailsham saw the sense of rejection which temporarily clouded the young man's swarthy face and felt slightly guilty. The little Uzbek had understood him on a level which went far beyond the mere translation of another language. For without wanting to spell it out, Hailsham knew that Safar's continued presence was no longer needed, and might even start to become a dangerous liability. The men had taken to him almost like a favourite pet, or a mascot. In a crisis situation any one of them might act instinctively rather than rationally to protect him, thus endangering their own lives and that of the others. It was not a risk Hailsham cared to take.

There was another factor, of course. Clad in his colourful swathing of blankets, Safar made a rather tempting target. If, as with many Arabic cultures, the pattern of those blankets carried some clue to ethnic identity, then parading Safar in their midst would be like a red rag to a bull. Hailsham had already seen enough evidence of the blind and instinctive hatred between the Uzbeks and the Kazakhs to know that Safar's presence was inviting attack. Without him, the possibility that the Kazakh forces would choose to leave them alone was increased.

With the instinctive racial knowledge of one whose people had been spurned and despised for generations,

Safar could tell all this from Hailsham's apologetic eyes. There was no attempt at argument. With a brief, deferential nod of his head, the little Uzbek complied meekly.

'I will leave you now,' he murmured simply. 'Just follow this path.'

He turned away without another word and began to walk past the file of men, who looked at him with fond, almost sorrowful expressions on their faces. The Thinker stepped out into the little Uzbek's path, holding out the AK-47 which he had picked up from the dead Kazakh in the cave, and thrust it into his hands. 'You might find this will come in useful,' he said quietly, even though Safar could not understand the words. It hardly mattered. It was a gesture which was universal. Safar grasped the weapon, cradling it against his chest with a thin smile on his face. Between friends of any culture, the traditional parting gift was recognized and appreciated.

The men stood in silence and watched him walk away for several seconds. He never turned to look back at them. Finally, their last respects paid, Hailsham called them all back to attention.

'Right, let's get moving,' he said brusquely. 'And keep your bloody eyes open.'

Weapons at the ready, and their senses on full alert, the column of men moved forward onto the ledge and began the gradual ascent to the narrow pass. Each footstep was more cautious now, carrying a new sense of urgency. Hailsham's fears had been communicated all too clearly. Fears which were totally justified, as it was shortly to turn out. For carried on the wind, and echoing through the valleys and ridges between the mountains, the sound of helicopter engines was about to reach their ears.

19

Tweedledee, in the Tail-end Charlie position and strung out some fifteen yards behind the main party, heard the sound first. He froze in his tracks, hissing ahead to Andrew, who was next in line.

'Psst. We got company, boss.'

'Jesus Christ,' Andrew spat out, his concern tinged with more than a hint of indignation, as though he took the unwelcome intrusion as a personal affront. 'That's all we bloody need right now.' He shouted a warning ahead to Hailsham, at the front. 'Incoming bandits.'

Hailsham had detected the faint sound of the choppers, and was already considering a suitable reaction. Not that there was much choice, he thought bitterly. Their position could hardly have been worse. Strung out along the ledge, with absolutely no cover at all, they might as well be waving welcome banners. He craned his neck upwards, his eyes sweeping the skies above. There was no visual sign yet, but the sound was definitely growing louder by the second. The helicopters – at least two of them, Hailsham reckoned – were headed in their direction sure enough, and with a particularly irksome sense of timing.

There was a Jewish expression which summed up

their position rather succinctly, Hailsham reflected with a sense of irony: 'Caught between a rock and a hard place.' It could have been specially commissioned for this very situation. Basically there were two choices – either make a break forward for the limited cover offered by the pass ahead or stay where they were. Both options were fraught with dangers. To rush forward blindly could be to run straight into an ambush, in which case they would probably be cut to shreds. To remain exposed invited the same fate. Hailsham's sense of frustration was almost like a physical pain inside his head. Indecision tore at him like a terrible guilt.

Then, suddenly, there was no decision to make any more. The matter was taken out of his hands as the two Hind-A choppers cleared a long ridge of hills to the east and came into view. Wheeling in the sky like a pair of scout bees performing a food dance, they homed in inexorably towards the troopers' position. Hailsham studied them stoically, a strange sense of calm creeping through his body like an anaesthetic. His only identifiable feeling was one of mild surprise, he realized. For some obscure reason, he had always expected to die in a hot climate.

These thoughts were not those of a defeatist, but of a realist. Hailsham was a born fighter, and would take a brave stand against whatever odds fate threw at him. But cold logic told him that six lightly armed troopers pinned against a bare rock face stood absolutely no chance of survival against two combat helicopters hell-bent on destroying them. It was as certain as night follows day.

Equally as certain was his duty. Hailsham dropped

to one knee on the rocky floor of the ledge, bringing his SA-80 up to his shoulder. He barked what he expected to be his last orders to the rest of the men.

'Fire at will when you think you've got a chance of hitting something worthwhile.'

There was little point in spelling it out any more plainly. Hailsham knew only too well that his men were as aware as he was of the awesome armour-plating specifications of the MIL Mi-24 series of helicopters. They were all tough — but the Hind-A assault version was perhaps the toughest of all. It had few vulnerable points, and it would take a very skilful or a very lucky shot at close range to bring one down.

Trooper Barry Naughton also reflected on the probability of death — but without the equanimity of his commanding officer. It wasn't supposed to be like this, a little voice screamed inside his head. Not so cold, so impersonal . . . so mechanical. All those hours spent in the 'killing house' at Hereford, pitting his brain and physical reflexes against recognizably human enemies, even if they were only cardboard pop-ups. All the months of training, of shared challenges and hardship, inherited foes and adopted friends. Comradeship, both group and individual pride, even the banter and the piss-taking. Everything the Army, and the SAS, had had led Barry to believe that an Army death would be like Army life. A matter of men pitted against men, an intense, close, and essentially living thing, somehow. Not hopelessly confronting two hunks of cold, grey metal in a cold, grey sky.

For the first time in his life, Barry wished that he

could be more articulate, if only in his own mind. He would have liked to explain his own thoughts to himself more clearly, sift through his own confusion and make sense of it. Disappointment, tinged with more than a hint of bitterness, crowded in on him. He only knew that this moment was wrong, and perhaps everything else had been wrong, too. Even his very reasons for choosing the Army as a career. Now, too late, he had begun to understand something about himself and his needs, realizing for the first time that the Army could never, and would never, satisfy them.

Barry glanced sideways at his companions in turn, the bitterness spilling out of him as helpless anger.

'Fuck you,' he screamed. 'Fuck you all.' His hand dropped to his hip, drawing his Browning. Raising the handgun to his temple, he shot himself through the head.

Hailsham registered the noise of the single shot, and the sight of the trooper's head exploding sideways in a spray of blood and white bone fragments, almost as subliminal images. They were not real – they were just snatches of somebody else's nightmare.

Reality was the two helicopters hovering like a pair of malevolent dragonflies waiting to close in on their prey. Only they were *not* closing in, Hailsham suddenly realized with a shock. Both craft had assumed and were holding a position immediately above the steeper side of the hog's back the troopers had traversed earlier. Watching and waiting. Hailsham shivered slightly, the sense of quiet menace was so acute.

Seconds ticked away into a minute, and then two.

To the men crouched on the exposed ledge, the tension was almost unbearable. Each of them knew that both of the choppers carried at least four 57mm rockets, and were well within range to launch them. Yet they did not fire. What the hell were they waiting for? Hailsham asked himself.

Andrew posed the question out loud. 'What the fuck are they playing at?' he exploded.

Hailsham could only shrug. 'Maybe they're just toying with us,' he suggested. 'Maybe they've radioed back to base and are waiting for specific orders. Who knows?'

'Or maybe they're scared of us,' the Thinker put in, with characteristic sarcasm. It was intended to be a joke, but it gave Hailsham food for serious thought.

'Actually, you might not be too far from the truth,' he muttered eventually, having analysed the situation and made possible sense of it. 'Neither of those pilots has any way of knowing we don't have the Stinger any more. To them, this could seem like a stand-off situation.'

'Which would explain why they're holding a position over that ridge,' Andrew agreed, following Hailsham's chain of thought. 'At the first sign of a missile launch, they can simply drop down behind it like a couple of concrete skylarks.'

At another time, Hailsham might have enjoyed Andrew's colourful imagery, even found it worthy of a smile. But the tension of the situation, and the horror of Naughton's death, had numbed everything except that which had been programmed into his subconscious by a lifetime of training. Several minutes had now passed, and expected death had not materialized. It was time to consider survival again.

'Someone's got to make a move to break this deadlock,' Hailsham said firmly. It might as well be us. I suggest we start to make a slow and very cautious bug-out back to the rocks at the base of the cliff. If the bastards let us get that far, we can at least break up and seek individual cover. That is, of course, unless anyone else has a better idea.'

The Thinker spoke for them all. 'Sounds pretty good to me, boss.'

Andrew also nodded his assent. Hailsham rose to his feet, stepping sideways over the dead trooper. Never taking his eyes from the two hovering helicopters, he executed the first of a series of slow, crab-like steps back down the slope of the ledge.

As though they were linked in some strange and invisible way, these small movements were picked up and copied by the two helicopters. Both craft rose perhaps thirty to forty feet higher in the sky, drifting to the left side of the hog's back as though carried on the wind. Hailsham froze; the choppers ceased their lateral movement and dropped back to the ridge again.

'This is fucking crazy,' Hailsham muttered. Galvanizing himself into movement once more, he took another dozen steps.

The two helicopters started to rise again, but this time they did not stop. Hardly daring to believe his own eyes, Hailsham watched the two craft climb steadily to a height of around two hundred feet above the ridge, then peel off and wheel away back in the direction they had come from. In a matter of minutes they had dwindled to gnat-like insignificance in the sky and then out of sight altogether behind the mountains. The chatter of their engines faded to a dim and distant echo, then fell below an audible level. They were gone.

Sheer relief, and a sense of incredulity, hit them all like a punch in the guts.

'Well what the hell do you make of that?' Cyclops asked finally, of no one in particular. He was not really expecting an answer, and was not surprised when none was offered. Now that the immediate threat of the helicopters was past, the men's thoughts were free to dwell on Barry again. They all looked back up the incline to where he lay as he had fallen, his shattered head surrounded by the dark stain of blood already congealing in the cold.

Andrew pulled Hailsham slightly to one side, sighing deeply. 'What a fucking waste,' he murmured. 'What the hell was he thinking?'

Hailsham shrugged helplessly, his face drawn and grim. 'Christ, we think we're so bloody clever, don't we?' he said bitterly. 'We kid ourselves that our selection and training techniques are foolproof – but they're not. Every now and again, some poor bastard like Naughton slips through the net somehow.' He looked at Andrew, his eyes heavy with unjustified guilt. 'Goddammit, Andrew, someone should have picked up that he was likely to crack like a rotten egg under the first crisis situation. The pathetic little bastard should never have been badged.'

Andrew attempted to reassure him. 'That was nothing to do with you, Mike,' he pointed out. 'It's not your fault.'

But Hailsham was not going to be consoled easily. He shook his head slowly from side to side. 'But I picked him for this mission, Andrew. I'm responsible for that.'

'You chose him from a shortlist because he had Arctic training under his belt and he was a good back-up sniper in case anything happened to Cyclops,' Andrew reminded him forcefully. 'On paper he was the right man for the job. Fuck it, Mike – if you want to start apportioning blame, then we all ought to collect our share. Nobody ever really *talked* to the kid, for Chrissake, apart from the bullshit and the piss-taking. Maybe that was the trouble – none of us ever really knew him.'

Hailsham digested this, glancing up at the body on the ledge again. 'The unknown soldier,' he murmured finally, an edge of savage irony in his voice. He looked up into the empty sky again, as if to completely reassure himself that the helicopters were gone.

'Think they'll be back?' Andrew asked, reading his thoughts.

'Christ knows,' Hailsham answered with a shrug. 'But I don't think it's a good idea to wait around here to find out. Let's get moving.'

He moved into point position again, ready to lead them all back up the ledge on their original course. There seemed to be little point in reminding the men about staying on their guard again. They were all as totally primed for action as a she-cat on heat. They passed Naughton's body, leaving it where it lay on the bare ledge. There were not even enough loose rocks around to build a cairn. If scavengers had not already taken it, they would remove the body for proper burial on the way back, Hailsham thought. That was if they got back.

They reached the point where the ledge cut round the side of the mountain into unknown territory. It sliced deeper into the rock face here, creating a sloping overhang of rock above their heads. Rather than walk upright on the outer edge, Hailsham led them deeper into the V-shaped gash – a manoeuvre which necessitated crouching over like a tribe of primitive ape-men. Rounding the bend, Hailsham was slightly dismayed to see that the ledge had largely crumbled away for about twenty feet, leaving only a thin shelf of rock no wider than a man's boot. However, the fissure in the rock face continued, although it now dropped in height to no more than a horizontal slit. There was no real choice but to drop down and slither through the next section on their bellies, pushing their bergens ahead of them.

'I suppose this ain't the best time to tell you about my claustrophobia, is it, boss?' the Thinker said dead-pan, immediately behind Hailsham. Nevertheless, he followed the major's lead in hitting the deck, although he preferred to progress on his back rather than his stomach.

Hailsham edged his way forwards until the fissure began to open up again. Ahead of him, he could now see that they had come round the edge of the mountain and would shortly be, as he had fully expected, totally exposed to any one of half a dozen vantage points from the other surrounding peaks. He stopped, craning his head around to hiss back to the men behind him.

'We go out singly, at twenty-second intervals. First sign of trouble, you get your heads back under cover, ASAP. Understood?' Raising himself onto his hands and knees, Hailsham crawled forward another few yards until he was able to climb to his feet again. He shrugged into his bergen and checked his SA-80. Now comes the nasty bit, he thought.

Squinting against the sudden shock of stepping out into full daylight again, Hailsham took a breath and moved out from beneath the cover of the overhang. He took in the immediate terrain quickly with practised and wary eyes. The ledge widened and flattened out in front of him, forming an open bowl at the foot of two steep and rocky slopes to his left and right. Both climbed for several hundred feet, at roughly the same sort of gradient, but it was the one on the right which immediately seemed to offer the most promise. Slightly broader than its companion, it faced north-east and so was constantly exposed to both the warmth of the daytime sun and the icy blasts of Arctic winds. Generations of sudden and dramatic temperature change, added to the ferocity of wind, storm and blizzard, had split and eroded the rock face into broken and channelled ridges and fissures which provided an almost stair-like ascent. Climbing it would present little difficulty, Hailsham thought with deep satisfaction. He took another few steps forward, clearing the way for the Thinker to come out behind him.

The sudden, sharp crack of a rifle shot and a small spurt of chipped rock and dust from the ground in front of him made Hailsham react with lightning speed. Without pausing to even consider from which direction the shot had been fired, he threw himself to the ground, scrabbling backwards to regain the cover of the overhang. The Thinker, who had just been climbing to his feet, had no chance to get out of the way as Hailsham backed hurriedly into his legs. Thrown off balance, the corporal stumbled and fell forwards, ending up hunched over his CO's back like a dog mounting a bitch.

'Jesus Christ, boss – we can't go on meeting like this,' he muttered, struggling to pull himself off into a more dignified position. Regaining his hands and knees, he crawled up to Hailsham's side. 'Looks like we've got a problem,' he said with typical understatement.

Hailsham nodded. 'I had a bad feeling about this all along. Don't you just hate it when you're always right?' He twisted his body round, curling into a near-foetal position so that he could call back to the rest of the men still making their way along the fissure. 'Everybody freeze where they are for the moment – only get ready to back off fast if I give the word.'

Andrew's voice echoed up to him. 'You got cover, boss?' There was genuine concern in his voice.

Hailsham looked upwards at the comforting solidity of the rock overhanging his head. They were protected well enough for the present, he reckoned. There was no way anyone outside could have a direct line of fire. In the longer term, however, their safety largely depended on the position, strength and fire-power of their unknown enemy. If they were in a position to get closer, and had a grenade launcher at their disposal, then Hailsham and the rest of his men could be in deep shit.

Hailsham neglected to make this particular point to Andrew as he called back his answer. 'We're OK here, but I need to get out there again to take a look-see at what we're up against.' He glanced aside at the Thinker. 'Reckon you can squeeze up close enough to give me covering fire without shooting me up the backside?'

The Thinker grinned. 'I can try,' he said. 'It largely depends on whether you can keep your arse and your head down at the same time.'

'Point taken,' Hailsham muttered, returning the grin. 'So let's do it.' He crawled forward until he could raise to a crouch and poised himself on the balls of his feet. 'Cover on my left,' he hissed at the Thinker. 'My gut tells me that's where they are.'

'You got it, boss.' Completely serious now, the big man cradled the bullpup in his arms and moved into position behind Hailsham.

'Now,' Hailsham hissed. He threw himself into the open, firing a short burst into the air.

Behind him, and to his left, the Thinker began a longer, raking burst along the top of the eastern ridge, counting off three seconds in his head before pulling back again to make room for Hailsham. Two individual rifle shots cracked out before Hailsham was safely back under the protection of the overhang.

'See anything?' the Thinker asked.

Hailsham nodded. 'I was right. They're up on the left sure enough. The arrogant bastards are so confident they've got us completely pinned down that they're standing right out in the open.'

The Thinker flashed him an apologetic smile. 'They could be right, boss.'

'Yeah,' Hailsham grunted. 'Anyway, go again. I need to get an accurate head count. Give me another three seconds, and concentrate your fire about eleven o'clock. Ready?'

'I'm with you.'

The two men poised themselves to repeat the first manoeuvre. This time, the Thinker saw a couple of figures as he opened fire, and had the brief satisfaction of seeing one of them topple sideways before he ducked back into cover.

'And then there were five,' Hailsham murmured as he retreated under the overhang. 'Nice one, Thinker.'

The Mancunian smiled proudly. 'We aim to please, boss. Reckon that's all of 'em?'

Hailsham considered for a few seconds, finally nodding. 'Sounds about right,' he said. 'Six up there, plus the two we encountered earlier. These guerrilla groups rarely operate much into double figures.' He allowed himself a thin smile. 'Encouraging, don't you think? If you look at it from the right perspective, we've already accounted for a third of the buggers.'

The Thinker was not impressed with the philosophical school of thought which said that a half-empty glass of beer was half full. 'You look at it that way if you like,' he said. 'Personally, I'm a half-empty man.' He gave Hailsham a quizzical look. 'So, what do we do now?'

'I think it's time to call a Chinese parliament,' Hailsham said.

20

Hailsham outlined their position as simply and as quickly as possible. 'So, gentlemen, that's the situation,' he finished off. 'Please consider yourselves free to make any suggestions.'

'There's the obvious, of course,' the Thinker said. 'We just shoot and scoot.'

'Yes, there's always that possibility,' Hailsham agreed with a nod. 'But that doesn't offer us very good odds. There's just about room for two men at a time out there, and damn-all cover. You were lucky the last time, picking one of them off while they were still out in the open. They'll have learned a lesson from that and taken up good defensive positions. It means we'd be out there, completely exposed and with no targets to shoot at. Sitting ducks. Even at a conservative estimate, I'd reckon our losses would be sixty per cent.'

'Suppose we loaded those odds a bit more in our favour,' Cyclops suggested. 'We could break out a mortar and one man could operate it from under the cover of the overhang. A nice pattern of shells laid down on that mountainside would give the bastards something to think about while the rest made a run for it.'

It was a sensible suggestion, which Hailsham thought about. 'OK, that's a good contender,' he admitted at last. 'The main drawback as far as I can see is that whoever is on the mortar is on a hiding to nothing. Sooner or later, he's going to have to run the gauntlet all on his own.'

'I'd thought about that, boss,' Cyclops said. 'Perhaps I didn't make it clear that I was volunteering for the job.'

'Noted and commended, Corporal,' Hailsham replied. 'But I'm still looking for the main chance which is going to get us all out of here in one piece.'

'Look, we don't really want to get into a fight at all, unless we have to,' Andrew pointed out. 'Like someone said before we started out on this crazy mission: this ain't our war. So, isn't it at least possible that these guys might feel the same way?'

'What are you suggesting, boss?' asked Tweedledee. 'We surrender to 'em?'

Andrew ignored the facetious comment, directing his attention to Hailsham. 'Well? Seriously, don't you think we ought to offer them the chance of a truce? What have we got to lose?'

It sounded like an eminently sensible suggestion, Hailsham thought, although he held out faint hopes of it succeeding. Experience so far had shown the guerrilla forces on both sides to be both nervous and trigger-happy. Fortunately for them in the latter case, Hailsham thought gratefully. If the over-eager rifleman had not loosed off that first, erratic shot, they might all now be dead. If the guerrillas had been a bit smarter, they would have waited for the entire patrol to get out into the open, and then picked them all off in one fell swoop.

Hailsham detached the white hood from his Arctic suit and draped it over the barrel of his SA-80. 'Think this will do for a white flag?' he asked. Without waiting for an answer, he moved out towards the lip of the overhang, holding the gun out at arm's length.

A fusillade of shots gave him the answer he had feared. Returning to the rest of the men, he smiled ruefully. 'Well, it was a nice idea, anyway,' he said to Andrew. 'Pity everyone doesn't share your pacifist inclinations.' He was silent for a few seconds. 'Well, has anyone else got any bright ideas?'

'Suppose we bug out and try to find another way up?' the Thinker put in. 'Maybe even a completely different route.'

There was a long silence during which it became clear that no more suggestions were forthcoming. Rather than let time waste any more, Hailsham decided to sum up the options for them.

'So, basically, we go out all gung-ho like the Light Brigade or we sneak back with our tails between our legs.' He paused for a second, the trace of a sparkle in his eyes. 'Or we go for a combination of the ideas we've already discussed.'

Hailsham had some sort of a plan, Andrew could tell. 'What are you thinking, boss?'

Hailsham did not answer him, turning to Cyclops instead. 'How's your climbing, Corporal? Ever manage to get past the giant-spider phase in the school playground?'

Cyclops shrugged. 'I managed the tree at the bottom of the garden once. Why do you ask?'

'The face at the bottom of this pass,' Hailsham said. 'It's nasty, but not impossible.'

Cyclops looked at him doubtfully. 'Christ, boss, we'd never make that loaded with all our equipment.'

'True,' Hailsham allowed. 'But one man, carrying only a rifle, might stand a bloody good chance.' For the moment, he said no more.

He had no need to, for Cyclops was already ahead of him. 'And if that just happened to be a sniping rifle, and the guy carrying it knew how to use it . . . we could be talking about a whole new game plan,' he finished off for Hailsham.

The major looked him squarely in the eyes. 'That man would have to volunteer, of course,' he murmured. 'He'd also have to be something of a prat to even consider such a hazardous mission.'

Cyclops grinned good-naturedly. 'The sort of prat who would offer to sit out in the open with a mortar, for instance?'

Hailsham nodded. 'Yes, someone like that might do quite nicely. Then, if another prat like myself were to operate the mortar . . .'

He did not bother to finish. It was, after all, a Chinese parliament. The rest of the men had to make their own decisions. Hailsham sat quietly, eyeing them all in turn as they digested the scheme he had outlined.

'It could work,' the Thinker muttered eventually. 'Dammit, boss, it could bloody well work.'

'It *will* work,' Cyclops said quietly. 'I could probably pick off two or even three of those bastards before they even knew what was happening. And once the whole mountainside under their feet starts going up like Guy Fawkes Night, they'll be too bloody busy running like fucking rabbits to worry about you guys.'

'But just in case, you'll be in position to cover the boss when he makes his run,' Andrew put in, his tone reflecting the general air of enthusiasm. 'I like it.'

Perhaps they were all getting a bit *too* carried away, Hailsham reflected. His face more serious, he looked at Cyclops again. 'Seriously, though, the whole thing hangs on you being able to get up that rock face. Can you make it, do you think?'

It was Cyclops's turn to review the whole scheme in the harsh light of reality. There was no point in making rash promises. 'I won't know until I try,' he said with complete honesty. He turned to Andrew. 'How much proper climbing equipment are we carrying?'

The sergeant's face suddenly fell as a terrible thought struck him. In the temporary euphoria, it was something they had all overlooked. 'It ain't good,' he said grimly. 'This whole jaunt was basically underequipped from the start, as you well know. Cutting weight seemed like a good idea at the time.' He paused for a moment, as if unwilling to release the really bad news. 'The trouble is, most of the gear was in Jimmy's bergen. He was our climbing expert.' He paused again, racking his memory for a complete inventory of the limited equipment he had requisitioned. 'We've still got ropes, of course, and there should be a few pitons and perhaps half a dozen spikes in your own pack. That's about it, I'm afraid.'

Cyclops accepted the news with a philosophical

shrug. 'Well, I suppose it will have to do,' he said. Stripping off his bergen, he began to rummage through it for the items in question.

'I just had an idea that might help,' the Thinker blurted out suddenly. He began to rummage through his own equipment, finally pulling out a small hand-ful of time fuses and detonator caps. Andrew and Hailsham looked at him with puzzled expressions on their faces. The Thinker grinned back sheepishly. 'Well, they do tell us to improvise,' he said quietly. 'So this is my contribution.' He held out the detonators to Cyclops. 'If you really got stuck, one of these might blast out just enough rock to give you a hand or toe hold in an emergency,' he suggested. 'Only don't blow your own fucking head off, that's all.'

Cyclops accepted the detonators gratefully. The Thinker was right. At a pinch, they might just work. It was worth taking them along, anyway. Every little helped. He unpacked the L96A1 sniper rifle, stroking the green plastic stock with the caress of a lover. He even whispered words of endearment to the sleek killing machine: 'It's just going to be me and you, my beauty. You won't let me down, will you?'

After assembling, carefully cleaning and checking the weapon, Cyclops packed a dozen of the heavy 7.62mm slugs into his escape belt and glanced up at Hailsham. 'Right, I'm ready,' he announced flatly.

Hailsham nodded, glancing at his watch. 'It should take you about twelve minutes to get back down to the face,' he said quietly. 'And hopefully no more than twenty to make the ascent. How long to set up once you reach a decent firing position?'

Cyclops thought over Hailsham's projected timings

carefully. They seemed reasonable enough. 'Give me another five minutes on top,' he suggested eventually. 'I'll need a couple of ranging shots to recalibrate the sights after humping this baby up a mountain. No point in blasting off blind if you're not going to hit what you're aiming at.'

Hailsham ran the figures through his head again. 'OK, so forty minutes tops,' he said. 'We'll set up for action well before that, but wait for your first two shots. Exactly thirty seconds after your second shot we'll fire a few bursts up the mountain to bring them out into the open. Then it's down to you. We'll give you exactly five clear shots before we open up with the mortar and make our break for it. If everything goes well, we'll RV with you up on the plateau Safar spoke about.'

For a makeshift plan, it all seemed pretty tight. 'You got it, boss,' Cyclops said, and prepared to move off. It took a certain amount of intricate shuffling and manoeuvring in the narrowest part of the fissure to let him through, but eventually he was clear and on his way. The Thinker and Tweedledee took advantage of the extra room to crowd up into the cover of the over-hang, taking it upon themselves to set up the mortar.

'Well, all we have to do now is wait, gentlemen,' Hailsham said, checking his watch again.

There was a long, strained silence before Tweedledee finally piped up. 'You know, boss – you never did get around to telling us that story about the whore and the donkey in Kuwait.'

Hailsham smiled thinly. 'Didn't I?' he replied with mock surprise. 'Well, in that case . . .'

* * *

Despite the luridness of the tale, which Hailsham embellished freely for the occasion, it was a long and agonizing wait for all of them. Everyone had seen the rock face on the way past, and was fully aware of the difficulties it posed. Their watches had rarely been used so much in such a short space of time.

Just over half an hour had passed when they heard the first, faint echo of a small explosion. It made them all jump, even though they were already on tenterhooks.

Three pairs of eyes flashed towards Hailsham's, questioningly.

'He can't have made it already,' Andrew murmured, glancing at his watch again for perhaps the twentieth time.

Hailsham shook his head slowly, looking aside at the Thinker. 'Looks like your little idea came in useful after all,' he observed. The sound they had heard had to be one of the detonator caps going off. The firing signature of the Accuracy International was loud, and distinctive. Even from a distance it had a sharp, unique quality.

They settled back to wait again. The allotted forty minutes passed. Hailsham's face was taut with strain as he realized a full hour had elapsed since Cyclops's departure.

'Dammit, he should have made it by now,' he hissed.

There was a pregnant pause; nobody seemed to want to voice the obvious. But somebody had to say it.

'Maybe he didn't make it,' Andrew said flatly at last, letting them all off the hook.

There it was, out in the open. There was almost a sense of relief underneath the depression which settled over them like a black cloud.

'Yeah,' Hailsham grunted, a deep sigh following the single word of resignation. He checked his watch again, his face grim. 'We'll give him another five minutes, and then we'll have to revert to Plan A.'

They all fell silent again, deliberately avoiding each other's gaze as the seconds continued to tick inexorably away.

Finally, reluctantly, Hailsham spoke again. 'It's time to make a move,' he announced gravely. He started to make for the mortar. 'Move out in your own time as soon as I start plastering that mountain. And good luck,' he added, trying vainly not to make it sound like a farewell.

The sudden, sharp report of a heavy-calibre rifle shattered the silence, cracking off the mountains in a series of spitting echoes.

Relief was not the word for the wave of near-exultation which seemed to sweep through the air of gloom like a storm wind charged with electricity. It hit Hailsham like a blow in the chest, driving air from his lungs up into his throat, where it lodged in a painful lump. Andrew felt like Saul on the road to Damascus, or a kid waking up to his first Christmas stocking. Miracles *did* happen, there really was magic in the world. The Thinker let out a loud whoop which was totally out of character.

'He made it. The beautiful bastard made it,' Tweedledee screamed out, the look on his face mirroring the sheer disbelief in his voice.

They all waited, picturing Cyclops's actions and

242

counting off the seconds in their heads. A minor adjustment with thumb and forefinger . . . another squint through the adjusted sights . . . another cartridge slipped into the breech . . . loaded and cocked. Finger on the trigger now . . . taking up the slight pressure of resistance . . . gently squeezing.

The second report was the signal for them all. Hailsham's eyes darted to his watch then back up to Andrew, counting under his breath as the Barbadian tensed himself for action.

'Thirty seconds,' he barked. 'Go.'

Andrew was already crouched and poised under the last safe area of cover. On Hailsham's command, he exploded from underneath the overhang, emptying the entire thirty-round magazine up into the mountains in less than three seconds. He was already well back in cover and getting ready to slam a new magazine into the SA-80 when the first of half a dozen rifle slugs chewed into the ground and rock face where he had stood. Almost simultaneously came the louder crack of the Accuracy International L96.

Hailsham dropped to his belly, slithering up to the mortar and sliding the base plate forward until the firing tube pointed clear of the overhang. Four 51mm bombs lay out in a neat line in readiness. Selecting the first, Hailsham cradled it in his hand, waiting for Cyclops's next four shots.

They came with remarkable speed – even for Cyclops. Even knowing the man's legendary skill, Hailsham found it hard to believe that any man could reload, select a target, aim and fire the single shot, bolt-action weapon so quickly. He could only pray that the shots were as accurate as they were fast.

He held the tail fins of the mortar bomb over the open mouth of the firing tube as the last of the five shots cracked out amid the still-reverberating echoes of its predecessor.

First-shot accuracy with the comparatively cheap and simple British 51mm mortar was never easy, and Hailsham was not even really trying. He dropped the first bomb into the tube, merely raking it down a couple of degrees and reloading as the first missile discharged with a dull whoosh. Firing the second shell, he twisted the base plate the merest faction of an inch and dropped in the third just as the first explosion boomed out from the mountainside above.

Hailsham notched the firing tube up again, holding the last missile in position. 'Get going,' he screamed without looking round. He waited perhaps two seconds until Andrew ran past his prone body and then dropped it into the tube.

Then the Thinker and Tweedledee were also past him and gone, breaking out from cover and running at full pelt, firing sideways from the hip. The chatter of three weapons, and the echoing rumble of the rest of the exploding mortar shells created a wall of noise through which it was impossible to pick out the sound of individual rifle fire. Hailsham thought that he heard two more shots from Cyclops's L96, but he could not be sure.

Then, abruptly, there was silence again. Hailsham sucked in a deep breath. So, this was it, he told himself, pushing himself to his feet and staring out into the open. He had estimated a twenty-second run to the bowl at the foot of the two hills. Once upon a time he might have done it in fifteen. Except he was no longer twenty-five, and they were probably already at an altitude of around 13,000 feet.

Neither was a factor that he cared to dwell on, even if there had been time to do so. 'Oh well, shit or bust time, Hailsham,' he told himself out loud, jumping off the balls of his feet and breaking into a run.

A single bullet smacked into the rock face in front of him, but Hailsham kept running. Up ahead, two of the SA-80s opened up in unison from inside the cover of a rock fissure with a couple of short bursts. Three or four single shots came from another location nearby. After that there was silence again. There was no more rifle fire.

Reaching the bowl, Hailsham threw himself into a diving roll and sought the scant cover of a shallow depression. He lay face down, catching his breath for several seconds before glancing up and attempting to get his bearings.

Andrew's grinning black face popped up from behind a long, flat rock to his right. 'Actually, I think we got 'em all, boss – but I'd keeni-meeni over here just to be on the safe side, if I were you.'

Hailsham took the advice to heart, adopting the slithering, snake-like belly crawl which the poached Swahili phrase suggested. Wriggling over to join Andrew, he heaved himself over the top of the rock and dropped into cover beside him.

'You really think we got the lot?' he asked.

Andrew nodded happily. 'Pretty sure,' he said confidently. 'I saw Cyclops take two out as we started running, and Thinker popped one just after we hit the bowl. One of your mortar rounds threw something up in the air that looked remarkably like the bottom two-thirds of a body, and I just hit that last bastard who took a shot at you. If your original head count was right, I figure we're home and dry. He broke off to shrug. 'Not that it really matters, anyway. If there is anyone left up there, Cyclops can pick 'em off while they're still squinting down the sights. So, do you want to move out again?'

Hailsham shook his head. 'No, we'll rest up for five or ten minutes. Just in case there are any stragglers left up on that mountain. By that time they'll have either shown themselves or got the fuck out to safer ground. Don't forget – they don't know we're not coming after them. Besides, we've got a long, hard climb ahead of us, and a poor old bastard like me needs all the rest he can get.'

'Jesus, boss, you hared along that ridge like a bloody nineteen-year-old,' Andrew told him, in what was supposed to be a compliment.

Hailsham laughed cynically. He could still feel his heart pumping in his chest like an antiquated steamhammer. 'Yeah, but a nineteen-year-old what?'

Just as Hailsham's initial recce of the northern slope had suggested, the climbing was hard enough, but not too difficult. It was more like advanced rock climbing than real mountaineering, and by taking it at a restrained but steady pace they could monitor their own progress almost minute by minute. Less than half an hour after leaving the bowl, they were starting to come more or less in line with the top of the face which Cyclops had taken, and were probably slightly over halfway to the summit.

Hailsham's belly was starting to rumble. It was

now nearly six hours since their last, meagre meal and they had all burned up a great deal of mental and physical energy. Although he was in no doubt that they could all hold out for a while yet, the need for food would become a priority soon enough, even if the reasonably bearable weather conditions persisted. But if the storms and the icy winds returned, it might be a completely different matter. For nothing drained the body's reserves as efficiently as bitter and sustained cold. Allied to hunger, it could be an equally efficient killer.

The route ahead offered at least some slim hopes, Hailsham thought optimistically, recalling his basic research into the topography of the region before the mission had got under way. The high mountain plateaux were invariably used as summer pasture areas by the semi-nomadic tribespeople of the region. It was more than possible that the droppings of grazing animals had enriched the ground over the years to the extent that it had set up its own limited life-chain. Beetles, insects or worms at the lowest and most unpalatable end of the spectrum, and perhaps small mammals at the more optimistic level. Allowing himself to pursue this line of reasoning to its eventual, if somewhat wishful, conclusion, Hailsham dared to imagine that the plateau areas might even be the source of the ground-burrowing marmots which seemed to make up the basic protein source of the locals.

With this thought in mind, Hailsham suddenly realized that he should have asked Safar for more details about the life-cycle of the creatures and how they were captured. Did they roam free in the winter months, and if so, what was the best way to trap them? Or did they hibernate, and have to be dug up from deep underground burrows? Cursing himself for his oversight, Hailsham reflected that he did not even know if the rodents were diurnal or nocturnal in their habits.

Forcing himself to snap out of a potential chain of negative thoughts again, Hailsham indulged in the most fanciful imaginings, picturing the plateau region populated by stray or abandoned goats which had somehow managed to establish feral colonies and survive the harsh winters. Fantasizing about a fresh goat steak brought the saliva bubbling to his palate and started his stomach rumbling again with renewed vigour. With a conscious effort, Hailsham pushed all thoughts of food from his mind and concentrated on his climbing once again as the going suddenly got tougher.

Dragging himself over the crest of a rocky ridge, Hailsham saw that the terrain immediately ahead changed dramatically. Quite abruptly the crags and crannies which had assisted their passage were no longer in evidence. It was as if a giant bulldozer had run amok down the mountainside at a crazy angle, sweeping away all surface features and leaving only a smooth, tilted plate of rock which was too steep to even retain snow. That had all slipped down the face into massive drifts at the left-hand corner, in depths it was impossible even to guess at.

Hailsham regarded this new obstacle morosely. To attempt a vertical climb of the tilted plane was obviously impractical, since the direct route up represented a gradient of perhaps sixty-five or seventy degrees. The only realistic approach was to traverse it at an obtuse angle, gaining height gradually. The smooth wall of rock stretched ahead for about a mile and a half, actually rising about six hundred feet to the mouth of a rocky gorge which split the next range into two near-vertical faces.

Skirting round the area of more obvious snowdrifts, Hailsham moved warily, checking each step foward with a cautious probe of his foot. Several times his leg sank almost up to the thigh in the soft, powdery snow before encountering something solid beneath it. Acute awareness of the dangers of plunging into a hidden crevasse at any moment made for agonizingly slow and gut-churning progress, and Hailsham was profoundly relieved when he finally reached the bare rock face and hauled himself up onto it. He sat back, watching the rest of his men as they followed his ploughed-out trail through the drifts.

Andrew perched himself on the rock beside Hailsham. 'Where now?'

Hailsham jerked his thumb over his shoulder towards the gorge. 'Hobson's Choice, from the look of things. It won't be easy,' he added, rather stating the obvious.

Andrew took in the daunting traverse across the rock face with a faint nod. 'I'm beginning to think we sent Cyclops up the easy route,' he muttered. 'From here, that looks like a job for Spiderman.'

Hailsham allowed himself a wry smile. 'We're supposed to be supermen – remember? Faster than a speeding bullet . . . clearing tall buildings at a single bound? Nothing's impossible for the SAS.'

Andrew grinned. 'Oh yes, I forgot. Well, that's all right, then.'

'However, as handy telephone boxes around here seem somewhat conspicuous by their absence,' Hailsham went on, 'I suggest a slightly more mortal approach. We'll just take it in very easy stages. Let's call it the Janet and John approach to mountaineering.' He half-turned, running his eyes along the inclined plane of the face and seeking out features which could be used to their advantage. Although there were no obvious fissures or projections, the seemingly smooth face was not uniformly bland. At varying heights and angles all the way up, the main mass of reddish-brown rock was striated by layers of a darker colour, like a multi-layered sponge cake. It was obviously composed of two compressed, but clearly different rock layers. And where two layers met, there was almost sure to be a slight imperfection caused by differing degrees of erosion, Hailsham knew. It might be no more than a few millimetres, but it would probably be enough for a man to get some sort of a grip on. Preferably a man unburdened by heavy equipment.

Hailsham extended one finger, tracing along the fault lines. 'There,' he said, pointing to one such layer. 'And there,' he added, running his finger back, tracing out a zigzag route across and up the face.

Andrew followed Hailsham's directions with keen eyes, nodding his approval. 'Yep, that's the way to do it,' he agreed finally. 'It's a bloody long way round to gain comparatively little height, but it's probably our best bet.'

'*My* best bet,' Hailsham corrected him. 'This one's

best tackled as a solo. I'll leave my equipment here and take a rope up. Once I reach the mouth of that gully I can secure it and you can all pull yourselves straight up. Then we haul up our gear and we're on our way again.'

'That's if there *is* a way,' Andrew pointed out. 'We don't know what that gully might lead into.'

'Party pooper,' Hailsham shot back. 'Let's face that one when we come to it.'

He began to strip off his bergen. Andrew's hand descended on his arm, restraining him. 'With the greatest respect, boss, have we got the best man for the job here? I'm younger than you.'

'And heavier,' Hailsham pointed out.

Andrew shrugged. 'Well, if age and weight are going to be the chief criteria here, then what about Tweedledee?' he asked.

Hailsham smiled grimly, nodding his head up the wall of rock. 'One slip up there and there's only the fast route down. It's got to be down to you or me, Andrew – and I've got the casting vote on this one.'

It was obvious that Hailsham had made his mind up, Andrew reflected. He was sorry now that he had even mentioned his age. The last thing the man needed at this moment was anything which could sap his confidence. 'Yeah. You're probably right,' he conceded, stepping back as Hailsham finished peeling off his equipment.

Hailsham coiled a length of nylon rope around his waist and secured it. 'Tie on extra lengths as you need them,' he said to Andrew. 'I'll give you a clear signal when it's safe to follow me up. Last man ropes on the excess gear and we can all haul it up together.'

Andrew nodded. 'Good luck, boss.'

Hailsham grinned, exuding more confidence than he really felt. 'I taught Peter Parker his tricks in the first place.'

Andrew did not understand. He looked at Hailsham blankly. 'Peter Parker? Who's Peter Parker?'

Hailsham clucked his teeth in a vaguely reproving gesture. 'Spiderman's alter ego,' he reminded the big Barbadian. 'Good Lord, Andrew, doesn't *anybody* read comic books any more?' He turned away and began to scramble along the sloping side of the rock face with a curious half-slithering, half-hopping motion which made Andrew think of a giant land-crab.

The sergeant watched him progress along the shallowest part of the incline towards the first strata fault, gaining a few precious inches in height for every few lateral feet. As the gradient increased, Hailsham pressed himself tightly against the face, his hands spread out wide and flat, and his feet splayed out at angles to gain the maximum possible amount of friction between his boots and the smooth rock. Every possible square inch of his body was glued against the unyielding surface, as though Hailsham was consciously willing his entire body to melt into the rock, fuse and become part of it.

He looked less like a land-crab now, Andrew thought idly. More like a tree-frog or a gecko.

Hailsham reached the darker layer of rock strata and pulled himself up until it was at eye level. With the side of his face pressed against the cold rock, he examined it carefully. If anything, it was slightly more promising than he had dared to hope. Granular and slightly pitted in texture like coarse sandpaper, it was obviously softer than the smooth and slab-like volcanic basalt trap-rock which had engulfed it a hundred million years ago. The eroding effects of wind and ice over the ages had done their slow but sure work, eating away at the rougher surface until it was distinctly impressed within the overall outer level of the main face. The tiny lip which it created was probably no more than a centimetre at its deepest parts, but it was enough to get a fingerhold against.

Easing himself into position, Hailsham began the tricky business of backtracking along the fault line. His cheek still pressed tightly against the rock face, he dared to turn his head slightly, rolling his eyes upwards. Seen from this perspective, the gradient above appeared almost vertical, although he knew it was not. It just looked that way – and felt that way! Hailsham marvelled at the sheer impossibility of his position. It seemed that his entire body-weight was being suspended on his fingernails alone. He was not sure that his boots had any kind of grip at all, and he did not feel disposed to put it to the test. His fingertips shrieked out with pain and cold as he edged, precariously along his zigzag path to the next strata, which slanted away again to his right.

He was now just over twenty-five feet above the heads of Andrew, Tweedledee and the Thinker, who were following every painful inch of his progress with hypnotic fascination.

'Dammit, boss, if you're going to slip, then do it now for Chrissake,' Andrew found himself saying under his breath. It was not a wish for failure, but a last plea for Hailsham's safety. He could probably survive a fall from this height with no more than a few nasty bruises. In a matter of a few more minutes, the choice would be between broken bones and death. Both probably more or less the same thing, Andrew reflected, given the vulnerability of their position. It would be almost impossible to carry a badly wounded man down out of the mountains again. And if they left him, he would never survive the first night in the cold.

But Hailsham did not slip, against all the odds. Reaching the second layer of pitted rock, he turned himself again and set out back across the face, now climbing about one vertical foot for every four gained sideways.

'He's a human fucking limpet,' the Thinker said, impressed.

Andrew tore his eyes away from the fly-like figure on the rock face and busied himself tying on another length of rope. He could not bear to watch any more.

Maybe he should have worn gloves, Hailsham thought. His fingers were completely numb now, despite the fact that several nails had been broken and torn away from the quick, leaving the sensitive flesh bleeding profusely. He shrugged off the thought, knowing that it was academic anyway. Besides, although gloves might have offered some protection from the cold and the roughness of the stone, they would have provided less grip. He might not have made it this far – and warm hands were not much use to a man with a broken spine lying at the bottom of a mountain. At least the numbness held the pain at bay, Hailsham told himself philosophically. He could only hope that his fingertips actually retained more feeling and sensitivity than his brain was registering. For at least ten minutes now, he had had the strangest feeling that he was clinging to the mountainside by sheer willpower.

Suddenly there was a small but deep vertical fissure in the main rock formation, just above his head to the right. And above that, a definite inward slant to the face, presenting a sloping shelf which culminated in a flat ridge. And that was it. Above that ridge lay an easy scramble over broken and pitted rock to the snow-filled mouth of the gorge. For the first time since starting the ascent, Hailsham actually dared to believe that he might just make it to the top.

Gratefully he reached up and jammed the heel of his hand into the crack, pulling himself up and feeling a sense of relief as the strain of his body-weight was transferred to his wrist and arm. He brought up his left foot, scraping the side of his sole tentatively against the face, feeling for the tell-tale roughness of the granular strata. Finding it, and probing for the support of the thin lip between the two layers, Hailsham poised himself both mentally and physically for the next, critical move.

Everything depended upon the security of that foothold now. It really was shit or bust time. With a silent prayer to a God he did not really believe in, Hailsham pulled his hand out of the fissure and let his weight drop onto his left foot.

It held. Holding his breath lest the slightest bodily movement could upset the delicate balance of things,

Hailsham tensed the muscles of his calves and thighs and pushed himself up until he could jam his elbow into the tiny cleft. Another upward heave, and he was free to throw his left arm onto the shelf and drag himself up to the ridge.

Hailsham lay there, face down, for several seconds. He still hardly dared to believe that he had made it. Finally he pushed himself up on to his hands and knees and scrambled to the mouth of the gorge, scooping away the deep drifts of snow until he had uncovered a rocky crag around which to secure the rope. Tying it off, he slithered back down to the ledge on his behind and called over the edge to the men waiting below.

'Come on up,' he yelled. 'The lift's working now.'

It was not much of a joke, but Hailsham found himself dissolving into childish giggles at his own wit.

The gorge ran deeper into the mountains than anyone had imagined. They had already covered at least a quarter of a mile, and although it had begun to narrow to a width of only a few feet, it showed little sign of ending. Equally, it showed little sign of leading to a negotiable pathway to the plateau above. On either side, the sixty-foot walls of rock were smooth and vertical. Their only hope so far, Hailsham thought, was that the ravine would eventually narrow to the extent that they could climb between its two sides like a chimney. In the meantime, they had no choice but to keep moving. Wading through the deep snow which sometimes came up to their chests, the team continued penetrating into the very heart of the mountains.

The gorge ended, eventually opening out into a huge, bowl-like canyon. They were now surrounded on all sides by sheer, unscalable faces of rock which all apparently ended abruptly in a flat rim no more than fifty feet above their heads.

Hailsham brought the party to a halt, swivelling his head around to take in the full panorama with a sinking heart. There was nothing to offer them even the remotest chance of a climb to the top. They had reached a dead-end, and they were trapped. They might as well be at the bottom of a well, Hailsham thought, heavily. He cursed silently, thinking of the plateau just those few tantalizing feet above. So bloody near – yet so bloody far!

Tweedledee put it even more succinctly. 'Now we're *really* fucked,' he groaned. No one argued.

God, but he hated to be beaten, Hailsham thought angrily. He continued to scan the sides of the canyon, convincing himself that there had to be something he had missed, some feasible route up he had overlooked.

He had missed nothing – nor did he miss the brief flash of movement at the rim of the canyon on his right.

It was crazy, impossible. Altitude sickness, Hailsham's brain told him, trying to find some rational explanation for the unexplainable. He was hallucinating. Or maybe it was a bird, a trick of the light, something plucked off the canyon rim by a freak gust of wind.

But a coil of nylon rope was a rare, and particularly bizarre, hallucination. And far too heavy to be carried on the wind. And birds did not drop from the sky like stones, unravelling themselves as they fell.

Andrew had also seen the coiled rope tossed out from the plateau above. With unbelieving eyes, he watched it fall to the canyon floor before looking across at Hailsham and exchanging a glance of total bemusement.

'Cyclops?' he breathed. It was the only possible explanation he could think of.

'Well it sure as hell wasn't God,' Tweedledee put in, as the rope crashed into the snow less than ten feet away from him.

Hailsham's eyes were fixed on the spot where the now dangling rope looped over the edge of the canyon. There was no further sign of movement. He continued staring for nearly a minute, finally realizing that their unknown benefactor was not going to show himself.

'Well, boss, what do we do now?' Andrew asked. 'Somebody up there obviously likes us.'

Hailsham could only shrug helplessly. The entire situation was just too bizarre for words. He trudged over to the dangling rope, seizing it and tugging at it heavily. It was clearly well secured at the top. With another helpless shrug at Andrew, he wedged one foot against the sheer cliff face and began to climb. For some reason, he had the curious feeling that he might disappear in a puff of blue smoke when he reached the end of the rope.

He was wrong. Hauling himself up to eye level with the rim of the canyon, Hailsham was immediately struck by several things. One was that the plateau was much vaster than he had imagined, stretching out in an unbroken white plain all the way to the foothills of the Sailyukem Mountains.

Unbroken, that was, but for the two black shapes

of the two Hind-A assault helicopters in the immediate foreground. Nearer still, and more immediately menacing was the line of a dozen soldiers, clad in heavy grey uniforms and greatcoats pensioned off from the Red Army and each cradling a Kalashnikov in his hands.

Hailsham's heart fell through his boots. He was caught like a fly on flypaper and there was nothing he could do about it. Cursing himself for his impetuosity, he finished hauling himself up to the safety of the plateau and stood stiffly, waiting for the next move.

A young man – no more than thirty-five, Hailsham estimated – stepped forward briskly. He wore the insignia of a captain, and was smiling.

'Major Hailsham? We've been expecting you,' he said, in a friendly tone, and in near-flawless English. 'What took you so long?'

Hailsham just could not take it all in. He gazed over towards the helicopters again, where another, smaller group of soldiers had set up tents, an ammunition and equipment dump, and a petrol-fired cooking stove. Cyclops was sitting next to it, basking in its warmth. He was grinning stupidly, and sipping hot soup from a tin mug.

21

'What the fuck is going on?' Hailsham demanded. Under the circumstances, he thought he was being rather restrained.

The young officer extended his hand in formal greeting. 'I am Captain Dmitri Yascovar, of the Kazakh Republican Army,' he said quietly. 'Please relax, Major. My men intend you no harm.'

To back up his words, Yascovar raised one hand in the air and clicked his fingers. The armed soldiers stood down at once, dropping their rifles butt down on the ground.

His question remained unanswered. Hailsham repeated it, this time a little more politely. 'Do you mind telling me exactly what is going on, Captain?'

Yascovar smiled warmly. 'All in good time, Major Hailsham. First, I suspect that you and your men could do with some hot food and a drink. If you would care to bring them up, we have a meal waiting for you.'

He stared into Hailsham's eyes, identifying the distrust there.

'But, of course, I am forgetting. You will need some sort of proof of our good intentions. Please forgive me.' Yascovar reached into the inside pocket of his greatcoat, drew out a thin, folded sheet of paper, and handed it across. It was a fax, Hailsham noticed as he unfolded the sheet. His sense of unreality increased. After their days of isolation in some of the wildest country on the face of the earth, it seemed totally incongruous to be receiving a faxed message on the top of a bloody mountain, he thought. Nevertheless, he began to read the single sheet.

It bore the unmistakable seal of the British Foreign Office, albeit slightly smudged by the old-style heat-sensitive paper which the East Europeans were obviously still using in their fax machines. Hailsham initially suspected a forgery, but the coded reference at the top left-hand corner of the sheet was letter-perfect, leaving little doubt that it was the genuine article.

The message was short and to the point:

'Major Hailsham. Until you receive further specific orders by direct radio link, you are expected to cooperate fully with officers of the official Kazakh Republican Army.'

The letter was signed by the Foreign Secretary, and countersigned by Lieutenant-Colonel Barney Davies.

Still no closer to understanding the strange new turn of events, Hailsham handed the letter back like a man in a dream. Only then did he accept Yascovar's proffered handshake, returning it curtly and without warmth. He moved back to the rim of the canyon and shouted over the side.

'Sergeant Winston. Bring the rest of the men up — and don't do anything hasty when you notice the reception committee up here.'

He turned back to Captain Yascovar. 'The letter mentioned a direct radio link to my superior officer. How soon can that be arranged?'

'As soon as you wish, Major,' Yascovar answered politely. 'Our base at Alma-Ata has been in virtually permanent contact for the last five hours. I can patch you through from one of the helicopters as soon as you are ready.'

The young Kazakh officer seemed perfectly sincere, even anxious to please. Despite his initial mistrust, and continued confusion, Hailsham found himself warming to the man. He wondered if Yascovar knew about the helicopter which Andrew had shot down. It seemed improbable that he should not, and yet that made his apparently genuine friendliness even more baffling.

This question, at least, was soon answered as Andrew, Tweedledee and the Thinker finally appeared over the rim of the plateau and assembled into a bemused and dispirited group. After a few meaningful gestures from the armed soldiers and a confirming nod from Hailsham, they dropped their weapons and equipment into an untidy heap in the snow. Yascovar's eyes flashed over the weaponry, betraying the faintest flicker of surprise. 'I was given to understand you were carrying an anti-aircraft missile system, Major. It would appear that I was misinformed.'

Hailsham flashed a quick glance at Andrew, warning him not to show any reaction. Under the circumstances, it seemed safest to give away as little as possible, Hailsham thought. Obviously Yascovar was aware that the helicopter had been shot down, but not totally sure who the culprits were. For the time being at least, that doubt might be best left unresolved.

Their own situation, however, definitely needed clarification.

'Are we to consider ourselves prisoners?' Hailsham asked, returning his attention to Captain Yascovar.

The man shook his head firmly. 'By no means, Major. More like allies. Perhaps unlikely ones, I admit – but allies nevertheless.' He seemed to take pity on Hailsham's continued confusion, and smiled sympathetically.

'I was not briefed to give you any great details, Major, but perhaps I can stretch my orders to at least give you an idea of the broader picture.'

Again Hailsham was struck by the man's sincerity. It seemed like a genuine offer – almost an attempt to establish mutual respect and understanding between two military officers. 'That would be nice,' he muttered.

'In simple terms, it would appear that you have rattled a large stick in a nest of rats,' Yascovar went on. He paused, looking somewhat apologetic. 'But no doubt you have a more descriptive phrase in the English language.'

Hailsham shook his head, smiling despite himself. 'No, I think that covers it quite adequately.'

'Ah, good.' Yascovar looked pleased. 'Anyway, your involvement, and that of the Chinese, has stirred up things which had been buried and forgotten for a long time. This may have been the intention of the Chinese all along, of course – it is often difficult to know how their devious minds work. But now that certain matters are out in the open, it has become clear that they can only be tackled at a diplomatic level. So our two governments are now working together, Major. You and I are mere servants of those governments.'

Hailsham was no nearer to understanding exactly what was going on, but he was beginning to get the general picture. 'Duty calls and no questions asked – is that it?' he asked.

Yascovar smiled. 'We are soldiers, Major Hailsham. Politicians make the wars – we only fight them.'

It was a simplistic view, Hailsham thought. Either that, or it suggested that matters had escalated to a much higher international level than Yascovar was prepared to admit. It was even possible that the Kazakh captain was just as confused as he was. Perhaps he was taking refuge in the position of simply following orders. Or perhaps it was no longer clear where, or from whom, those orders were coming.

'I take it that individual heads are rolling?' he said, probing the man.

Yascovar's smile turned to an open grin. 'The sharks are in a feeding frenzy, Major,' he replied. 'But I really cannot tell you any more. I think I may have already exceeded my authority.'

Hailsham thought that he understood a little better now, but he would know a whole lot more when he spoke to Barney Davies. 'Your frankness is appreciated, Captain,' he said politely. 'But I think I would like to make that call now.'

'Of course,' Yascovar said, nodding. 'But perhaps you and your men would care to join your comrade while I set up the necessary link. I think you will find he is quite complimentary about our hospitality. He certainly seemed to appreciate the food.' He then turned away and began to lead the way across to the camp.

Andrew fell into step beside Hailsham. 'What the hell is this all about, boss?' he hissed in Hailsham's ear.

Hailsham shrugged, lacking an adequate answer. 'For the moment, it appears to be food,' he muttered obliquely.

The smell of hot, spicy stew and freshly brewed thick, black, Turkish-style coffee proved irresistible as they neared the camp. Hailsham allowed himself and his men to be ushered into one of the tents, where they squatted down on a soft carpet of thick army blankets and waited for the food to be served. The interior of the tent was cosy and warm, heated by flexible metal pipes which carried hot water from the petrol stove outside.

It was all very efficient, Hailsham thought – suggesting that the whole operation had been fully equipped and prepared for a full-scale mission. After making sure that they were comfortable, Captain Yascovar made his polite excuses and left, promising to establish the radio link while the meal was being served. The men were left alone, and, glancing outside the tent, Hailsham could see no sign that any sort of guard had been posted. On the face of it, at least, Yascovar's assurance that they were not prisoners seemed to be borne out.

Cyclops came into the tent to join them. He grinned at Hailsham sheepishly. 'I hope you don't think I was collaborating with the enemy, boss, but I was bloody hungry,' he said. 'Anyway, there's been no attempt to interrogate me in any way, and they didn't even insist on taking my handgun.' He patted his holstered

Browning High Power to back up the statement. 'So I figured the best way to play it was to just go along with them until you got here. I hope I did the right thing.'

Hailsham nodded, putting the trooper at his ease. 'That's what we're all doing, until I can find out exactly what's going on. They're trying to patch me through to Lieutenant-Colonel Davies at the moment.' He turned to face Andrew and the others. 'So, gentlemen, until I have some hard information, you might as well keep your questions on ice. I suggest you try to relax and make the most of the hospitality which is being offered to us.'

The speech effectively pre-empted the barrage of questions which Hailsham had been expecting – exactly as it was supposed to.

'So what's the bloody grub like?' the Thinker asked Cyclops.

'Just like your mum used to make,' Cyclops assured him.

The Thinker grimaced. 'Shit. My old lady was the worst fucking cook I ever knew. The only reason I joined the bloody army was to get some decent scran.'

It was a wild enough exaggeration to raise a smile all round. The mood was almost jovial by the time two soldiers eventually turned up, bearing trays of hot stew with great chunks of bread, proper eating utensils and a big pot of coffee and tin mugs.

The Thinker regarded the food with obvious relish. 'This is as good as the bloody Ritz,' he muttered. 'Pity about the waitresses, though.'

The soldiers put down the trays and left. Hailsham and his men set about the food voraciously. They had all forgotten how hungry they actually were. The metal plates were all wiped and licked clean by the time Captain Yascovar returned.

'Major Hailsham? Everything is ready for you now,' he announced.

Hailsham jumped to his feet expectantly. At last he might get some answers he would understand, he thought. He followed Yascovar outside and across to the nearest helicopter.

The craft's radio officer handed him a pair of earphones and a mike, then stepped into the background and stayed there. It seemed to Hailsham that he was hovering about not so much to monitor the conversation as to be ready to offer help if it was needed. In any case, he was only a private, and it was unlikely that he understood much English. Not that Hailsham had expected privacy anyway.

Slipping on the headset, Hailsham thumbed the mike button. 'Hello, this is Major Mike Hailsham, 22 SAS. Reporting for briefing as ordered.'

Despite the distance of the radio link, and the fact that it was being patched through at least one intermediate base, Barney Davies's voice was unmistakable.

'Mike? I expect you have a question or two.'

Hailsham laughed cynically. 'That's a fucking understatement, Barney, and you know it,' he said. 'Here's question one for starters. What the fuck is going on? Question two – is this supposed to be an open conversation? I have visitors.'

'Don't worry about that, Mike,' Davies assured

him. 'This link is scrambled at this end and patched through GCHQ. There's full and open cooperation between our government and the government of the Kazakhstan Republic. Over and above that, it should be safe from outside ears. As far as you are concerned, Captain Yascovar is as fully briefed by his people as you're about to be.' Davies paused for a second. 'Oh, and be nice to him, by the way. He'll probably be a general by tomorrow.'

'Jesus!' Hailsham hissed, making the obvious inference. 'It really is the Night of the Long Knives, is it?'

'Now who's dealing in understatements?' Davies asked. 'A three-way hotline between Moscow, Alma-Ata and London has been buzzing almost continuously for the past thirty-six hours, the Chinese delegation has stormed out of the Hong Kong talks and is threatening a total boycott, the Kazakh Republican military chief Osipov is under close arrest, and there are some very embarrassing questions being asked in the House of Commons. Yes, I think one might reasonably say that the shit has well and truly hit the fan. Does that answer your question?'

'Eloquently,' Hailsham said. 'So where does that leave us?'

'Surprisingly, smelling of roses,' Davies told him. 'Having tipped over the slops bucket, the Kazakh authorities seem quite anxious to have us help clean up the mess. However, the Foreign Secretary has insisted I point out that you do have a choice.'

'Choice?' Hailsham queried. He did not quite understand.

'You can abort this mission right now,' Davies said, spelling it out for him. 'If you do decide to pull out, Captain Yascovar will make sure that you are all safely escorted back to Alma-Ata and transferred to a neutral base. No questions asked, no complications. However, if you want to stick around, then the Kazakhs would appreciate your help. They're not too experienced in this sort of situation.' Davies paused for a few seconds to let it all sink in. 'Well?' he demanded eventually. 'Do you want out?'

Hailsham almost exploded into the mike. 'No bloody way,' he said vehemently. 'No way am I prepared to abort this one, Barney. Not now. I've lost three men, and I've dragged the others through hell and out the other side again.'

It was the answer which Lieutenant-Colonel Davies had fully expected. Knowing Hailsham as he did, it could hardly have been otherwise. 'That's what I thought, Mike,' he said. 'But I was asked to give you the choice, and I did.'

'So, when are you going to fill me in with the details?' Hailsham asked, growing impatient. 'How much more do we know about this mountain complex and what we might face up there?'

There was a long pause at the other end as Davies assembled his thoughts. 'Right, are we sitting comfortably?' he asked eventually. 'Then pin your ears back, Mike. This gets kind of complicated.'

Another, shorter pause, and Barney Davies began to launch into a story of horror, intrigue, conspiracy and double-dealing that soon had Hailsham's head spinning.

'Well, now you know as much as I do,' Captain Yascovar said, as they walked back towards the tents rom the helicopter. 'It's all rather incredible, don't you think?'

Hailsham let out a derisive grunt halfway between a laugh and a snort. 'What I find incredible is that all this could have remained buried for so many years,' he muttered.

'Simply because no one wanted to dig for the truth,' Yascovar pointed out. 'Until your mission stirred things up, nobody had asked any questions. Once they did, of course, the whole thing snowballed.'

'But what the hell were our various governments doing all that time? American intelligence . . . our own security services?'

Yascover shrugged. 'They didn't call it the Cold War for nothing, Major. The Iron Curtain was a lot thicker than many people ever realized. And don't forget that it worked both ways – or would you have me believe that neither British or American scientists were involved in warfare research projects during those thirty years? I don't know if you're aware of it, Major Hailsham, but the rumour still persists throughout the Eastern bloc that AIDS was originally developed by the Americans as a biological weapon for use in Vietnam.'

Hailsham smiled thinly. 'And we thought it was the Russians in Afghanistan.'

'So you see,' Yascovar went on. 'The world continues to hold unpleasant mysteries and secrets. People such as you and I are always the last to know, Major.'

Hailsham nodded. 'You make your point, Captain.' He stopped in mid-stride, turning towards the Kazakh officer. There was a slightly embarrassed look on his face. 'Look, do you think we could start again?' He held out his hand.

It was more than just a conciliatory gesture. Barney Davies had made it clear that they were to work together. Although each officer would be responsible for his own men, the planning and execution of the raid on the Phoenix complex was very much a joint mission. And, in typical SAS fashion, rank was virtually suspended. To all intents and purposes Hailsham and Yascovar were equal.

The Russian took Hailsham's hand in a firm grip. This time, there was real warmth, even friendship, in their handshake.

They began to walk on towards the tents again. 'So, when do we move in?' Hailsham asked after a while.

'Just before first light tomorrow,' Yascovar answered him. 'I thought that the element of surprise might work in our favour. The complex was designed to withstand the full fury of the elements, and it is heavily protected against attack. Breaking into it will not be easy.'

Hailsham nodded.

'Which is why you and I have a busy night ahead of us. There's a lot of planning to be done,' Yascovar added.

Both men were silent again for a while. Finally Yascovar said: 'By the way, what did happen to your SAM system, Major?'

There did not seem much point in trying to lie. 'We had to abandon it,' Hailsham said. He eyed Yascovar cautiously. 'Look, it was unfortunate, but we thought we were under attack.'

Yascovar dismissed the matter with a wave of his

hand. 'Such things happen,' he said quietly. 'As I said earlier, Major Hailsham – we are soldiers. We leave politics to the politicians.'

'Yes,' Hailsham murmured thoughtfully. The matter ended there.

22

Captain Yascovar seemed to have given himself the
shitty end of the stick, Hailsham thought initially. By
opting for a frontal assault on the main body of the
complex, he was exposing himself and his men to the
full fury of the facility's defensive shield. Their actual
knowledge of those defences was sketchy, to say the
least, but even their limited intelligence suggested that
it posed an awesome threat.

The research building itself, built six subterranean
levels deep into the very bedrock of the mountain, was
constructed of steel-mesh reinforced concrete. The top
eight feet which actually showed above the ground
was of even more robust construction, a windowless
and virtually featureless block of eighteen-inch-thick
concrete built around a cage of sheet-metal plating.
The only indication that the structure was anything
more than a solid and inaccessible monolith was the
single access port at ground level, designed like a
bank vault door and controlled only by sophisticated
electronic coding from deep within the lower levels.

All four sides of the roughly square building were
protected by video-sighted 7.62mm heavy machine-
guns and the slightly domed roof was virtually
bomb-proof. Externally an area of somewhere in the

region of thirty square metres in the immediate vicinity of the access port was heavily seeded with electronic proximity mines, controlled by well-protected sensors built into the structure of the roof. Internally the facility boasted a complement of thirty-two well-armed security staff. On paper, the complex seemed impregnable.

Yet that was what Yascovar had set himself and his men up against. Compared with that task, his own job was a doddle, Hailsham told himself. Breaking into buildings was, after all, the SAS's stock in trade.

Seen in this light, Captain Yascovar's plan made logical sense, Hailsham realized. A full-scale frontal assault would give the security forces something to think about while the real invasion took place. It was all about having the right men for the right job – and having them in the right place at the right time.

Curiously enough, it was the very design and structure of the complex which gave it its one weakness. For the sheer size of the subterranean building demanded a vast intake of fresh air which had to be sucked in, filtered and purified and then pumped around the labyrinth of laboratories, offices and corridors. Three massive intake vents higher up in the surrounding mountains took care of this inflow, although all of them were armoured and protected against explosives. Even if access could have been effected, there would still have been no way through the whirling intake turbine blades, or the impassable wall of filtering and pumping machinery.

But air sucked in also has to be pumped out again – and it was here that the original designers had created the single, vital flaw in the system. Perhaps it had been just an oversight, or perhaps a simple and human psychological error which suggested that an inlet demanded more security than an outlet. It did not really matter either way. The important thing was that the single exhaust vent for the entire complex was protected only by a grille of half-inch metal bars. And it was here that Hailsham and his men would make their entry.

The first faint rays of the early morning sun glinted on the whirling rotor blades of the two helicopters as they lifted from the plateau and rose towards the mountains.

The Hind-As were designed for a crew of four and a passenger capability of eight fully equipped combat troops. Packing Hailsham, Cyclops, Andrew, Tweedledee and the Thinker in on top of Captain Yascovar's complement of eighteen men was a bit of a squeeze, but then they had not been expecting to fly Ambassador Class. Clad as they were in heavy NBC suits and S6 respirators, comfort was hardly a matter for consideration.

Cyclops glanced at Tweedledee. 'Bet you never thought we'd be going in by private air-taxi service,' he said, his voice distorted and blurred by the respirator. 'Makes you feel like a VIP, doesn't it?'

Tweedledee grunted. 'All I feel like is a bloody Star Wars trooper,' he said.

Cyclops nodded. 'Yeah, you look like one,' he confirmed.

It was time for last-minute orders. Hailsham pulled his mask away from his face so that he could speak clearly.

'Right. Now the important thing to remember is that once we do get inside that complex there must be no wild and indiscriminate shooting,' he reminded them all. 'Aim specifically and directly at human targets only – and make sure that there is no scientific equipment of any sort either in or behind your line of fire. I don't need to point out that there could be anything in there, from bacteriological agents to nerve gas. We don't know what's in there, or how deadly it might be. The last thing we can afford is to go spraying bullets around the place. If you're in any doubt at all, hold your fire. Dive for the nearest protection and wait for someone else to cover you from a safe line of fire. Understood?'

The men nodded gravely, all well aware of the potential horrors which might greet them once they reached the laboratory areas.

'And secondly, don't open fire at all unless fired upon,' Hailsham went on. 'We want to make this assault as much of a surprise as possible. Hopefully, Captain Yascovar and his men will be keeping the security forces well occupied on the complex perimeters. We want to keep them from knowing we're sneaking in the back door for as long as we can.'

A slight lurching feeling in the pit of his belly told Hailsham that the Hind-A was starting to go down again. It had been agreed that the two choppers would swoop in low, dropping Hailsham's team off about fifty yards below the complex before climbing again to circle round and make a final approach down from the mountains. If no one had already heard them coming, it might at least suggest that the attack was from one direction only, and focus the defences at a single point.

Even if this small advantage was only a temporary one it would help — and they needed all the help they could get.

Hailsham slipped his respirator back in place and checked it. He glanced over at Yascovar, jerking one thumb into the air. Reaching up, Yascovar punched a control button and the bottom section of the horizontally divided door at the front of the passenger cabin began to drop down like a ramp. With another sickening lurch, the Hind-A sank to within four feet of the ground and hovered just long enough for Hailsham and his men to drop over the side and into the thick snow. Then the helicopter was off again to join its companion in a smooth and almost unbroken movement.

Hailsham watched them both climb and wheel away for a few seconds before returning his eyes to the ground. He unfolded the sketched plan of the complex he had been carrying in his hand and studied it quickly. Tapping Andrew lightly on the shoulder, he pointed up ahead to the right, where the exhaust ventilation shaft could be seen as a black, igloo-shaped hole against a white background. Pausing only to check their weapons, the troopers began to plough through the snow towards it.

The sound of heavy machine-guns opening up from higher up the mountain made Hailsham's head snap up, a curse forming on his lips. The dark mound which had been all he could see of the complex was now twinkling with flashes of light as the roof-mounted machine-guns spat out a hail of fire at the approaching helicopters.

'Damn!' Hailsham grated out, realizing that their

chance of a surprise attack was gone. He had hoped to get at least as far as the ventilation shaft entrance before the action started. Obviously the complex boasted an efficient early detection and warning system. They had probably picked up the approach of the helicopters at a range of a mile or more. Hailsham's heart sank. If their surveillance was that good, then they had probably monitored the close approach of the drop-off helicopter as well. In which case, it would not take a genius to figure out the probability of a primary assault force. Or indeed roughly where they were likely to be.

Hailsham certainly did not intend to stick around long enough to test out this observation to its logical conclusion. With a warning yell to the others, he threw himself forward through the thick snow, desperately trying to break into a run. The best he could manage was an ungainly, floundering struggle, but it sufficed. The distance between him and the dark mouth of the ventilation shaft began to dwindle, yard by precious yard.

So, the expected attack had come at last, Tovan Leveski realized as the internal alarms started to pulse out their incessant warning bleeps. It was no surprise. He had been primed for it for two days and nights now, ever since the coded messages had started coming in over the radio. He was prepared; he knew what he had to do. The tension of waiting had focused his attention, channelling the wanderings of his muddled brain into unusual clarity.

He rose from his desk, walked calmly across his office towards the shredding machine and switched it on. The files were already piled beside it, in readiness. Every scrap of paperwork, laboratory note or requisition slip which referred to the Phoenix Project was there. The computer records had already been erased, the hard drives taken out and destroyed so that there would never be the faintest chance of retrieval. Slowly, painstakingly, Leveski started feeding the files into the shredder. Finally he pulled a cigar and lighter from his pocket. Lighting the cigar, he sucked on it for a few seconds. Then, using a twisted bundle of shredded paper as a spill, he lit that and dropped it into the waste bag and watched the flames spread greedily.

Phoenix would keep its dark secrets from the outside world. There remained only the physical evidence, but soon that too would be destroyed. As, indeed, the whole complex would be destroyed.

Hailsham threw himself into the tunnel of the ventilation shaft, pressing himself against one wall so that the others could crowd in behind him. Exactly as the plans had shown, there was just the single barrier of the metal grille, recessed about three feet inside the mouth of the shaft. Beyond that the tunnel ran straight ahead at a steady incline for about fifty yards, before branching off into several smaller shafts which Hailsham assumed went to the various different levels. The fact that he could see clearly was something of a bonus, he reasoned. He had expected the tunnel to be as black as pitch, since one would not expect an exhaust vent to be illuminated. As it happened, none of the upper levels or outer corridors had been supplied with power for several months, ever since Leveski had sealed and isolated them. It was only now that the complex's alarm system had been activated that emergency lighting had cut in automatically.

'Right, Thinker, this is your department,' Hailsham grunted, but the burly corporal had already set himself to work. Dropping to his knees and opening his bergen, the Thinker took out and unwrapped two bundles of Semtex and began to knead the malleable substance in his hands. Rolling it out into long, thin sausages, he pressed it into place at strategic points where the grille was embedded in the walls of the shaft. Explosives were his speciality, and he was good at his job. He worked quickly and efficiently, knowing instinctively how much to use and where to place it. The entire operation took less than forty seconds. Finally he stuck in the pencil fuses and detonators and nodded his head at Hailsham. 'Fifteen seconds,' he said quietly, deftly setting the timers.

It was more than enough time to retreat and take shelter around the outside of the shaft. They did so – although in truth they could probably have safely stayed exactly where they were. With his typical expertise, the Thinker had used no more explosive than was strictly necessary to do the job. The blast which blew the grille clear out of the tunnel wall did not even disturb the snow outside the mouth of the shaft.

They were back inside and running down the ventilation tunnel before the small amount of smoke from the explosion had cleared. If the original plans still held good, and the air-conditioning system had not been modified in recent years, it was a clear run to the exhaust pumping station. From there they should be able to use the maintenance access directly into the storage bays, and thence get into the internal security area. With luck, most of the guards would still be occupied with the frontal assault, and they could expect only minimal resistance. That was the plan, anyway.

The front access port of the Phoenix Complex had been designed to withstand the most violent of storms and any normal ground-level military attack. Over four decades previously, its makers had not been able to foresee the devastating effects of the steady stream of 'Swatter' anti-tank missiles and 57mm rockets which were being delivered by the two still-circling Hind-A helicopters. Under such a blistering attack, even a door made of eight-inch steel armour plate is still just a door.

As the surrounding concrete walls blew in with a final roar, Captain Yascovar ordered the two helicopters to rake the minefield with a hail of shells from their undernose heavy machine-guns. It was a matter of minutes now before he could safely bring them both in to land and discharge his troops. He wondered how Hailsham and his men were getting on.

The Thinker inspected the heavy steel shutter which sealed off the loading bay from the storage area. 'No problem,' he said confidently to himself, preparing to set another couple of explosive charges.

'Stop wasting time, you plonker,' Cyclops yelled out at him through the intake of his respirator. Pushing past the big man, he bent over and pulled up the bottom of the shutter. It slid up effortlessly, the open padlock dangling impotently.

A burst of gunfire from an AK-47 took him in the legs and abdomen as the shutter slammed into the ceiling above. He screamed horribly and fell back at the Thinker's feet, convulsing and twitching violently for a few seconds before finally lying still.

The Thinker hardly moved, other than to step slightly to one side and bring his SA-80 up into the business position. The single security guard in charge of the loading bay never got a chance to fire a second burst. The Thinker's first four slugs opened his chest up like a split watermelon. The next twelve slid his corpse jerkily across the loading-bay floor, leaving a glistening trail of blood. The Thinker did not even blink.

The very walls of the complex were echoing and vibrating with the sounds of gunfire now, as Yascovar's troops poured into the breached building. Guided by the sound, Hailsham led the rest of his men towards the scene of battle, prepared for further opposition but never encountering it. Perhaps overawed at the ferocity of the assault that had been mounted against them, or dispirited by their months of isolation, Leveski's security guards maintained only a token resistance for a few more minutes, and then put down their weapons and surrendered to the inevitable. Captain Yascovar was already interrogating them by the time Hailsham joined him in the central control room.

The door to Leveski's office was ajar. Hailsham sent one of the captured guards through it first, just in case. Nothing happened. Cautiously, Hailsham kicked the door fully open with his boot and fired a warning burst from his SA-80 up into the ceiling. Only then did he step forward, flanked by Andrew and Tweedledee.

Leveski sat at his desk, facing the open door. He smiled chillingly as Hailsham entered. 'I've been expecting someone,' he said quietly. 'Although the British SAS is something of a surprise.'

'Your men have already surrendered,' Hailsham told him calmly. 'Now I must ask you to do the same.'

The Russian pushed himself stiffly to his feet, clicking his heels together in a curiously old-fashioned gesture. 'Of course, Major. You must ask — just as I must refuse.' He leaned forward, pressing a small red button set into the surface of his desk.

He smiled again, and Hailsham thought that the man's face was possibly the most evil thing he had ever seen.

'And now we all die together,' Leveski said. 'I have just initiated the auto-destruct sequence which will blow this entire complex apart in just over thirty seconds. There is no way that you and your men can escape in time, Major.'

Hailsham's face was impassive. 'Wrong,' he said quietly. 'We have already disarmed it.'

His hand dropped to his hip, drawing his Browning. Raising it, he put a double tap cleanly through Leveski's forehead.

'That's for Piggy Baker,' Hailsham muttered. 'Never trust a fucking Russian.'